THE BOOK OF A
THOUSAND THRILLS

All-Star Stories
of Mystery, Crime
and Romance

ALLIED NEWSPAPERS LTD.
200 GRAY'S INN ROAD
LONDON, W.C.1

THE BOOK OF A THOUSAND THRILLS

All-Star Stories
of Mystery, Crime
and Romance

ALLIED NEWSPAPERS LTD.
200 GRAY'S INN ROAD
LONDON, W.C.1

CONTENTS

7

8 *Contents*

I*

Contents

1*

LIST OF ILLUSTRATIONS

INTRODUCTION

The Thrill-story through the Ages

THE vogue of the thrill-story began earlier than the dawn of history, has continued through the ages, and will probably endure to the end of time.

Long before the art of writing was invented, before nations began to exist, when men wandered over the face of the earth in scattered families and tribes, mighty hunters sat by the camp fire in the misty evening and boasted how they had fought victoriously against boar or tiger or lured the mammoth to his doom in the marsh. They were the tellers of the first thrill-stories—the John Buchans, Rider Haggards, and Edgar Wallaces of their prehistoric day.

One can imagine the fierce delight with which the barbarian audience in those shades of antiquity would listen to such stories of mystery, horror, fear, and courage.

But it is not only to the barbarian that the thrill-story appeals. Mystery, horror, fear, and courage—the thrill-writer's stock-in-trade throughout the ages—are elemental things that strike a responsive chord in all of us, and must continue to do so while human nature endures.

The Golden Age of ancient Greece, that most cultured epoch of long ago, was remarkable for some of the most wonderful thrill-stories ever written. You may be sure that the citizens of Athens read the *Odyssey* and the *Iliad* of Homer as much for their stories of magic and mystery, of high adventure and warlike deeds as for the poetry of their sonorous lines.

Great writers in all lands and in all times have produced thrillers for the delight of their contemporaries. What was Shakespeare doing when he wrote *Macbeth*, if he was not writing a thriller ?   Or Dickens when he penned his gorgeous narrative of the murder of Mr. Pecksniff by Jonas Chuzzlewit ?

Dumas, Victor Hugo, Sir Walter Scott, Edgar Allan Poe, Charles Dickens, Lord Lytton, Wilkie Collins—how they revelled in thrills, and how their readers delighted in the thrills they provided.

And so we come to yesterday and to-day—to Le Queux, Orczy, Wallace, Oppenheim, Mason, Sapper, and the rest.

Modern publishers and booksellers have long known that it is to the most intelligent section of the public that the thrill-story makes its appeal.   Statesmen, lawyers, doctors, scientists, turn for relaxation, when the day's work is done, not to the egotistical introspective novels of the Bloomsbury and Chelsea schools, but to the sane and healthy excitement provided by those masters of the thrill-story whose work is contained in this volume.

Here you will find some of the best stories that have come from the pens of such master purveyors of thrills as John Buchan, William Le Queux, A. E. W. Mason, E. Phillips Oppenheim, Baroness Orczy, Eden Phillpotts, " Sapper," Dorothy Sayers, Edgar Wallace, " Seamark," Valentine Williams, Ian Hay, and many other authors whose work is in the authentic tradition of the great masters.

NOTE

The characters in all the stories in this book are entirely imaginary, and are not intended to portray any living person

RUBY M. AYRES

The Lady who loved a King

RUBY M. AYRES started writing
stories when she was about twenty-five
years old, and has since written serials
which have been published in a great
many newspapers and magazines, and
numerous volumes in book form. She
has also done work for the films in
London and America.

It has been said that her novels have
been more widely read than those of
any other living authoress.

THE LADY WHO LOVED A KING

THE Lady who loved a King lived in a Bloomsbury boarding-house, and uncomplainingly ate and drank of the over-cooked meat and underdone meat and watery rice puddings and stewed tea, and slept on a hard mattress in an attic room with a sloping ceiling, because it was all cheap and because she had hardly any money.

Nobody in the Bloomsbury boarding-house had any money worth talking about, and for the most part they were a sour, cross-grained lot who talked about one another and envied and hated one another—all that is, except the Lady who loved a King, and she was just the sweetest, most contented, happiest lady who ever wore old-fashioned clothes and went to church regularly twice on Sunday.

The other people in the Bloomsbury boarding-house said she was mad, not dangerously mad, of course, but just foolish, and they looked at one another meaningly, and tapped their foreheads with deep significance whenever she chipped into the conversation with one of her bright, birdlike remarks. Otherwise they contented themselves by ignoring her or by treating her as if she were a child. And the Lady who loved a King submitted to being pushed into the background, and was quite contented with her knitting and the colonel's newspapers, and her thoughts !

But in spite of all this, she was the one person who caught Penny's attention when she first walked nervously into the dining-room to supper, and she was also the one person who made any attempt to put Penny at her ease.

Now Penny had run away from home with a very unhappy heart and about five pounds in her pocket, and she was thinking that the Bloomsbury boarding-house was the most awful place she had ever seen, when across the bare, badly-lit room she caught the sweet, friendly smile of the Lady who loved a King. And that smile comforted her and gave her courage, so that when the unappetising meal of stale cheese and dry bread and woolly radishes was ended, they drifted together quite naturally and began to talk, and the Lady who loved a King said :

" It is not often anyone so young and pretty as you are comes to cheer us up, my dear."

And Penny answered tremulously : " Oh, I don't think I *should* have come if I had known what it was really like. Is it always as bad as this ? "

The Lady who loved a King looked surprised. " What do you mean by ' bad ' ? " she asked a trifle offendedly. " I have lived here for nearly fourteen years and I am quite happy."

Penny cast a despairing look around her at the narrow, airless hall through which they had just passed, to the so-called drawing-room, where a broken-springed couch, for the possession of which people fought twice nightly (before and after supper), was drawn up to a smoky fire, and a dusty aspidistra on a bamboo table struggled for existence behind a draughty window which was draped in cheap lace curtains.

" Fourteen years !   Oh, how could you have borne it all that time ? " she faltered, closing her eyes with a little sick feeling as against her lids she visualised once more the rows of disagreeable, inquisitive faces that had been turned to her half an hour before when she entered the dining-room.

" Does it seem so strange to you ? " the old lady asked wonderingly.   " Well, perhaps it did to me at first, but it is so long ago now I almost forget, and at any rate you will soon get used to it.   The people really are all very kind.   You will like them when you know them well."

Penny shivered.   " They all stared at me so rudely," she faltered.   " Especially that horrid man who sat next to you with the bald head and shaggy eyebrows."

The Lady who loved a King bridled a little.   " That is Colonel Swift," she said with dignity.   " And he is the kindest friend I have, *quite* the kindest.   He lends me his *Times* when he had read it himself, and he sometimes brings me flowers when he has a little money to spare."

" But is he really a colonel ? " Penny asked amazed. " He doesn't look a bit as if he had been in the Army."

The Lady who loved a King shook her head.   " I don't for a moment suppose that he has," she agreed simply. " But he has always called himself a colonel, and so we

have always called him that, too, and now we are quite
used to it." She lowered her voice. " You will find that
a great many of us here are not really at all what we pretend
to be, and some "—she smiled, a queer little " fey " smile—
" and some are a great deal better and grander than anyone
dreams of. For instance "—she drew her hard, uncomfortable chair a little closer to Penny's—" you will probably
not believe me if I tell you that nearly every night I am
visited by a king."

Penny's eyes opened wide. " By a king ! What king ? "
she asked, mystified.

The little old lady smoothed a crease in the old-fashioned
black silk apron which she always wore to protect her frock.

" A real king," she explained triumphantly. " He
always wears his crown, and his robes of state, and he comes
to the side of my bed, and kneels down and kisses my hand
as if I were his queen." The strange smile came again.
" You see, we loved one another years ago when I was
young," she went on ; " but as I was not of royal blood,
we were not allowed to marry, and although he is dead he
always finds out where I live, and nearly every night about
twelve o'clock—that is when departed spirits are free to
visit their loved ones on earth, you know, my dear—he
comes to my room—I sleep on the top floor—and kisses me
good night."

Penny said nothing, but her pretty eyes widened blankly,
and the old lady laughed.

" I told you you would not believe me," she said reproachfully. " Never mind, some night you shall come
along to my room and see for yourself."

She rose to her feet as a wheezy clock out in the airless
hall began to strike ten. " I will say good night," she
said. She touched the girl's cheek with her slender finger.
" Pleasant dreams, my dear."

She walked slowly from the room, her old-fashioned,
voluminous skirts trailing behind her, and Penny watched
her go with a dazed feeling of unreality.

Into what sort of a place had she wandered, she asked
herself, and what was the meaning of the pretty nonsense
to which she had just listened ?

A tall girl with a permanent wave and horn-rimmed
glasses crossed the room and paused for a moment beside her.

" Say, has our Cleopatra been telling you the tale ? " she asked with a Yankee drawl. " Gee, but she must be tickled to death to have got a brand new audience."

Penny looked up with bewildered eyes. " But what does it all mean ? " she gasped. " She told me some impossible story about a king who comes to visit her ! A real live king in robes and a crown ! "

Miss America burst out laughing. " Sure, she's told us all that," she said with good-natured tolerance. " She believes it, too, poor lamb !" She tapped her bony forehead above the horn-rimmed spectacles. " That's where she wants it, bless her," she explained.

Penny caught her breath. " Do you mean she's mad ? " she asked.

" Sure she is ! Mad as a hatter," Miss America said cheerfully. " But quite harmless, you bet your life, or we shouldn't have her here." She looked at Penny consideringly for a moment, then drew up a rickety chair and sat down beside her.

" Gee, don't look so scared, honey ! " she said in kindly fashion. " She's got a history, poor old darling. I've heard it a score of times and so will you if you stay long enough. No, not from her, she's forgotten it herself, but the others in this Noah's Ark are fond of telling the story to all newcomers. She was hitched up to some boy years ago when they were kids, and they were at a dance—a fancy ball— and he was dressed as a king, and there was an accident— someone spilt a lamp and set the show alight and his robe was all trimmed with cotton-wool and so——" She stopped as she saw Penny shiver. " Yes, it must have been real nasty," she agreed pleasantly.

" And so the poor little lady went mad ? " Penny said pityingly.

Miss America nodded. " So history tells us. Lost her memory—can't remember a thing." She sat still for a moment, then sprang up suddenly. " Well, I'm making tracks." She took a step towards the door, then stopped and glanced back over her shoulder. " Guess you won't be staying here long ? " she hazarded.

Penny hesitated. " I don't know," she said cautiously.

Miss America went on her way, shutting the door behind her with sufficient finality to call forth a storm of complaint from the chilly crowd round the fire, and under cover of it the bald-headed man with the shaggy brows (who, the Lady who loved a King had agreed with Penny, was very probably not a real colonel at all) sidled up to Penny. "Er—good evening," he said in rather a husky voice. Penny looked up in alarm, flushing a little, then she saw that his eyes beneath their fierce brows were kind, and she smiled timidly.

"Good evening," she answered. She glanced at the chair vacated by Miss America. "Won't you sit down?" she asked.

She felt that he would be less formidable sitting than he was towering above her, for he was a very tall man.

But the colonel shook his head. "Thank you, but I am just going out. I always go out at ten o'clock and walk twice round the Square before going to bed."

He cleared his throat. "I just wanted to say that our friend, the American lady, is rather apt to exaggerate. I know what she has been telling you. I should have told you myself if the opportunity had come my way before it came hers—only I should have told you differently—I should not have said, as I am sure Miss America did, that the very charming lady whom we know here as Cleopatra, is —mad!" He gave a little shudder of distaste at the word. "I should have quoted from our greatest poet, the quotation which, of course, you know, about ' sweet bells jangled out of tune ' ! "

He waited, but Penny made no comment, and he said again with a curious softening in his harsh voice : " You see, I have known her all my life—only she has forgotten me."

Then he bowed and left her. to take his solitary prowl round the dingy Square.

Penny had been in the dingy boarding-house for a week when one evening the Lady who loved a King came tapping at her bedroom door.

Penny had not gone downstairs to supper that night because she knew there was only tripe to be had, and she detested tripe, so she stayed in her own room with a bag of biscuits, and read by the light of a candle, for it was forbidden to burn the gas during hours when the sitting-rooms could be occupied.

She was feeling cold and miserable, and the tears were not far away when the gentle tapping sounded on her door, and the Lady who loved a King walked into the room.

" I was afraid you might be ill," she apologised as Penny rose to greet her, " or is it only that you don't care for tripe ? "

" I wasn't hungry," Penny explained, " and I wanted to read so——" She paused. " Won't you sit down ? " she asked.

The little lady hesitated.

" I didn't mean to stay," she said, " but perhaps just for a few minutes." The soft eyes sought the girl's face. " My dear, have you been crying ? " she asked in concern.

Penny shook her head, but the tears started to her eyes, and suddenly she covered her face with her hands.

" Oh, I'm so unhappy ! " she whispered desolately.

The little lady sat down beside her, and for a moment she did not speak, then she said softly : " Would you like to tell me about him ? Is it that he does not love you, or that you have lost him, or that he has married someone else ? "

Penny cried out : " He is my husband ! "

The Lady who loved a King laid a white hand on the girl's lap.

" Then perhaps it is you who do not love him ? " she asked.

Penny shook her head.

" Oh, no, no ! But we quarrelled. He said I was extravagant, or too fond of pleasure. He said—oh, he said a great many cruel things which I shall never forget, and he told me if I was not satisfied with the home he had given me and with him, I could go. And so——"

She stopped, and the Lady who loved a King said simply : " And so you ran away. Is that it ? "

" Yes."

There was a little silence, then the lady laughed, a silvery little laugh of pure enjoyment and amusement.

" Well, then, my dear child, instead of sitting up here in the cold crying about it, put on your hat and run back to him again."

Penny's hands fell from her face and she looked up with resentful eyes.

" Haven't *you* ever cried about anyone ? " she asked.

The old lady shook her head.

" Never," she said gravely, " but then I am one of those wonderfully lucky women who have never lost the man they love. And I never can lose him now, although he is dead, and I am old. He still comes to me every night faithfully, and when I die, he will just take me by the hand and help me across the Dark River." She smiled with serene happiness.

" And so I am not at all afraid," she added, " and if you and your husband love one another, you need not be afraid either. Just go back to him."

Penny's tear-stained face hardened.

" I will never go back," she said ; " he told me to go away, and I will never go back. My pride will not let me."

The Lady who loved a King was silent for a moment. Then she rose to her feet.

" Then do not cry, because you are wilfully hurting yourself," she said.

She began to cross the room, but stopped in front of the glass and looked at her reflection, such a dainty reflection. Slim figure in voluminous skirts, silvery hair smoothly parted on either side of an ivory pale face, and gentle, happy eyes.

Penny watched her enviously.

" If she is really mad," was her thought, " I wish I were, if it means being as happy as she."

The Lady who loved a King spoke again.

" I really came to give you an invitation," she said with her most regal air. " I don't suppose you have ever seen a real king, my dear, have you ? "

Penny shook her head.

" I once saw King George in the distance," she said, " but he had on a frock coat and a tall hat. He didn't look very much like a king."

The little lady looked delighted.

" Then my invitation will please you very much," she said, " for it is an invitation to come to my room at twelve o'clock to-night and see *my* king. Don't come before twelve, and be very careful not to make a noise. Not that he would mind, but the other people in the boarding-house don't like to be disturbed, you know."

For a moment Penny looked almost frightened.

"But shall I really see him ? Will he really come ? " she asked.

The Lady who loved a King drew up her slender figure with great dignity.

" He always comes," she said.

But at five minutes to twelve the house was so dark and silent that Penny was afraid.

She stood at her bedroom door for a long moment, shading the candle-flame with her hand, and looking up the winding staircase to the attic where the Lady who loved a King slept, afraid of the darkness, and of her own fast-beating heart.

Then with a little smile at herself, she stepped out on to the landing, closing the door softly behind her and began to ascend the stairs.

The house seemed alive with silent, unknown things. Penny was sure that they were all about her, crowding round, resenting her intrusion in this, their one midnight hour of freedom. But she went on, until she stood outside the door which the Lady who loved a King had left ajar. There was a faint light burning within, and as Penny put out her hand to push the door wider, far below, down in the hall, the wheezy clock began to strike twelve.

Penny counted the strokes by her heartbeats.

" Nine, ten, eleven, twelve."

Then she closed her eyes with a feeling of real fear and went forward into the room.

But it was empty save for the little figure of the Lady who loved a King, lying peacefully in the bed, her soft white hair scattered over the pillow, her cheek resting on her hand.

Fast asleep she was in the dim candle-light with a happy smile on her lips, but there was no king in his crown and robes of State, nobody at all, though Penny waited in the shadows till she was chilled through, and nearly half an hour had passed before she crept back shivering to her own bed.

" Poor little lady, she *is* mad," she told herself. " Oh, poor little lady."

Then she fell asleep to dream of the man whom she adored, but from whom in a foolish moment of anger she had run away.

And in the morning the Lady who loved a King whispered to Penny. " Well, my dear, what did you think of him ? Isn't he wonderful ?   Isn't he a king indeed ? "

Penny flushed and stammered.   No ready answer would come until at last she managed to say : " I'm so sorry.   I fell asleep.   I did not go to your room.   I fell asleep."

The old lady looked disappointed.

" This is not a very polite way to treat an invitation," she said with dignity, and swept away.

The Lady who loved a King was ill. Not seriously ill, but she had a nasty cold and a temperature, and so she stayed in bed.

" I have my suspicions that my clean sheet this week was not sufficiently aired," she confided to Penny, who devotedly visited her half a dozen times a day.   " However, it's nothing very serious.   I shall soon be up and about again."

But that is just what did not happen, and at the end of a week her place at the dinner-table next to Colonel Swift was still empty.

Everyone was very concerned. The colonel bought bunches of violets and snowdrops (it was spring) every day, and sent his *Times* upstairs for her to read before he had even glanced at it himself, and even Miss America softened her heavy tread about the house and lowered her voice so as not to disturb the little lady upstairs.

And a dozen times a day the colonel stopped Penny and asked in a voice that tried hard to disguise his anxiety :

" Well, and how are we to-day ? "

And one evening Penny told him that the Lady who loved a King had been crying.

Colonel Swift looked very fierce.

" Crying ! " he said, in a voice that would have been just the thing for a parade ground.   " What's she been crying for ?   Is there anything she wants ?   If so, tell me what it is, and I'll get it for her this minute."

And half laughing, half crying, Penny told him.

" It's foolish, I know, and yet pathetic, so pathetic because nothing can be done about it, but she says that since she's been ill, the king—*her* king, you know, has not once been to see her."

Her tears overflowed. " Oh, I think it's so sad, because to her it's all so *real*, and she really believes that a king does come to see her."

The colonel scowled till his bushy eyebrows quite hid his eyes.

" Stuff and nonsense ! All imagination," he growled, " and if that's the trouble, I'm afraid I can't help her. I'm sorry, but I'm afraid I can't."

And he walked off for his nightly constitutional round the Square grumbling to himself at the foolishness of women and the inclemency of the weather.

And the next day the Lady who loved a King was worse. Her ivory white face was flushed, and her eyes had a curiously glazed look, and when she spoke her voice was high-pitched as if with fever.

And the colonel's *Times* lay unopened beside her bed ; and when the doctor came, he shook his head, and looked grave and said he should call in again that evening.

And Penny stayed with her all day long, holding the restless hands that seemed to be eternally groping, groping for something which was not there, and sometimes those hands lay passive for a little while, only to be wrenched away again as if unsatisfied.

But when the doctor came for the second time he said she was better, her pulse quieter, her temperature down.

" If she lives through the night she may recover," he told Penny. " But I am afraid. Shall you stay with her ? "

" Of course," she answered. She went back to the bed when he had gone and found the little lady with wide-open eyes staring at her.

" I heard what the doctor said," she whispered weakly. " But he is wrong—quite wrong. I couldn't die, how could I die, until the king comes for me. And he will not come yet. He has not been for so long." There was a sound of tears and weariness in her voice. " He has not been for so long, and I am so tired of waiting," she whispered again.

Penny took her hands. " He will come when you get well," she said firmly. " He will come at once then. So you will try to get well, dear, won't you ? "

She seemed to fall into an easier sleep towards midnight, and Penny seized the opportunity to slip downstairs for more coal with which to replenish the dying fire. Coal was guarded as religiously as if it were gold in the Bloomsbury boarding-house, and it was only through the generosity of Miss America that the Lady who loved a King had been able to have a fire in her room night and day.

" Sakes ! What's a few scuttles of coal," she said heartily when she heard of the trouble. " I'll find the dollars and be tickled to death."

So Penny crept down in her stockinged feet to the much-guarded cellar, feeling tired and sad and more in want of the dear, but angry husband with whom she had quarrelled than ever in her life before, and she was dropping a few tears amongst the precious knobs of coal when overhead in the hall the wheezy clock began to strike midnight.

And a sudden feeling of apprehension filled her heart, and she began to tremble so much that she had to put the scuttle down, and in putting the scuttle down, she dropped the candle and found herself in darkness.

And then a panic came to her, so that she turned and fled up the cellar steps and across the hall and up two more flights of stairs and past her own door, and then up the winding staircase to the attics, her stockinged feet making no sound, so that she came noiselessly to the door of the room where the Lady who loved a King lay so ill, and then she stopped dead, catching her breath, one hand going out to the wall for support.

For inside the room was a strange sight, so strange that for a moment Penny thought she must either be mad like the poor little lady, or dreaming, for there by the bed, in the wavering candle-light, stood a noble romantic figure, poor little Cleopatra's King.

His back was turned to Penny, but the yellow candle-light gleamed on the points of his gold crown, and on the splendour of his embroidered sleeves.

A long velvet train edged with ermine hung from his fine shoulders and swept the floor behind him, and as Penny stared half wondering, half frightened, she saw him go down on his knees beside the bed and kiss the white slender hand of the Lady who loved him, which lay outside the coverlet.

Then Penny looked at the face on the pillow, framed in its scattered silvery hair, at its closed eyes, and happily smiling lips, and a stifled sob broke from her, for she knew that the Lady who had loved a King was dead.

And at the sound of that sob the King rose hurriedly to his feet, and turned round towards Penny, and the face beneath the golden crown was the face of Colonel Swift.

And for a moment he and Penny looked at one another silently, and she saw how his mouth was quivering and that his eyes beneath their shaggy brows were filled with tears, then gently, and very reverently, he released the slim white hand from his own and laid it down on the coverlet before, with bowed head, he stumbled from the room, the long velvet train gathered up clumsily beneath his arm.

In the morning he and Penny had a few moments together. The colonel's fierce eyes were red as if with crying and he held that day's *Times* unopened in his hand.

" I'm not going to explain anything," he said to Penny angrily, and at once began to explain it all. " But I told you that I'd known her all her life . . . all her life . . . and loved her, too," he added fiercely. " Loved her as the other man never did. And last night . . . well, it was all I could do to help her. . . . You said it was what she wanted . . . so I hired the gimcracks from the theatrical man. It made her happy . . . I was with her when she died."

And now the tears stood unashamedly on his rugged cheeks.

" She told me about you," he said presently, more gently. " We were good friends, she and I, so she told me about you."

He held out his hand. " You go home to that husband of yours and say you're sorry," he admonished her fiercely. " Life's so infernally short."

Penny laid her hand in his.

" I'm going to-day, colonel," she said.

He squeezed her hand hard.

" That's right. That's right. Good girl."

He turned to go, then came back again. " I'm not really a colonel," he said gruffly. " I was never in the Army at all. It's all humbug."

She tried to smile.

" *She* knew, and didn't mind," he added proudly.

Penny tried to speak, but she could not find her voice,

and he turned away once more and began slowly to climb the stairs.

Penny watched him silently, and somehow at that moment he no longer looked as she had always seen him, just a big clumsily-built man, with a bald head and fierce eyes beneath shaggy brows, but instead there was something noble, something dignified, something of a real King about this man who had loved a lady.

CAMERON BLAKE

The Troubles of an Old Ship-mate
The Irishman Olsabuk

¶ CAMERON BLAKE—a name assumed by the author only for his works of fiction—has travelled in most of the uninhabited quarters of the world. Under his own name he has published travel books about his wanderings in the Yukon and Africa, Spain and South America, which have received general praise. Those who are in the secret of his real identity often wonder whether the ships' captains and hard-bitten adventurers of his stories are not real-life companions and acquaintances of the traveller rather than the pure creations of the fiction-writer.

2

THE TROUBLES OF AN OLD SHIP-MATE

"Seamen are always complainin' of 'aving to be at sea, but afore they bin ashore very long, with all their money spent and very like the D.T.'s a-comin' on, they very soon look for another ship." Hanks was giving forth this dictum to Lamont, whom he had found, in a complacent mood, sitting upon the forward hatch-cover.

"No, sir!" he went on, in answer to a question from the Westerner. "No, sir! If I was left a fortin, which ain't not at all likely, I don't think as I would leave the sea. If the fortin were a big one I'd become a shipowner and go to sea as master o' me own craft. Now that'd be somethink like, that would; and knowin' wot I does about the sea and the ways o' sailormen I'd make a good thing of it. I knowed one cove wot was left a fortin and it didn't do 'im no good at all. Brought 'im a lot of trouble, and very little else. It wasn't exackly a fortin, but it was an 'undred quid. 'Undred quid's a lot o' money for an A.B. to find in 'is pockets all at once! Lot 'o money, 'undred quid!

"It all started from this chap, George 'Ampson 'is name was, pickin' up of an old gent wot 'ad fallen down in front of a big waggon o' barrels wot was comin' down 'ill somewhere in Chatham. George was a big strong chap. 'E was just standin' on the pavement, in Chatham, when 'e see this old gent tread on a bit of orange peel and down 'e went, right in front o' this 'ere dray wot was comin' down the 'ill at an 'orrible rate. Another minute and the old gent would 'a' been either squashed by the wheels or trod on by the 'orses or both. Maybe it don't make much difference if you 'ave to be killed by a barrel waggon, whether you're cut in 'alf or trod on. Anyway this old gent 'e come pretty near it and the next thing as 'e knows was George a clutchin' of 'im by the collar and 'auling 'im back on to the pavement.

"'Gord strewth!' says the old gent, 'you just 'ad me out o' that in time! Another 'arf tick and that waggon

would 'ave 'ad me as flat as a kipper ! ' 'e says. Talked very
refined, 'e did. You could see as 'e was a reel gent, gold
watch chain an' all. 'E said 'e thought 'e needed a drink
to pull 'im round. 'E let George old 'is arm to the nearest
pub and 'e pushed into the saloon bar as if it belonged to
'im. 'E told the barmaid to give 'im a double Scotch, and
to let George 'ave w'atever 'e liked. George 'ad a double
Scotch too. After that they both 'ad another, the old gent
payin' for it all, and then 'e up an' give George a golden
sovering for savin' of his life. George saw the old gent to
the train 'e 'ad to catch to London and the old gent wrote
down George's name and George's mother's address in
Gravesend.

" It must ha' been five year arter that when George next
'eard about that old gent. 'Im an' me was ship-mates, then,
just back from a v'y'ge to Australia round the Cape in a
barque called the *Mouette*. Good ship, she was ; pleasure to
sail in 'er. Not many like 'er on the sea nowadays. Ran
ashore off Tasmania, she did, and broke up. Well, sir,
George got a letter from some lawyers in London called
Bolton, Symes, Bolton and Bolton. Why they couldn't ha'
called theirselves Bolton and Co., and been done with it, I
don't know. They said in their letter as Mr. Arthur
Shaddock 'ad been an' died and as George was left one
'undred pounds in 'is last Will and Testament !

" 'Gor lummy ! ' says George, ' one 'undred pounds !
Look 'ere,' 'e says to the rest of us, wot was gazin' at 'im
round the forecastle, ' is this 'ere some o' your perishin'
fun ? '

" We said it wasn't nothink to do with us, an' pretty
soon George see as we was pretty near as excited about it
as wot 'e was 'imself.

" ' One 'undred quid ! ' says George. ' But 'oo the 'ell
is Mr. Arthur Shaddock ? I never 'eard o' no Mr. Arthur
Shaddock ! '

" ' It don't matter to you 'oo 'e was,' says one o' the chaps,
' so long as you gets your 'undred quid. You go along and
get it afore they finds out as you're the wrong chap. They
probably been and got you all mixed up with someone else.
That's wot they done,' 'e says.

" Of course that made George see there might be somethink in wot 'e said, and then George started a-worryin' about

wot would 'appen if they found out as 'e was the wrong chap after 'e'd spent the 'undred quid.

" ' Why, I might go to quod for years,' says pore George, 'orrified. But a seaman called Bill North, wot knew a whole lot about the law, 'im avin' been in trouble more'n once, said as the lawyers 'd 'ave to go to quod, and not George.

" ' You go and get your money,' says Bill. ' When you get it that'll be time to worry about a losin' of it.'

" Well, George 'e said 'e'd like me and Bill to come with 'im to see 'im through. George was a big strong chap, but simple. 'E said 'e was frightened to go alone, never 'avin' seen a lawyer, and 'e was fair tremblin' with excitement, partly at 'avin' a 'undred quid all at once, and partly 'cos 'e was afraid 'e might 'ave it took away from 'im when 'e got it.

" So Bill and me we went to see 'im through with the Bolton lot. Bill combed 'is 'air and I put on a collar, and 'avin' just been paid off we all 'ad plenty o' money, so George 'e bought a collar too. We 'ad some drinks in a pub and Bill and me we paid for 'em all.

" ' You can stand us some when you've got your 'undred quid, old pal,' says Bill.

" Well, sir, we found Bolton, Symes, Bolton and Bolton's shop at larst, with their names wrote on a big brass plate and ' Solicitors and Commissionaires of Oaths ' wrote underneath.

" ' Lor lummy ! ' says George, 'arf afraid to go in, ' wot the 'ell's a commissionaire of oaths ? Somethink to do with bad language ? '

" ' Naow ! ' sez Bill, very scornful. ' 'E's a chap wot makes you swear as you 'aven't done somethink when you 'ave. Kind o' lawyer.'

" So we pushes in at the door and a big old chap in uniform 'e pushes us back again.

" ' Wot do you want ? ' asks the big chap.

" ' We've come to see our laywer,' says Bill North, lookin' very 'aughty at 'im, and George 'e pulls out the letter and shows 'im the name printed at the top of it. So the old chap 'e lets us in and we looks round till I sees a door marked ' Enquiries,' and a little dark chap with specs and a pen behind 'is ear says,' Wot do you want 'ere ? 'Ave you come to mend that stove-pipe ? '

" ' None o' your blasted lip ! ' says George, very fierce. ' I've come to see my lawyers, I 'ave ; three gents called Bolton and one called Symes.'

" ' Ho ! ' says the little chap, ' Ho, you 'ave, 'ave you ? And wot do you want to see them about ? ' 'e says.

" George shows 'im the letter and the chap says 'e'll go and see if Mr. Pringle will see 'im.

" ' Pringle ! ' says George, ' I don't want to see no Pringle ! I want to see Mr. Symes or one o' the Mr. Boltons,' 'e says.

" ' Well, they're all dead,' says the chap, ' so you carn't ! ' And 'e goes out with the letter into a room beyond.

" ' All dead ! ' says Bill. ' Wot, all of 'em ? Lor lummy, and that brass plate looks new as can be ! Ah,' 'e says, ' that shows 'ow un'ealthy it is to live in an orfice like lawyers do ! Plate not six months old and the 'ole bloomin' lot dead ! '

" ' I 'ope we don't catch wot it was they all died of ! ' says pore George, lookin' round all frightened. George never 'avin' been ill in 'is life was mortal frightened of dying. That's the way with lots of 'ealthy men, ain't it, sir ? " Hanks looked down at Lamont, who had lain back on the canvas of the hatch cover and closed his eyes.

" You're dead right," he said, sleepily, opening one eye to look at the chief steward and shutting it again.

" Well, sir," went on the little man. " We was still waiting when the clerk chap come back and says as Mr. Pringle would see Mr. 'Ampson. So we all gets up, and Bill 'itches up 'is trousers a bit, and the clerk 'e says : ' 'Ere,' 'e says, ' all of you ain't goin' in,' e' says.

" ' Ho, yes, we is,' says Bill, pushin' 'im out o' the way. So we all goes in.

" Mr. Pringle was a little old dried up chap with white 'air and gold spectacles, and 'e was sitting with another chap wot looked as if 'e'd swallowed a lot of somethink as didn't agree with 'im.

" ' This is my partner, Mr. Bright,' says Mr. Pringle, nodding 'is 'ead towards the melancholy lookin' chap. ' Which of you gentlemen is Mr. 'Ampson ? '

" ' Me,' says George.

" ' And 'oo may be your friends, if you don't objeck to my arskin' ? ' says Mr. Pringle.

" ' These are my pals, Mr. North and Mr. 'Anks, wot 'ave come along to see as everything's above board, and 'as I don't get done out o' my 'undred quid,' says George.

" ' You won't get done out o' nothink 'ere,' says Mr. Pringle, larfin', and Mr. Bright looked more melancholic than ever. Funny thing, ain't it," continued Hanks in meditative tone, " 'ow a name don't always suit a man at all. Chaps called ' Bright ' are dull and chaps called ' Black ' are fair-'aired ; I knew a cove in Bonus Erries," he went on in reminiscent parenthesis, " called Angel White. 'E was as black as a nigger and the biggest rascal unhung ! "

Lamont grunted but kept his eyes closed.

" So Mr. Pringle arsked a lot o' questions to make shore as George was 'imself and not somebody else, and then 'e explained as Mr. Shaddock, who'd been a coal-merchant in Rochester, 'ad been the old gent wot George 'ad pulled out from in front of the barrel waggon in Chatham, five years afore.

" ' Gawd strike me blind ! ' says George, when 'e seen as 'e reely was agoin' to get the money. And Mr. Pringle made George sign 'is name on a bit o' paper and asked wot 'e wanted done with the 'undred quid.

" ' Done with it ? ' says George, surprised. ' Why, I want it, of course ! '

" ' All right,' says Mr. Pringle, ' I'll give you a cheque for it,' and 'e wrote one and 'anded it to George, 'oo put it in 'is pocket.

" ' Now you must sign your name on this receipt,' said Mr. Pringle, ' to show as you've got the money,' 'e says.

" ' Got the money ? But I haven't got it yet ! '

Mr. Pringle explained what the cheque was and George took it out of 'is pocket and kept on turnin' it round and lookin' at it as if 'e'd never stop. So Mr. Pringle said 'e'd send the clerk with us to the bank, to make shore George got the money, and George signed 'is name again, and, being excited and clumsy, trod right on pore Mr. Pringle's foot, wot 'ad corns on it. Then we shook 'ands with 'im and Mr. Bright, and Bill North, 'oo was as strong as a bull, gave Mr. Pringle's 'and such a squeeze that 'e fair 'owled with the pain. But Bill never noticed and leaned over to shake 'ands with Mr. Bright and made 'im 'owl even worse. Then we got down to the bank with the clerk chap and, first thing we knew, George 'ad the 'undred quid in 'is pocket all safe and sound.

" Well, the next thing was to think wot George was goin' to do with the money. I said 'e ought to take a pub with it. Bill thought a sheep farm in Australia. The only sensible one was George 'imself, and 'e said we'd all go and 'ave a drink. 'E pushed 'is way into the saloon bar of a nice public-'ouse, with me whisperin' to 'im not to say nothink about 'is money.

" ' Public bar's round to the left,' said the gel behind the bar. Red-'eaded gel with green eyes and an orange dress. Proper snappish, she spoke.

" ' Wot if it is ? ' says George, 'aughty. ' Three port wines, please, miss.' And 'e pulled out a five pound note and chucked it on the bar.

" The gel brought the port wines and smiled hamiable, when she seen the money, and we drank it off.

" ' This 'ere stuff tastes all right,' says George, ' but there ain't enough of it. Bring me the 'ole bottle,' 'e says to the gel. We drank it up and then we 'ad another and drank that too. By the time we'd finished the second one George was leanin' over the bar telling the red-'eaded gel all about 'is 'undred quid and Bill was crying because there wasn't anyone better worth lickin' than Jack Johnson. Bill never did take 'is liquor well. We went out and then 'ad a bit o' trouble owin' to Bill punching a Lascar fireman in the Mile End Road, thinking 'e was Jack Johnson. Then 'e punched two policemen and next morning 'e 'ad to pay fifteen bob to the beak.

" Well, sir, for a week everythink went lovely. George wouldn't 'ear of Bill and me leavin' 'im and 'e wouldn't let us put our 'ands in our pockets for so much as 'arf a pint. We took a charybang ride to Windsor and George 'ired a rowboat for eighteen pence, and we got in the way of the Eton and 'Arrer boat race. Bill was rowing and finding fault with the leather studs they 'ad on the oars, and the boys was running along the bank 'ollering like mad, and an old chap with a megaphone was screechin' at Bill to get out o' the way. Bill got out o' the way o' the first three, but the fourth chap run right into us and rammed us amidships. The bow of 'is little racing boat was all crumpled up and the young toff 'e just stood off from us, swimmin' easy as a fish, and called Bill every bad name pore Bill 'ad ever 'eard, and some as 'e 'adn't. When 'e'd finished 'e swam off to the bank and Bill mopped 'is face.

" ' Gord strewth ! ' says Bill, ' did you ever 'ear the like in all your born days ? Not an 'air on 'is face and I never 'eard even the mate of a dredger use such langwidge to a dago greaser ! There's somethink in these colleges after all ! ' says Bill.

" As I said, things went fine for a week. George stood us drinks and bus rides and cab-rides, and we went to music 'alls and theayters and then 'ad more drinks. We 'ad a nice lodging, all three together. But George 'e kep' on going back to the pub with the red-'eaded gel, and though the pub was all right we didn't like the way George and the gel was getting on together.

" ' You mark my words, George,' I says, ' she's after your 'undred quid ! You didn't oughter told 'er you 'ad it ! '

" The second day she was a-callin' 'im George and the third day she was 'olding 'is 'and in the back room. Afore that she'd told 'im she was a widder and that the pub belonged to 'er, and afore the week was up she'd been and got pore George into thinking that 'avin' a red-'eaded wife and a pub at the same time would be better than being at sea. It was 'ard for me to argify agin it,' cos 'o what I'd said to 'im before about keepin' a pub. The pub was all right, but the red'-eaded gel wasn't to my way o' likin', nor Bill's neither, only every time me or Bill said as we didn't like green eyes, or that red 'air went with bad temper, or somethink tackful like that, George 'e'd flare up and say if we didn't like 'er we didn't 'ave to go into the place at all. And at the end of a week 'e'd married 'er—rather she'd married 'im.

" So Bill and me we didn't see much o' George after that until the *Mouette* sailed again and we went in 'er. Ah ! she was a lovely craft, that *Mouette* ! It was over six months afore we were back in London, and first thing Bill and me done was go along to the ' Crown and Anchor ' to see 'ow George was gettin' on. We pushed into the private bar, same as afore George got married, and the first thing we see was pore George bending down to empty the spittoons into a pail. 'E was in 'is shirt-sleeves, and it wasn't 'ard to see

2*

'as the last thing 'e'd been doing 'ad somethink to do with coal.

" ' Wot cheer, George ? ' says Bill. George drops the spittoons and pail on the floor and comes over and shakes 'ands with Bill and me as if 'e'd never stop. 'E'd fell away somethink awful ! Wot 'ad been a big young chap, full o' fun and with a jolly round face, was now as 'arassed a lookin' cove as I ever see : 'is face 'ad fell away and 'e was thinner and 'ad bags under 'is eyes and one'd ha' thought 'e was a-going to be 'ung by the look on 'is face. But 'e cheered up wunnerful to see us and was just arskin' after 'is old mates in the *Mouette* when Mrs. 'Ampson come into the private bar and stood lookin' at us. Easy to see as she wasn't pleased to see us there.

" ' Lizzie,' says George, 'umble as could be, ' I was going to ask my old mates to 'ave a drink on the 'ouse.'

" ' Why, shorely,' says Mrs. 'Ampson. ' George, give 'em each 'arf a pint of bitter.'

" 'Arf a pint ! George looked as though she'd 'it 'im, but 'e dursn't speak back to 'er. When 'e brought us our arf pints she'd gone into the public bar and George kep' listenin', like an 'unted hanimal, while 'e talked to us.

" ' She don't let me 'ave no money,' says pore George, ' so I can't buy you a drink, and I dursn't take it on the 'ouse. Wot's more, she don't let me touch a drop o' beer meself ! If a customer stands me a pot, I draw it and 'old it up and then pour it back again be'ind the bar. She don't let me go out and she don't like my pals except when they're pushin' money over the bar. She don't keep a barman nor she don't keep any 'elp except a girl. 'Cos why ? 'Cos I'm the barman and the sweeper-up and the coal man and the gas man and the wood chopper and the carpenter and the plumber ! ' says pore George. And 'e went on tellin' us 'ow 'is wife ruled 'im and wot a time 'e 'ad, until 'is wife came back again to see if we'd gorn. As soon as we see 'er we asked for a couple o' pots of ale, and asked 'er if she wouldn't 'ave a bit of somethink 'erself. But she said she 'adn't time, wot with 'avin' to go back to the bar, and old George to get on with the cleanin' up 'e'd left off when we come in. So Bill and me drank up our ale and went out quick. 'Eartrendin'.

" ' Wot George wants to do,' says Bill, ' is to give that woman a good clip on the side o' the 'ead ! '

" ' I expeck as 'e does, Bill,' I says, mournful, ' but 'e won't never do it. She's got 'im in 'and proper ! Like a little dorg 'e is ! ' We was so upset to see pore George that way that it spoilt our first evening ashore.

" The *Mouette* 'ad gorn down and was lying off Gravesend when we went back to the ' Crown and Anchor ' next time. She was sailing again in a week. George wasn't very good company, not bein' able to drink with us or go out for the evening, but 'e asked in a casual way where we was lodging and we told 'im when we was goin' to sail again. Bill and me went out to a music 'all and Bill 'ad a row with a Scotch-man and I 'ad a row with a chap as said 'e was the Scotchman's brother, and wot with makin' up the quarrel with whisky and 'avin' to carry the Scotchman's brother 'ome for about two miles and past about twenty policemen 'oo wanted to know if 'e was dead, we didn't get 'ome till pretty late. And when we went into our room we found as the landlady 'ad pulled another bed into it, and 'oo was sittin' on the chair but good old George 'Ampson !

" When we come in George stood up and larfed. 'E was dressed in 'is old sailor's slops and the same old cap on 'is 'ead, and 'e stood up and threw out 'is chest and 'eld up 'is 'ead and looked no more like the pore chap we'd spoke to that same afternoon than I did.

" ' Five quid ! ' says George, pulling out a lot 'o silver an' a few 'arf soverings and slapping them down on the table. ' Five quid ; my own money and I 'ad to steal it out o' my own bar ! To-morrer I go down to sign aboard the *Mouette*, and I don't care if she don't come back to Lunnon for twenty years ! '

" A week arter that George was 'aulin' on the mainsheet as the *Mouette* turned 'er nose into the tide on 'er way to China. I see 'im from the galley door, and of all the 'appy faces aboard that ship, George's face was the 'appiest ! That shows, don't it, sir ? that a seaman may not be the better for 'avin' money left 'im. Been the same with George 'Ampson if the 'undred quid 'ad been a thousand ; that woman would 'ave 'ad the lot ! "

Lamont made no sign of having heard and, on looking closely, Hanks saw that the American was fast asleep. For a moment his feelings suffered ; then his sharp little face brightened up and he smiled.

"It's drinking Bass as done it," he said to himself. " Bottle o' Bass and the 'ot sunshine ; send anyone to sleep, that will." He walked back towards the pantry and, forgetting Lamont, remembered the *Mouette* and his sailing ship days as a younger man : the creaking of the oaken timbers as the tall ships leaped in the wind, the seamen's chanties and the full wet sails ; the thunder of the captains and the shouting.

THE IRISHMAN OLSABUK

THE air seemed to hang heavy and leaden in that part of the tropic evening which should have been cool and pleasant. It left the passengers sweating and fidgeting upon the bridge at the time when normally, after their six o'clock " sundowner " they would have been cutting cards for their turns at the bath.

Lamont sniffed at the following wind and made a wry face.

" I don't know nothin' about tropical meteorology," he drawled, " nor I ain't in any manner o' speakin' a seafaring man, but if I was on the prairie, and translated hot to cold, I'd say it was going to snow to beat the band with a change of wind."

" I think you'd have made a good seaman, Mr. Lamont." Captain Sismey got up and sniffed to windward. " I think it's going to storm. It'll be from the North, I should think. We're just about opposite Bahia, now, and pointing our course very little west of south, so it'll come right in our stern."

They had another tot apiece, taking whisky instead of gin, and the talk veered round from pearl-fishery to boot-leggers, from boot-leggers to taxidermy, from taxidermy to white slavery, and from Lake Ontario to the Arab nomad tribes. Hadjadlian, who had probably forgotten more about Arabs than they had ever known, was below changing his clothes. Stewart, the sun-dried Anglo-African, took up the conversation.

" I can't say I know much about them, really," he said, puffing at his pipe between the words, " but I lived with them for a while. In fact, I led a crew of desert bandits. It was after I got into difficulties with the Congo Belgiques. I can't stand a Belgique ! They took a dislike to me on account of some traffic in ivory that didn't fit in with their law. I'd been elephant hunting in the southern Congo and had run foul of Belgian and Portuguese officials at the same

45

time. Well, an elephant hunter is an elephant hunter. That may sound like a damned silly remark, but the fact remains that he's generally a public enemy as far as the State officials are concerned. Unless he's a sporting chap on a big-game tour ; but then he's not an elephant hunter—he's just a chap who shoots a bull when he sees one. Be that as it may : I was in hot water in Angola, the Belgian Congo and Deutsch Ostafrika at that time. The Deutscher part of it was because I'd been gold-mining in the Mwanza country as a Boer called Smit. It was easier to be Dutch than English under the German regime. But someone found out I was English and spilled the beans and I only got across into the Congo in time to avoid a lot of awkward questions. So after all three of those roomy territories became too warm for comfort I automatically drifted up into the French Congo and, eventually, into the French Sudan.

" All this was long before the War. I was very young, pretty well fever-proof and correspondingly reckless. I somehow got up into the semi-desert and desert country north and east of Lake Chad. I knew a fair amount of Arabic. I'd learnt it on the breakwater in Port Said and used it in Zanzibar and Somaliland. And now it came back and stood me in good stead. I'm not a bad linguist for an Englishman. I suppose that's my original Scotch descent, though I've never been in Scotland. Anyway I got in with this tribe of Arab bandits simply because they were anti-French, anti-law, anti-everything and pro-loot. I made ample profession of the same faith when I found myself a sort of prisoner among them.

" I lived among them for about three years. It was a queer life. By God, it was a damned queer life ! When I go back to England I always spend a few days with a sister of mine who married a solicitor in Reading. I never find myself in Reading but I somehow begin thinking about that Arab band in the Sudanese desert—their harsh voices, their pious oaths, their bloody slaughterings and their scrupulous division of spoil from the caravans we looted.

" At the end of a couple of years I found myself the leader of the band. I never aspired to omniscience in tactics, be-cause a desert Arab knows his desert better than any white man can ever learn it, but I generally thought a bit ahead in general strategy, and perhaps I led a bolder hand in attack.

Also I made a treaty with another tribe who acted as rivals in the same line of business. After that we worked together and did much better that way.

"It may seem a queer or perhaps degraded way for a white man to spend three years. I can look back on it now, from the Reading solicitor's brother-in-law's point of view, and see that it looks very improper. But I never have loved the French. I don't love them now. I hated them then, and I was more or less a fugitive. I took my toll from the fat merchants and their *hamlas* that strung through the desert in single file of baggage camels. We would scout and spy. We would reckon on the strength of the caravans from the east and we laid our ambushes to catch them when they were disorganised amid the turmoil of camp-making, or perhaps pick a place where we could charge from some steep height into their midst unexpectedly. Their baggage camels would groan and roar and turn to fly when the guns began to shoot and they smelt the blood ; the thoroughbred *hegâna* on which we were mounted would pour silently upon them, as swift as greyhounds and as biddable as mares ; the merchants would howl and curse and shoot and call upon God and run to stand over the most costly of their merchandise. Sometimes this was pearls, gold, silk, girls, carpets or spices. If going West to East, it was male slaves, ivory, ebony, ostrich feathers, gold and rare woods. So where they made most row there we attacked in greatest force and we seldom got beaten back. Sometimes we let the caravan go forward, without further bloodshed, after taking a ransom in goods or girls. The girls seemed very content as a rule. They seemed to prefer capture by picturesque young brigands to being sold to frowzy old traders in Timbuktu. Sometimes we got badly hammered in the pursuit of banditry. When we did we left our wounded lying, as a rule, for the Arab has an abhorrence of killing a man to save him from a slower and more painful death. He can't see the white man's point of view that way. I used to do some crude surgery among our wounded, but they never quite understood the spirit of it."

"Is that how you got that slug in your neck, Stewart ? Excuse my asking." Moreton was speaking.

"It isn't a slug. I know it looks like a slug, or a chunk of shrapnel or something, but as a matter of fact it was a

Masai spear. But that is all another story, of a different place and at a different time."

" Tell it us. Have another spot and keep on jawing. None of the rest of us have got the energy."

Moreton settled himself more deeply in the bight of his canvas chair and half-closed his eyes.

" I got that in Tanganyika, since the War." Stewart swallowed half the whisky in a gulp. " I was back not far from the same part of the country that the Bosch had chased me out of in 1909. This time I was a highly respectable English prospector. Not that a prospector is ever respectable, but at any rate I wasn't especially suspect. And up in that hill country I found the most extraordinary bird that perhaps I ever met. He lived among the Masai. You all know what the Masai are : they are nomad herdsmen, and great warriors. Also they have little respect for white men. The English officials have not given them cause for much. Well, this fellow was living among them and yet not with them. He took no part in their tribal life nor any account of their circular nomadic movements. He built himself a damned great grass house, imported a couple of Swahili servants from the coast, bought some cattle from the Masai and lived the life of an independent being, all alone among the most inflammable, fearless devils on God's earth. He was an Irishman. His name was actually McKenna, and I believe he came from Monaghan, but the Masai called him Olsabuk because his huge moustaches looked like the horns of a buffalo. His servants called him Bwana Mbogo, which means the same thing in Swahili.

" Olsabuk's house was very big and very dirty. He lived rather like a pig, but he had no especial inducement to live otherwise. All round the house and the various huts and storehouses he had built the deuce of a big stockade of great limbs and trunks of trees, so strongly built and nailed together that only a monkey or a leopard could have got over them. And inside the stockade he had about a hundred of the finest dogs I have ever seen in my life. He let them breed pretty well haphazard, and there were quite a few weeds among them, but for the most part they were great hard thirty-inch devils with teeth like wolves, vicious as wild dogs and with great stiff ruffs of hair all down their spines. Olsabuk used them for hunting lion.

" I've always been a good hand with tykes, and that was how Olsabuk and I got acquainted first. I'd been prospecting not far off his place and walked in there one day. His stockade gate was open and all the dogs rushed out on me. Olsabuk came sauntering out to see that they didn't eat me up. I don't think he cared a damn whether they did or not. But when he saw the big savage brutes chumming up to me he said I must be a good chap or they'd have torn me to pieces. Then he asked me to make his place my headquarters, and I did.

" Olsabuk was entirely self-supporting and scarcely ever did a stroke of work. He had his two Swahili servants. He killed eland and buffalo meat for his dogs ; his needs were simple ; he had his herd of cows and a couple of herdsmen, and he killed three elephants a year on his resident's hunting licence. I don't know how many elephants he really killed, but I know he never sold a tusk weighing less than eighty pounds. That kept him in everything he wanted and left something pretty substantial over. He was a big strong man, though no longer a youngster. There must have been something about him that appealed to the Masai girls. Anyway they used to come round to his place pretty regularly. Olsabuk told me that was the only kind of liberality he ever accepted from the Masai. I can't say that they ever appealed to me at all, although they were of good shape and very young, but their stinking-dyed hair and heavily bangled arms made them rather revolting. But Olsabuk seemed to like them.

" Just once in a while the Masai warriors would work themselves up into something of a frenzy about the way the girls used to call on Olsabuk. In that tribe, as a general rule, the very young girls live with the warriors until they are old enough for motherhood. Then they are married off to the ' old men.' Anything over thirty is an ' old man.' He ceases to be a warrior and becomes a cattle owner and a councillor in the tribal councils. So the young fellows used to come round to argue with Olsabuk. They had only one argument and that was with the spear. Olsabuk had his one argument, and that was to get inside his stockade, turn all his dogs loose inside it, and wait until their wrath had died down. Sometimes he would harangue them from inside the stockade, and he had the Irish gift of the gab in

Masai as well as most Irishmen have it in English. He'd
play on them as he liked and wait as long as they liked.
Then he'd go out, tell his dogs to keep quiet, and everything
would be friendly until next time. A precarious sort of
existence. I asked him once what would happen if he was
attacked while he was out alone and unprotected. He
laughed and said : ' Why, then I wud be desthroyed entirely.
Unless it might be that I cud find some argymint to convince
them.' Then he laughed again.

" I asked him that question before one of these periodical
attacks caught the both of us outside the stockade. They
only happened about twice a year and it was the only one I
saw. We'd been hunting and had killed an eland and two
hartebeest for the dogs and ourselves. Two nights before
that there had been a considerable invasion of Masai girls.
Olsabuk had sent them all away quite satisfied ; he was an
adequate old bird. Well, that started the young men on
the warpath, and they caught us just outside the stockade.
They came at us with spears, all ready for slaughter without
explanation. A Masai looks an ugly devil when he comes
at you with uplifted spear. The thing has a long thin blade
and is very heavy, and he can kill a lion with it every time.
His eyes flash white in the brown face and his red pigtail
makes him look devilish. We both had guns, but Olsabuk
hollered out : ' Whatever ye do, dinnot shoot ! ' So I
grabbed a damned great pole that lay handy and laid about
me with that. Olsabuk took his ·401 by the muzzle and
swung it like a club. We fought our way back to the mouth
of the stockade, and when we got inside he fired a shot over
their heads to give us time to bar the entrance. The Masai
don't like bullets. Then he turned all the dogs loose inside.
Before we got clear I got the spear through my neck that's
left this ugly mark.

" Then Olsabuk got up on the roof of a hut and talked to
those blood-mad devils outside. The Masai don't throw their
spears, so he was safe enough away outside stabbing range.
He talked to them and talked to them, and I could hear the
Irish tone coming out in that Masai lingo that I didn't
understand. And by and by an occasional deep-chested
chuckle would come from one warrior or another ; finally
he had the whole lot laughing uproariously. Then they
lifted their spears, cried out something with flashing grins,

and went back to their camp. I asked Olsabuk, while he was cleaning out my wound, what he had said to switch their tempers round so completely. He said he had been describing, in hideous detail, the ravages of the blow-flies that would certainly get into the spear-wound they had given me. Then he had called upon the God of the Masai and any man present to bear witness that no blow-flies had ever resulted from his more gentle dealings with their girls. That touched their sense of humour. Knowing what I do know about the native African, that was the best if not the only line of diplomacy he could have taken. I left the district not long after that. The Masai have probably killed Olsabuk long ago. And they have probably been mourning his death ever since."

"How like an Irishman," said Moreton.

VICTOR BRIDGES

The Ordeal by Water
Full-back for England
The Nadir Bandar

 VICTOR BRIDGES has been a bank
clerk, an actor, a journalist, an editor,
and secretary of the Boy Scouts, before
taking to novel-writing. As a novelist,
his greatest successes have generally
been connected with the sea, and his
popularity is shown by the fact that
his works have been translated into
ten languages.

THE ORDEAL BY WATER

WHEN I pushed open the door of the restaurant, the first person I saw was Tommy. He was lunching with another man, and, as usual, conversing with such vigorous cheerfulness that he failed to notice my arrival. I walked up to him, and laid my hand on his shoulder.

" Hallo, Tommy," I said. " I thought you were in Timbuctoo."

He spun round.

" Well I'm jiggered ! " he cried. Then, with that artless directness that so endears him to strangers, he added impetuously, " What the dickens are you doing in this Godforsaken place ? "

An eminent Bristolian at the next table snorted audibly.

" I was just going to ask you the same question," I replied, " only in rather more tactful language. I'm here on business."

" Sit down," said Tommy, clutching me by the wrist and dragging me into a vacant chair. " This is Mortimer— Jimmy Mortimer, of the Gold Coast. We're motoring and you've got to join us."

" May I have some lunch first ? " I asked, bowing politely to Mr. Mortimer.

" Why, of course," said Tommy cheerfully. " You're feeding with us. Here, waiter, waiter, get this gentleman some lunch."

" Look here," he added, as the waiter slid off to fulfil the order, " do you know anything about salmon fishing ? "

" In theory," I said, " I know everything. Why ? "

" Because as soon as you've finished we're going to take you up to Hereford for a couple of days on the best salmon river in England."

I turned to Mortimer.

" Much lager," I said, " has made him mad."

Tommy chuckled.

55

" I'm not joking. I've got two miles of the finest private fishing on the Wye from Saturday to Monday, and a bungalow chucked in."

Mortimer nodded his head.

" That's right," he added.

I gazed at Tommy in mingled amazement and admiration.

" My dear Tommy," I said, " no one appreciates your powers of acquisition more than I do, but how the devil did you manage it ? "

Tommy lit a cigar with some contentment.

" It was a reward for a kind action," he explained. " The place belongs to an old boy called Quinn—Sir Cuthbert Quinn. I ran across him last week in a country lane near Bedford, trying to find out what was the matter with his car. He'd been trying for some time. Well, I hopped out and put things straight—it was only a choked jet, but he was so grateful that he insisted on my coming back to lunch with him. While we were lunching, we got on the subject of salmon fishing. I happened to say how keen I was, and then he trotted out the fact that he owned an island with a bungalow on it and two miles of the best fishing above Symond's Yat. ' Would you like a week-end there ? ' he said. ' I should,' said I, ' very much.' Well, to cut a long yarn short, he handed me over the key, and told me I could come up for a couple of days and bring another rod with me. I couldn't think of anyone else at the time, so I wired for Mortimer."

" Thanks," said Mortimer dryly.

" Well, as you've got Mortimer," I observed, " you can't take me."

" Oh, that's all right," put in Mortimer ; " I don't fish. I've only come for the charm of Tommy's conversation."

" I haven't got a rod," I objected.

" That doesn't matter," said Tommy, " neither have I. But there are two up there which old Quinn said we could use."

" How are we going to manage about grub ? " I asked.

Mortimer laughed.

" The car's stuffed with it," he said, " especially drink."

That decided me.

" I'll come," I said, " but you'll have to call for my traps. I'm staying up in Clifton, so it's all on the way."

" Good ! " cried Tommy. " You buck up and finish your lunch, while we go round to the garage and get the car."

The car, when it arrived, proved to be a 12–14 De Dion, which had apparently been a stranger to the sunny land of France for many strenuous years. In colour it had once been green.

" Not much to look at," said Tommy apologetically ; " but she goes—eh, Mortimer ? "

" She would if I had her," admitted Mortimer, " for what she'd fetch."

Knowing, however, of Tommy's amazing genius for coaxing motion out of discarded scrap-iron, I got in behind without a qualm. With a fanfare on the horn, we slid out of the garage, and then, clanking like an ironmonger's shop in an earthquake, pounded bravely up Park Street at a surprising velocity.

It only took me about five minutes to cast my week-end trappings into a Gladstone bag and square accounts with the worthy lady at whose house I had been staying. Then off we thundered again through the peaceful respectabilities of Clifton and Redland, out on to the far-flung road that wanders northwards up the Severn Valley.

If the *Zeitgeist* had any particular purpose when it tossed Tommy's atoms together, it must have been the production of a super-chauffeur. Amazingly erratic as he is in other things, his driving and handling of a car more nearly approaches perfection than any human effort I know. In other hands the hired wreckage that bore our fortunes would, I feel sure, have collapsed hopelessly long before we reached Gloucester. But Tommy, who, according to Mortimer, had pored lovingly over it with a spanner for several hours that morning, lifted it triumphantly, if complainingly, through all demands. At half-past six, dusty and incredibly vociferous, it clattered into Ross, and, practically speaking, our journey was accomplished.

We had a cup of tea at the hotel there, and then in the cool of the evening clanked on cheerfully through the thickly wooded lanes that led to Sir Cuthbert Quinn's bungalow. The distance must have been about six miles, and it was while we were covering this that we got on to the question of how great a strain a salmon rod would stand. Tommy had been telling us some yarn about how a man he knew had jerked a fifteen-pound salmon clean out of the water, and I had ventured to cast a little mild doubt on the accuracy of the tale. Tommy had been quite indignant.

" Why, of course it's possible," he had declared. " A salmon rod will stand almost any strain. The best swimmer in the world would be quite helpless if you hooked him by a belt round his middle."

" Get out, Tommy," I said derisively ; " he'd break you every time."

" I bet you he wouldn't," said Tommy. " Look here, you get a good swimmer—anyone you like, I don't care who he is—and I'll bet you five pounds I'll land him in under half an hour."

" Done with you," I replied. " And what's more, I'll bet you another fiver he breaks your line inside of five minutes."

Mortimer chuckled.

" There's money in this," he observed. " We'd better advertise it in the *Sportsman* and charge for seats. We might make quite a decent thing out of it."

As he spoke we rattled round the corner of a deeply embedded lane, and, of a sudden, the Wye lay before us, gleaming like silver in its cool green valley.

" That's the bungalow," said Tommy, pointing to a low, red-tiled building which one could just catch a glimpse of through the trees. " The boat-house must be just below us."

We trundled delicately down the hill, for the road rather resembled the traditional highway to Zion, and pulled up outside a solid-looking building on the banks of the river.

Tommy stopped the engine, and we all clambered out. The island lay exactly opposite, its neatly painted landing-stage facing us across the water.

" Why, there's the boat ! " exclaimed Mortimer suddenly. " Over there by the steps—look ! "

He pointed towards the island, and following his gesture, we all saw a small dinghy apparently tied up to one of the willows that fringed the bank.

We stared at it in amazement.

" Well, that's funny," I said. " How did it get there ? There must be someone on the island."

" Oh no," said Tommy. " Why, I had a card from old stick-in-the-mud only yesterday saying that it was all clear. There's probably another boat of some kind in the shed."

He took the key out of his pocket, and, thrusting it into the lock, flung open the door. The place was as empty as a barn.

Mortimer laughed.

" Your aged friend seems to be a bit of a humorist, Tommy."

" There *must* be someone there," I said. " Most likely it's the gardener. Let's go outside and give him a hail."

We stepped out on to the bank, where Tommy let off a vigorous yell, while I played an impressive voluntary on the horn.

" That ought to bring him out of his shell," observed Mortimer with approval.

As a matter of fact, it did nothing of the kind. The island remained as blissfully untroubled as the garden of Proserpine.

" Try again," suggested Mortimer encouragingly, and we repeated our efforts with the same result.

" I'm getting fed up with this," broke out Tommy. " There's only one thing to do, and that's to swim across and fetch the boat."

" What a pity we haven't got a salmon rod," I remarked. " We might kill two birds with one stone."

" Don't you worry," retorted Tommy. " We'll try that later."

He stripped off his clothes, and going to the edge of the bank, inspected the water.

" Seems clear enough," he observed ; " here goes."

There was a mighty splash, and he disappeared from view, emerging a few moments later well out in the river. Mortimer and I gave him an encouraging cheer, and then watched him with some anxiety as he ploughed his way across the strongly running current. It seemed at first as though he would be swept past the island, but, with a big effort, he just managed to get clear of the stream in time and clutch an overhanging bough some way below the landing-stage. Then he drew himself out, and answering our hail with a triumphant wave of the hand, picked his way gingerly along the bank to where the boat was tethered.

Unhitching the rope, he climbed in, and with a few strong pulls, sculled back across the river.

" Bravo, Leander ! " sung out Mortimer, as the boat

bumped up against the bank. " How are you feeling after your great effort ? "

" Deuced sore," returned Tommy, shipping his oars and stepping out on to the grass. " That seat's as hard as a millstone."

" Never mind," I said consolingly. " You'll be too busy cooking the dinner to want to sit down. What shall we do with the car ? "

" Oh, run her into the boat-house," said Tommy. " There's plenty of room there. And then you might shove the grub into the boat."

Mortimer and I carried out his instructions. With the expenditure of considerable energy and language, we trundled that decayed scrap-iron into the shed, and then began to transfer its contents to the bottom of the dinghy.

By this Tommy had resumed his clothes and come to our assistance.

" I can't make it out, all the same," said Mortimer reflectively. " If there's no one on the island, how the devil did the boat get there ? Old Quinn must have got off somehow last time he left."

" Perhaps he's a Christian Scientist, and just wished himself ashore," suggested Tommy. " Anyhow it's no good worrying about miracles. Catch on to this, and that's the lot."

He pushed over a bulky case of soda-water, which Mortimer, still frowning thoughtfully to himself, tucked under one arm, and carrying the remaining stores between us, we made our way down to the dinghy.

" I'll take the oars," I said ; " it's just my distance."

" Don't overtire yourself," put in Tommy kindly. " Remember there's a stiff stream running."

" If you find it too much for you," added Mortimer, " we can always get out and walk."

Disregarding such ragged efforts at humour, I pushed off from the bank ; and then, setting a course well up against the current, slowly tugged my precious freight over to the island. With the true instinct of a waterman, I hit the landing-stage exactly ; in fact, I hit it so hard that Tommy, who was injudiciously standing up, was as nearly as possible precipitated into the water.

" He thinks it's a bumping race," said Mortimer. " That's the worst of these 'Varsity men. Here, catch hold."

He flung the rope to Tommy, who had jumped out on to the step, and in half a minute the boat was hitched up tight to a convenient post.

Mortimer and I handed out the goods, which Tommy received and piled up on the shore. When we were finally unloaded we also disembarked, and, picking up as much as we could carry, mounted the wooden steps that led to the front door of the bungalow. Tommy inserted the key, and flung it open.

" Here we are," he said. " Not such a dusty sort of shanty, is it ? "

The eulogy was by no means excessive. Whatever else Mr. Quinn may have lacked, he certainly had a nice eye for his surroundings. The large, low-ceilinged apartment, with its white walls, old-fashioned furniture, and big, green-tiled hearth, combined in the happiest degree the claims of comfort and good taste. From the main room a door on the left led into the kitchen, while at the back an arched space gave access to a passage from which the three bedrooms opened off.

" What's the programme now ? " asked Mortimer.

" I don't know what you chaps feel like," said Tommy, " but I'm uncommon hungry. I vote we start by having some grub right away."

Mortimer held up his hand.

" Carried unanimously," I said.

" Right-ho ! " responded Tommy. " There's a cold chicken somewhere in the baggage. You chaps might unpack while I forage about the kitchen and get things ready."

He disappeared through the door, taking off his coat, and Mortimer and I set to work upon the various packages which we had brought with us. We unearthed an appetising-looking fowl, a ham, two or three nice crusty loaves, a jar of butter, and numerous other aids to successful salmon fishing, including enough beer and whisky to stock a modest hotel.

We were contemplating the latter in a kind of pleased reverie, when Tommy came back with a tablecloth under his arm, and a trayload of accessories.

" I say," he began, " it's deuced funny, but I can't find any forks and spoons. Plenty of glasses and plates and knives, but not another bally thing in the place."

Mortimer burst out laughing.

" I expect your aged friend eats with his fingers," he said.

" Or else someone's been in and cleared the lot," I suggested.

" Oh, they can't have done that," said Tommy ; " or else the boat wouldn't be here."

" Well, we shall have to do what we can without," remarked Mortimer. " You fellows can tear off a leg each, and I'll have the pickings."

We pulled out a table into the centre of the room, and while I helped Mortimer arrange the feast, Tommy went into the kitchen to have another look for the missing silver.

His efforts proved as barren as before, and finally abandoning the attempt, we settled ourselves down to do as well as we could with knives and fingers.

" Here's to our week-end," said Tommy, holding up a glass of Bass. " And death to the salmon."

" Death to the salmon," I repeated hopefully, raising my glass in turn.

We were just drinking the toast, when Mortimer suddenly sat bolt upright in his chair and glanced quickly round behind him.

" What's the matter ? " I asked.

" 'Sh ! " he whispered. " Go on talking loudly. Don't stop whatever you do."

We followed his instructions, watching him with amazement as he jumped up noiselessly from his chair, and crept like a cat across the room as far as the archway. Here he stopped, bending down and listening intently, with his hand to his ear.

When he turned, his face was alight with excitement. He came swiftly back, signalling to us to keep up the conversation.

" There's someone getting out of one of the bedroom windows," he whispered across the table. " Don't stop talking, but get to the door, and make a sudden rush for it. We're bound to catch him."

A smile of holy joy irradiated Tommy's countenance. Next to wrestling with a motor-car, a physical difference of opinion with a fellow-creature appeals to him more than anything else in the world. He leapt up, and instantly assumed command.

" You and Mortimer take the left ; I'll go the other way. Buck up, or the blighter will have scooted."

Before he had finished speaking he had reached the door, clearing the steps with a single jump and bursting his way through the shrubs like a rather reckless rhinoceros.

Further strategy being apparently out of place, Mortimer and I followed as rapidly as we could. Darting up the path that ran round the other side of the house, we emerged into the clearing behind, just in time to see an unknown gentleman hurl himself frantically into the fringe of undergrowth that lined the opposite bank.

In a moment Tommy, who was hard on his heels, had plunged in after him. There was a shout, and then the dull thud of two heavily falling bodies.

" Come on," roared Tommy. " I've got him."

As he spoke, Mortimer tripped over the root of a tree and went sprawling full length on the grass. I did not wait, but, leaping over a tangle of blackberry bush that barred the path, pressed on gallantly to Tommy's assistance.

I found him tied up in an amazing network of agitated arms and legs. As far as I could see, the stranger was underneath, and from the somewhat unpleasant sounds which were rising into the air, I gathered that he was finding some difficulty in breathing.

" Sit on his head," hissed Tommy's voice. " Take care he doesn't bite you. He's as strong as a horse."

I was attempting to carry out his instructions when, with a mighty effort, our visitor jerked himself clear enough to speak.

" All right, guv'nor," he gasped. " I gives in."

He ceased to struggle, and, panting but triumphant, we released our respective grips.

At that moment Mortimer arrived on the scene. He looked down on us with a smile.

" Well, you seem to have got him all right," he said. " Who is it ? "

Tommy mopped his forehead with the back of his hand.

" I think it's Sandow," he replied. " Get up, my friend, and let's have a squint at you."

The stranger rose rather stiffly into a sitting posture. " You've 'alf choked me, guv'nor," he said reproachfully, putting his hand to his neck. " You 'adn't no call to 'andle me like that."

We all three burst out laughing.

" I'm sorry," said Tommy gravely. " I was under the impression that you were trying to kick me in the stomach."

The stranger grinned, and somewhat painfully clambered to his feet.

He was a massively built man of about forty, swarthy and black-bearded, and clothed in the conventional rags of a case-hardened tramp.

" Suppose we adjourn to the bungalow," I suggested. " I'm sure we all want a drink after this little romp."

Tommy took the stranger's arm and tucked it affectionately under his in that unbreakable clasp invented by the Japanese. Then, dishevelled and slightly out of breath, we retraced our steps to the house.

" Where will Mr. Sandow sit ? " I inquired, as soon as we were all assembled in the front room.

" I would suggest somewhere not too near the door," said Mortimer. " I'm getting too old for these sudden bursts of speed."

" This will do," said Tommy, pulling up a rush-seated wooden chair with his foot. " Take a pew, my friend."

He dumped the stranger down into the seat, and as he did so there came from the latter's pocket the muffled but quite distinct chink of silver.

" There is music in the air," observed Mortimer thoughtfully.

" By gad," cried Tommy, " those must be our spoons. Trot 'em out, my son ; the game's up, you know."

Somewhat reluctantly, the stranger inserted his hand into the gaping orifice which served him as a pocket, and drew out a large number of spoons wrapped up in a duster. He laid them on the table.

" Thank you," said Tommy ; " and now if we may trouble you for the forks—ah, much obliged."

The forks followed, similarly protected, the stranger all

the time throwing little furtive glances round the room, first
at one of us and then at the other.

While this interesting operation was in progress I had been
occupying myself mixing drinks. I offered one to Tommy,
but he waved it aside.

" A guest," he said, " especially an uninvited one, should
always be served first."

I handed the tumbler to the stranger, who accepted it
with a grin and a nod.

" And now," said Tommy, when we were all three similarly
equipped, " I think it would be more friendly if we knew
something about each other." He turned to the stranger.
" Wouldn't you like to tell us your name, old sport ? "

Our visitor looked at him cunningly.

" Me, guv'nor ? " he said. " I'm the Dook o' Wellington."

" Ah ! " replied Tommy politely. " I was sure I'd seen
your face somewhere. If you won't think me inquisitive,
may I ask what brought you to the island ? "

The duke took a long drink. Then he jerked his thumb
towards the steps.

" That there ruddy boat, guv'nor," he replied casually.

" I said so," cried Mortimer. " Now perhaps you'll
apologise, Tommy."

" What I want to know," I interrupted, " is why you
didn't clear out when you heard us on the bank."

The duke eyed me contemptuously.

" And 'ave you raisin' the 'ole bloomin' country on me.
I *don't* think ! "

" No, no," broke in Mortimer ; " his grace is a sound
tactician. If he could have cut off with the boat and left
us here, he'd have been in clover."

" As it is," I observed, " he's in the soup."

" Still, it wasn't much good your making for the other
side of the island," went on Mortimer, addressing our guest.
" You couldn't get off that way."

" Ho, couldn't I ? " remarked the duke, with some scorn.
" If I'd 'a' got to the bank fust you'd 'ave know'd all about
that. It'd take six o' your sort to ketch me in the
water."

Tommy brought his hand down on the table with a sudden
bang that made us all jump.

" By Jove," he cried, " here's the very man we want !

3

Listen here, Whiskers. Suppose we find a way of settling this little business without handing you over to the police, eh ? "

The duke blinked at him without any visible sign of emotion.

" Wotjer gettin' at ? " he inquired imperturbably.

" Well, the fact is," explained Tommy, " I've got a little wager with the distinguished-looking gentleman in the arm-chair. I've bet him that I could land the best swimmer in the world with a salmon rod inside of half an hour."

" 'Ave yer, guv'nor ? " observed the duke. " Then ye can 'take it from me yer on a loser."

I gave a gentle laugh, which obviously nettled Tommy.

" Perhaps you think you could get away ? " he said.

The duke finished his whisky with some deliberation, and set down the empty glass on the floor.

" Think ! " he repeated. " I'm blinking well sure as no blinking salmon rod would 'old me 'arf a blinking minit." (" Blinking " was not the precise word that he used, but it will serve.)

Tommy turned to me with a grin.

" D'you feel like taking it on ? " he asked.

I looked the duke over with a critical eye.

" Yes," I said ; " I'll risk it."

" Well, let's put it to him," said Tommy. " Look here, my friend, if you're so cocksure I can't land you, what d'you say to my having a shot at it ? "

The duke glanced suspiciously round the circle.

" Wot do I get out of it ? " he demanded.

" You get out of going to quod,"replied Tommy. " What-ever happens, we'll land you on the bank afterwards and let you clear off. That's a bargain."

" And what's more," I put in, " I'll lay you a pound to nothing that you don't break the line."

" Ye might make it a couple o' quid, guv'nor," observed his grace pathetically. " It's worth that to 'ave a damn great salmon 'ook shoved in yer."

There was a roar of laughter from all three of us.

" Well, he's a sportsman," I said, " whatever else he is." Then, turning to the duke, I explained that the performance would not be of quite such a realistic nature as he imagined. " We'll lend you a belt," I said, " and fasten the line to that.

Then all you'll have to do will be to dive in and see if you can get clear."

He rose with some alacrity.

" Ho, if that's all, I'm bloomin' well on ! It's a walk over, guv'nor—that's wot it is, a ruddy walk over."

" He can have my belt," said Tommy, unstrapping the article in question and tossing it across. " I'll go and get a salmon rod. They're hanging up in the passage."

He stepped through the archway, and took down a rod from the row of pegs, carrying it out through the side door into the garden, where we all three joined him.

Both Mortimer and I felt hugely excited, but neither the duke nor Tommy betrayed any special emotion.

" You'd better take your Sunday suit off," said the latter. " It'll give you a better chance."

The duke shook his head.

" I'll just shift me boots," he announced. " The water won't 'urt these 'ere duds."

" On the contrary," said Mortimer unkindly, " it ought to do 'em a bit of good. But you'll find it devilish wet walking afterwards."

" They'll dry quick enough," replied the duke, " with this 'ere sun."

He sat down on the bank and removed the decayed shreds of leather that decorated his feet. Then with some care he fastened Tommy's belt round his waist.

" How are you going to fix the line ? " I inquired.

" That's simple enough," said Tommy. " There's a ring at the back, you see. I'll take off the hook and fasten the gut to that."

He suited the action to the word, and in about five minutes the operation was completed. Tommy tested his handiwork with two or three stiff jerks, which the duke resisted by sitting peacefully on the ground.

" Can he have the benefit of the stream ? " I asked. " If so, this side of the island is the best."

" Oh yes," said Tommy. " I'll give you every chance. All I bargain is that Mortimer stands by with a walking-stick. If I get him close in enough to be touched, I've won the bet."

" Right you are," I agreed. " That's fair."

The duke got up and inspected the stream.

" You can choose your own place," said Tommy. " Only
let's know when you're going to dive."

" Hold on," I said suddenly. " I'd better bring the boat
round. We don't want the chap to drown, and if he gets
loose in this stream he'll never fetch the island again."

I ran back to the steps, and, getting into the dinghy,
tugged her round to where the others were standing. There
I caught hold of a branch and steadied myself against
the bank.

" When you're ready," I called out.

With delightful coolness the duke sauntered to the edge,
where the river was deepest.

" All right, guv'nor ? " he inquired, looking back over his
shoulder at Tommy.

The latter nodded, planting himself firmly on the grass,
with his legs well apart.

There was a short pause, and then suddenly the tattered
figure on the bank shot outwards and downwards, taking
the water with a splash that sent the spray flying in all
directions. Tommy took a step forward, and the line went
screaming out like an angry wasp.

Tense with excitement, Mortimer and I stared at the spot
where the duke had disappeared. He came up some ten
yards farther on. The line was still fastened to his back,
but without a moment's hesitation he set off downstream,
swimming with a vigorous overhand stroke that carried him
along rapidly in the swift-running water.

He must have covered about twenty-five yards before
Tommy made his first attempt to check him. We saw the
line tighten suddenly, and the point of the rod bend double
beneath the strain. The effect on the duke was instantaneous. Ceasing to swim, he spun round in the water,
and lay on his back apparently as helpless as a floating log.

Very carefully Tommy began to wind him in. Nearer
and nearer he came, jerking along through the broken water,
and making no attempt to resist. For a moment I thought
it was all over, and then, just as Mortimer was creeping
down the bank with the stick in his hand, there came another
sharp " whir " from the reel, and away went the quarry
down the stream as vigorously as a fresh-run salmon.

" Look out ! " yelled Mortimer. " He's making for the
rock ! "

Away to the left a crest of grey stone reared itself above swirling waters. Towards this the duke was swimming rapidly with the evident intention of fouling the line.

Tommy saw the danger, and just at the right moment put on the check. The duke halted abruptly, paused for a moment just where he was, then, suddenly rising high in the water, dived beneath the surface like a dog-otter. There was a sharp snick, the rod jerked back with a swirl of flying line, and Tommy sat down abruptly on the bank.

With a shout of triumph I grabbed my oars, and, shoving off the boat from the bank, sped hastily to the rescue.

I was just in time. Exhausted apparently by his great effort, the duke was drifting feebly down the current, devoting his remaining energies to keeping his head above water. I grabbed him by the collar, and, with a mighty haul succeeded in lifting him up like some enervated porpoise over the side of the dinghy. With a grunt he collapsed on the seat, and, putting all my strength into it, I tugged our craft back to the island.

Tommy, who is a sportsman to the backbone, was standing on the bank with a stiff whisky and soda, which he had secured from the bungalow.

" Here you are, Captain Webb," he said. " Get this down your neck, and you'll feel better."

The duke took the glass and shifted its contents without a tremor.

" I'm all right, guv'nor," he said ; " but you nearly 'ad me."

Tommy laughed and shook his head.

" Let's see where it broke," he said, turning his late quarry round so as to examine the belt. " By Jove ! Just about the ring, and as clean as a whistle ! Well, we'd better fix you up with a dry shirt before you go. I've got one I can spare you."

" Thank ye, guv'nor," said the duke. " I could do with a shirt."

Tommy disappeared into the house, returning a moment later with the garment and a bottle of whisky.

" Take this too," he said ; " it'll keep the cold out."

I groped in my pocket and produced a sovereign.

" Here you are," I added, handing it to my guest. " I'll row you ashore."

We got back into the boat, the duke hugging his whisky and his shirt ; and, steering a course a little upstream, I pulled him over to the opposite bank. Tommy and Mortimer stood on the island waving us farewell.

When we reached our destination, I stood up and offered him my hand.

" Good-bye, old friend," I said. " Thank you for winning my bet."

Very slowly he withdrew a hand from his pocket, and with a sideways glance at the island opened it so that I could see its contents.

" I'd never 'ave done it, guv'nor," he said hoarsely, " if it 'adn't 'a' bin for these 'ere wire-nippers."

FULL-BACK FOR ENGLAND

VERY quietly the long reeds that hedged the Okestock football field were parted aside, and a face peered cautiously
through, taking a long and careful survey of the immediate
neighbourhood. The face belonged to Mr. William Yard,
known to his more intimate friends in London as " Pills,"
and to the police as one of the most daring and successful
burglars of the day.

A reason for Mr. Yard's prudence was not hard to find :
the briefest glance at his khaki-coloured clothes, plentifully
dotted with broad arrows, made it quite evident that for the
time, at all events, any form of publicity would be painful
to him.

The fact was that on the previous afternoon Mr. Yard
had accomplished the remarkable feat of escaping from
Dartmoor. An unexpected mist sweeping down over the
granite-studded hill-side when he was at work had suddenly inspired him with the idea of making a dash for liberty.
Without further thought he had flung down his spade and
bolted into its shelter, before either of the nearest warders
had been able to stop him. It is true that a couple of charges
of buckshot had whistled by, unpleasantly close to his legs,
but they had only served to add to his already useful turn
of speed. By the time the other convicts had been collected,
and the mist had lifted sufficiently for the warders to see
what they were doing, Mr. Yard was some two miles away
in the opposite direction from which he had started, safely
hidden in a small plantation that fringed the main road to
Okestock.

Here he had stayed until nightfall, expecting any minute
to be routed out by a party of pursuing warders. No one
had turned up, however, his ingenious idea of throwing a
circle while the mist still concealed him having apparently
put them temporarily off the scent.

Under cover of darkness he had stolen from his hiding-

place, and, following the main road at a judicious distance,
tramped doggedly on mile after mile, until the lights of
Okestock some hundred feet below him had shown him that
he had reached the boundaries of the moor.

Utterly dead beat, he had felt tempted to throw himself
down on the open heather and snatch a few hours' rest.
But the dread of discovery had urged him on, and, clamber-
ing cautiously down the hill-side, he had made his way along
the deserted road until he had reached the wire fence which
bounded the Okestock football ground. Here a stray gleam
of moonlight coming out between the clouds had shown him
the patch of long, reedy grass behind the goal-posts. With a
last effort he had crept into its shelter, and dropped almost
instantly into a profound sleep.

It was the sun which had woke him up eventually, a
bright yellow winter sun shining down out of a sky of
cloudless blue. For a moment Mr. Yard had rubbed his
eyes and stared at it with amazement ; then with a sudden
shock he had remembered he was no longer a guest of the
Government. He had tried to scramble up, but his numbed
limbs had refused to support him, and with a groan he had
fallen back again, feeling rather like a trapped rabbit waiting
the arrival of the keeper.

A few minutes' energetic rubbing, however, had been
sufficient to restore both his circulation and his confidence,
and it was then that he had pulled aside the reeds and
peered out in the discreet manner already described.

The first thing that met his eyes was the football pavilion,
a small wooden building on the left of the ground. Instantly
the possibilities of a change of clothes jumped into his mind.

" There's bound to be some clobber kicking about in
there," he muttered to himself. " Wonder if I can get in
without bein' nabbed ? "

That, as Hamlet would have said, was the question. The
public road, as he remembered from last night, ran right
alongside the ground, and, to judge by the sun, the time
was already past ten o'clock. Still, it was no good lying
like a hunted rat among the reeds. It was a case of neck or
nothing, and Mr. Yard was not the man to fail at a crisis.

Licking his blue lips, he raised himself to a crouching
position, and then, with a care which would have done credit
to a Boy Scout, elevated his head above the top of the reeds.

So far as he could see in each direction, the road was empty. Hesitating no longer, he crept out from his hiding-place, and, bending almost double, covered the distance between the goal and the pavilion in almost the same time that it takes to read these words.

The door was in front, facing the yard; but Mr. Yard did not trouble about this recognised means of entrance. He hurried round to the back, where he found a small window just large enough to admit a man's body. It was shut, of course; but this was a trifling obstacle to a gentleman of his experience. In about half a minute he had forced it open, and, pulling himself up by the sill, scrambled through and dropped on to the floor.

He found himself in a small matchboard apartment, set round with wooden lockers. There were also various pegs from which were suspended one or two mud-stained jerseys and sweaters, an old greatcoat, and a couple of pairs of blue football shorts, distinctly the worse for wear.

To Mr. Yard's eyes, however, they were more welcome and attractive than the flowers in May. Stripping himself of his broad-arrowed costume with feverish rapidity, he hastily arrayed himself in the somewhat less conspicuous costume of a British footballer, minus the stockings and boots. A hurried search through the lockers revealed both these luxuries, with the aid of which he promptly proceeded to complete his outfit.

" Lor' ! " he chuckled, surveying himself with satisfaction in the broken bit of looking-glass that hung from the wall. " I never thought I should be wearin' footer kit again. It's like old days ! "

There was no time for sentiment, however, and Mr. Yard was not slow in realising the fact. Grabbing the greatcoat from its peg, he was just about to make for the window when a sudden shout outside brought him to an abrupt halt.

" Hallo, Tubby ! " sang out a cheery voice.

Like a cat Mr. Yard stole to the window. Some thirty yards away a young man with a bag in his hand was advancing towards the pavilion across the next field.

Swiftly and noiselessly the convict crossed the floor to the other side of the apartment, and peeped through a crack in the boards. Another young man with another bag in his hand was approaching from the roadway.

3*

Mr. Yard swore, softly but fervently.

" Pipped ! " he said ; " pipped on the post ! "

For a second he hesitated, and then, returning to the spot where he had dressed, picked up his late garments and stuffed them into one of the lockers and shut the lid.

Having done this he sat down and waited events.

" I've got the key, Tubby ! " called out the same aggressively jovial voice.

" Righto ! " responded the other. " D'you know this bally window's open ? "

There was a grating in the lock.

" That's that old ass Smith again ! " said the cheerful voice. " I told him to shut it."

Mr. Yard rose to his feet. If he had to be captured he would at least enjoy the memory of one really magnificent scrap. There was a sharp click, a bump, and then the door swung open.

" Hallo ! " exclaimed the young man with the bag.

" Hallo ! " returned Mr. Yard coolly.

The new-comer stared at him for a moment in amazement, and then, with a sudden smile, put down his bag and advanced towards him.

" Mr. Logan, I suppose," he said. " This is awfully good of you. I'd just made up my mind we should have to play one short."

He put out his hand, which Mr. Yard grasped and shook heartily.

At that moment the other young man entered.

" This is Logan, Tubby ! " exclaimed the first. " He's turned up, after all."

" Good man ! " exclaimed Tubby. " But how the dickens did you get in ? "

" Through the window," explained Mr. Yard truthfully.

" That's the style," laughed the other. " Jack, why weren't you here to receive your guests ? I suppose you came over in Sam's cart ? "

Mr. Yard, who was trying desperately hard to get his bearings, contented himself with a nod.

" Well, I'm mostly awf'ly obliged to you for turning up," said Jack. " Old Morton had heard you were at Rundle-stone, and suggested my sending you a wire first thing this

morning, when Collins cried off. I never thought you'd be
able to come."

" It was just chance," admitted Mr. Yard frankly. " I
got away unexpected."

" We're jolly glad to see you, anyhow," broke in Tubby.
" The Battery are sending over a beastly hot team, and we
should have been absolutely snookered without a back."

Mr. Yard suppressed a start. In more innocent days,
before the stern career of burglary had claimed him for its
own, he had figured as a full-back of some local renown for
a famous Yorkshire club. And now apparently it was in
the same capacity that he was being so hospitably received
by these two unsuspicious young men. Who the missing
Logan might be he could only guess. Evidently some well-
known player who was staying in the district, and had
been invited over to assist Okestock at the eleventh
hour. " If he turns up," thought Mr. Yard, " things'll
be a bit hot."

His reflections were broken in upon by Jack.

" These morning matches are the deuce, you know, Logan.
Half our fellows are in business, and it's a rare job to get a
team together."

" One can't always get off when one wants to," said Mr.
Yard sympathetically ; " I've found that meself."

" I shouldn't have taken them on," continued the other,
stripping off his shirt, and groping in his bag for a jersey,
" if it hadn't been that they're leaving Plymouth on Friday.
The Colonel was very keen to have a cut at us first, as we
haven't been beaten this year. The old beggar thought he'd
catch us on the hop if he could fix up a mid-week match.
He'll be awfully sick when he finds you're playing for us.
I expect there are a lot of people after you when you're on a
holiday, aren't there ? "

" Quite enough," confessed Mr. Yard.

A sudden sound of laughter and voices outside became
audible, and Tubby, walking to the door, flung it open.

" Here are the others ! " he said.

Some seven or eight young fellows, most of them already
changed, came straggling across the field. When they saw
Tubby at the door they raised a cheerful " Coo-ee ! "

" The Campbells are coming ! " called out one.

The words had hardly left his lips when a big brake,

packed with men, rumbled along the road and drew up at the entrance to the ground.

As the soldiers were disembarking themselves, Mr. Yard was being introduced to the new arrivals on his own side. On every hand he was greeted with the warmest of welcomes.

" I saw you play a couple of years ago for Devon," said one youngster admiringly. " My word, you were in form ! Hadn't you a moustache then, by the way ? "

Mr. Yard nodded.

" I had it shaved off last year," he said.

By this time the slightly mistaken impression as to his identity had become public property, and the visitors, who had all arrived in their footer kit, were standing viewing him with mingled expressions of curiosity and respect.

The Colonel, who had brought the Battery over, a jolly-looking, fat old man with a white moustache, came up and introduced himself.

" Glad to have the chance of seeing you play, Mr. Logan," he said, " but it's a low-down trick of young Mortimer here roping you in. We weren't expecting to run up against an international full-back."

" You'll run up against him all right," interrupted Jack, with a laugh. " That's what he's here for."

Mr. Yard, who was beginning to get a little nervous about his growing reputation, smiled uneasily. He had not played for at least five years, and although, thanks to the healthy limitations of Dartmoor, he was in excellent condition, he could not help feeling grave doubts as to whether he would be able to live up to Mr. Logan's formidable fame. However, there was nothing to do now but to go through with it.

Tubby, fully changed, came running out from the pavilion with a ball, followed by several other members of the team.

" Here you are," he sang out, passing it to Yard ; " have a shot at goal ! "

The convict caught the leather, and somehow or other the once-familiar feel of it restored his waning spirits. Taking a couple of short steps, he sent it soaring away towards the goal, a beautiful drop-kick that only fell short of the crossbar by a couple of inches.

" Bravo ! " shouted Jack, gazing after it admiringly. " What do you think of that, Colonel ? "

" Too damned good altogether ! " grunted the old soldier. " I shall take my boys back to barracks if he does it again."

There was a general laugh, cut short by a sharp whistle from the referee.

The two sides lined up. As far as looks went they seemed fairly equally matched, the superior weight of the soldiers in the scrum being pretty well counter-balanced by the youth and speedy appearance of the Okestock three-quarters and halves.

From the solitary glory of his position at full-back, Mr. Yard cast a critical eye over his opponents. A tall, fair-haired man who was playing on the right wing seemed especially to rivet his attention.

" Who's that chap ? " he asked Tubby, as the latter fell back in preparation for the kick-off.

" Private Buckle," answered the latter, glancing in the direction he indicated. " You'll have to look out for him ; he's about their best man."

The full-back smiled unpleasantly.

" I'll look out for him all right," he answered.

For eighteen months Mr. Yard had been under the immediate charge of a warder of the same name, whose striking resemblance to the tall three-quarter proclaimed their relationship beyond doubt.

Mr. Yard spat on his hands.

" I only hope they're twins," he said to himself.

Another sharp whistle, a general movement forward amongst the line of stalwart soldiers, and the ball came soaring through the air straight into Tubby's hands. The game had started.

For the first ten minutes the play remained more or less confined to the centre of the ground. The Okestock forwards, settling down quicker than their adversaries, were more than holding their own in the scrum, and only the very keen tackling of the soldier three-quarters prevented Tubby and his companions from coming away with the ball.

At last the former got his chance. Taking a swift pass from the half, he cut right through the opposition line, and dashed off down the field, with only the back between himself and the goal. As the latter leaped at him, he transferred the ball neatly to Jack, who was racing along a yard and a half to his left. Catching it in his stride, that genial young man swerved round the disgruntled soldier, and, galloping over the line, placed it fair and square between the goal-posts.

Picking it up again, he leisurely retraced his steps. Some twenty yards out he halted, and beckoned to Mr. Yard.

" Will you take the kick, Logan ? " he shouted.

Mr. Yard modestly shook his head.

" Oh, but you must ! " protested three or four of the others. " We've all heard about your goal-kicking."

The whole field was waiting, and, seeing that there was no help for it, Mr. Yard strode reluctantly forward.

" Where would you like it ? " inquired Jack.

" Oh, any old place ! " answered the unhappy convict. " This'll do."

He viciously dug out a hole with his heel. Jack, carefully poising the ball in his hands, stretched himself out full length, and a painful moment of silence prevailed over the field.

Mr. Yard retired two or three steps.

" Down ! " he cried hoarsely ; and then, running forward, hacked at the ball with amazing ferocity. Up it flew high over the crossbar, and, describing a graceful curve in the air, settled down in the next field.

There was a wild outburst of applause from the delighted Okestock team ; and Mr. Yard, mopping his forehead with his sleeve, retired to his former position.

" If I hadn't have said to myself it was a warder's head," he muttered, " I'd never have done it."

The game was resumed even more vigorously than before. Determined to draw level, the soldiers hurled themselves into their task with unsparing energy, and their extra weight and strength in the scrum began to tell its tale.

On one occasion four stalwart privates broke right through the Okestock pack, and came thundering down the field with the ball at their feet. A score seemed certain, but Mr. Yard, whose arduous training as a burglar had taught him the value of strategy, saved the situation. Just as the quartette were drawing up to him, he suddenly rasped out in excellent imitation of a drill-sergeant the one magic word : " Halt ! "

His opponents instinctively checked themselves, and, before they could recover, Mr. Yard had flung himself at the ball and with a flying kick sent it hurtling into touch.

He was surprised, and for a moment alarmed, at the indignation which his ingenious idea provoked among its immediate victims. All four of them were appealing angrily to the referee, who, speechless with laughter, could only shake his head and sign to them to proceed.

It was not until Mr. Yard realised that even the other members of the regimental team were hugely enjoying their companions' discomfiture that his fear lest he should have given himself away completely vanished.

" Git on with the game, ye fat'eads," roared the bully corporal who was skippering the team. Then, turning to Jack, he added admiringly: " 'Ot stuff ! That what 'e is—'ot stuff ! "

Jack, who was struggling between mirth and amazement, thought it wiser to say nothing. A moment later, however, finding himself alongside of Tubby, he whispered hurriedly :

" I say, that was a bit thick, wasn't it ? "

Tubby grinned.

The soldiers' revenge was not long in coming. From the line-out one of them caught the ball, and flung it back to the tall, fair-haired three-quarter, who was standing unmarked. In a moment the latter had cut through and was galloping along the touch-line towards the Okestock goal.

With a grunt of joy, Mr. Yard came hurrying across, and leaped at his quarry like a tiger at a stag. In the splendour of his emotions, however, he committed the unpardonable error of going a shade too high.

The soldier's muscular hand shot out, and, catching his assailant fair and square under the chin, sent him spinning backwards on the grass. Then, amidst roars of delight from his companions, he ran round and deposited the ball halfway between the goal-posts.

Mr. Yard sat up and looked after him.

" You swine ! " he said softly. " You wait ! "

Jack and Tubby came hurrying up.

" Not hurt, Logan, are you ? " inquired the former anxiously.

" Only in me feelings ! " answered Mr. Yard.

Tubby laughed.

" Well, it's a new sensation for you to miss any one ! " he said, as they walked back towards the goal. " I always thought Buckle was a pretty stiff proposition ; now I'm sure."

Mr. Yard made no audible answer. To himself, however, he remarked bitterly : " He'll be stiffer still before I've done with him."

A successful place-kick put the two sides level, and immediately afterwards the whistle went for half-time.

When they resumed, Mr. Yard had quite recovered from the effects of his tumble. He was standing in his place, luxuriously pondering over his next meeting with Private Buckle, when he suddenly observed a telegraph-boy opening the gate which led into the field.

Great minds work quickly. In a flash, Mr. Yard realised his danger. It was a hundred to one that the missing Logan had wired to explain his absence.

Casting a hasty glance at the game, which gave no sign of requiring his immediate services, he hurried down to the touch-line and held out his hand.

" For Mr. Mortimer, sir," said the lad.

" All right, my son," answered Mr. Yard pleasantly. " I'll give it him."

The boy handed over the yellow envelope, and then slowly began to retrace his steps, walking backwards and keeping a longing eye on the game. His inclinations, fortunately for Mr. Yard, were at variance with the Government's views as to how long a telegraph-boy might take over a message, and, seeing that the full-back had no opportunity as yet of passing on the wire, he at length vanished round the corner, unsuspicious as to its ultimate delivery.

It was not until he had completely disappeared that Mr. Yard opened the envelope.

" Sorry can't play to-day. Away last night ; only just received letter.—LOGAN."

The convict barely had time to master the message when a sudden shout of " Look out, there ! " recalled him abruptly to his environment.

The soldiers' three-quarters were in full movement ; the ball travelling neatly up the line towards the right wing.

It finally came to rest in the hands of Private Buckle, who, avoiding the well-meant but somewhat belated attentions of Jack, came racing away down the touch-line.

"The soldier's muscular hand shot out and sent him spinning
backwards on the grass."

"The soldier's muscular hand shot out and sent him spinning backwards on the grass."

Mr. Yard almost sobbed with pleasure.

He darted across the ground, timing his arrival to perfection. The three-quarter saw him coming, and, shifting the ball to his right arm, prepared to repeat his successful hand-off. But, like many other good intentions, his purpose was destined never to bear fruit.

Dropping his bullet head, Mr. Yard propelled himself through the air on the lines of a Whitehead torpedo, and with an appalling crash the two men hurtled to the ground and rolled over, locked in each other's arms.

" Gad, what a collar ! " roared Jack, as the ball, after leaping high into the air, dropped safely into touch.

Mr. Yard was the first to rise. In that exquisite moment he seemed to have worked off all the bottled resentment of eighteen soul-searing months.

" Hope you're not hurt ? " he grinned, extending a hand to the unfortunate Buckle, who lay on the ground gasping like a recently landed salmon.

The latter accepted it, and scrambled painfully to his feet. " 'Urt ! " he stammered ironically. " Ho n-n-no, I ain't 'urt ! I shouldn't a' known you'd c-c-collared me if you 'adn't mentioned it."

There was a general laugh, which the corporal capped by inquiring gravely :

" You don't 'appen to be wanting a job as a six-inch shell, I s'pose, Mr. Logan ? We could do with a few more."

Mr. Yard shook his head.

" I've had enough o' working for the Government ! " he remarked dryly.

Only ten minutes more remained for play, and the fun became fast and furious. Both sides laid themselves out to score, magnificently indifferent to anything approaching defensive tactics. On one occasion Jack was hurled into touch when only a couple of feet from the soldiers' line, while, on another, nothing but an untimely stumble on the part of the big corporal prevented that gentleman from dribbling over and touching down.

It was left to Mr. Yard to put the crowning touch on the day's work. One minute from time, the Battery's full-back picked up the ball in front of his own goal, and took a huge punt straight up the field. It dropped right into the hands of the convict, who was standing in a line with the centre flag.

The rushing forwards paused to give him five yards' law, and Mr. Yard gripped the occasion with commendable promptness.

Instead of kicking, he suddenly launched himself forward right into the thick of his waiting adversaries. In a moment he had bullocked his way through, his sudden run taking the opposition utterly by surprise.

There was a roar of " Collar him ! " and from both sides the halves and three-quarters came thundering in to cut off his advance. Mr. Yard took in the situation at a glance. In a flash he had measured the distance between himself and the goal, and then, dropping the ball, sent it soaring away with a terrific kick straight for the bar.

There was a moment of painful silence. The ball pitched fair and square bang on the centrepiece, bounded up into the air, and then trickled gently over on the farther side.

A howl of joy from the Okestock team, the referee whistled, and the game was over.

Mr. Yard found himself surrounded by a throng of his fellow-players, each endeavouring to outvie the other in compliments and gratitude. With a sudden inspiration, he thrust his way through, and made a dash for the pavilion. It could not have been more than forty-five seconds before the foremost of his laughing pursuers ran in after him, but that priceless interval had not been wasted. In Mr. Yard's breeches-pocket reposed practically the entire stock of loose cash which had previously enriched the hanging line of waistcoats and trousers.

" I must be off ! " he said hastily, picking up his adopted coat and cap.

" Oh, hang it all ! " cried Jack. " I was going to suggest that you should come back and have some lunch with us."

Mr. Yard shook his head. The thought of food was a very fragrant one, but the money in his pocket clamoured for instant retreat.

" Can't," he said regretfully. " It's uncommon good of you, but I've got to get into Plymouth as quickly as possible."

" Plymouth ! " exclaimed the Colonel, who had just come up. " If you want to go to Plymouth you'd better pack in with us. We can drop you at the Halfpenny Gate, and you can pick up a tram from there."

" Thanks ! " said Mr. Yard gratefully. " That'll do me fine."

" Come along, then," said the Colonel ; " we're off right away."

" Will you be on the moor next Saturday ? " cried Jack, pressing forward with the others to shake the hand of their parting guest.

" It's quite possible," admitted Mr. Yard.

" Well, you'll come and play for us again, won't you ? "

" I'd like to," said Mr. Yard, " if I can get away."

He clambered into the brake with the soldiers, and waved a parting farewell to his late colleagues, who set up a ringing cheer as the big vehicle slowly rumbled off.

" Good set of lads," said the Colonel.

Mr. Yard, thoughtfully fingering the money in his pocket, nodded his head.

The eight-mile drive into Plymouth was not without its anxieties. At every turn in the road Mr. Yard half expected to find a mounted warder holding up his hands to stop the horses. No such untimely incident, however, marred the harmony of the day, and just as the clocks were striking half-past one the brake was clattering through the ill-paved, straggling streets of Devonport.

At the junction of Dockyard Road and Broadway, Mr. Yard's eyes detected a second-hand clothes shop of particularly disreputable aspect. He waited until they reached the next corner, and then turning to the Colonel, remarked casually : " This'll do all right for me ; I want to get some 'baccy."

" Right you are," said the Colonel, giving the order to stop. " You know where the bridge is—first to the left, then straight on."

Mr. Yard nodded, and climbed down. " Thank ye for the lift," he said.

" Not at all," answered the Colonel. " Delighted ! The Battery will always be proud to think that they had the honour of playing against you and scoring a try—eh, men?"

There was a general chorus of " Yes, sir," and a hearty salute, which Mr. Yard gracefully returned.

Then the driver cracked his whip, and the brake rolled away, leaving Mr. Yard standing in the roadway.

. . . .

It was three days later, when Jack, folding up the *Western Morning News*, tossed it across to Tubby.

" There you are," he said, " picture and everything. We shall never hear the last of this as long as we live."

Tubby caught the paper, and, unfolding it, read out the heavily leaded headlines :

ASTOUNDING AUDACITY OF ESCAPED CONVICT

THE NOTORIOUS BILL YARD PLAYS FOOTBALL
FOR OKESTOCK

FULL STORY AND INTERVIEWS

He skimmed quickly through the three columns of description, and then, with a grin, dropped the paper on the floor.

" We *do* look a pretty tidy lot of idiots," he admitted. " I wonder where he is ? "

Jack shrugged his shoulders. " So do the police. They've no idea what happened to him after he got the clothes. He's simply vanished—disappeared, and my ten shillings with him." Then he paused. " I only wish it had been a quid," he added.

" Mine was," said Tubby softly.

THE NADIR BANDAR

I HAD known Bruce for about fifteen years before this amazing thing happened.

He was a nephew of Mervyn Bruce, the famous traveller, and we had turned up the same day at Haileybury—two forlorn new boys. I can see him now with his shock of red hair, his friendly grin, and that funny little habit of scratching the back of his right ear which has never left him.

He came up and spoke to me in the quad. Some big fellow had just asked me my name, and when in all innocence I had said : " Bridges—what's yours ? " I had been answered with a clip over the head that had sent me sprawling on the asphalt.

" Why did he hit you ? " asked Bruce.

I explained, trying not to blubber.

" You'll know him again, won't you ? " said Bruce.

I nodded.

" That's all right," he said cheerfully. " Then you can poison his food."

I remember this struck me as being a very comforting reflection, and from that moment Bruce and I have always been the best of friends.

Later on we shared a study together, the corner study next " the big school," and one summer holiday I went and stayed with his people in that big, ivy-covered house near Goring that you can see from the railway line.

When we left school our paths separated for a time. I started at journalism in London, while Bruce was sent to France " to learn the language." I think his father had some idea that he would make a good Prime Minister.

When the old man died, Bruce came home and settled in London. He had come into about £800 a year, and had no intention at all of going into politics.

Since then we have always seen a good deal of each other. He is just the same cheery, irresponsible, adven-

87

turous, good-natured chap that he was at school. I don't think we ever had anything approaching a quarrel in our lives.

I have told you all this so that you can see exactly what sort of people we are. It's really quite unnecessary, because you won't believe my story in any case. Still, unless Bruce and I are insane, the thing really happened ; and as there is absolutely no reason to suppose we are, I intend to tell it and get it off my chest.

I will begin right at the beginning. It was on the 9th of February that I first learned of Mervyn Bruce's death. I saw it in the *Daily Mail* while I was having breakfast. There was a portrait of him in rough shooting clothes and a cork helmet—it must have been taken many years before—and a full column about his life and adventures. He had died at Etretat, where the paper said he had been living for some time.

I didn't bother myself about it, because I knew that he and Bruce had not been on speaking terms for years. There had been some silly family squabble somewhere back in the dark ages and the old explorer was one of those fatuous people who think it a point of honour to keep a thing like that up for ever. So, after making an ineffectual attempt at a reconciliation when he was in France, Bruce had simply let matters slide.

I was therefore a little surprised to get a line from him on the 11th, saying that he was just off to Etretat, to see about his uncle's funeral. " The fact is," he wrote, " the old chap had quarrelled with everyone by the time he died, and as I'm his nearest relation I suppose I ought to see him through. I shall be back by the end of the week."

It was six days before I heard anything more. Then, late on Tuesday evening, I received a wire from him at the office :

" Please come Hampstead to-morrow—lunch. Important."

Bruce lives in one of those old-fashioned three-storey houses away to the right off the top of Haverstock Hill. I expect you know them if you have ever been up in that direction. Standing back from the road, with balconies, long windows, and creeper-covered fronts, they seem to shrink in a kind of desolate dismay from the new red-brick splendour which has gradually hemmed them in.

Heath View, the end one, is where Bruce hangs out. It belongs to an ex-police sergeant and his wife, called Jones, and Bruce has the whole of the two top floors. They make him very comfortable, but I have often wondered why he doesn't take a flat. He says it is because Mrs. Jones is the only woman in London who can cook a mushroom omelette.

When I rang the bell the possessor of this unique talent opened the door herself. She is a tall, good-looking woman of about forty, with that sort of grave, respectful manner you don't often meet nowadays.

Yes, Mr. Bruce was in, she said, and expecting me. Would I go straight up ?

Bruce heard me coming, and flung open the door. He had just jumped up from his desk, which was littered with papers and bundles of deeds tied up by red tape. He looked flushed and a little excited.

" Come along in," he said. " I was just beginning to be afraid you couldn't turn up."

I discarded my coat, and followed him into the room.

" I couldn't neglect such a poignant wire," I said. " What's the matter ? Have you come into a fortune ? "

He laughed in a curious, jerky sort of way, and just then Mrs. Jones came in and began to lay the table for lunch.

As soon as she had gone down again, Bruce walked across to the fireplace, and threw down his cigarette in the grate.

" I didn't get any money," he said abruptly. " The old chap left every cent he had to Reardon, the man who published his book of travels."

" I should dispute the will," I said. " An author who leaves money to a publisher is obviously mad."

Bruce scratched his ear for a moment in silence.

" I've got something else, though," he said at last. Then he stepped to his desk, pulled open the drawer, and took out a small, dark green object.

" What do you make of it ? " he said, handing it to me.

I took it, and crossed to the window so as to get it in a better light.

I am not a particularly impressionable person, but when I saw it at close quarters I as nearly as possible dropped it.

" Good heavens," I said, " what a loathsome thing ! What is it ? A monkey or a devil ? "

Bruce laughed uneasily. " It's the Nadir Bandar,"
he said.

At that moment the door opened and Mrs. Jones came
in again with a mushroom omelette. I stuffed the infernal
piece of jade away in my pocket, and we sat down at the
table. It was not until she had shut the door behind her
that I took it out.

" And what the devil is the Nadir Bandar when it's at
home ? " I asked, setting the horrible thing up on the
tablecloth in front of me.

Bruce laid down his fork, and, putting his hand in his
pocket, pulled out a couple of sheets of dirty folded foolscap.
" You'd better read that," he said.

I took them with no little curiosity. They were written
in a very fine sloping hand, and were headed : " An Account
of the Finding of the Nadir Bandar. Not to be published
until after my death.—MERVYN BRUCE."

Here is the whole thing as it was written :

" I first heard of the Nadir Bandar when I was at Nikh
in '73. I was told of it by the Sheikh Al-Abbas, who claimed
himself to be descended from Nadir Shah.

" Al-Abbas had been wounded in the rebellion against
Nasr-ed-Din, and had fled to Nikh, where I found him
dying and in disguise. I took him into my house and
looked after him as well as I could, for the man was a
great man of noble blood, and not an accursed Turkish dog
like Nasr-ed-Din.

" On the night before he died he spoke to me of the Nadir
Bandar.

" ' If I had it,' he said, ' I would wish to be well, and I
would also wish that Nasr-ed-Din should be eaten of worms.'

" Myself : ' What is the Nadir Bandar, Sheikh Al-Abbas ?
I have not heard of it.'

" The Sheikh : ' There is but one who has heard of it,
and he will die with the coming of the sun.'

" Myself : ' It is a great power if it can grant such wishes
as you name.'

" The Sheikh : ' There is no wish that it cannot grant.
Four times may a man call upon it and four times will it
answer. With its aid my ancestor, Nadir Shah, conquered
the entire world.'

" Myself : ' If he possessed such a power, Sheikh Al-Abbas, why did he allow himself to be slain ? ''

" The Sheikh : ' Four times had he called on it and four times had it answered.'

" Myself : ' You mean that its power had passed away ? '

" The Sheikh : ' He had buried it at the meeting of the waters. His last wish had been that he might win the world and gain the mountain of light. When this was granted he buried it beneath the great sun stone at the meeting of the waters. After that he was slain.'

" Myself : ' And where is the meeting of the waters, Sheikh Al-Abbas ? '

" The Sheikh : ' I cannot say. All that I know I was told by my father, who had had it from his father before him.'

" When I rose next morning the Skeikh Al-Abbas was dead. I buried him, pondering greatly over his story. Some would have dismissed it from their minds as the babbling of a dying man, but I have seen many strange things in this world, and I knew well that the Sheikh Al-Abbas had spoken what he believed to be true.

" So soon as I could get away from Nikh in safety I travelled through to Quetta, and, there procuring a map, I traced out the marches of Nadir Shah, as he came back from the ravishing of Delhi. So far as I could see there was but one place to which the phrase used by the Sheikh Al-Abbas could be applied. That was a few miles to the east of Jelalabad, where the Chitral and Kabul rivers mingle together and flow down to the great lakes.

" I made my way up to Peshawar, and in the disguise of an Afghan hillman crossed the border. At Lalpura I fell in with a travelling merchant, who was in much fear of being waylaid by robbers. ' Two,' said he, ' are better company than one.' And together we set out on the road to Jelalabad.

" We passed through Kila Akhund before the sun was high in the sky, and halted for our midday rest on the bank of the Kabul river. It was there that I learned of the Temple of the Sun Stone.

" It stood before us at the meeting of the waters, a low stone building set on an island in mid-stream.

"When my companion spoke of it by its name my heart leaped suddenly within me, for I recalled the words of the Sheikh Al-Abbas.

" ' It is very sacred,' said my companion. ' No one but the priests of the Sun are allowed to enter or even to land on the island.'

" I made no reply to him, and later on we continued our journey to Jelalabad, where we parted.

" That night I rode out from the city, and tied up my horse in a thicket on the bank of the river opposite to the temple. Then, stripping myself of my clothes, I entered the water and swam to the island, having some matches and a loaded pistol in my turban. These I took out on landing, and advanced very carefully towards the gate of the temple.

" It was shut, and I could find no means of opening it save by breaking it in with a stone. This I did, waiting in some anxiety to see what might happen. There was no sound or movement, and I entered. The temple was quite dark inside ; so, halting and striking a match, I held it up above my head and looked about me.

" The floor was of beaten earth, and at the further end I beheld a large red stone, as red as blood, and guarded by golden rails. There were two candles, one each side, set in brass candlesticks.

" These I lighted, and then without more ado set to work digging out the earth under the stone with the aid of my knife. I must have laboured for the best part of an hour before the steel struck upon something hard, and the blade snapped in my hand. In another minute I had dragged to light an ancient iron box, which had rusted fully as red as the stone above. The cover fell off as I lifted it, and inside I beheld the Nadir Bandar.

" Scarcely had I taken it in my hand, when the door of the temple opened. I looked up quickly. In the gloom I could see three figures—tall men robed in white, and carrying swords.

" I raised my pistol, but as I did so the words of the Sheikh Al-Abbas came flooding into my mind. ' I wish,' said I clearly and without hesitation, ' that I was in Peshawar.'

" For a moment my eyes closed. When I opened them

I was standing outside the house in Peshawar where I had
lately lodged."

At this point I laid down the manuscript and burst into
a shout of laughter.

Bruce leaned across and picked it up.   " You think it's
all nonsense ? " he said.

" I think," said I, " that as an explorer your uncle can
give points to Louis de Rougemont and Dr. Cook.   The
picture of him suddenly appearing naked in the main street
of Peshawar, with a pistol in one hand and the Nadir Bandar
in the other, is about the richest touch of imagination I've
ever struck."

" You think it's all a lie ? " persisted Bruce.

I stared at him.

" My dear chap," I said, " it's either a lie or else the old
boy was as mad as a March hare.   Considering he left his
money to a publisher, I personally incline to the latter
theory."

Bruce sat silent for a minute, scratching his ear.   Then
he laughed in a rather apologetic sort of fashion.

" You'll think I'm dotty, too," he said, " but do you
know, upon my soul, I believe there's something in it."

" Oh, get out ! " I said ; " and pass me the whisky."

Bruce handed over the bottle.

" I'm not joking," he went on obstinately.   " I've got a
funny sort of feeling that the old chap was speaking the
truth."

" You ought to take something for it," I said.   " Mother
Seigel or Dr. Williams' Pink Pills for Neurotic Nephews."

Bruce got up, and, crossing to the mantelpiece, began to
fill a pipe.   For some moments we both remained silent.

" Well, look here," he broke out at last rather awkwardly,
" I'm going to have a wish and see what happens."

I shook my head with a kind of mock disapproval.

" You're sure to be sorry," I said.   " These things always
turn out badly.   Think of ' Uncle Peter's Fairy Story.' "

" What's that ? " asked Bruce.

" It's a book," I replied, " a book that delighted my early
childhood.   As far as I can recollect, everyone in it was
allowed to have one wish, and the results were—well, not
quite what they expected.   I remember one kind-hearted

lady wishing that the blacksmith's baby, who was dying of consumption, should be as well and strong as its father. In about three minutes the baby was decimating the village with the sledge-hammer."

" I shall be very careful," remarked Bruce, a little uncomfortably. " I——"

" By the way," I interrupted, " what happened to your uncle? You took away his masterpiece before I'd finished it."

" He never had any more wishes," said Bruce. " That first shot seems to have frightened him off it."

I laughed.

" I don't wonder," I said. " One experience like that would be enough to make me sign the pledge for ever."

Bruce came to the table and picked up the Nadir Bandar.

" What are you going to wish? " I asked mischievously. " For goodness' sake be careful."

" It's all right," he answered. " I've got four wishes, so I can always unwish one if it goes wrong."

Then he paused.

" I wish," he said, very slowly and distinctly, " that I may be irresistible to all women."

I burst out laughing.

" Good heavens," I said, " you've done it now! Think what will happen if you run up against a girls' school! What on earth made you wish that? "

An obstinate look came into Bruce's face.

" It's Cynthia," he said. " Cynthia West, you know. I want to marry her, and she won't give up the stage."

" Well, you needn't have indulged in quite such a sweeping demand," I protested.

Bruce looked a little ashamed.

" I thought I'd be on the safe side," he explained. " You see, I might get tired of Cynthia one day, and then it would save wasting a second wish."

" Well, I'm blessed ! " I said. " For a lover I think you're about the most cold-blooded cynic I ever stiuck. What are you going to wish next? "

" I must have some money," Bruce said thoughtfully.

" You must," I agreed, " plenty ! Eight hundred a year won't go far with Cynthia, to say nothing of the others."

" What about a billion in Consols ? " suggested Bruce.

I shook my head.

" Too much," I said. " Think what *The Clarion* and *Reynolds'* would say about it ! You'd have no peace."

" I know," exclaimed Bruce suddenly. " I'll wish that I had as much money as John P. Fox, the American Rubber King."

" That ought to see you through all right," I remarked approvingly. " The papers say he is worth six millions."

Bruce again held up the Nadir Bandar.

" I wish," said he, " that I had as much money as John P. Fox, the American Rubber King."

" Two up and one to play," I said, laughing. " You may as well have a third while you're about it ; that will still leave you one to hedge with."

Bruce thought a moment.

" I wish that I may live for ever," he said.

" Good ! " I cried. " You'll be able to read Hall Caine's next novel right through."

With this hopeful reflection I got up from my chair and walked to the window.

" Now this tomfoolery's over," I observed, with a yawn, " what are we going to do ? "

Bruce scratched his ear.

" I shall go and call on Cynthia, I think," he said in a rather apologetic voice. " After all, you know," he added lamely, " there might be something in it."

" Superstition," I began, " when coupled with——"

Then I stopped abruptly. The excellent aphorism that I was about to utter was never completed.

" What's up ? " asked Bruce, turning to me in surprise.

I pointed to the door of the room.

" Look at that," I said.

It was opening, slowly and stealthily, without a sound.

We stared at it in amazement.

" Who's there ? " called out Bruce sharply.

There was a moment's pause, and then, very quietly, Mrs. Jones slipped into the room and shut the door behind her. She was breathing quickly, and her face was curiously flushed.

For several seconds we all three stood facing each other. Then Bruce spoke.

" What's the matter, Mrs. Jones ? Are you ill ? " he asked.

The woman made no reply. With her eyes half-closed, she rocked slowly from side to side as if about to fall.

" Look out ! " I cried. " She's going to faint ! "

We both sprang forward together, but Bruce got there first and caught her by the shoulders. In a flash she had clutched him, winding her arms round his waist, and burying her face in his coat with a little cry, half-way between a laugh and a sob.

For a moment Bruce was too dumbfounded to resist. Then, with frantic energy, he made a vain attempt to disentangle himself from her embrace.

" Here, let me go ! " he stammered. " What are you doing ? What's the matter ? Pull her off, Bridges—pull her off ! "

I hastened to his assistance, feeling as if I were taking part in some exceptionally spirited nightmare.

To and fro we swayed, pulling, struggling, and banging against the table. At last, with a mighty heave, I managed to unfasten one of her hands, and, ducking down, Bruce tore himself free.

" She's mad ! " he gasped. " Shove her outside, and lock the door, quick ! "

" Well, give us a hand, then ! " I panted, for the woman was twisting and writhing in a manner that made it almost impossible to hold her.

Watching his opportunity, Bruce leaped in and seized her disengaged wrist. She fought furiously, but together we half-pushed, half-carried her into the passage, and then, wrenching ourselves loose, leaped back into the room and slammed and locked the door.

I sank down on the sofa and gazed at Bruce, who leaned against a table, mopping his forehead with a handkerchief.

Presently he found his voice.

" Lord ! " he muttered in an awe-struck whisper. " I never thought the darn thing would work like this ! "

That revived me.

" Don't be an idiot ! " I cried sharply. " You don't suppose it's got anything to do with your beastly green monkey ? The wretched woman's gone clean off her head. Something must be done at once."

At that moment there came a savage hammering on the panels of the door.

"I know what I'm going to do!" exclaimed Bruce hastily, "and that's get out of the window. She'll have Jones up in a moment if she goes on like that, and the man's as jealous as Satan. He'd kill me for a certainty before I had time to explain."

"Well, I'm not going to be left here with a couple of gibbering lunatics!" I protested, jumping up from the sofa.

He caught me by the sleeve.

"Come on then; we can get out on the balcony and climb down by the ivy. Anything's better than waiting for Jones."

By this time I was so bewildered that I think I should have fallen in with any suggestion, however ludicrous. I remember some vague wonder passing through my mind as to what the next-door people would think if they saw us swarming down the front of the house; but with the door threatening to yield every instant before Mrs. Jones's frantic assault, there was no opportunity for detached reflection. Grabbing my hat from the table, I followed Bruce out on to the balcony, shutting the window behind me. One glance up and down showed us that the road was empty.

"You go first," I said unselfishly; "you're in most danger."

He climbed the rail, and, clutching the stems of the ivy with both hands, slid off into space. Leaning over, I watched him swaying downwards in short, spasmodic jerks.

Suddenly from within the room came the crash of a splintering panel.

"Look out!" I yelled hurriedly. "I'm coming!" And, scrambling over the rail, I, too, committed myself to that inadequate creeper.

I know that in books of adventure people swarm up and down an ivy-clad house without the faintest inconvenience, but as one who has tried it, I can only say that it's about the most poisonously impossible feat ever attempted.

Bruce was luckier than I. He was within four feet of the ground when the stuff gave way; I must have fallen at least twelve. And I landed in a rose bush.

4

Bruce, who had scrambled to his feet, rushed up and pulled me out of the wreckage.

" Hurt ? " he inquired eagerly.

" Oh no," I replied, with some bitterness, " not in the least ! I love to come down sitting on a rose bush. It's a kind of hobby of mine."

We had no time to squabble, however. Before Bruce could answer, we heard the window above flung violently open, and the furious panting of Mrs. Jones as she climbed out on to the balcony.

That was enough. With incredible celerity we dashed for the garden gate, and nearly killed ourselves trying to get out at the same moment. Then, turning to the right, we raced down the road towards Haverstock Hill.

We must have covered at least half the distance before I regained sufficient sanity to realise what we were doing. Then I clutched Bruce by the arm.

" Steady on ! " I gasped. " If there's anyone looking they'll think we're mad ! "

Even as I spoke there came a sharp " teuf teuf ! " and instinctively we pulled up. Round the corner of FitzJohn Villas bowled a solitary taxi, the driver leaning back comfortably in his seat and smoking a big cigar.

" Hi ! " we yelled in unison.

Some note of unusual urgency in our summons must have attracted him, for he at once applied his brakes. Having done this, however, he recollected himself, and, removing his cigar, spat pleasantly in the roadway.

" Nothin' doin', guv'nor ! " he said, with a kind of gloomy satisfaction. " Just orf to the garrige."

" You must ! " I said desperately. " We're in a hurry, we can't wait ! I'll give you a sovereign ! "

" A suvrin ! " he repeated dully. " Where d'yer want to go to ? "

" Piccadilly Circus," I blurted out. It was the first place that came into my head.

He stared at me, and then something like a look of sympathy crept into his face.

" Ar ! " he said. " Git in."

For about three minutes after the taxi started neither of us spoke. Then Bruce broke the silence.

" Well," he said, " d'you believe it now ? "

I turned on him angrily.

" Look here," I cried, " don't talk blithering rot ! The thing's impossible ! You know it as well as I do ! "

He shook his head.

" Well, what about Mrs. Jones ? " he said obstinately.

" Mrs. Jones," I repeated, " is the victim of the same disease that you're suffering from—common or garden hysteria. No doubt she was listening at the door, and overheard your tomfool nonsense with that ridiculous monkey. Being a highly strung, passionate sort of woman——"

Bruce cut me short.

" Jones," he said, " is always complaining that she's too cold."

" Cold ! " I groaned. " Oh, Lord ! "

" So it couldn't be that," he added.

" Well, if it isn't that," I said, " what the blazes is it ? You don't seriously expect me to believe in black magic and Mumbo Jumbo and all that sort of bunkum, do you ? "

Bruce scratched his ear.

" I don't know," he said unhappily.

We sat in silence as the cab ran on, each of us staring out of the window on our respective sides. It was not until we were half-way up Tottenham Court Road that I suddenly noticed the time. There was a big clock outside one of the furniture shops, and the hands were pointing to half-past two. I called Bruce's attention to the fact.

" Cynthia won't have finished her lunch yet," I said. " We had better get out at Piccadilly Circus and walk up. Or perhaps you'd rather go alone ? "

" No," he answered eagerly ; " I want you to come. You needn't stay, you know, but I'd like you just to come and see what happens."

" All right," I said, with a laugh. " I may as well see you through now I've begun. If Cynthia starts embracing you, I'll leave the room."

" Oh, don't joke about it ! " Bruce said nervously.

The cab swerved its way through the traffic in Piccadilly Circus, and drew up with a jerk opposite Swan and Edgar's. We got out, and I handed the man a sovereign which I had ready.

He took it with a friendly smile.

" Thank ye, sir," he said, " an' good luck."

" It's my cab," said Bruce, as we turned into Regent Street.

" Very well," I answered, " we won't fight about it. You can pay me as soon as your green monkey pushes along those six millions."

By this time we were just opposite the entrance to the Piccadilly Hotel. As we passed, the door swung open, and a handsome woman, dressed in a long sable cloak, stepped out on to the pavement. In the roadway opposite, a liveried manservant was holding open the door of a smart electric brougham.

At the sight of us she paused, and her lips parted in one of the sweetest smiles I have ever seen. We both took off our hats, but as Bruce made no attempt to stop I walked on with him.

" Who is she ? " I whispered.

He stared at me.

" I don't know," he said. " I thought she was a friend of yours."

" Never seen her in my life," I answered. " I wonder who she took us for ? "

I looked round, and then touched his arm.

" Bruce," I said, " she's following us."

He glanced back over his shoulder, and I saw him start as though something had stung him.

" Come on ! " he muttered, suddenly quickening his pace.

" Why, what does it matter ? " I protested.

" Others, too," he whispered, " just behind her ! Three, or four of 'em ! It's that infernal charm ! "

" Bosh ! " I said incredulously, and then turned round to take another look. For a moment I felt as if someone had suddenly placed a large piece of ice inside my waistcoat. At least five women were following us along the pavement, headed by the lady in sables. There could be no possible doubt about it. Even as I looked two girls who had been walking in the other direction suddenly pulled up, and then, turning round, came hurriedly in pursuit of the rest. We seemed to be clearing Regent Street.

" This is awful ! " I gasped. " What are we to do ? "

" We must t-take a taxi ! " stammered Bruce, looking wildly about him.

Of course, as luck would have it, there was not a cab of any kind passing. We couldn't wait, for every moment things were growing worse. Women were appearing suddenly out of shops, and hurrying over from the other side of the street in twos and threes, recklessly indifferent to the traffic. In less than a minute a jostling crowd of about fifty or sixty were sweeping after us up the pavement.

" Run ! " gasped Bruce. " Run."

It was, of course, about as mad a thing as we could have done ; but panic, stark, blind panic, had gripped hold of us, and our only feeling was a frantic desire to escape. Without another word we took to our heels.

Of what followed I have a somewhat confused recollection. I remember a terrific uproar all round us, yells of " Suffragettes ! " " Stop 'em ! " " Police ! " And then two helmeted figures in dark blue suddenly leaped across our path. I suppose they must have taken us for Cabinet Ministers, for they opened out to let us go through, and without hesitation hurled themselves into the wild avalanche of pursuing women.

The check was only a momentary one, but it saved us. Before the shattered column could reform we had reached the corner of Vigo Street, where a taxi—a thrice-blessed taxi with an excited, beckoning driver at the wheel—was standing in readiness.

" Jump in ! " he roared, as we hurled ourselves panting at the door.

Willing hands banged it behind us, someone raised a cheer as we sank back on the seat, and there we were spinning past the Bodley Head, with the tumult and shouting dying away behind us.

There are some emotions which words are quite inadequate to express. At that moment Bruce and I were suffering from about six of them.

It was the taxi-driver who first broke the silence. At the bottom of Bond Street he pulled up, and, projecting his head round the side of the cab, signified his desire to speak with us. Mechanically I pulled down the window.

" The 'Ouse of Commons, guv'nor ? " he inquired.

" No," I said dully ; " Cynthia's flat."

He stared at me, and I recollected myself.

" Manor Court, Marylebone Road," I observed harshly.

He spun round and we retraced our way up Bond Street.

Just as we were emerging from the bottom of Harley Street, Bruce leaned across and laid his hand on my arm.

" After I've seen Cynthia," he said brokenly, " I shall unwish that first wish."

I nodded.

The taxi drew up at the gate of Manor Court and we got out.

The driver looked at us with interest.

" Just in time, I was," he observed ; " they'd 'ave 'ad you in another minit."

Bruce handed him half a sovereign.

" Thank ye, sir," he said, " thank ye." Then he paused. " I knows wot them suffrinjettes wants," he added, " and if I 'ad my way I'd give it 'em."

With this dark saying he slipped in his clutch and left us.

Side by side we walked up the gravelled drive and stepped in through the main entrance.

Cynthia's flat is on the ground floor on the right-hand side, the one with the green door and the copper knocker. Bruce laid his hand on the latter, and then hesitated.

" Go on," I said bitterly. " Think what we've been through."

His face hardened and he gave two sharp rat-tats.

A minute's pause, a sound of footsteps, and then the door swung open. A pretty, dark girl in the dress of a parlour-maid was standing before us.

Bruce cleared his throat.

" Is Miss West at home ? " he asked huskily.

She looked at him curiously for a moment without replying, then suddenly she said : " Yes, sir," and stepped back from the door.

We followed her into the hall, laying our hats and sticks on the table inside. Bruce's hands were shaking like leaves.

Without looking at us the girl led the way down the passage and opened a door on the left-hand side.

" Will you please come in here, sir ? " she said gently.

Bruce, who was about two paces ahead of me, stepped in first. In a flash the girl had followed him, slamming the door in my face with a bang that echoed through the flat.

I pulled up short, and as I did so there came a stifled cry from Bruce :

" Help, help, Bridges, help ! "

Flinging open the door again, I rushed in. As far as I could see, Bruce and the parlourmaid were engaged in a rather strenuous waltz. They were swaying down the room wreathed in each other's arms, splendidly regardless of the furniture. Even as I entered, they fetched up against the end of the sofa, and collapsed into a tangled heap.

At that instant something heavy struck me violently in the back and sent me reeling against the wall. A big woman in a print dress, her arms covered with flour, and a rolling-pin in her hand, brushed violently past me. In two strides she reached the sofa, and, seizing hold of the dark girl, began to drag her away from Bruce. If the latter's collar had not given way he would certainly have been choked. As it was, the stud broke just in the nick of time.

The two women reached the floor together with a loud thud, the rolling-pin clattering away across the room. Next moment, collarless and dishevelled, Bruce was leaping for the door.

I followed him, grabbing the handle, and slamming it behind me. As luck would have it, there was a lock outside ; and while Bruce snatched up his hat and fumbled with the front door, I turned the key with a savage force and broke it off short in my hand. Then, like two drunken men, we fell rather than staggered out into the main hall.

Fortunately, there was no one about. Panting and exhausted, we leaned against the foot of the lift, while Bruce, by turning up his collar and brushing his coat with one hand, made a feeble attempt to regain some semblance of respectability.

We were interrupted by the crunch of footsteps on the drive outside.

" Look out," I whispered hastily ; " here's someone coming."

Bruce straightened himself just as a burly porter in uniform swung in through the doorway. He evidently recognised us as friends of Cynthia, for he saluted with a friendly but respectful smile.

" Good-day, gen'lemen," he remarked. " I'm afraid Miss West ain't in town. Gone to Reigate, so I understand. P'r'haps you've seen the parlourmaid ? "

I nodded my head.

" Yes," I said ; " we've seen the parlourmaid. Could you get us a cab ? "

" Certainly, sir ; taxi, sir ? "

" It doesn't matter," interrupted Bruce in a dazed voice, " as long as there are no women in it."

I nudged him warningly, but the porter, evidently taking him for a humorist, laughed heartily.

" Very well, sir," he said briskly ; " I'll see to that, sir." Then, pulling a whistle from under his uniform, he stepped outside and blew a shrill blast. Almost immediately a taxi rolled up the drive.

The porter opened the door ; and as we came down the steps to get in, a small boy with a bundle of newspapers under his arm dashed up and thrust one out before me.

" 'Ere y'are, sir ; two-thirty winner. Death of a well-known millionaire, sir."

" Push off, me lad," said the porter grandly.

I had pulled a penny out of my pocket, however, before he spoke, and with an *Evening News* in my hand I followed Bruce into the taxi.

" Where to, sir ? " inquired the porter.

For a moment I was floored.

" The Bachelors' Club," said Bruce, handing him a shilling.

The porter saluted and passed on the instructions.

" Bruce," I said dully, " do you realise what we're spending in cabs ? "

Bruce shook his head with an air of utter weariness.

" It doesn't matter," he said. " I've got six million somewhere."

Half an hour earlier I should have laughed. As it was I only stared at him stupidly.

" Yes," I said. " I suppose you have."

Then, in a sort of mechanical way, I opened the paper. For a moment I gazed at it like a man in a trance.

" What's the matter ? " asked Bruce.

I was past speaking. I could only point with a trembling

finger to the three huge headlines which seemed to dance mockingly across the page :

SUICIDE OF JOHN P. FOX

RUINED RUBBER KING BLOWS OUT HIS BRAINS

PAUPER FOR THE PAST SIX WEEKS

Bruce read them aloud in a strange, dry voice. Then he burst out into a horrid, cackling, mad sort of laugh.

" That's done it ! " he cried. " No money, and this nightmare of a day for ever ! " His voice rose to a scream. " I'm damned if I do ! " he yelled.

Thrusting his hand into his pocket, he pulled out the Nadir Bandar.

" I wish," he sobbed, " that I'd never had a wish at all ! "

JOHN BUCHAN

The Wind in the Portico
Sing a Song of Sixpence

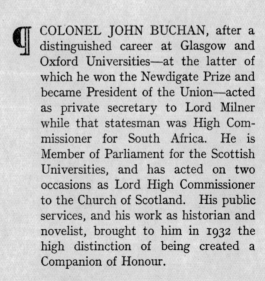

COLONEL JOHN BUCHAN, after a distinguished career at Glasgow and Oxford Universities—at the latter of which he won the Newdigate Prize and became President of the Union—acted as private secretary to Lord Milner while that statesman was High Commissioner for South Africa. He is Member of Parliament for the Scottish Universities, and has acted on two occasions as Lord High Commissioner to the Church of Scotland. His public services, and his work as historian and novelist, brought to him in 1932 the high distinction of being created a Companion of Honour.

THE WIND IN THE PORTICO

A dry wind of the high places . . . not to fan nor to cleanse, even a full wind from those places shall come unto me.

Jeremiah iv. 11–12.

NIGHTINGALE was a hard man to draw. His doings with the Bedawin had become a legend, but he would as soon have talked about them as claimed to have won the War. He was a slim dark fellow about thirty-five years of age, very short-sighted, and wearing such high-powered double glasses that it was impossible to tell the colour of his eyes. This weakness made him stoop a little and peer, so that he was the strangest figure to picture in a burnous leading an army of desert tribesmen. I fancy his power came partly from his oddness, for his followers thought that the hand of Allah had been laid on him, and partly from his quick imagination and his flawless courage. After the War he had gone back to his Cambridge fellowship, declaring that, thank God, that chapter in his life was over.

As I say, he never mentioned the deeds which had made him famous. He knew his own business, and probably realised that to keep his mental balance he had to drop the curtain on what must have been the most nerve-racking four years ever spent by man. We respected his decision and kept off Arabia. It was a remark of Hannay's that drew from him the following story. Hannay was talking about his Cotswold house, which was on the Fosse Way, and saying that it always puzzled him how so elaborate a civilisation as Roman Britain could have been destroyed utterly and left no mark on the national history beyond a few roads and ruins and place-names. Peckwether, the historian, demurred, and had a good deal to say about how much the Roman tradition was woven into the Saxon culture. " Rome only sleeps," he said ; " she never dies."

Nightingale nodded. " Sometimes she dreams in her sleep and talks. Once she scared me out of my senses."

After a good deal of pressing he produced this story.
He was not much of a talker, so he wrote it out and read it
to us.

There is a place in Shropshire which I do not propose to
visit again. It lies between Ludlow and the hills, in a
shallow valley full of woods. Its name is St. Sant, a village
with a big house and park adjoining, on a stream called the
Vaun, about five miles from the little town of Faxeter.
They have queer names in those parts, and other things
queerer than the names.

I was motoring from Wales to Cambridge at the close of
the long vacation. All this happened before the War, when
I had just got my fellowship and was settling down to
academic work. It was a fine night in early October, with
a full moon, and I intended to push on to Ludlow for supper
and bed. The time was about half-past eight, the road was
empty and good going, and I was trundling pleasantly along
when something went wrong with my headlights. It was a
small thing, and I stopped to remedy it beyond a village
and just at the lodge-gates of a house.

On the opposite side of the road a carrier's cart had drawn
up, and two men, who looked like indoor servants, were
lifting some packages from it on to a big barrow. The moon
was up, so I didn't need the feeble light of the carrier's lamp
to see what they were doing. I suppose I wanted to stretch
my legs for a moment, for when I had finished my job I
strolled over to them. They did not hear me coming, and
the carrier on his perch seemed to be asleep.

The packages were the ordinary consignments from some
big shop in town. But I noticed that the two men handled
them very gingerly, and that, as each was laid in the barrow,
they clipped off the shop label and affixed one of their own.
The new labels were odd things, large and square, with some
address written on them in very black capital letters.
There was nothing in that, but the men's faces puzzled me.
For they seemed to do their job in a fever, longing to get it
over and yet in a sweat lest they should make some mistake.
Their commonplace task seemed to be for them a matter of
tremendous importance. I moved so as to get a view of
their faces, and I saw that they were white and strained.
The two were of the butler or valet class, both elderly, and

I could have sworn that they were labouring under something like fear.

I shuffled my feet to let them know of my presence and remarked that it was a fine night. They started as if they had been robbing a corpse. One of them mumbled something in reply, but the other caught a package which was slipping, and in a tone of violent alarm growled to his mate to be careful. I had a notion that they were handling explosives.

I had no time to waste, so I pushed on. That night, in my room at Ludlow, I had the curiosity to look up my map and identify the place where I had seen the men. The village was St. Sant, and it appeared that the gate I had stopped at belonged to a considerable demesne called Vauncastle. That was my first visit.

At that time I was busy on a critical edition of Theocritus, for which I was making a new collation of the manuscripts. There was a variant of the Medicean Codex in England, which nobody had seen since Gaisford, and after a good deal of trouble I found that it was in the library of a man called Dubellay. I wrote to him at his London club, and, to my surprise, got a reply from Vauncastle Hall, Faxeter. It was an odd letter, for you could see that he longed to tell me to go to the devil, but couldn't quite reconcile it with his conscience. We exchanged several letters, and the upshot was that he gave me permission to examine his manuscript. He did not ask me to stay, but mentioned that there was a comfortable little inn in St. Sant.

My second visit began on the 27th of December, after I had been home for Christmas. We had had a week of severe frost, and then it had thawed a little ; but it remained bitterly cold, with leaden skies that threatened snow. I drove from Faxeter, and as we ascended the valley I remember thinking that it was a curiously sad country. The hills were too low to be impressive, and their outlines were mostly blurred with woods ; but the tops showed clear, funny little knolls of grey bent that suggested a volcanic origin. It might have been one of those backgrounds you find in Italian primitives, with all the light and colour left out. When I got a glimpse of the Vaun in the bleached meadows it looked like the " wan water " of the Border ballads. The woods, too, had not the friendly bareness of

English copses in winter-time. They remained dark and
cloudy, as if they were hiding secrets. Before I reached
St. Sant, I decided that the landscape was not only sad, but
ominous.

I was fortunate in my inn. In the single street of one-
storied cottages it rose like a lighthouse, with a cheery glow
from behind the red curtains of the bar parlour. The inside
proved as good as the outside. I found a bedroom with a
bright fire, and I dined in a wainscoted room full of preposterous old pictures of lanky hounds and hollow-backed
horses. I had been rather depressed on my journey, but
my spirits were raised by this comfort, and when the house
produced a most respectable bottle of port I had the landlord in to drink a glass. He was an ancient man who had
been a gamekeeper, with a much younger wife, who was
responsible for the management. I was curious to hear
something about the owner of my manuscript, but I got
little from the landlord. He had been with the old squire,
and had never served the present one. I heard of Dubellays
in plenty—the landlord's master, who had hunted his own
hounds for forty years; the Major his brother, who had fallen
at Abu Klea ; Parson Jack, who had had the living till he
died, and of all kinds of collaterals. The " Deblays " had
been a high-spirited, open-handed stock, and much liked
in the place. But of the present master of the Hall he could
or would tell me nothing. The Squire was a " great schol-
ard," but I gathered that he followed no sport and was not
a convivial soul like his predecessors. He had spent a mint
of money on the house, but not many people went there.
He, the landlord, had never been inside the grounds in the
new master's time, though in the old days there had been
hunt breakfasts on the lawn for the whole countryside, and
mighty tenantry dinners. I went to bed with a clear
picture in my mind of the man I was to interview on the
morrow. A scholarly and autocratic recluse, who collected
treasures and beautified his dwelling and probably lived in
his library. I rather looked forward to meeting him, for
the bonhomous sporting squire was not much in my line.

After breakfast next morning I made my way to the Hall.
It was the same leaden weather, and when I entered the
gates the air seemed to grow bitterer and the skies darker.
The place was muffled in great trees which even in their

winter bareness made a pall about it. There was a long avenue of ancient sycamores, through which one caught only rare glimpses of the frozen park. I took my bearings, and realised that I was walking nearly due south, and was gradually descending. The house must be in a hollow. Presently the trees thinned, I passed through an iron gate, came out on a big untended lawn, untidily studded with laurels and rhododendrons, and there before me was the house front.

I had expected something beautiful—an old Tudor or Queen Anne façade or a dignified Georgian portico. I was disappointed, for the front was simply mean. It was low and irregular, more like the back parts of a house, and I guessed that at sometime or another the building had been turned round, and the old kitchen door made the chief entrance. I was confirmed in my conclusion by observing that the roofs rose in tiers like one of those recessed New York sky-scrapers, so that the present back parts of the building were of an impressive height.

The oddity of the place interested me, and still more its dilapidation. What on earth could the owner have spent his money on ? Everything—lawn, flower-beds, paths—was neglected. There was a new stone doorway, but the walls badly needed pointing, the window woodwork had not been painted for ages, and there were several broken panes. The bell did not ring, so I was reduced to hammering on the knocker, and it must have been ten minutes before the door opened. A pale butler, one of the men I had seen at the carrier's cart the October before, stood blinking in the entrance.

He led me in without question, when I gave my name, so I was evidently expected. The hall was my second surprise. What had become of my picture of the collector ? The place was small and poky, and furnished as barely as the lobby of a farmhouse. The only thing I approved was its warmth. Unlike most English country houses there seemed to be excellent heating arrangements.

I was taken into a little dark room with one window that looked out on a shrubbery, while the man went to fetch his master. My chief feeling was of gratitude that I had not been asked to stay, for the inn was paradise compared with this sepulchre. I was examining the prints on the wall, when I heard my name spoken and turned round to greet Mr. Dubellay.

He was my third surprise. I had made a portrait in my mind of a fastidious old scholar, with eye-glasses on a black cord, and a finical *weltkind*-ish manner. Instead I found a man still in early middle age, a heavy fellow dressed in the roughest country tweeds. He was as untidy as his demesne, for he had not shaved that morning, his flannel collar was badly frayed, and his finger-nails would have been the better for a scrubbing brush. His face was hard to describe. It was high-coloured, but the colour was not healthy; it was friendly, but it was also wary; above all, it was *unquiet*. He gave me the impression of a man whose nerves were all wrong, and who was perpetually on his guard.

He said a few civil words, and thrust a badly tied brown paper parcel at me.

" That's your manuscript," he said jauntily.

I was staggered. I had expected to be permitted to collate the codex in his library, and in the last few minutes had realised that the prospect was distasteful. But here was this casual owner offering me the priceless thing to take away.

I stammered my thanks, and added that it was very good of him to trust a stranger with such a treasure.

" Only as far as the inn," he said. " I wouldn't like to send it by post. But there's no harm in your working at it at the inn. There should be confidence among scholars." And he gave an odd cackle of a laugh.

" I greatly prefer your plan," I said. " But I thought you would insist on my working at it here."

" No, indeed," he said earnestly. " I shouldn't think of such a thing. . . . Wouldn't do at all. . . . An insult to our freemasonry. . . . That's how I should regard it."

We had a few minutes' further talk. I learned that he had inherited under the entail from a cousin, and had been just over ten years at Vauncastle. Before that he had been a London solicitor. He asked me a question or two about Cambridge—wished he had been at the University—much hampered in his work by a defective education. I was a Greek scholar ?—Latin, too, he presumed. Wonderful people the Romans. . . . He spoke quite freely, but all the time his queer restless eyes were darting about, and I had a strong impression that he would have liked to say something to me very different from these commonplaces—that he was longing to broach some subject but was held back by shyness or fear. He had such an odd appraising way of looking at me.

I left without his having asked me to a meal, for which I was not sorry, for I did not like the atmosphere of the place. I took a short cut over the ragged lawn, and turned at the top of the slope to look back. The house was in reality a huge pile, and I saw that I had been right and that the main building was all at the back. Was it, I wondered, like the Alhambra, which behind a front like a factory concealed a treasure-house ? I saw, too, that the woodland hollow was more spacious than I had fancied. The house, as at present arranged, faced due north, and behind the south front was an open space in which I guessed that a lake might lie. Far beyond I could see in the December dimness the lift of high dark hills.

That evening the snow came in earnest, and fell continuously for the better part of two days. I banked up the fire in my bedroom and spent a happy time with the codex. I had brought only my working books with me and the inn boasted no library, so when I wanted to relax I went down to the tap-room, or gossiped with the landlady in the bar parlour. The yokels who congregated in the former were pleasant fellows, but, like all the folk on the Marches, they did not talk readily to a stranger and I heard little from them of the Hall. The old squire had reared every year three thousand pheasants, but the present squire would not allow a gun to be fired on his land and there were only a few wild birds left. For the same reason the woods were thick with vermin. This they told me when I professed an interest in shooting. But of Mr. Dubellay they would not speak, declaring that they never saw him. I daresay they gossiped wildly about him, and their public reticence struck me as having in it a touch of fear.

The landlady, who came from a different part of the shire, was more communicative. She had not known the former Dubellays and so had no standard of comparison, but she was inclined to regard the present squire as not quite right in the head. " They do say," she would begin, but she, too, suffered from some inhibition, and what promised to be sensational would tail off into the commonplace. One thing apparently puzzled the neighbourhood above others, and that was his rearrangement of the house. " They do say," she said in an awed voice, " that he have built a great church." She had never visited it—no one in the parish had, for Squire Dubellay did not allow intruders—but from Lyne Hill you could see it through a gap in the woods. " He's no good Christian," she told me, " and him and Vicar has quarrelled this many a day. But they do say as he worships summat there." I learned that there were no women servants in the house, only the men he had brought from London. " Poor benighted souls, they must live in a sad hobble," and the buxom lady shrugged her shoulders and giggled.

On the last day of December I decided that I needed exercise and must go for a long stride. The snow had ceased that morning, and the dull skies had changed to a clear blue. It was still very cold, but the sun was shining, the snow was firm and crisp underfoot, and I proposed to survey the country. So after luncheon I put on thick boots and gaiters, and made for Lyne Hill. This meant a considerable circuit, for the place lay south of the Vauncastle park. From it I hoped to get a view of the other side of the house.

I was not disappointed. There was a rift in the thick woodlands, and below me, two miles off, I suddenly saw a strange building, like a classical temple. Only the entablature and the tops of the pillars showed above the trees, but they stood out vivid and dark against the background of snow. The spectacle in that lonely place was so startling that for a little I could only stare. I remember that I glanced behind me to the snowy line of the Welsh mountains, and felt that I might have been looking at a winter view of the Apennines two thousand years ago.

My curiosity was now alert, and I determined to get a nearer view of this marvel. I left the track and ploughed through the snowy fields down to the skirts of the woods. After that my troubles began. I found myself in a very good imitation of a primeval forest, where the undergrowth had been unchecked and the rides uncut for years. I sank into deep pits, I was savagely torn by briers and brambles, but I struggled on, keeping a line as best I could. At last the trees stopped. Before me was a flat expanse which I knew must be a lake, and beyond rose the temple.

It ran the whole length of the house, and from where I stood it was hard to believe that there were buildings at its back where men dwelt. It was a fine piece of work—the first glance told me that—admirably proportioned, classical, yet not following exactly any of the classical models. One could imagine a great echoing interior dim with the smoke of sacrifice, and it was only by reflecting that I realised that the peristyle could not be continued down the two sides, that there was no interior, and that what I was looking at was only a portico.

The thing was at once impressive and preposterous. What madness had been in Dubellay when he embellished his house with such a grandiose garden front ? The sun was setting and the shadow of the wooded hills darkened the interior, so I could not even make out the back wall of the porch. I wanted a nearer view, so I embarked on the frozen lake.

Then I had an odd experience. I was not tired, the snow lay level and firm, but I was conscious of extreme weariness. The biting air had become warm and oppressive. I had to drag boots that seemed to weigh tons across that lake. The place was utterly silent in the stricture of the frost, and from the pile in front no sign of life came.

I reached the other side at last and found myself in a frozen shallow of bulrushes and skeleton willow-herbs. They were taller than my head, and to see the house I had to look upward through their snowy traceries. It was perhaps eighty feet above me and a hundred yards distant, and, since I was below it, the delicate pillars seemed to spring to a great height. But it was still dusky, and the only detail I could see was on the ceiling, which seemed either to be carved or painted with deeply-shaded monochrome figures.

Suddenly the dying sun came slanting through the gap in the hills, and for an instant the whole portico to its farthest recesses was washed in clear gold and scarlet. That was wonderful enough, but there was something more. The air was utterly still with not the faintest breath of wind— so still that when I had lit a cigarette half an hour before the flame of the match had burned steadily upward like a candle in a room. As I stood among the sedges not a single frost crystal stirred. . . . But there was a wind blowing in the portico.

I could see it lifting feathers of snow from the base of the pillars and fluffing the cornices. The floor had already been swept clean, but tiny flakes drifted on to it from the exposed edges. The interior was filled with a furious movement, though a yard from it was frozen peace. I felt nothing of the action of the wind, but I knew that it was hot, hot as the breath of a furnace.

I had only one thought, dread of being overtaken by night near that place. I turned and ran. Ran with labouring steps across the lake, panting and stifling with a deadly hot oppression, ran blindly by a sort of instinct in the direction of the village. I did not stop till I had wrestled through the big wood, and come out on some rough pasture above the highway. Then I dropped on the ground, and felt again the comforting chill of the December air.

The adventure left me in an uncomfortable mood. I was ashamed of myself for playing the fool, and at the same time hopelessly puzzled, for the oftener I went over in my mind the incidents of that afternoon the more I was at a loss for an explanation. One feeling was uppermost, that I did not like this place and wanted to be out of it. I had already broken the back of my task, and by shutting myself up for two days I completed it ; that is to say, I made my collation as far as I had advanced myself in my commentary on the text. I did not want to go back to the Hall, so I wrote a civil note to Dubellay, expressing my gratitude and saying that I was sending up the manuscript by the landlord's son, as I scrupled to trouble him with another visit.

I got a reply at once, saying that Mr. Dubellay would like to give himself the pleasure of dining with me at the inn before I went, and would receive the manuscript in person.

It was the last night of my stay in St. Sant, so I ordered the best dinner the place could provide, and a magnum of claret, of which I discovered a bin in the cellar. Dubellay appeared promptly at eight o'clock, arriving to my surprise in a car. He had tidied himself up and put on a dinner jacket, and he looked exactly like the city solicitors you see dining in the Junior Carlton.

He was in excellent spirits, and his eyes had lost their air of being on guard. He seemed to have reached some conclusion about me, or decided that I was harmless. More, he seemed to be burning to talk to me. After my adventure

I was prepared to find fear in him, the fear I had seen in the faces of the men-servants. But there was none ; instead there was excitement, overpowering excitement.

He neglected the courses in his verbosity. His coming to dinner had considerably startled the inn, and instead of a maid the landlady herself waited on us. She seemed to want to get the meal over, and hustled the biscuits and the port on to the table as soon as she decently could. Then Dubellay became confidential.

He was an enthusiast, it appeared, an enthusiast with a single hobby. All his life he had pottered among antiquities, and when he succeeded to Vauncastle he had the leisure and money to indulge himself. The place, it seemed, had been famous in Roman Britain—Vauni Castra—and Faxeter was a corruption of the same. " Who was Vaunus ? " I asked. He grinned, and told me to wait.

There had been an old temple up in the high woods. There had always been a local legend about it, and the place was supposed to be haunted. Well, he had had the site excavated and he had found—— Here he became the cautious solicitor, and explained to me the law of treasure trove. As long as the objects found were not intrinsically valuable, not gold or jewels, the finder was entitled to keep them. He had done so—had not published the results of his excavations in the proceedings of any learned society—did not want to be bothered by tourists. I was different, for I was a scholar.

What had he found ? It was really rather hard to follow his babbling talk, but I gathered that he had found certain carvings and sacrificial implements. And—he sunk his voice—most important of all, an altar, an altar of Vaunus, the tutelary deity of the vale.

When he mentioned this word his face took on a new look —not of fear but of secrecy, a kind of secret excitement. I have seen the same look on the face of a street-preaching Salvationist.

Vaunus had been a British god of the hills, whom the Romans in their liberal way appear to have identified with Apollo. He gave me a long confused account of him, from which it appeared that Mr. Dubellay was not an exact scholar. Some of his derivations of place-names were absurd—like St. Sant from Sancta Sanctorum—and in quoting a line of Ausonius he made two false quantities. He seemed to hope that I could tell him something more about Vaunus, but I said that my subject was Greek, and that I was deeply ignorant about Roman Britain. I mentioned several books, and found that he had never heard of Haverfield.

One word he used, " hypocaust," which suddenly gave me a clue. He must have heated the temple, as he heated his house, by some very efficient system of hot air. I know little about science, but I imagined that the artificial heat of the portico, as contrasted with the cold outside, might create an air current. At any rate that explanation satisfied me, and my afternoon's adventure lost its uncanniness. The reaction made me feel friendly towards him, and I listened to his talk with sympathy, but I decided not to mention that I had visited his temple.

He told me about it himself in the most open way. " I couldn't leave the altar on the hillside," he said. " I had to make a place for it, so I turned the old front of the house into a sort of temple. I got the best advice, but architects are ignorant people, and I often wished I had been a better scholar. Still the place satisfies me."

" I hope it satisfies Vaunus," I said jocularly.

" I think so," he replied quite seriously, and then his thoughts seemed to go wandering, and for a minute or so he looked through me with a queer abstraction in his eyes.

" What do you do with it now you've got it ? " I asked.

He didn't reply, but smiled to himself.

" I don't know if you remember a passage in Sidonius Apollinaris," I said, " a formula for consecrating pagan altars to Christian uses. You begin by sacrificing a white cock or something suitable and tell Apollo with all friendliness that the old dedication is off for the present. Then you have a Christian invocation——"

He nearly jumped out of his chair.

" That wouldn't do—wouldn't do at all ! . . . Oh Lord, no ! . . . Couldn't think of it for one moment ! "

It was as if I had offended his ears by some horrid blasphemy, and the odd thing was that he never recovered his composure. He tried, for he had good manners, but his ease and friendliness had gone. We talked stiffly for another half-hour about trifles, and then he rose to leave.

I returned him his manuscript neatly parcelled up, and
expanded in thanks, but he scarcely seemed to heed me.
He stuck the thing in his pocket, and departed with the
same air of shocked absorption.

After he had gone I sat before the fire and reviewed the
situation. I was satisfied with my hypocaust theory, and
had no more perturbation in my memory about my afternoon's adventure. Yet a slight flavour of unpleasantness
hung about it, and I felt that I did not quite like Dubellay.
I set him down as a crank who had tangled himself up with
a half-witted hobby, like an old maid with her cats, and I
was not sorry to be leaving the place.

My third and last visit to St. Sant was in the following
June—the midsummer of 1914. I had all but finished my
Theocritus, but I needed another day or two with the
Vauncastle manuscript, and, as I wanted to clear the whole
thing off before I went to Italy in July, I wrote to Dubellay
and asked if I might have another sight of it. The thing
was a bore, but it had to be faced, and I fancied that the
valley would be a pleasant place in that hot summer.

I got a reply at once, inviting, almost begging me to come,
and insisting that I should stay at the Hall. I couldn't
very well refuse, though I would have preferred the inn.
He wired about my train, and wired again saying he would
meet me. This time I seemed to be a particularly welcome
guest.

I reached Faxeter in the evening, and was met by a car
from a Faxeter garage. The driver was a talkative young
man, and, as the car was a closed one, I sat beside him for
the sake of fresh air. The term had tired me, and I was
glad to get out of stuffy Cambridge, but I cannot say that I
found it much cooler as we ascended the Vaun valley. The
woods were in their summer magnificence but a little dulled
and tarnished by the heat, the river was shrunk to a trickle,
and the curious hill-tops were so scorched by the sun that
they seemed almost yellow above the green of the trees.
Once again I had the feeling of a landscape fantastically
unEnglish.

"Squire Dubellay's been in a great way about your
coming, sir," the driver informed me. "Sent down three
times to the boss to make sure it was all right. He's got a

car of his own, too, a nice little Daimler, but he don't seem
to use it much. Haven't seen him about in it for a month
of Sundays."

As we turned in at the Hall gates he looked curiously
about him. "Never been here before, though I've been in
most gentlemen's parks for fifty miles round. Rum old-
fashioned spot, isn't it, sir ? "

If it had seemed a shuttered sanctuary in mid-winter, in
that June twilight it was more than ever a place enclosed
and guarded. There was almost an autumn smell of decay,
a dry decay like touchwood. We seemed to be descending
through layers of ever-thickening woods. When at last we
turned through the iron gate I saw that the lawns had
reached a further stage of neglect, for they were as shaggy
as a hayfield.

The white-faced butler let me in, and there, waiting at
his back, was Dubellay. But he was not the man whom I
had seen in December. He was dressed in an old baggy suit
of flannels, and his unwholesome red face was painfully
drawn and sunken. There were dark pouches under his
eyes, and these eyes were no longer excited, but dull and
pained. Yes, and there was more than pain in them—there
was fear. I wondered if his hobby were becoming too much
for him.

He greeted me like a long-lost brother. Considering that
I scarcely knew him, I was a little embarrassed by his
warmth. "Bless you for coming, my dear fellow," he
cried. "You want a wash and then we'll have dinner.
Don't bother to change, unless you want to. I never do."
He led me to my bedroom, which was clean enough, but small
and shabby like a servant's room. I guessed that he had
gutted the house to build his absurd temple.

We dined in a fair-sized room which was a kind of library.
It was lined with old books, but they did not look as if they
had been there long ; rather it seemed like a lumber-room
in which a fine collection had been stored. Once no doubt
they had lived in a dignified Georgian chamber. There was
nothing else, none of the antiques which I had expected.

"You have come just in time," he told me. "I fairly
jumped when I got your letter, for I had been thinking of
running up to Cambridge to insist on your coming down
here. I hope you're in no hurry to leave."

"As it happens," I said, "I *am* rather pressed for time,
for I hope to go abroad next week. I ought to finish my
work here in a couple of days. I can't tell you how much
I'm in your debt for your kindness."

"Two days," he said. "That will get us over midsummer. That should be enough." I hadn't a notion what
he meant.

I told him that I was looking forward to examining his
collection. He opened his eyes. "Your discoveries, I
mean," I said, "the altar of Vaunus . . ."

As I spoke the words his face suddenly contorted in a
spasm of what looked like terror. He choked and then
recovered himself. "Yes, yes," he said rapidly. "You
shall see it—you shall see everything—but not now—not
to-night. To-morrow—in broad daylight—that's the time."

After that the evening became a bad dream. Small talk
deserted him, and he could only reply with an effort to my
commonplaces. I caught him often looking at me furtively,
as if he were sizing me up and wondering how far he could
go with me. The thing fairly got on my nerves, and to
crown all, it was abominably stuffy. The windows of the
room gave on a little paved court with a background of
laurels, and I might have been in Seven Dials for all the air
there was.

When coffee was served I could stand it no longer.
"What about smoking in the temple?" I said. "It should
be cool there with the air from the lake."

I might have been proposing the assassination of his
mother. He simply gibbered at me. "No, no," he
stammered. "My God, no!" It was half an hour before
he could properly collect himself. A servant lit two oil
lamps, and we sat on in the frowsty room.

"You said something when we last met," he ventured
at last, after many a sidelong glance at me. "Something
about a ritual for rededicating an altar."

I remembered my remark about Sidonius Apollinaris.

"Could you show me the passage? There is a good
classical library here, collected by my great-grandfather.
Unfortunately my scholarship is not equal to using it
properly."

I got up and hunted along the shelves, and presently
found a copy of Sidonius, the Plantin edition of 1609. I

turned up the passage, and roughly translated it for him. He listened hungrily and made me repeat it twice.

"He says a cock," he hesitated. "Is that essential?"

"I don't think so. I fancy any of the recognised ritual stuff would do."

"I am glad," he said simply. "I am afraid of blood."

"Good God, man," I cried out, "are you taking my nonsense seriously? I was only chaffing. Let old Vaunus stick to his altar!"

He looked at me like a puzzled and rather offended dog.

"Sidonius was in earnest . . ."

"Well, I'm not," I said rudely. "We're in the twentieth century and not in the third. Isn't it about time we went to bed?"

He made no objection, and found me a candle in the hall. As I undressed I wondered into what kind of lunatic asylum I had strayed. I felt the strongest distaste for the place, and longed to go straight off to the inn; only I couldn't make use of a man's manuscripts and insult his hospitality. It was fairly clear to me that Dubellay was mad. He had ridden his hobby to the death of his wits and was now in its bondage. Good Lord! he had talked of his precious Vaunus as a votary talks of a god. I believed he had come to worship some figment of his half-educated fancy.

I think I must have slept for a couple of hours. Then I woke dripping with perspiration, for the place was simply an oven. My window was as wide open as it would go, and, though it was a warm night, when I stuck my head out the air was fresh. The heat came from indoors. The room was on the first floor near the entrance and I was looking on to the overgrown lawns. The night was very dark and utterly still, but I could have sworn that I heard wind. The trees were as motionless as marble, but somewhere close at hand I heard a strong gust blowing. Also, though there was no moon, there was somewhere near me a steady glow of light; I could see the reflection of it round the end of the house. That meant that it came from the temple. What kind of saturnalia was Dubellay conducting at such an hour?

When I drew in my head I felt that if I was to get any sleep something must be done. There could be no question about it; some fool had turned on the steam heat, for the room was a furnace. My temper was rising. There was no bell to be found, so I lit my candle and set out to find a servant.

I tried a cast downstairs and discovered the room where we had dined. Then I explored a passage at right angles, which brought me up against a great oak door. The light showed me that it was a new door, and that there was no apparent way of opening it. I guessed that it led into the temple, and, though it fitted close and there seemed to be no key-hole, I could hear through it a sound like a rushing wind. . . . Next I opened a door on my right and found myself in a big store cupboard. It had a funny, exotic, spicy smell, and arranged very neatly on the floor and shelves was a number of small sacks and coffers. Each bore a label, a square of stout paper with very black lettering. I read " *Pro servitio Vauni.*"

I had seen them before, for my memory betrayed me if they were not the very labels that Dubellay's servants had been attaching to the packages from the carrier's cart that evening in the past autumn. The discovery made my suspicions an unpleasant certainty. Dubellay evidently meant the labels to read " For the service of Vaunus." He was no scholar, for it was an impossible use of the word " servitium," but he was very patently a madman.

However, it was my immediate business to find some way to sleep, so I continued my quest for a servant. I followed another corridor, and discovered a second staircase. At the top of it I saw an open door and looked in. It must have been Dubellay's, for his flannels were tumbled untidily on a chair, but Dubellay himself was not there and the bed had not been slept in.

I suppose my irritation was greater than my alarm— though I must say I was getting a little scared—for I still pursued the evasive servant. There was another stair which apparently led to attics, and in going up it I slipped and made a great clatter. When I looked up the butler in his nightgown was staring down at me, and if ever a mortal face held fear it was his. When he saw who it was he seemed to recover a little.

" Look here," I said, " for God's sake turn off that infernal hot air. I can't get a wink of sleep. What idiot set it going ? "

He looked at me owlishly, but he managed to find his tongue.

"I beg your pardon, sir," he said, "but there is no heating apparatus in this house."

There was nothing more to be said. I returned to my bedroom and it seemed to me that it had grown cooler. As I leaned out of the window, too, the mysterious wind seemed to have died away, and the glow no longer showed from beyond the corner of the house. I got into bed and slept heavily till I was roused by the appearance of my shaving water about half-past nine. There was no bathroom, so I bathed in a tin pannikin.

It was a hazy morning, which promised a day of blistering heat. When I went down to breakfast I found Dubellay in the dining-room. In the daylight he looked a very sick man, but he seemed to have taken a pull on himself, for his manner was considerably less nervy than the night before. Indeed, he appeared almost normal, and I might have reconsidered my view but for the look in his eyes.

I told him that I proposed to sit tight all day over the manuscript, and get the thing finished. He nodded. "That's all right. I've a lot to do myself, and I won't disturb you."

"But first," I said, "you promised to show me your discoveries."

He looked at the window where the sun was shining on the laurels and on a segment of the paved court.

"The light is good," he said—an odd remark. "Let us go there now. There are times and seasons for the temple."

He led me down the passage I had explored the previous night. The door opened not by a key but by some lever in the wall. I found myself looking suddenly at a bath of sunshine with the lake below as blue as a turquoise.

It is not easy to describe my impressions of that place. It was unbelievably light and airy, as brilliant as an Italian colonnade in midsummer. The proportions must have been good, for the columns soared and swam, and the roof (which looked like cedar) floated as delicately as a flower on its stalk. The stone was some local limestone, which on the floor took a polish like marble. All around was a vista of sparkling water and summer woods and far blue mountains. It should have been as wholesome as the top of a hill.

And yet I had scarcely entered before I knew that it was a prison. I am not an imaginative man, and I believe my nerves are fairly good, but I could scarcely put one foot before the other, so strong was my distaste. I felt shut off from the world, as if I were in a dungeon or on an ice-floe. And I felt, too, that though far enough from humanity, we were not alone.

On the inner wall there were three carvings. Two were imperfect friezes sculptured in low-relief, dealing apparently with the same subject. It was a ritual procession, priests bearing branches, the ordinary *dendrophori* business. The faces were only half-human, and that was from no lack of skill, for the artist had been a master. The striking thing was that the branches and the hair of the hierophants were being tossed by a violent wind, and the expression of each was of a being in the last stage of endurance, shaken to the core by terror and pain.

Between the friezes was a great roundel of a Gorgon's head. It was not a female head, such as you commonly find, but a male head, with the viperous hair sprouting from chin and lip. It had once been coloured, and fragments of a green pigment remained in the locks. It was an awful thing, the ultimate horror of fear, the last dementia of cruelty made manifest in stone. I hurriedly averted my eyes and looked at the altar.

That stood at the west end on a pediment with three steps. It was a beautiful piece of work, scarcely harmed by the centuries, with two words inscribed on its face—APOLL. VAUN. It was made of some foreign marble, and the hollow top was dark with ancient sacrifices. Not so ancient either, for I could have sworn that I saw there the mark of recent flame.

I do not suppose I was more than five minutes in the place. I wanted to get out, and Dubellay wanted to get me out. We did not speak a word till we were back in the library.

"For God's sake give it up!" I said. "You're playing with fire, Mr. Dubellay. You're driving yourself into Bedlam. Send these damned things to a museum and leave this place. Now, now, I tell you. You have no time to lose. Come down with me to the inn straight off and shut up this house."

He looked at me with his lip quivering like a child about to cry.

"I will. I promise you I will. . . . But not yet. . . . After to-night. . . . To-morrow I'll do whatever you tell me. . . . You won't leave me ? "

"I won't leave you, but what earthly good am I to you if you won't take my advice ? "

"Sidonius . . ." he began.

"Oh, damn Sidonius ! I wish I had never mentioned him. The whole thing is arrant nonsense, but it's killing you. You've got it on the brain. Don't you know you're a sick man ? "

"I'm not feeling very grand. It's so warm to-day. I think I'll lie down."

It was no good arguing with him, for he had the appalling obstinacy of very weak things. I went off to my work in a shocking, bad temper.

The day was what it had promised to be, blisteringly hot. Before midday the sun was hidden by a coppery haze, and there was not the faintest stirring of wind. Dubellay did not appear at luncheon—it was not a meal he ever ate, the butler told me. I slogged away all the afternoon, and had pretty well finished my job by six o'clock. That would enable me to leave next morning, and I hoped to be able to persuade my host to come with me.

The conclusion of my task put me into a better humour, and I went for a walk before dinner. It was a very close evening, for the heat haze had not lifted ; the woods were as silent as a grave, not a bird spoke, and when I came out of the cover to the burnt pastures the sheep seemed too languid to graze. During my walk I prospected the environs of the house, and saw that it would be very hard to get access to the temple except by a long circuit. On one side was a mass of outbuildings, and then a high wall, and on the other the very closest and highest quickset hedge I have ever seen, which ended in a wood with savage spikes on its containing wall. I returned to my room, had a cold bath in the exiguous tub, and changed.

Dubellay was not at dinner. The butler said that his master was feeling unwell and had gone to bed. The news pleased me, for bed was the best place for him. After that I settled myself down to a lonely evening in the library.

I browsed among the shelves and found a number of rare editions which served to pass the time. I noticed that the copy of Sidonius was absent from its place.

I think it was about ten o'clock when I went to bed, for I was unaccountably tired. I remember wondering whether I oughtn't to go and visit Dubellay, but decided that it was better to leave him alone. I still reproach myself for that decision. I know now I ought to have taken him by force and haled him to the inn.

Suddenly I came out of heavy sleep with a start. A human cry seemed to be ringing in the corridors of my brain. I held my breath and listened. It came again, a horrid scream of panic and torture.

I was out of bed in a second, and only stopped to get my feet into slippers. The cry must have come from the temple. I tore downstairs expecting to hear the noise of an alarmed household. But there was no sound and the awful cry was not repeated.

The door in the corridor was shut, as I expected. Behind it pandemonium seemed to be loose, for there was a howling like a tempest—and something more, a crackling like fire. I made for the front door, slipped off the chain, and found myself in the still, moonless night. Still, except for the rending gale that seemed to be raging in the house I had left.

From what I had seen on my evening's walk I knew that my one chance to get to the temple was by way of the quickset hedge. I thought I might manage to force a way between the end of it and the wall. I did it, at the cost of much of my raiment and my skin. Beyond was another rough lawn set with tangled shrubberies, and then a precipitous slope to the level of the lake. I scrambled along the sedgy margin, not daring to lift my eyes till I was on the temple steps.

The place was brighter than day with a roaring blast of fire. The very air seemed to be incandescent and to have become a flaming ether. And yet there were no flames—only a burning brightness. I could not enter, for the waft from it struck my face like a scorching hand and I felt my hair singe. . . .

I am short-sighted as you know, and I may have been mistaken, but this is what I think I saw. From the altar a great tongue of flame seemed to shoot upwards and lick the roof, and from its pediment ran flaming streams. In front of it lay a body—Dubellay's—a naked body, already charred and black. There was nothing else, except that the Gorgon's head in the wall seemed to glow like a sun in hell. I suppose I must have tried to enter. All I know is that I found myself staggering back, rather badly burned. I covered my eyes, and as I looked through my fingers I seemed to see the flames flowing under the wall, where there may have been lockers, or possibly another entrance. Then the great oak door suddenly shrivelled like gauze, and with a roar the fiery river poured into the house.

I ducked myself in the lake to ease the pain, and then ran back as hard as I could by the way I had come. Dubellay, poor devil, was beyond my aid. After that I am not very clear what happened. I know that the house burned like a haystack. I found one of the men-servants on the lawn, and I think I helped to get the other down from his room by one of the rain-pipes. By the time the neighbours arrived the house was ashes, and I was pretty well mother-naked. They took me to the inn and put me to bed, and I remained there till after the inquest. The coroner's jury were puzzled, but they found it simply death by misadventure ; a lot of country houses were burned that summer. There was nothing found of Dubellay ; nothing remained of the house except a few blackened pillars ; the altar and the sculptures were so cracked and scarred that no museum wanted them. The place has not been rebuilt, and for all I know they are there to-day. I am not going back to look for them.

Nightingale finished his story and looked round his audience.

"Don't ask me for an explanation," he said, "for I haven't any. You may believe if you like that the god Vaunus inhabited the temple which Dubellay built for him, and, when his votary grew scared and tried Sidonius's receipt for shifting the dedication, became angry and slew him with his flaming wind. That wind seems to have been a perquisite of Vaunus. We know more about him now, for last year they dug up a temple of his in Wales."

"Lightning," someone suggested.

"It was a quiet night, with no thunderstorm," said Nightingale.

"In front of it lay a body."

" Isn't the countryside volcanic ? " Peckwether asked. " What about pockets of natural gas or something of the kind ? "

" Possibly. You may please yourself in your explanation. I'm afraid I can't help you. All I know is that I don't propose to visit that valley again ! "

" What became of your Theocritus ? "

" Burned, like everything else. However, that didn't worry me much. Six weeks later came the War, and I had other things to think about."

Reprinted with the Author's permission from *The Runagates Club*.

SING A SONG OF SIXPENCE

LEITHEN'S face had that sharp chiselling of the jaw and that compression of the lips which seem to follow upon high legal success. Also an overdose of German gas in 1918 had given his skin a habitual pallor, so that he looked not unhealthy, but notably urban. As a matter of fact he was one of the hardest men I have ever known, but a chance observer might have guessed from his complexion that he rarely left the pavements.

Burminster, who had come back from a month in the grass countries with a face like a deep-sea mariner's, commented on this one evening.

"How do you manage always to look the complete Cit, Ned?" he asked. "You're as much a Londoner as a Parisian is a Parisian, if you know what I mean."

Leithen said that he was not ashamed of it, and he embarked on a eulogy of the metropolis. In London you met sooner or later everybody you had ever known; you could lay your hand on any knowledge you wanted; you could pull strings that controlled the innermost Sahara and the topmost Pamirs. Romance lay in wait for you at every street corner. It was the true City of the Caliphs.

"That is what they say," said Sandy Arbuthnot sadly, "but I never found it so. I yawn my head off in London. Nothing amusing ever finds me out—I have to go and search for it, and it usually costs the deuce of a lot."

"I once stumbled upon a pretty generous allowance of romance," said Leithen, "and it cost me precisely sixpence."

Then he told us this story.

It happened a good many years ago, just when I was beginning to get on at the Bar. I spent busy days in court and chambers, but I was young and had a young man's appetite for society, so I used to dine out most nights and go to more balls than were good for me. It was pleasant after

134

a heavy day to dive into a different kind of life. My rooms at the time were in Down Street, the same house as my present one, only two floors higher up.

On a certain night in February I was dining in Bryanston Square with the Nantleys. Mollie Nantley was an old friend, and used to fit me as an unattached bachelor into her big dinners. She was a young hostess and full of ambition, and one met an odd assortment of people at her house. Mostly political, of course, but a sprinkling of art and letters, and any visiting lion that happened to be passing through. Mollie was a very innocent lion-hunter, but she had a partiality for the breed.

I don't remember much about the dinner, except that the principal guest had failed her. Mollie was loud in her lamentations. He was a South American President who had engineered a very pretty *coup d'état* the year before, and was now in England on some business concerning the finances of his state. You may remember his name—Ramon Pelem—he made rather a stir in the world for a year or two. I had read about him in the papers, and had looked forward to meeting him, for he had won his way to power by extraordinary boldness and courage, and he was quite young. There was a story that he was partly English and that his grandfather's name had been Pelham. I don't know what truth there was in that, but he knew England well and Englishmen liked him.

Well, he had cried off on the telephone an hour before, and Mollie was grievously disappointed. Her other guests bore the loss with more fortitude, for I expect they thought he was a brand of cigar.

In those days dinners began earlier and dances later than they do to-day. I meant to leave soon, go back to my rooms and read briefs, and then look in at Lady Samplar's dance between eleven and twelve. So at nine-thirty I took my leave.

Jervis, the old butler, who had been my ally from boyhood, was standing on the threshold, and in the square there was a considerable crowd now thinning away. I asked what the trouble was.

" There's been an arrest, Mr. Edward," he said in an awestruck voice. " It 'appened when I was serving coffee in the dining-room, but our Albert saw it all. Two foreigners, he said—proper rascals by their look—were took away by the police just outside this very door. The constables was very nippy and collared them before they could use their pistols—but they 'ad pistols on them and no mistake. Albert says he saw the weapons."

" Did they propose to burgle you ? " I asked.

" I cannot say, Mr. Edward. But I shall give instructions for a very careful lock-up to-night."

There were no cabs about, so I decided to walk on and pick one up. When I got into Great Cumberland Place it began to rain sharply, and I was just about to call a prowling hansom, when I put my hand into my pocket. I found that I had no more than one solitary sixpence.

I could of course have paid when I got to my flat. But as the rain seemed to be slacking off, I preferred to walk. Mollie's dining-room had been stuffy, I had been in court all day, and I wanted some fresh air.

You know how in little things, when you have decided on a course, you are curiously reluctant to change it. Before I got to the Marble Arch it had begun to pour in downright earnest. But I still stumped on. Only I entered the Park, for even in February there is a certain amount of cover from the trees.

I passed one or two hurried pedestrians, but the place was almost empty. The occasional lamps made only spots of light in a dripping darkness, and it struck me that this was a curious patch of gloom and loneliness to be so near to crowded streets, for with the rain had come a fine mist. I pitied the poor devils to whom it was the only home. There was one of them on a seat which I passed. The collar of his thin, shabby overcoat was turned up, and his shameful old felt hat was turned down so that only a few square inches of pale face were visible. His toes stuck out of his boots, and he seemed sunk in a sodden misery.

I passed him and then turned back. Casual charity is an easy dope for the conscience, and I indulge in it too often. When I approached him he seemed to stiffen, and his hands moved in his pockets.

" A rotten night," I said. " Is sixpence any good to you ? " And I held out my solitary coin.

He lifted his face, and I started. For the eyes that looked at me were not those of a waster. They were bright, penetrating, authoritative—and they were young. I was conscious that they took in more of me than mine did of him.

"Thank you very much," he said, as he took the coin, and the voice was that of a cultivated man. "But I'm afraid I need rather more than sixpence."

"How much ? " I asked. This was clearly an original.

"To be accurate, five million pounds."

He was certainly mad, but I was fascinated by this wisp of humanity. I wished that he would show more of his face.

"Till your ship comes home," I said, "you want a bed, and you'd be the better of a change. Sixpence is all I have on me. But if you come to my rooms I'll give you the price of a night's lodging, and I think I might find you some old clothes."

"Where do you live ? " he asked.

"Close by—in Down Street." I gave the number.

He seemed to reflect, and then he shot a glance on either side into the gloom behind the road. It may have been fancy, but I thought that I saw something stir in the darkness.

"What are you ? " he asked.

I was getting abominably wet, and yet I submitted to be cross-examined by this waif.

"I am a lawyer," I said.

He looked at me again, very intently.

"Have you a telephone ? " he asked.

I nodded.

"Right," he said. "You seem a good fellow and I'll take you at your word. I'll follow you. . . . Don't look back, please. It's important. . . . I'll be in Down Street as soon as you. . . . *Marchons.*"

It sounds preposterous, but I did exactly as I was bid. I never looked back, but I kept my ears open for the sound of following footsteps. I thought I heard them and then they seemed to die away. I turned out of the Park at Grosvenor Gate and went down Park Lane. When I reached the house which contained my flat, I looked up and down the street, but it was empty except for a waiting four-wheeler. But just as I turned in I caught a glimpse of someone running at the Hertford Street end. The runner

5*

came to a sudden halt, and I saw that it was not the man I had left.

To my surprise I found the waif on the landing outside my flat. I was about to tell him to stop outside, but as soon as I unlocked the door he brushed past me and entered. My man, who did not sleep on the premises, had left the light burning in the little hall.

"Lock the door," he said in a tone of authority. "Forgive me taking charge, but I assure you it is important."

Then to my amazement he peeled off the sopping overcoat, and kicked off his disreputable shoes. They were odd shoes, for what looked like his toes sticking out was really part of the make-up. He stood up before me in underclothes and socks, and I noticed that his underclothing seemed to be of the finest material.

"Now for your telephone," he said.

I was getting angry at these liberties.

"Who the devil are you?" I demanded.

"I am President Pelem," he said, with all the dignity in the world. "And you?"

"I?—oh, I am the German Emperor."

He laughed. "You know you invited me here," he said. "You've brought this on yourself." Then he stared at me. "Hullo, I've seen you before. You're Leithen. I saw you play at Lord's. I was twelfth man for Harrow that year. . . . Now for the telephone."

There was something about the fellow, something defiant and debonair and young, that stopped all further protest on my part. He might or might not be President Pelem, but he was certainly not a wastrel. Besides, he seemed curiously keyed up, as if the occasion were desperately important, and he infected me with the same feeling. I said no more, but led the way into my sitting-room. He flung himself on the telephone, gave a number, was instantly connected, and began a conversation in monosyllables.

It was a queer jumble that I overheard. Bryanston Square was mentioned, and the Park, and the number of my house was given—to somebody. There was a string of foreign names—Pedro and Alejandro and Manuel and Alcaza—and short breathless inquiries. Then I heard— "a good fellow—looks as if he might be useful in a row," and I wondered if he was referring to me. Some rapid

Spanish followed, and then, " Come round at once—they
will be here before you. Have policemen below, but don't
let them come up. We should be able to manage alone.
Oh, and tell Burton to ring up here as soon as he has news."
And he gave my telephone number.

I put some coals on the fire, changed into a tweed jacket,
and lit a pipe. I fetched a dressing-gown from my bedroom
and flung it on the sofa. " You'd better put that on," I
said when he had finished.

He shook his head.

" I would rather be unencumbered," he said. " But I
should dearly love a cigarette . . . and a liqueur brandy,
if you have such a thing. That Park of yours is infernally
chilly."

I supplied his needs, and he stretched himself in an arm-
chair, with his stockinged feet to the fire.

" You have been very good-humoured, Leithen," he said.
" Valdez—that's my aide-de-camp—will be here presently,
and he will probably be preceded by other guests. But I
think I have time for the short explanation which is your
due. You believe what I told you ? "

I nodded.

" Good. Well, I came to London three weeks ago to raise
a loan. That was a matter of life or death for my big stupid
country. I have succeeded. This afternoon the agreement was signed. I think I mentioned the amount to you—
five million sterling."

He smiled happily and blew a smoke-ring into the air.

" I must tell you that I have enemies. Among my happy
people there are many rascals, and I had to deal harshly
with them. ' So foul a sky clears not without a storm '—
that's Shakespeare, isn't it ? I learned it at school. You
see, I had Holy Church behind me, and therefore I had
against me all the gentry who call themselves liberators.
Red Masons, anarchists, communists, that sort of crew. A
good many are now reposing beneath the sod, but some of
the worst remain. In particular, six followed me to England
with instructions that I must not return.

" I don't mind telling you, Leithen, that I have had a
peculiarly rotten time the last three weeks. It was most
important that nothing should happen to me till the loan
was settled, so I had to lead the sheltered life. It went

against the grain, I assure you, for I prefer the offensive to the defensive. The English police were very amiable, and I never stirred without a cordon, your people and my own. The Six wanted to kill me, and as it is pretty easy to kill anybody if you don't mind being killed yourself, we had to take rather elaborate precautions. As it was, I was twice nearly done in. Once my carriage broke down mysteriously, and a crowd collected, and if I hadn't had the luck to board a passing cab, I should have had a knife in my ribs. The second was at a public dinner—something not quite right about the cayenne pepper served with the oysters. One of my staff is still seriously ill."

He stretched his arms.

" Well, that first stage is over. They can't wreck the loan, whatever happens to me. Now I am free to adopt different tactics and take the offensive. I have no fear of the Six in my own country. There I can take precautions, and they will find it difficult to cross the frontier or to live for six hours thereafter if they succeed. But here you are a free people and protection is not so easy. I do not wish to leave England just yet—I have done my work and have earned a little play. I know your land and love it, and I look forward to seeing something of my friends. Also I want to attend the Grand National. Therefore, it is necessary that my enemies should be confined for a little, while I take my holiday. So for this evening I made a plan. I took the offensive. I deliberately put myself in their danger."

He turned his dancing eyes towards me, and I have rarely had such an impression of wild and mirthful audacity.

" We have an excellent intelligence system," he went on, " and the Six have been assiduously shadowed. But as I have told you, no precautions avail against the fanatic, and I do not wish to be killed on my little holiday. So I resolved to draw their fire—to expose myself as ground bait, so to speak, that I might have the chance of netting them. The Six usually hunt in couples, so it was necessary to have three separate acts in the play, if all were to be gathered in. The first——"

" Was in Bryanston Square," I put in, " outside Lady Nantley's house ? "

" True. How did you know ? "

" I have just been dining there, and heard that you were

expected. I saw the crowd in the square as I came away."

" It seems to have gone off quite nicely. We took pains to let it be known where I was dining. The Six, who mistrust me, delegated only two of their number for the job. They never put all their eggs in one basket. The two gentlemen were induced to make a scene, and, since they proved to be heavily armed, were taken into custody and may get a six months' sentence. Very prettily managed, but unfortunately it was the two that matter least—the ones we call Little Pedro and Alejandro the Scholar. Impatient, blundering children, both of them. That leaves four."

The telephone bell rang, and he made a long arm for the receiver. The news he got seemed to be good, for he turned a smiling face to me.

" I should have said two. My little enterprise in the Park has proved a brilliant success. . . . But I must explain. I was to be the bait for my enemies, so I showed myself to the remaining four. That was really rather a clever piece of business. They lost me at the Marble Arch and they did not recognise me as the scarecrow sitting on the seat in the rain. But they knew I had gone to earth there, and they stuck to the scent like terriers. Presently they would have found me, and there would have been shooting. Some of my own people were in the shadow between the road and the railings."

" When I saw you, were your enemies near ? " I asked.

" Two were on the opposite side of the road. One was standing under the lamp-post at the gate. I don't know where the fourth was at that moment. But all had passed me more than once. . . . By the way, you very nearly got yourself shot, you know. When you asked me if sixpence was any good to me. . . . That happens to be their password. I take great credit to myself for seeing instantly that you were harmless."

" Why did you leave the Park if you had your trap so well laid ? " I asked.

" Because it meant dealing with all four together at once, and I do them the honour of being rather nervous about them. They are very quick with their guns. I wanted a chance to break up the covey, and your arrival gave it me. When I went off two followed, as I thought they would. My car was in Park Lane, and gave me a lift ; and one of

them saw me in it. I puzzled them a little, but by now
they must be certain. You see, my car has been waiting
for some minutes outside this house."

" What about the other two ? " I asked.

" Burton has just telephoned that they have been
gathered in. Quite an exciting little scrap. To your police
it must have seemed a bad case of highway robbery—two
ruffianly looking fellows hold up a peaceful elderly gentleman
returning from dinner. The odds were not quite like that,
but the men I had on the job are old soldiers of the Indian
wars and can move softly. . . . I only wish I knew which
two they have got. Burton was not sure. Alcaza is one,
but I can't be certain about the other. I hope it is not the
Irishman."

My bell rang very loud and steadily.

" In a few seconds I shall have solved that problem," he
said gaily. " I am afraid I must trouble you to open the
door, Leithen."

" Is it your aide-de-camp ? "

" No. I instructed Valdez to knock. It is the residuum
of the Six. Now, listen to me, my friend. These two,
whoever they are, have come here to kill me, and I don't
mean to be killed. . . . My first plan was to have Valdez
here—and others—so that my two enemies should walk
into a trap. But I changed my mind before I telephoned.
They are very clever men and by this time they will be
very wary. So I have thought of something else."

The bell rang again and a third time insistently.

" Take these," and he held out a pair of cruel little bluish
revolvers. " When you open the door, you will say that the
President is at home and, in token of his confidence, offers
them these. *'Une espèce d'Irlandais, Messieurs. Vous
commencez trop tard, et vous finissez trop tôt.'* Then bring
them here. Quick now. I hope Corbally is one of them."

I did exactly as I was told. I cannot say that I had any
liking for the task, but I was a good deal under the spell of
that calm young man, and I was resigned to my flat being
made a rendezvous for desperadoes. I had locked and
chained and bolted the door, so it took me a few moments
to open it.

I found myself looking at emptiness.

" Who is it ? " I called. " Who rang ? "

I was answered from behind me. It was the quickest thing I have ever seen, for they must have slipped through in the moment when my eyes were dazzled by the change from the dim light of the hall to the glare of the landing. That gave me some notion of the men we had to deal with.

" Here," said the voice. I turned and saw two men in waterproofs and felt hats, who had kept their hands in their pockets and had a fraction of an eye on the two pistols I swung by the muzzles.

" M. le Président will be glad to see you, gentlemen," I said. I held out the revolvers, which they seemed to grasp and flick into their pockets with a single movement. Then I repeated slowly the piece of rudeness in French.

One of the men laughed. " Ramon does not forget," he said. He was a young man with sandy hair and hot blue eyes and an odd break in his long drooping nose. The other was a wiry little fellow, with a grizzled beard and what looked like a stiff leg.

I had no guess at my friend's plan, and was concerned to do precisely as I was told. I opened the door of my sitting-room, and noticed that the President was stretched on my sofa facing the door. He was smoking and was still in his under-clothes. When the two men behind me saw that he was patently unarmed they slipped into the room with a quick cat-like movement, and took their stand with their backs against the door.

" Hullo, Corbally," said the President pleasantly. " And you, Manuel. You're looking younger than when I saw you last. Have a cigarette ? " and he nodded towards my box on the table behind him. Both shook their heads.

" I'm glad you have come. You have probably seen the news of the loan in the evening papers. That should give you a holiday, as it gives me one. No further need for the hectic oversight of each other, which is so wearing and takes up so much time."

" No," said the man called Manuel, and there was something very grim about his quiet tones. " We shall take steps to prevent any need for that in the future."

" Tut, tut—that is your old self, Manuel. You are too fond of melodrama to be an artist. You are a priest at heart."

The man snarled. "There will be no priest at your death-bed." Then to his companion. "Let us get this farce over."

The President paid not the slightest attention, but looked steadily at the Irishman. "You used to be a sportsman, Mike. Have you come to share Manuel's taste for potting the sitting rabbit ? "

"We are not sportsmen, we are executioners of justice," said Manuel.

The President laughed merrily. "Superb! The best Roman manner." He still kept his eyes on Corbally.

"Damn you, what's your game, Ramon ? " the Irishman asked. His freckled face had become very red.

"Simply to propose a short armistice. I want a holiday. If you must know, I want to go to the National."

"So do I."

"Well, let's call a truce. Say for two months or till I leave England—whichever period shall be the shorter. After that you can get busy again."

The one he had named Manuel broke into a spluttering torrent of Spanish, and for a little they all talked that language. It sounded like a commination service on the President, to which he good-humouredly replied. I had never seen this class of ruffian before, to whom murder was as simple as shooting a partridge, and I noted curiously the lean hands, the restless, wary eyes, and the ugly lips of the type. So far as I could make out, the President seemed to be getting on well with the Irishman but to be having trouble with Manuel.

"Have ye really and truly nothing on ye ? " Corbally asked.

The President stretched his arms and revealed his slim figure in its close-fitting pants and vest.

"Nor him there ? " and he nodded towards me.

"He is a lawyer ; he doesn't use guns."

"Then I'm damned if I touch ye. Two months it is. What's your fancy for Liverpool ? "

This was too much for Manuel. I saw in what seemed to be one movement his hand slip from his pocket, Corbally's arm swing in a circle, and a plaster bust of Julius Cæsar tumble off the top of my bookcase. Then I heard the report.

" Ye nasty little man," said Corbally as he pressed him to his bosom in a bear's hug.

" You are a traitor," Manuel shouted. " How will we face the others ? What will Alejandro say and Alcaza—— ? "

" I think I can explain," said the President pleasantly. " They won't know for quite a time, and then only if you tell them. You two gentlemen are all that remain for the moment of your patriotic company. The other four have been the victims of the English police—two in Bryanston Square, and two in the Park close to the Marble Arch."

" Ye don't say ! " said Corbally, with admiration in his voice. " Faith, that's smart work ! "

" They too will have a little holiday. A few months to meditate on politics, while you and I go to the Grand National."

Suddenly there was a sharp rat-tat at my door. It was like the knocking in *Macbeth* for dramatic effect. Corbally had one pistol at my ear in an instant, while a second covered the President.

" It's all right," said the latter, never moving a muscle. " It's General Valdez, whom I think you know. That was another argument which I was coming to if I hadn't had the good fortune to appeal to Mr. Corbally's higher nature. I know you have sworn to kill me, but I take it that the killer wants to have a sporting chance of escape. Well, there wouldn't have been the faintest shadow of a chance here. Valdez is at the door, and the English police are below. You are brave men, I know, but even brave men dislike the cold gallows."

The knocker fell again. " Let him in, Leithen," I was told, " or he will be damaging your valuable door. He has not the northern phlegm of you and me and Mr. Corbally."

A tall man in an ulster, which looked as if it covered a uniform, stood on the threshold. Someone had obscured the lights on the landing so that the staircase was dark, but I could see in the gloom other figures. " President Pelem," he began . . .

" The President is here," I said. " Quite well and in great form. He is entertaining two other guests."

The General marched to my sitting-room. I was behind him and did not see his face, but I can believe that it showed surprise when he recognised the guests. Manuel stood sulkily defiant, his hands in his waterproof pockets, but Corbally's light eyes were laughing.

"I think you know each other," said the President graciously.

"My God!" Valdez seemed to choke at the sight. "These swine? . . . Excellency, I have——"

"You have nothing of the kind. These are friends of mine for the next two months, and Mr. Corbally and I are going to the Grand National together. Will you have the goodness to conduct them downstairs and explain to the inspector of police below that all has gone well and that I am perfectly satisfied, and that he will hear from me in the morning? . . . One moment. What about a stirrup-cup? Leithen, does your establishment run to a whisky and soda all round?"

It did. We all had a drink, and I believe I clinked glasses with Manuel.

. . . . . .

I looked in at Lady Samplar's dance as I had meant to. Presently I saw a resplendent figure arrive—the President, with the ribbon of the Gold Star of Bolivar across his chest. He was no more the larky undergraduate, but the responsible statesman, the father of his country. There was a considerable crowd in his vicinity when I got near him and he was making his apologies to Mollie Nantley. She saw me and insisted on introducing me. "I so much wanted you two to meet. I had hoped it would be at my dinner—but anyhow I have managed it." I think she was a little surprised when the President took my hand in both of his. "I saw Mr. Leithen play at Lord's in '97," he said. "I was twelfth man for Harrow that year. It is delightful to make his acquaintance, I shall never forget this meeting."

"How English he is!" Mollie whispered to me as we made our way out of the crowd.

They got him next year. They were bound to, for in that kind of business you can have no real protection. But he managed to set his country on its feet before he went down. . . . No, it was neither Manuel nor Corbally. I think it was Alejandro the Scholar.

Reprinted with the Author's permission from *The Runagates Club*.

REGINALD CAMPBELL

The Humbling of Ai Poy and Ai Soo
Even Justice

⁋ After serving in the Navy in the World
War, Mr. CAMPBELL went to Siam
as a forest assistant with a British firm
leasing teak forests. Here he gained
that familiar knowledge of the jungle
that is so often manifested in his
best-known literary work. Probably
no novelist writing to-day knows more
about elephants than Reginald Campbell.

THE HUMBLING OF AI POY AND AI SOO

RAYMOND MANNERING, rafting assistant of the Siam Wood Company, was camped in a forest clearing some four miles to the north of his bungalow at Ban Huat. One by one the company elephants were filing past his tent for their monthly inspection, and the last to roll up to him was old Me Keo Me Wan. As Mannering's eyes took in her sunken cheeks and the great overflap at the top of the ears, he knew that her period of servitude to man was over, and that the only merciful course for him was to let her loose, unhobbled, in the forest, there to pass her last remaining years in peace and quietude.

Her departure from his force would be a great loss to the company, for not only was she a magnificent timber-working elephant, but she ruled the other animals of the firm with an authority that was unquestioned. Fractious youngsters, shirking their fair share of dragging in the River Me Toom, were promptly brought to book by blows from her powerful trunk, and even fierce tuskers had been known to quail before the onrush of this terrible old lady. But now that part of her life was over, and only the peace of the jungle remained.

" Throw down the hobbles," ordered Raymond Mannering to Ai Poy, her mahout.

The steel chains suspended round the elephant's neck clattered to the ground, then slowly, majestically, the vast bulk rolled out of the clearing, free at last from the humans she had served so faithfully for seventy long years. . . .

Twenty minutes later the mahout reappeared on foot from the surrounding forest and salaamed to Mannering.

" Lord," said he, " Me Keo Me Wan is free, and now I have no elephant to ride. If the lord could give me a fierce elephant. . . ."

" Ai Poy must wait his turn," answered the white man, " for have not the fierce elephants of the company already got their mahouts ?   Ai Poy will be given another female elephant."

With a look of disgust Ai Poy returned to the coolie lines, where he relapsed into sullen meditation.   For many moons had he cherished the wish to become a fierce-elephant rider, since for riding fierce elephants mahouts drew as much as fifteen whole silver ticals a month instead of the paltry eight or ten the other mahouts received, and they also came in for much admiration from the dark-eyed Lao girls of the little jungle villages.   He, Ai Poy, would fain have that admiration one day, but, since the Lord Mannering had told him that there were no fierce elephants available, his only chance lay in one of their mahouts either falling sick or being dismissed.

Being dismissed.   Ai Poy dwelt on the thought and eventually, round about noon, he rose to his feet and walked swiftly away from the camp in the direction of the north.

After two miles' tramping he passed a tiny jungle village, and another two miles beyond that he arrived at a small attap-roofed hut built in the very heart of the forest.

Now the hut was the abode of one Ai Soo, the mahout of Poo Oo, and Poo Oo was one of the fiercest elephants in Mannering's company, being a real and veritable killer who would obey none other than his own mahout.   The white man had therefore decreed that when Poo Oo was not working in the River Me Toom, he should graze by himself in a lonely part of the forest at a goodly distance from villages and plantations.   Thus did Ai Soo live for a great part of his time in a small jungle shanty two miles away from the nearest haunts of men.

Arrived at this shanty, Ai Poy found Ai Soo resting in the heat of the day.

" Not for many ticals would I live here, Ai Soo," he said after the greetings were over.   " To live in the forest, alone save for forest devils and a very fierce elephant—*meh wooi*, I would not dare."

" I am a man," said the other importantly.

" That is so indeed, and doubtless Ai Soo receives as much as twenty-five ticals a month from the Lord Mannering."

" But fifteen," admitted Ai Soo.

" *But fifteen ?* " exclaimed his companion in astonishment. There followed much earnest conversation, with the result that soon Ai Soo was boiling with righteous indignation. He, Ai Soo, the greatest mahout in all the world—(had not Ai Poy said so ?)—was receiving the absurd sum of fifteen ticals a month, when he should be receiving twenty-five at least. He would go forthwith and tell the Lord Mannering, who would without doubt agree with him that great injustice had been done.

Thus at four o'clock in the afternoon Ai Poy found himself back in camp awaiting, in pleasant anticipation, the re-appearance of Ai Soo from his lord and master's tent.

The mahout was not kept on tenterhooks for long, for shortly Ai Soo came striding towards him.

" Leukarn," exclaimed Ai Soo, " the Lord Mannering has refused me even one single tical's advance in wages."

" Why ? "

" He did say that no other fierce-elephant driver receives more than fifteen ticals, wherefore was it against the custom."

" And what will Ai Soo do now ? "

" I return to my elephant," muttered Ai Soo sullenly.

When the man disappeared, Ai Poy did some more hard thinking, and eventually, when evening was approaching, he too stole out of the clearing and hastened along the path that led away to the north.

.   .   .   .   .   .

The following morning serious news came to Raymond Mannering. Poo Oo had slipped his hobbles during the night and, as though bent on mischief, was approaching the little village that lay two miles to the north of the camp.

Dismissing the perspiring native who had brought the information, Mannering caused his swiftest pony to be saddled, and then he rode hell-for-leather for the village.

Arrived at the outskirts, he dismounted and, after tying the pony's reins to a branch that overhung the path, pushed forward on foot, to meet a moment later the entire population of the village hastening in the opposite direction.

Youths, maidens, married women with children on their hips, old men and old women, streamed past him in one mad jostle of fright, but, undaunted, Mannering strode on. On rounding a corner he came to the beginning of the village, whereupon he halted abruptly, for, some fifty yards ahead of him, right in the centre of the market-place, Poo Oo was standing in solitary grandeur.

The elephant, as yet unaware of the white man's presence, was engaged in lunching off the sweetmeats and rice cakes on the market stalls, and when these were finished he began demolition work. To the accompaniment of bellows of wrath, hut after hut dissolved into thin air, and in five minutes' time Poo Oo had worked himself up into a rage that was terrible to behold.

Now Mannering knew that his company would be liable for many hundreds of ticals' worth of damage should this devastation continue for long, and so he nerved himself to do a very brave thing. Without any attempt at concealment, he walked openly towards the great, roaring, bellowing Death, and shouted the command to kneel.

At the sound of his voice the elephant swung his bulk round and then, with a blaring trumpet, charged.

Mannering turned and ran down the path again. He rounded the corner and his frightened pony, prancing in circles, came into view. In a flash he reached it, ripped the reins from the overhanging branch, and then flung himself on to the animal's back.

He galloped furiously till he judged a full mile separated him from the village, whereupon he pulled his sweating pony on to its haunches and listened intently. Soon he heard the sound of trumpeting, followed by the noise of falling trees, which told him that he had succeeded in luring the elephant away from the village and that even now it was following up his track along the path that led directly to his camp.

Now this was precisely what Mannering had wished for, since once in the camp fierce-elephant riders might be found to round up the brute, and if the worst came to the worst there was always the heavy rifle in his tent to be resorted to.

He therefore rode in more leisurely fashion the remaining mile to his camp, and on arrival there found an excited mob of coolies and mahouts awaiting his appearance. Among them was Ai Soo, the mahout of Poo Oo, and Mannering's eyes narrowed, for he shrewdly suspected that dusky gentleman of loosing the elephant's hobbles and then bolting to a far distant part of the forest. But now here was Ai Soo advancing, as bold as brass, out of the crowd to meet him.

" So," said Mannering curtly, " and why hast thou not been near thy elephant ? "

" Lord," answered Ai Soo, " I know nought of the affair,

for last night I was visiting my mother, who lives in a village very far from here. When I return to my shanty this morning, I see Poo Oo is missing, so I hasten to the lord's camp to let him know, only to find the lord already gone."

" Thou art a liar and a knave," said Mannering icily.

" Master," the mahout Ai Poy was salaaming before him, " if I tame Poo Oo before he reach the camp, can I have him for always ? "

Mannering nodded, and a moment later Ai Poy, his features flushed with triumph, hastened out of the camp clearing and along the path by which Poo Oo was approaching.

As soon as the mahout had disappeared, Mannering strode into his tent, seized his heavy rifle, loaded it, then waited for developments.

They soon came, for shortly an ear-splitting trumpet sounded from somewhere along the hidden path, to be followed by the sudden return of Ai Poy, whose face was now the colour of grass. With arms and legs working like pistons, he literally shot through the astonished spectators and then dived into the thickest part of the jungle on the farther side of the clearing.

So much for Mr. Poy, thought Mannering grimly, as the apparition vanished, and now for the next !

Ai Soo came forward. " Pah ! " said he, " Ai Poy is fit only to ride butcha elephants. I, Ai Soo, will go, lord, for am I not the best mahout in all the world ? "

He went, to return three minutes later travelling at an even greater speed if possible than the vanished Ai Poy. He did not, however, bolt into the surrounding jungle as the other had done ; instead, he shot up a large teak tree, from which point of vantage he peered down at the Lord Mannering.

" Master," he croaked with ashen lips, " have a care. Nothing living can stop Poo Oo now, for the blood-lust is upon him."

The mention of blood-lust was enough, for at the words every remaining coolie and mahout sought the safety of the tree-tops that encircled the camp, leaving the white man standing alone by his tent.

Hardly had the last coolie climbed up into position, when Poo Oo himself rolled into the clearing, and halting, glared round the arena. Standing thus, with the brilliant tropical

sunshine streaming over his gleaming tusks and massive
head, his very magnificence made Raymond Mannering's
heart miss a beat. Six thousand pounds or more of brawn
and muscle, enclosing the soul of a tiger, is something that
is not easy to forget, and Mannering, as he slowly raised
weapon to shoulder, was loath to shoot such a magnificent
creature. But—his eye ran along the barrel and on to the
thick root of the trunk that hides the brain—Poo Oo had
now become unmanageable, and for this he must pay with
his life.

With one finger he squeezed lightly on the trigger of his
rifle, for now the elephant was charging towards him. The
pressure on the trigger increased. One ounce more, and
Poo Oo's career would have ended, but suddenly there
came a rending of bushes from one side of the clearing,
and next second a gigantic form blurred across Mannering's
vision.

Crash . . . two enormous bodies met with a shock that
literally jarred the earth, and Mannering, lowering his
weapon, found himself gazing in amazement at the spectacle
of old Me Keo Me Wan hurling, with prodding head and
flaying trunk, a veritable broadside of blows upon the
man-killer's neck, head and shoulders.

The punishment did not last long, for soon Poo Oo, terrified and humbled by a fierce old dame he had strength to
slay a dozen times over, fled panic-stricken from the clearing,
leaving the old lady snorting with rage and somewhat out
of breath.

. . . .

That evening Raymond Mannering was seated in his tent,
with Ai Soo and Ai Poy crouching before him.

" Lord," said Ai Soo, " I have done well, for Poo Oo is
now quieter and him have I caught and shackled."

" And I also have done well, master," chimed in Ai Poy.
" When I run away from Poo Oo I think hard all the time.
I know Me Keo Me Wan still graze very near the camp ;
I also know that even fierce elephants are very much afraid
of her, wherefore did I seek her out quickly and bring her to
the clearing."

" Then why," snapped Mannering, " were you not on her
back when she came into the clearing ? "

" Lord, I was very much afraid. Therefore did I slip

off her back at the edge of the jungle, knowing that she would do the rest."

" Then of a truth Ai Poy is no fierce-elephant rider," said the white man.   " But enough of that, for there is the escape of Poo Oo to be considered.   Now I have heard it said by the coolies that yesterday Ai Poy was twice seen going through the village that leads to Ai Soo's shanty, once in the morning and once late in the evening.   Had Ai Poy urgent business up there ? "

" Lord, I go walking," replied the man addressed.

" Without doubt you did, but for what reason ?   Now it would appear to me that Ai Poy wished to become the mahout of Poo Oo, and that he also knew of my refusal to raise the wages of Ai Soo.   He *might* then think thus : I will go secretly and loose the elephant with the result that the Lord Mannering will suspect Ai Soo of revenge and dismiss him.   Thus will I, Ai Poy, become Poo Oo's mahout and gain much thereby."

Mannering paused, and flashed a quick glance at Ai Soo, upon whose dusky features he noted a certain expression. He then turned to Ai Poy again, who was fidgeting uneasily.

" Lord," muttered Ai Poy, " you are all-wise, but I swear I did not loose the elephant last night."

Mannering grinned openly now, since this was exactly what he had been working for.

" No, Ai Poy, you did not," he said icily.   " What actually happened was that you went up north yesterday for the purpose of freeing Poo Oo, only to find that he had already been loosed. . . . Ai Soo," the speaker swung round to the second mahout, " why didst thou loose the elephant ? "

" Lord," said the latter, " I know nought of the affair."

But Mannering, remembering the look of surprise that had flitted across Ai Soo's face, was adamant.

" Ai Soo," said he, " thy countenance can I read like an open book.   The fact that Ai Poy had gone up secretly to unhobble Poo Oo was news to thee, therefore do I know well that it was thou who loosed the elephant."

" Lord," whispered Ai Soo nervously, " how you do know this is beyond my understanding, but—yes, master, it was I who loosed the elephant."

" Ha !   And how would Ai Soo gain over the affair ? "

" Lord, I think I unhobble Poo Oo, and say he escape by accident. Then I pretend I away with my mother, and wait till he do some damage. Then I go to the Lord Mannering and tell him I will catch the elephant again. Then I do this, and the lord, seeing that no other mahout can tame Poo Oo but me, will be pleased. Thus will he raise my wages after all."

" A delightfully simple plan," breathed Mannering to himself, " which didn't exactly come off."

Then he addressed the others aloud : " There has been evil work here," he told them. " Also much foolishness. There will therefore be punishments. Thou, Ai Soo, shalt have thy wages reduced to ten ticals a month, yet still ride Poo Oo. Thou shalt also, with thine own hands, help to rebuild the market stalls of the village."

" Lord, the punishment is too great. I will ride Poo Oo no longer."

" In that case," said Mannering briskly, " I go tell the villagers the whole truth about Ai Soo. And they, knowing their lives have been in danger by reason of his action, will be very angry, so that extremely unpleasant things may happen to Ai Soo."

" Lord, I ride Poo Oo and do all that you say," replied Ai Soo hastily.

" And now in the matter of an elephant for Ai Poy," said Mannering. " I have one for him."

" The lord is good," remarked Ai Poy gratefully.

Mannering smiled grimly, then shouted for his headman, to whom he gave a certain order. The headman disappeared, to return shortly with a tiny elephant barely six years old. Normally this little creature would have been ridden by some young mahout who was learning his job, but now the white man motioned Ai Poy towards it.

" This shall be thy elephant, Ai Poy," said he, " and thy pay four ticals a month."

A roar of laughter went up from a group of drivers nearby, and Ai Poy flushed darkly. He, a full mahout, and destined to be a fierce-elephant rider, was reduced to this !

" I refuse, master," he said sullenly, " and shall leave the company. And is this my reward for saving the lord's life ? "

" Ai Poy is good at tales," said Mannering sternly, " and

maybe that is another tale.   Whether it is or not, the fact
remains that Ai Poy, like Ai Soo, has done much evil.   Now
supposing the villagers were to hear that Ai Poy had even
thought of loosing . . ."

"I take the little elephant, master," said Ai Poy quickly.

. . . . . .

Later that evening Raymond Mannering caused his headman to bring Me Keo Me Wan into the clearing again, for he
knew that she still was grazing in the vicinity of the camp.

"Now I wonder," he whispered, as he handed her some
of the soft, crushed tamarind that she loved, "I wonder
whether Ai Poy has ever slung leg across thee since thou left
us ?   I wonder whether Me Keo Me Wan, on hearing the
uproar of Poo Oo, did not come of her own accord to humble
him, the while Ai Poy cowered in the thickest part of the
jungle ?   Yes, I wonder, old lady."

But Me Keo Me Wan could only rumble with satisfaction.
She had done a good deed that day, and the tamarind tasted
good to her.

EVEN JUSTICE

RAYMOND MANNERING, rafting assistant of the Siam Wood Company, stood at the threshold of his tent one brilliant March morning, swearing roundly. His best new saddle, which had but recently come up to the head of the railway from distant Bangkok, and which had cost him the large sum of two hundred and fifty ticals, had been spirited away from his camp the previous night, and well he knew that the chances of its recovery were small.

Mannering peered into the encircling jungle, as if to search out its secrets. The hot weather being at its worst, the forest, sucked dry by the fiery rays of the sun, was bare and leafless. Even the little watercourse that ran behind his tent was now a dry, tumbled mass of shining stones, and no green was to be seen anywhere, save for some coco-nut palms that grew a few hundred yards to the right of his camp.

At the sight of the palms Mannering's steely blue eyes hardened, for they denoted the beginning of the little native village of Ban Onn, of which Ai Luang the deceitful was the headman.

Now Ai Luang was the oldest and most cunning village headman in all Northern Siam, and Mannering shrewdly suspected that the ancient was responsible for stealing the saddle, but to bring the theft home on Ai Luang would, in view of the old scoundrel's cunning, be well-nigh impossible.

Mannering was none too happy at being camped so close to Ban Onn, but on the previous evening two of his baggage elephants had gone dead lame, with the result that he had been compelled to halt forthwith and make a temporary resting-place near the village, where he must remain for at least two days until his elephants should be fit to travel again.

There was also an added reason for Mannering's wishing to leave the locality as soon as possible. This was the presence in his tent of ten small, square wooden boxes, nestling underneath his bed. And each of these boxes contained an average of two thousand silver ticals in specie, or twenty thousand ticals in all. It was a lot of money with which to be travelling in a wild, rolling country, far away from civilisation, but banks being non-existent in Upper Siam, the only method of obtaining cash from Bangkok for the working expenses of Mannering's company was for the white man to meet the north-bound train at the nearest railway station, take delivery of the boxes, and with them travel back to the firm's rafting premises at Ban Huat, six days' march away.

So now here was he, half-way back on his return journey, with two of his elephants lame, his saddle stolen, and twenty thousand ticals' worth of specie lying within a few hundred yards of a wily old village headman.

Mannering frowned and, as by now the heat was intense, called to his cook for a drink. The servant handed it him, then coughed and shifted his feet uneasily, as though some matter were on his mind.

" Well, what is it ? " demanded Mannering.

" Lord," whispered the cook uneasily, " in the camp it is said that the Ka Mooi gang has been following us these last two days. Lord, it is feared that there is bad business afoot."

At the mention of the gang Mannering whistled, for he had heard of them. They were five robbers who, working together, had for the last few weeks harried many peaceful, defenceless jungle villages. Indeed, only the village of Ban Onn had up till now been spared, though Mannering guessed this was from no motive of mercy on the part of the robbers, but because they feared the old villain who acted as its headsman. They had not, indeed, committed actual murder to date, consequently a price of only fifty ticals had been placed on each of their heads, a sum for which no villager, save perhaps Ai Luang, would dare to betray them.

But now—Mannering's frown deepened—the robbers were near Ban Onn, and should they join forces with Ai Luang in order to rob him of the specie, he would be up against a very formidable combination indeed. He did not, certainly, suspect them of the theft of the saddle—Ai Luang was responsible for that, he was sure—no, they were out for larger game in the shape of the boxes, and it behoved him to tread warily.

For a while he remained deep in thought, then, in the absence of his boy, who had been left behind to take care of the company's bungalow at Ban Huat, he shouted for the cook and ordered him to summon Ai Luang immediately to his tent.

. . . . .

At noon, the old man, white-haired, wizened, a mere dried-up rattle of bones and skin, crawled into the tent and salaamed profoundly before Mannering.

" Ai Luang," snapped Mannering, " I have lost a saddle. It was a very good saddle."

The ancient spread deprecatory hands. It was terrible, unthinkable, unbelievable to hear of the Lord's misfortune. Perhaps a devil . . . but Mannering cut him short.

" In my tent," said he slowly, " as doubtless Ai Luang knows, I have much money belonging to the great company."

" Lord, I know nought of this."

" Which is strange," replied Mannering. " Are boxes of silver, carried on elephant-back, so small and so light that no one knows of their presence ? "

" As the Lord wills," said Ai Luang meekly.

" Now supposing," resumed Mannering, " that this money is stolen while I am still near your village, Ai Luang will come to great trouble."

The headman shifted on his haunches, and his wrinkled features wore an air of pained surprise. The Lord Mannering was not fair to him ; the Lord was speaking in parables, which were difficult to understand ; the Lord was playing with him, Ai Luang, who would not touch a hair of the Great Master's head ; perhaps the Lord would explain.

Mannering proceeded to do so. " In the Great City, in Bangkok," he said, " lives the Big Man of my Great Company. He is a very, very Big Man, so much so that he is friends with the King. Every evening they have meat and rice together."

" Wooi," exclaimed Ai Luang, awe-struck at mention of the King of Siam.

" If," continued Mannering, " my Big Man hear that his company's money has been stolen near Ban Onn, he tell the

King. The King will send up soldiers, many soldiers, to Ban Onn, and suspicion will fall upon Ai Luang, for is he not headman of the district? They will then take Ai Luang to the Great City, where he have to give evidence. He spend many moons in prison there, *even if he not found guilty.*"

Mannering's tones were hard and icy-cold, and Ai Luang's hams quivered ever so slightly as he heard the words.

" The talk is finished," snapped Mannering after a short pause, and, turning his back on the ancient, he picked up a six weeks' old newspaper. The interview was at an end.

Back in the attap-roofed shanty that served Ai Luang for a home, the headman sank into profound meditation. The brief interview with the Lord Mannering had shaken him more than he cared to admit, and, now he came to think upon the matter, these white lords were, indeed, exceedingly powerful, and to meddle in their affairs was courting danger.

Still, it was a pity not to go through with the plot he had hatched, for the coup had been so nicely arranged for this very night. He had met the robbers secretly, and for his help he was to receive one of the boxes as commission, which wouldn't be so bad, as from their reported size he was certain they held at least two thousand ticals apiece.

And his part in the affair was so simple. All he had to do was to arrange that when the Lord Mannering's camp followers should visit his village in the cool of the evening, they would be provided with free rice spirit. They would then, he knew, drink until none of them could stand, and sleep the rest of the night amidst the market stalls. Thus would the white man's camp be unguarded, save for the cook, and the cook could easily be overpowered should he give the alarm.

True, there was the little matter of ensuring that the Lord Mannering should sleep well during the night, but after that all would be easy.

When the sun was on the wane Ai Luang came to a decision. First, he ordered the largest, freshest, and most juicy coco-nut in the village to be brought to him. Having whittled off the thick fibre that surrounded the shell, he cunningly pierced a hole in one end of the nut and, without

6

allowing any of the fluid to escape, blew, with the aid of a thin bamboo pipe, a quantity of fine white powder into the milk. He then closed up the hole with great care, so that no one should know the shell had been tampered with, after which he summoned his eldest son.

" Here is a coco-nut," wheezed Ai Luang. " Now this coco-nut, together with some bananas and eggs, thou shalt take to the Lord Mannering after he has had his evening meal. Thou shalt say that Ai Luang sends gifts, and hopes that the Lord is well. Thou shalt further say that the night is hot, and that this coco-nut is the best coco-nut in all the country. Wherefore is its milk cool and pleasant to the taste, especially since the night is hot. Does my son understand ? "

" He understands."

" Then go."

The son, a strapping, full-blooded, swarthy Lao, disappeared, and shortly afterwards another visitor slunk into Ai Luang's home. The new-comer was the chief of the robber gang, and with him the old man held much earnest converse.

An hour after dawn Mannering awoke. He stretched his arms, which ached unaccustomedly, as if he had toiled much the previous evening, and then he slid through his mosquito-net on to the ground, after which he glanced under the bed, to find that the space there was empty, and that not one box remained out of the ten.

He dressed hurriedly, then swung out into the clearing. As he did so the figures of some of his coolies and mahouts came slinking back to camp from the direction of Ban Onn, and one glance assured Mannering that their heads were sore and their throats extremely parched. He ignored them, however, and began striding up the path that led to the village. When half-way there a Lao, whom he recognised as one of Ai Luang's sons, came hurrying towards him.

" Take me to thy father," snapped Mannering.

Five minutes later the white man climbed up the rickety bamboo ladder leading to the shanty, and stepped inside.

Squatting in a circle on the cane flooring were six figures, five of whom were securely bound with creeper. In the centre of the circle were ten wooden boxes, entirely intact.

" The Lord has slept well ? " inquired the sixth figure, who was Ai Luang.

" Not well, not bad," answered Mannering. " Would Ai Luang kindly explain ? "

" Master," began the old man, " soon after midnight I dreamed a dream that the white lord's boxes were in danger. I wake from this dream, and I send my sons and my strongest villagers quick to your camp. On the way they see five robbers, their arms heavy with two boxes each, going through the jungle. They catch them and bring them to me, and I keep them here."

" And Ai Luang did not tell me ? " asked Mannering, speaking in tones that were different from his wont. The quick, merciless decision in his voice was lacking, and his mien was almost servile as he addressed the old native.

" Master, I send one son back to the Lord's tent, where he listen. Then he return, saying the Lord still sleep. So I think it better not wake the Lord, for he wish to rest and the money safe anyhow. It is good ? "

" It is good," said Mannering brokenly. " How can I ever repay Ai Luang ? Of a truth, he is all-wise and all-powerful."

Though the headman's face remained a black, wrinkled mask, he grinned inwardly. These white lords : they were fools after all, and not to be feared in the least. However . . . he cleared his throat and was about to speak again when a restless movement came from one of the bound robbers, whereupon Ai Luang turned his head and gave the man one glance.

Now the glance was outwardly one of benign tranquillity, but apparently the robber thought otherwise, for he froze again into immobility and his sullen eyes sought the floor. He and his four friends had been betrayed by Ai Luang, but, though his soul was seething in righteous anger, he knew well that Ai Luang would provide his escort for the journey to the distant gendarmerie station, and on the way accidents might happen, especially if he endeavoured to enlighten the white man with regard to certain events of the previous night. Prison, therefore, being preferable to an accident occurring on the way to it, the robber maintained a gloomy silence, and eventually Ai Luang, having transferred his gaze to Raymond Mannering, spoke again.

" The Lord will give me a reward ? Have I not saved him much money ? "

The white man pointed to the largest of the boxes that lay on the floor. " For thy great services, half the contents of that box shall be thine, Ai Luang."

The old man's eyes flashed greedily, for here was good business indeed. One thousand ticals at least, not to speak of the extra two hundred and fifty he would be given as a reward for capturing the robbers, was a sum which well-nigh staggered the imagination. Rosy dreams came to him, which were interrupted by the sound of the white man's voice :

" Since Ai Luang is so wise and so powerful, could not he have another dream ? " the white man was pleading. " A dream about the saddle. It was a very good saddle, and if it could be found the other half of the box is Ai Luang's also."

The headman shifted on his hams and purred mentally. He also swelled visibly, for the normal masterfulness of the Lord Mannering had broken down, and the great white man was bowing to him, a native. *Two* thousand two hundred and fifty ticals ! He rose to his feet.

" It may be done," he said to Mannering, omitting the word " Lord." " I go see smoke dreams."

He vanished into an adjoining partition, where, highly pleased with his own importance, he left Raymond Mannering for one whole hour alone with the robbers. At the end of this time he returned to the first compartment, where he found the white man waiting in absolute humility for his reappearance.

" Ai Luang has had a dream ? " asked Mannering in an anxious voice.

" He has," replied the other importantly. " I see man who stole the saddle, and I go find him."

This time the headman climbed down the bamboo ladder and walked into the village market-place, where he remained one more hour before he retrieved the saddle from the spot where he had hidden it. By noon he was back in the shanty again and handing the stolen property to its rightful owner.

" Here is the saddle," he wheezed, being somewhat out of breath. " I find it after much trouble, and the thief I have punished. It is well ? "

" It is well," echoed Mannering. Then the white man stooped and with his own hands lifted the largest and heaviest of the boxes, which he placed at Ai Luang's feet.

The old man's eyes glinted with mingled greed and excitement, and, seizing his jungle knife, he eagerly prized open the lid. Inside the box, firmly embedded between large stones, was an enormous coco-nut.

.   .   .   .   .   .

" What . . . what is the meaning of this ? " stuttered Ai Luang, after a pause that spoke for itself.

" What is the meaning of this, *Lord* ! " prompted Mannering very softly.

" Lord," quavered Ai Luang, as a pair of steely, cold eyes seemed to bore right through his head.

" The meaning," said Mannering icily, " is that thou art a fool as well as a knave. Open all the other boxes, dog ! ".

Though the bowels melted within him and his hands trembled like teak leaves in the wind, the old man hastily complied, and when he had finished he stared in dumb amazement at nine more boxes filled to the brim with round, dry, shining stones.

" So," breathed Mannering, " justice is even. I have back my saddle, and thou wilt have two hundred and fifty ticals in payment for much rice toddy expended and the trouble of escorting the robbers to the gendarmerie station. It is good ? "

" It is good, Lord," quavered Ai Luang. " The Lord is beyond the understanding of such a one as me."

" The Lord is tired now," remarked Mannering, yawning. " He not sleep till *late* last night, for he wait and listen till certain visitors come and go. Now he return to camp. Meanwhile, villain, take out the stones and bring the empty boxes back to the tent."

Without another word Mannering walked out into the sunshine. Ten minutes later he was entering his tent, behind which ran the dry watercourse dotted with round, shining stones.

He yawned again, then stretched his arms. They still ached with the toil he had performed when, after the arrival of the coco-nut the previous evening, he had with great haste taken the silver out of all the boxes and buried it in the earth below his ground-sheet.

Not for nothing had Raymond Mannering suspected that Ai Luang might double-cross both him and the thieves.

LESLIE CHARTERIS

The Million Pound Day

The Blind Spot •

Mr. CHARTERIS, whose stories of that modern d'Artagnan, Simon Templar, otherwise known as " the Saint," have been praised by, among others, Edgar Wallace and P. G. Wodehouse, first thought that he wanted to be a barrister ; but at the age of nineteen he shipped as an ordinary sailor, and began to wield his pen in his spare time. Others of his spare-time occupations are painting, writing comic verse, composing dance numbers, boxing with a police heavyweight champion, and travelling leisurely through Europe.

THE MILLION POUND DAY

I

THE scream pealed out at such point-blank range, and was strangled so swiftly and suddenly, that Simon Templar opened his eyes and wondered for a moment whether he had dreamed it.

The darkness inside the car was impenetrable ; and outside, through the thin mist that a light frost had etched upon the windows, he could distinguish nothing but the dull shadows of a few trees silhouetted against the flat pallor of the sky. A glance at the luminous dial of his wrist watch showed that it was a quarter to five : he had slept barely two hours.

A week-end visit to some friends who lived on the remote margin of Cornwall, about thirteen inches from Land's End, had terminated a little more than seven hours earlier, when the Saint, feeling slightly limp after three days in the company of two young souls who were convalescing from a recent honeymoon, had pulled out his car to make the best of a clear night road back to London. A few miles beyond Basingstoke he had backed into a side lane for a cigarette, a sandwich, and a nap. The cigarette and the sandwich he had had ; but the nap should have lasted until the hands of his watch met at six-thirty and the sky was white and clear with the morning—he had fixed that time for himself, and had known that his eyes would not open one minute later.

And they hadn't. But they shouldn't have opened one minute earlier, either. . . . And the Saint sat for a second or two without moving, straining his ears into the stillness for the faintest whisper of sound that might answer the question in his mind, and driving his memory backwards into those last blank moments of sleep to recall the sound that had woken him.

And then, with a quick stealthy movement, he turned the handle of the door and slipped out into the road.

Before that, he had realised that that scream could never have been shaped in his imagination. The sheer shrieking horror of it still rang between his eardrums and his brain : the hideous high-pitched sob on which it had died seemed still to be quivering on the air. And the muffled patter of running feet which had reached him as he listened had served only to confirm what he already knew.

He stood in the shadow of the car with the cold damp smell of the dawn in his nostrils, and heard the footsteps coming closer. They were coming towards him down the main road—now that he was outside the car, they tapped into his brain with an unmistakable clearness. He heard them so distinctly, in the utter silence that lay all around, that he felt he could almost see the man who made them. And he knew that that was the man who had screamed. The same stark terror that had gone shuddering through the very core of the scream was beating out the wild tattoo of those running feet—the same stomach-sinking dread translated into terms of muscular reaction. For the feet were not running as a man ordinarily runs. They were kicking, blinding, stumbling, hammering along in the mad muscle-binding, heart-bursting flight of a man whose reason has tottered and cracked before a vision of all the tortures of the Pit. . . .

Simon felt the hairs on the nape of his neck prickling. In another instant he could hear the gasping agony of the man's breathing, but he stayed waiting where he was. He had moved a little way from the car, and now he was crouched right by the corner of the lane, less than a yard from the road, completely hidden in the blackness under the hedge.

The most elementary process of deduction told him that no man would run like that unless the terror that drove him on was close upon his heels—and no man would have screamed like that unless he had felt cold upon his shoulder the clutching hand of an intolerable doom. Therefore the Saint waited.

And then the man reached the corner of the lane.

Simon got one glimpse of him—a man of middle height and build, coatless, with his head back and his fists working. Under the feebly lightening sky his face showed thin and hollow-cheeked, pointed at the chin by a small peaked beard, the eyes starting from their sockets.

He was done in—finished. He must have been finished two hundred yards back. But as he reached the corner the ultimate end came. His feet blundered again, and he plunged as if a trip-wire had caught him across the knees. And then it must have been the last instinct of the hunted animal that made him turn and reel round into the little lane ; and the Saint's strong arms caught him as he fell.

The man stared up into the Saint's face. His lips tried to shape a word, but the breath whistled voicelessly in his throat. And then his eyes closed and his body went limp, and Simon lowered him gently to the ground.

The Saint straightened up again, and vanished once more in the gloom. The slow bleaching of the sky seemed only to intensify the blackness that sheltered him, while beyond the shadows a faint light was beginning to pick out the details of the road. And Simon heard the coming of the second man.

The footfalls were so soft that he was not surprised that he had not heard them before. At the moment when he picked them up they could only have been a few yards away, and to anyone less keen of hearing they would still have been inaudible. But the Saint heard them—heard the long-striding ghostly sureness of them padding over the macadam —and a second tingle of eerie understanding crawled over his scalp and glissaded down his spine like a needle-spray of ice-cold water. For the feet that made those sounds were human, but the feet were bare. . . .

And the man turned the corner.

Simon saw him as clearly as he had seen the first—more clearly.

He stood huge and straight in the opening of the lane, gazing ahead into the darkness. The wan light in the sky fell evenly across the broad black primitive-featured face, and stippled glistening silver high-lights on the gigantic ebony limbs. Except for a loosely knotted loin-cloth he was naked, and the gleaming surfaces of his tremendous chest shifted rhythmically to the mighty movements of his breathing. And the third and last thrill of comprehension slithered clammily into the small of the Saint's back as he saw all these things—as he saw the savage ruthlessness of purpose behind the mere physical presence of that magnificent brute-man, sensed the primeval lust of cruelty in the parting of the thick lips and the glitter of the eyes. Almost he seemed to smell the sickly stench of rotting jungles seeping its fetid breath into the clean cold air of that English dawn, swelling in hot stifling waves about the figure of the pursuing beast that had taken the continents and the centuries in its barefoot loping strides.

And while Simon watched, fascinated, the eyes of the negro fell on the sprawling figure that lay in the middle of the lane, and he stepped forward with the snarl of a beast rumbling in his throat.

And it was then that the Saint, with an effort which was as much physical as mental, tore from his mind the steely tentacles of the hypnotic spell that had held him paralysed for those few seconds—and also moved.

" Good morning," spoke the Saint politely, but that was the last polite speech he made that day. No one who had ever heard him talk had any illusions about the Saint's opinion of Simon Templar's physical prowess, and no one who had ever seen him fight had ever seriously questioned the accuracy of those opinions ; but this was the kind of occasion on which the Saint knew that the paths of glory led but to the grave. Which may help to explain why, after that single preliminary concession to the requirements of his manual of etiquette, he heaved the volume over the horizon and proceeded to lapse from grace in no uncertain manner.

After all, that encyclopædia of all the social virtues, though it had some cheering and helpful suggestions to offer on the subject of addressing letters to archdeacons, placing Grand Lamas in the correct relation of precedence to Herzegovinian Grossherzöge, and declining invitations to open bazaars in aid of Homes for Ichthyotic Vulcanisers' Mates, had never even envisaged such a situation as that which was then up for inspection ; and the Saint figured that the rules allowed him a free hand.

The negro, crouching in the attitude in which the Saint's gentle voice had frozen him, was straining his eyes into the darkness. And out of that darkness, like a human cannon-ball, the Saint came at him.

He came in a weird kind of twisting leap that shot him out of the obscurity with no less startling a suddenness than if he had at that instant materialised out of the fourth dimension.

And the negro simply had no time to do anything about it. For that suddenness was positively the only intangible quality about the movement. It had, for instance, a very tangible momentum, which must have been one of the most painfully concrete things that the victim of it had ever encountered. That momentum started from the five toes of the Saint's left foot ; it rippled up his left calf, surged up his left thigh, and gathered to itself a final wave of power from the big muscles of his hips. And then, in that twisting action of his body, it was swung on into another channel : it travelled down the tautening fibres of his right leg, gathering new force in every inch of its progress, and came right out at the end of his shoe with all the smashing violence of a ten-ton stream of water cramped down into the finest nozzle of a garden hose. And at the very instant when every molecule of shattering velocity and weight was concentrated in the point of that right shoe, the point impacted precisely in the geometrical centre of the negro's stomach.

If there had been a football at that point of impact, a rag of shredded leather might reasonably have been expected to come to earth somewhere north of the Aberdeen Providential Society Buildings. And the effect upon the human target, colossus though it was, was just as devastating, even if a trifle less spectacular.

Simon heard the juicy *whuck* ! of his shoe making contact, and saw the man travel three feet backwards as if he had been caught in the full fairway of a high-speed hydraulic battering-ram. The wheezy *phe-e-ew* of electrically emptied lungs merged into the synchronised sound effects, and ended in a little grunting cough. And then the negro seemed to dissolve on to the roadway like a statute of sculptured butter caught in the blast of a superheated furnace. . . .

Simon jerked open one of the rear doors of the car, picked the bearded man lightly off the ground, heaved him in upon the cushions, and slammed the door again.

Five seconds later he was behind the wheel, and the self-starter was whirring over the cold engine.

The headlights carved a blazing chunk of luminance out of the dimness as he touched a switch, and he saw the negro bucking up on to his hands and knees. He let in the clutch, and the car jerked away with a spluttering exhaust. One running-board rustled in the long grass of the banking as he lashed through the narrow gap ; and then he was spinning round into the wide main road.

Ten yards ahead, in the full beam of the headlights, a uniformed constable tumbled off his bicycle and ran to the middle of the road with outstretched hands ; and the Saint almost gasped.

Instantaneously he realised that the scream which had woken him must have been audible for some considerable distance—the policeman's attitude could not more clearly have indicated a curiosity which the Saint was at that moment instinctively disinclined to meet.

He eased up, and the constable guilelessly fell round to the side of the car.

And then the Saint revved up his engine, let in the clutch again with a bang, and went roaring on through the dawn with the policeman's shout tattered to futile fragments in the wind behind him.

II

It was full daylight when he turned into Upper Berkeley Mews and stopped before his own front door, and the door opened even before he had switched off the engine.

" Hullo, boy ! " said Patricia. " I wasn't expecting you for another hour."

" Neither was I," said the Saint.

He kissed her lightly on the lips, and stood there with his cap tilted rakishly to the back of his head and his leather coat swinging back from wide square shoulders, peeling off his gloves and smiling one of his most cryptic smiles.

" I've brought you a new pet," he said.

He twitched open the door behind him, and she peered puzzledly into the back of the car. The passenger was still unconscious, lolling back like a limp mummy in the travelling rug which the Saint had tucked round him, his white face turned blankly to the roof.

" But—who is he ? "

" I haven't the faintest idea," said the Saint blandly. " But for the purposes of convenient reference I have christened him Beppo. His shirt has a Milan tab on it— Sherlock Holmes himself could deduce no more. And up to the present, he hasn't been sufficiently compos to offer any information."

Patricia Holm looked into his face, and saw the battle glint in his eye and a ghost of Saintliness flickering in the corners of his smile, and tilted her sweet fair head.

" Have you been in some more trouble ? "

" It was rather a one-sided affair," said the Saint modestly. " Sambo never had a break—and I didn't mean him to have one, either. But the Queensberry Rules were strictly observed. There was no hitting below belts, which were worn loosely around the ankles——"

" Who's this you're talking about now ? "

" Again, we are without information. But again for the purpose of convenient reference, you may call him His Beatitude the Negro Spiritual. And now listen."

Simon took her shoulders and swung her round.

" Somewhere between Basingstoke and Wintney," he said, " there's a gay game being played that's going to interest us a lot. And I came into it as a perfectly innocent party, for once in my life—but I haven't got time to tell you about it now. The big point at the moment is that a cop who arrived two minutes too late to be useful got my number. With Beppo in the back, I couldn't stop to hold converse with him, and you can bet he's jumped to the worst conclusions. In which he's damned right, but not in the way he thinks he is. There was a 'phone box twenty yards away, and unless the Negro Spiritual strangled him first he's referred my number to London most of an hour ago, and Teal will be snorting down a hot scent as soon as they can get him out of bed. Now, all you've got to know is this : I've just arrived, and I'm in my bath. Tell the glad news to anyone who rings up and anyone who calls ; and if it's a call, hang a towel out of the window."

" But where are you going ? "

" The Berkeley—to park the patient. I just dropped in to give you your cue." Simon Templar drew the end of a cigarette red, and snapped his lighter shut again. " And I'll be right back," he said, and wormed in behind the wheel.

A matter of seconds later the big car was in Berkeley Street, and he was pushing through the revolving doors of the hotel.

" Friend of mine had a bit of a car smash," he rapped at a

sleepy reception clerk. " I wanna room for him now, and a
doctor at eleven. Will you send a coupla men out to carry
him in ? Car at the door."

" One four eight," said the clerk, without batting an
eyelid.

Simon saw the unconscious man carried upstairs, shot
half-crowns into the hands of the men who performed the
transportation, and closed the door on them.

Then he whipped from his pocket a thin nickelled case
which he had brought from a pocket in the car. He snapped
the neck of a small glass phial and drew up the colourless
fluid it contained into the barrel of a hypodermic syringe.
His latest protégé was still sleeping the sleep of sheer exhaustion, but Simon had no guarantee of how long that sleep
would last. He proceeded to provide that guarantee himself, stabbing the needle into a limp arm and pressing home
the plunger until the complete dose had been administered.

Then he closed and locked the door behind him and went
quickly down the stairs.

Below, the reception clerk stopped him.

" What name shall I register, sir ? "

" Teal," said the Saint, with a wry flick of humour. " Mr.
C. E. Teal. He'll sign your book later."

" Yes, sir. . . . Er—has Mr. Teal no luggage, sir ? "

" Nope." A new ten-pound note drifted down to the desk.
" On account," said the Saint. " And see that that doctor's
waiting here for me at eleven, or I'll take the roof off your
hotel and crown you with it."

He pulled his cap sideways and went back to his car.
As he turned into Upper Berkeley Mews for the second time,
he saw that his first home-coming had only just been soon
enough. But that did not surprise him, for he had figured
out his chances on that schedule almost to a second. A
warning blink of white from an upper window caught his
expectant eye at once, and he locked the wheel hard over and
pulled up broadside on across the mews. In a flash he was
out of his seat unlocking a pair of garage doors right at the
street end of the mews, and in another second or two the car
was hissing back into that garage with the cut-out firmly
closed.

The Saint, without advertising the fact, had recently
become the owner of one complete side of Upper Berkeley

Mews, and he was in process of making some interesting structural alterations to that block of real estate of which the London County Council had not been informed and about which the District Surveyor had not even been consulted. The great work was not yet by any means completed, but even now it was capable of serving part of its purposes.

Simon went up a ladder into the bare empty room above. In one corner, a hole had been roughly knocked through the wall; he went through it into another similar room, and on the far side of this was another hole in a wall; thus he passed in quick succession through numbers 1, 3, and 5, until the last plunge through the last hole and a curtain beyond it brought him into No. 7 and his own bedroom.

His tie was already off and his shirt unbuttoned by that time, and he tore off the rest of his clothes in little more than the time it took him to stroll through to the bathroom. And the bath was already full—filled long ago by Patricia.

" Thinks of everything ! " sighed the Saint, with a wide grin of pure delight.

He slid into the bath like an otter, head and all, and came out of it almost in the same movement with a mighty splash, tweaking the plug out of the waste pipe as he did so. In another couple of seconds he was hauling himself into an enormously woolly blue bath-robe and grabbing a towel . . . and he went paddling down the stairs with his feet kicking about in a pair of gorgeously dilapidated moccasins, humming the hum of a man with a copper-plated liver and not one solitary little baby sin upon his conscience.

And thus he rolled into the sitting-room.

" Sorry to have kept you waiting, old dear," he murmured ; and Chief Inspector Claud Eustace Teal rose from an arm-chair and surveyed him heavily.

" Good morning," said Mr. Teal.

" Beautiful, isn't it ? " agreed the Saint affably. Patricia was smoking a cigarette in another chair. She should, according to the book of etiquette, have been beguiling the visitor's wait with some vivacious topical chatter ; but the Saint, who was sensitive to atmosphere, had perceived nothing but a glutinously expanding silence as he entered the room. The perception failed to disturb him. He lifted the silver cover from a plate of bacon and eggs, and sniffed appreciatively. "You don't mind if I eat, do you, Claud?" he murmured.

The detective swallowed. If he had never been required to interview the Saint on business, he could have enjoyed a tolerably placid life. He was not by nature an excitable man, but these interviews never seemed to take the course which he intended them to take.

"Where were you last night?" he blurted.

"In Cornwall," said the Saint. "Charming country—full of area. Know it?"

"What time did you leave?"

"Nine-fifty-two pip."

"Did anybody see you go?"

"Everyone who had stayed the course observed my departure," said the Saint carefully. "A few of the male population had retired hurt a little earlier, and others were still enthusiastic but already blind. Apart from seven who had been ruled out earlier in the week by an epidemic of measles——"

"And where were you between ten and five minutes to five this morning?"

"I was on my way."

"Were you anywhere near Wintney?"

"That would be about it."

"Notice anything peculiar around there?"

Simon wrinkled his brow.

"I recall the scene distinctly. It was the hour before the dawn. The sleeping earth, still spellbound by the magic of the night, lay quiet beneath the paling skies. Over the peaceful scene brooded the expectant hush of all the mornings since the beginning of these days. The whole world, like a bride listening for the footfall of her lover, or a breakfast sausage hoping against hope——"

The movement with which Teal clamped a battered piece of spearmint between his molars was one of sheer ferocity.

"Now listen," he snarled. "Near Wintney, between ten and five minutes to five this morning, a Hirondel with your number-plates on it was called on to stop by a police officer—and it drove straight past him!"

Simon nodded.

"Sure, that was me," he said innocently. "I was in a hurry. D'you mean I'm going to be summoned?"

" I mean more than that. Shortly before you came past the constable heard a scream——"

Simon nodded again.

" Sure, I heard it too. Weird noises owls make sometimes. Did he want me to hold his hand ? "

" That was no owl screaming——"

" Yeah ? You were there as well, were you ? "

" I've got the constable's telephoned report——"

" You can find a use for it." The Saint opened his mouth, inserted egg, bacon, and buttered toast in suitable proportions, and stood up. " And now *you* listen, Claud Eustace." He tapped the detective's stomach with his forefinger. " Have you got a warrant to come round and cross-examine me at this ungodly hour of the morning—or any other hour, for that matter ? "

" It's part of my duty——"

" It's part of the blunt end of the pig of the aunt of the gardener. Let that pass for a minute. Is there one single crime that even your pop-eyed imagination can think of to charge me with ? There is not. But we understand the functioning of your so-called brain. Some loutish cop thought he heard someone scream in Hampshire this morning, and because I happened to be passing through the same country you think I must have had something to do with it. If somebody tells you that a dud shilling has been found in a slot machine in Blackpool, the first thing you want to know is whether I was within a hundred miles of the spot within six months of the event. A drowned man is fished out of the ocean at Boston, and if you hear a rumour that I was staying beside the same ocean at Biarritz two years before——"

" I never——"

" You invariably. And now get another earful. You haven't a search-warrant, but we'll excuse that. Would you like to go upstairs and run through my wardrobe and see if you can find any bloodstains on my clothes ? Because you're welcome. Would you like to push into the garage and take a look at my car and see if you can find a body under the back seat ? Shove on. Make yourself absolutely at home. But digest this first." Again that dictatorial forefinger impressed its point on the preliminary concavity of the detective's waistcoat. " Make that search—accept my invitation—and if you can't find anything to justify it, you're going to wish your father had died a bachelor, which he may have done for all I know. You're becoming a nuisance, Claud, and I'm telling you that this is where you get off. Give me the small half of less than a quarter of a break, and I'm going to roast the hell out of you. I'm going to send you up to the sky on one big balloon ; and when you come down you're not going to bounce—you're going to spread yourself out so flat that a short-sighted man will not be able to see you sideways. Got it ? "

Teal gulped.

His cherubic countenance took on a slightly redder tinge, and he shuffled his feet like a truant schoolboy. But that, to do him justice, was the only childish thing about his attitude, and it was beyond Teal's power to control. For he gazed deep into the dancing, mocking, challenging blue eyes of the Saint standing there before him, lean and reckless and debonair even in that preposterous bath-robe outfit ; and he understood the issue exactly.

And Chief Inspector Claud Eustace Teal nodded.

" Of course," he grunted, " if that's the way you take it, there's nothing more to be said."

" There isn't," agreed the Saint concisely. " And if there was, I'd say it."

He picked up the detective's bowler hat, dusted it with his towel, and handed it over. Teal accepted it, looked at it, and sighed. And he was still sighing when the Saint took him by the arm and ushered him politely but firmly to the door.

III

" And if that," remarked the Saint, blithely returning to his interrupted breakfast, " doesn't shake up Claud Eustace from the Anzora downwards, nothing short of an earthquake will."

Patricia lighted another cigarette.

" So long as you didn't overdo it," she said. " *Qui s'excuse, s'accuse*——"

" And *honi soit qui mal y pense*," said the Saint cheerfully. " No, old sweetheart—that outburst had been on its way for a long while. We've been seeing a great deal too much of Claud Eustace lately, and I have a feeling that the Teal-baiting season is just getting into full swing."

" But what *is* the story about Beppo ? "

Simon embarked upon his second egg.

" Oh, yes ! Well, Beppo. . . ."

He told her what he knew, and it is worth noting that she believed him. The recital, with necessary comment and decoration, ran out with the toast and marmalade ; and at the end of it she knew as much as he did, which was not much.

" But in a little while we're going to know a whole lot more," he said.

He smoked a couple of cigarettes, glanced over the headlines of a newspaper, and went upstairs again. For several minutes he swung a pair of heavy Indian clubs with cheerful vigour ; then a shave, a second and longer immersion in the bath with savon and vox humana accompaniment, and he felt ready to punch holes in three distinct and different heavyweights. None of which being available, he selected a fresh outfit of clothes, dressed himself with leisurely care, and descended once more upon the sitting-room looking like one consolidated ray of sunshine.

" Cocktail at the Bruton at a quarter to one," he murmured, and drifted out again.

By that time, which was 10.44 precisely, if that matters a damn to anyone, the floating population of Upper Berkeley Mews had increased by one conspicuous unit ; but that did not surprise the Saint. Such things had happened before, they were part of the inevitable paraphernalia of the attacks of virulent detectivosis which periodically afflicted the ponderous lucubrations of Chief Inspector Teal ; and after the brief but comprehensive exchange of pleasantries earlier that morning, Simon Templar would have been more disappointed than otherwise if he had seen no symptoms of a fresh outbreak of the disease.

Simon was not perturbed. . . . He raised his hat politely to the sleuth, was cut dead, and remained unperturbed. . . . And he sauntered imperturbably westwards through the smaller streets of Mayfair until, in one of the very smallest streets, he was able to collar the one and only visible taxi, in which he drove away, fluttering his handkerchief out of the window, and leaving a fuming plain-clothes man standing on the kerb glaring frantically around for another cab in which to continue the chase—and finding none.

At the Dover Street corner of Piccadilly, he paid off the

driver and strolled back to the Piccadilly entrance of the Berkeley. It still wanted a few minutes to eleven, but the reception clerk, spurred on perhaps by the Saint's departing purposefulness, had a doctor already waiting for him.

Simon conducted the move to the patient's room himself, and had his first shock when he helped to remove the man's shirt.

He looked at what he saw in silence for some seconds; and then the doctor, who had also looked, turned to him with his ruddy face gone a shade paler.

" I was told that your friend had had an accident," he said bluntly, and the Saint nodded.

" Something unpleasant has certainly happened to him. Will you go on with your examination ? "

He lighted a cigarette and went over to the window, where he stood gazing thoughtfully down into Berkeley Street until the doctor rejoined him.

" Your friend seems to have been given an injection of scopolamine and morphia—you have probably heard of ' twilight sleep.' His other injuries you've seen for yourself—I haven't found any more."

The Saint nodded.

" I gave him the injection myself. He should be waking up soon—he had rather less than one-hundredth of a grain of scopolamine. Will you want to move him to a nursing home ? "

" I don't think that will be necessary, unless he wishes it himself, Mr. —— "

" Travers."

" Mr. Travers. He should have a nurse, of course—— "

" I can get one."

The doctor inclined his head.

Then he removed his pince-nez and looked the Saint directly in the eyes.

" I presume you know how your friend received his injuries ? " he said.

" I can guess." The Saint flicked a short cylinder of ash from his cigarette. " I should say that he had been beaten with a raw-hide whip, and that persuasion by hot irons had also been applied."

The doctor put his finger-tips together and blinked.

"You must admit, Mr. Travers, that the circumstances are—er—somewhat unusual."

"You could say all that twice, and no one would accuse you of exaggerating," assented the Saint, with conviction. "But if that fact is bothering your professional conscience, I can only say that I'm as much in the dark as you are. The accident story was just to satisfy the birds below. As a matter of fact, I found our friend lying by the roadside in the small hours of this morning, and I sort of took charge. Doubtless the mystery will be cleared up in due course."

"Naturally, you have communicated with the police."

"I've already interviewed one detective, and I'm sure he's doing everything he can," said the Saint veraciously. He opened the door, and propelled the doctor decisively along the corridor. "Will you want to see the patient again to-day?"

"I hardly think it will be necessary, Mr. Travers. His dressings should be changed to-night—the nurse will see to that. I'll come in to-morrow morning——"

"Thanks very much. I shall expect you at the same time. Good-bye."

Simon shook the doctor warmly by the hand, swept him briskly into the waiting elevator, and watched him sink downwards out of view.

Then he went back to the room, poured out a glass of water, and sat down in a chair by the bedside. The patient was sleeping easily; and Simon, after a glance at his watch, prepared to await the natural working-off of the drug.

A quarter of an hour later he was extinguishing a cigarette when the patient stirred and groaned. A thin hand crawled up to the bare throat, and the man's head rolled sideways with his eyelids flickering. As Simon bent over him, a husky whisper of a word came through the relaxed lips.

"*Acqua....*"

"Sure thing, brother." Simon propped up the man's head and put the glass to his mouth.

"*Mille grazie.*"

"*Prego.*"

Presently the man sank back again. And then his eyes opened, and focussed on the Saint.

For a number of seconds there was not the faintest glimmer of understanding in the eyes: they stared at and through their object like the eyes of a blind man. And then, slowly, they widened into round pools of shuddering horror, and the Italian shrank away with a thin cry rattling in his throat.

Simon gripped his arm and smiled.

" *Non tema. Sono un amico.* "

It was some time before he was able to calm the man into a dully incredulous quietness ; but he won belief before he had finished, and at last the Italian sank back again among the pillows and was silent.

Simon mopped his brow and fished out his cigarette-case.

And then the man spoke again, still weakly, but in a different voice.

" *Quanti ne abbiamo quest'oggi ?* "

" *È il due ottobre.* "

There was a pause.

" *Vuol favorire di dirmi il suo nome ?* "

" Templar—Simon Templar. "

There was another pause. And then the man rolled over and looked at the Saint again. And he spoke in almost perfect English.

" I have heard of you. You were called——"

" Many things. But that was a long time ago. "

" How did you find me ? "

" Well—I rather think that you found me. "

The Italian passed a hand across his eyes.

" I remember now. I was running. I fell down. Some-one caught me. . . ." Suddenly he clutched the Saint's wrist. " Did you see—*him* ? "

" Your gentleman friend ? " murmured Simon lightly. " Sure I did. He also saw me, but not soon enough. Yes, we certainly met. "

The grip of the trembling fingers loosened slowly, and the man lay still, breathing jerkily through his nose.

" *Voglia scusarmi,* " he said at length. " *Mi vergogno.* "

" *Non ne val la pena.* "

" It is as if I had awoken from a terrible dream. Even now——" The Italian looked down at the bandages that swathed the whole of the upper part of his body, and shivered uncontrollably. " Did you put on these ? " he asked.

" No—a doctor did that. "

The man looked round the room.

" And this——"

" This is the Berkeley Hotel, London."

The Italian nodded. He swallowed painfully, and Simon refilled his glass and passed it back. Another silence fell, which grew so long that the Saint wondered if his patient had fallen asleep again. He rose stealthily to his feet, and the Italian roused and caught his sleeve.

" Wait." The words came quite quietly and sanely. " I must talk to you."

" Sure." Simon smiled down at the man. " But do you want to do it now ? Hadn't you better rest for a bit—maybe have something to eat——"

The Italian shook his head.

" Afterwards. Will you sit down again ? "

And Simon Templar sat down.

And he listened, almost without movement, while the minute hand of his watch voyaged unobserved once round the dial. He listened in a perfect trance of concentration, while the short, precise sentences of the Italian's story slid into the atmosphere and built themselves up into a shape that he had never even dreamed of.

It was past one o'clock when he walked slowly down the stairs with the inside story of one of the most stupendous crimes in history whirling round in his brain like the armature of a high-powered dynamo.

Wrapped up in the rumination of what he had heard, he passed out like a sleep-walker into Berkeley Street. And it so happened that in his abstraction he almost cannoned into a man who was at the moment walking down towards Piccadilly. He stepped aside with a muttered apology, absent-mindedly registering a kind of panoramic impression of a brilliantly purple suit, lemon-coloured gloves, a gold-mounted cane, a lavender shirt, spotted tie, and——

Just for an instant the Saint's gaze rested on the man's face. And then they were past each other, without a flicker of recognition, without the batting of an eyelid. But the Saint knew. . . .

He knew that that savagely arrogant face, like a mask of black marble, was like no other black face that he had ever seen in his life before that morning. And he knew, with the same certainty, that the eyes in the black face had recognised him in the same moment as he had recognised them—and with no more betrayal of their knowledge. And as he wandered up into Berkeley Square, and the portals of the Bruton Club received him, he knew, though he had not looked back, that the black eyes were still behind him, and had seen where he went.

IV

BUT the smile with which the Saint greeted Patricia was as gay and carefree as she had ever seen.

" I should like," said the Saint, sinking into an arm-chair, " three large double Martinis in a big glass. Just to line my stomach. After which, I shall be able to deal respectfully with a thirst which can only be satisfactorily slaked by two gallons of bitter beer."

" You will have one Martini, and then we'll have some lunch," said Patricia ; and the Saint sighed.

" You have no soul," he complained.

Patricia put her magazine under the table.

" What's new, boy ? " she asked.

" About Beppo ? . . . Well, a whole heap of things are new about Beppo. I can tell you this, for instance : Beppo is no smaller a guy than the Duke of Fortezza, and he is the acting President of the Bank of Italy."

" He's—what ? "

" He's the acting President of the Bank of Italy—and that's not the half of it. Pat, old girl, I told you at the start that there was some gay game being played, and, by the Lord, it's as gay a game as we may ever find ! " Simon signed the chit on the waiter's tray with a flourish and settled back again, surveying his drink dreamily. " Remember reading in some paper recently that the Bank of Italy was preparing to put out an entirely new and original line of paper currency ? " he asked.

" I saw something about it."

" It was so. The contract was placed with Crosby Dorman, one of our own biggest printing firms—they do the thin cash and postal issues of half a dozen odd little countries. Beppo put the deal through. A while ago he brought over the plates and gave the order, and one week back he came on his second trip to take delivery of three million pounds' worth of coloured paper in a tin-lined box."

" And then ? "

" I'll tell you what then. One whole extra million pounds' worth of mazuma is ordered, and that printing goes into a separate box. Ordered on official notepaper, too, with Beppo's own signature in the south-east corner. And meanwhile Beppo is indisposed. The first crate of spondulix departs in the golden galleon without him, completely surrounded by soldiers, secret service agents, and general detectives, all armed to the teeth and beyond. Another of those nice letters apologises for Beppo's absence, and instructs the guard to carry on ; a third letter explains the circumstances, ditto and ditto, to the Bank——"

Patricia sat up.

" And the box is empty ? "

" The box is packed tight under a hydraulic press, stiff to the sealing-wax with the genuine articles as per invoice."

" But——"

" But obviously. That box had got to go through. The new issue had to spread itself out. It's been on the market three days already. And the ground bait is now laid for the big haul—the second box, containing approximately one million hundred-lire bills convertible into equivalent sterling on sight. And the whole board of the Bank of Italy, the complete staff of cashiers, office-boys, and outside porters, the entire vigilance society of soldiers, secret service agents, and general detectives, all armed to the teeth and beyond, are as innocent of the existence of that million as the unborn daughter of the Caliph's washerwoman."

The girl looked at him with startled eyes.

" And do you mean Beppo was in this ? "

" Does it seem that way ? " Simon Templar swivelled round towards her with one eyebrow inquisitorially cocked and a long wisp of smoke training through his lips. " I wish you could have seen him. . . . Sure he's in it. They turned him over to the Negro Spiritual, and let that big black swine pet him till he signed. If I told you what they'd done to him you wouldn't be in such a hurry for your lunch." For a moment the Saint's lips thinned fractionally. " He's just shot to pieces, and when you see him you'll know why. Sure, that bunch are like brothers to Beppo ! "

Patricia sat in a thoughtful silence, and the Saint emptied his glass.

Then she said : " Who are this bunch ? "

Simon slithered his cigarette round to the corner of his mouth.

" Well, the actual bunch are mostly miscellaneous, as you might say," he answered. " But the big noise seems to be a bird named Kuzela, whom we haven't met before, but whom I'm going to meet darned soon."

" And this money——"

" Is being delivered to Kuzela's men to-day." The Saint glanced at his watch. " Has been, by now. And within twenty-four hours parcels of it will be burning the sky over to his agents in Paris, Berlin, Vienna, and Madrid. Within the week it will be gravitating back to him through the same channels—big bouncing wads of it, translated into authentic wads of francs, marks, and pesetas—while one million perfectly genuine hundred-lire bills whose numbers were never in the catalogue are drifting home to a Bank of Italy that will be wondering whether the whole world is falling to pieces round its ears. . . . Do you get me, Pat ? "

The clear blue eyes rested on her face with the twist of mocking hell-for-leather delight that she knew so well, and she asked her next question almost mechanically.

" Is it your party ? "

" It is, old Pat. And not a question asked. No living soul must ever know—there'd be a panic on the international exchanges if a word of it leaked out. But every single one of those extra million bills has got to be taken by the hand and led gently back to Beppo's tender care—and the man who's going to do it is ready for his lunch."

And lunch it was without further comment, for the Saint was like that. . . . But about his latest meeting with the Negro Spiritual he did not find it necessary to say anything at all—for, again, the Saint was that way. . . . And after lunch, when Patricia was ordering coffee in the lounge, yet another incident which the Saint was inclined to regard as strictly private and personal clicked into its appointed socket in the energetic history of that day.

Simon had gone out to telephone a modest tenner on a horse for the 3.30, and he was on his way back through the hall when a porter stopped him.

" Excuse me, sir, but did you come here from the Berkeley ? "

The Saint fetched his right foot up alongside his left and lowered his brows one millimetre.

" Yeah—I have been in there this morning."

" A coloured gentleman brought these for you, sir. He said he saw you drop them as you came out of the hotel, but he lost you in the crowd while he was picking them up. And then, as he was walking through Lansdowne Passage, he happened to look up and see you at one of the windows, so he brought them in. From the description he gave me it seemed as if it must have been you, sir——"

" Oh, it was certainly me."

The Saint, who had never owned a pair of lemon-coloured gloves in his life, accepted the specimens gingerly, folded them, and slipped them into his pocket.

" Funny coincidence, sir, wasn't it ? " said the porter chattily. " Him happening to pass by, and you happening to be in the window at that time."

" Quite remarkable," agreed the Saint gravely, recalling the care he had taken to avoid all windows ; and, turning back, he retired rapidly to a remote sanctuary.

There he unfolded the gloves in an empty wash-basin, contriving to work them cautiously inside out with his fountain pen in one hand and his propelling pencil in the other.

He had not the vaguest idea what kind of creeping West African frightfulness might be waiting for him in those citron-hued misdemeanours, but he was certainly a trifle surprised when he saw what fell out of the first glove that he tackled.

It was simply a thin splinter of wood, pointed at both ends, and stained with some dark stain.

For a moment or two he looked at it expressionlessly.

Then he picked it up between two matches and stowed it carefully in his cigarette-case.

He turned his attention to the second glove, and extracted from it a soiled scrap of paper. He read :

If you will come to 85, Vandermeer Avenue, Hampstead, at midnight to-night, we may be able to reach some mutually satisfactory agreement. Otherwise, I fear that the consequences of your interference may be infinitely regrettable.

K.

Simon Templar held the message at arm's length, well up to the light, and gazed at it wall-eyed.

" And whales do so lay eggs," he articulated at last, when he could find a voice sufficiently impregnated with emotion.

And then he laughed and went back to Patricia.

" If Monday's Child comes home, you shall have a new hat," he said, and the girl smiled.

" What else happens before that ? " she asked.

" We go on a little tour," said the Saint.

They left the club together, and boarded a taxi that had just been paid off at the door.

" Piccadilly Hotel," said the Saint.

He settled back, lighting a cigarette.

" I shook off Teal's man by Method One," he explained. " You are now going to see a demonstration of Method Two. If you can go on studying under my supervision, all the shadowers you will ever meet will mean nothing to you. . . . The present performance may be a waste of energy "—he glanced back through the rear window—" or it may not. But the wise man is permanently suspicious."

They reached the Piccadilly entrance of the hotel in a few minutes, and the Saint opened the door. The exact fare, plus bonus, was ready in the Saint's hand, and he dropped it in the driver's palm and followed Patricia across the pavement—without any appearance of haste, but very briskly. As he reached the doors, he saw in one glass panel the reflection of another taxi pulling in to the kerb behind him.

" This way."

He steered the girl swiftly through the main hall, swung her through a short passage, across another hall, and up some steps, and brought her out through another door into Regent Street. A break in the traffic let them straight through to the taxi rank in the middle of the road.

" Berkeley Hotel," said the Saint.

He lounged deep in his corner and grinned at her.

" Method Two is not for use on a trained sleuth who knows you know he's after you," he murmured. " Other times, it's the whelk's knee-cap." He took her bag from her hands, slipped out the little mirror, and used it for a periscope to survey the south side pavement as they drove away. " This is one of those whens," he said complacently.

" Then why are we going to the Berkeley ? "

" Because you are the nurse who is going to look after Beppo. His number is 148, and 149 is already booked for you.

Incidentally, you might remember that he's registered in the name of Teal—C. E. Teal. I'll pack a bag and bring it along to you later ; but once you're inside the Berkeley Arms you've got to stay put so long as it's daylight. The doctor's name is Branson and mine is Travers, and if anyone else applies for admission you will shoot him through the binder and ring for the bell-hop to remove the body."

" But what will you be doing ? "

" I am the proud possessor of a Clue, and I'm going to be very busy tying a knot in its tail. Also I have an ambition to be humorous, and that will mean that I've got to push round to a shop I wot of and purchase one of those mechanical jokes that are said to create roars of laughter. I've been remembering my younger days, and they've brought back to me the very thing I need. . . . And here we are."

The cab had stopped at its destination, and they got out. Patricia hesitated in the doorway.

" When will you be back ? " she asked.

" I shall be along for dinner about eight," said the Saint. " Meanwhile, you'll be able to get acquainted with Beppo. Really, you'll find him quite human. Prattle gently to him, and he'll eat out of your hand. When he's stronger, you might even be allowed to sing to him—I'll ask the doctor about that to-morrow. . . . So long, lass ! "

And the Saint was gone.

And he did exactly what he had said he was going to do. He went to a shop in Regent Street and bought a little toy and took it back with him to Upper Berkeley Mews ; and a certain alteration which he made to its inner functionings kept him busy for some time and afforded him considerable amusement.

For he had not the slightest doubt that there was going to be fun and games before the next dawn. The incident of those lemon-coloured gloves was a distinct encouragement. It showed a certain thoroughness on the part of the opposition, and that sort of thing always gave the Saint great pleasure.

"If one glove doesn't work, the other is expected to oblige," he figured it out, as he popped studs into a snowy white dress shirt. " And it would be a pity to disappoint anyone."

He elaborated this latter idea to Patricia Holm when he rejoined her at the Berkeley, having shaken off his official watcher again by Method Three. Before he left, he told her nearly everything.

" At midnight, all the dreams of the ungodly are coming true," he said. " Picture to yourself the scene. It will be the witching hour. The menace of dark deeds will veil the stars. And up the heights of Hampstead will come toiling the pitiful figure of the unsuspecting victim, with his bleary eyes bulging and his mouth hanging open and the green moss sprouting behind his ears ; and that will be Little Boy. . . ."

V

SOME men enjoy trouble ; others just as definitely don't. And there are some who enjoy dreaming about the things they would do if they only dared—but they need not concern us.

Simon Templar came into Category A—straight and slick, with his name in a panel all to itself, and a full stop just where it hits hardest.

For there is a price ticket on everything that puts a whiz into life, and adventure follows the rule. It's distressing, but there you are. If there was no competition, everything would be quite all right. If you could be certain that you were the strongest man in the world, the most quick-witted, the most cunning, the most keen sighted, the most vigilant, and simultaneously the possessor of the one and only lethal weapon in the whole wide universe, there wouldn't be much difficulty about it. You would just step out of your hutch and hammer the first thing that came along.

But it doesn't always pan out like that in practice. When you try the medicine on the dog, you are apt to discover some violent reactions which were not arranged for in the prescription. And then, when the guns give tongue, and a spot of fur beings to fly, you are liable to arrive at the sudden and soul-shattering realisation that a couple of ounces of lead travelling with a given velocity will make precisely as deep an impression on your anatomical system as they will on that of the next man.

Which monumental fact the Saint had thoroughly digested a few days after mastering his alphabet. And the effect it had registered upon his unweaned peace of mind had been so near to absolute zero that a hair-line could not have been drawn between them—neither on the day of the discovery nor on any subsequent day in all his life.

In theory. . . .

In theory, of course, he allowed the artillery to pop, and the fur to become volatile, without permitting a single lock of his own sleek, dark hair to aberrate from the patent-leather discipline in which he disposed it ; and thereby he became the Saint. But it is perfectly possible to appreciate and acknowledge the penetrating unpleasantness of high-velocity lead, and forthwith to adopt a debonairly philosophical attitude towards the same, without being in a tearing hurry to offer your own carcase for the purposes of practical demonstration ; this also the Saint did, and by doing it with meticulous attention contrived to be spoken of in the present tense for many years longer than the most optimistic insurance broker would have backed him to achieve.

All of which has not a little to do with 85, Vandermeer Avenue, Hampstead.

Down this road strolled the Saint, his hands deep in the pockets of knife-edged trousers, the crook of his walking-stick hooked over his left wrist, and slanting sidelong over his right eye a filibustering black felt hat which alone was something very like a breach of the peace. A little song rollicked on his lips, and was inaudible two yards away. And as he walked, his lazy eyes absorbed every interesting item of the scenery.

> " *Aspidistra, little herb,*
> *Do you think it silly*
> *When the botaniser's blurb*
> *Links you with the lily ?* "

Up in one window of the house, he caught the almost imperceptible sway of a shifting curtain, and knew that his approach had already been observed. " But it is nice," thought the Saint, " to be expected." And he sauntered on :

> " *Up above your window-ledge*
> *Streatham stars are gleaming :*
> *Aspidistra, little veg,*
> *Does your soul go dreaming ?* "

A low iron gate opened from the road. He pushed it wide with his foot, and went up the steps to the porch.

7

Beside the door was a bell-push set in a panel of polished brass tracery.

The Saint's fingers moved towards it . . . and travelled back again. He stooped and examined the filigree more closely, and a little smile lightened his face.

Then he cuddled himself into the extreme houseward corner of the porch, held his hat over the panel, and pressed the button with the ferrule of his stick. He heard a faint hiss, and turned his hat back to the light of a street lamp. A stained splinter of wood quivered in the white satin lining of the crown; and the Saint's smile became blindingly seraphic as he reached into a side pocket of his jacket for a pair of tweezers. . . .

And then the door was opening slowly.

Deep in his angle of shadow, he watched the strip of yellow light widening across the porch and down the short flagged passage to the gate. The silhouette of a man loomed into it and stood motionless for a while behind the threshold.

Then it stepped out into full view—a big, heavy-shouldered, close-cropped man, with thick bunched fists hanging loosely at his sides. He peered outwards down the shaft of light, and then to right and left, his battered face creasing to the strain of probing the darkness on either side. The Saint's white shirt-front caught his eye, and he licked his lips and spoke like an automaton.

" Comin' in ? "

" Behind you, brother," said the Saint.

He stepped across the light, taking the bruiser by the elbows and spinning him adroitly round. They entered the house in the order of his own arrangement, and Simon kicked the door shut behind him.

There was no machine-gun at the far end of the hall, as he had half expected ; but the Saint was unashamed.

" Windy ? " sneered the bruiser, as the Saint released him ; and Simon smiled.

" Never since taking soda-mint," he murmured. " Where do we go from here ? "

The bruiser glanced sideways, jerking his head :

" Upstairs."

" Oh, yeah ? "

Simon slanted a cigarette into his mouth and followed the

glance. His eyes weaved up the banisters and down the separate steps of the stairway.

" After you again," he drawled. " Just to be certain."

The bruiser led the way, and Simon followed discreetly. They arrived in procession at the upper landing, where a second bruiser, a trifle shorter than the first, but even heavier of shoulder, lounged beside an open door with an unlighted stump of cigar in his mouth.

The second man gestured with his lower jaw and the cigar.

" In there."

" Thanks," said the Saint.

He paused for a moment in the doorway and surveyed the room, one hand ostentatiously remaining in the pocket of his coat.

Facing him, in the centre of the rich brown carpet, was a broad flat-topped desk. It harmonised with the solid simplicity of the book-cases that broke the panelling of the bare walls, and with the long austere lines of the velvet hangings that covered the windows—even, perhaps, with the squat square materialism of the safe that stood in a corner behind it. And on the far side of the desk sat the man whom the Saint had come to see, leaning forward out of a straight-backed oak chair.

Simon moved forward, and the two bruisers closed the door and ranged themselves on either side of him.

" Good evening, Kuzela," said the Saint.

" Good evening, Mr. Templar." The man behind the desk moved one white hand. " Sit down."

Simon looked at the chair that had been placed ready for him. Then he turned, and took one of the bruisers by the lapels of his coat. He shot the man into the chair, bounced him up and down a couple of times, swung him from side to side, and yanked him out again.

" Just to make *quite* certain," said the Saint sweetly. He beamed upon the glowering pugilist, felt his biceps, and patted him encouragingly on the shoulder. " You'll be a big man when you grow up, Cuthbert," he said affably.

Then he moved the chair a yard to one side and sat in it himself.

" I'm sure you'll excuse all these formalities," he remarked conversationally. " I have to be so careful these days. The most extraordinary things happen to me. Only the other day, a large spotted hypotenuse, overtaking on the wrong side——"

" I have already observed that you possess a well-developed instinct of self-preservation, Mr. Templar," said Kuzela suavely.

He clasped his well-kept hands on the blotter before him, and studied the Saint interestedly.

Simon returned the compliment.

He saw a man in healthy middle age, broad-shouldered and strongly built. A high, firmly modelled forehead rose into a receding setting of clipped iron-grey hair. With his square jaw and slightly aquiline nose, he might have posed for a symbolical portrait of any successful business man. Only his eyes might have betrayed the imposture. Pale blue, deep-set and unwinking, they levelled themselves upon the object of their scrutiny in a feline stare of utter ruthlessness. . . . And the Saint looked into the eyes and laughed.

" You certainly win on the exchange," he said ; and a slight frown came between the other's eyebrows.

" If you would explain—— ? "

" I'm good-looking," said the Saint easily, and centred his tie with elegance.

Kuzela leaned back.

" Your name is known to me, of course ; but I think this is the first time we have had the pleasure of meeting."

" This is certainly the first time you've had the pleasure of meeting me," said the Saint carefully.

" Even now, the responsibility is yours. You have elected to interfere with my affairs——"

Simon shook his head sympathetically.

" It's most distressing, isn't it ? " he murmured. " And your most strenuous efforts up to date have failed to dispose of the interference. Even when you sent me a pair of gloves that would have given a rhinoceros a headache to look at, I survived the shock. It must be Fate, old dear."

Kuzela pulled himself forward again.

" You are an enterprising young man," he said quietly. " An unusually enterprising young man. There are not many men living who could have overcome Ngano, even by the method which you adopted. The mere fact that you were able to enter this house is another testimony to your foresight—or your good luck."

" My foresight," said the Saint modestly.

" You moved your chair before you sat down—and that again showed remarkable intelligence. If you had sat where I intended you to sit, it would have been possible for me, by a light movement of my foot, to send a bullet through the centre of your body."

" So I guessed."

" Since you arrived, your hand has been in your pocket several times. I presume you are armed——"

Simon Templar inspected the finger-nails of his two hands.

" If I had been born the day before yesterday," he observed mildly, " you'd find out everything you wanted to know in approximately two minutes."

" Again, a man of your reputation would not have communicated with the police——"

" But he would take great care of himself." The Saint's eyes met Kuzela's steadily. " I'll talk or fight, Kuzela, just as you like. Which is it to be ? "

" You are prepared to deal ? "

" Within limits—yes."

Kuzela drummed his knuckles together.

" On what terms ? "

" They might be—one hundred thousand pounds."

Kuzela shrugged.

" If you came here in a week's time——"

" I should be very pleased to have a drink with you," said the Saint pointedly.

" Suppose," said Kuzela, " I gave you a cheque which you could cash to morrow morning——"

" Or suppose," said the Saint calmly, " you gave me some cash with which I could buy jujubes on my way home."

Kuzela looked at him with a kind of admiration.

" Rumour has not lied about you, Mr. Templar," he said. " I imagine you will have no objection to receiving this sum in—er—foreign currency ? "

" None whatever," said the the Saint blandly.

The other stood up, taking a little key from his waistcoat pocket. And the Saint, who for the moment had been looking at the delicately painted shade of the lamp that stood on one side of the desk, which was the sole dim illumination of the room, slewed round with a sudden start.

He knew that there was going to be a catch somewhere—that, with a man of Kuzela's type, a man who had sent those gloves and who had devised that extremely ingenious bell-push on the front door, a coup could never be quite so easy. How that last catch was going to be worked he had no idea ; nor was he inclined to wait and learn it. In his own way, he had done as much as he had hoped to do ; and, all things considered——

" Let me see that key ! " he exclaimed.

Kuzela turned puzzledly.

" Really, Mr. Templar—— "

" Let me see it ! " repeated the Saint excitedly.

He reached over the desk and took the key out of Kuzela's hands. For a second he gazed at it ; and then he raised his eyes again with a dancing devil of mischief glinting out of their blueness.

" Sorry I must be going, souls," he said ; and with one smashing sweep of his arm he sent the lamp flying off the desk and plunged the room into inky blackness.

'VI

THE phrase is neither original nor copyright, and may be performed in public without fee or licence. It remains, however, an excellent way of describing that particular phenomenon.

With the extinction of the single source of luminance, the darkness came down in all the drenching suddenness of an unleashed cataract of Stygian gloom. For an instant, it seemed to blot out not only the sense of sight, but also every other active faculty ; and a frozen, throbbing stillness settled between the four walls. And in that stillness the Saint sank down without a sound upon his toes and the tips of his fingers. . . .

He knew his bearings to the nth part of a degree, and he travelled to his destination with the noiseless precision of a cat. Around him he could hear the sounds of tensely restrained breathing, and the slithering caress of wary feet creeping over the carpet. Then, behind him, came the vibration of a violent movement, the thud of a heavy blow, a curse, a scuffle, a crashing fall, and a shrill yelp of startled anguish . . . and the Saint grinned gently.

" I got 'im," proclaimed a triumphant voice, out of the dark void. " Strike a light, Bill."

Through an undercurrent of muffled yammering sizzled the crisp kindling of a match. It was held in the hand of Kuzela himself, and by its light the two bruisers glared at each other, their reddened stares of hate aimed upwards and downwards respectively. And before the match went out the opinions of the foundation member found fervid utterance.

" You perishing bleeder," he said, in accents that literally wobbled with earnestness.

" Peep-bo," said the Saint, and heard the contortionist effects blasphemously disentangling themselves as he closed the door behind him.

A bullet splintered a panel two inches east of his neck as he shifted briskly westwards. The next door stood invitingly ajar : he went through it as the other door reopened, slammed it behind him, and turned the key.

In a few strides he was across the room and flinging up the window. He squirmed over the sill like an eel, curved his fingers over the edge, and hung at the full stretch of his arms. A foot below the level of his eyes there was a narrow stone ledge running along the side of the building : he transferred himself to it, and worked rapidly along to the nearest corner. As he rounded it, he looked down into the road, twenty feet below, and saw a car standing by the kerb.

Another window came over his head. He reached up, got a grip of the sill, and levered his elbows above the sill level with a skilful kick and an acrobatic twist of his body. From there he was able to make a grab for the top of the lower sash. . . . And in another moment he was standing upright on the sill, pushing the upper sash cautiously downwards.

A murmur of dumbfounded voices drifted to his ears.

" Where the 'ell can 'e 'ave gorn to ? "

" Think 'e jumped for it ? "

" Jumped for it, yer silly fat-'ead ? . . ."

And then the Saint lowered himself cat-footed to the carpet on the safe side of the curtains in the room he had recently left.

Through a narrow gap in the hangings he could see Kuzela replacing the shattered bulb of the table lamp by the light of a match. The man's white efficient hands were perfectly steady ; his face was without expression. He accomplished his task with the tremorless tranquillity of a patient middle-aged gentleman whom no slight accident could seriously annoy—tested the switch. . . .

And then, as the room lighted up again, he raised his eyes to the convex mirror panel on the opposite wall, and had one distorted glimpse of the figure behind him. . . .

Then the Saint took him by the neck.

Fingers like bands of steel paralysed his larynx and choked back into his chest the cry he would have uttered. He fought like a maniac ; but though his strength was above the average, he was as helpless as a puppet in that relentless grip. And almost affectionately Simon Templar's thumbs sidled round to their mark—the deadly pressure on the carotid arteries which is to crude ordinary throttling what foil play is to sabre work. . . .

It was all over in a few seconds. And Kuzela was lying limply spread-eagled across the desk, and Simon Templar was fitting his key into the lock of the safe.

The plungers pistoned smoothly back, and the heavy door swung open. And the Saint sat back on his heels and gazed in rapture at what he saw.

Five small leather attaché cases stood in a neat row before his eyes. It was superb—splendiferous—it was just five times infinitely more than he had ever seriously dared to hope. That one hundred million lire were lying around somewhere in London he had been as sure as a man can be of anything—Kuzela would never have wasted time transporting his booty from the departure centre to the country house where the Duke of Fortezza had been kept—but that the most extempore bluff should have led him promptly and faultlessly to the hiding-place of all that merry mazuma was almost too good to be true. And for a few precious seconds the Saint stared entranced at the vision that his everlastingly preposterous luck had ladled out for his delight. . . .

And then he was swiftly hauling the valises out on to the floor.

He did not even have to attempt to open one of them. He knew. . . .

Rapidly he ranged the bags in a happy little line across

the carpet. He picked up his stick ; and he was adjusting his hat at its most effective angle when the two men who had pursued him returned through the door. But there was a wicked little automatic pivoting round in his free hand, and the two men noticed it in time.

" Restrain your enthusiasm, boys," said the Saint. " We're going on a journey. Pick up your luggage, and let's be moving."

He transferred one of the bags to his left hand, and his gun continued to conduct the orchestra. And under its gentle supervision the two men obeyed his orders. The delirious progress of events during the past couple of minutes had been a shade too much for their ivorine uptakes : their faces wore two uniformly blank expressions of pained bewilderment, vaguely reminiscent of the registers of a pair of precocious goldfish photographed immediately after signing their first talking picture contract. Even the power of protest had temporarily drained out of their vocal organs. They picked up two bags apiece, and suffered themselves to be shepherded out of the room in the same bovine vacuity of acquiescence.

In the hall, Simon halted the fatigue party for a moment.

" Before we pass out into the night," he said, " I want you to be quite clear about one thing. Those bags you're carrying, as you may or may not know, are each supposed to contain the equivalent of two hundred thousand pounds in ready money ; and I want you to know that anything you may be prepared to do to keep all those spondulix for yourselves is just so much tadpole-gizzard beside what I'm prepared to do to prise it off you. So you should think a long while before you do anything rash. I am the greatest gun artist in the world," said the Saint persuasively, but with a singular lack of honesty, " and I'm warning you here and now that at the first sign I see of any undue enterprise, I shall shoot each of you through the middle of the eleventh spinal vertebra, counting from the bottom. Move on, my children."

The procession moved on.

It went down the porch steps and through the iron wicket gate to the road ; and the Saint brought up the rear with his right hand in his pocket. The comedy was played without witnesses : at that hour Vandermeer Avenue, a quiet

7*

backwater even at the height of the day, was absolutely deserted. A sum total of four lighted windows was visible along the whole length of the thoroughfare, and those were too far away to provide the slightest inconvenience in any conceivable circumstances. Hampstead was being good that night. . . .

The car which Simon had observed on his prowl round the exterior of the house was parked right opposite the gate—which was where he had expected it to be. As the two men paused outside the gate, waiting for further instructions, a door of the car opened, and a slim supple figure decanted itself lightly on to the sidewalk. Patricia. . . . She came forward with her swinging long-limbed stride.

" O.K., Simon ? "

" O.K., lass."

" Gee, boy, I'm glad to see you ! "

" And I you. And the whole Wild West show was just a sitting rabbit, believe it or believe it not." The Saint's hand touched her arm. " Get back behind the wheel, Pat, start her up, and be ready to pull out so soon as the boodle's on board. It isn't every day we ferry a cool million across London, and I don't see why the honour of being the pilot shouldn't be your share of the act."

" Right-ho. . . ."

The girl disappeared, and Simon opened another door.

He watched the cases being stowed one by one in the back of the car, and the forefinger of his right hand curled tensely over the trigger of his gun. He had meant every word of his threat to the two men who were doing the job ; and they must have known it, for they carried out his orders with commendable alacrity.

And yet Simon felt a faint electric tingle of uneasiness fanning up his back and into the roots of his hair like the march of a thousand ghostly needle-points. He could not have described it in any other way, and he was as much at a loss to account for it as if the simile had been the actual fact. It was sheer blind instinct, a seventh sense born of a hundred breathless adventures, that touched him with that single thrill of insufficient warning—and left it at that. And for once in his life he ignored the danger-sign. He heard the whine of the self-starter, followed by the low-pitched powerful pulsing of the eight cleanly balanced cylinders, and saw the door closed upon the last of the bags ; and he turned smiling to the two bruisers. He pointed.

" If you keep straight on down that road," he said, " it ought to land you up somewhere near Birmingham—if you travel far enough. You might make that your next stop."

One of the men took a pace towards him.

" You just listen a minute——"

" To what ? " asked the Saint politely.

" I'm tellin' yer——"

" A bad habit," said the Saint disapprovingly. " You must try and break yourself of that. And now I'm sorry, but I can't stop. I hope you'll wash the back of your neck, see that your socks are aired, say your prayers every night, and get your face lifted at the first opportunity. . . . Now push your ears back, my cherubs, and let your feet chase each other."

His right hand moved significantly in his pocket, and there was an instant's perilous silence. And then the man who had spoken jerked his head at the other.

" Come on," he said.

The two men turned and lurched slowly away, looking back over their shoulders.

And the Saint put one foot on the running-board.

And somewhere, far away, he heard the sound of his own head being hit. It was as extraordinary an experience as any that had ever happened to him. Patricia was looking ahead down the road, while her hand eased the gears quietly into mesh ; and the Saint himself had not heard the slightest movement that might have put him on his guard. And the premonitory crawling of his nerves which he had felt a few seconds earlier had performed what it considered to be its duty, and had subsided. . . . He could have believed that the whole thing was an incredibly vivid hallucination—but for the sickening sharp stab of sudden agony that plunged through his brain like a spurt of molten metal and paralysed every milligram of strength in his body.

A great white light swelled up and exploded before his eyes ; and after it came a wave of whirling blackness shot with rocketing flashes of dizzy, dazzling colour, and the blackness was filled with a thin high singing note that drilled into his eardrums. His knees seemed to melt away beneath him. . . .

And then, from somewhere above the vast dark gulf into which he was sinking, he heard Patricia's voice cry out.

" *Simon !* "

The word seemed to spell itself into his dulled brain letter by letter, as if his mind read it off a slowly uncoiling scroll. But it touched a nerve centre that roused him for one fractional instant of time to fight back titanically against the numbing oblivion that was swallowing him up.

He knew that his eyes were open, but all he could see was one blurred segment of her face, as he might have seen her picture in a badly-focused fade-out that had gone askew. And to that isolated scrap of vision in the overwhelming blackness he found the blessed strength to croak two words :

" Drive on."

And then a second surge of darkness welled up around him and blotted out every sight and sound, and he fell away into the infinite black void.

VII

" So even your arrangements can break down, Templar— when your accomplice fails you," Kuzela remarked silkily. " My enterprising young friend, when you are older you will realise that it is always a mistake to rely upon a woman. I have never employed a woman myself for that reason."

" I'll bet that broke her heart," said the Saint.

Once again he sat in Kuzela's study, with his head still throbbing painfully from the crashing welt it had received, and a lump on the back of it feeling as if it were growing out of his skull like a great auk's egg. His hair was slightly disarranged, and the straps on his wrists prevented him from rearranging it effectively ; but the Saintly smile had not lost one iota of its charm.

" It remains, however, to decide whether you are going to be permitted to profit by this experience—whether you are going to live long enough to do so. Perhaps it has not occurred to you that you may have come to the end of your promising career," continued the man on the other side of the desk dispassionately ; and the Saint sighed.

" What, not again ? " he pleaded brokenly, and Kuzela frowned.

" I do not understand you."

" Only a few months ago I was listening to those very words," explained the Saint. " Alas, poor Wilfred ! And he meant it, too. ' Wilf, old polecat,' I said, ' don't you realise that I can't be killed before page three hundred and twenty ? ' He didn't believe me. And he died. They put a rope round his neck and dropped him through a hole in the floor, and the consequences to his figure were very startling. Up to the base of the neck he was not so thin—but oh, boy, from then on. . . . It was awfully sad."

And Simon Templar beamed around upon the congregation—upon Kuzela, and upon the two bruisers who loafed about the room, and upon the negro who stood behind his chair. And the negro he indicated with a nod.

" One of your little pets ? " he inquired ; and Kuzela's lips moved in the fraction of a smile.

" It was fortunate that Ngano heard some of the noise," he said. " He came out of the house just in time."

" To soak me over the head from behind ? " drawled the Saint genially. " Doubtless, old dear. But apart from that——"

" Your accomplice escaped, with my property. True. But my dear Templar, need that prove to be a tragedy ? We have your own invaluable self still with us—and you, I am quite sure, know not only where the lady has gone, but also where you have hidden a gentleman whom I should very much like to have restored to me."

Simon raised languid eyebrows.

" When I was the Wallachian Vice-Consul at Pfaffenhausen," he said pleasantly, " our diplomacy was governed by a picturesque little Pomeranian poem, which begins :

" *Der Steiss des Elephanten*
Ist nicht, ist nicht so klein.

If you get the idea——"

Kuzela nodded without animosity. His deliberate, ruthless white hands trimmed the end of a cigar.

" You must not think that I am unused to hearing remarks like that, Templar," he said equably. " In fact, I remember listening to a precisely similar speech from our friend the Duke of Fortezza. And yet——" He paused to blow a few minute flakes of tobacco leaf from the shining top of the desk, and then his pale bland eyes flicked up again to the Saint's face. . . . " The Duke of Fortezza changed his mind," he said.

Simon blinked.

" Do you know," he said enthusiastically, " there's one of the great songs of the century there ! I can just feel it. Something like this :

> " *The Duke of Fortezza*
> *Quite frequently gets a*
> *Nimpulse to go blithering off on the blind.*
> *But the Duchess starts bimbling*
> *And wambling and wimbling*
> *And threatens to wallop his ducal behind ;*
> *And her Ladyship's threats are*
> *So fierce that he sweats a*
> *Nd just sobs as he pets her*
> *With tearful regrets—Ah !*
> *The Duke of Fortezza*
> *Is changing his mind.*

We could polish up the idea a lot if we had time, but you must admit that for an impromptu effort——"

" You underrate my own sense of humour, Templar." Unemotionally Kuzela inspected the even reddening of the tip of his cigar, and waved his match slowly in the air till it went out. " But do you know another mistake which you also make ? "

" I haven't the foggiest notion," said the Saint cheerfully.

" You underrate my sense of proportion."

The Saint smiled.

" In many ways," he murmured, " you remind me of the late Mr. Garniman. I wonder how you'll get on together ? "

The other straightened up suddenly in his chair. For a moment the mask of amiable self-possession fell from him.

" I shall be interested to bandy words with you later—if you survive, my friend." He spoke without raising his voice ; but two little specks of red burned in the cores of his eyes, and a shimmering marrow of vitriolitic savagery edged up through his unalteringly level intonation. " For the present, our time is short, and you have already wasted more than your due allowance. But I think you understand me." Once again, a smooth evanescent trickle of honey glossed over the bitingly measured syllables. " Come, now, my dear young friend, it would be a pity for us to quarrel. We have crossed swords, and you have lost. Let us reach an amicable armistice. You have only to give me a little information ; and then, as soon as I have verified it, and have finished my work—say after seven days, during which time you would stay with me as an honoured guest— you would be as free as air. We would shake hands and go our ways." Kuzela smiled, and picked up a pencil. " Now firstly : where has your accomplice gone ? "

" Naturally, she drove straight to Buckingham Palace," said the Saint.

Kuzela continued to smile.

" But you are suspicious. Possibly you think that some harm might befall her, and perhaps you would be unwilling to accept my assurance that she will be as safe as yourself. Well, it is a human suspicion after all, and I can understand it. But suppose we ask you another question. . . . Where is the Duke of Fortezza ? " Kuzela drew a small memorandum block towards him, and poised his pencil with engaging expectancy. " Come, come ! That is not a very difficult question to answer, is it ? He is nothing to you—a man whom you met a few hours ago for the first time. If, say, you had never met him, and you had read in your newspaper that some fatal accident had overtaken him, you would not have been in the least disturbed. And if it is a decision between his temporary inconvenience and your own promising young life . . ." Kuzela shrugged. " I have no wish to use threats. But you, with your experience and imagination, must know that death does not always come easily. And very recently you did something which has mortally offended the invaluable Ngano. It would distress me to have to deliver you into his keeping. . . . Now, now, let us make up our minds quickly. What have you done with the Duke ? "

Simon dropped his chin and looked upwards across the desk.

" Nothing that I should be ashamed to tell my mother," he said winningly ; and the other's eyes narrowed slowly.

" Do I, after all, understand you to refuse to tell me ? "

The Saint crossed his left ankle over on to his right knee.

" You know, laddie," he remarked, " you should be on the movies, really you should. As the strong silent man you'd be simply great, if you were a bit stronger and didn't talk so much."

For some seconds Kuzela looked at him.

Then he threw down his pencil and pushed away the pad.

" Very well," he said.

He snapped his fingers without turning his head, and one of the two bruisers came to his side. Kuzela spoke without giving the man a glance.

" Yelver, you will bring round the car. We shall require it very shortly."

The man nodded and went out ; and Kuzela clasped his hands again on the desk before him.

" And you, Templar, will tell us where we are going," he said, and Simon raised his head.

His eyes gazed full and clear into Kuzela's face, bright with the reckless light of their indomitable mockery, and a sardonically Saintly smile curved the corners of his mouth.

" You're going to hell, old dear," he said coolly ; and then the negro dragged him up out of his chair.

Simon went meekly down the stairs, with the negro gripping his arm and the second bruiser following behind ; and his brain was weighing up the exterior circumstances with lightning accuracy.

Patricia had got away—that was the first and greatest thing. He praised the Lord who had inspired her with the sober far-sightedness and clearness of head not to attempt any futile heroism. There was nothing she could have done, and mercifully she'd had the sense to see it. . . . But having got away, what would be her next move ?

" Claud Eustace, presumably," thought the Saint ; and a wry little twist roved across his lips, for he had always been the most incorrigible optimist in the world.

So he reached the hall, and there he was turned round and hustled along towards the back of the house. As he went, he stole a glance at his wrist watch. . . . Patricia must have been gone for the best part of an hour, and that would have been more than long enough for Teal to get busy. Half of that time would have been sufficient to get Teal on the 'phone from the nearest call box and have the house surrounded by enough men to wipe up a brigade—if anything of that sort were going to be done. And not a sign of any such developments had interrupted the playing of the piece. . . .

Down from the kitchen a flight of steps ran to the cellar ; and as the Saint was led down them he had a vivid appreciation of another similarity between that adventure and a concluding episode in the history of the late Mr. Garniman. The subterranean prospects in each case had been decidedly uninviting ; and now the Saint held his fire and wondered what treat was going to be offered him this time.

The cigar-chewing escort stopped at the foot of the steps, and the Saint was led on alone into a small bare room. From the threshold, the negro flung him forward into a far corner, and turned to lock the door behind him. He put the key in his pocket, took off his coat, and rolled up his sleeves ; and all the time his dark blazing eyes were riveted upon the Saint.

And then he picked up a great leather whip from the floor, and his thick lips curled back from his teeth in a ghastly grin.

" You will not talk, no ? " he said.

He swung his arm ; and the long lash whistled and crackled through the air, and snaked over the Saint's shoulders like the recoiling snap of an overstrained hawser.

VIII

SIMON reeled away in a slash of agony that ate into his chest as if a thin jet of boiling acid had been sprayed across his back.

And he went mad.

Never, otherwise, could he have accomplished what he did. For one blinding instant, which branded itself on his optic nerves with such an eye-aching clarity that it might have stood for an eternity of frozen stillness, he saw everything there was to see in that little room. He saw the stained grey walls and ceiling and the dusty paving underfoot ; he saw the locked door ; he saw the towering figure of the gigantic hate-vengeful negro before him, and the cyclopean muscles swelling and rippling under the thin texture of the lavender silk shirt ; and he saw himself. Just for that instant he saw those things as he had never

14

seen anything before, with every thought of everything else and every other living soul in the world wiped from his mind like chalk marks smeared from a smooth board. . . .

And then a red fog bellied up before his eyes, and the stillness seemed to burst inwards like the smithereening of a great glass vacuum bulb.

He felt nothing more—in that white heat of berserk fury the sense of pain was simply blotted out. He dodged round the room by instinct, ducking and swerving mechanically, and scarcely knew when he succeeded and when he failed.

And at his wrists he felt nothing at all.

The buckle of the strap there was out of reach of his teeth, but he twisted his hands inwards, one over the other, tightening up the leather with all his strength, till his muscles ached with the strain. He saw the edges of the strap biting into his skin, and the flesh swelling whitely up on either side ; the pain of that alone should have stopped him, but there was no such thing. . . . And he stood still and twisted once again, with a concentrated passion of power that writhed over the whole of his upper body like the stirring of a volcano ; and the leather broke before his eyes like a strip of tissue paper. . . .

And the Saint laughed.

The whip sang around again, and he leapt in underneath it and caught it as it fell. And what he had intuitively expected happened. The negro jerked at it savagely—and Simon Templar did not resist. But he kept his hold fast, and allowed all the vicious energy of that jerk to merge flowingly into his own unchecked rush ; and it catapulted him to his mark like a stone from a sling. His right fist sogged full and square into the negro's throat with a force that jarred the Saint's own shoulder, and Simon found the whip hanging free in his hand.

He stepped back and watched the grin melting out of the contorted black face. The negro's chest heaved up to the encompassing of a great groaning breath, but the shattering mule-power of that pent-up super-auxiliated swipe in the gullet had stunned his thyro-arytenoids as effectively as if a bullet had gone through them. His mouth worked wildly, but he could produce nothing more than an inaudible whisper. And the Saint laughed again, gathering up the whip.

" The boys will be expecting some music," he said, very gently. " And you are going to provide it."

Then the negro sprang at him like a tiger.

That one single punch which had reversed the situation would have sent any living European swooning off into hours of tortured helplessness, but in this case the Saint had never expected any such result from it. It had done all that he had ever hoped that it would do—obliterated the negro's speaking voice, and given the Saint himself the advantage of the one unwieldy weapon in the room. And with the red mists of unholy rage still swilling across his vision, Simon Templar went grimly into the fight of his life.

He side-stepped the negro's first maniac charge as smoothly and easily as a practised pedestrian evading a two-horse dray, and as he swerved he brought the whip cracking round in a stroke that split the lavender silk shirt as crisply as if a razor had been scored across it.

The negro fetched up against the far wall with an animal scream, spun round, and sprang at him again. And again the Saint swayed lightly aside, and made the whip lick venomously home with a report like a gunshot. . . .

He knew that that was the only earthly hope he had—to keep his opponent tearing blindly through a hazing madness of pain and fury that would scatter every idea of scientific fighting to the four winds. There were six feet eight inches of the negro, most of three hundred pounds pitiless, clawing, blood-mad primitive malignity caged up with Simon Templar within those blank damp-blotched walls ; and Simon knew, with a quiet cold certainty, that if once those six feet eight inches, those three hundred odd pounds of bone and muscle, resolved themselves into the same weight and size of logical, crafty, fighting precision, there was no man in the world who could have stood two minutes against them. And the Saint quietly and relentlessly crimped down his own strength and speed and fighting madness into the one narrow channel that would give it a fighting chance.

It was a duel between brute strength and animal ferocity on the one hand, and on the other hand the lithe swiftness and lightning eye of the trickiest fighting man alive—a duel with no referee, in which no foul was barred. Tirelessly the Saint went round the room, flitting airily beyond, around, even under the massive arms that grappled for him, bobbing and swooping and turning, up on his toes and supple as a dancer, as elusive as a drop of quicksilver on a plate ; and always the tapered leather thong in his hand was whirling and hissing like an angry fer-de-lance, striking and coiling and striking again with a bitter deadliness of aim. Once the negro grabbed at the whip and found it, and the Saint broke his hold with a kick to the elbow that opened the man's fingers as if the tendons had been cut ; once the Saint's foot slipped, and he battered his way out of a closing trap in a desperate flurry of rib-creaking body blows that made even the negro stagger for a sufficient moment ; and the fight went on.

It went on till the negro's half-naked torso shone with a streaming lather of sweat and blood, and a sudden kicking lurch in his step shot into Simon's taut-strung brain the wild wide knowledge that the fight was won.

And for the first time the Saint stood his ground, with his back to one wall, holding the negro at bay by the flailing sweep of the lash alone.

Then Simon pressed forward, and the negro went back. . . .

The Saint drove him into the opposite corner and beat him whimpering to his knees. And then, as the man spilled forward on to his face, Simon leapt in and got an ankle hold.

" Get your hands right up behind your back," he rasped incisively, " or I'll twist the leg off you ! "

He applied his leverage vigorously, and the man obeyed him with a yelp. Simon locked the ankle with his knee and bent his weight over it. With quick deft fingers he knotted the tail of the whip round the negro's wrists, and passed the stock over one shoulder, round the neck, and back over the other shoulder into a slip-knot. A draught of air gulped noisily into the negro's straining lungs, and Simon gave the noose a yank.

" One word from you, and you graze in the Green Pastures," he stated pungently, and heard the lungful choke sibilantly out again. " And get this," said the Saint, with no increase of friendliness : " if you move the half of an inch in that hog-tie, you'll bowstring your own sweet self. That's all."

He fished the key of the door out of the negro's pocket and stood up, breathing deeply.

He himself was starting to look as if he had recently taken

a warm shower-bath in his clothes ; and now that the anæsthetic red mists were thinning out, a large part of his back was beginning to stiffen itself up into an identical acreage of ache ; but he was not yet ready to sit down and be sorry about such minor discomforts. With the key snapping over in the lock, he brushed the hair back off his forehead and opened the door ; and the cigar-chewer at the foot of the steps crawled upright like a slow-motion picture, with his jaw sagging nervelessly and his eyes popping from their orbits, gaping at the Saint as he might have gaped at his own ghost. . . .

Smiling, and without any haste, Simon walked towards him.

And the man stood there staring at him, watching him come on, numbed with a bone-chilling superstitious terror. It was not until the Saint was within two yards of him that a sobbing little wail gurgled in his throat and he reached feebly round to his hip pocket.

And of the rest of the entertainment he knew little. He knew that a grip about which there was nothing ghostly seized upon his right wrist before he had time to draw, while another metallic clutch closed round his knees ; he knew that the weight came suddenly off his feet ; and then he seemed to go floating ethereally through space. Somewhere in the course of that flight an astonishingly hard quantity of concrete impinged upon his skull, but it did not seem an important incident. His soul went bimbering on, way out into the land of blissful dreams. . . .

And the Saint went on up the steps.

He was half-way up when a bell jangled somewhere overhead, and he checked involuntarily. And then a tiny skew-eyed grin skimmed over his lips.

" Claud Eustace for the hell of it," he murmured, and went upwards very softly.

Right up by the door at the top of the stairs he stopped again and listened. He heard slow and watchful footsteps going down the hall, followed by the rattle of a latch and the cautious whine of slowly turning hinges. And then he heard the most perplexing thing of all, which was nothing more or less than an expansive and omnipotent silence.

The Saint put up one hand and gently scratched his ear, with a puzzled crease chiselling in between his eyebrows.

He was prepared to hear almost anything else but that.
And he didn't. The silence continued for some time, and
then the front door closed again and the footsteps started
back solo on the return journey.

And then, in the very opposite direction, the creak of a
window-sash sliding up made him blink.

Someone was wriggling stealthily over the sill. With his
ear glued to a panel of the door, he could visualise every
movement as clearly as if he could have seen it. He heard
the faint patter of the intruder's weight coming on to the
floor, and then the equally faint sound of footsteps creeping
over the linoleum. They connected up in his mind with the
footsteps of the man who had gone to the door like the other
part of a duet. Then the second set of footsteps died away,
and there was only the sound of the man returning from the
hall. Another door opened. . . . And then a voice uttered
a corrosively quiet command.

" Keep still ! "

Simon almost fell down the steps. And then he wind-
milled dazedly back to his balance and hugged himself.

" Oh, Pat ! " he breathed. " Mightn't I have known it ?
And you ring the bell to draw the fire, and sprint round and
come in the back way. . . . Oh, you little treasure ! "

Grinning a great wide grin, he listened to the dialogue.

" Put your hands right up. . . . That's fine. . . . And
now, where's Kuzela ? "

Silence.

" Where is Kuzela ? "

A shifting of feet, and then the grudging answer :

" Upstairs."

" Lead on, sweetheart."

The sounds of reluctant movement. . . .

And the whole of Simon Templar's inside squirmed with
ecstasy at the pure poetic Saintliness of the technique. Not
for a thousand million pounds would he have butted in just
then—not one second before Kuzela himself had also had
time to appreciate the full ripe beauty of the situation. He
heard the footsteps travelling again : they came right past
his door and went on into the hall, and the Saint pointed
his toes in a few movements of an improvised cachucha.

And then, after a due pause, he opened the door and
followed on.

He gave the others time to reach the upper landing, and then he went whisking up the first flight. Peeking round the banisters, he was just in time to get a sight of Patricia disappearing into Kuzela's study. Then the door slammed behind her, and the Saint raced on up and halted outside it.

While after the answering of the dud front door call there had certainly been a silence, the stillness to which he listened now made all previous efforts in noiselessness sound like an artillery barrage. Against that background of devastating blankness, the clatter of a distant passing truck seemed to shake the earth, and the hoot of its klaxon sounded like the Last Trump.

And then Patricia spoke again, quite calmly, but with a lethal clearness that was hedged around on every side with the menace of every manner of murder.

" Where is the Saint ? " she asked.

And upon those words Simon Templar figured that he had his cue.

He turned the handle soundlessly and pushed the door wide open.

Patricia's back was towards him. A little further on to one side the second bruiser stood by with his hands high in the air. And behind the desk sat Kuzela, with his face still frozen in an expression of dumb, incredulous stupefaction.
. . . And as the door swung back, and the Saint advanced gracefully into the limelight, the eyes of the two men revolved and centred on him, and dilated slowly into petrified staring orbs of something near to panic.

" Good morning," said the Saint.

Patricia half turned. She could not help herself—the expressions on the faces of the two men in front of her were far too transparently heart-felt to leave her with any mistrust that they were part of a ruse to put her off her guard.

But the result of her movement was the same ; for as she turned her eyes away, the smallest part in the cast had his moment. He awoke out of his groping comatosity, saw his chance, and grabbed it with both fists.

The automatic was wrested violently out of the girl's hands, and she was thrown stumbling back into the Saint's arms. And the Saint's gentle smile never altered.

He passed Patricia to one side, and cocked a derisive eye

at the gun that was turned against him. And with no more heed for it than that, he continued on towards the desk.

" So nice to see you again," he said.

IX

KUZELA rose lingeringly to his feet.

There was a perceptible pause before he gained control of the faculty of speech. The two consecutive smacks that had been jolted into the very roots of his being within the space of the last forty seconds would have tottered the equilibrium of any man—of any man except, perhaps, the Saint himself. . . . But the Saint was not at all disturbed. He waited in a genteel silence, while the other schooled the flabby startlement out of his face and dragged up his mouth into an answering smile.

" My dear young friend ! "

The voice, when Kuzela found it, had the same svelte timbre as before, and Simon bowed a mocking compliment to the other's nerve.

" My dear old comrade ! " he murmured, open-armed.

" You have saved us the trouble of fetching you, Templar," Kuzela said blandly. " But where is Ngano ? "

" The Negro Spiritual ? " The Saint aligned his eyebrows banteringly. " I'm afraid he—er—met with a slight accident."

" Ah ! "

" No—not exactly. I don't think he's quite dead yet, though he may easily have strangled himself by this time. But he hasn't enjoyed himself. I think, if the circumstances had been reversed, he would have talked," said the Saint, with a glacial inclemency of quietness.

Kuzela stroked his chin.

" That is unfortunate," he said.

And then he smiled.

" But it is not fatal, my friend," he purred. " The lady has already solved one problem for us herself. And now that she is here, I am sure you would do anything rather than expose her to the slightest danger. So let us return to our previous conversation at once. Perhaps the lady will tell us herself where she went to when she drove away from here ? "

Simon put his hands in his pockets.

" Why, yes," he said good-humouredly. " I should think she would."

The girl looked at him as if she could not quite believe her ears. And Simon met her puzzled gaze with blue eyes of such a blinding Saintly innocence that even she could read no enticement to deception in them.

" Do you mean that ? " she asked.

" Of course," said the Saint. " There are one or two things I shouldn't mind knowing myself."

Patricia put a hand to her head.

" If you want to know—when I left here I drove straight to——"

" Buckingham Palace," drawled the Saint. " And then ? "

" I had the bags taken up to Beppo's room, and I saw him myself. He was quite wide awake and sensible. I told him I was coming back here to get you out, and said that if I wasn't back by four o'clock, or one of us hadn't rung him up, he was to get in touch with Teal. I gave him Teal's private number. He didn't want me to go at all, but I insisted. That's all there is to tell. I picked up a puncture on the second trip out here, and that held me up a bit——"

" But who cares about that ? " said the Saint.

He turned back to the desk.

The man with the gun stood less than a yard away on his right front ; but the Saint, ignoring his very existence, leaned a little forward and looked from the distance of another yard into the face of Kuzela. The loose poise of his body somehow centred attention even while it disarmed suspicion. But the mockery had gone out of his eyes.

" You heard ? " he asked.

Kuzela nodded. His mouth went up at one corner.

" But I still see no reason for alarm, my friend," he said, in that wheedling voice of slow malevolence. " After all, there is still time for much to happen. Before your friend Mr. Teal arrives——"

" Before my friend Chief Inspector Teal arrives with a squad of policemen in a plain van, I shall be a long way from here," said the Saint.

Kuzela started.

" So you have invoked the police ? " he snapped. And then again he recovered himself. " But that is your affair.

By the time they arrive, as you say, you will have left here. But where do you think you will have gone ? "

" Home, James," said the Saint.

He took one hand out of its pocket to straighten his coat, and smiled without mirth.

" Fortunately, the argument between us can be settled to-night," he said, " which will save me having to stage any reunions. Your black torturer has been dealt with. I have given him a dose of his own medicine which will, I think, put him in hospital for several weeks. But you remain. You are, after all, the man who gave Ngano his orders. I have seen what you did to the Duke of Fortezza, and I know what you wanted to have done to me. . . . I hope you will get on well with Wilfred."

" And what do you think you are going to do to me ? " asked Kuzela throatily ; and Simon held him with his eyes.

" I'm going to kill you, Kuzela," he said simply.

" Ah ! And how will you do that ? "

Simon's fingers dipped into his pocket. They came out with an ordinary match-box, and he laid it on the desk.

" That is the answer to all questions," he said.

Kuzela stared down at the box. It sat there in the middle of his clean white blotter, yellow and oblong and angular, as commonplace a thing as any man could see on his desk— and the mystery of it seemed to leer up at him malignantly. He picked it up and shook it : it weighed light in his hand, and his mind balked at the idea that it could conceal any engine of destruction. And the Saint's manner of presenting it had been void of the most minute scintilla of excitement—and still was. He eyed Kuzela quizzically.

" Why not open it ? " he suggested.

Kuzela looked at him blankly. And then, with a sudden impatience, he jabbed his thumb at the little sliding drawer. . . .

In a dead silence, the box fell through the air and flopped half-open on the desk.

" What does this mean ? " asked Kuzela, almost in a whisper.

" It means that you have four minutes to live," said the Saint.

Kuzela held up his hand and stared at it.

In the centre of the ball of his right thumb a little globule of blood was swelling up in the pinky-white of the surrounding skin. He gazed stupidly from it to the matchbox and back again. In imagination, he felt a second time the asp-like prick that had bitten into his thumb as he moved the drawer of the box—and understood. " The answer to all questions. . . ."

He stood there as powerless to move as a man in a nightmare, and watched the infinitely slow distension of the tiny crimson sphere under his eyes, his face going ashen with the knowledge of inescapable doom. The drop of blood hypnotised him, filled his vision till he could see nothing else but the microscopic reflections glistening over the surface of it— until all at once it seemed to grow magically into a coruscating red vesicle of enormous size, thrusting in upon him, bearing him down, filling the whole universe with the menace of its smothering scarlet magnitude. A roaring of mighty waters seethed up about his ears. . . .

The others saw him brace himself on his feet as if to resist falling ; and he remained quite still, with his eyes fixing and going dim. And then he took one step sideways, swayed, and crumpled down on to the floor with his limbs twitching convulsively and his chest labouring. . . .

Quite calmly and casually the Saint put out a hand and clasped it on the gun wrist of the man who stood beside him.

The man seemed to come alive out of a dream. And without any noticeable interregnum of full consciousness, he seemed to pass right on into another kind of dream—the transition being effected by the contingence upon the point of his jaw of a tearing uppercut that started well below the Saint's waistline and consummated every erg of its weight and velocity at the most vital angle of the victim's face. With the results aforementioned. He went down in a heap and lay very still, even as his companion had done a little earlier ; and Simon picked up the gun.

" Which finishes that," said the Saint, and found Patricia looking down again at Kuzela.

" What happened to him ? " she asked, a trifle unsteadily.

" More or less what he tried to make happen to me. Ever come across those trick match-boxes that shoot a needle into you when you try to open them ? I bought one last afternoon, and replaced the needle with something that was sent to me along with the message you know about. And I don't know that we shall want it again."

He took the little box of death over to the fireplace, dropped it in the grate, and raked the glowing embers over it. Then he took up his hat and stick, which he saw lying in a chair, and glanced around for the last time. Only Kuzela's fingers were twitching now, and a wet froth gleamed on his lips and dribbled down one cheek. . . . Simon put an arm round the girl's shoulders.

" I guess we can be going," he said, and led her out of the room.

It was in the hall that the expression on the face of a clock caught his eye and pulled him up with a jerk.

" What time did you say Beppo was going to get in touch with Teal ? " he inquired.

" Four o'clock." Patricia followed his gaze, and then looked at her wrist. " That clock must be fast——"

" Or else you've stopped," said the Saint pithily. He turned back his sleeve and inspected his own watch. "And stopped you have, old darling. It's thirty-three minutes after four now—and to give Claud Eustace even a chance to think that he'd pulled me out of a mess would break my heart. Not to include another reason why he mustn't find us here. Where did you leave the car ? "

" Just one block away."

" This is where we make greyhounds look lazy," said the Saint, and opened the front door.

They were at the gate when Simon saw the lights of a car slowing up and swinging in to the kerb on his left. Right in front of him, Kuzela's car was parked ; and the Saint knew clairvoyantly that that was their only chance.

He caught Patricia's arm and flipped up the collar of her coat.

" Jump to it," he crisped.

He scudded round to the driving seat, and the girl tumbled in beside him as he let in the clutch. He shot right past the police car with his head well down and his shoulders hunched. A tattered shout reached him as he went by ; and then he was bucking off down a side street with the car heeling over on two wheels as he crammed it round the corner. The police car would have to be turned right round in a narrow road before it could get after him, and he knew he was well away. He dodged hectically south-east, and kept hard at it till he was sure he had left any pursuit far behind.

Somewhere in the northern hinterlands of the Tottenham Court Road, he stopped the car and made some hurried repairs to his appearance with the aid of the driving mirror, and ended up looking distinctly more presentable than he had been when they left Hampstead. He looked so presentable, in fact, that they abandoned the car on that spot, and walked boldly on until they met a taxi, which took them to Berkeley Square.

" For the night isn't nearly over yet," said the Saint, as they walked down Upper Berkeley Mews together after the taxi had chugged off out of sight.

It was one of those fool-proof prophecies which always delighted his sense of the slickness of things by the brisk promptness with which they fulfilled themselves. He had hardly closed the door of his house when the telephone bell began to ring, and he went to answer the call with a feeling of large and unalloyed contentment.

" Hullo-o ? . . . Speaking. . . . That's which ? . . . Teal ? . . . Well, blow me, Claud Eustace, this is very late for you to be out ! Does your grandmother allow you—— What ? . . . What have I been doing to-night ? I've been drinking beer with Beppo. . . . No, not a leper— BEPPO. B for bdellium, E for eiderdown, P for psychology, P for pneumonia, O for a muse of fire that would ascend the brightest heaven of . . . I beg your pardon ? . . . You were called up and told I was in trouble ? . . . Someone's been pulling your leg, Claud. I'm at peace with the world. . . . Whassat ? . . . Why, sure. I was just going to bed, but I guess I can stay up a few minutes longer. Will you be bringing your own gum ? . . . Right-ho. . . ."

He listened for a moment longer ; and then he hung up the receiver and turned to Pat.

" Claud's coming right along," he said gleefully, and the laughter was lilting in his voice. " We're not to try to get away, because he'll have an armed guard at every sea and air port in the British Isles ten minutes after he gets here and finds we've done a bunk. Which will be tremendous fun for all concerned. . . . And now, get through to Beppo as fast as you can spin the dial, old sweetheart, while I sprint upstairs and change my shirt—for there's going to be a great day ! "

X

CHIEF INSPECTOR CLAUD EUSTACE TEAL fixed his pudgy hands in the belt of his overcoat, and levelled his unfriendly gaze on the superbly elegant young man who lounged against the table in front of him.

" So that message I had was a fake, was it ? " he snarled.

" It must have been, Claud."

Teal nodded fatly.

" Perhaps it was," he said. " But I went to the address it gave me—and what do you think I found ? "

" The Shah of Persia playing ludo," hazarded Simon Templar, intelligently ; and the detective glowered.

" In the cellar I found a nigger tied up with the whip that had beaten half the hide off his back. Outside, there was a white man with a fractured skull—he's gone to hospital as well. In a room upstairs there was another man laid out with a broken jaw, and a fourth man in the same room—dead."

The Saint raised his eyebrows.

" But, my dear old sturgeon ! " he protested reasonably— " what on earth do you think I am ? A sort of human earthquake ? "

" Both the nigger and the man with the broken jaw," Teal continued stonily, " gave me a description of the man responsible, and it fits you like a glove. The man with the broken jaw also added the description of a woman who couldn't be distinguished apart from Miss Holm."

" Then we obviously have doubles, Claud."

" He also heard the woman say : ' Where is the Saint ? ' "

Simon frowned.

" That's certainly odd," he admitted. " Where did you say this was ? "

" You know darned well where it was ! And I'll tell you some more. Just as I got there in the police car, a man and a woman dashed out of the house and got away. And who do you suppose they looked like ? "

" The same doubles, obviously," said the Saint with great brilliance.

" And just one block away from that house we found a blue saloon Hirondel, which the two people I saw would have got away in if they'd had time to reach it. The number of it was ZX1257. Is that the number of your car ? "

The Saint sat up.

" Claud, you're a blessing in disguise ! That certainly is my car—and I was thinking I'd lost her ! Pinched outside the May Fair only yesterday afternoon, she was, in broad daylight. I was meaning to ring up Vine Street before, but what with one thing and another——"

Teal drew a deep breath—and then he exploded.

" Now would you like to know what I think of your defence ? " he blurted out, in a boiling gust of righteous wrath. And he went on without waiting for encouragement. " I think it's the most weak-kneed tangle of moonshine I've ever had to listen to in my life. I think it's so drivelling that if any jury will listen to it for ten minutes, I'll walk right out of the court and have myself certified. I've got two men who'll swear to you on their dying oaths, and another one to put beside them if he recovers, and I know what I saw myself and what the men who were with me saw ; and I think everything you've got to say is so maudlin that I'm going to take you straight back to Scotland Yard with me and have it put in writing before we lock you up. I think I've landed you at last, Mr. Saint, and after what you said to me this morning I'm damned glad I've done it."

The Saint took out his cigarette-case and flopped off the table into an armchair, sprawling one long leg comfortably over the arm.

" Well, that does express your point of view quite clearly," he conceded. He lighted a cigarette, and looked up brightly. " Claud, you're getting almost fluent in your old age. But you've got to mind you don't let your new-found eloquence run away with you."

" Oh, have I ? " The detective took the bait right down into his œsophagus, and clinched his teeth on the line. " Very well. Then while all these extraordinary things were being done by your double—while half a dozen sober men were seeing you and listening to you and being beaten up by you and getting messages from you—maybe you'll tell me what you were doing and who else knows it besides yourself ? "

Simon inhaled luxuriously, and smiled.

" Why, sure. As I told you over the 'phone, I was drinking beer with Beppo."

" And who's he ? "

" The Duke of Fortezza."

" Oh, yes ? " Teal grew sarcastic. " And where was the King of Spain and the Prime Minister of Jugo-Slavia ? "

" Blowed if I know," said the Saint ingenuously. " But there were some other distinguished people present. The Count of Montalano, and Prince Marco d'Ombria, and the Italian Ambassador——"

" The Italian *what* ? "

" Ambassador. You know. Gent with top hat and spats."

" And where was this ? "

" At the Italian embassy. It was just a little private party, but it went on for a long time. We started about midnight, and didn't break up till half-past four—I hadn't been home two minutes when you 'phoned."

Teal almost choked.

" What sort of bluff are you trying to pull on me now ? " he demanded. " Have you got hold of the idea that I've gone dotty ? Are you sitting there believing that I'll soak up that story, along with everything else you've told me, and just go home and ask no questions ? " Teal snorted savagely. " You must have gone daft ! " he blared.

The Saint came slowly out of his chair. He posed himself before the detective, feet astraddle, his left hand on his hip, loose-limbed and smiling and dangerous ; and the long dictatorial forefinger which Teal had seen and hated before drove a straight and peremptory line into the third button of the detective's waistcoat.

" And now you listen to me again, Claud," said the Saint waspily. " Do you know what you're letting yourself in for ? "

" Do I know what I'm——"

" Do you know what you're letting yourself in for ? You burst into my house and make wild accusations against me. You shout at me, you bully me, you tell me I'm either lying or dippy, and you threaten to arrest me. I'm very sensitive,

Claud," said the Saint, " and you hurt me. You hurt me so much that I've a damned good mind to let you run me in— and then, when you'd put the rope right round your own neck and drawn it up as tight as it'd go, I'd pull down such a shemozzle around your bat ears that you'd want nothing more in life than to hand in your resignation and get away to some forgotten corner of the earth where they've never seen a newspaper. That's what's coming your way so fast that you're going to have to jump like a kangaroo to get from under it. It's only because I'm of a godly and forgiving disposition," said the Saint virtuously, " that I'm giving you a chance to save your skin. I'm going to let you verify my alibi before you arrest me, instead of having it fed into you with a stomach-pump afterwards ; and then you are going to apologise to me and go home," said the Saint.

He picked up a telephone directory, found a place, and thrust the book under Teal's oscillating eyes.

" There's the number," he said. " Mayfair three two three O. Check it up for yourself now, and save yourself the trouble of telling me I'm just ringing up an accomplice."

He left the detective blinking at the volume, and went to the telephone.

Teal read off the number, put down the book, and pulled at his collar.

Once again the situation had passed out of his control. He gazed at the Saint purply, and the beginnings of a despondent weariness pouched up under his eyes. It was starting to be borne in upon him, with a preposterous certitude, that he had just been listening to something more than bluff. And the irony of it made him want to burst into tears. It was unfair. It was brutal. It outraged every canon of logic and justice. He knew his case was watertight, knew that against the evidence he could put into a witness-box there could simply be no human way of escape—he would have sworn to it on the rack, and would have gone to his death still swearing it. And he knew that it wasn't going to work.

Through a haze of almost homicidal futility, he heard the Saint speaking.

" Oh, is that you, Signor Ravelli ? . . . Simon Templar speaking. Listen : there's some weird eruption going on in the brains of Scotland Yard. Some crime or other was com-

8

mitted somewhere to-night, and for some blithering reason they seem to think I was mixed up in it. I'm sorry to have to stop you on your way to bed, but a fat policeman has just barged in here——"

" Give me that telephone ! " snarled Teal.

He snatched the instrument away and rammed the receiver up against his ear.

" Hullo ! " he barked. " This is Chief Inspector Teal, Criminal Investigation Department, speaking. I have every reason to believe that this man Templar was concerned in a murder which took place in Hampstead shortly after four o'clock this morning. He's tried to tell me some cock-and-bull story about . . . What ? . . . But damn it—. . . . I beg your pardon, sir, but I definitely know . . . From twelve o'clock till half-past four ? . . . But . . . But . . . But oh, hell, I . . . No, sir, I said . . . But he . . . Who ? . . ."

The diaphragm of the receiver clacked and chattered, and Teal's round red face sagged sickly.

And then :

" All right, sir. Thank you very much, sir," he said in a strangled voice, and slammed the microphone back on its bracket.

The Saint smoothed his hair.

" We might get on to Beppo next," he suggested hopefully. " He's staying at the Berkeley. Then you can have a word with Prince d'Ombria——"

" Can I ? " Teal had eaten wormwood, and his voice was thick and raw with the bitterness of it. " Well, I haven't got time. I know when I'm licked. I know where I am when half a dozen princes and ambassadors will go into the witness-box and swear that you're chasing them round the equator at the very moment when I know that I'm talking to you here in this room. I don't even ask how you worked it. I expect you rang up the President of the United States and got him to fix it for you. But I'll be seeing you another time—don't worry."

He hitched his coat round, and grabbed up his hat.

" Bye-bye," sang the Saint.

" And you remember this," Teal gulped out. " I'm not through with you yet. You're not going to sit back on your laurels. You wouldn't. And that's what's going to be the

finish of you. You'll be up to something else soon enough
—and maybe you won't have the entire Italian Diplomatic
Service primed to lie you out of it next time. From this
minute, you're not even going to blow your nose without I
know it. I'll have you watched closer than the Crown
Jewels, and the next mistake you make is going to be the
last."

" Cheerio, dear heart," said the Saint, and heard the
vicious bang of the front door before he sank back into his
chair in hysterics of helpless laughter.

.   .   .   .   .   .

But the epilogue of that story was not written until some
weeks later, when a registered packet bearing an Italian
postmark was delivered at No. 7, Upper Berkeley Mews.

Simon opened it after breakfast.

First came a smaller envelope, which contained a draft on
the Bank of Italy for a sum whose proportions made even
Simon Templar blink.

And then he took out a small shagreen case, and turned it
over curiously. He pressed his thumb-nail into the little
spring catch, and the lid flew up and left him staring.

Patricia put a hand on his shoulder.

" What is it ? " she asked, and the Saint looked at her.

" It's the medallion of the Order of the Annunziata—and
I think we shall both have to have new hats on this," he said.

THE BLIND SPOT

IT is rather trite to remark that the greatest and sublimest characters always have concealed in them somewhere a speck of human jelly that wobbles furtively behind the imposing armour-plate, as if Nature's sense of proportion refused to tolerate such a thing as a perfect superman. Achilles had his heel. The hard-boiled hoodlum of the Volstead Act weeps openly to the strains of a syncopated Mammy song. The learned judge gravely inquires : " What is a gooseberry ? " The Cabinet Minister prances pontific-ally about the badminton court. The professor of theology knows the Saint Saga as well as the Epistle to the Ephesians. These things are familiar to every student of the popular newspapers.

But to Simon Templar they were more than mere curious facts, to be ranked with " Believe-it-or-not " strips or cigarette-cards describing the architectural principles of the igloo. They were the very practical psychology of his profession.

" Every man on earth has at least one blind spot some-where," Simon used to say, " and once you've found that spot you've got him. There's always some simple little thing that'll undermine his resistance, or some simple little trick that he's never heard of. A high-class cardsharper might never persuade him to play bridge for more than a halfpenny a hundred, and yet a three-card man at Brook-lands might take a fiver off him in five minutes. Develop that into a complete technique, and you can live in luxury without running any risks of getting brain fever."

One of Simon Templar's minor weaknesses was an in-satiable curiosity. He met Patricia at Charing Cross under-ground station one afternoon with a small brown bottle.

" A man at the Irving Statue sold me this for a shilling," he said.

The broad reach of pavement around the Irving Statue, at

228

the junction of Green Street and Charing Cross Road, is one of the greatest open-air theatres in London. Every day, at lunch-time, idle crowds gather there in circles around the performers on the day's bill, who carry on their work simultaneously like a three-ring circus. There is the Anti-Socialist tub-thumber, the numerologist, the strong man, the negro selling outfits to enable you to do the three-card trick in your own home, the handcuff escape king, the patent medicine salesman, every kind of huckster and street show-man takes up his pitch there on one day or another and holds his audience spellbound until the time comes for passing round the hat. Simon rarely passed there without pausing to inspect the day's offerings, but this was the first occasion on which he had been a buyer.

His bottle appeared to contain a colourless fluid like water, with a slight sediment of brownish particles.

" What is it ? " asked Patricia.

" Chromium plating for the home," he said. " The greatest invention of the century—according to the sales-man. Claimed to be the same outfit sold by mail order firms for three bob. He was demonstrating it on a brass shell-case and an old Primus and brass door-knobs and what not, and it looked swell. Here, I'll show you."

He fished a penny out of his pocket, uncorked the bottle, and poured a drop of the liquid on to the coin. The tarn-ished copper cleared and silvered itself under her eyes, and when he rubbed it with his handkerchief it took a silvery polish like stainless steel.

" Boy, that's marvellous ! " breathed Patricia dreamily. " You know that military sort of coat of mine, the one with the brass buttons ? We were wanting to get them chromiumed——"

The Saint sighed.

" And that," he said, " is approximately what the cave woman thought of first when her battle-scarred Man dragged home a vanquished leopard. My darling, when will you realise that we are first and foremost a business organisa-tion ? "

But at that moment he had no clear idea of the profitable purposes to which his purchase might be put. The Saint had an instinct and a collecting passion for facts and gadgets that " might come in useful," but at the times when he acquired them he could rarely have told you what use they were ever likely to be.

He corked the bottle and put it away in his pocket. The train they were waiting for was signalled, and the rumble of its approach could be felt underfoot. Down in the blackness of the tunnel its lights swept round a bend and drove towards the platform ; and it was quite by chance that the Saint's wandering glance flickered over the shabbily-dressed elderly man who waited a yard away on his left, and fixed on him with a sudden razor-edged intentness that was more intuitive than logical. Or perhaps the elderly man's agitation was too transparent to be ordinary, his eyes too strained and haggard to be reassuring. . . . Simon didn't know.

The leading draught of the train fanned on his face ; and then the elderly man clenched his fists and jumped. A woman screamed. " You blithering idiot ! " snapped the Saint, and jumped also.

His feet touched down neatly inside the track. By some brilliant fluke the shabby man's blind leap had missed the live rail, and he was simply cowering where he had landed with one arm covering his eyes. The train was hardly more than a yard away when the Saint picked him up and heaved him back on to the platform, flinging himself off the line in the opposite direction as he did so. The train whisked by so close to him that it brushed his sleeve, and squeaked to a standstill with hissing brakes.

The Saint slid back the nearest door on his side, swung himself up from the track, and stepped through the coach to the platform. A small crowd had gathered round the object of his somewhat sensational rescue, and Simon shouldered a path through them unceremoniously. He knew that one of the many sublimely intelligent laws of England ordains that any person who attempts to take his own life shall, if he survives, be prosecuted and at the discretion of the Law imprisoned, in order that he may be helped to see that life is after all a very jolly business and thoroughly worth living ; and such a flagrant case as the one Simon had just witnessed seemed to call for some distinctly prompt initiative.

" How d'you feel, old chap ? " asked the Saint, dropping on one knee beside the man.

" And then the man jumped."

" I saw him do it," babbled a fat woman smugly. " With me own eyes I saw it. Jumped in front of the train as deliberate as you please. I saw him."

" I'm afraid you're mistaken, madam," said the Saint quietly. " This gentleman is a friend of mine. He's subject to rather bad fits, and one of them must have taken him just as the train was coming in. He was standing rather close to the edge of the platform, and he simply fell over."

" A very plucky effort of yours, sir, getting him out of the way," opined a white-whiskered retired colonel. " Very plucky, by Gad ! "

Simon Templar, however, was not looking for bouquets. The shabby man was sitting motionlessly with his head in his hands : the desperation that had driven him into that spasmodic leap had left him, and he was trembling silently in a helpless reaction. Simon slipped an arm round him and lifted him to his feet ; and as he did so the guard broke through the crowd.

" I shall 'ave to make a report of this business, sir," he said.

" Lord—I'm not going to be anybody's hero ! " said the Saint. " My name's Abraham Lincoln, and this is my uncle, Mr. Christopher Columbus. You can take it or leave it."

" But if the gentleman's going to make any claim against the company I shall 'ave to make a report, sir," pleaded the guard plaintively.

" There'll be no complaints except for wasting time, Ebenezer," said the Saint. " Let's go."

He helped his unresisting salvage into a compartment, and the crowd broke up. The District Railway resumed its day's work ; and Simon Templar lighted a cigarette and glanced whimsically at Patricia.

" What d'you think we've picked up this time, old dear ? " he murmured.

The girl's hand touched his arm, and she smiled.

" When you went after him I was wondering what I'd lost," she said.

The Saint's quick smile answered her ; and he returned to a scrutiny of his acquisition. The shabby man was recovering himself slowly, and Simon thought it best to leave him to himself for a while. By the time they had reached

8*

Mark Lane station he seemed to have become comparatively normal, and Simon stood up and jerked a thumb.

" C'mon, uncle.   This is as far as I go."

The shabby man shook his head weakly.

" Really, I don't——"

" Step out," said the Saint.

The man obeyed listlessly ; and Simon took his arm and piloted him towards the exit.   They turned into a convenient café and found a deserted corner.

" I took a bit of trouble to pull out of a mess, uncle, and the story of your life is the least you can give me in return."

" Are you a reporter ? " asked the other wearily.

" I have a conscience," said the Saint.   " What's your name, and what do you do ? "

" Inwood.   I'm a chemist and—a sort of inventor."   The shabby man gazed apathetically at the cup of coffee which had been set before him.   " I ought to thank you for saving my life, I suppose, but——"

" Take it as a gift," said the Saint breezily.   " I was only thinking of our lines.   I've got a few shares in the company, and your method of suicide makes such a mess.   Now tell me why you did it."

Inwood looked up.

" Are you going to offer me charity ? "

" I never do that.   My charity begins at home, and stays on with Mother like a good girl."

" I suppose you've got some sort of right to an answer," said Inwood tiredly.   " I'm a failure, that's all."

" And aren't we all ? " said the Saint.   " What did you fail at, uncle ? "

" Inventing.   I gave up a good job ten years ago to try and make a fortune on my own and I've been living from hand to mouth ever since.   My wife had a small income of her own, and I lived on that.   I did one or two small things, but I didn't make much out of them.   I suppose I'm not such a genius as I thought I was, but I believed in myself then.   A month or so ago, when we were right at the end of our tether, I did make a little discovery.

The shabby man took from his pocket a small brass tube like a girl's lipstick case, and tossed it across the table. Simon removed the cap, and saw something like a crayon— it was white outside, with a pink core.

" Write something—with your pen, I mean," said Inwood.

Simon took out his fountain pen and scribbled a couple of words on the back of the menu. Inwood blew on it till it dried, and handed it back.

" Now rub it over with that crayon."

Simon did so, and the writing disappeared. It vanished quite smoothly and easily, at a couple of touches, without any hard rubbing, and the paper was left without a trace of discoloration or roughness.

" Just a useful thing for banks and offices," said Inwood. " There's nothing else like it. An ink eraser tears up the paper. You can buy a chemical bleacher, and several firms use it, but that's liquid—two reagents in separate bottles, and you have to put on drops of first one and then the other. That thing of mine is twice as simple and three times quicker."

Simon nodded.

" You're not likely to make a million out of it, but it ought to have quite a reasonable sale."

" I know that," said Inwood bitterly. " I didn't want a million. I'd have been glad to get a thousand. I've told you—I'm not such a genius as I thought I was. But a thousand pounds would have put us on our feet again—given me a chance to open a little shop or find a steady job or something. But I'm not going to get a penny out of it. It isn't my property—and I invented it ! . . . We've been living on capital as well as income. This would have put us straight. It had to be protected." The old man's faded eyes blinked at the Saint pitifully. " I don't know anything about things like that. I saw a patent agent's advertisement in a cheap paper, and took it to him. I gave him all my formulæ—everything. That was a fortnight ago. He told me he'd have to make a search of the records before any patent could be taken out. I had a letter from him this morning, and he said that a similar specification had been filed three days ago."

The Saint said nothing ; but his blue eyes were suddenly very clear and hard.

" You see what it was ? " In his weakness the shabby inventor was almost sobbing. " He swindled me. He gave my specifications to a friend of his and let him file them in his own name. I couldn't believe it. I went to the Patent Office myself this morning : a fellow I found there helped me to find what I wanted. Every figure in the specification was mine. It *was* my specification. The coincidence couldn't possibly have been so exact, even if somebody else *had* been working on the same idea at the same time as I was. But I can't prove anything. I haven't a shilling to fight him with. D'you hear ? He's ruined me——"

" Steady on, uncle," said the Saint gently. " Have you seen this bird again ? "

" I'd just left his office when—when you saw me at Charing Cross," said Inwood shakily. " He threw me out. When he found he couldn't bluff me he didn't bother to deny anything. Told me to go on and prove it, and be careful I didn't give him a chance to sue me for libel. There weren't any witnesses. He could say anything he liked——"

" Will you tell me his name ? "

" Parnock."

" Thanks." Simon made a note on the back of an envelope. " Now will you do something else for me ? "

" What is it ? "

" Promise not to do anything drastic before Tuesday. I'm going away for the week-end, but Parnock won't be able to do anything very villainous either. I may be able to do something for you—I have quite a way with me," said the Saint bashfully.

This was on a Friday—a date that Simon Templar had never been superstitious about. He was on his way to Burnham for a week-end's bumping about in a ten-ton yawl, and the fact that Mr. Inwood's misadventure had made him miss his train was a small fee for the introduction to Mr. Parnock. He caught a later train with plenty of time to spare ; but before he left the elderly chemist he obtained an address and telephone number.

He had another surprise the next morning, for he was searching for a certain penny to convince his incredulous host and owner of the yawl about a statement he had made at the breakfast table, and he couldn't find it.

" You must have spent it," said Patricia.

" I know I haven't," said the Saint. " I paid our fares yesterday afternoon out of a pound note ; and I bought a magazine for a bob—I didn't spend any coppers."

" What about those drinks at the pub last night ? " said the host and owner, who was Monty Hayward.

" We had one round each, at two-and-a-tanner a time. I changed a ten-bob note for my whack."

Monty shrugged.

" I expect you put it in a slot machine to look at rude pictures," he said.

Simon found his bottle and silvered another penny for demonstration purposes. It was left on a shelf in the saloon, and Simon thought no more about it until the following morning. He was looking for a box of matches after breakfast when he came across it ; and the sight of it made him scratch his head, for there was not a trace of silver on it.

" Is anyone being funny ? " he demanded ; and after he had explained himself there was a chorus of denial.

" Well, that's damned odd," said the Saint.

He plated a third penny on the spot, and put it away in his pocket with a piece of paper wrapped round it. He took it out at six o'clock that evening, and the plating had disappeared.

" Would you mind putting me ashore at Southend, Monty ? " he said. " I've got some business I must do in London."

He saw Inwood that night ; and after the chemist had sniffed at the bottle and tested its remarkable properties he told the Saint certain things which had been omitted from the syllabus of Simon Templar's variegated education. Simon paced the shabby inventor's shabby little lodging for nearly an hour afterwards, and went back to his own flat in a spirit of definite optimism.

At eleven o'clock the next morning he presented himself at Mr. Parnock's office in the Strand. The inscription on the frosted-glass panel of the door informed him that Mr. Parnock's baptismal name was Augustus, and an inspection of Mr. Parnock himself showed that there had been at least one parent with a commendable prescience in the matter of names. Mr. Parnock was so august a personage that it was impossible to think of anyone abbreviating him to " Gus." He was a large and very smooth man, with a smooth convex face and smooth clothes and smooth hair and a smooth voice —except for the voice, he reminded Simon of a well-groomed seal.

" Well, Mr.—er——"

" Smith," said the Saint—he was wearing a brown tweed coat and creaseless grey flannel trousers, and he looked agitated. " Mr. Parnock—I saw your advertisement in the *Inventor's Weekly*—is it true that you help inventors ? "

" I'm always ready to give any assistance I can, Mr. Smith," said Mr. Parnock smoothly. " Won't you sit down ? "

The Saint sat down.

" It's like this, Mr. Parnock. I've invented a method of chromium plating in one process—you probably know that at present they have to nickel-plate first. And my method's about fifty per cent. cheaper than anything they've discovered up to the present. It's done by simple immersion, according to a special formula." The Saint ruffled his hair nervously. " I know you'll think it's just another of these crazy schemes that you must be turning down every day, —but—— Look here, will this convince you ? "

He produced a letter and handed it across the desk. It bore the heading of one of the largest motor-car manufacturers in the country, and it was signed with the name of the managing director. Mr. Parnock was not to know that among Simon Templar's most valued possessions were a portfolio containing samples of notepaper and envelopes from every important firm in the kingdom, surreptitiously acquired at considerable trouble and expense, and an autograph album in which could be found the signatures of nearly every Captain of Industry in Europe. The letter regretted that Mr. Smith did not consider five thousand pounds a suitable offer for the rights in his invention, and invited him to lunch with the writer on the following Friday in the hope of coming to an agreement.

" You seem to be a very fortunate young man," said Mr. Parnock almost enviously, returning the document. " I take it that the firm has already tested your discovery ? "

" It doesn't need any tests," said the Saint. " I'll show it to you now."

He produced his little brown bottle, and borrowed Mr. Parnock's brass ash-tray for the experiment. Before Mr. Parnock's eyes it was silvered all over in a few seconds.

" This bottle of stuff cost about a penny," said the Saint ; and Mr. Parnock was amazed.

" I don't wonder you refused five thousand for it, Mr. Smith," he said, as smoothly as he could. " Now, if you had come to me in the first place and allowed me to act as your agent——"

" I want you to do even more than that."

Mr. Parnock's eyebrows moved smoothly upwards for about an eighth of an inch.

" Between ourselves," said the Saint bluntly, " I'm in the hell of a mess."

The faintest gleam of expression flitted across Mr. Parnock's smooth and fish-like eyes, and gave way to a gaze of expectant sympathy.

" Anything you wanted to tell me, Mr. Smith, would of course be treated confidentially."

" I've been gambling—living beyond my means—doing all sorts of silly things. You can see for yourself that I'm pretty young ; I suppose I ought to have known better. . . . I've stopped all that now, but—two months ago I tried to get out of the mess. I gave a dud cheque. I tried to stay in hiding—I was working on this invention, and I knew I'd be able to pay everyone when I'd got it finished. But they found me last Friday. They've been pretty decent, in a way. They gave me till Wednesday noon to find the money. Otherwise——"

The Saint's voice broke, and he averted his face despairingly.

Mr. Parnock gazed down at the silvered ash-tray, then at the letter, which was still spread open on his blotter, and rubbed his smooth chin thoughtfully. He cleared his throat.

" Come, come ! " he said paternally. " It isn't as bad as all that. With an asset like this invention of yours, you ought to have nothing to worry about."

" I told them about it. They were just polite. Wednesday noon or nothing, and hard cash—no promises. I suppose they're right. But it's all so wrong ! It's unjust ! "

Simon stood up and shook his fists frantically at the ceiling ; and Mr. Parnock coughed.

" Perhaps I could help," he suggested.

The Saint shook his head.

" That's what I came to see you about. It was just a

desperate idea. I haven't got any friends who'd listen to me—I owe them all too much money. But now I've told you all about it it all sounds so feeble and unconvincing. I wonder you don't send for the police right away."

He shrugged, and picked up his hat. Mr. Parnock, a cumbersome man, moved rather hastily to take it away from him and pat him soothingly on the shoulder.

" My dear old chap, you musn't say things like that. Now let's see what we can do for you. Sit down." He pressed the Saint back towards his chair. " Sit down, sit down. We can soon put this right. What's the value of this cheque ? "

" A thousand pounds," said the Saint listlessly. " But it might as well be a million for all the chance I've got of finding the money."

" Fortunately that's an exaggeration," said Mr. Parnock cheerfully. " Now this invention of yours—have you patented it ? "

Simon snorted harshly.

" What with ? I haven't had a shilling to call my own for weeks. I had to offer it to those people just as it stood, and trust them to give me a square deal."

Mr. Parnock chuckled with great affability. He opened a drawer and took out his cheque book.

" A thousand pounds, Mr. Smith ? And I expect you could do with a bit over for your expenses. Say, twenty pounds. . . . One thousand and twenty pounds." He inscribed the figures with a flourish. " I'll leave the cheque open so that you can go round to the bank and cash it at once. That'll take a load off your mind, won't it ? "

" But how do you know you'll ever see it back, Mr. Parnock ? "

Mr. Parnock appeared to ponder the point, but the appearance was illusory.

" Well, suppose you left me a copy of your formula ? That'd be good enough security for me. Of course, I expect you'll let me act as your agent, so I'm not really running any risk. But just as a formality. . . ."

The Saint reached for a piece of paper.

" Do you know anything about chemistry ? "

" Nothing at all," confessed Mr. Parnock. " But I have a friend who understands these things."

Simon wrote on the paper and passed it over. Mr. Parnock studied it wisely, as he would have studied a Greek text.

$$Cu + Hg + HNO_3 + Bf = CuHgNO_3 + H_2O + NO_2$$

" Aha ! " said Mr. Parnock intelligently. He folded the paper and stowed it away in his pocket-book, and stood up with his smooth fruity chuckle. " Well, Mr. Smith, you run along now and attend to your business, and come and have lunch with me on Thursday and let's see what we can do about your invention."

" I can't tell you how grateful I am to you, Mr. Parnock," said the Saint almost tearfully, as he shook the patent agent's smooth fat hand ; but for once he was speaking nothing but the truth.

He went down to see Inwood again later that afternoon. He had one thousand pounds with him, in crisp new Bank of England notes ; and the shabby old chemist's gratitude was worth all his trouble. Inwood swallowed several times, and blinked at the money dazedly.

" I couldn't possibly take it," he said.

" Of course you could, uncle," said the Saint. " And you will. It's only a fair price for your invention. Just do one thing for me in return."

" I'd do anything you asked me to," said the inventor.

" Then never forget," said Simon deliberately, " that I was with you the whole of this morning—from half-past ten till one o'clock. That might be rather important." Simon lighted a cigarette and stretched himself luxuriously in his chair. " And when you've got that thoroughly settled into your memory, let us try to imagine what Augustus Parnock is doing right now."

It was at that precise moment, as a matter of history, that Mr. Augustus Parnock and his friend who understood those things were staring at a brass ash-tray on which no vestige of plating was visible.

" What's the joke, Gus ? " demanded Mr. Parnock's friend at length.

" I tell you it isn't a joke ! " yelped Mr. Parnock. " That ash-tray was perfectly plated all over when I put it in my pocket at lunch-time. The fellow gave me his formula and everything. Look—here it is ! "

The friend who understood those things studied the scrap

of paper, and dabbed a stained forefinger on the various items.

" *Cu* is copper," he said. " *Hg* is mercury, and *HNO₃* is nitric acid. What it means is that you dissolve a little mercury in some weak nitric acid ; and when you put it on copper the nitric acid eats a little of the copper, and the mercury forms an amalgam. *CuHgNO₃* is the amalgam— it'd have a silvery look which might make you think the thing had been plated. The other constituents resolve themselves into *H₂O*, which is water, and *NO₂*, which is a gas. Any schoolboy could have told you that. Of course, the nitric acid goes on eating, and after a time it destroys the amalgam and the thing looks like copper again. That's all there is to it."

" But what about the *Bf* ? " asked Mr. Parnock querulously.

His friend shrugged.

" I can't make that out at all—it isn't any chemical symbol," he said ; but it dawned on Mr. Parnock later.

J. S. FLETCHER

The Earl, the Warder and the Wayward Heiress
Extra-Judicial

⁋ Mr. J. S. FLETCHER, in addition to
his journalistic activities under the
pseudonym " A Son of the Soil," has
written every type of novel, but he is
perhaps most famous for such detective
stories as *The Stolen Budget* and *Murder
in the Squire's Pew*. He has also
published some collected verse, and his
recreations include travelling, cricket,
and book collecting.

THE EARL, THE WARDER AND THE
WAYWARD HEIRESS

I

THE TEN THOUSAND POUNDS WAGER

THE Earl of Normanstowe flung away the newspaper which had just been handed to him, and looked defiantly round the semi-circle of faces, all eager and youthful as his own, which surrounded his armchair, set in a corner of the smoking-room which at that, his pet club, was regarded as the peculiar preserve of himself and his set.

" I will lay any man an even ten thousand pounds," he said in calm but forceful accents, " that I walk out of this club to-night and hide myself in London for the space of one month without being found, let whatever efforts to find me be made by whoever likes to make 'em ! Who takes me ? "

The attendant faces slowly withdrew themselves from the contemplation of Lord Normanstowe's healthy countenance and gave themselves to turning elsewhere. From the lips of one came a deep sigh.

" Wish I'd got ten thousand to lay at that game," said their owner. " I guess I'd ferret you out in less than a month, Normanstowe."

" I repeat that I'll lay any man ten thousand pounds," said Lord Normanstowe. " But—there'll be conditions."

" What conditions ? " asked a member of the group. " Stiff 'uns, of course."

" No, easy ones. All I would ask is 16 hours' start. To be plain and matter-of-fact, I'll put it like this : I'll engage to walk out of this room at precisely 8 o'clock this evening and disappear in my own way. Whoever takes my bet engages not to do anything in the way of searching for me until 12 noon to-morrow. That's giving me the 16 hours' start I asked for, isn't it ? "

" And when the search begins, is the searcher to have a

free hand ? Can he do what he pleases ? Employ the police, for instance," asked somebody else. " Can he offer a reward ? Can he stick up bills, placards ? "

" He can do whatever he jolly well likes ! He can offer a reward in hundreds or in thousands. He can subsidise all the private detectives, inquiry agents and investigation offices in London. He can get the whole of Scotland Yard at his back if it's possible. All I say is that I'll lay ten thousand to his ten thousand that I disappear at 8 o'clock to-night, and that I'm not found until I walk into this room at 8 o'clock in the evening precisely one month hence."

" And you wouldn't go out of town."

" I wouldn't go out of town."

" What's town to mean ? " inquired a dark-visaged young gentleman who sat in a tilted chair in the corner. " Radius of one mile from St. James's Street, say ? "

" Rot ! " answered Lord Normanstowe. " Radius of five miles from Charing Cross."

" That's a lot of country to cover," remarked the young man in the corner. " There are thick coverts and deep woods within that bit."

" It's London, anyhow," said Normanstowe. " What is it we've been talking about ? Here's an account in the newspaper about a chap walking out of a club in Pall Mall and disappearing so effectually that he can't be found. You fellows say it's impossible for any man of note to disappear in London except by collusion and design. I say that's nonsense. I believe I'm pretty well known in more ways than one. Very good. But I say that without any help from anybody I will disappear for the space of a month. That's my conviction. And I'll back it to the extent of ten thousand."

The dark-visaged young gentleman tilted his chair a little more.

" I'll take you," he said.

The semblance of a gentle sigh ran round the semi-circle. Normanstowe, phlegmatic as ever, half-turned towards a table furnished with writing materials.

" Good ! " he said. " We'll put it down in formal fashion. Chisholm, how did they do these things in the days of our grandfathers ? "

" In the days of our grandfathers," replied the man

addressed, who was also the eldest of the group, " they kept a book in these places and entered up individual bets. As we don't possess such an iniquitous thing here, we must make a half-sheet of the club notepaper suffice."

He reached over to the table, and took paper and pen and laid a blotting pad on his knee.

" I'll write it down," he said. " I think I remember the phrasing of the old-time wagers. This is about it." And he read slowly, as he wrote :

" ' Lord Normanstowe bets Sir Charles Wrigge ten thousand pounds that he, Lord Normanstowe, walks out of the Melatherium Club at 8 o'clock p.m., on October 20, 1904, disappears, and is not found by Sir Charles Wrigge nor by any person Sir Charles Wrigge employs to search for him, before he walks into the club at 8 o'clock p.m. on November 20, 1904. Lord Normanstowe engages not to go out of a radius of five miles from Charing Cross during the time of his disappearance.' How's that ? " concluded Chisholm.

" All right, as regards me," replied Normanstowe. " But now for Wrigge."

" Oh, that's similarly worded, with small differences," said Chisholm, continuing to write, " This is it : ' Sir Charles Wrigge bets Lord Normanstowe ten thousand pounds that he, Sir Charles, or persons employed by him, will find Lord Normanstowe, dead or alive, within the time and under the conditions specified in the bet made by Lord Normanstowe with him. Sir Charles Wrigge engages to give Lord Normanstowe 16 hours start, dating from 8 o'clock p.m. on October 20, 1904.' Now, if you'll both initial this sheet of paper," concluded Chisholm, " I'll put it in my pocketbook, and the thing's done."

Wrigge laughed as he took and carefully put away his bit of paper.

" I shall find you before a fortnight's up, Normanstowe," he said, confidently.

" I'll lay you another ten thousand you don't," exclaimed Normanstowe, with equal confidence. " Won't have it ? All right." He pulled out his watch. " It's 6.30. I'm going to make my preparations. When they are made, I shall dine here, comfortably, quietly. At precisely 8 o'clock I shall walk out of the dining-room and the house and into the street. And you will see me no more for one month."

"During which time all London will ring with your name and fame," remarked Chisholm. "Get your preparations made and we'll all dine together."

II

DROPPED OUT

LORD NORMANSTOWE'S preparations were of a simple and an elementary character. He went over to a quiet corner and wrote a note to his sister, Lady Trementower, who enjoyed a widespread reputation as being the most gossipy woman in London. It was a brief and a characteristic epistle.

"MY DEAR GABBLE : For reasons of my own, I am about to disappear from the world—I mean our world—for the space of one month from to-night. My disappearance will naturally cause much comment. It will also give you something new to talk about. You may expatiate on several hypotheses—that I may have gone into retreat, to meditate on my sins, or be writing an epic poem in a Bloomsbury attic, or have disguised myself as a crossing sweeper in order to study life. The only reason I have for writing this note, is to privately assure you that I shall be quite well and happy, and that I shall reappear to a much-concerned world at 8 o'clock on the evening of November 20 next.

"Your affectionate brother,

"CARROTS."

This communication Lord Normanstowe laid aside for posting later in the evening. Meanwhile he proceeded upstairs to a bedroom, which was perpetually reserved for him, and wherein he kept various suits of clothes, changes of linen, and articles of toilet. Before dressing for dinner he looked out a small and well-worn kit bag, and into this he packed an old tweed suit of a nondescript grey which he had carefully preserved from the hands of his valet because it possessed certain sentimental associations. Also he packed in the kit bag a shaving outfit, a pair of brogues and a couple of fairly heavy dumb-bells. Locking up the bag he made his evening toilet. And that accomplished, he went downstairs to take an early dinner.

It was remarked by those who dined with Lord Norman-stowe that evening that his appetite was noticeable. He ate with great gusto ; he was particular in selecting a certain burgundy for which the cellar of the Melatherium is justly famous. Yet while he ate and drank with such relish, he was careful to leave himself time to smoke an excellent cigar after dinner. He sighed once or twice as he sniffed its fragrance and sipped his coffee. But at precisely five minutes to 8 o'clock he jumped to his feet with alacrity, threw away the cigar, and left the room. At one minute to eight he reappeared at the door, wearing a dark coat over his evening dress, and carrying the small kit bag. The men who were in the secret, headed by Sir Charles Wrigge and Chisholm, joined him in the hall.

" It seems, somehow," said one, " as if we were about to assist at an execution. You are really off, Normanstowe ? "

Normanstowe smiled affectionately upon the group, gripped his kit bag, and, as the hall clock struck eight, walked down the steps into St. James's Street. The men whom he left behind saw him disappear in the shadows. One of them remarked, quite unnecessarily : " He's gone ! "

III

MALICIOUS DAMAGE

NORMANSTOWE, carrying his kit bag, walked up the street in leisurely fashion until he reached Piccadilly. At the corner he signalled to the driver of a passing taxicab.

" Take me," said Normanstowe, as he entered, " to Paddington railway station."

The driver observed nothing in his fare's manner or speech that could cause him to hesitate. To him the young earl seemed to be no more than an ordinary young gentleman of the superior classes who might be inclined to put half-a-crown into his hand at the end of the journey, without any unnecessary words or reference to the state of the meter. In this pleasant conjecture the driver proved to be right ; when he pulled up at the first class booking office at Paddington, his fare duly presented him with the coin in question before lounging slowly into the station. A porter standing near suddenly started, and, touching his cap, made for the small kit bag.

" No, thank you, my man," said Normanstowe.

He passed forward, and the rebuffed porter looked at the driver, who was pouching his half-crown before attending to his meter.

" Know 'im ? " asked the porter.

" Not from Adam," answered the driver.

" Lord Normanstowe, thet is," said the porter with pride. " Hearl of Normanstowe, y'know—'im wot done thet there charge with the Imperial Yeomanry at one of them scraps in the Boe-er war. Know him well 'ere, we do—got a plice dahn the line."

" Oh—that 'im ? " said the driver. He pulled out the half-crown and spat on it before returning it to his pocket and moving off. And the porter, looking round and into the booking office, saw Lord Normanstowe approach the ticket window.

Normanstowe had purposely thrown open his overcoat as he entered the booking office.

The clerk who dispensed first class tickets, and knew him well, recognised him as he demanded a first single for a certain station beyond Newbury, which was in close proximity to Normanstowe Park. He saw him stroll off in the direction of the train—he remembered all this, two days later, when the news of the young peer's unaccountable disappearance began to be noised abroad. It was the opinion of that clerk that his lordship went to join a train which was about to leave for the West of England.

Normanstowe, however, joined no trains. He went out of the booking office by its western exit, lingered a moment at the bookstall, passed along the platform, and going downstairs to the dressing rooms, engaged one, paid for it, and locked himself within its privacy. That done, he set down his bag on the toilet table, and took a careful look at himself.

What Normanstowe saw in the glass was the apparition of a very ordinary type of young man. He had neither grace of figure nor distinction of feature. His hair was inclined—very much inclined—to be red ; his face was a homely one ; he possessed a snub nose and a wide smile, and his eyes were of that indefinite blue which is commonly associated with people who are called Smith or Robinson. He wore a moustache which was rather lighter in colour than his hair ; he also wore small side whiskers—a vulgar habit which he had adopted out of sheer contrariness. And as he looked at himself in the dressing mirror, he grinned with what might have seemed to a beholder (had there been one present) a fatuous and a foolish delight.

" Common ! " he murmured. " As common as ever they make 'em ! The sort of young man who calls with a note book and a pencil to inspect the gas meter or take orders for the grocer. And the whiskers and moustache—or, rather, the disappearance of them—will make all the difference in the world."

These conclusions led him to divest himself of his dinner jacket, waistcoat, and dress shirt, and to shave his face as clean as that of a schoolboy who has been asked out to dinner. The disappearance of the moustache and the whiskers made him a very inconspicuous person indeed ; with them all suggestion of a long line of ancestors seemed to disappear. He grinned again—more fatuously than before. That done, he drew off his trousers, kicked off his elegant boots, and took the old tweed suit, a coloured shirt, and a noncommittal necktie from the kit bag.

In ten minutes Normanstowe, looking at the results of his labours in the mirror, saw the reflection of a good typical specimen of the very ordinary young man. He had kept his eyes open in his journey through his twenty-eight years of life, and he knew that you could meet just such a young man as he now looked to be by the thousand ; you passed them in the streets, you saw them in the pits of the theatres, they were massed together in the shilling enclosures of the football fields ; they huddled against the railings on the race-courses. He grinned again with increased delight.

" A very ordinary type indeed ! " he said. " Excellent ! "

Then, with a last glance at himself, he turned to the garments which he had discarded. He packed every one of them into the kit bag. There was money in the pockets of the trousers—gold, silver and copper. He took it in his hand and gazed thoughtfully at it. In the end he selected a shilling, a sixpence, four pennies and a halfpenny, and put them in the watch pocket of his vest ; the rest of the money he restored to his dress clothes. Then he packed up the

shaving outfit and the discarded white shirt and tie ; finally
he crammed the overcoat and the two dumb-bells into the
kit bag, which he proceeded to lock. He glanced around
him ; no, he had not overlooked anything. Normanstowe's
idea had been to walk out of Paddington Station to the canal
which runs at the side of it and to drop his weighted bag into
that part of the dismal waterway which is spanned by a
bridge at the end of Warwick Avenue. He had once or
twice been up that way, seeing home a sprightly lady who was
associated with musical comedy, and who lived in that
neighbourhood, and it had struck him as being a likely spot
for getting rid of his present encumbrances. But, upon
reflection, he thought that he might go one better—he would
deposit his bag at the cloak room. They had a trick, these
fellows, he said to himself, of dragging canals for dead bodies,
and though the kit bag had neither name nor initials upon it,
he knew that its contents would speedily be recognised.
But it would remain in the cloak room, comfortably lost, for
a long time.

Through sheer habit Normanstowe pulled out his watch.
At the sight of it he whistled, not from any surprise in
connection with the time, but because he suddenly recognised his own stupidity. Go where he meant to go with a
valuable watch on which his initials and crest were enamelled !
That would never do ! He hastily took it off, and, unlocking
the bag once more, put the watch safely inside. Then he
remembered that the sleeve links in the cuffs of his coloured
shirt were also ornamented with his initials, and he took
them off, too. But when he had relocked the bag, he
breathed freely, for he remembered that his undergarments
and his shirt and his handkerchief and collar were all unmarked—he had once sent out for a supply of such things
from the club in a hurry and these were part of that supply,
and there was nothing upon them that could betray him.
He was denuded of everything.

He presently opened the door, looked cautiously around
him, and, seeing nobody about, seized the bag and marched
off. He passed two men and one lady on the platform with
whom he was on intimate terms of friendship—not one of
them knew him. So he marched still more confidently
forward and slammed the bag down on the counter of the
cloak room.

" Name ? " demanded the person in attendance, beginning to fill out the ticket.

" Smith—John," answered Normanstowe, readily enough. He put down sixpence and presently took up fourpence in coppers, and walked off. " Now for it ! " he muttered, and turned out of the station into the covered entrance-way.

Normanstowe knew exactly what he was going to do. For a young gentleman of his rank his knowledge of London was extensive and peculiar. Knowing what he wanted, he went straight to his object. That was the police station in the Harrow Road, close to Paddington Green. Five minutes walk brought him to it. He put his hands in his pockets and looked at its lighted windows. He sauntered past the open door and saw uniformed individuals moving about inside. And, having thus prospected, he walked around the corner by Paddington town hall and filled the pockets of his jacket with stones which he kicked out of the road surface with the help of toe and heel.

Then Normanstowe went back, ready to carry out his nefarious design upon the innocent tenants of the police station. Just then the Harrow Road was fairly quiet at that point. There was no great stream of traffic ; only a few people were about on the pavements. But amongst the few were two police constables, one on duty, the other off, who were exchanging remarks in close proximity to the door of the station. That was precisely what Normanstowe wanted ; he desired to draw attention to himself as quickly as possible. Wherefore, having carefully selected three of his largest stones, he took a deliberate aim and threw one of them through a window of the charge office. As the crash aroused the attention of everybody who was near he threw a second stone through another window.

The two constables started into sudden activity, caught sight of the aggressor, saw him cast the second stone, and made a heavy dart for him. And Normanstowe, drawing back with a laugh, threw the third stone, with even more effect, just as various uniformed individuals came tumbling over each other out of the front door and down the steps of the station. Then, for the first time in his life, Normanstowe knew what it was to be forcibly grasped by the hands of authority. He became aware that they were no very gentle hands, and his ideas grew mixed and confused. It reminded him, this event, of a rough-and-tumble loose scrimmage in a hotly-contested football match, in which he appeared to be taking all the kicks and bruises. He came out of it mauled and breathless, to find himself within the building which he had so shamelessly attacked, the cynosure of many pairs of indignant eyes and the object of attention by a particularly truculent-looking inspector, who glared at him as if he meant to order his immediate execution.

" Now, then," demanded this awful being, " what did you do that for ? "

" Fun ! " answered Normanstowe unblushingly, and not without impudence.

The high official glared at him still more fiercely. In a purely official voice he asked his name and address. Normanstowe rudely bade him to find out these particulars for himself.

" Not that they matter," he added, still more impudently.

The inspector motioned to those who held the prisoner in a firm grip.

" Go through him," he commanded.

Somebody went through Normanstowe in thorough and systematic fashion, but they found nothing but the very small amount of small change which he had placed in his pocket at the railway station. For Normanstowe had kept his wits about him all through his adventures, and having made a tiny hole in the lining of his jacket, he had thrust into it the cloak room ticket which he had taken out for his kit bag. Wherefore there was not a scrap of paper upon him. All that was upon him, as an official voice presently announced, was one shilling and eightpence halfpenny, in silver and bronze, and five stones, obviously picked up from the road outside.

Three minutes later Normanstowe, seventh earl of his line, and owner of one of the finest estates in England, to say nothing of a town house, a Highland shooting-box and a stud of race horses, found himself in a police station cell. In the light of a feeble gas jet, placed where he could not interfere with it, he looked around him and grinned in his characteristic fashion, and his mind turned to sundry experiences in South Africa, not unconnected with want of food and with shelter that a respectable dog would have shaken its ears at.

" All a matter of taste," he observed calmly.

Then he sat down on the plain wooden bench, and, folding his arms, listened attentively to an inebriated lady, who, in the next cell, was cheering her present circumstances with hearty song.

IV

THE BIRTHMARK

IN the grey gloom of a dull October morning Normanstowe entered the dock of the police court, and afforded its habitués some occasion of interest and merriment. Officialdom could make nothing of him. He pleaded guilty with alacrity. He refused to give any name or address. The police were unanimous in testifying to his sobriety ; nothing but his extraordinary conduct of the previous night suggested any doubts as to his sanity. Incidentally, it was reported, that when he was asked why he had done this thing, he answered that he had done it for fun. But at that the magistrate shook his head, and looked at the prisoner with a certain amount of speculative inquisitiveness.

" Did you break these windows for fun ? " he asked.

" No," answered Normanstowe, " not at all ! "

The magistrate looked down at the charge sheet, and then at Normanstowe.

" Why did you break them, then ? " he inquired mildly.

" Why did I ? Oh, by way of protest ! " replied Normanstowe. " Protest, of course ! "

" Protest against what ? " inquired the magistrate.

Normanstowe looked at the edge of the dock, and then at the ceiling of the court, and then at a point somewhere between the top and bottom buttons of the magistrate's waistcoat.

" Oh, I don't know ! " he answered. " Anything— everything ! The Government, you know ! "

The magistrate looked at the policeman who had brought Normanstowe to the seat of justice.

" Have you noticed anything about this man ? " he inquired.

" Nothing, your worship," answered the policeman. " Excepting that, when he had eaten his breakfast this morning, he asked if he couldn't have another."

" Well, I offered to pay for it," interjected the prisoner. " You have one-and-eightpence-halfpenny of mine."

The magistrate favoured Normanstowe with a look which a very observant person would have taken to mean many things.

" Fined twenty shillings and costs, and you will have to pay for the damage you have done," he said tersely, " or you will go to prison for twenty-eight days."

" I am much obliged to you," said Normanstowe. " I will go to prison for twenty-eight days. Unless you like to take my one-and-eightpence-halfpenny as a first instalment, and——"

The magistrate made a slight motion of his pen, and Normanstowe found himself ushered out of the dock by a gruff-voiced person who asked him pertinently how long he wanted to keep the next gentleman waiting.

After that, Normanstowe himself waited at other people's pleasure in a comfortless, whitewashed receptacle, until such time as a cargo of evil-doers was ready for conveyance to Wormwood Scrubs. Some of his fellow passengers sang as Black Maria carried them westward. Normanstowe occupied himself in speculating on the best method of profitably spending the moments of what he was determined to regard as a rest cure.

For the various little preliminary rites of prison life Normanstowe was rigidly resolved to feel no distaste ; certainly he would die before he would show any. He cheerfully did all that he was ordered to do. He looked confidingly and in quite a polite manner at the various officials with whom he now commenced acquaintanceship. And suddenly he saw a face of which he had some curious recollection. It was the face of a warder ; a youngish, good-looking, smartly-set-up fellow, who moved about with alert steps.

" Where have I seen that man before ? " asked Normanstowe of himself. " I certainly remember his face. Suppose now, that he remembers mine."

But then he comforted himself by his shorn-off moustache. Oh no, not even Wrigge nor Chisholm would know him now, attired as he was. For at that moment he was wearing no more than a shirt, and the obligatory bath was literally at the end of his toes.

" In with you ! " commanded the voice of authority.

That particular voice happened to be the voice of the warder whom Normanstowe was sure he had seen somewhere, and who was just then in charge of the ablutions. He was about to make some further remarks or orders when they were suddenly arrested. And, if Normanstowe had looked around he would have seen the warder's eyes fixed, as if they were fascinated, upon a certain mark which showed distinct and conspicuous upon the prisoner's left shoulder. But Normanstowe was just then engaged in a punctilious discharge of the duty required of him, and if he had thought to spare it was in the direction of thankfulness that the water was fresh and clean. He obeyed the prison regulations with scrupulous fidelity. When he had accomplished them in that instance he glanced at the warder of the somewhat familiar face, and became aware that he was looking at his prisoner with puzzled eyes.

" I hope to goodness that chap doesn't think he recognises me as somebody he's known ! " thought Normanstowe. " It may be awkward if he gets ideas of that kind into his head."

It fell to the lot of that particular warder to march Normanstowe to his cell, and to instruct him as to rules and routine. All the time that he talked, the warder was staring at the prisoner in disconcerting fashion ; and it required much self-control on Normanstowe's part to refrain from requesting him to look elsewhere.

When the man had departed, Normanstowe sat down on his stool and considered matters. Supposing he was recognised ! It would be unpleasant. It might lead to complications which would result in his losing his bet. But renewed confidence came to him.

" No, he can't know me," he decided. " It's impossible. All the same, I'm sure I've seen that chap before somewhere. In which case, he may have seen me."

During the next two or three days Normanstowe caught that warder looking at him narrowly. He looked at him as a man looks at something which puzzles him very much. Sometimes he looked at him when Normanstowe was on his way to and from the prison chapel ; sometimes when he was taking the air in the exercise yard ; sometimes when he visited his cell. Normanstowe began to feel as a highly sensitive insect may feel which is kept in a glass-covered receptacle by an inquisitive scientist who takes uncertain and speculative glances at it from time to time, wondering what it really is. He grew a little uneasy under these searching looks, and he got to be afraid of meeting the warder's eyes.

And on the fourth day, at a quiet hour of the afternoon, Normanstowe being busily engaged in sewing stout sacks together, the warder stole gently into the cell, and closed the door behind him. Normanstowe bent his head over his work ; the warder coughed lightly.

" Er—my lord ! " he whispered. " My—er—lord ! "

Normanstowe looked up. The warder was winking mysteriously, and his right hand held out to the prisoner a scrap of paper. Once more his lips shaped themselves to emit another tremulous whisper !

" Your—er—lordship ! "

V

SOCIAL AMBITIONS

NORMANSTOWE possessed the family temper. He forgot where he was, and he snarled angrily.

" Don't talk damned rot ! " he said snappily.

The warder shook his head.

" Beg pardon, my lord, but I felt sure I knew your lordship from the very first," he said. " It was the—the birthmark, my lord. When your lordship was—beg pardon for mentioning it—stripped."

Then Normanstowe remembered the birthmark, and felt inclined to kick himself for having forgotten it. It was a birthmark that ran in the family—a definite strawberry mark, and Normanstowe had always affirmed that it meant that he was some day to get two steps in the peerage, and be a duke. But how should this man know he had it ?

He suddenly dashed his sacking and his needle on the floor of his cell.

" Who the devil are you ? " he demanded. " Why do you come and interfere in this way ? You're exceeding your duties, my man ! "

The warder made signs which besought hushed conversation.

" Beg your pardon, I'm sure, my lord, but—the birth-mark ! Your lordship doesn't remember me—I was in your troop, my lord, during the war. Doesn't your lordship remember that awful hot day when we all bathed in the Orange River, near Bethulie ? I saw the birthmark then. My name's Copper, my lord—ex-Trooper Copper."

Normanstowe resignedly picked up his work. That had got to be done, at any rate.

" Oh, all right, Copper," he said. " Sorry I spoke sharply. Thought I knew you, too, only I couldn't place you. Well, what do you want, Copper—I mean, sir ? "

For he suddenly remembered what he was, and that it was his duty to address warders with respect.

" Sir—of course," he repeated. " I'd forgotten, of course, Copper—I mean, sir."

" Just so, my lord," said Copper. " Er—I'm a bit mixed, my lord."

" So am I," said Normanstowe, stitching away at his sack.

Copper looked all round him, as if he sought inspiration.

" To see you here ! " he murmured. " Sewing sacks ! "

" Seems a bit odd, doesn't it ? " replied Normanstowe. " Ups and downs of life, you know. What's that scrap of newspaper ? "

Copper brightened. He handed the scrap over.

" That's just it, my lord," he whispered. " That's what I came for. Read it."

Normanstowe read. What he read was just what he would have expected to read had newspapers come in his way. It was an excited announcement of his own disappear-ance. Half the world seemed to be searching for him. Also, three thousand pounds were being offered for news of him.

" That's Wrigge ! " he muttered to himself. " He might have made it five. Well, Copper," he said aloud, " you see I'm at your mercy. Between ourselves, this is all because of a bet. I thought I should be safe here. But I never foresaw that anyone who could recognise that birthmark would be here ! "

" But—but the life, my lord ! " exclaimed Copper.

" It is quiet, certainly," said Normanstowe. " I like it. It's a rest cure."

" And this grub, my lord ! "

" Plain—very, Copper. But wholesome and regular—and there were times in South Africa, Copper—when——"

" Yes, I know," said Copper. " I've not forgotten, my lord. Well, this is a rum go. And your lordship really means to stick it out ? "

" I mean to stick it out, Copper, and I shall stick it out, unless——"

But the warder suddenly opened the door of the cell, poked his head out into the corridor, looked up and down, withdrew his body after his head, and vanished as rapidly as he had come. Normanstowe sighed.

" An entirely unforeseen contingency," he murmured.

Two days later Copper again appeared, bearing a second scrap of newspaper.

" The reward's gone up to five thousand pounds now," he whispered. Then his face became gloomy. " Five thousand pounds is an awful lot of money," he said.

Normanstowe laid down his needle.

" Copper," he said, " let's talk business. As our opportunities are limited, let us be business-like. I don't want to leave this peaceful retreat until my time is up. Now, then, can't I square you to hold your tongue ? "

Copper flushed.

" I—I shouldn't like to do anything low, my lord," he said. " I wouldn't give your lordship away for anything. I'm sure. But five thousand——"

" I stand to win ten thousand if I'm not found for a month," said Normanstowe. " You hold your tongue and I'll set you up for life. Look here, do you think there's anybody else in this hole who might recognise me ? Has anybody any suspicion ? "

Copper shook his head with decision. No, he was certain there was no suspicion and no danger. If it hadn't been for the birthmark——"

" All right," said the prisoner. " Now we come to business." He cocked a shrewd and whimsical eye at Copper, and the warder began to fidget under its inspection. " What's your idea, Copper ? " he asked.

Copper suddenly grew bold and found his tongue.

" To get a better job than this," he answered promptly and firmly.

" What, for instance ? " asked Normanstowe.

" Well, I'd like to go back to South Africa with money in my pocket," replied Copper. " I could make a fortune out there, if I'd capital."

" You shall have it," replied the prisoner. " Only keep your mouth shut until my time is up, and I'll see to you. Anything else, Copper ? "

The warder rubbed his chin and smiled.

" Well," he said, half coyly, " there is a little of something else. The fact is, I've always had a sort of desire to see a bit of high life, just to—to see what it's really like, my lord. If your lordship could give me a taste of it, now——"

Normanstowe laid down his needle and his sack, and after staring at the warder, laughed, as loudly as he dared.

" Social ambitions, eh, Copper ? " he said. Then he looked the man over. " You're an uncommonly good-looking chap, too," he continued. " You look much more like a peer of the realm than I do. All right—before you depart for South Africa I'll show you round a bit. And now go away, Copper, and let me get on with my daily task. There was one thing that I learnt in my soldiering days, Copper, and that was to obey orders. And while I'm here I mean to do my duty like a man. Well, that's settled. Hold your tongue, and hand in your notice, or resignation, or whatever it is."

So the warder went away and the prisoner resumed his stitching as if his life depended on it.

VI

THE WELL-FEATHERED NEST

THE reappearance of the Earl of Normanstowe in the merry world of Mayfair roused almost as much commotion as his sudden quitting of that fascinating stage had aroused precisely a month before.

His disappearance had set up a nine-days' wonder ; the newspaper reporters, the police, the private inquiry agents, had racked their brains and used up all their energies in their attempts to find him. Certainly, said those who were acquainted with the youthful nobleman's career, there was nothing surprising about Normanstowe's sudden disappearance ; it was like him to set everybody talking. His whole life, from his Eton days onward, had been a succession of episodes of the noticeable order.

It was he who painted the Provost's door a brilliant vermilion. It was he who drove a zebra and a dromedary, tandem fashion, round the park, himself attired in Arab costume, and accompanied by a gigantic Zulu, clothed to the manner, desperately armed. It was he who made a daring parachute descent at Ranelagh. It was he who, dressed up in wonderful garments of the East, and accompanied by a suite of singularly disguised friends, presented himself at the Mansion House, and introduced his person and company to the Lord Mayor as an Oriental potentate from the undiscovered regions of Asia. It was he who organised the famous hoax on the Prime Minister, whereby Downing Street and Whitehall were filled one afternoon with the equipages of all the ambassadors, diplomatists, and political luminaries of London. It was he who sent four Punch and Judy shows, a merry-go-round, and a travelling circus to the garden party at Lambeth Palace, which garden party was being given by the Archbishop of Canterbury to the Colonial bishops and their ladies.

Most people who kept themselves acquainted with things knew of Lord Normanstowe and his eccentricities : his disappearance merely seemed to them to be another of his little ways. The probability was, said they, that he was enjoying himself in Paris or Vienna, and would return again, with more mischief in his head, when he was least expected.

But Normanstowe presented himself at the Melatherium to the moment, loudly demanding his £10,000 as soon as he had greeted the select coterie which awaited his coming with suppressed excitement. They stared at him, wonderingly. That he had shaved off his famous whiskers, and even got rid of his moustache, was at once apparent ; it was also apparent that he was a little thin. But he brought in with him an alert manner and bright, clear eyes, and he looked uncommonly fit as if he had been in strict training. And then everybody wanted to know where he had hidden himself.

"That," replied Normanstowe, carefully putting Wrigge's cheque away in his pocket, "is my secret. I have, of course, remained within the circumscribed area provided for in the terms of our wager. But as to where I have been, how I got there, what I did there, how I came away from there—that, my friends, is a secret which will never be revealed by me from now to Doomsday."

" Well, you've done it, anyway," said Chisholm.

" Didn't I say I'd do it ? " replied Normanstowe. " Of course I've done it. I'll do it again next year on similar terms. It's easy as lighting this cigar. But in the meantime I return to the calm and quiet routine of my usual life."

It was speedily noticed that in pursuing this routine Lord Normanstowe was accompanied almost everywhere by a quiet young man whom he introduced to his set and circle as Mr. John Copperthwaite. According to Normanstowe he had made the acquaintance in South Africa, and had been greatly delighted to renew it. Mr. Copperthwaite proved to be a quiet, well-behaved person, who united modest manners with eminently good looks ; it was evident that on his recent arrival in this country he had patronised the best tradesmen in Savile Row and Bond Street, and his well-set-up, irreproachably garbed and groomed figure, handsome features, and quiet air impressed everybody who met him. And Normanstowe, who was entertaining him royally in the family mansion in Mount Street, used to laugh heartily when they were alone at night.

" 'Pon my honour, Copper," he would say, " this is great fun ! You're a consummate actor, by gad ! "

" No," answered Copper, " I'm only perfectly natural— I never could act. I just take things as they come."

Whereupon Normanstowe would laugh more than ever in his high falsetto voice, and slap his guest on the back and declare that he was the best fun he had had for ages, and that they would keep things up. For Lord Normanstowe was never happy unless he was playing some mischievous game, and it delighted him to take the ex-trooper, ex-warder, out to dinners and dances—all to see him solemnly " playing pretty," as Normanstowe phrased it.

" Gad ! " he used to say, " it's better than a play ! " And he enjoyed it all the more—a characteristic of his—because he had the secret all to himself.

But one morning when Normanstowe was alone, occupied in the engrossing task of seeing how much his racing establishment had cost him that year, there entered to him his sister, Lady Trementower, who was some twelve years older than himself, and in addition to being an incurable gossip, was also a lady of observation and penetration. She closed the door of her brother's study, sacred to the serious reading of Ruff's Guide to the Turf and the latest French fiction, and dropped into a chair by his desk. Normanstowe took a sly glance at her, and saw signs of bad weather.

" Look here, Normanstowe," said her ladyship abruptly, " who is this man Copperthwaite ? "

" Chap I knew in South Africa," answered Normanstowe, promptly and truthfully.

" I dare say you knew a lot of chaps, as you call them, in South Africa," observed his sister. " But who is he ? "

" Name's John Copperthwaite," said Normanstowe. " Come from Windebusch, Orange Free State."

" That conveys nothing to me. I want to know who he is. Is he a gentleman ? " demanded Lady Trementower.

" What's he look like ? " asked Normanstowe.

" He is certainly a very well-mannered young man," replied his sister thoughtfully. " And much more modest than most of you young men are nowadays. But that doesn't explain him, and such strange people come from South Africa."

" Yes, live in Park Lane, most of 'em," said Normanstowe.

" I'm not talking of that sort," said Lady Trementower. " I want to know who this man is."

" What's the matter ? " asked Normanstowe.

Lady Trementower coughed.

" Well, of course you introduced him as a friend of yours——"

" Excellent friend, thoroughly dependable, keeps his word," murmured Normanstowe. " Yes, go on."

" And so, of course I received him as such," continued her ladyship. " And he's come to us and we've been here, and we meet him at a great many places to which you take him, and, well, I'm uneasy about Alma Stuvesant."

Normanstowe lifted his hands in the air, opened his large mouth to its widest extent, and then pursed his lips in a shrill whistle.

" Whew ! What—the heiress ? " he exclaimed.

" That's just it," replied Lady Trementower. " Alma Stuvesant has a quarter of a million in her own right, Normanstowe. Not even her father can touch it. And think of what she expects to get from him—one of the richest men in Chicago ! "

" But I thought you and she were fishing for nothing under a Marquis ? " said Normanstowe. " You both gave me the frozen eye, anyhow."

" What girl do you suppose would marry you until you've settled down ? " demanded Lady Trementower. " But, really, Normanstowe, I do believe the girl is in love with this Copperthwaite. And she's of age, and her own mistress, and you know what these American girls are ! "

" Well, not quite, but I don't want to know any more," answered Normanstowe. " You—you surprise me greatly, I had no idea that Alma's amorous propensities——"

" When is this young man going back to South Africa ? " asked Lady Trementower hastily.

" Don't know. I'll ask him," replied Normanstowe. " I think—yes, I believe—soon."

" Well, I hope so," said his sister, rising. " I hope so. The fact is that he and Alma are meeting every day—in the park, or in Kensington Gardens, or at one or other of the museums. I know. I've had her watched."

" What horrible depravity ! " exclaimed Normanstowe. " Ah, these American manners. Sad, aren't they ? So different to ours. However, I'll speak to Copper—I mean Mr. Copperthwaite."

That night in the privacy of the smoking-room, Normanstowe addressed his guest in fatherly fashion.

" I say, Copper, I had my sister here this morning," he said. " She was on to me like a thousand of bricks—about you."

" I trust I have done nothing to give her ladyship pain," answered the guest modestly.

" You'll give her ladyship an apoplectic fit if you don't mend your manners," answered the host. " You've been playing the meet-me-by-moonlight-alone game with the packed-pork maiden."

Copper drew himself up.

" My father was more than equal in rank to Miss Stuvesant's father," he said. " He was a clergyman, though a poor one—and if family reverses——"

" Oh, chuck that," said Normanstowe. " Miss Stuvesant is over here to marry a duke, or something of the sort. Why,

9*

man, she wouldn't have me! And don't you see, my sister would get into an awful hole if—but there, what's the use of talking? When do you think of leaving England to start that South African game, Copper?"

"I'm leaving England almost at once," replied Copper tersely.

"That's all right," said Normanstowe. "Well, you've kept, and I'm sure you'll keep, your word to me. You're never to let it out about where we met, you know. Half the fun of my recent adventure is that all these fellows who were in at it are biting their tongues with vexation because they can't find out where I put myself. And here's the five thousand I promised you, Copper, and I hope you'll turn it into a million. And now let's have a turn at billiards, and you leave the Chicago beauty to espouse strawberry leaves."

Copper pocketed the cheque with a single word of thanks, and said no more. He went out of the house very early next morning, and Normanstowe formed the opinion that he had gone to book his passage to South Africa. But just about noon, as he was thinking of strolling out to one of his clubs, Lady Trementower rang him up on the telephone, and as soon as she had got his ear, poured out a breathless flood into it.

"Normanstowe!" she screamed, "is that you? That headstrong girl has married that Copperthwaite person— married him, I tell you! At the Kensington Registry Office this morning. She's just sent me a note. Stay in, Normanstowe, do you hear? I'm coming round to see you at once. You must do something to have it annulled or——"

Normanstowe calmly dropped the receiver and rang off. Presently the bell rang again sharply; he took no notice. Instead he rang another bell for his valet.

"Beevers," he said, "we go to Paris, on our way South, by the 2.20 from Charing Cross. Pack all I shall immediately want, and all that you want, and meet me at the train. And oh, Beevers, tell Johnson that if anybody calls this morning—Lady Trementower, for instance—I'm out, and nobody knows when I shall be in."

Then Normanstowe walked out of the house and began to shake the dust of Mayfair off his feet.

EXTRA-JUDICIAL

I

THIS was the first time that the judge, recently raised to the Bench, had ever pronounced the death sentence, and his voice trembled a little as he came to the final words. But he spoke them at last, and his accents became firmer as he added their complement.

". . . And may the Lord have mercy upon your soul."

" Amen ! " said the chaplain, in a faint whisper.

The man in the dock, who had never taken his eyes off the judge during the couple of minutes during which the black square had rested on the grey wig, suddenly smiled— a cynical, half-sneering smile.   And, shrugging his shoulders as the warders on either side touched his elbows, he spoke— his voice as hard and steady as the judge's had been un- certain and faltering.

" If I get no better mercy from them above than I've had from them below I shall do badly ! " he said.   " How- ever, there's none of you'll know what chances up yonder. Damn the lot of you ! "

Then, with a harsh laugh that grated badly on at least one set of nerves, he turned and disappeared, and the judge, who had already risen from his seat, disappeared, too, behind the heavy curtains over which hung the insignia of Justice. He went slowly to his room, and the high sheriff went with him, zealous in the performance of the duties of his office. A pompous and punctilious man, he shook his head as he and the judge looked at each other.

" A hardened sinner—a bad fellow ! " said the high sheriff solemnly.   " Sad—very sad, to hear such sentiments on such an occasion."

The judge took off his wig with a sigh of weariness.

" I'm not at all satisfied about that case," he remarked. " Not at all ! "

The high sheriff started. He himself was very well satisfied ; in his opinion, the case had ended very properly.

" Not—satisfied ? " he exclaimed. " I—ahem !—the evidence——"

" On the evidence," said the judge quietly, " the jury could not possibly have found any other verdict, and the trial could not have come to any other end. But—I am not at all sure, in my own mind, that this unfortunate fellow is guilty."

" Dear me ! " said the high sheriff. " Um ! Oh, well, of course, I suppose we all have——"

" Our secret impressions ! " broke in the judge, with a sly smile. " Just so. And, you see, that happens to be mine. In spite of—what has just happened—I am not satisfied. Judicially, of course, I am. But——"

" Oh, quite so, quite so ! " said the high sheriff, who was not a brilliant man, and who called black black and white white. " I understand. But, of course, such things happen."

The judge slowly took off his robes and looked at his marshal with a whimsical smile.

" They happen," he said—" yes, they happen."

Then he began to talk of something else ; and presently he drove away in state to the judge's lodgings outside the little town, and the high sheriff was glad to see the last of him for that day. Mr. Justice Machin had had a reputation for slight eccentricity and whimsicality before his elevation from bar to bench, and, in the high sheriff's opinion, he was bidding fair to deepen it.

" Not guilty, indeed ! " mused the high sheriff, as he himself drove off to his country seat. " God bless my soul ! Why, the case was as plain as a pikestaff. Never heard clearer evidence in my life—Machin himself said so."

Mr. Justice Machin had certainly said so in his summing-up of the case, and his reminder to the jury that the evidence before them was purely circumstantial had not influenced them on the prisoner's behalf. Everything pointed to the prisoner's guilt, and as the judge slowly dressed for dinner that night he once more reviewed the whole testimony, point by point, and he knew that no conscientious jury could have arrived at any other conclusion. And yet——

" And after all," mused Mr. Justice Machin—" after all,

there is such a thing as intuition. I suppose I possess a certain share of it, and my intuition, whatever it's worth, tells me that the poor fellow is innocent. Innocent ! Yet found guilty on the strongest circumstantial evidence ! "

For the evidence in what was known as the Muirdale case was strong enough. It was a somewhat sordid tragedy of primitive passions. In Muirdale, a lonely, far-away valley amongst the wild hills that shut in that side of the country in which Mr. Justice Machin was then holding the Spring Assize, two men, young farmers, were in love with the same girl, and the sad fact that one of them was now lying in a murdered man's grave, and the other sitting in his cell, awaiting execution for the murder, was largely due to another fact no less certain—that the girl had played fast and loose with each in turn. The mere details of the case, which had seemed so plain to the high sheriff—a good representative of popular opinion—were few. Michael Cruddas, a well-to-do young farmer, of Muirdale, culti- vating his own land, had been engaged to the daughter of a neighbour, Avice Thormthwaite, who evidently had a reputation as the beauty of the district. Suddenly the engagement was broken off, and the girl immediately entered into another with James Garth, tenant of an adjacent farm. Michael Cruddas, undoubtedly a man of violent and ungovernable passions, had suspected Garth of underhand work, and, after a fierce quarrel with him at Highland Market, had publicly threatened to shoot him. Early next morning a shepherd, setting out across the hills from Muirdale, had found Garth's dead body lying in a lonely place near Michael Cruddas's farm, with half the head blown off. He had been dead some hours and had presumably been shot as he made his way home from market—shot, too, at close quarters. And close by the cottage was a cartridge which was new and had evidently been withdrawn from a fowling-piece as soon as it had been fired. Here had occurred a damning piece of evidence— Michael Cruddas was the only man in the neighbourhood who used that particular make of cartridge, and an examina- tion of his gun by the police on the morning after the murder . showed that it had been very recently discharged.

Considering the circumstances, and the savage threat made, said the witnesses, in apparent dead earnest, there seemed to be no reasonable doubt that Cruddas had been so obsessed by his passion for vengeance that, regardless of consequences, he had laid in wait for his successful rival and killed him.

But Michael Cruddas, promptly arrested, immediately declared his innocence. He said then what he afterwards said before the magistrates and at his trial. He had certainly threatened to shoot Garth, and he meant to shoot him if he came across him. But he had not shot him. Confronted with the facts of the cartridge, of the recently-discharged gun, and the clear proof that no other gun in this district—a very thinly-populated one—could be used for such a cartridge, he merely replied that he knew nothing about the affair. He had returned from market somewhat the worse for drink ; he had drunk heavily in his own house, and had gone to bed drunk. Of that night he remembered no more than that. But out of this the prosecution made much ; Michael Cruddas, it urged, had been drunk when he shot James Garth in the lonely lane near his farm ; he had gone home and drunk more ; drunk so much, in fact, that his mind had become a blank. And, in the opinion of everybody in court, this theory was a correct one. No one doubted that Michael Cruddas was a murderer.

Nevertheless, Mr. Justice Machin doubted whether, in this case, justice was being done. He was unable to account to himself for his notions—they were vague, formless, but they were there. Something in the accused man's bitter, cynical, almost indifferent conduct in dock and witness-box had impressed him—the last remark, made with the death sentence still ringing in his ears, had convinced him that there was an element in the Muirdale case which so far had escaped notice. And late that night, as he smoked a last cigar in company with the smart young barrister—his nephew—who acted as his marshal, Mr. Justice Machin suddenly clenched a resolution that had been slowly forming.

" We shall finish all the business by noon to-morrow," he observed. " And we shall get away by an early afternoon train. And as I have no further duties for a week I am going—somewhere. The fact is I am going—keep the fact to yourself—to Muirdale."

The young man on the other side of the hearth glanced quickly at the keen face and watchful eyes.

"Muirdale!" he exclaimed. "The place of the murder?"

"Just so," replied Mr. Justice Machin. "The truth is—though I don't want it talked about—I am not satisfied about that case, and I propose to perform a little extra-judicial work upon it. I am going to Muirdale to have a look round."

"You'll be spotted—known," pointed out the marshal.

"I think not," said the judge. "If you remember, there were very few witnesses and persons concerned. Muirdale is one of the loneliest valleys in the North, I understand. Also I hear you can get a little fishing there. I shall put on an old tweed suit and take my rod. I don't think that the people who only saw me in court will recognise me in shabby mufti. Anyway, I am going."

When Mr. Justice Machin said he was going to do anything those who knew him best were well aware that he would do it, and his companion accordingly made no comment beyond remarking that the proposed excursion was rather unusual.

"I said I proposed to do a little extra-judicial work," answered the judge, with a dry smile. "I am not going to Muirdale in a professional capacity, but as, say, Mr. Maxwell, a quiet, elderly gentleman who wishes for a few days' rest amongst the hills. If anybody in the shape of, perhaps, police, recognises me—well, I dare say a quiet word will ensure silence."

Then Mr. Justice Machin threw away his cigar and went to bed, and before retiring he packed a knapsack and laid a fishing-rod at its side, and as he glanced at himself in the mirror he smiled to think what a difference a judge's wig and stately robes can make to a pleasant-faced, rather country-squire-looking gentleman.

"I don't believe anybody will know me from Adam!" he mused.

II

AT a late hour of the following afternoon an elderly gentleman in a well-worn suit of grey tweed, whose shoulders supported a small knapsack and whose left hand carried a fishing-rod, came to the head of a winding pass which zigzagged up a heath-clad hillside, and, pausing, looked down into a valley which lay, lost amongst the hills, far beneath him. And he laughed gently, but cynically, as he looked at the narrow streak of winding stream, the tiny spire of a little church, the cluster of stone-roofed cottages about a grey bridge, the sparsely dotted farmsteads on the hillsides and in the ravines which lay dipped in black shadow—this, according to the poets and painters, should be a haunt of idyllic peace.

"But, unfortunately," mused the judge, as he began to descend into the valley, "unfortunately the human passions run in as fierce tides in Arcadia as in Babylon. And if the spirit of Nature seems divine enough on the surface here in Muirdale, I had enough proof yesterday that man's spirit is not appreciably different here among pastoral prettiness from what it is in Seven Dials or Whitechapel. Primitive! Primitive! I suppose my accommodation will also be primitive—if there is any."

He found accommodation at a little wayside inn, whose landlord told him that he occasionally lodged chance tourists and strolling artists, and could give his visitors a decent room, clean sheets, plain food and a bit of fishing in the stream.

"Nothing better," said the judge, and went upstairs to wash away the dust of his journey.

He looked out of a tiny window on the lonely houses of the hillside, and wondered which of them was that across whose threshold Michael Cruddas would never again set foot—unless something extraordinary occurred to save him from the hangman. He wondered, too, in which of those patches of green standing out against the blue and purple of the hillsides James Garth had met his death. And before he went down to the little parlour to eat the bacon and eggs which he had ordered his mind was filled with wonder that, in such solitudes as these, men and women should so forget the impressiveness of the great silence, the far-stretching skies, the hush of the nights and glory of the sunsets, as to let their passions carry them to deeds of blood.

But the judge was soon to learn that the folk who live amongst the finer things of Nature are as much concerned with personalities as the people of towns. He sat in a shadowed corner of the little parlour that night and watched and listened. Men came and went—men passing along the dale who stayed a few minutes, men who sat down for half an hour over a pint of ale, men who stayed longer, sitting in accustomed places. And there was but one topic of conversation—the result of the local murder case. Also there was but one opinion upon it—James Garth had undoubtedly been shot by Michael Cruddas.

But there was a difference of opinion as to the state of Michael Cruddas's mind when the murder took place. The judge, although unused to the north country dialect, easily made out what the difference was. One set of critics held that Michael Cruddas shot his victim in cold blood ; the other set held that he was drunk when he did the deed, and never knew that he had done it. And they were arguing these differences, each side supporting its arguments by recalling interesting characteristics in Michael Cruddas, when a young man strode into the place, at sight of whom everybody became suddenly silent.

The observant watcher in the shadowy corner, seeing the effect which the newcomer's entrance had produced, looked at him with interest as he went up to the bar and demanded a glass of ale. He saw a tall, lumpish-looking fellow, heavy of face, cold of eye. His whole air and attitude showed a species of surly shyness, and when he looked around with a general nod at the company his expression was furtive and almost suspicious. He was evidently in no mood for conversation, and he flushed awkwardly when one of the men sitting near the bar addressed him.

" Been a fair day for t' time o' year, Mr. Cruddas," he observed.

The newcomer turned away sullenly.

" Reight enough," he muttered.

He drank off his ale and strode quickly out without further word, and the men looked at each other.

" Allus short o' speech, is Marshall Cruddas," observed one. " Ye nivver can get much out of him."

" Happen he feels that a time like this it's best to say naught," remarked another man. " It's none a pleasant reflection to know that a relative's goin' to be hanged by t' neck till he's dead, now, is it ? "

The landlord, who was leaning over the bar in his shirt sleeves, smiled and scratched his elbows.

"Well, it's an old saying that it's an ill wind that blows nobody any good," he remarked. "It's a bad thing for Michael Cruddas to come under t' hangman's hands, so to speak, but it's a good thing for Marshall Cruddas yonder. Marshall'll come in for all 'at Michael leaves."

There was a murmur of assent from the small company.

"Ay, that's right enough, that is," said an elderly man. "Land, at any rate. Marshall's all the man-relative that Michael's got. Oh, ay, he'll come in for a nice thing, will Marshall!"

"So you see 'at that old saying's right," observed the landlord. "T' wind's blowin' bad for Michael—he'll be hanged—but good for Marshall—he'll get what Michael leaves."

Then ten o'clock struck, and the two or three late sitters clumped away, and the landlord, having fastened the front door, returned to the parlour and looked at his guest. He was obviously inclined for a chat.

"Yon young feller that was in a bit since," he said, "is cousin to him that was sentenced to death at th' 'sizes yesterday. As them men were saying, he'll come in for all 'at t' poor chap leaves."

"And that," asked the judge, "is it much?"

"Nicish thing," answered the landlord. He supplied himself with a drink, and began to fill his pipe. "Michael's none badly off. There's happen 150 acres of land 'at's been in the Cruddas family many a hundred year; it's their own freehold, so it's bound to come to Marshall—him that was in just now. Then I should think Michael has money put by. He's allus done well, and, though he drank heavy of late over this love affair, he wasn't a waster or a spender. And there's nobody much for it but Marshall, 'ceptin' an old aunt or two 'at he might leave a few pounds for."

"Were the two cousins on friendly terms?" asked the judge.

"Oh, they were right enough with each other!" replied the landlord. "Neither of 'em the sort for makin' much display o' family feelin', as you might say, but still the sort to reckon 'at blood's thicker than water."

"Live together?" inquired the judge.

"Nay, they didn't," said the landlord, "though single men both. No; Michael, his place is High Gill. You can see it from your bedroom window. Marshall, he runs a mill lower down in the valley. He'd be on his way home, would Marshall, when he called in just now."

" I read this case in the newspaper this morning," remarked the judge. " I suppose there is no doubt in the opinion of the people hereabouts that Michael was guilty ? "

" None ! " answered the landlord, with decision. " None whatever ! But, as you heard to-night, there's some hold that Michael never knew he'd done it. Did it when he was drunk, they say."

" Is that possible ? " said the judge, more to himself than his companion. " Could he really have shot this man and never known anything of it ? "

" In my opinion he could," said the landlord calmly, " for I've known men do some queer things when they were in drink and have no recollection of doin' them when they grew sober. Anyway, they've found Michael guilty, and I reckon he'll hang, and Marshall yonder'll step into his shoes."

" There was a girl mentioned in the case," said the judge.

The landlord nodded, and then shook his head.

" Avice Thormthwaite," he said. " Ay, just so ! There gen'ally is a woman i' them cases, mister, isn't there ? "

" What about this woman ? " asked the judge.

" Why, she played fast and she played loose," answered the landlord. " She's a beauty—no denyin' that—but she's skittish. First she was on with Michael Cruddas, and then with Jim Garth ; then she'd change about again. What drove Michael mad in the end was that he got it into his head that Jim Garth had tricked him. But what is likely is that what trickery was done was done by her. And," concluded the landlord, dropping his voice as he glanced round at his kitchen door, behind which sat his women folk—" and they do say—some of 'em—that Avice was tricking both of 'em, and that, instead of quarrelling over her, they'd ha' done well to ha' shaken hands and had no more to do wi' her. See, mister ? "

" I see," said the judge.

Then he took his candle and went to bed ; and as the murmur of the stream soothed him to sleep, he mused on the fact that when Michael Cruddas dropped into eternity through that gruesome hole in the floor of the scaffold, Marshall Cruddas would succeed to a very desirable bit of property, which would be none the less valuable because it had belonged to a murderer.

" That is," murmured the judge sleepily—" that is, if Michael really is a murderer. Now, I wonder——"

But then sleep overcame him.

III

NEXT morning found Mr. Justice Machin, in his character of holiday-maker, exploring in the neighbourhood of High Gill. He came across an ancient woodman, who showed him where James Garth's body was found, and he was able to trace for himself all the details of the scene on which the sordid tragedy was enacted. And as he looked about him he formed a new opinion—that in cases like this it would be an excellent thing if judge and jury took the trouble to visit the scene of a crime and make a study of its geography.

The woodman was inclined to be talkative ; it was seldom that he had a chance of playing the part of showman. From a slight eminence in the road on which the judge met him, he pointed out one place after another.

" Ay," he said, indicating a lonely farmstead in a deep dell just below, " yon's High Gill Farm, as belongs to Michael Cruddas, him as is to die for murderin' Jim Garth. Ye see yon little clump o' trees, master—there a' t' end o' the farm garden ? That's where they say Michael laid i' wait to shoot him ; that's where t'body was found, and that there cart- ridge that the lawyers made so much fuss about. Ye see, Jim Garth he were bound to pass that garden end on his way home—yon's his house, up t' hillside there. And yon cottage as ye see among t' trees in t' end o' this valley, that's where the lass lives 'at they quarrelled over—Avice Thorm- thwaite they call her."

" Is her father a farmer, too ? " asked the judge.

The woodman laughed drily.

" It 'ud take a cleverer man nor me to tell you what Thormthwaite is, master," he answered. " He reckons to be a game watcher, but there's them as would say he poaches a great deal more nor what he preserves. Queer lot is them Thormthwaites."

The judge made no reply to this. He was examining the landscape.

" Which is the way to the market town—Highdale ? " he suddenly asked.

The woodman raised his hand and pointed.

" Go down this lane to t' corner of Cruddas's garden— where I told yer Jim Garth was shot," he said. " Turn there to your left and go straight over t' shoulder o' yon hill—ye'll see Highdale then. That," he added, " is t' way 'at Jim Garth walked to his death—he were coming back fro' market when Cruddas laid i' wait for him wi' t' gun."

Mr. Justice Machin gave his informant a shilling, and set out in the direction indicated. He paused a moment at the clump of trees by which Garth had met his death. Certainly that was a likely place for a murder. The trees made good cover, and the murderer could easily slip away amongst them when the deed was done. And the judge was conjuring up the scene for his own benefit when the hasp of a gate snapped close by, and out of the farm garden came two people in such close converse that they did not see the stranger until they were close upon him.

One of these two was the man whom the judge had seen in the little inn on the previous evening—Marshall Cruddas. The other was a tall, finely-developed, black-haired, black-eyed, bold-looking young woman, whose beauty blazed out in those Arcadian surroundings like a peony in a garden of quiet colour. Both looked up sharply as the stranger moved ; Marshall Cruddas, recognising him as the visitor at the inn, dropped his eye and turned his head. The girl stared the judge through and through, and when he had passed her for some distance and purposely glanced back, she was still staring.

" Avice Thormthwaite, of course," murmured the judge, as he walked leisurely forward. " A bold beauty."

He went on his way, lounging about as a holiday-maker would, until he topped the shoulder of the hill pointed out by the woodman. There, two miles off, he saw Highdale, a cluster of grey houses around a square-towered church. But Mr. Justice Machin had no intention of going into the little town ; the only people who would be likely to recognise him lived there. They were not many—a police official or

two, a solicitor or two, two or three witnesses who had heard
Michael Cruddas use the threatening words. Still, the judge
had an object in his walk. In the map of the district which
had been laid before him at the trial, there was marked, on
the roadside leading from Highdale to High Gill, an inn
called the Pigeon Pie. And he had a certain notion concerning that inn, and he went forward until he found it, a queer,
half ramshackle old place standing lonely amidst pine and
fir ; and he went in and asked for a glass of ale from a
landlord who had obviously little to do.

It was an easy thing to lure this man into talking of the
murder ; he, in fact, was reading of it in a day-old newspaper when the judge entered the house.

" I suppose," said the caller, " that you know all the
parties concerned in this affair ? "

The landlord shook his head with the knowingness of the
man who believes himself unusually conversant with things.

" Know 'em, mister ? Ay, all on 'em ! " he answered.
" I weren't called as a witness, but I was one o' them that
heerd Michael Cruddas use them threats to Jim Garth. In
the Three Crowns at Highdale yonder it war—market day.
Drunk, of course, was Michael—but not drunk enough to
know nowt about what he said. ' Next time I come across
yer when I've a gun in my hand,' he says, ' I'll shoot yer as
I'd shoot a mad dog,' he says them words."

" I read the case," remarked the judge. " This house of
yours would be on the way home for these men. Did
Cruddas call here that night ? "

" No, he didn't," replied the landlord. " I saw him go
past, mutterin' and talkin' to hisself, just as it come dark
like. But Jim Garth come in—I've allus said, since, that
I reckon I was the last he ever spok' to. An' I warned him
agen Michael—'cause Michael had murder in him when he
spok' them words—ye could see it ? "

" And what did Garth say ? " said the judge.

" He said summit 'at I've puzzled and studied over ever
since," answered the landlord, scratching his head. " It
were this here—and he said it as he was sitting i' that very
chair 'at you're in now. ' If Michael Cruddas knew t' truth,'
he says, ' he'd be for shakin' hands wi' me, i'stead o' shootin'
me.' ' Why don't you tell him t' truth, then ? ' I says.
' 'Cause he's one o' them 'at'll listen to nowt when he's

mad wi' rage an' drink,' says Garth. 'All t' same,' he says,
'it'll come out.'"

"What do you think he meant?" said the judge.

The landlord shook his head and stared at the smoke-
blackened rafters.

"Don't know, mister," he said. "But—very—like—
summat about yon lass. She played fast and loose wi' Jim,
and she played t' same wi' Michael—and if she could do
that wi' t' two on 'em, separate like, she could do it wi'
i' both put together."

"But you don't know anything?" suggested the judge.

"Nowt," said the landlord. "Nowt! All t' same, that
were what Garth said, sittin' in' that chair an hour afore he
met his end."

The judge said no more, and presently he rose to depart,
and the landlord, following him to the door, looked critically
at the lowering sky.

"There's goin' to be a heavy rain," he remarked. "It'll
come within twelve hours. Stayin' i' these parts, mister?"

"For a day or two," answered the judge.

"Then ye'll see what ye've very like never seen afore,"
said the landlord. "When it rains here—it rains."

The judge went slowly back to Muirdale, thinking of
anything but weather.

He was chiefly wondering if the evidence brought before
men in his capacity is always as carefully prepared as it
might be. If he had known of James Garth's remark to the
landlord of the Pigeon Pie during the course of Michael
Cruddas's short trial, he would have insisted on knowing
more. But—of what—of whom?

"There is time yet, however," he mused.

He spent that afternoon in pottering around the neighbourhood of the inn; in the evening, after his simple meal,
he once more repaired to the quiet corner of the parlour in
which he had sat the previous night. And as he became
accustomed to the gloom, he saw in another corner a strange
face, which when he looked at it was fixed attentively on his
own. Mr. Justice Machin knew when he saw that face that
he had seen it before; he knew, too, that he had cause to
remember it. But, in spite of an instant searching of
memory, he could neither remember where he had seen it
or when or why he preserved a recollection of it. It was a

face that suggested gipsy blood—very dark, sinister, crafty ;
even in that dim light the judge could make out the black
locks which framed it, and the gleam of the black eyes
looking out from beneath shaggy eyebrows. And as he
looked, it moved out of the shadow, and its owner, a wiry,
muscular-looking fellow of middle age, clad in velveteens
and whipcord, came across to him, pulling at his fur cap with
an affectation of almost servile politeness.

"Begging your pardon, sir," said the man. "Gentleman as is stopping in the house, I think, sir ? "

"Well ? " said the judge quietly.

"I hear as how you were after a bit o' fishing, sir," continued the other. "The landlord mentioned of it. If you
like, sir, I can take you to a spot to-morrow, after the rain—
it's coming to-night, sir—where you'll enjoy yourself.
Grand spot, sir."

"Is it a place you have a right to fish in ? " asked the
judge.

"Oh, yes, sir ; all right. Common fishing, sir—not
preserved," answered the man, readily enough. "But,"
he added, with a knowing wink, "there ain't many as
knows of it."

The judge reflected a moment.

"Very good," he said. "Come for me to-morrow when
you think fit. It will rain to-night, you say ? "

"Rain within half an hour, sir," replied the other confidently. "To-morrow, then, sir ? It'll be towards
evening."

The judge nodded and the man, again pulling his forelock,
moved off and presently left the inn. The landlord entered
as he went out, and exchanged a word with him at the door.

"The man who has just gone out," remarked the judge
presently, "is not, I think, a North countryman ? "

"You're right, sir—he isn't," answered the landlord.
"Comes from southern parts, though he's been here, game
watching, these six or seven years. That's Thormthwaite.
Father," he continued, drawing nearer to the judge and
whispering, "of her that was talked of in the murder case."

"Ah, indeed," said the judge indifferently. "He has
promised to show me a bit of good fishing to-morrow. Will
he be all right ? "

The landlord laughed.

" Nobody better, sir," he answered. " Although he's not a native, there's nobody knows these parts better than Dan Thormthwaite. He'll take you where you can pull 'em out fast as you can throw in. There'll be good fishing after this rain—it's coming."

The rain came almost as the landlord finished speaking— came as it only can come in a mountainous country, with a suddenness of fury that swept all before it ere settling down into a steady, continuous, letting loose of the moisture that had been gathering all day around the hilltops in great masses of ominous cloud. It was still pouring down on roof and road when the judge went to bed ; it was as heavy as ever when he woke in the night ; the ceaseless rattle of it was there when he half woke in the grey dawn. Nor was there any sign of its cessation when he drew his blind at last and saw that the little river had already overflowed and that the meadow which flanked it had been transformed into a miniature lake.

All the morning and through half the afternoon the rain fell, never staying, and the valley resounded with the noise of many waters. Far up the dark hillsides the judge, staring out of the inn windows, saw long, white streaks come into being against the blackness of the rocks and the purple of the heather, and recognised them for newly-formed cascades pouring down from the moors above.

Now and then a soaked traveller came in and spoke of flooded and impassable ways. It seemed to the judge that he was being cut off from the outer world. And then, towards the close of the afternoon, the rain ceased as suddenly as it had begun, and a weak sun struggled out of the clouds and shot fitful gleams on the swirling brown waters in the valley. And presently, as the judge drank a cup of tea in the parlour, a dark face showed itself at the door, and Thormthwaite's voice hoped the gentleman was ready for his bit of sport.

" Is it possible to make one's way anywhere ? " asked the judge, glancing at the window. " Aren't we water-locked ? "

" Leave that to me, sir," answered Thormthwaite knowingly. " If you'll follow me you shan't as much as wet your ankles."

The judge set out without demur. He had his good reasons

for making this excursion. For one thing, he was a good sportsman and the adventure appealed to him ; for another, he wanted to find out quietly—where and when he had seen this man Thormthwaite before ; and lastly, it was in his mind that during this excursion he might learn something which would throw some light on the business which had brought him to Muirdale. He would ask no questions, he would make no reference, but his nearly thirty years' legal experience would stand him in good stead if a dropped word, a mere phrase, came in his way.

Thormthwaite led the way out of the valley by a rocky path which ran along the side of the ravine over which High Gill Farm stood. Muirdale was filled with these ravines. They penetrated deeply into the hillsides, and when the trees were in full leaf, as they were at that time, they were black as night till unaccustomed eyes grew used to their gloom.

The judge looked curiously about him as they progressed. Below the shelving rock and loose boulders over which they scrambled, a swollen cataract poured down into the valley, carrying loose debris of plants and branches on its swirling waters. There was little prospect of successful fishing amidst such a tumult, and he pointed the fact out to his guide. But Thormthwaite pointed into the further recesses of the gloomy ravine, and the judge, straining his eyes, saw what looked like the ruins of an ancient water-mill.

" There's a pool behind those walls," said Thormthwaite, " where we shall find as many trout as I can carry. And there—it's quiet."

He led the way forward until they came up to the mill and to a door which stood in an angle of the wall. This he pushed open and stood aside, motioning his companion to enter. And the judge entered, and saw at once that he was in strange and curious surroundings.

The place he had walked into so unsuspectingly was a cavernous vault, formed by high, naked walls, open to the sky. Half-way up one of these walls water trickled freely through what was obviously a hatch, long unused ; on the flagged floor on which the judge stood water lay in shallow pools. He was a man of remarkably quick perception and he saw instantly what this place was—the wheelhouse of a mill, from which the wheel itself had been removed. And he saw, too, that if the hatch in the wall above him gave way under the pressure of water in the dam behind it, the whole place would be submerged in a few minutes—or seconds.

All this Mr. Justice Machin recognised in an instant. And in the same instant he heard a mocking laugh and a hurried step on the wet stones. Then the door was slammed and a bolt shot into a socket without. He was alone—a prisoner.

" Now I know that this man and I have met before," he said suddenly. " This is his revenge."

The immediate presence of what might be danger—might, indeed, be death—nerved the judge to an apparently imperturbable composure. And when Thormthwaite's face, sneering and evil, suddenly appeared in an opening high above him, he looked up steadily and even commandingly.

" My man," he said calmly, " you will come down and open that door at once ! "

Thormthwaite laughed. He was leaning out of a ruinous trap-door in the side wall some twelve or fifteen feet above his prisoner, and he folded his arms on the ledge and sneered again as he watched the proud face below.

" You forget, Mr. Justice Machin, that I'm up and you're down this time," he said. " You're a good hand at forgetting. I ain't—I remember all that I want to remember. I remember you—knew you as soon as I set eyes on you last night. Hang me if I ever expected such luck—after all these years ! "

The judge had been making a violent effort to exercise his memory to the full. And suddenly a certain day of the past came to him, and he nodded quietly.

" I remember you," he said. " You came before me at the quarter sessions at Malgrave—many years ago—when I was recorder. But your name was not Thormthwaite at that time."

" 'Tain't now, for that matter," sneered the man, " but I'm the same chap. Yes, I did come before you, as you says, and you give me five years—five awful years ! I wish I could keep you where you are now for five years. I would if I could ! "

" And I also remember that you richly deserved your sentence," continued the judge calmly. " You are evidently still inclined to wickedness. What are you intending to do now ? "

"I'm intending to make an end of you," answered Thormthwaite insolently. "You're going to drown—like a rat in a cage. I'm going to knock a timber or two out of that sluice up there presently, and give you a bath. You'll never want another. Look round ; there's no getting out of where you are."

But the judge kept his keen eyes fixed on his captor.

"Let me point out to you," he said, as quietly as if he were arguing some legal quibble, "that you're putting a noose round your own neck. It is known that I am in Muirdale ; the people at the inn also know that I have come out with you. If——"

"There's no 'if' about it," was the reply. "I reckoned it all out last night—especially after I saw what a lot o' rain we should have. My tale'll be straight enough to suit any crowner's jury, anyhow. You come out fishing with me—I show you a good place at back of the old mill, and I leave you there, fishing peaceable, while I go to get my supper. When I come back you've fallen into the mill-weir and drowned yourself. Eh ? "

"I'm not in the mill-weir," said the judge.

Thormthwaite laughed once more ; this time he seemed to be genuinely amused.

"You will be—when I find you," he said. "I tell you I've worked it all out. I shall watch you drown, and when you're done I shall let the water off by that sluice behind you—it only opens from the outside, so you needn't try it—and then I shall pull you out and put you in the weir. Plain and simple, eh ? You fell in owing to the bank being rotten with the heavy rain. What d'ye say to that ? "

"I say you are a murderer," answered the judge, "and I hope you have no other murders on your conscience. But I doubt it ! "

"You're a rotten liar ! " said Thormthwaite. "I've none. And there'll be no murder done on you, only justice. I'd a wife and three youngsters to keep when you put me away for five years—all I'd left when I came out was the lass you saw this morning. And what—what," he suddenly burst out with a flash of ungovernable fury—"what did you come spying around here for ? A judge ! You didn't come here by no accident, I'll warrant. Happen you think I killed Jim Garth ? "

" I am beginning to think it very possible," said the judge coldly.

" Then you're wrong ! " sneered Thormthwaite, laughing evilly. " For I didn't. All the same, as you're going where you can't tell secrets, I don't mind telling you that I know who did. And it wasn't Michael Cruddas ! "

The judge's own danger was suddenly swept out of his mind. He turned a beseechingly eager face to his tormentor.

" Thormthwaite ! " he cried. " Stop this foolishness ! Take me out of this. Tell me who killed Garth, and I'll give you a thousand—two thousand pounds ! I won't say a word about this business—it shall be a secret between us. Cash, Thormthwaite—down in good gold ! Come, man, be sensible, be—my God, what's that ? "

High above both of them, high above the sluice to which Thormthwaite had kept pointing so threateningly, a sudden cracking of the gaunt, bare wall showed itself, and a great spurt of brown water shot through, forming a gleaming arch, and hit the stone flags at the judge's feet. And before either man could cry out again the crack wavered, deepened, widened, the big wall seemed to be torn in two by giant hands, and, with a roar that startled the folk down in Muirdale, a mighty mass of seething water leaped out above them. The mill-weir had burst, and the judge just realised the horror of it as he was caught up, buffeted, crushed, swept away into stifling darkness amongst a whirling wreckage of wood and stone.

It seemed to him that he heard a human cry of shrill agony, and he was vaguely wondering if it was his own, when a great blank rushed over him and he knew no more. The blankness and blackness came so suddenly that he had scarcely time to wonder if death were also at hand.

When Mr. Justice Machin next knew anything, he found himself lying in a soft, warm bed, in a slightly darkened room. Near him he heard voices—hushed, murmuring. He lay still and listened.

" Bound to happen sooner or later," said a voice which had a professional ring in it. " The turning of that old mill-weir into a big fish-pond was a most foolish thing to do. I warned Sir Thomas myself of what might happen when an unusually heavy rain came—and here's the result ! "

Half the village swept away, eight lives lost. Our patient here had a most lucky escape—and, by the by, when he comes round we must get to know who he really is."

The judge turned his head and spoke, and was frightened to hear the feebleness of his own voice.

" I will tell you that," he said, " if you will tell me how much I am damaged and when I can get about again."

The two doctors came forward and became busy, and the judge watched both.

" I must request an immediate and unequivocal answer," he said sharply. " Shall I be able to travel to London within a week ? Yes or no ? "

" No ! " replied the elder doctor. " Certainly not ! Nor within a fortnight."

" Thank you," said the judge. " Then I must trouble you to take down a telegraphic message for me, and I must ask you to personally see to its immediate transmission. The fact is, I am Sir Francis Machin, and the telegram is to the Home Secretary."

Two days later the Home Secretary sat in his private room listening to the report made to him by the very high official whom he had sent down to Muirdale on receipt of the judge's telegram. He smiled a little when the report came to an end.

" So it really comes to this," he said, rising and pacing the room. " On the strength of his own intuitive feeling in the matter, and on that chance remark of the man Thorm-thwaite, made to him just before the accident happened—that he, Thormthwaite, knew who murdered James Garth, and it was not Michael Cruddas—Machin wants me to stay execution in this case ? That it ? "

" That is it," answered the official. " What is more, I'm quite certain that he'll be in a fever until he knows that you've done what he wants. I never saw a man so earnest about anything in my life ! He's confident that this man Michael Cruddas is innocent."

" And pray whom does he think is—or was—guilty ? " asked the Home Secretary.

" His theory," answered the official, " is that the cousin, Marshall Cruddas, shot Garth, and that the girl Avice Thormthwaite was accessory, and possibly instigator."

" And those two, you say, are dead ; drowned in the

flood, as the girl's father also was ? " said the Home Secretary.

" Marshall Cruddas and the girl were drowned together in Cruddas's house," replied the official. " The father was killed by falling masonry."

The Home Secretary smiled enigmatically.

" Machin," he observed, " was always a man of queer whims and fancies, but I don't think he's very likely to be wrong. Oh, well, send Machin a wire. A word will do. Send it now and set his mind at rest."

The official rose and moved to the door.

" The word ? " he asked.

The Home Secretary had already reseated himself, and was absent-mindedly staring at the papers. He looked up, half vacantly.

" Eh ? " he said. " Oh ! Why, of course, there is only one—Reprieved."

R. AUSTIN FREEMAN

The Apparition of Burling Court
The Case of the White Foot-prints

¶ Dr. R. AUSTIN FREEMAN—once an
assistant Colonial Surgeon in the Gold
Coast Colony—is famous as the creator
of Dr. John Thorndyke, perhaps the
most famous fiction sleuth since Sherlock Holmes. His medical experience
has been of enormous service to him
since he decided to take up authorship
upon the appearance in 1907 of *The
Red Thumb Mark*; for the technical
knowledge gained from first-hand
sources during the author's early life
in England and Africa is a feature of
all the Thorndyke investigations.

THE APPARITION OF BURLING COURT

THORNDYKE seldom took a formal holiday. He did not seem to need one. As he himself put it, " A holiday implies the exchange of a less pleasurable occupation for one more pleasurable. But there is no occupation more pleasurable than the practice of Medical Jurisprudence." Moreover, his work was less affected by terms and vacations than that of an ordinary barrister, and the Long Vacation often found him with his hands full. Even when he did appear to take a holiday the appearance tended to be misleading, and it was apt to turn out that his disappearance from his usual haunts was associated with a case of unusual interest at a distance.

Thus it was on the occasion when our old friend, Mr. Brodribb, of Lincoln's Inn, beguiled him into a fortnight's change at St. David's-at-Cliffe, a seaside hamlet on the Kentish coast. There was a case in the background, and a very curious case it turned out to be, though at first it appeared to me quite a commonplace affair ; and the manner of its introduction was as follows.

One hot afternoon in the early part of the Long Vacation the old solicitor dropped in for a cup of tea and a chat. That, at least, was how he explained his visit ; but my experience of Mr. Brodribb led me to suspect some ulterior purpose in the call, and as he sat by the open window, tea-cup in hand, looking, with his fine pink complexion, his silky white hair and his faultless " turn out," the very type of the courtly, old-fashioned lawyer, I waited expectantly for the matter of his visit to transpire. And, presently, out it came.

" I am going to take a little holiday down at St. David's," said he. " Just a quiet spell by the sea, you know. Delightful place. So quiet and restful and so breezy and fresh. Ever been there ? "

" No," replied Thorndyke. " I only just know the name."

" Well, why shouldn't you come down for a week or so ?

Both of you. I shall stay at Burling Court, the Lumleys' place. I can't invite you there, as I'm only a guest, but I know of some comfortable rooms in the village that I could get for you. I wish you would come down, Thorndyke," he added after a pause. " I'm rather unhappy about young Lumley—I'm the family lawyer, you know, and so were my father and my grandfather, so I feel almost as if the Lumleys were my own kin—and I should like to have your advice and help."

" Why not have it now ? " suggested Thorndyke.

" I will," he replied ; " but I should like your help on the spot too. I'd like you to see Lumley and have a talk with him and tell me what you think of him."

" What is amiss with him ? " Thorndyke asked.

" Well," answered Brodribb, " it looks uncomfortably like insanity. He has delusions—sees apparitions and that sort of thing. And there is some insanity in the family. But I had better give you the facts in their natural order.

" About four months ago Giles Lumley of Burling Court died ; and as he was a widower without issue, the estate passed to his nearest male relative, my present client, Frank Lumley, who was also the principal beneficiary under the will. At the time of Giles' death Frank was abroad, but a cousin of his, Lewis Price, was staying at the house with his wife as a more or less permanent guest ; and as Price's circumstances were not very flourishing, and as he is the next heir to the estate, Frank—who is a bachelor—wrote to him at once telling him to look upon Burling Court as his home for as long as he pleased."

" That was extremely generous of him," I remarked.

" Yes," Brodribb agreed ; " Frank is a good fellow ; a very high-minded gentleman and a very sweet nature ; but a little queer—very queer just now. Well, Frank came back from abroad and took up his abode at the house ; and for a time all went well. Then, one day, Price called on me and gave me some very unpleasant news. It seemed that Frank, who had always been rather neurotic and imaginative, had been interesting himself a good deal in psychical research and—and balderdash of that kind, you know. Well, there was no great harm in that, perhaps. But just lately he had taken to seeing visions and—what was worse— talking about them ; so much so that Price got uneasy and privately invited a mental specialist down to lunch ; and the specialist, having had a longish talk with Frank, informed Price confidentially that he (Frank) was obviously suffering from insane delusions.   Thereupon Price called on me and begged me to see Frank myself and consider what ought to be done ; so I made an occasion for him to come and see me at the office."

" And what did you think of him ? " asked Thorndyke.

" I was horrified—horrified," said Mr. Brodribb.   " I assure you, Thorndyke, that that poor young man sat in my office and talked like a stark lunatic.   Quite quietly, you know.   No excitement, though he was evidently anxious and unhappy.   But there he sat gravely talking the damnedest nonsense you ever heard."

" As, for instance——? "

" Well, his infernal visions.   Luminous birds flying about in the dark, and a human head suspended in mid-air—upside down, too.   But I had better give you his story as he told it.   I made full shorthand notes as he was talking, and I've brought them with me, though I hardly need them.

" His trouble seems to have begun soon after he took up his quarters at Burling Court.   Being a bookish sort of fellow, he started to go through his library systematically ; and presently he came across a small manuscript book, which turned out to be a sort of family history, or rather a collection of episodes.   It was rather a lurid little book, for it apparently dwelt chiefly on the family crime, the family spectre and the family madness."

" Did you know about these heirlooms ? " Thorndyke asked.

" No ; it was the first I'd heard of 'em.   Price knew there was some sort of family superstition, but he didn't know what it was ; and Giles knew about it—so Price tells me—but didn't care to talk about it.   He never mentioned it to me."

" What is the nature of the tradition ? " inquired Thorndyke.

" I'll tell you," said Brodribb, taking out his notes. " I've got it all down, and poor Frank reeled the stuff off as if he had learned it by heart.   The book, which is dated 1819, was apparently written by a Walter Lumley ; and the story of the crime and the spook runs thus : About 1720 the property passed to a Gilbert Lumley, a naval officer, who then gave up the sea, married and settled down at Burling Court. A year or two later some trouble arose about his wife and a man named Glynn, a neighbouring squire. With or without cause, Lumley became violently jealous, and the end of it was that he lured Glynn to a large cavern in the cliffs and there murdered him. It was a most ferocious and vindictive crime. The cavern, which was then used by smugglers, had a beam across the roof bearing a tackle for hoisting out boat cargoes, and this tackle Lumley fastened to Glynn's ankles— having first pinioned him—and hoisted him up so that he hung head downwards a foot or so clear of the floor of the cave. And there he left him hanging until the rising tide flowed into the cave and drowned him.

" The very next day the murder was discovered, and as Lumley was the nearest justice of the peace, the discoverers reported to him and took him to the cave to see the body. When he entered the cave the corpse was still hanging as he had left the living man, and a bat was flittering round and round the dead man's head. He had the body taken down and carried to Glynn's house and took the necessary measures for the inquest. Of course, everyone suspected him of the murder, but there was no evidence against him. The verdict was murder by some person unknown, and as Gilbert Lumley was not sensitive, everything seemed to have gone off quite satisfactorily.

" But it hadn't. One night, exactly a month after the murder, Gilbert retired to his bedroom in the dark. He was in the act of feeling along the mantelpiece for the tinder-box, when he became aware of a dim light moving about the room. He turned round quickly and then saw that it was a bat— a most uncanny and abnormal bat that seemed to give out a greenish ghostly light—flitting round and round his bed. On this, remembering the bat in the cavern, he rushed out of the room in the very deuce of a fright. Presently he returned with one of the manservants and a couple of candles ; but the bat had disappeared.

" From that time onward, the luminous bat haunted Gilbert, appearing in dark rooms, on staircases and in passages and corridors, until his nerves were all on edge and he did not dare to move about the house at night without a candle or a lantern. But that was not the worst. Exactly two months after the murder the next stage of the haunting began. He had retired to his bedroom and was just about to get into bed when he remembered that he had left his watch in the little dressing-room that adjoined his chamber. With a candle in his hand he went to the dressing-room and flung open the door. And then he stopped dead and stood as if turned to stone ; for, within a couple of yards of him, suspended in mid-air, was a man's head hanging upside down.

" For some seconds he stood rooted to the spot, unable to move. Then he uttered a cry of horror and rushed back to his room and down to the hall. There was no doubt whose head it was, strange and horrible as it looked in that unnatural, inverted position ; for he had seen it twice before in that very position hanging in the cavern. Evidently he had not got rid of Glynn.

" That night, and every night henceforth, he slept in his wife's room. And all through the night he was conscious of a strange and dreadful impulse to rise and go down to the shore ; to steal into the cavern and wait for the flowing tide. He lay awake, fighting against the invisible power that seemed to be drawing him to destruction, and by the morning the horrid impulse began to weaken. But he went about in terror, not daring to go near the shore and afraid to trust himself alone.

" A month passed. The effect of the apparition grew daily weaker and an abundance of lights in the house protected him from the visitation of the bat. Then, exactly three months after the murder, he saw the head again. This time it was in the library, when he had gone to fetch a book. He was standing by the bookshelves and had just taken out a volume, when, as he turned away, there the hideous thing was, hanging in that awful, grotesque posture, chin upwards and the scanty hair dropping down like wet fringe. Gilbert dropped the book that he was holding and fled from the room with a shriek ; and all that night invisible hands seemed to be plucking at him to draw him away to where the voices of the waves were reverberating in the cavern.

" This second visitation affected him profoundly. He could not shake off that sinister impulse to steal away to the shore. He was a broken man, the victim of an abiding terror, clinging for protection to the very servants, creeping abroad with shaking limbs and an apprehensive eye towards

the sea. And ever in his ears was the murmur of the surf and
the hollow echoes of the cavern.

"Already he had sought forgetfulness in drink ; and
sought it in vain. Now he took refuge in opiates. Every
night, before retiring to the dreaded bed, he mingled laudanum with the brandy that brought him stupor if not repose.
And brandy and opium began to leave their traces in the
tremulous hand, the sallow cheek and the bloodshot eye.
And so another month passed.

"As the day approached that would mark the fourth
month, his terror of the visitation that he now anticipated
reduced him to a state of utter prostration. Sleep—even
drugged sleep—appeared that night to be out of the question,
and he decided to sit up with his family, hoping by that
means to escape the dreaded visitor. But it was a vain
hope. Hour after hour he sat in his elbow-chair by the fire,
while his wife dozed in her chair opposite, until the clock in
the hall struck twelve. He listened and counted the strokes
of the bell, leaning back with his eyes closed. Half the
weary night was gone. As the last stroke sounded and a
deep silence fell on the house, he opened his eyes—and looked
into the face of Glynn within a few inches of his own.

"For some moments he sat with dropped jaw and dilated
eyes staring in silent horror at this awful thing ; then with an
agonised screech he slid from his chair into a heap on the
floor.

"At noon on the following day he was missed from the
house. A search was made in the grounds and in the neighbourhood, but he was nowhere to be found. At last someone thought of the cavern, of which he had spoken in his wild
mutterings, and a party of searchers made their way thither.
And there they found him when the tide went out, lying on the
wet sand with the brown sea-tangle wreathed about his
limbs and the laudanum bottle—now full of sea water—by
his side.

"With the death of Gilbert Lumley it seemed that the
murdered man's spirit was appeased. During the lifetime
of Gilbert's son, Thomas, the departed Glynn made no sign.
But on his death and the succession of his son Arthur—then
a middle-aged man—the visitations began again, and in the
same order. At the end of the first month the luminous bat
appeared ; at the end of the second, the inverted head made

its entry, and again at the third and the fourth months ; and within twenty-four hours of the last visitation, the body of Arthur Lumley was found in the cavern. And so it has been from that time onward. One generation escapes untouched by the curse ; but in the next, Glynn and the sea claim their own."

" Is that true, so far as you know ? " asked Thorndyke.

" I can't say," answered Brodribb. " I am now only quoting Walter Lumley's infernal little book. But I remember that, in fact, Giles' father was drowned. I understood that his boat capsized, but that may have been only a story to cover the suicide.

" Well, now, I have given you the gruesome history from this book that poor Frank had the misfortune to find. You see that he had it all off by heart and had evidently read it again and again. Now I come to his own story, which he told me very quietly but with intense conviction and very evident forebodings.

" He found this damned book a few days after his arrival at Burling Court, and it was clear to him that, if the story was true, he was the next victim, since his predecessor, Giles, had been left in peace. And so it turned out. Exactly a month after his arrival, going up to his bedroom in the dark —no doubt expecting this apparition—as soon as he opened the door he saw a thing like a big glow-worm or firefly flitting round the room. It is evident that he was a good deal upset, for he rushed downstairs in a state of great agitation and fetched Price up to see it. But the strange thing was— though perhaps not so very strange, after all—that, although the thing was still there, flitting about the room, Price could see nothing. However, he pulled up the blind—the window was wide open—and the bat flopped out and disappeared.

" During the next month the bat reappeared several times in the bedroom, in corridors and once in a garret, when it flew out as Frank opened the door."

" What was he doing in the garret ? " asked Thorndyke.

" He went up to fetch an ancient coffin-stool that Mrs. Price had seen there and was telling him about. Well, this went on until the end of the second month. And then came the second act. It seems that by some infernal stupidity, he was occupying the bedroom that had been used by Gilbert. Now on this night, as soon as he had gone up, he must needs

10*

pay a visit to the little dressing-room, which is now known as ' Gilbert's cabin '—so he tells me, for I was not aware of it—and where Gilbert's cutlass, telescope, quadrant and the old navigator's watch are kept."

" Did he take a light with him ? " inquired Thorndyke.

" I think not. There is a gas-jet in the corridor and presumably he lit that. Then he opened the door of the cabin ; and immediately he saw, a few feet in front of him, a man's head, upside down, apparently hanging in mid-air. It gave him a fearful shock—the more so, perhaps, because he half expected it—and, as before, he ran downstairs, all of a tremble. Price had gone to bed, but Mrs. Price came up with him, and he showed her the horrible thing which was still hanging in the middle of the dark room.

" But Mrs. Price could see nothing. She assured him that it was all his imagination ; and in proof of it, she walked into the room, right through the head, as it seemed, and when she had found the matches, she lit the gas. Of course, there was nothing whatever in the room.

" Another month passed. The bat appeared at intervals and kept poor Frank's nerves in a state of constant tension. On the night of the appointed day, as you will anticipate, Frank went again to Gilbert's cabin, drawn there by an attraction that one can quite understand. And there, of course, was the confounded head as before. That was a fortnight ago. So, you see, the affair is getting urgent. Either there is some truth in this weird story—which I don't believe for a moment—or poor old Frank is ripe for the asylum. But in any case something will have to be done."

" You spoke just now," said Thorndyke, " of some insanity in the family. What does it amount to, leaving these apparitions out of the question ? "

" Well, a cousin of Frank's committed suicide in an asylum."

" And Frank's parents ? "

" They were quite sane. The cousin was the son of Frank's mother's sister ; and she was all right, too. But the boy's father had to be put away."

" Then," said Thorndyke, " the insanity doesn't seem to be in Frank's family at all, in a medical sense. Legal inheritance and physiological inheritance do not follow the same lines. If his mother's sister married a lunatic, he might inherit that lunatic's property, but he could not inherit his insanity. There was no blood relationship."

"No, that's true," Brodribb admitted, "though Frank certainly seems as mad as a hatter. But now, to come back to the holiday question, what do you say to a week or so at St. David's ? "

Thorndyke looked at me interrogatively. "What says my learned friend ? " he asked.

"I say : Let us put up the shutters and leave Polton in charge," I replied ; and Thorndyke assented without a murmur.

Less than a week later, we were installed in the very comfortable rooms that Mr. Brodribb had found for us in the hamlet of St. David's, within five minutes' walk of the steep gap-way that led down to the beach. Thorndyke entered into the holiday with an enthusiasm that would have astonished the denizens of King's Bench Walk. He explored the village, he examined the church, inside and out, he sampled all the footpaths with the aid of the Ordnance map, he foregathered with the fishermen on the beach and renewed his acquaintance with boat-craft, and he made a pilgrimage to the historic cavern—it was less than a mile along the shore—and inspected its dark and chilly interior with the most lively curiosity.

We had not been at St. David's twenty-four hours before we made the acquaintance of Frank Lumley—Mr. Brodribb saw to that. For the old solicitor was profoundly anxious about his client—he took his responsibilities very seriously, did Mr. Brodribb. His "family" clients were to him as his own kin, and their interests his own interests—and his confidence in Thorndyke's wisdom was unbounded. We were both very favourably impressed by the quiet, gentle, rather frail young man, and for my part, I found him, for a certifiable lunatic, a singularly reasonable and intelligent person. Indeed, apart from his delusions—or rather hallucinations— he seemed perfectly sane ; for a somewhat eager interest in psychical and supernormal phenomena (of which he made no secret) is hardly enough to create a suspicion of a man's sanity.

But he was clearly uneasy about his own mental condition. He realised that the apparitions might possibly be the products of a disordered brain, though that was not his own view of them ; and he discussed them with us in the most open and ingenuous manner.

" You don't think," Thorndyke suggested, " that these apparitions may possibly be natural appearances which you have misinterpreted or exaggerated in consequence of having read that very circumstantial story ? "

Lumley shook his head emphatically. " It is impossible," said he. " How could I ? Take the case of the bat. I have seen it on several occasions quite distinctly. It was obviously a bat ; but yet it seemed full of a ghostly, greenish light like that of a glow-worm. If it was not what it appeared, what was it ? And then the head. There it was, perfectly clear and solid and real, hanging in mid-air within three or four feet of me. I could have touched it if I had dared."

" What size did it appear ? " asked Thorndyke.

Lumley reflected. " It was not quite life-size. I should say about two-thirds the size of an ordinary head."

" Should you recognise the face if you saw it again ? "

" I can't say," replied Lumley. " You see, it was upside down. I haven't a very clear picture of it—I mean as to what the face would have been like the right way up."

" Was the room quite dark on both occasions ? " Thorndyke asked.

" Yes, quite. The gas-jet in the corridor is just above the door and does not throw any light into the room."

" And what is there opposite the door ? "

" There is a small window, but that is usually kept shuttered nowadays. Under the window is a small folding dressing-table that belonged to Gilbert Lumley. He had it made when he came home from sea."

Thus Lumley was quite lucid and coherent in his answers. His manner was perfectly sane ; it was only the matter that was abnormal. Of the reality of the apparitions he had not the slightest doubt, and he never varied in the smallest degree in his description of their appearance. The fact that they had been invisible both to Mr. Price and his wife he explained by pointing out that the curse applied only to the direct descendants of Gilbert Lumley, and to those only in alternate generations.

After one of our conversations, Thorndyke expressed a

wish to see the little manuscript book that had been the cause
of all the trouble—or at least had been the forerunner ; and
Lumley promised to bring it to our rooms on the following
afternoon. But then came an interruption to our holiday,
not entirely unexpected ; an urgent telegram from one of
our solicitor friends asking for a consultation on an important
and intricate case, that had just been put into his hands,
and making it necessary for us to go up to town by an early
train on the following morning.

We sent a note to Brodribb, telling him that we should be
away from St. David's for perhaps a day or two, and on our
way to the station he overtook us.

" I am sorry you have had to break your holiday," he said ;
" but I hope you will be back before Thursday."

" Why Thursday, in particular ? " inquired Thorndyke.

" Because Thursday is the day on which that damned
head is due to make its third appearance. It will be an
anxious time. Frank hasn't said anything, but I know
his nerves are strung up to concert pitch."

" You must watch him," said Thorndyke. " Don't let
him out of your sight if you can help it."

" That's all very well," said Brodribb, " but he isn't a
child, and I am not his keeper. He is the master of the house
and I am just his guest. I can't follow him about if he wants
to be alone."

" You mustn't stand on politeness, Brodribb," rejoined
Thorndyke. " It will be a critical time and you must keep
him in sight."

" I shall do my best," Brodribb said anxiously, " but I do
hope you will be back by then."

He accompanied us dejectedly to the platform and stayed
with us until our train came in. Suddenly, just as we were
entering our carriage, he thrust his hand into his pocket.

" God bless me ! " he exclaimed, " I had nearly forgotten
this book. Frank asked me to give it to you." As he spoke,
he drew out a little rusty calf-bound volume and handed it to
Thorndyke. " You can look through it at your leisure,"
said he, " and if you think it best to chuck the infernal thing
out of the window, do so. I suspect poor Frank is none the
better for conning it over perpetually as he does."

I thought there was a good deal of reason in Brodribb's
opinion. If Lumley's illusions were, as I suspected, the

result of suggestion produced by reading the narrative, that suggestion would certainly tend to be reinforced by conning it over and over again. But the old lawyer's proposal was hardly practicable.

As soon as the train had fairly started, Thorndyke proceeded to inspect the little volume ; and his manner of doing so was highly characteristic. An ordinary person would have opened the book and looked through the contents, probably seeking out at once the sinister history of Gilbert Lumley.

Not so Thorndyke. His inspection began at the very beginning and proceeded systematically to deal with every fact that the book had to disclose. For he made an exhaustive examination of the cover ; scrutinised the corners ; inspected the bottom edges and compared them with the top edges ; and compared the top and bottom head-caps. Then he brought out his lens and examined the tooling, which was simple in character and worked in " blind "—i.e. not gilt. He also inspected the head-bands through the glass, and then he turned his attention to the interior. He looked carefully at both end-papers, he opened the sections and examined the sewing-thread, he held the leaves up to the light and tested the paper by eye and by touch and he viewed the writing in several places through his lens. Finally he handed the book and the lens to me without remark.

It was a quaint little volume, with a curiously antique air, though it was but a century old. The cover was of rusty calf, a good deal rubbed, but not in bad condition ; for the joints were perfectly sound ; but then it had probably had comparatively little use. The paper—a laid paper with very distinct wire-lines but no water-mark—had turned with age to a pale, creamy buff ; the writing had faded to a warm brown, but was easily legible and very clearly and carefully written. Having noted these points, I turned over the leaves until I came to the story of Gilbert Lumley and the ill-fated Glynn, which I read through attentively, observing that Mr. Brodribb's notes had given the whole substance of the narrative with singular completeness.

" This story," I said, as I handed the book back to Thorndyke, " strikes me as rather unreal and unconvincing. One doesn't see how Walter Lumley got his information."

"No," agreed Thorndyke. "It is on the plane of fiction. The narrator speaks in the manner of a novelist, with complete knowledge of events and actions which were apparently known only to the actors."

"Do you think it possible that Walter Lumley was simply romancing?"

"I think it quite possible, and in fact very probable, that the whole narrative is fictitious," he replied. "We shall have to go into that question later on. For the present, I suppose, we had better give our attention to the case that we have in hand at the moment."

The little volume was accordingly put away, and for the rest of the journey our conversation was occupied with the matter of the consultation that formed our immediate business. As this, however, had no connection with the present history, I need make no further reference to it beyond stating that it kept us both busy for three days and that we finished with it on the evening of the third.

"Do you propose to go down to St. David's to-night or to-morrow?" I asked, as we let ourselves into our chambers.

"To-night," replied Thorndyke. "This is Thursday, you know, and Brodribb was anxious that we should be back some time to-day. I have sent him a telegram saying that we shall go down by the train that arrives about ten o'clock. So if he wants us, he can meet us at the station or send a message."

"I wonder," said I, "if the apparition of Glynn's head will make its expected visitation to-night."

"It probably will if there is an opportunity," Thorndyke replied. "But I hope that Brodribb will manage to prevent the opportunity from occurring. And, talking of Lumley, as we have an hour to spare, we may as well finish our inspection of his book. I snipped off a corner of one of the leaves and gave it to Polton to boil up in weak caustic soda. It will be ready for examination by now."

"You don't suspect that the book has been faked, do you?" said I.

"I view that book with the deepest suspicion," he replied, opening a drawer and producing the little volume.

"Just look at it, Jervis. Look at the cover, for instance."

"Well," I said, turning the book over in my hand, "the

cover looks ancient enough to me ; typical old, rusty calf with a century's wear on it."

" Oh, there's no doubt that it is old calf," said he ; " just the sort of leather that you could skin off the cover of an old quarto or folio. But don't you see that the signs of wear are all in the wrong places ? How does a book wear in use ? Well, first there are the bottom edges, which rub on the shelf. Then the corners, which are the thinnest leather and the most exposed. Then the top head-cap, which the finger hooks into in pulling the book from the shelf. Then the joint or hinge, which wears through from frequent opening and shutting. The sides get the least wear of all. But in this book, the bottom edges, the corners, the top head-cap and the joints are perfectly sound. They are not more worn than the sides ; and the tooling is modern in character, looks quite fresh and the tool-marks are impressed on the marks of wear instead of being themselves worn. The appearances suggest to me a new binding with old leather.

" Then look at the paper. It professes to be discoloured by age. But the discoloration of the leaves of an old book occurs principally at the edges, where the paper has become oxidised by exposure to the air. The leaves of this book are equally discoloured all over. To me they suggest a bath of weak tea rather than old age.

" Again, there is the writing. Its appearance is that of faded writing done with the old-fashioned writing-ink—made with iron sulphate and oak-galls. But it doesn't look quite the right colour. However, we can easily test that. If it is old iron-gall ink, a drop of ammonium sulphide will turn it black. Let us take the book up to the laboratory and try it—and we had better have a ' control ' to compare it with."

He ran his eye along the book-shelves and took down a rusty-looking volume of *Humphry Clinker*, the end-paper of which bore several brown and faded signatures. " Here is a signature dated 1803," said he. " That will be near enough " ; and with the two books in his hand he led the way upstairs to the laboratory. Here he took down the ammonium sulphide bottle, and dipping up a little of the liquid in a fine glass tube, opened the cover of *Humphry Clinker* and carefully deposited a tiny drop on the figure 3 in the date. Almost immediately the ghostly brown began to darken until it at length became jet black. Then, in the same way, he opened Walter Lumley's manuscript book and on the 9 of the date, 1819, he deposited a drop of the solution. But this time there was no darkening of the pale brown writing ; on the contrary, it faded rapidly to a faint and muddy violet.

" It is not an iron ink," said Thorndyke, " and it looks suspiciously like an aniline brown. But let us see what the paper is made of. Have you boiled up that fragment, Polton ? "

" Yes, sir," answered our laboratory assistant, " and I've washed the soda out of it, so it's all ready."

He produced a labelled test-tube containing a tiny corner of paper floating in water, which he carefully emptied into a large watch-glass. From this Thorndyke transferred the little pulpy fragment to a microscope slide and, with a pair of mounted needles, broke it up into its constituent fibres. Then he dropped on it a drop of aniline stain, removed the surplus with blotting-paper, added a drop of glycerine and put on it a large cover-slip.

" There, Jervis," said he, handing me the slide, " let us have your opinion on Walter Lumley's paper."

I placed the slide on the stage of the microscope and proceeded to inspect the specimen. But no exhaustive examination was necessary. The first glance settled the matter.

" It is nearly all wood," I said. " Mechanical wood fibre, with some esparto, a little cotton and a few linen fibres."

" Then," said Thorndyke, " it is a modern paper. Mechanical wood-pulp—prepared by Keller's process—was first used in paper-making in 1840. ' Chemical wood-pulp ' came later ; and esparto was not used until 1860. So we can say with confidence that this paper was not made until more than twenty years after the date that is written on it. Probably it is of quite recent manufacture."

" In that case," said I, " this book is a counterfeit—presumably fraudulent."

" Yes. In effect it is a forgery."

" But that seems to suggest a conspiracy."

" It does," Thorndyke agreed ; " especially if it is considered in conjunction with the apparitions. The suggestion is that this book was prepared for the purpose of inducing a state of mind favourable to the acceptance of supernatural appearances. The obvious inference is that the apparitions themselves were an imposture produced for fraudulent purposes. But it is time for us to go."

We shook hands with Polton, and, having collected our suit-cases from the sitting-room, set forth for the station.

During the journey down I reflected on the new turn that Frank Lumley's affairs had taken. Apparently, Brodribb had done his client an injustice. Lumley was not so mad as the old lawyer had supposed. He was merely credulous and highly suggestible. The " hallucinations " were real phenomena which he had simply misinterpreted. But who was behind these sham illusions ? And what was it all about ? I tried to open the question with Thorndyke ; but though he was willing to discuss the sham manuscript book and the technique of its production, he would commit himself to nothing further.

On our arrival at St. David's, Thorndyke looked up and down the platform and again up the station approach.

" No sign of Brodribb or any messenger," he remarked, " so we may assume that all is well at Burling Court up to the present. Let us hope that Brodribb's presence has had an inhibitory effect on the apparitions."

Nevertheless, it was evident that he was not quite easy in his mind. During supper he appeared watchful and preoccupied, and when, after the meal, he proposed a stroll down to the beach, he left word with our landlady as to where he was to be found if he should be wanted.

It was about a quarter to eleven when we arrived at the shore, and the tide was beginning to run out. The beach was deserted with the exception of a couple of fishermen who had apparently come in with the tide and who were making their boat secure for the night before going home. Thorndyke approached them, and addressing the older fisherman, remarked : " That is a big, powerful boat. Pretty fast, too, isn't she ? "

" Ay, sir," was the reply ; " fast and weatherly, she is. What we calls a galley-punt. Built at Deal for the hovelling trade—salvage, you know, sir—but there ain't no hovelling nowadays, not to speak of."

" Are you going out to-morrow ? " asked Thorndyke.

" Not as I knows of, sir. Was you thinking of a bit of fishing ? "

" If you are free," said Thorndyke, " I should like to

charter the boat for to-morrow. I don't know what time I
shall be able to start, but if you will stand by ready to put
off at once when I come down we can count the waiting as
sailing."

"Very well, sir," said the fisherman ; "the boat's yours
for the day to-morrow. Any time after six, or earlier, if
you like, if you come down here you'll find me and my mate
standing by with a stock of bait and the boat ready to push
off."

"That will do admirably," said Thorndyke ; and the
morrow's programme being thus settled, we wished the
fishermen good-night and walked slowly back to our lodgings,
where, after a final pipe, we turned in.

On the following morning, just as we were finishing a
rather leisurely breakfast, we saw from our window our friend
Mr. Brodribb hurrying down the street towards our house.
I ran out and opened the door, and as he entered I conducted him into our sitting-room. From his anxious and
flustered manner it was obvious that something had gone
wrong, and his first words confirmed the sinister impression.

"I'm afraid we're in for trouble, Thorndyke," said he.
"Frank is missing."

"Since when ? " asked Thorndyke.

"Since about eight o'clock this morning. He is nowhere
about the house and he hasn't had any breakfast."

"When was he last seen ? " Thorndyke asked. "And
where ? "

"About eight o'clock, in the breakfast-room. Apparently
he went in there to say ' good-bye ' to the Prices—they have
gone on a visit for the day to Folkestone and were having an
early breakfast so as to catch the eight-thirty train. But he
didn't have breakfast with them. He just went in and
wished them a pleasant journey and then it appears that he
went out for a stroll in the grounds. When I came down to
breakfast at half-past eight, the Prices had gone and Frank
hadn't come in. The maid sounded the gong, and as Frank
still did not appear, she went out into the grounds to look for
him ; and presently I went out myself. But he wasn't there
and he wasn't anywhere in the house. I don't like the look
of it at all. He is usually very regular and punctual at meals.
What do you think we had better do, Thorndyke ? "

My colleague looked at his watch and rang the bell.

" I think, Brodribb," said he, " that we must act on the obvious probabilities and provide against the one great danger that is known to us. Mrs. Robinson," he added, addressing the landlady, who had answered the bell in person, " can you let us have a jug of strong coffee at once ? "

Mrs. Robinson could, and bustled away to prepare it, while Thorndyke produced from a cupboard a large vacuum flask.

" I don't quite follow you, Thorndyke," said Mr. Brodribb. " What probabilities and what danger do you mean ? "

" I mean that, up to the present, Frank Lumley has exactly reproduced in his experiences and his actions the experiences and actions of Gilbert Lumley as set forth in Walter Lumley's narrative. The overwhelming probability is that he will continue to reproduce the story of Gilbert to the end. He probably saw the apparition for the third time last night, and is even now preparing for the final act."

" Good God ! " gasped Brodribb. " What a fool I am ! You mean the cave ? But we can never get there now. It will be high water in an hour and the beach at St. David's Head will be covered already. Unless we can get a boat," he added despairingly.

" We have got a boat," said Thorndyke. " I chartered one last night."

" Thank the Lord ! " exclaimed Brodribb. " But you always think of everything—though I don't know what you want that coffee for."

" We may not want it at all," said Thorndyke, as he poured the coffee, which the landlady had just brought, into the vacuum flask, " but on the other hand we may."

He deposited the flask in a hand-bag, in which I observed a small emergency-case, and then turned to Brodribb.

" We had better get down to the beach now," said he.

As we emerged from the bottom of the gap-way we saw our friends of the previous night laying a double line of planks across the beach from the boat to the margin of the surf ; for the long galley-punt, with her load of ballast, was too heavy to drag over the shingle. They had just got the last plank laid as we reached the boat, and as they observed us they came running back with half a dozen of their mates.

" Jump aboard, gentlemen," said our skipper, with a slightly dubious eye on Mr. Brodribb—for the boat's gunwale was a good four feet above the beach. " We'll have her afloat in a jiffy."

We climbed in and hauled Mr. Brodribb in after us. The tall mast was already stepped—against the middle thwart in the odd fashion of galley-punts—and the great sail was hooked to the traveller and the tack-hook ready for hoisting. The party of boatmen gathered round ; and each took a tenacious hold of gunwale or thole. The skipper gave time with a jovial " Yo-ho ! " his mates joined in with a responsive howl and heaved as one man. The great boat moved forward, and gathering way, slid swiftly along the greased planks towards the edge of the surf. Then her nose splashed into the sea ; the skipper and his mate sprang in over the transom ; the tall lug-sail soared up the mast and filled, and the skipper let the rudder slide down its pintles and grasped the tiller.

" Did you want to go anywheres in particklar ? " he inquired.

" We want to make for the big cave round St. David's Head," said Thorndyke, " and we want to get there well before high water."

" We'll do that easy enough, sir," said the skipper, " with this breeze. 'Tis but about a mile and we've got three-quarters of an hour to do it in."

He took a pull at the main sheet and, putting the helm down, brought the boat on a course parallel to the coast. Quietly but swiftly the water slipped past, one after another fresh headlands opened out till, in about a quarter of an hour, we were abreast of St. David's Head with the sinister black shape of the cavern in full view over the port bow. Shortly afterwards the sail was lowered and our crew, reinforced by Thorndyke and me, took to the oars, pulling straight towards the shore with the cavern directly ahead.

As the boat grounded on the beach Thorndyke, Brodribb and I sprang out and hurried across the sand and shingle to the gloomy and forbidding hole in the white cliff. At first, coming out of the bright sunlight, we seemed to be plunged in absolute darkness, and groped our way insecurely over the heaps of slippery sea-tangle that littered the floor. Presently our eyes grew accustomed to the dim light, and we could trace faintly the narrow, tunnel-like passage with its slimy green walls and the jagged roof nearly black with age.

At the farther end it grew higher ; and here I could see the small, dark bodies of bats hanging from the roof and clinging to the walls, and one or two fluttering blindly and noiselessly like large moths in the hollows of the vault above. But it was not the bats that engrossed my attention. Far away, at the extreme end, I could dimly discern the prostrate figure of a man lying motionless on a patch of smooth sand ; a dreadful shape that seemed to sound the final note of tragedy to which the darkness, the clammy chill of the cavern and the ghostly forms of the bats had been a fitting prelude.

" My God ! " gasped Brodribb, " we're too late ! "

He broke into a shambling run and Thorndyke and I darted on ahead. The man was Frank Lumley, of course, and a glance at him gave us at least a ray of hope. He was lying in an easy posture with closed eyes and was still breathing, though his respiration was shallow and slow. Beside him on the sand lay a little bottle and near it a cork. I picked up the former and read on the label " Laudanum : Poison " and a local druggist's name and address. But it was empty save for a few drops, the appearance and smell of which confirmed the label.

Thorndyke, who had been examining the unconscious man's eyes with a little electric lamp, glanced at the bottle.

" Well," said he, " we know the worst. That is a two-drachm phial, so if he took the lot his condition is not hopeless."

As he spoke he opened the hand-bag, and taking out the emergency-case, produced from it a hypodermic syringe and a tiny bottle of atropine solution. I drew up Lumley's sleeve while the syringe was filled and Thorndyke then administered the injection.

" It is opium poisoning, I suppose ? " said I.

" Yes," was the answer. " His pupils are like pin-points ; but his pulse is not so bad. I think we can safely move him down to the boat."

Thereupon we lifted him, and with Brodribb supporting his feet, we moved in melancholy procession down the cave. Already the waves were lapping the beach at the entrance and even trickling in amongst the seaweed ; and the boat, following the rising tide, had her bows within the cavern. The two fishermen, who were steadying the boat with their

oars, greeted our appearance, carrying the body, with exclamations of astonishment. But they asked no questions,
simply taking the unconscious man from us and laying him
gently on the grating in the stern-sheets.

" Why, 'tis Mr. Lumley ! " exclaimed the skipper.

" Yes," said Thorndyke ; and having given them a few
words of explanation, he added : " I look to you to keep this
affair to yourselves."

To this the two men agreed heartily, and the boat having
been pushed off and the sail hoisted, the skipper asked :

" Do we sail straight back, sir ? "

" Yes," replied Thorndyke, " but we won't land yet.
Stand on and off opposite the gap-way."

Already, as a result of the movement, the patient's stupor
appeared less profound. And now Thorndyke took definite
measures to rouse him, shaking him gently and constantly
changing his position. Presently Lumley drew a deep sighing breath, and opened his eyes for a moment. Then
Thorndyke sat him up, and producing the vacuum-flask,
made him swallow a few teaspoonfuls of coffee. This procedure was continued for over an hour while the boat cruised
up and down opposite the landing-place half a mile or so
from the shore. Constantly our patient relapsed into
stuporous sleep, only to be roused again and given a sip of
coffee.

At length he recovered so far as to be able to sit up—
lurching from side to side as the boat rolled—and drowsily
answer questions spoken loudly in his ear. A quarter of an
hour later, as he still continued to improve, Thorndyke
ordered the skipper to bring the boat to the landing-place.

" I think he could walk now," said he, " and the exercise
will rouse him more completely."

The boat was accordingly beached and Lumley assisted
to climb out ; and though at first he staggered as if he would
fall, after a few paces he was able to walk fairly steadily,
supported on either side by me and Thorndyke. The effect
of ascending the steep gap-way revived him further ; and
by the time we reached the gate of Burling Court—half a
mile across the fields—he was almost able to stand alone.

But even when he had arrived home he was not allowed to
rest, earnestly as he begged to be left in peace. First
Thorndyke insisted on his taking a light meal, and then

proceeded to question him as to the events of the previous night.

" I presume, Lumley," said he, " that you saw the apparition of Glynn's head ? "

" Yes. After Mr. Brodribb had seen me to bed, I got up and went to Gilbert's cabin. Something seemed to draw me to it. And as soon as I opened the door, there was the head hanging in the air within three feet of me. Then I knew that Glynn was calling me, and—well, you know the rest."

" I understand," said Thorndyke. " But now I want you to come to Gilbert's cabin with me and show me exactly where you were and where the head was."

Lumley was profoundly reluctant and tried to postpone the demonstration. But Thorndyke would listen to no refusal, and at last Lumley rose wearily and conducted his tormentor up the stairs, followed by Brodribb and me.

We went first to Lumley's bedroom and from that into a corridor, into which some other bedrooms opened. The corridor was dimly lighted by a single window, and when Thorndyke had drawn the thick curtain over this, the place was almost completely dark. At one end of the corridor was the small, narrow door of the " cabin," over which was a gas bracket. Thorndyke lighted the gas and opened the door and we then saw that the room was in total darkness, its only window being closely shuttered and the curtains drawn. Thorndyke struck a match and lit the gas and we then looked curiously about the little room.

It was a quaint little apartment, to which its antique furniture and contents gave an old-world air. An ancient hanger, quadrant and spy-glass hung on the wall, a large dropsical-looking watch, inscribed " Thomas Tompion, Londini fecit," reposed on a little velvet cushion in the middle of a small, black mahogany table by the window, and a couple of Cromwellian chairs stood against the wall. Thorndyke looked curiously at the table, which was raised on wooden blocks, and Lumley explained :

" That was Gilbert's dressing -table. He had it made for his cabin on board ship."

" Indeed," said Thorndyke. " Then Gilbert was a rather up-to-date gentleman. There wasn't much mahogany furniture before 1720. Let us have a look at the interior arrangements."

He lifted the watch, and having placed it on a chair, raised the lid of the table, disclosing a small wash-hand basin, a little squat ewer and other toilet appliances. The table lid, which was held upright by a brass strut, held a rather large dressing-mirror enclosed in a projecting case.

"I wonder," said I, "why the table was stood on those blocks."

"Apparently," said Thorndyke, "for the purpose of bringing the mirror to the eye level of a person standing up."

The answer gave Brodribb an idea. "I suppose, Frank," said he, "it was not your own reflection in the mirror that you saw?"

"How could it be?" demanded Lumley. "The head was upside down, and besides, it was quite near to me."

"No, that's true," said Brodribb; and turning away from the table he picked up the old navigator's watch. "A queer old timepiece, this," he remarked.

"Yes," said Lumley; "but it's beautifully made. Let me show you the inside."

He took off the outer case and opened the inner one, exhibiting the delicate workmanship of the interior to Brodribb and me, while Thorndyke continued to pore over the inner fittings of the table. Suddenly my colleague said:

"Just go outside, you three, and shut the door. I want to try an experiment."

Obediently we all filed out and closed the door, waiting expectantly in the corridor. In a couple of minutes Thorndyke came out and before he shut the door I noticed that the little room was now in darkness. He walked us a short distance down the corridor and then, halting, said:

"Now, Lumley, I want you to go into the cabin and tell us what you see."

Lumley appeared a little reluctant to go in alone, but eventually he walked towards the cabin and opened the door. Instantly he uttered a cry of horror, and closing the door, ran back to us, trembling, agitated, wild-eyed.

"It is there now!" he exclaimed. "I saw it distinctly."

"Very well," said Thorndyke. "Now you go and look, Brodribb."

Mr. Brodribb showed no eagerness. With very obvious trepidation he advanced to the door and threw it open with a jerk. Then, with a sharp exclamation, he slammed it to, and came hurrying back, his usually pink complexion paled down to a delicate mauve.

" Horrible ! Horrible ! " he exclaimed. " What the devil is it, Thorndyke ? "

A sudden suspicion flashed into my mind. I strode forward, and turning the handle of the door, pulled it open. And then I was not surprised that Brodribb had been startled. Within a yard of my face, clear, distinct and solid, was an inverted head, floating in mid-air in the pitch-dark room. Of course, being prepared for it, I saw at a glance what it was ; recognised my own features, strangely and horribly altered as they were by their inverted position. But even now that I knew what it was, the thing had a most appalling, uncanny aspect.

" Now," said Thorndyke, " let us go in and explode the mystery. Just stand outside the door, Jervis, while I demonstrate."

He produced a sheet of white paper from his pocket, and smoothing it out, let our two friends into the room.

" First," said he, holding the paper out flat at the eye-level, " you see on this paper a picture of Dr. Jervis's head upside down."

" So there is," said Brodribb ; " like a magic-lantern picture."

" Exactly like," agreed Thorndyke ; " and of exactly the same nature. Now let us see how it is produced."

He struck a match and lit the gas ; and instantly all our eyes turned towards the open dressing-table.

" But that is not the same mirror that we saw just now," said Brodribb.

" No," replied Thorndyke. " The frame is reversible on a sliding hinge and I have turned it round. On one side is the ordinary flat looking-glass which you saw before ; on the other is this concave shaving-mirror. You observe that, if you stand close to it, you see your face the right way up and magnified ; if you go back to the door, you see your head upside down and smaller."

" But," objected Lumley, " the head looked quite solid and seemed to be right out in the room."

" So it was, and is still. But the effect of reality is destroyed by the fact that you can now see the frame of the mirror enclosing the image, so that the head appears to be in the mirror. But in the dark, you could only see the image; the mirror was invisible."

Brodribb reflected on this explanation. Presently he said :

" I don't think I quite understand it now."

Thorndyke took a pencil from his pocket and began to draw a diagram on the sheet of paper that he still held.

" The figure that you see in an ordinary flat looking-glass," he explained, " is what is called a ' virtual image.' It appears to be behind the mirror, but of course it is not there. It is an optical illusion. But the image from a concave mirror is in front of the mirror and is a real image like that of a magic-lantern or a camera, and, like them, inverted. This diagram will explain matters. Here is Lumley standing at the open door of the room. His figure is well lighted by the gas over the door (which, however, throws no light into the room) and is clearly reflected by the mirror, which throws forward a bright inverted image. But, as the room is dark and the mirror invisible, he sees only the image, which looks like—and in fact is—a real object standing in mid-air."

" But why did I see only the head ? " asked Lumley.

" Because the head occupied the whole of the mirror. If the mirror had been large enough you would have seen the full-length figure."

Lumley reflected for a moment. " It almost looks as if this had been arranged," he said at length.

" Of course it has been arranged," said Thorndyke ; " and very cleverly arranged, too. And now let us go and see if anything else has been arranged. Which is Mr. Price's room ? "

" He has three rooms, which open out of this corridor," said Lumley ; and he conducted us to a door at the farther end, which Thorndyke tried and found locked.

" It is a case for the smoker's companion," said he, producing from his pocket an instrument that went by that name, but which looked suspiciously like a pick-lock. At any rate, after one or two trials—which Mr. Brodribb watched with an appreciative smile—the bolt shot back and the door opened.

We entered what was evidently the bedroom, around which Thorndyke cast a rapid glance and then asked :

" What are the other rooms ? "

" I think he uses them to tinker in," said Lumley, " but I don't quite know what he does in them. All three rooms communicate."

We advanced to the door of communication and, finding it unlocked, passed through into the next room. Here, on a large table by the window, was a litter of various tools and appliances.

" What is that thing with the wooden screws ? " Brodribb asked.

" A bookbinder's sewing-press," replied Thorndyke. " And here are some boxes of finishing tools. Let us look over them."

He took up the boxes one after the other and inspected the ends of the tools—brass stamps for impressing the ornaments on book covers. Presently he lifted out two, a leaf and a flower. Then he produced from his coat pocket the little manuscript book, and laying it on the table, picked up from the floor a little fragment of leather. Placing this also on the table, he pressed each of the tools on it, leaving a clear impression of a leaf and a flower. Finally he laid the scrap of leather on the book, when it was obvious that the leaf and flower were identical replicas of the leaves and flowers which formed the decoration of the book cover.

" This is very curious," said Lumley. " They seem to be exactly alike."

" They are exactly alike," said Thorndyke. " I affirm that the tooling on that book was done with these tools, and the leaves sewn on that press."

" But the book is a hundred years old," objected Lumley.

Thorndyke shook his head. " The leather is old," said he, " but the book is new. We have tested the paper and found it to be of recent manufacture. But now let us see what is in that little cupboard. There seem to be some bottles there."

He ran his eye along the shelves, crowded with bottles and jars of varnish, glair, oil, cement and other material.

" Here," he said, taking down a small bottle of dark-coloured powder, " is some aniline brown. That probably produced the ancient and faded writing. But this is more illuminating—in more senses than one." He picked out a little, wide-mouthed bottle labelled, " Radium Paint for the hands and figures of luminous watches."

" Ha ! " exclaimed Brodribb ; " a very illuminating discovery, as you say." •

" And that," said Thorndyke, looking keenly round the
room, " seems to be all there is here. Shall we take a glance
at the third room ? "

We passed through the communicating doorway and found
ourselves in a small apartment, practically unfurnished and
littered with trunks, bags and various lumber. As we stood
looking about us, Thorndyke sniffed suspiciously.

" I seem to detect a sort of mousy odour," said he, glancing
round inquisitively. " Do you notice it, Jervis ? "

I did ; and with the obvious idea in my mind began to
prowl round the room in search of the source. Suddenly my
eye lighted on a smallish box, in the top of which a number
of gimlet-holes had been bored. I raised the lid and peered
in. The interior was covered with filth and on the bottom
lay a dead bat.

We all stood for a few seconds looking in silence at the
little corpse. Then Thorndyke closed the box and tucked it
under his arm.

" This completes the case, I think," said he. " What
time does Price return ? "

" He is expected home about seven o'clock," said Lumley.
Then he added with a troubled expression :

" I don't understand all this. What does it mean ? "

" It is very simple," replied Thorndyke. " You have a
sham ancient book containing an evidently fabulous story
of supernatural events ; and you have a series of appliances
and arrangements for producing illusions which seem to
repeat those events. The book was planted where it was certain to be found and read, and the illusions began after it was
known that it actually had been read. It is a conspiracy."

" But why ? " demanded Lumley. " What was the
object ? "

" My dear Frank," said Brodribb, " you seem to forget
that Price is the next of kin and the heir to your estate on
your death."

Lumley's eyes filled. He seemed overcome with grief and
disgust.

" It is incredible," he murmured huskily. " The baseness
of it is beyond belief."

Price and his wife arrived home at about seven o'clock. A meal had been prepared for them, and when they had finished, a servant was sent in to ask Mr. Price to speak with Mr. Brodribb in the study. There we all awaited him, Lumley being present by his own wish ; and on the table were deposited the little book, the scrap of leather, the two finishing tools, the pot of radium paint and the box containing the dead bat. Presently Price entered, accompanied by his wife ; and at the sight of the objects on the table they both turned deadly pale. Mr. Brodribb placed chairs for them, and when they were seated he began in a dry, stern voice :

" I have sent for you, Mr. Price, to give you certain information. These two gentlemen, Dr. Thorndyke and Dr. Jervis, are eminent criminal lawyers whom I have commissioned to make certain investigations and to advise me in this matter. Their investigations have disclosed the existence of a forged manuscript, a dead bat, a pot of luminous paint and a concave mirror. I need not enlarge on these discoveries. My intention is to prosecute you and your wife for conspiracy to procure the suicide of Mr. Frank Lumley. But, at Mr. Lumley's request, I have consented to delay the proceedings for forty-eight hours. During that period you will be at liberty to act as you think best."

For some seconds there was a tense silence. The two crestfallen conspirators sat with their eyes fixed on the floor, and Mrs. Price choked down a half-hysterical sob. Then they rose ; and Price, without looking at any of us, said in a low voice :

" Very well. Then I suppose we had better clear out."

" And the best thing, too," remarked Brodribb, when they had gone ; " for I doubt if we could have carried our bluff into court."

On the wall of our sitting-room in the Temple there hang, to this day, two keys. One is that of the postern gate of Burling Court, and the other belongs to the suite of rooms that were once occupied by Mr. Lewis Price ; and they hang there, by Frank Lumley's wish, as a token that Burling Court is a country home to which we have access at all hours and seasons as tenants in virtue of an inalienable right.

Reprinted with the Author's permission from *The Thorndyke Omnibus*.

THE CASE OF THE WHITE FOOT-PRINTS

"WELL," said my friend Foxton, pursuing a familiar and apparently inexhaustible topic, "I'd sooner have your job than my own."

"I've no doubt you would," was my unsympathetic reply. "I never met a man who wouldn't. We all tend to consider other men's jobs in terms of their advantages and our own in terms of their drawbacks. It is human nature."

"Oh, it's all very well for you to be so beastly philosophical," retorted Foxton. "You wouldn't be if you were in my place. Here, in Margate, it's measles, chicken-pox and scarlatina all the summer, and bronchitis, colds and rheumatism all the winter. A deadly monotony. Whereas you and Thorndyke sit there in your chambers and let your clients feed you up with the raw material of romance. Why, your life is a sort of everlasting Adelphi drama."

"You exaggerate, Foxton," said I. "We, like you, have our routine work, only it is never heard of outside the Law Courts ; and you, like every other doctor, must run up against mystery and romance from time to time."

Foxton shook his head as he held out his hand for my cup. "I don't," said he. "My practice yields nothing but an endless round of dull routine."

And then, as if in commentary on this last statement, the housemaid burst into the room and, with hardly dissembled agitation, exclaimed :

"If you please, sir, the page from Beddingfield's Boarding House says that a lady has been found dead in her bed and would you go round there immediately."

"Very well, Jane," said Foxton, and as the maid retired, he deliberately helped himself to another fried egg and, looking across the table at me, exclaimed : "Isn't that always the way ? Come immediately—now—this very instant, although the patient may have been considering for a day or two whether he'll send for you or not. But directly he decides, you must spring out of bed, or jump up from your breakfast, and run."

" That's quite true," I agreed : " but this really does seem to be an urgent case."

" What's the urgency ? " demanded Foxton. " The woman is already dead. Anyone would think she was in imminent danger of coming to life again and that my instant arrival was the only thing that could prevent such a catastrophe."

" You've only a third-hand statement that she is dead," said I. " It is just possible that she isn't ; and even if she is, as you will have to give evidence at the inquest, you don't want the police to get there first and turn out the room before you've made your inspection."

" Gad ! " exclaimed Foxton. " I hadn't thought of that. Yes. You're right. I'll hop round at once."

He swallowed the remainder of the egg at a single gulp and rose from the table. Then he paused and stood for a few moments looking down at me irresolutely.

" I wonder, Jervis," he said, " if you would mind coming round with me. You know all the medico-legal ropes, and I don't. What do you say ? "

I agreed instantly, having, in fact, been restrained only by delicacy from making the suggestion myself ; and when I had fetched from my room my pocket camera and telescopic tripod, we set forth together without further delay.

Beddingfield's Boarding House was but a few minutes' walk from Foxton's residence, being situated near the middle of Ethelred Road, Cliftonville, a quiet, suburban street which abounded in similar establishments, many of which, I noticed, were undergoing a spring-cleaning and renovation to prepare them for the approaching season.

" That's the house," said Foxton, " where that woman is standing at the front door. Look at the boarders, collected at the dining-room window. There's a rare commotion in that house, I'll warrant."

Here, arriving at the house, he ran up the steps and accosted in sympathetic tones the elderly woman who stood by the open street door.

" What a dreadful thing this is, Mrs. Beddingfield ! Terrible ! Most distressing for you ! "

" Ah, you're right, Dr. Foxton," she replied. " It's an

awful affair. Shocking. So bad for business, too. I do hope and trust there won't be any scandal."

" I'm sure I hope not," said Foxton. " There shan't be if I can help it. And as my friend, Dr. Jervis, who is staying with me for a few days, is a lawyer as well as a doctor, we shall have the best advice. When was the affair discovered ? "

" Just before I sent for you, Dr. Foxton. The maid noticed that Mrs. Toussaint—that is the poor creature's name—had not taken in her hot water, so she knocked at the door. As she couldn't get any answer, she tried the door and found it bolted on the inside, and then she came and told me. I went up and knocked loudly, and then, as I couldn't get any reply, I told our boy, James, to force the door open with a case-opener, which he did quite easily as the bolt was only a small one. Then I went in, all of a tremble, for I had a presentiment that there was something wrong ; and there she was, lying stone dead, with a most 'orrible stare on her face and an empty bottle in her hand."

" A bottle, eh ! " said Foxton.

" Yes. She'd made away with herself, poor thing ! and all on account of some silly love affair—and it was hardly even that."

" Ah," said Foxton. " The usual thing. You must tell us about that later. Now we'd better go up and see the patient—at least the—er—perhaps you'll show us the room, Mrs. Beddingfield."

The landlady turned and preceded us up the stairs to the first-floor back, where she paused, and softly opening a door, peered nervously into the room. As we stepped past her and entered, she seemed inclined to follow, but, at a significant glance from me, Foxton persuasively ejected her and closed the door. Then we stood silent for a while and looked about us.

In the aspect of the room there was something strangely incongruous with the tragedy that had been enacted within its walls ; a mingling of the commonplace and the terrible that almost amounted to anticlimax. Through the wide-open window the bright spring sunshine streamed in on the garish wall-paper and cheap furniture ; from the street below, the periodic shouts of a man selling " sole and mack-ro ! " broke into the brisk staccato of a barrel-organ, and both sounds

mingled with a raucous voice close at hand, cheerfully trol-
ling a popular song, and accounted for by a linen-clad elbow
that bobbed in front of the window and evidently apper-
tained to a house painter on an adjacent ladder.

It was all very commonplace and familiar and discord-
antly out of character with the stark figure that lay on the
bed like a waxen effigy symbolic of tragedy.   Here was none
of that gracious somnolence in which death often presents
itself with a suggestion of eternal repose.   This woman was
dead ; horribly, aggressively dead.   The thin, sallow face
was rigid as stone, the dark eyes stared into infinite space
with a horrid fixity that was quite disturbing to look on.
And yet the posture of the corpse was not uneasy, being, in
fact, rather curiously symmetrical, with both arms outside
the bed-clothes and both hands closed, the right grasping, as
Mrs. Beddingfield had said, an empty bottle.

" Well," said Foxton, as he stood looking down on the dead
woman, " it seems a pretty clear case.   She appears to have
laid herself out and kept hold of the bottle so that there
should be no mistake.   How long do you suppose this woman
has been dead, Jervis ? "

I felt the rigid limbs, and tested the temperature of the
body surface.

" Not less than six hours," I replied.   " Probably more.
I should say that she died about two o'clock this morning."

" And that is about all we can say," said Foxton, " until
the post-mortem has been made.   Everything looks quite
straightforward.   No signs of a struggle or marks of violence.
The blood on the mouth is probably due to her biting her
lip when she drank from the bottle.   Yes ; here's a little cut
on the inside of the lip, corresponding to the upper incisors.
By the way, I wonder if there is anything left in the
bottle."

As he spoke, he drew the small, unlabelled, green glass
phial from the closed hand—out of which it slipped quite
easily—and held it up to the light.

" Yes," he exclaimed, " there's more than a drachm left ;
quite enough for an analysis.   But I don't recognise the
smell.   Do you ? "

I sniffed at the bottle and was aware of a faint unfamiliar
vegetable odour.

" No," I answered.   " It appears to be a watery solution

of some kind, but I can't give it a name. Where is the cork ? "

" I haven't seen it," he replied. " Probably it is on the floor somewhere."

We both stooped to look for the missing cork and presently found it in the shadow, under the little bedside table. But, in the course of that brief search, I found something else, which had indeed been lying in full view all the time—a wax match. Now a wax match is a perfectly innocent and very commonplace object, but yet the presence of this one gave me pause. In the first place, women do not, as a rule, use wax matches, though there was not much in that. What was more to the point was that the candlestick by the bedside contained a box of safety matches, and that, as the burned remains of one lay in the tray, it appeared to have been used to light the candle. Then why the wax match ?

While I was turning over this problem Foxton had corked the bottle, wrapped it carefully in a piece of paper which he took from the dressing-table and bestowed it in his pocket.

" Well, Jervis," said he, " I think we've seen everything. The analysis and the post-mortem will complete the case. Shall we go down and hear what Mrs. Beddingfield has to say ? "

But that wax match, slight as was its significance, taken alone, had presented itself to me as the last of a succession of phenomena each of which was susceptible of a sinister inter-pretation, and the cumulative effect of these slight sugges-tions began to impress me somewhat strongly.

" One moment, Foxton," said I. " Don't let us take any-thing for granted. We are here to collect evidence, and we must go warily. There is such a thing as homicidal poison-ing, you know."

" Yes, of course," he replied, " but there is nothing to suggest it in this case ; at least, I see nothing. Do you ? "

" Nothing very positive," said I ; " but there are some facts that seem to call for consideration. Let us go over what we have seen. In the first place, there is a distinct discrepancy in the appearance of the body. The general easy, symmetrical posture, like that of a figure on a tomb, suggests the effect of a slow painless poison. But look at the face. There is nothing reposeful about that. It is very strongly suggestive of pain or terror or both."

"Yes," said Foxton, "that is so. But you can't draw any satisfactory conclusions from the facial expression of dead bodies. Why, men who have been hanged, or even stabbed, often look as peaceful as babes."

"Still," I urged, "it is a fact to be noted. Then there is that cut on the lip. It may have been produced in the way you suggest ; but it may equally well be the result of pressure on the mouth."

Foxton made no comment on this beyond a slight shrug of the shoulders, and I continued :

"Then there is the state of the hand. It was closed, but it did not really grasp the object it contained. You drew the bottle out without any resistance. It simply lay in the closed hand. But that is not a normal state of affairs. As you know, when a person dies grasping any object, either the hand relaxes and lets it drop, or the muscular action passes into cadaveric spasm and grasps the object firmly. And lastly, there is this wax match. Where did it come from ? The dead woman apparently lit her candle with a safety match from the box. It is a small matter, but it wants explaining."

Foxton raised his eyebrows protestingly. "You're like all specialists, Jervis," said he. "You see your speciality in everything. And while you are straining these flimsy suggestions to turn a simple suicide into murder, you ignore the really conclusive fact that the door was bolted and had to be broken open before anyone could get in."

"You are not forgetting, I suppose," said I, "that the window was wide open and that there were house painters about and possibly a ladder left standing against the house."

"As to the ladder," said Foxton, "that is a pure assumption ; but we can easily settle the question by asking that fellow out there if it was or was not left standing last night."

Simultaneously we moved towards the window ; but halfway we both stopped short. For the question of the ladder had in a moment become negligible. Staring up at us from the dull red linoleum which covered the floor were the impressions of a pair of bare feet, imprinted in white paint with the distinctness of a woodcut. There was no need to ask if they had been made by the dead woman : they were unmistakably the feet of a man, and large feet at that. Nor could there be any doubts as to whence those feet had come.

Beginning with startling distinctness under the window, the tracks diminished rapidly in intensity until they reached the carpeted portion of the room, where they vanished abruptly ; and only by the closest scrutiny was it possible to detect the faint traces of the retiring tracks.

Foxton and I stood for some moments gazing in silence at the sinister white shapes ; then we looked at one another.

" You've saved me from a most horrible blunder, Jervis," said Foxton. " Ladder or no ladder, that fellow came in at the window ; and he came in last night, for I saw them painting these window-sills yesterday afternoon. Which side did he come from, I wonder ? "

We moved to the window and looked out on the sill. A set of distinct, though smeared impressions on the new paint gave unneeded confirmation and showed that the intruder had approached from the left side, close to which was a cast-iron stack-pipe, now covered with fresh green paint.

" So," said Foxton, " the presence or absence of the ladder is of no significance. The man got in through the window somehow, and that's all that matters."

" On the contrary," said I, " the point may be of considerable importance in identification. It isn't everyone who could climb up a stack-pipe, whereas most people could make shift to climb a ladder even if it were guarded by a plank. But the fact that the man took off his boots and socks suggests that he came up by the pipe. If he had merely aimed at silencing his foot-falls he would probably have removed his boots only."

From the window we turned to examine more closely the foot-prints on the floor, and while I took a series of measurements with my spring tape, Foxton entered them in my note-book.

" Doesn't it strike you as rather odd, Jervis," said he, " that neither of the little toes has made any mark ? "

" It does indeed," I replied. " The appearances suggest that the little toes were absent, but I have never met with such a condition. Have you ? "

" Never. Of course one is acquainted with the supernumerary toe deformity, but I have never heard of congenitally deficient little toes."

Once more we scrutinised the foot-prints, and even examined those on the window-sill, obscurely marked on the fresh paint ; but, exquisitely distinct as were those on the linoleum, showing every wrinkle and minute skin-marking, not the faintest hint of a little toe was to be seen on either foot.

" It's very extraordinary," said Foxton. " He has certainly lost his little toes, if he ever had any. They couldn't have failed to make some mark. But it's a queer affair Quite a windfall for the police, by the way ; I mean for purposes of identification."

" Yes," I agreed, " and having regard to the importance of the foot-prints, I think it would be wise to get a photograph of them."

" Oh, the police will see to that," said Foxton. " Besides, we haven't got a camera unless you thought of using that little toy snapshotter of yours."

As Foxton was no photographer I did not trouble to explain that my camera, though small, had been specially made for scientific purposes.

" Any photograph is better than none," I said, and with this I opened the tripod and set it over one of the most distinct of the foot-prints, screwed the camera to the gooseneck, carefully framed the foot-print in the finder and adjusted the focus, finally making the exposure by means of an Antinous release. This process I repeated four times, twice on a right foot-print and twice on a left.

" Well," Foxton remarked, " with all those photographs the police ought to be able to pick up the scent."

" Yes, they've got something to go on ; but they'll have to catch their hare before they can cook him. He won't be walking about bare-footed, you know."

" No. It's a poor clue in that respect. And now we may as well be off as we've seen all there is to see. I think we won't have much to say to Mrs. Beddingfield. This is a police case, and the less I'm mixed up in it the better it will be for my practice."

I was faintly amused at Foxton's caution when considered by the light of his utterances at the breakfast table. Apparently his appetite for mystery and romance was easily satisfied. But that was no affair of mine. I waited on the doorstep while he said a few—probably evasive—words to the landlady and then, as we started off together in the direction of the police station, I began to turn over in my mind the salient features of the case. For some time we walked on in silence, and must have been pursuing a parallel train of thought, for, when he at length spoke, he almost put my reflections into words.

" You know, Jervis," said he, " there ought to be a clue in those foot-prints. I realise that you can't tell how many toes a man has by looking at his booted feet. But those unusual foot-prints ought to give an expert a hint as to what sort of man to look for. Don't they convey any hint to you ? "

I felt that Foxton was right ; that if my brilliant colleague, Thorndyke, had been in my place, he would have extracted from those foot-prints some leading fact that would have given the police a start along some definite line of inquiry ; and that belief, coupled with Foxton's challenge, put me on my mettle.

" They offer no particular suggestion to me at this moment," said I, " but I think that, if we consider them systematically, we may be able to draw some useful deductions."

" Very well," said Foxton, " then let us consider them systematically. Fire away. I should like to hear how you work these things out."

Foxton's frankly spectatorial attitude was a little disconcerting, especially as it seemed to commit me to a result that I was by no means confident of attaining. I therefore began a little diffidently.

" We are assuming that both the feet that made those prints were from some cause devoid of little toes. That assumption—which is almost certainly correct—we treat as a fact, and, taking it as our starting-point, the first step in the inquiry is to find some explanation of it. Now there are three possibilities, and only three : deformity, injury, and disease. The toes may have been absent from birth, they may have been lost as a result of mechanical injury, or they may have been lost by disease. Let us take those possibilities in order.

" Deformity we exclude since such a malformation is unknown to us.

" Mechanical injury seems to be excluded by the fact that the two little toes are on opposite sides of the body and could not conceivably be affected by any violence which left the intervening feet uninjured. This seems to narrow the possibilities down to disease ; and the question that arises is, What diseases are there which might result in the loss of both little toes ? "

I looked inquiringly at Foxton, but he merely nodded encouragingly. His rôle was that of listener.

" Well," I pursued, " the loss of both toes seems to exclude local disease, just as it excluded local injury ; and as to general diseases, I can think only of three which might produce this condition—Raynaud's disease, ergotism, and frost-bite."

" You don't call frost-bite a general disease, do you ? " objected Foxton.

" For our present purpose, I do. The effects are local, but the cause—low external temperature—affects the whole body and is a general cause. Well, now, taking the diseases in order, I think we can exclude Raynaud's disease. It does, it is true, occasionally cause the fingers or toes to die and drop off, and the little toes would be especially liable to be affected as being the most remote from the heart. But in such a severe case the other toes would be affected. They would be shrivelled and tapered, whereas, if you remember, the toes of these feet were quite plump and full, to judge by the large impressions they made. So I think we may safely reject Raynaud's disease. There remain ergotism and frost-bite ; and the choice between them is just a question of relative frequency. Frost-bite is more common ; therefore frost-bite is more probable."

" Do they tend equally to affect the little toes ? " asked Foxton.

" As a matter of probability, yes. The poison of ergot acting from within, and intense cold acting from without, contract the small blood-vessels and arrest the circulation. The feet, being the most distant parts of the body from the heart, are the first to feel the effects ; and the little toes, which are the most distant parts of the feet, are the most susceptible of all."

Foxton reflected awhile, and then remarked :

" This is all very well, Jervis, but I don't see that you are much forrader. This man has lost both his little toes, and on your showing, the probabilities are that the loss was due either to chronic ergot poisoning or to frost-bite, with a balance of probability in favour of frost-bite. That's all.

No proof, no verification. Just the law of probability applied to a particular case, which is always unsatisfactory. He may have lost his toes in some totally different way. But even if the probabilities work out correctly, I don't see what use your conclusions would be to the police. They wouldn't tell them what sort of man to look for."

There was a good deal of truth in Foxton's objection. A man who has suffered from ergotism or frost-bite is not externally different from any other man. Still, we had not exhausted the case, as I ventured to point out.

" Don't be premature, Foxton," said I. " Let us pursue our argument a little farther. We have established a probability that this unknown man has suffered either from ergotism or frost-bite. That, as you say, is of no use by itself ; but supposing we can show that these conditions tend to affect a particular class of persons, we shall have established a fact that will indicate a line of investigation. And I think we can. Let us take the case of ergotism first.

." Now, how is chronic ergot poisoning caused ? Not by the medicinal use of the drug, but by the consumption of the diseased rye in which ergot occurs. It is therefore peculiar to countries in which rye is used extensively as food. Those countries, broadly speaking, are the countries of North-Eastern Europe, and especially Russia and Poland.

" Then take the case of frost-bite. Obviously, the most likely person to get frost-bite is the inhabitant of a country with a cold climate. The most rigorous climates inhabited by white people are North America and North-Eastern Europe, especially Russia and Poland. So you see, the areas associated with ergotism and frost-bite overlap to some extent. In fact they do more than overlap ; for a person even slightly affected by ergot would be specially liable to frost-bite, owing to the impaired circulation. The conclusion is that, racially, in both ergotism and frost-bite, the balance of probability is in favour of a Russian, a Pole, or a Scandinavian.

" Then in the case of frost-bite there is the occupation factor. What class of men tend most to become frost-bitten ? Well, beyond all doubt, the greatest sufferers from frost-bite are sailors, especially those on sailing ships, and, naturally, on ships trading to arctic and sub-arctic countries. But the bulk of such sailing ships are those engaged in the

Baltic and Archangel trade ; and the crews of those ships are almost exclusively Scandinavians, Finns, Russians, and Poles.   So that, again, the probabilities point to a native of North-Eastern Europe, and, taken as a whole, by the overlapping of factors, to a Russian, a Pole, or a Scandinavian."

Foxton smiled sardonically.   " Very ingenious, Jervis," said he.   " Most ingenious.   As an academic statement of probabilities, quite excellent.   But for practical purpose absolutely useless.   However, here we are at the police station.   I'll just run in and give them the facts and then go on to the coroner's office."

" I suppose I'd better not come in with you ? " I said.

" Well, no," he replied.   " You see, you have no official connection with the case, and they mightn't like it.   You'd better go and amuse yourself while I get the morning's visits done.   We can talk things over at lunch."

With this he disappeared into the police station, and I turned away with a smile of grim amusement.   Experience is apt to make us a trifle uncharitable, and experience had taught me that those who are the most scornful of academic reasoning are often not above retailing it with some reticence as to its original authorship.   I had a shrewd suspicion that Foxton was at this very moment disgorging my despised " academic statement of probabilities " to an admiring police-inspector.

My way towards the sea lay through Ethelred Road, and I had traversed about half its length and was approaching the house of the tragedy when I observed Mrs. Beddingfield at the bay window.   Evidently she recognised me, for a few moments later she appeared in outdoor clothes on the doorstep and advanced to meet me.

" Have you seen the police ? " she asked as we met.

I replied that Dr. Foxton was even now at the police station.

" Ah ! " she said, " it's a dreadful affair ; most unfortunate, too, just at the beginning of the season.   A scandal is absolute ruin to a boarding-house.   What do you think of the case ?   Will it be possible to hush it up ?   Dr. Foxton said you were a lawyer, I think, Dr. Jervis ? "

" Yes, I am a lawyer, but really I know nothing of the circumstances of this case.   Did I understand that there had been something in the nature of a love affair ? "

" Yes—at least—well, perhaps I oughtn't to have said that. But hadn't I better tell you the whole story ?—that is, if I am not taking up too much of your time."

" I should be interested to hear what led to the disaster," said I.

" Then," she said, " I will tell you all about it. Will you come indoors, or shall I walk a little way with you ? "

As I suspected that the police were at that moment on their way to the house, I chose the latter alternative and led her away seawards at a pretty brisk pace.

" Was this poor lady a widow ? " I asked as we started up the street.

" No, she wasn't," replied Mrs. Beddingfield, " and that was the trouble. Her husband was abroad—at least, he had been, and he was just coming home. A pretty home-coming it will be for him, poor man ! He is an officer in the civil police at Sierra Leone, but he hasn't been there long. He went there for his health."

" What ! To Sierra Leone ! " I exclaimed, for the " White Man's Grave " seemed a queer health resort.

" Yes. You see, Mr. Toussaint is a French Canadian, and it seems that he has always been somewhat of a rolling stone. For some time he was in the Klondyke, but he suffered so much from the cold that he had to come away. It injured his health very severely ; I don't quite know in what way, but I do know that he was quite a cripple for a time. When he got better he looked out for a post in a warm climate and eventually obtained the appointment of Inspector of Civil Police at Sierra Leone. That was about ten months ago, and when he sailed for Africa his wife came to stay with me, and has been here ever since."

" And this love affair that you spoke of ? "

" Yes, but I oughtn't to have called it that. Let me explain what happened. About three months ago a Swedish gentleman—a Mr. Bergson—came to stay here, and he seemed to be very much smitten with Mrs. Toussaint."

" And she ? "

" Oh, she liked him well enough. He is a tall, good-looking man—though for that matter he is no taller than her husband, nor any better looking. Both men are over six feet. But there was no harm so far as she was concerned, excepting that she didn't see the position quite soon enough. She wasn't very discreet, in fact, I thought it necessary to give her a little advice. However, Mr. Bergson left here and went to live at Ramsgate to superintend the unloading of the ice ships (he came from Sweden in one), and I thought the trouble was at an end. But it wasn't, for he took to coming over to see Mrs. Toussaint, and of course I couldn't have that. So at last I had to tell him that he mustn't come to the house again. It was very unfortunate, for on that occasion I think he had been " tasting," as they say in Scotland. He wasn't drunk, but he was excitable and noisy, and when I told him he mustn't come again he made such a disturbance that two of the gentlemen boarders—Mr. Wardale and Mr. Macauley —had to interfere. And then he was most insulting to them, especially to Mr. Macauley, who is a coloured gentleman ; called him a ' buck nigger' and all sorts of offensive names."

" And how did the coloured gentleman take it ? "

" Not very well, I am sorry to say, considering that he is a gentleman—a law student with chambers in the Temple. In fact, his language was so objectionable that Mr. Wardale insisted on my giving him notice on the spot. But I managed to get him taken in next door but one ; you see, Mr. Wardale had been a Commissioner at Sierra Leone—it was through him that Mr. Toussaint got his appointment—so I suppose he was rather on his dignity with coloured people."

" And was that the last you heard of Mr. Bergson ? "

" He never came here again, but he wrote several times to Mrs. Toussaint, asking her to meet him. At last, only a few days ago, she wrote to him and told him that the acquaintance must cease."

" And has it ceased ? "

" As far as I know, it has."

" Then, Mrs. Beddingfield," said I, " what makes you connect the affair with—with what has happened ? "

" Well, you see," she explained, " there is the husband. He was coming home, and is probably in England already."

" Indeed ! " said I.

" Yes," she continued. " He went up into the bush to arrest some natives belonging to one of these gangs of murderers—Leopard Societies, I think they are called—and he got seriously wounded. He wrote to his wife from hospital, saying that he would be sent home as soon as he was fit to travel, and about ten days ago she got a letter from him saying that he was coming by the next ship.

" I noticed that she seemed very nervous and upset when she got the letters from hospital, and still more so when the last letter came. Of course, I don't know what he said to her in those letters. It may be that he had heard something about Mr. Bergson, and threatened to take some action. Of course, I can't say. I only know that she was very nervous and restless, and when we saw in the paper four days ago that the ship he would be coming by had arrived in Liverpool, she seemed dreadfully upset. And she got worse and worse until—well, until last night."

" Has anything been heard of the husband since the ship arrived ? " I asked.

" Nothing whatever," replied Mrs. Beddingfield, with a meaning look at me which I had no difficulty in interpreting. " No letter, no telegram, not a word. And you see, if he hadn't come by that ship he would almost certainly have sent a letter by her. He must have arrived in England, but why hasn't he turned up, or at least sent a wire ? What is he doing ? Why is he staying away ? Can he have heard something ? And what does he mean to do ? That's what kept the poor thing on wires, and that, I feel certain, is what drove her to make away with herself."

It was not my business to contest Mrs. Beddingfield's erroneous deductions. I was seeking information—it seemed that I had nearly exhausted the present source. But one point required amplifying.

" To return to Mr. Bergson, Mrs. Beddingfield," said I. " Do I understand that he is a seafaring man ? "

" He was," she replied. " At present he is settled at Ramsgate as manager of a company in the ice trade, but formerly he was a sailor. I have heard him say that he was one of the crew of an exploring ship that went in search of the North Pole and that he was locked up in the ice for months and months. I should have thought he would have had enough of ice after that."

With this view I expressed warm agreement, and having now obtained all the information that appeared to be available, I proceeded to bring the interview to an end.

" Well, Mrs. Beddingfield," I said, " it is a rather mysterious affair. Perhaps more light may be thrown on it at the inquest. Meanwhile, I should think that it will be wise of you to keep your own counsel as far as outsiders are concerned."

The remainder of the morning I spent pacing the smooth stretch of sand that lies to the east of the jetty, and reflecting on the evidence that I had acquired in respect of this singular crime. Evidently there was no lack of clues in this case. On the contrary, there were two quite obvious lines of inquiry, for both the Swede and the missing husband presented the characters of the hypothetical murderer. Both had been exposed to the conditions which tend to produce frost-bite ; one of them had probably been a consumer of rye meal, and both might be said to have a motive—though, to be sure, it was a very insufficient one—for committing the crime. Still, in both cases the evidence was merely speculative ; it suggested a line of investigation, but it did nothing more.

When I met Foxton at lunch I was sensible of a curious change in his manner. His previous expansiveness had given place to marked reticence and a certain official secretiveness.

"I don't think you know, Jervis," he said, when I opened the subject, "that we had better discuss this affair. You see, I am the principal witness, and while the case is *sub judice*—well, in fact, the police don't want the case talked about."

"But surely I am a witness, too, and an expert witness, moreover——"

"That isn't the view of the police. They look on you as more or less of an amateur, and as you have no official connection with the case, I don't think they propose to subpœna you. Superintendent Platt, who is in charge of the case, wasn't very pleased at my having taken you to the house. Said it was quite irregular. Oh, and by the way, he says you must hand over those photographs."

"But isn't Platt going to have the foot-prints photographed on his own account ? " I objected.

"Of course he is. He is going to have a set of proper photographs taken by an expert photographer—he was mightily amused when he heard about your little snapshot affair. Oh, you can trust Platt. He is a great man. He has had a course of instruction at the Finger-print Department in London."

"I don't see how that is going to help him, as there aren't

any finger-prints in this case." This was a mere fly-cast on my part, but Foxton rose at once at the rather clumsy bait. "Oh, aren't there?" he exclaimed. "You didn't happen to spot them, but they were there. Platt has got the prints of a complete right hand. That is in strict confidence, you know," he added, with somewhat belated caution.

Foxton's sudden reticence restrained me from uttering the obvious comment on the superintendent's achievement. I returned to the subject of the photographs.

"Suppose I decline to hand over my film?" said I.

"But I hope you won't—and, in fact, you mustn't. I am officially connected with the case, and I've got to live with these people. As the police-surgeon, I am responsible for the medical evidence, and Platt expects me to get those photographs from you. Obviously you can't keep them. It would be most irregular."

It was useless to argue. Evidently the police did not want me to be introduced into the case, and after all, the superintendent was within his rights, if he chose to regard me as a private individual and to demand the surrender of the film.

Nevertheless I was loath to give up the photographs, at least, until I had carefully studied them. The case was within my own speciality of practice, and was a strange and interesting one. Moreover, it appeared to be in unskilled hands, judging from the finger-print episode, and then experience had taught me to treasure up small scraps of chance evidence, since one never knew when one might be drawn into a case in a professional capacity. In effect, I decided not to give up the photographs, though that decision committed me to a ruse that I was not very willing to adopt. I would rather have acted quite straightforwardly.

"Well, if you insist, Foxton," I said, "I will hand over the film or, if you like, I will destroy it in your presence."

"I think Platt would rather have the film uninjured," said Foxton. "Then he'll know, you know," he added with a sly grin.

In my heart, I thanked Foxton for that grin. It made my own guileful proceedings so much easier; for a suspicious man invites you to get the better of him if you can.

After lunch I went up to my room, locked the door and took the little camera from my pocket. Having fully wound up the film, I extracted it, wrapped it up carefully and bestowed it in my inside breast-pocket. Then I inserted a fresh film, and going to the open window, took four successive snapshots of the sky. This done, I closed the camera, slipped it into my pocket and went downstairs. Foxton was in the hall, brushing his hat, as I descended, and at once renewed his demand.

" About those photographs, Jervis," said he; " I shall be looking in at the police station presently, so if you wouldn't mind——"

" To be sure," said I. " I will give you the film now, if you like."

Taking the camera from my pocket, I solemnly wound up the remainder of the film, extracted it, stuck down the loose end with ostentatious care, and handed it to him.

" Better not expose it to the light," I said, going the whole hog of deception, " or you may fog the exposures."

Foxton took the spool from me as if it were hot—he was not a photographer—and thrust it into his handbag. He was still thanking me quite profusely when the front-door bell rang.

The visitor who stood revealed when Foxton opened the door was a small, spare gentleman with a complexion of the peculiar brown-papery quality that suggests long residence in the Tropics. He stepped in briskly and introduced himself and his business without preamble.

" My name is Wardale—boarder at Beddingfield's. I've called with reference to the tragic event which——"

Here Foxton interposed in his frostiest official tone. " I am afraid, Mr. Wardale, I can't give you any information about the case at present."

" I saw you two gentlemen at the house this morning," Mr. Wardale continued, but Foxton again cut him short.

" You did. We were there—or at least, I was—as the representative of the law, and while the case is *sub judice* ——"

" It isn't yet," interrupted Wardale.

" Well, I can't enter into any discussion of it——"

" I am not asking you to," said Wardale, a little impatiently. " But I understand that one of you is Dr. Jervis."

" I am," said I.

" I must really warn you," Foxton began again ; but Mr. Wardale interrupted testily :

" My dear sir, I am a lawyer and a magistrate and understand perfectly well what is and what is not permissible. I have come simply to make a professional engagement with Dr. Jervis."

" In what way can I be of service to you ? " I asked.

" I will tell you," said Mr. Wardale. " This poor lady, whose death has occurred in so mysterious a manner, was the wife of a man who was, like myself, a servant of the Government of Sierra Leone. I was the friend of both of them ; and in the absence of the husband, I should like to have the inquiry into the circumstances of this lady's death watched by a competent lawyer with the necessary special knowledge of medical evidence. Will you or your colleague, Dr. Thorndyke, undertake to watch the case for me ? "

Of course I was willing to undertake the case and said so.

" Then," said Mr. Wardale, " I will instruct my solicitor to write to you and formally retain you in the case. Here is my card. You will find my name in the Colonial Office List, and you know my address here."

He handed me his card, wished us both good-afternoon, and then, with a stiff little bow, turned and took his departure.

" I think I had better run up to town and confer with Thorndyke," said I. " How do the trains run ? "

" There is a good train in about three-quarters of an hour," replied Foxton.

" Then I will go by it, but I shall come down again to-morrow or the next day, and probably Thorndyke will come down with me."

" Very well," said Foxton. " Bring him in to lunch or dinner, but I can't put him up, I am afraid."

" It would be better not," said I. " Your friend, Platt, wouldn't like it. He won't want Thorndyke—or me either, for that matter. And what about those photographs ? Thorndyke will want them, you know."

" He can't have them," said Foxton doggedly, " unless Platt is willing to hand them back ; which I don't suppose he will be."

I had private reasons for thinking otherwise, but I kept them to myself ; and as Foxton went forth on his afternoon round, I returned upstairs to pack my suit-case and write the telegram to Thorndyke informing him of my movements.

It was only a quarter past five when I let myself into our chambers in King's Bench Walk. To my relief I found my colleague at home and our laboratory assistant, Polton, in the act of laying tea for two.

" I gather," said Thorndyke as we shook hands, " that my learned brother brings grist to the mill ? "

" Yes," I replied. " Nominally a watching brief, but I think you will agree with me that it is a case for independent investigation."

" Will there be anything in my line, sir ? " inquired Polton, who was always agog at the word " investigation."

" There is a film to be developed. Four exposures of white foot-prints on a dark ground."

" Ah ! " said Polton, " you'll want good strong negatives and they ought to be enlarged if they are from the little camera. Can you give me the dimensions ? "

I wrote out the measurements from my notebook and handed him the paper together with the spool of film, with which he retired gleefully to the laboratory.

" And now, Jervis," said Thorndyke, " while Polton is operating on the film and we are discussing our tea, let us have a sketch of the case."

I gave him more than a sketch, for the events were recent and I had carefully sorted out the facts during my journey to town, making rough notes, which I now consulted. To my rather lengthy recital he listened in his usual attentive manner, without any comment, excepting in regard to my manœuvre to retain possession of the exposed film.

" It's almost a pity you didn't refuse," said he. " They could hardly have enforced their demand, and my feeling is that it is more convenient as well as more dignified to avoid direct deception unless one is driven to it. But perhaps you considered that you were."

As a matter of fact I had at the time, but I had since come to Thorndyke's opinion. My little manœuvre was going to be a source of inconvenience presently.

" Well," said Thorndyke, when I had finished my recital, " I think we may take it that the police theory is, in the main, your own theory derived from Foxton."

" I think so, excepting that I learn from Foxton that Superintendent Platt has obtained the complete finger-prints of a right hand."

Thorndyke raised his eyebrows. " Finger-prints ! " he exclaimed. "Why, the fellow must be a mere simpleton. But there," he added, " everybody—police, lawyers, magistrates and even judges—seems to lose every vestige of common sense as soon as the subject of finger-prints is raised. But it would be interesting to know how he got them and what they are like. We must try to find that out. However, to return to your case, since your theory and the police theory are probably the same, we may as well consider the value of your inferences.

" At present we are dealing with the case in the abstract. Our data are largely assumptions, and our inferences are largely derived from an application of the mathematical laws of probability. Thus we assume that a murder has been committed, whereas it may turn out to have been suicide. We assume the murder to have been committed by the person who made the foot-prints, and we assume that that person has no little toes, whereas he may have retracted little toes which do not touch the ground and so leave no impression. Assuming the little toes to be absent, we account for their absence by considering known cases in the order of their probability. Excluding—quite properly, I think—Raynaud's disease, we arrive at frost-bite and ergotism. But two persons, both of whom are of a stature corresponding to the size of the foot-prints, may have had a motive—though a very inadequate one—for committing the crime, and both have been exposed to the conditions which tend to produce frost-bite, while one of them has probably been exposed to the conditions which tend to produce ergotism. The laws of probability point to both of these two men ; and the chances in favour of the Swede being the murderer rather than the Canadian would be represented by the common factor—frost-bite—multiplied by the additional factor, ergotism. But this is purely speculative at present. There is no evidence that either man has ever been frost-bitten or has ever eaten spurred rye. Nevertheless, it is a perfectly sound method at this stage. It indicates a line of investigation. If it should transpire that either man has suffered from frost-bite or ergotism, a definite advance would have been made. But here is Polton with a couple of finished prints. How on earth did you manage it in the time, Polton ? "

"Why, you see, sir, I just dried the film with spirit," replied Polton. "It saves a lot of time. I will let you have a pair of enlargements in about a quarter of an hour."

Handing us the two wet prints, each stuck on a glass plate, he retired to the laboratory, and Thorndyke and I proceeded to scrutinise the photographs with the aid of our pocket lenses. The promised enlargements were really hardly necessary excepting for the purpose of comparative measurements, for the image of the white foot-print, fully two inches long, was so microscopically sharp that, with the assistance of the lens, the minutest detail could be clearly seen.

"There is certainly not a vestige of little toe," remarked Thorndyke, "and the plump appearance of the other toes supports your rejection of Raynaud's disease. Does the character of the foot-print convey any other suggestion to you, Jervis?"

"It gives me the impression that the man had been accustomed to go bare-footed in early life and had only taken to boots comparatively recently. The position of the great toe suggests this, and the presence of a number of small scars on the toes and ball of the foot seems to confirm it. A person walking bare-foot would sustain innumerable small wounds from treading on small, sharp objects."

Thorndyke looked dissatisfied. "I agree with you," he said, "as to the suggestion offered by the undeformed state of the great toes ; but those little pits do not convey to me the impression of scars produced as you suggest. Still, you may be right."

Here our conversation was interrupted by a knock on the outer oak. Thorndyke stepped out through the lobby and I heard him open the door. A moment or two later he re-entered, accompanied by a short, brown-faced gentleman whom I instantly recognised as Mr. Wardale.

"I must have come up by the same train as you," he remarked as we shook hands, "and to a certain extent, I suspect, on the same errand. I thought I would like to put our arrangement on a business footing, as I am a stranger to both of you."

"What do you want us to do?" asked Thorndyke.

"I want you to watch the case, and, if necessary, to look into the facts independently."

"Can you give us any information that may help us?"

Mr. Wardale reflected. " I don't think I can," he said at length. " I have no facts that you have not, and any surmises of mine might be misleading. I had rather you kept an open mind. But perhaps we might go into the question of costs."

This, of course, was somewhat difficult, but Thorndyke contrived to indicate the probable liabilities involved to Mr. Wardale's satisfaction.

" There is one other little matter," said Wardale as he rose to depart. " I have got a suit-case here which Mrs. Beddingfield lent me to bring some things up to town. It is one that Mr. Macauley left behind when he went away from the boarding-house. Mrs. Beddingfield suggested that I might leave it at his chambers when I had finished with it ; but I don't know his address, excepting that it is somewhere in the Temple, and I don't want to meet the fellow if he should happen to have come up to town."

" Is it empty ? " asked Thorndyke.

" Excepting for a suit of pyjamas and a pair of shocking old slippers." He opened the suit-case as he spoke and exhibited its contents with a grin.

" Characteristic of a negro, isn't it ? Pink silk pyjamas and slippers about three sizes too small."

" Very well," said Thorndyke. " I will get my man to find out the address and leave it there."

As Mr. Wardale went out, Polton entered with the enlarged photographs, which showed the foot-prints the natural size. Thorndyke handed them to me, and as I sat down to examine them he followed his assistant to the laboratory. He returned in a few minutes, and after a brief inspection of the photographs, remarked :

" They show us nothing more than we have seen, though they may be useful later. So your stock of facts is all we have to go on at present. Are you going home to-night ?"

" Yes, I shall go back to Margate to-morrow."

" Then, as I have to call at Scotland Yard, we may as well walk to Charing Cross together."

As we walked down the Strand we gossiped on general topics, but before we separated at Charing Cross, Thorndyke reverted to the case.

" Let me know the date of the inquest," said he, " and try to find out what the poison was—if it was really a poison."

" The liquid that was left in the bottle seemed to be a watery solution of some kind," said I, " as I think I mentioned."

" Yes," said Thorndyke. " Possibly a watery infusion of strophanthus."

" Why strophanthus ? " I asked.

" Why not ? " demanded Thorndyke. And with this and an inscrutable smile, he turned and walked down Whitehall.

Three days later I found myself at Margate sitting beside Thorndyke in a room adjoining the Town Hall, in which the inquest on the death of Mrs. Toussaint was to be held. Already the coroner was in his chair, the jury were in their seats and the witnesses assembled in a group of chairs apart. These included Foxton, a stranger who sat by him—presumably the other medical witness—Mrs. Beddingfield, Mr. Wardale, the police superintendent and a well-dressed coloured man, whom I correctly assumed to be Mr. Macauley.

As I sat by my rather sphinx-like colleague my mind recurred for the hundredth time to his extraordinary powers of mental synthesis. That parting remark of his as to the possible nature of the poison had brought home to me in a flash the fact that he already had a definite theory of this crime, and that his theory was not mine nor that of the police. True, the poison might not be strophanthus, after all, but that would not alter the position. He had a theory of the crime, but yet he was in possession of no facts excepting those with which I had supplied him. Therefore those facts contained the material for a theory, whereas I had deduced from them nothing but the bald, ambiguous mathematical probabilities.

The first witness called was naturally Dr. Foxton, who described the circumstances already known to me. He further stated that he had been present at the autopsy, that he had found, on the throat and limbs of the deceased, bruises that suggested a struggle and violent restraint. The immediate cause of death was heart failure, but whether that failure was due to shock, terror, or the action of a poison he could not positively say.

The next witness was a Dr. Prescott, an expert pathologist and toxicologist. He had made the autopsy and agreed with

Dr. Foxton as to the cause of death. He had examined the liquid contained in the bottle taken from the hand of the deceased and found it to be a watery infusion or decoction of strophanthus seeds. He had analysed the fluid contained in the stomach and found it to consist largely of the same infusion.

" Is infusion of strophanthus seeds used in medicine ? " the coroner asked.

" No," was the reply. " The tincture is the form in which strophanthus is administered unless it is given in the form of strophanthine."

" Do you consider that the strophanthus caused or contributed to death ? "

" It is difficult to say," replied Dr. Prescott. " Strophanthus is a heart poison, and there was a very large poisonous dose. But very little had been absorbed, and the appearances were not inconsistent with death from shock."

" Could death have been self-produced by the voluntary taking of the poison ? " asked the coroner.

" I should say, decidedly not. Dr. Foxton's evidence shows that the bottle was almost certainly placed in the hands of the deceased after death, and this is in complete agreement with the enormous dose and small absorption."

" Would you say that appearances point to suicidal or homicidal poisoning ? "

" I should say that they point to homicidal poisoning, but that death was probably due mainly to shock."

This concluded the expert's evidence. It was followed by that of Mrs. Beddingfield, which brought out nothing new to me but the fact that a trunk had been broken open and a small attaché case belonging to the deceased abstracted and taken away.

" Do you know what the deceased kept in that case ? " the coroner asked.

" I have seen her put her husband's letters into it. She had quite a number of them. I don't know what else she kept in it except, of course, her cheque book."

" Had she any considerable balance at the bank ? "

" I believe she had. Her husband used to send most of his pay home and she used to pay it in and leave it with the bank. She might have two or three hundred pounds to her credit."

As Mrs. Beddingfield concluded Mr. Wardale was called, and he was followed by Mr. Macauley. The evidence of both was quite brief and concerned entirely with the disturbance made by Bergson, whose absence from the court I had already noted.

The last witness was the police superintendent, and he, as I had expected, was decidedly reticent. He did refer to the foot-prints, but, like Foxton—who presumably had his instructions—he abstained from describing their peculiarities. Nor did he say anything about finger-prints. As to the identity of the criminal, that had to be further inquired into. Suspicion had at first fastened upon Bergson, but it had since transpired that the Swede sailed from Ramsgate on an ice-ship two days before the occurrence of the tragedy. Then suspicion had pointed to the husband, who was known to have landed at Liverpool four days before the death of his wife and who had mysteriously disappeared. But he (the superintendent) had only that morning received a telegram from the Liverpool police informing him that the body of Toussaint had been found floating in the Mersey, and that it bore a number of wounds of an apparently homicidal character. Apparently he had been murdered and his corpse thrown into the river.

" This is very terrible," said the coroner. " Does this second murder throw any light on the case which we are investigating ? "

" I think it does," replied the officer, without any great conviction, however, " but it is not advisable to go into details."

" Quite so," agreed the coroner. " Most inexpedient. But are we to understand that you have a clue to the perpetrator of this crime—assuming a crime to have been committed ? "

" Yes," replied Platt. " We have several important clues."

" And do they point to any particular individual ? "

The superintendent hesitated. " Well——" he began, with some embarrassment, but the coroner interrupted him.

" Perhaps the question is indiscreet. We mustn't hamper the police, gentlemen, and the point is not really material to our inquiry. You would rather we waived that question, superintendent ? "

" If you please, sir," was the emphatic reply.

" Have any cheques from the deceased woman's cheque-book been presented at the bank ? "

" Not since her death. I inquired at the bank only this morning."

This concluded the evidence, and after a brief but capable summing-up by the coroner, the jury returned a verdict of " wilful murder against some person unknown."

As the proceedings terminated, Thorndyke rose and turned round, and then to my surprise I perceived Superintendent Miller, of the Criminal Investigation Department, who had come in unperceived by me and was sitting immediately behind us.

" I have followed your instructions, sir," said he, addressing Thorndyke, " but before we take any definite action I should like to have a few words with you."

He led the way to an adjoining room, and as we entered we were followed by Superintendent Platt and Dr. Foxton.

" Now, doctor," said Miller, carefully closing the door, " I have carried out your suggestions. Mr. Macauley is being detained, but before we commit ourselves to an arrest, we must have something to go upon. I shall want you to make out a prima facie case."

" Very well," said Thorndyke, laying upon the table the small, green suit-case that was his almost invariable companion.

" I've seen that prima facie case before," Miller remarked with a grin, as Thorndyke unlocked it and drew out a large envelope. " Now, what have you got there ? "

As Thorndyke extracted from the envelope Polton's enlargements of my small photographs, Platt's eyes appeared to bulge, while Foxton gave me a quick glance of reproach.

" These," said Thorndyke, " are the full-sized photographs of the foot-prints of the suspected murderer. Superintendent Platt can probably verify them."

Rather reluctantly Platt produced from his pocket a pair of whole-plate photographs, which he laid beside the enlargements.

" Yes," said Miller, after comparing them, " they are the same foot-prints. But you say, doctor, that they are Macauley's foot-prints. Now, what evidence have you ? "

Thorndyke again had recourse to the green case, from which

he produced two copper plates mounted on wood and coated with printing ink.

" I propose," said he, lifting the plates out of their protecting frame, " that we take prints of Macauley's feet and compare them with the photographs."

" Yes," said Platt. " And then there are the finger-prints that we've got. We can test those, too."

" You don't want finger-prints if you've got a set of toe-prints," objected Miller.

" With regard to those finger-prints," said Thorndyke. " May I ask if they were obtained from the bottle ? "

" They were," Platt admitted.

" And were there any other finger-prints ? "

" No," replied Platt. " These were the only ones."

As he spoke he laid on the table a photograph showing the prints of the thumb and fingers of a right hand.

Thorndyke glanced at the photograph and, turning to Miller, said :

" I suggest that those are Dr. Foxton's finger-prints."

" Impossible ! " exclaimed Platt, and then suddenly fell silent.

" We can soon see," said Thorndyke, producing from the case a pad of white paper. " If Dr. Foxton will lay the finger-tips of his right hand first on this inked plate and then on the paper, we can compare the prints with the photograph."

Foxton placed his fingers on the blackened plate and then pressed them on the paper pad, leaving on the latter four beautifully clear, black finger-prints. These Superintendent Platt scrutinised eagerly, and as his glance travelled from the prints to the photographs he broke into a sheepish grin.

" Sold again ! " he muttered. " They are the same prints."

" Well," said Miller in a tone of disgust, " you must have been a mug not to have thought of that when you knew that Dr. Foxton had handled the bottle."

" The fact, however, is important," said Thorndyke. " The absence of any finger-prints but Dr. Foxton's not only suggests that the murderer took the precaution to wear gloves, but especially it proves that the bottle was not handled by the deceased during life. A suicide's hands will usually be pretty moist and would leave conspicuous, if not very clear, impressions."

"Yes," agreed Miller, "that is quite true. But with regard to these foot-prints. We can't compel this man to let us examine his feet without arresting him. Don't think, Dr. Thorndyke, that I suspect you of guessing. I've known you too long for that. You've got your facts all right, I don't doubt, but you must let us have enough to justify our arrest."

Thorndyke's answer was to plunge once more into the inexhaustible green case, from which he now produced two objects wrapped in tissue paper. The paper being removed, there was revealed what looked like a model of an excessively shabby pair of brown shoes.

"These," said Thorndyke, exhibiting the " models " to Superintendent Miller—who viewed them with an undisguised grin—" are plaster casts of the interiors of a pair of slippers—very old and much too tight—belonging to Mr. Macauley. His name was written inside them. The casts have been waxed and painted with raw umber, which has been lightly rubbed off, thus accentuating the prominences and depressions. You will notice that the impressions of the toes on the soles and of the ' knuckles ' on the uppers appear as prominences ; in fact we have in these casts a sketchy reproduction of the actual feet.

"Now, first as to dimensions. Dr. Jervis's measurements of the foot-prints give us ten inches and three-quarters as the extreme length and four inches and five-eighths as the extreme width at the heads of the metatarsus. On these casts, as you see, the extreme length is ten inches and five-eighths—the loss of one-eighth being accounted for by the curve of the sole—and the extreme width is four inches and a quarter—three-eighths being accounted for by the lateral compression of a tight slipper. The agreement of the dimensions is remarkable, considering the unusual size. And now as to the peculiarities of the feet. You notice that each toe has made a perfectly distinct impression on the sole, excepting the little toe, of which there is no trace in either cast. And, turning to the uppers, you notice that the knuckles of the toes appear quite distinct and prominent—again excepting the little toes, which have made no impression at all. Thus it is not a case of retracted little toes, for they would appear as an extra prominence. Then, looking at the feet as a whole, it is evident that the little toes are absent ; there is a distinct hollow where there should be a prominence."

" M'yes," said Miller dubiously, " it's all very neat. But isn't it just a bit speculative ? "

" Oh, come, Miller," protested Thorndyke ; " just consider the facts. Here is a suspected murderer known to have feet of an unusual size and presenting a very rare deformity ; and here are a pair of feet of that same unusual size and presenting that same rare deformity ; and they are the feet of a man who had actually lived in the same house as the murdered woman and who, at the date of the crime, was living only two doors away. What more would you have ? "

" Well, there is the question of motive," objected Miller.

" That hardly belongs to a prima facie case," said Thorndyke. " But even if it did, is there not ample matter for suspicion ? Remember who the murdered woman was, what her husband was, and who this Sierra Leone gentleman is."

" Yes, yes ; that's true," said Miller somewhat hastily, either perceiving the drift of Thorndyke's argument (which I did not), or being unwilling to admit that he was still in the dark. " Yes, we'll have the fellow in and get his actual foot-prints."

He went to the door and, putting his head out, made some sign, which was almost immediately followed by a trampling of feet, and Macauley entered the room, followed by two large plain-clothes policemen. The negro was evidently alarmed, for he looked about him with the wild expression of a hunted animal. But his manner was aggressive and truculent.

" Why am I being interfered with in this impertinent manner ? " he demanded in the deep, buzzing voice characteristic of the male negro.

"We want to have a look at your feet, Mr. Macauley," said Miller. " Will you kindly take off your shoes and socks ? "

" No," roared Macauley. " I'll see you damned first."

" Then," said Miller, " I arrest you on a charge of having murdered——"

The rest of the sentence was drowned in a sudden uproar. The tall, powerful negro, bellowing like an angry bull, had whipped out a large, strangely shaped knife and charged furiously at the superintendent. But the two plain-clothes men had been watching him from behind and now sprang upon him, each seizing an arm. Two sharp, metallic clicks in quick succession, a thunderous crash and an ear-splitting yell, and the formidable barbarian lay prostrate on the floor with one massive constable sitting astride his chest, and the other seated on his knees.

" Now's your chance, doctor," said Miller. " I'll get his shoes and socks off."

As Thorndyke re-inked his plates, Miller and the local superintendent expertly removed the smart patent shoes and the green silk socks from the feet of the writhing, bellowing negro. Then Thorndyke rapidly and skilfully applied the inked plates to the soles of the feet—which I steadied for the purpose—and followed up with a dexterous pressure of the paper pad, first to one foot and then—having torn off the printed sheet—to the other. In spite of the difficulties occasioned by Macauley's struggles, each sheet presented a perfectly clear and sharp print of the sole of the foot, even the ridge-patterns of the toes and ball of the foot being quite distinct. Thorndyke laid each of the new prints on the table beside the corresponding large photograph, and invited the two superintendents to compare them.

" Yes," said Miller—and Superintendent Platt nodded his acquiescence—" there can't be a shadow of a doubt. The ink-prints and the photographs are identical, to every line and skin-marking. You've made out your case, doctor, as you always do."

" So you see," said Thorndyke, as we smoked our evening pipes on the old stone pier, " your method was a perfectly sound one, only you didn't apply it properly. Like too many mathematicians, you started on your calculations before you had secured your data. If you had applied the simple laws of probability to the real data, they would have pointed straight to Macauley."

" How do you suppose he lost his little toes ? " I asked.

" I don't suppose at all. Obviously it was a case of double ainhum."

" Ainhum ! " I exclaimed with a sudden flash of recollection.

" Yes ; that was what you overlooked. You compared the probabilities of three diseases either of which only very rarely causes the loss of even one little toe and infinitely rarely causes the loss of both, and none of which conditions is confined to any definite class of persons ; and you ignored ainhum, a disease which attacks almost exclusively the little toe, causing it to drop off, and quite commonly destroys both little toes—a disease, moreover, which is confined to the black-skinned races. In European practice ainhum is unknown, but in Africa, and to a less extent, in India, it is quite common. If you were to assemble all the men in the world who have lost both little toes, more than nine-tenths of them would be suffering from ainhum ; so that, by the laws of probability, your foot-prints were, by nine chances to one, those of a man who had suffered from ainhum, and therefore a black-skinned man. But as soon as you had established a black man as the probable criminal, you opened up a new field of corroborative evidence. There was a black man on the spot. That man was a native of Sierra Leone and almost certainly a man of importance there. But the victim's husband had deadly enemies in the native secret societies of Sierra Leone. The letters of the husband to the wife probably contained matter incriminating certain natives of Sierra Leone. The evidence became cumulative, you see. Taken as a whole, it pointed plainly to Macauley, apart from the new fact of the murder of Toussaint in Liverpool, a city with a considerable floating population of West Africans."

" And I gather from your reference to the African poison, strophanthus, that you fixed on Macauley at once when I gave you my sketch of the case ? "

"Yes ; especially when I saw your photographs of the foot-prints with the absent little toes and those characteristic chigger-scars on the toes that remained. But it was sheer luck that enabled me to fit the keystone into its place and turn mere probability into virtual certainty. I could have embraced the magician Wardale when he brought us the magic slipper. Still, it isn't an absolute certainty, even now, though I expect it will be by to-morrow."

And Thorndyke was right. That very evening the police entered Macauley's chambers in Tanfield Court, where they discovered the dead woman's attaché case. It still contained Toussaint's letters to his wife, and one of those letters mentioned by name, as members of a dangerous secret society, several prominent Sierra Leone men, including the accused David Macauley.

Reprinted with the Author's permission from *The Thorndyke Omnibus*.

GEORGE GOODCHILD

The Death of Signor Lotto

Séance

A Microbe Murder

¶ Mr. GOODCHILD started as a publisher, but drifted into journalism, and
finally into authorship. In the World
War he served as an artillery officer, and
wrote a number of War books while
hostilities were in progress. H claims
to be one of the most prolific writers
alive, and has over a hundred books to
his name, besides short stories, films and
plays. His books are available in nine
languages.

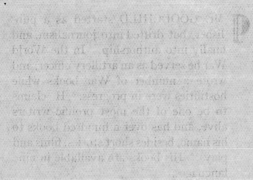

THE DEATH OF SIGNOR LOTTO

McLEAN was on holiday—a month of well-earned respite from the world of crooks and murderers in which he habitually moved. In relaxation McLean was just as thorough as in the moments of his professional activity. Every morning he left the small hotel in the Highlands, with a book and some sandwiches packed in a rucksack, and tramped to some delectable spot where he could recline and laze away that day. His attire was the very opposite of the well-cut and well-creased clothes which he habitually wore, and few would have recognised the brilliant inspector of the C.I.D. in his shapeless felt hat, baggy trousers and heavy boots.

He had an innate love for nature, and as he walked his observant eyes took in details that most men would have missed. A crawling insect in his path was enough to bring him to a halt, and cause him to stoop down and examine it, catalogue it in its correct species and blow it into mid-air.

In truth he had forgotten the very existence of Scotland Yard. Scotland was quite enough ! On this particular day he lounged by a musical stream, read his book, dozed at intervals and let Time have her fling. When the sun declined he walked back to the hotel, with his mind at peace with the world, and a splendid hunger gnawing at his vitals. But on reaching his haven of rest he was informed that a gentleman named Searle wished to see him.

" Searle—Searle ! No. I'm not available."

He went upstairs, took a bath, changed into evening dress, as if he were staying at the Ritz instead of a remote hostelry at which he was the sole guest, and came down to dinner. And still the pugnacious Mr. Searle was waiting.

" Didn't you tell him I was not available ? " he inquired of the waiter.

" Yes, sir, but he said he would wait."

" All right—I'll see him."

It then transpired that his visitor was not named Searle

but Tearle—a man known to McLean, and at this moment holding a prominent position in a big Scottish insurance company.

" So it's you," said McLean. " I was told your name was Searle. What's the trouble ? "

" I have been trying to find you since yesterday morning. Will you help us ? You are the only man to solve——"

" I'm on holiday."

" I know—I met your sister in Glasgow. It was she who put me on your trail. This isn't a police matter—I mean, that I am begging you in a private capacity to save us from being swindled out of ten thousand pounds."

" You think I can perform miracles ? Who is the swindler, anyway ? "

" A dead man."

" Rather clever of him. Look here, since you've ruined my holiday by distracting my mind, you had better have a meal with me, and run over the points."

Tearle was more than agreeable, having waited with the patience of Job since lunch. They repaired to the small dining-room and the waiter brought an extra plate.

" Now," said McLean, " what's all the fuss about ? "

" Did you see yesterday's newspaper ? "

" No. I never read newspapers when I'm on holiday."

" Well, a man insured with the Company was found asphyxiated in his garage—an Italian named Lotto. A year ago he took up a life policy for £10,000."

" Most thoughtful of him."

" Very. So far as we can see, the coroner is bound to bring in a verdict of accidental death—in which case we pay up to his nearest relative—in Italy. But suicide is barred in the policy."

" Ah—I get you."

" Wait ! The Company is absolutely straight. But there are some curious facts connected with this business. For instance, we have an engineer who swears that the exhaust-pipe of the car was deliberately disconnected under the footboards, thus permitting the dangerous carbon-monoxide gases to excape into the interior of the car. Secondly, the doors of the garage were closed—shut tight."

" Won't the coroner's jury take those facts into consideration ? "

" There's contrary evidence. The chauffeur has already
stated that the exhaust pipe came adrift two days ago, and
that he intended having it repaired on the day after the
tragedy occurred."

" And the closed doors ? "

" Both Lotto and the chauffeur were in the habit of entering the garage by the small door in the garden, starting up
the car, and letting the engine warm up while they opened the
big doors. Anyway, we aren't quite satisfied about it, and
you know what these juries are ? If they can bring it in
' accidental death ' they will—to spare his relatives."

" H'm ! What do you want me to do ? "

" Come and have a look at the place."

" Great Scott ! I'm going fishing to-morrow."

" It isn't far from here—just over the border. I have
a car on hand and could run you over there early to-morrow
morning. We only want to do the right thing. But we
don't feel like being swindled."

" Evidently you have made up your mind that swindling
was contemplated ? "

" Yes—for various reasons. I know for a fact that Lotto
has been living beyond his means—that he has poor relatives
in Italy to whom he was greatly attached. The suicide
clause was inserted deliberately because he seemed rather a
strange fellow. Will you come, and help us through this
trouble ? "

McLean agreed to do so, without displaying any of the
zest that he felt. In truth he could never resist a mystery—
and small as this one appeared to be on the surface, experience told him that on innumerable occasions big things
emerged from apparently simple cases.

The house of the dead man was remotely situated, and
standing in an acre of timbered grounds. McLean had
begged Tearle to keep his name and object quiet, and to
present him as a friend of Lotto. To the butler he gave his
name as Singleton, and expressed a desire to see the corpse.

" Certainly, sir. His death was a great blow to me, for he
was the best of masters."

He spoke with an accent that revealed his origin at once—
Italian, and was a dark, suave individual of about fifty years
of age. He led McLean to the bedroom, and left him alone

with the dead man for a few minutes. McLean had seen several asphyxiated men in his time, and Lotto carried all the symptoms. Tearle came in while McLean was nosing around.

" What's the butler's name ? " asked McLean.

" Loretti. He has been with Lotto for a number of years, and was devoted to him."

" Did Lotto live alone ? "

" Yes. A rather reserved man. I believe he sprang from nothing. Made a little money by some mysterious means and settled down here."

" Any will ? "

" I don't know. I think the matter is in the hands of the Public Trustee."

" His private papers are gone ? "

" I suppose so. Loretti will know. The chauffeur is outside. Do you want to see him ? "

" Yes. Italian ? "

" No—English."

The chauffeur was named Spillings, and had been with Lotto for one year—ever since Lotto bought his first car. He was well-spoken, polite, and apparently very upset at what had taken place.

" This gentleman is an old friend of your master's," said Tearle. " He cannot understand how Mr. Lotto came to meet with his misadventure."

" Nor I, sir. I take a good deal of blame upon myself, for not mending the exhaust-pipe sooner."

" Is this the car ? " asked McLean.

" Yes, sir."

" Exactly as it was when the tragedy took place ? "

" Yes. I have not touched it. I can show you the cause of all the trouble."

He lifted the ill-fitting footboard, and revealed the broken joint. McLean craned his head forward, and saw the break. It was, as Tearle had said, a little suspicious, for there were a few minute marks which might well have been caused by the use of a tool.

" That was broken on the road ? " he said.

" Yes, sir. We hit a big pot-hole and I heard immediately an increase in the sound of the exhaust. I told Mr. Lotto what had happened."

" You told him—and yet he sat in this enclosed car, with all the windows up—on that evening ? "

" It was foolish. He must have forgotten."

McLean wandered over to the big doors—and pulled them aside. Then he came back and examined the window.

" Who found Mr. Lotto ? "

" I did, sir. It was my evening off and I went into Carlisle. I returned at eleven o'clock and, to my surprise, heard the engine running. I came in and found Mr. Lotto sitting in the car, with his hands on the steering-wheel—dead."

" Did you detect poisonous gas ? "

" The place was full of smoke and the radiator was boiling over. But of course I had opened the big doors—so I wasn't affected by the fumes."

" Did Mr. Lotto have an appointment on that evening ? "

" I didn't know he had, or I should have stayed. But Loretti told me he was rung up after I left—about eight o'clock, and he told Loretti he had to run into Carlisle to see a friend."

McLean shook his head sadly, playing the part of interested and grieved friend.

" I suppose you will be wanted at the inquest to-morrow ?" he inquired.

" Yes, sir."

" You think it was all an accident ? "

" Why, of course, sir. If you knew Mr. Lotto you must know that he was not the sort of man to take his—— That is just a wicked rumour."

" But why didn't he open the doors before he started up the engine ? "

" I don't think he paid much attention to what people said about the danger of carbon-monoxide gas. The engine would never run well until it was warmed up. No, sir—there is only one possible verdict."

McLean spent another hour about the place. In the library he found a bureau with some documents in it, and before he left he stuffed some of these into his pocket—while the butler's eagle eyes were elsewhere.

" When does the interment take place ? " he asked.

" The day after to-morrow, sir—at Carlisle."

" I shall try to be present. It is a very sad business, Mr. Loretti."

" Very sad, sir. We have wired to his sister in Italy, but it is doubtful whether she will arrive in time for the interment. He was very fond of her."

" You speak excellent English."

" I have travelled a great deal, sir. Mr. Lotto could scarcely speak a word."

McLean and Tearle ultimately made their departure, and all the way to his hotel McLean was silent. Now and again he would consult the papers and documents which he had taken without permission, and then it was that fishing and lounging were completely forgotten.

" Well," said Tearle at length. " What do you make of it ? "

" Interesting—very interesting."

" You don't think it was suicide ? "

" I know it wasn't."

" Then you must give evidence——"

" Oh, no. The verdict is a foregone conclusion. You will never get away with the suicide story."

" If we don't—we pay."

" That remains to be seen. I am coming to the Court to-morrow—merely out of interest. But I want you to meet me at Lotto's house to-morrow night at nine o'clock."

" I don't quite understand. Once that verdict is uttered there is nothing left to do but pay up."

" I beg to differ. There are some strange facts in this case. But I have no intention of trying to upset the kindly verdict. Meet me there at nine o'clock, and have two policemen in the offing."

" What ! "

" That is my advice."

" Then, by Jove, I'll follow it, though I don't understand what you are driving at."

He went off and McLean spent the rest of the day working up an engrossing theory—nay, more than a theory. Among the things which he had filched was a small photograph—a curious thing that, taken in conjunction with a newspaper cutting, was of the gravest importance.

" Clever ! " mused McLean. " Damned clever—if it is true ! "

On the following day he motored into Carlisle and attended

the inquest. Things went very smoothly. A jury had been empanelled because of the slight element of doubt as between a verdict of accidental death and suicide, but the evidence supported the former view, and as Mr. Lotto was known and respected locally he was given the benefit of the doubt. As to the cause of death, that left no shadow of doubt. Tearle was slightly dejected despite McLean's absolute composure.

" Accident ! " he said. " That was no accident."

" I am inclined to agree."

" Then what——? "

" Nine o'clock," reminded McLean. " I fancy your Company will have no need to write that substantial cheque."

Punctually at nine o'clock McLean turned up at the meeting-place, and found Tearle there in the darkness. Close by were two plain-clothes men from the local police. McLean went to them.

" I am Inspector McLean of Scotland Yard," he whispered. " I want you to remain here in the mean-time. If what I suspect is true, I may have need of you. If you hear a shot or a whistle, enter the house, without delay."

" Very good, Inspector."

" You have two sets of handcuffs ? "

" Yes."

" Good ! "

He and Tearle then made up the drive and rang the front-door bell. A long time elapsed before it was answered. Loretti came to the door and blinked at them.

" I find I cannot attend the funeral," said McLean. " But I should like to bid a last farewell to my old friend. Is that convenient ? "

" I am afraid not, sir. The undertaker screwed down the coffin this evening."

" Ah. Then I will pay my respects—just the same, if I may ? "

Loretti was agreeable. Tearle waited in the hall and McLean entered the library where the coffin lay. Loretti withdrew and McLean immediately went to the window, and slipped back the latch. A minute later he was in the hall—looking distressed.

" Thank you, Mr. Loretti," he said. " I am very sorry to trouble you so late at night. But I have to go to London early in the morning."

" No trouble at all, sir. Good night ! "

" Well ? " gasped Tearle, when they reached a sheltered part of the garden. " What happened ? "

" Nothing much. But something soon will. I have unfastened the library window. We will go through it in a few minutes."

They waited a while, and then stole towards the house. At last McLean reached the window and gently opened it. Tearle followed him into the big room, and shuddered when McLean flashed an electric torch full on to the coffin.

" S-sh ! Now we shall know the truth."

He put the torch into Tearle's hand, and produced a screwdriver from his pocket. Then, to Tearle's amazement, he began to remove the many screws. At last the lid was loose. McLean lifted it, and a low exclamation broke from Tearle's lips. *The coffin was filled with—earth.*

" S-sh ! You didn't expect that—eh ? "

" Great heavens—no. What does it mean ? Why is there no body in the coffin ? "

" There was when the undertaker screwed it down. But I rather fancy it has been removed—for a certain purpose. I think we will endeavour to locate it. Better remove your shoes. I have rubber on mine."

Tearle did this, but he was a little nervous all the time. Keen as he was to do his duty to his Company, this adventure overawed him. But McLean was as eager as a greyhound on the leash. So far everything had transpired as he had expected, and he had no doubt about the finale.

" Tread warily," he whispered. " Mr. Loretti has good ears, if I am any judge."

" Loretti ! "

" Sh ! Come ! "

They passed into the hall, which was now in darkness, and began to investigate the rooms, one at a time. The ground floor was quite deserted, and on looking through the window McLean saw that the chauffeur's quarters over the garage were unlighted.

" There was a maid," he mused. " Appears to be out. Yes, they would see to that. Let us go upstairs."

The house comprised two stories only, and all the rooms upstairs led from one central corridor. One by one they were entered, and still no living soul was seen. At length McLean came to the end room. It was locked, but the key was present. He turned it and switched on the light.

" Ah—Loretti's ! "

The butler's clothes were spread over the bed, and on the floor close by was a very large travelling trunk, already half filled with clothing and sundry articles.

" Our friend intends to make an early departure," he mused. " Probably after the funeral."

" I'm still in the dark."

" That is astonishing. I think we have time to make ourselves acquainted with Mr. Loretti's possessions. Leave the door slightly ajar, and if you hear him approaching warn me."

He thereupon commenced to turn out the contents of the trunk. In the bottom of it was a toilet-bag, containing a safety-razor, shaving-brush, and a few oddments. Among the last was a small blue bottle, with a glass stopper. On the side of it was a fragment of red label. McLean removed the stopper and smelt it warily.

" Got it ! " he exclaimed.

" Poison ? "

" Chloroform. I wish I had the label, but it is not vital. Now we will look up our two friends."

" But where are they ? "

" Where is the body ? Find that and we find them."

" Great Scott ! This is getting gruesome."

" I am afraid it is. I ought to warn you, Tearle, that it is possible they may object to any intrusion on our part. Would you prefer to join the officers outside—until they are wanted ? "

" Not likely. I'm going to see this thing through. Lead on, Macduff ! "

McLean went down the stairs, and passed through the kitchen. Beyond was a door which gave access to a flight of stone steps. Silently he descended them. They found themselves in a big basement, at the windows of which were bars and shutters—now closed. A door lay on the right, and from the other side of it came the sound of low voices. With an automatic in one hand and the torch in the other,

McLean crept towards it. He removed the key and squinted through the keyhole. Then he slipped the torch into his pocket and caught Tearle's arm, indicating the key-hole with the muzzle of the automatic. Tearle bent down and squinted. Inside was a long table, and on it was stretched a human shape—under a sheet. Nearby was Loretti, clad in a long smock, with a knife in his hand—and opposite him the chauffeur, looking pallid.

" My God ! " he whispered.

McLean pressed a whistle into his hand.

" Go upstairs and blow it," he whispered. " There is no way out for them."

Tearle mopped his brow and went off. McLean guessed that the door was bolted on the other side, so he went back and put all the strength of his leg into one blow at the lock. The inside staple went, and the door flew open. Loretti swung round, and his face went black with baffled rage.

" You ! " he snarled. " What the devil—— ? "

Quick as lightning a revolver appeared from the pocket of the smock and a bullet whistled dangerously close to McLean's head. The next moment McLean fired and Loretti dropped his weapon and clutched his right arm with contorted features.

" Put up your hands, Spillings ! " rapped McLean. " I shouldn't be surprised if you, too, collected firearms—as well as jewels."

Spillings obeyed, and McLean went forward and ran his free hand through the chauffeur's pockets. But he found nothing more dangerous than a knife. Then Tearle's whistle pealed out. Loretti dived for the fallen revolver, but McLean got there first and bowled the Italian over with his foot.

" I arrest you both for murder," he said.

Loretti scowled, but Spillings broke down.

" I didn't do it," he cried. " I only helped to carry him—— I knew nothing until——"

" Rat ! " snarled Loretti.

Through the door came the two officers with Tearle. McLean pointed to his prisoners and in twenty seconds both were handcuffed.

" Take them away," said McLean. " I will come to the station immediately."

Tearle winced as he stared at the form on the table, and the box of surgical instruments on the dresser.

" What—what was the idea ? " he inquired.

" A little post-mortem operation."

" But with what object ? "

McLean produced an old news-cutting from his pocket. But it was from an Italian newspaper and Tearle could not read it. McLean thereupon translated it.

" To-day the strange case of Signor Lotto came before Judge Matioli at Naples. Signor Lutz, a wealthy diamond merchant of Naples, deposed that on the twentieth instant, Lotto, who was employed by him as a diamond-cutter, swallowed a stone the value of £6,000. The theft was suspected, and Lotto was taken into custody. When the stone failed to appear, an X-ray photograph was taken, and it was shown that the jewel had become lodged in the prisoner's intestine. Signor Lutz now begged that the Judge make an order for an operation to be performed on the man, but this the Judge refused to do. After a long debate the prisoner was sentenced to one year's imprisonment."

" That was twenty years ago," said McLean. " Here is another cutting from the same newspaper—three years later."

" We learn that since his release from prison Signor Lotto, who figured so prominently in the Lutz diamond case, has suffered from attack on the part of professional thieves. Three attempts have been made on his life in order to secure the jewel which he still carries inside his body."

" Well ! " gasped Tearle.

" The third document is a receipt from Signor Lutz—dated two years ago. It is a receipt for a sum of money equal to the value of the diamond. Evidently Lotto made enough money to settle that old debt, but he was afraid to go back to Italy. Crooks have long memories. With these documents was an X-ray photograph—taken after Lotto's release, I presume, and attached to a letter from an English surgeon who does not advise an operation. That is the whole grim story."

" By Jove ! Who would have dreamed of it ! Then they drugged him and carried him into the car—after tinkering with the exhaust pipe ? "

" Undoubtedly, and I dare say that they saw to it that he stood no chance of recovering from the drug. Doubtless he lived long enough to inhale quite a quantity of carbon-monoxide gas, and the smell of the stuff was enough to drown the chloroform. Rather ingenious—what ? "

" But what made you suspect them, when there was no question of murder at that time ? "

" There were quite a number of suspicious points. In the first place, it is unusual for an Italian to settle down in a northerly climate, when he could scarcely speak a word of the language, and all his interests are in Italy. Obviously he had something to fear—some reason for living a lonely life. Then there was Loretti. He was too eager with his explanations—too free with his assumed emotions. I suspected Loretti from the first. But the first real light came when I found that photographic print of Lotto's internals, with a cross marking the diamond. That and the press-cuttings provided a solid motive."

" It was one that never occurred to me."

" Probably not, but then, my dear Tearle, you have not spent so many years of your priceless youth in the pursuit of the unrighteous. I have come to look upon every person as dishonest until it is proved otherwise. Lord, what a mess-up you have made of my holiday ! "

But his twinkling eyes gave that assertion the lie. McLean was a man-hunter all the time. Even fishing and the collection of wee beasties had to take second place.

SÉANCE

SYLVIA DUNNING ran into the library, her pretty face aglow with excitement. On bursting through the doorway, she gasped to see her father and uncle apparently in the throes of a violent altercation. But at her entrance the trouble ceased, and Richard Dunning—her uncle—smiled at her with his usual charm.

" We were just having an argument, Sylvia," he said. " Usual subject—Politics."

Sylvia blinked, for she had never seen her father looking so agitated. But he, too, smiled now, and inquired after the cause of her headlong entry into his retreat.

" Mrs. Wren is here, father, and the Pollards have also turned up. Can we hold it in here ? "

" Hold—what ? "

" Have you forgotten ? The séance, of course."

Richard Dunning turned to his brother.

" What's all this, James ? "

" I had forgotten. Sylvia has got the Spiritualism bug, and I agreed to let them hold a séance here—apparently this evening."

" What rubbish ! " grunted Richard.

" It isn't rubbish," protested Sylvia hotly. " Mrs. Wren is one of the best mediums in England. I've heard wonderful stories about her."

Her father shrugged his shoulders, and then nodded his head.

" I suppose it must take place," he said. " Is George at home ? "

" Why, of course ! " replied Sylvia. " George is as keen as I am. Then we *can* have this room ? That will be fine. Mrs. Wren believes in the atmosphere of books, and there is that old harmonium to provide the music."

" Music ! "

" There must be music. Oh, here's George ! "

Her brother sailed in. He was a well-built fellow of about twenty-one, the living image of his father—a pugnacious jaw, keen blue eyes, and a head that showed considerable mental development.

"The spooks are here," he said. "Mrs. Wren has appointed me musician-in-chief. I am to spank the dominoes——"

"George, you oughtn't to be so flippant," said Sylvia. "Nothing ever happens unless everyone is serious. We are going to take this seriously, aren't we ? "

"It depends upon what happens. Sylvia, you have left Mrs. Wren all alone."

"She knows the Pollards. But I will go. Get the table ready, will you ? "

A few minutes later the visitors entered. The medium was a pallid little woman, with bird-like eyes, and silvery hair. She had met the two brothers before, but never in a professional capacity. The Pollards were neighbours, and mildly interested in the subject. They represented four of the party—John Pollard, his wife, son, and son-in-law. All chatted together for a few minutes, and then Mrs. Wren took command.

"I think that will do," she said finally. "I will sit here, you there, Sylvia—between Mr. Pollard and your uncle. Nothing may happen for some time, but I beg you to be patient—and serious. Will you switch off the lights, George, and then open with a hymn."

This was done. The wheezy little harmonium started to play "Abide with Me," and the sitters were reduced to silence. Time passed, and then the silence was suddenly broken by the sound of a weak voice.

"James ! "

The harmonium stopped, and James Dunning muttered something.

"It—it is mother's voice," said Sylvia. "Father—answer her—why don't you answer her ? "

"Is—it—Rose ? " quavered Dunning.

"Yes—your wife, who passed over three years ago. I have been trying for so long to get into touch with you and my beloved children."

"If—if this is true—if it is really Rose that speaks—give me proof. I want to be—sure."

" What proof can I give but what you hear now ? Is not my voice proof enough ? "

" Can't I see you ? Isn't it possible to show me your face— just your dear face ? "

" The conditions are not too good. But I will try."

Came a long and anxious silence, in which could be heard the heavy breathing of the medium, and the shorter gasps of the somewhat scared sitters.

" Rose ! " called Dunning in a strained voice. " Aren't you—coming back ? "

" Father," begged Sylvia. " Give her time."

Then the most amazing thing happened. There was a slight noise, a sort of suppressed ejaculation, and then the flash and thundering report of a firearm.

" Great God ! " cried a voice.

" The lights ! Switch on the lights ! "

Half a minute passed while George sought for the switch. Then the lights blazed up. A piercing shriek came from Sylvia, and exclamations of horror from the other sitters. James Dunning was sitting with his head drooping forward, and the table was stained with blood. His brother raised the drooping head. Dunning was dead—shot through the heart !

" The window ! " gasped George. " Look, the window is open ! "

He ran to the casement and leapt through it, but outside was the quiet garden—no sign of a living soul. He came back, with haggard face.

" All—here ! " he gasped. " Who could shoot him— like that—in the dark ? "

" Better call the police," said Pollard. " And the ladies had better retire. What a shocking business ! Come, Sylvia—don't give way."

The medium was still in a trance, from which she was slowly recovering. At last she was led away to join the other ladies. The men sat and stared at each other, until the police arrived, with the doctor. It only needed one look at the dead man to satisfy the doctor.

" Dead ! " he said. " What has been going on here ? "

The fussy little inspector then took control of the situa- tion. The ladies were brought in, and they and the men were closely questioned. But no clue of any sort emerged, and the revolver, or pistol, remained missing. It was the most baffling case the local police had ever had to deal with, and before a week was out they called in Scotland Yard.

McLean drifted into the house one morning, with his devoted assistant hot on his heels. His presence was announced to Richard Dunning, and the two met in the fatal room, while Sergeant Brook wandered along the terrace.

" You are the brother of the dead man ? " asked McLean.

" Yes."

" I am Inspector McLean. I think I am possessed of all the details. I presume that is the window which was found open after the tragedy ? "

" That is so."

" Do you remember if it was locked before the séance took place ? "

" It was certainly closed, but I cannot say whether it was latched or not."

" Hm ! You heard no sound of anyone entering the room ? "

" No. There was a slight noise, as if the window had blown open, but no sound of feet."

McLean put his hand into his pocket and produced a small revolver.

" Have you ever seen this weapon before ? "

" No. Is that—— ? "

" It was found in the grounds—under a bush exactly opposite this window."

" Then someone did enter ! "

" It looks like it. Nothing has been touched in this room since the tragedy ? "

" Absolutely nothing. There is the table exactly as it was. I gave instructions that not a thing should be moved in any way."

" Good ! There were footprints immediately outside the window—on a flower-bed."

" My nephew made them. He ran to the window when he saw it was open, and descended into the garden. Seeing no one, he came back."

" Who sat opposite your brother ? "

" Mr. Pollard, senior, with his son on one side of him, and his wife on the other."

" You are aware that your brother was shot from the front ? "

" Yes."

" I presume the Pollards were great friends of the family?"

" Well, neighbours of long standing—but perfectly trust-worthy people."

" Had your brother any enemies ? "

" No—at least not in this country. Many years ago he lived in Java, and there he got himself mixed up in a murder case. He was called upon to give evidence for the prosecution, and some time afterwards an attempt was made on his life."

" Hm ! Your brother was not very keen about this séance ? "

" Not at first—but afterwards, when he heard—or thought he heard—his wife's voice——"

" You heard it, too. Could you recognise that voice ? "

" I wouldn't care to swear to it. There was certainly a marked resemblance, but we were all so strung up we might have imagined anything."

" And the medium—how long have you known her ? "

" Six months."

" She was paid to come here ? "

" No. She was eager to convince us that there was life beyond the grave. She gave her services for nothing."

" Thank you. I should like to examine this room at my leisure. May I see you later ? "

" Certainly. My nephew and niece are in the house if you should need to question them."

" I will—later on."

Richard Dunning left the room, and McLean commenced his investigations. After a while he called in Brook, and bade him sit at the table where the dead man had sat. Brook put his fourteen stone into the chair, and was promptly covered by the revolver from the opposite side.

" All right," drawled McLean. " I was just wondering ——"

" I hope the cartridges are out."

" They are. Brook, this is a queer case."

" That's how it strikes me. Evidently someone came through that window and shot that poor devil clean through the heart—in pitch blackness, too."

" You think so ? "

" Well, isn't it clear ? He slipped away and got rid of the gun where the police found it."

" Your logic is sadly at fault. Mr. Dunning was shot by someone who was in this room all the time."

" But the men were searched, and the ladies——"

" The ladies were not. Leaving them out of the problem—there was nothing to prevent the murderer from flinging the revolver through the window afterwards."

" But only one man went to the window—and that was Master George—the dead man's own son."

" That, my dear Brook, is where the case is difficult. Dunning was known to be a man of wealth—his son is doubtless his heir. Thus he would benefit from his father's death—also the girl, and possibly the brother. There appears to be nothing against the Pollards at the moment—nor the medium. We must search deeper if we are going to clear up this matter."

" I wouldn't be surprised if it is never cleared up."

McLean shook his head. His was not the temperament to admit defeat so early in the quest. He sent Brook to take a statement from the servant who was in the house at the time of the tragedy, and continued to examine everything in detail. At last he came to the window. On trying the latch he found that the window would not close without the latch being fastened. It was a small but important discovery, for it meant that the window must have been latched before the séance, and that no person could have entered that way. The harmonium was so placed that it was extremely doubtful whether anyone could enter by the door without being seen by the player, for the open door would have permitted light to enter the room from the hall. It clinched one point—Dunning was shot by someone in the house—in that room !

The casement window was provided with blue plush curtains, now pulled well back. McLean closed them a trifle, and as the folds came out his eagle eyes saw something. It was several well-defined blood-stained finger-prints just where the silk lining was stitched to the curtain proper. His heart bounded—and yet there was a flaw. How could the murderer get blood on his hands ? An hour later a good photograph was taken.

Two days passed, and McLean cudgelled his fine brains to solve the mystery. He had cross-examined all the parties connected with the séance, and their statements contained nothing that conflicted. Brook was losing heart, for McLean had told him very little, and Brook was still of the opinion that someone from outside, with eyes like a cat, had come in, done the bloody deed, and vanished after discarding the revolver. McLean knew different, and devised a scheme to learn the truth.

" We are going to have a full-dress rehearsal to-night," he said.

" A what ? "

" I have asked the medium to come here, also all the others who were present at that séance. We'll have it all over again. Get rid of that blood-stained table. It may arouse horrible feelings. This mahogany one will do."

Brook was mystified, but that was nothing unusual. McLean had a tantalising habit of keeping his plans to himself. All the afternoon he was playing about with bottles and other things, and by the evening he was quite cheerful.

" Things are looking up, Brook."

" I don't get you."

" But you will. I may make an arrest to-night."

" You know who it was ? "

" No, but I shall do in less than an hour. At least I shall know—— But we are wasting time. I want you to play a dramatic part. At eight o'clock you will stand outside that window with your face masked and a pistol in your hand. When I whistle you will blunder through the door noisily, and hold them all up—drive them from the table. Leave the rest to me."

Brook went to dress for his part, and later McLean welcomed the visitors and also the members of the household. They were all looking somewhat nervous at having to go through that ordeal again, and Pollard in particular protested.

" I naturally presume you are all anxious to get this dreadful business cleared up," said McLean. " I am anxious to know exactly what took place on that night. I want you all to sit at this table in exactly the same positions as you occupied then. I will take that place—the vacant chair."

" Am I to play the harmonium ? " inquired George.

" Yes—exactly as you did that night."

As he sat down Richard Dunning looked very agitated, and McLean, who was next to him, shot him a swift glance.

" Is a real séance intended ? " asked Richard.

" I merely want a repetition of what happened before."

" Is it your intention to try and get through Spiritualism the truth about—my brother ? "

" You think that is possible ? "

" Well—I don't know. But none of us want any more ghostly voices. Sylvia is distraught."

" I'm not," said Sylvia in a firm voice. " If mother could help us she would do so."

" Well, let us see," said McLean. " Mr. Dunning, will you please switch off the lights ? "

George obeyed, and a few seconds later the harmonium started to play.

" Hands on the table—as before," said McLean.

In the darkness he felt his little finger touching Richard's thumb on his right. A few minutes of dead silence passed, save for the low whining of the harmonium, and then a whistle pealed out.

" Oh ! "

The music suddenly stopped. The window was pushed violently open, and McLean groped for the switch. The lights came on, revealing a masked figure standing about two yards from the table with a pistol in his hand.

" Great heavens ! " ejaculated Richard Dunning.

" Stand back ! " cried Brook. " All of you—into the corner ! "

They backed before the weapon—all except McLean, who went to the table.

" All right, Brook," he said. " You can put that pop-gun away."

" What is the meaning of this ? " gasped the irate Pollard. " How dare you play this trick on us ? "

" To learn the truth," snapped McLean. " If I am not mistaken, the table will tell it unerringly."

Amazed, they watched him take a small print from his pocket, and also a large reading-glass. Pulling the electric pendant lower, he examined the face of the table through the magnifying-glass, and at last found what he wanted—in the place where Richard Dunning had put his two hands.

" Finger-prints ! " ejaculated George.

" Yes," replied McLean. " I had the table prepared. The results are better than I expected."

" But why——? Great heavens—you don't suspect it was one of us—— ? " gasped George.

McLean made no answer, but went to the window and folded back the curling edge of the plush curtain so that the imprint on the lining came to view.

" Bloodstains ! "

" Aye, the finger-prints of the man who threw the revolver into the garden."

Sylvia's horrified eyes went to George, and George's face became ashen.

" I never did," he gasped. " I went to the window to see if I could catch a glimpse of the murderer. Do you imagine I would shoot my—my own father—the best man in the world ? "

" Not for one moment," replied McLean. " Nevertheless the person who left his finger-prints on that curtain is in this room—at this moment. I will give him one minute to confess."

They all looked at each other, wide-eyed and nervous. Richard Dunning gulped and shook his head.

" It is a trick," he said. " You have no right to descend to such trickery, Inspector."

" I have every right—when I know who it was who went to that window and threw the pistol outside."

" Then tell us," cried Pollard. " Great God, don't leave us in suspense. Who was it ? "

" Yes—who ? " quavered Sylvia.

McLean produced a pair of handcuffs and looked straight at Richard Dunning.

" Not—not Uncle Dick ! " almost screamed Sylvia.

" Rot ! " said George.

" I arrest you, Richard Dunning, for the murder of your brother James," said McLean grimly.

" No—no," said Sylvia, coming forward and wringing her hands. " There is a dreadful mistake."

" Wait ! " begged McLean. " Let him speak if he wishes to, but I must warn him that anything——"

This was too much for George. He came forward, taking no heed of McLean's gesture.

" This is too much," he said. " My uncle and my father were the best of friends. Why, it was Uncle Dick who saved father's life in Java many years ago. Anyone who knows them will tell you that they never had a single quarrel during all the years they have worked and lived together."

Sylvia started as she recalled the scene in the library, when Richard had stated that he and his brother had been having a political argument. McLean saw the look of dawning terror in her eyes. He waved George aside.

" Put out your hands, Mr. Dunning," he said.

Richard pulled himself together.

" I am innocent," he said in a clear voice. " I never fired that revolver."

" You went to that window—in the darkness ? "

" Yes."

" You had the revolver in your hand ? "

" Yes."

" Uncle," cried George. " You are incriminating yourself. You need not——"

" I know what I am saying, George. I—I am afraid the truth must be told."

" It is always advisable," agreed McLean. " Tell me why you disposed of that weapon ? "

" Because—because my poor brother shot himself."

" What ! " ejaculated George.

" It is true."

" That might be a clever invention," mused McLean.

" It might. But I think I have the means to clear myself. On the evening of the séance my brother received—this."

He handed a cablegram to McLean. McLean read it aloud. It was to the effect that James Dunning's bank in Java had gone broke—that he was ruined.

" I found him in the library, with a revolver in his hand. He had been ill and was still in a low state of health, otherwise he would never have contemplated so dreadful a thing as suicide. I argued with him, and there was a bit of a struggle. But I did not secure the revolver. Sylvia came in to tell us that the medium had arrived."

" Yes—yes," put in Sylvia. " That is true."

" After that I had no chance of getting him into a better frame of mind, nor of taking the weapon from him, but I thought that the worst was over for the moment, and resolved to take the revolver from him after the séance." His eyes flashed. " It was this unhealthy business that brought about his end. He thought he heard his wife's voice. He asked her to appear before him. When—when she failed to do so he—— You know the rest. I realised immediately what had happened, and found the revolver on the table. My fingers must have touched blood. I clung to the curtain, for I was shocked and unsteady."

" Why did you not let matters stay as they were instead of attempting to hide the truth ? "

" There I was guilty of subterfuge. In a flash I realised that my brother's life insurance policy did not cover an act of suicide. I—I wanted to save his children from poverty. For that abortive act may God forgive me."

Sylvia went to him and caught his hand, and McLean put the handcuffs into his pocket.

" You—you believe him, Inspector ? " asked George anxiously.

" Yes. Murder would have been entirely motiveless, and extremely difficult. I suspected suicide, but wanted proof. The cablegram has furnished that. You must forgive me for subjecting you all to such an ordeal as you have gone through. Brook, if you have those notes completed, we will make our departure. I am badly needed elsewhere."

A MICROBE MURDER

AMONG certain cases which were never completely cleared up, but for which McLean possessed solutions that satisfied him, was that of Count Leo Ronke, for some time attached to the Russian Foreign Office. Soon after the outbreak of the revolution Ronke managed to make his way to England, and took a large house in the neighbourhood of Richmond.

McLean's first meeting with the swarthy Russian took place at Scotland Yard, whither Ronke had come, in a state of great nervous stress, to beg an interview with the Assistant Commissioner. He was passed on to McLean, who sized him up at once as a gentleman of mystery, and at that moment suffered from a " blue funk."

The ex-Attaché was immaculately attired, in morning coat, light trousers and spats, and a silk hat. He was round about sixty years of age, slightly corpulent, and above average height. His hair was dark and luxuriant, and he wore a short, pointed beard and neat moustache. As he sat down in the chair offered him by Sergeant Brook he mopped his expansive brow with a silk handkerchief, and his large white fingers closed and unclosed on the gold knob of his malacca cane.

" You are Inspector McLean ? " he asked in a deep, but rather shaky voice.

" At your service, sir."

" You—you have my card ? "

" Yes. Count Ronke, I believe ? "

" So—as you will doubtless perceive, I am very—very disturbed in my mind. To-day I saw a spectre."

" A what ? "

" A man from the past—one who hates me, and who will leave no stone unturned to avenge himself on me."

" Who is this—spectre ? "

" A Doctor Volsky. It is twenty years since I saw him last. The circumstances which gave rise to this bad feeling do not matter much. He—he was condemned to Siberia for the rest of his life, and I thought I had seen the last of him. But this morning—I met him face to face. I—I was startled, but thought he did not recognise me. I was mistaken."

He moistened his lips and again made use of the handkerchief—for his brow was clammy with perspiration born of deeply rooted fear.

" Go on," said McLean.

" I took a taxi home, and he must have followed me. Ten minutes after my arrival I was rung up on the telephone. It—it was Volsky speaking. He said he had been looking for me, for eight years, and that now he had found me, and would finish me off in a few days."

" Well ? "

" That is all. He gave me no time to make any response. I heard him laugh as he hung up the receiver—that hideous, cynical laugh that has never ceased to ring in my ears since I first heard it, over twenty years ago."

" And you take this threat seriously ? "

" Yes. I am not naturally a nervous man, for I have been through much trouble ; but Volsky is a fiend. I could tell you terrible stories about him. He will watch me now. I shall not be able to move without his knowledge. I—I need help—or I am doomed."

" What do you fear ? "

" Death—subtle, mysterious death, planned by the most cunning brain in the world. I am not exaggerating. He means what he says. Even at this moment he——"

He gulped and looked round the room, as if he feared that his bitter enemy might be concealed there. McLean wrinkled his brows, for the story was too much like melodrama.

" It is not so easy to commit murder, if the intended victim is warned and takes reasonable precautions. Your house has bolts and bars, I presume ? "

" You don't know Volsky. Bolts and bars will not keep him out. I—I need a bodyguard—someone who will watch over me—keep him from me. Isn't that possible ? "

" It might be, temporarily, but it could not go on indefinitely. The police have quite enough work on their hands in connection with crimes already committed——"

" The business of the police is to prevent crime also," he cut in with asperity. " Isn't it better to save a life than to hang a murderer ? "

" Assuredly. But it is possible you take too serious a view of the threat that was uttered."

" I tell you that unless something is done to prevent it, I shall be dead within a week."

This conviction was certainly reflected in his countenance, and McLean could not help but be interested, for it was evident that his visitor was not a neurasthenic or hysterical type of person.

" I will see what can be done," he promised. " To-night, at any rate, your house will be watched."

" Thank you ! "

" This man—Volsky—what is he like ? "

" Tall and lean, about sixty-five years of age. When I saw him this morning he was wearing a light overcoat, dark trousers, and black felt hat. He is thin, and lean in the face—dark, sunken eyes."

Brook wrote down the description, and ultimately Count Ronke took his departure. McLean turned to Brook, who was scratching his head reflectively.

" What do you make of that, Brook ? "

" Bad wind-up about nothing. If Doctor What's-his-name meant to do him in, would he ring him up to tell him so ? "

" He might. That is no argument either way. Well, as a proof of our hospitality to aliens we ought to do something. Would you like to run down to Richmond, Brook ? "

" To-night ? "

" Yes. Go home and have a rest now, and watch the house from dusk onwards. We'll give him protection for a night or two. After that he must look after himself."

Brook was not in the least interested in the case, and he wondered that McLean, with all his experience, should be willing to waste the time of the force on such a project. But McLean was impressed by Ronke's story. He did not look the type of man to get alarmed over trifles.

That night McLean was called away to the north of England, where a suspect had been detained. Two days were spent in Newcastle taking statements in reference to the detained man, and just before McLean left the police-station to catch the London train a telegram came from Brook :

Count Ronke dead.

McLean stroked his chin reflectively and wished Brook had been a little more communicative. But from those three words he concluded that the cause of death was not yet settled. On arriving at the office he found Brook there.

" You got my wire, Inspector ? "

" Yes. What has happened ? "

" I watched the house as instructed, for two nights. There was no unusual occurrence of any kind. It's a big house, lying off the terrace that overlooks the river, and there are no obstructions of any kind."

" When did Ronke die ? "

" This morning. About eleven o'clock last night his valet came out in a hurry. I asked him if anything was wrong, and he said his master was terribly ill. He had tried to get on to the doctor, but the telephone had gone wrong. The doctor lived only a few minutes away, so he went on foot. When he came back with the doctor I told him who I was, and asked permission to see the Count."

" Well ? "

" He was in a terrible state. Looked like a fit to me—or some violent poison. He couldn't speak, and the doctor was evidently puzzled. I waited for hours and then the doctor came down and told me the Count was dead."

" He didn't tell you the cause ? "

" He didn't know. At least, he wasn't sure."

McLean decided to pay a visit to the doctor immediately, and half an hour later was sitting in the surgery of a young medical man named Winterton.

" You know why the police are interested, Doctor ? "

" Yes. I understand that the Count feared an attempt on his life ? "

" That is so. Are there any grounds for such a belief ? "

" I think not. The symptoms might possibly be brought on by a violent poison, but I am inclined to suspect a seizure of some kind. A very uncommon case."

" There will be an autopsy ? "

" Yes. I should not care to give a certificate—in the peculiar circumstances."

When McLean left him he visited the house of the dead Russian. It was a well-run establishment, employing a butler and a personal servant—the latter a Russian named Lodz, who have been valet to the Count for close upon twenty years. Apparently he knew nothing about the mysterious Doctor Volsky, and was convinced that his master had died from a stroke.

" When was he first taken ill ? "

" Two days ago. I begged him to see the doctor, but he said it was just a temporary indisposition, and would pass."

" There has been no unusual occurrence here ? "

" In what way ? "

" No attempt at—shall we say burglary ? "

Lodz started, stroked his chin for a few seconds, and then shook his head.

" Why do you hesitate ? "

" A little thing did happen, but it was of a trifling nature. A few days ago—last Thursday to be exact—I heard a noise from the direction of the bathroom, which adjoins my poor master's bedroom. My master was out at the time, and I went to investigate. But I found nothing to cause the noise. It was on the following morning that I discovered one of the panes of frosted glass was cracked from top to bottom. There is a large garden beyond the room— belonging to our neighbour, and I have seen a boy there with a catapult at various times. I taxed him with doing the damage, but he swore he was in bed half an hour before the thing happened."

" Did you inform the Count ? "

" Oh, no. He has been worried for some time—about some business matter, I think, and the incident was not of sufficient importance to mention it. I had a new pane put in."

" The Count used to take most of his meals here ? "

" Yes. Occasionally he would lunch in town, but not very often. He was rather particular about his food."

" There is a trustworthy cook ? "

" Quite. She has been with the Count for many years."

McLean went round the house, and interviewed the cook

and the other servants. He discovered nothing that
aroused his suspicions in that direction. They were all old
and trusted servants, and seemed to be deeply affected by
the sudden strange death of their employer.

" What callers have you had during the past few days—
since the breaking of the window ? "

" Only two—apart from the tradesmen. They were
both friends of the Count."

" And the tradesmen ? "

" The regular callers, except for the glazier. His was a
chance call. I employed him to replace the broken pane of
glass."

McLean immediately became interested. He went to the
bathroom and examined the mended window. It was
frosted glass, and the work was badly carried out. On the
right edge the glass was obviously short, and the space filled
up with putty.

" Tell me about that glazier," he said. " Do I understand he called on the morning following the breakage ? "

" Yes. He had a small hand-truck, and asked if there were
any windows that needed replacement."

" A tall man ? "

" Yes."

" What kind of speech ? "

" Rather refined, I thought, but with a slight accent."

" And it so happened that he had with him a pane of glass
almost exactly like that used for these windows ? "

" Yes. It was not quite the same, as you will notice, but
I told him it would do."

" You have never seen this man before ? "

" No."

" How long did he stay ? "

" About half an hour, I think."

" He had access to the bathroom ? "

" Yes. That was necessary."

" The Count's bedroom—adjoining—was that locked ? "

" Yes. I locked it purposely and took away the key."

McLean put a few more questions and then made a
minute survey of the room. Half an hour later he returned
to Scotland Yard, and there wrestled with the problem.
The incident of the glazier was too important to be overlooked. Was it merely a coincidence which brought an

itinerant glazier to that house immediately following the mysterious breaking of a window, and that that glazier should carry with him glass almost identical with the cracked pane ? Such men did not usually frequent the better-class neighbourhoods, nor did they make so poor a job as this man had. Also he was tall, with a foreign accent !

But he remembered that this incident had taken place some days before the dead man had seen his enemy—before the threat had been made ! Presuming that the glazier was Volsky, why had he smashed that window ? What exactly was his object in entering the house ? And why had he let several days pass before uttering his threat ? There seemed but one possible answer. The Count was doomed before the threat was made. Whatever had been administered was in process of doing its deadly work before the threat was made. Volsky had boasted only when he knew that death was on the wing, and it might have been that meeting with the Count which had revealed the fact to his murderer.

An autopsy was subsequently made, and it failed to reveal any trace of poison in the body. After some deliberation the coroner's jury found a verdict of death from natural causes. But McLean was not satisfied. He had seen the body, and had discovered a very small puncture behind the left ear. The doctor, too, had observed it, but attached no great importance to it.

" So the Count cheated his enemy by having a stroke," mused Sergeant Brook. " Well, that saves Doctor Volsky from risking his neck."

" You think so, Brook ? "

" Well, the verdict makes that clear."

" All that it makes clear is that Ronke is dead. He was doomed when he entered this office, and there was never any need for you to watch his house."

" You mean—Volsky did get him, after all ? "

" I feel certain, and it is only five minutes since I hit upon a possible solution. I am going down to Richmond again. If what I believe is true, then we may have to find Doctor Volsky."

But McLean's trip to Richmond was vain of results. The bathroom had been cleaned out, and the whole place was in the hands of the executors. The inspiration had come

too late to permit him to retain a single possible exhibit.
He went back to his office bitterly disappointed.

" No luck ? " asked Brook.

" No. But I want Volsky—if I can find him."

" Isn't the case dropped, sir ? "

" Officially, yes, but I hope to secure information that will
cause it to be reopened. The first thing is to locate Volsky."

" Is there any such person ? "

" There is. He visited that house as a glazier, with a
barrow containing sheets of glass and other things. We
have to find that glazier."

" Where do we start ? "

" In the neighbourhood of Richmond. It is certain that
he would not push a barrow a longer distance than he could
possibly help. He probably hired it. We will make a
start this afternoon."

Aided by the local police, they scoured the neighbourhood,
but without the slightest success. McLean was about to
return to headquarters when news came to the effect that a
park-keeper in Richmond Park had found a barrow containing glass and some tools, hidden among some undergrowth.

McLean stayed on while the barrow was brought to the
station, and then the dead man's valet was sent for. He
averred that the contraption was identical with the thing
which the glazier had brought with him, and now there was
no doubt that the man had disposed of it immediately after
the execution of his job. But it gave no clue to his whereabouts, nor of the person from whom it had been bought or
borrowed.

" Stumped again ! " muttered McLean.

Volsky's description was circulated to all police-stations
over a wide area, and two days later a woman who appeared
at Bow Street, on a charge of disorderly conduct, volunteered information which raised McLean's hopes once
more.

" My name's Soake," she said. " Kate Soake, and I let
lodgings at Pringle Street. Over a month ago a gentleman
called and asked to see my rooms. He was dark and lean—
skinny, I should call him, and he spoke like a foreigner. I
showed him my best rooms and told him the price. He
paid me a week's rent in advance, and took two of them. I

asked him if he was a single gentleman, and he said he was, but he had a niece. He asked me to move one of the beds into the second room. That night him and the girl turned up. All they had was a large trunk and a small bag."

" Did he give you his name ? "

" Yes. Mr. Groll. He called the girl Nadia. She couldn't speak much English."

" He is not with you now ? "

" No. They left suddenly over a week ago. I don't know where he went to, but the girl told me she had got a job in an Italian restaurant up West."

" How did this Mr. Groll behave ? "

" Oh, he was a quiet gentleman. Never seemed to do any work. But he used to go out a lot—at odd times. Once I asked the girl what her uncle did for a living. She said he had a doctor's degree, but found it difficult to get a practice—in England."

" Have you ever heard the name—Volsky ? "

" Yes. He knew a man named Volsky. Some letters came in that name, and he told me this friend of his was using my address, and hoped I didn't mind."

It started McLean off on a new tack. That Groll was Volsky he had no doubt. The next step was to find the girl. Every Italian restaurant in the West-End was visited, and at last McLean found a small place off Seven Dials where a girl named Nadia Groll had been employed until a few days previously. The manager had two addresses—one at the house of Kate Soake, and another in a mean street in Islington.

" Why did she leave ? " asked McLean.

" I don't know. She just didn't turn up, and I engaged another girl. She was in the cash desk. A nice girl, too—well-bred."

Slowly the thing was being narrowed down. McLean decided to pay a visit to the Islington address, and he took Brook with him in case of trouble, for the neighbourhood was a rough one, and Doctor Volsky seemed to be the sort of person well able to take care of himself.

" Are you going to make an arrest ? " asked Brook.

" It depends upon many things. As a matter of fact the evidence against Volsky is scanty. The autopsy rather queered our pitch, unless I can find——"

" What ? "

" The stuff which Volsky used to kill Ronke."

" Poison ? "

" Oh, no."

Brook screwed up his face. McLean had that annoying habit of feeding his interest up to a point, and then closing up like an oyster.

" Suppose you find—what you hope to find, will that help to bring a conviction, after a verdict of death from natural causes ? "

McLean grunted something inaudible. He scarcely liked to admit that he had scarcely a dog's chance of getting a conviction against Volsky in the circumstances, and that his real object was to satisfy himself that murder of a ghastly kind had really been committed.

" Here's the house," he said. " Not exactly a palace, what ? "

It was a tall brick building, fast falling into decay. There was scarcely a window on the whole of its five floors which was not broken, and half of them were boarded up. The entrance was narrow and dark, and the stairs broken and bare of covering. Farther up the street a barrel-organ was playing, and some poorly-clad children were squatting on the kerb close to it.

" Problem—is she here ? " mused McLean.

" Shall I inquire ? Here comes a fellow who looks as if he lives close by."

McLean nodded and stepped into the doorway while Brook inquired of the street lounger whether he knew a man named Groll or Volsky. The man shook his head.

" He's a tall man—a Russian, and he has a niece——"

" Oh, 'im ! 'E lives in there—number six—top floor."

He indicated the doorway where McLean was standing, and Brook thanked him and joined the inspector.

" We're all right. Top floor."

" Good ! We'll go up."

They mounted the steep staircase, and ultimately reached the fifth floor. McLean rapped on the door, and after a minute's delay it was opened by a tall, shapely girl. Her face was thin and sad, and her eyes seemed to be red from weeping.

13

"Is Mr. Groll in?" asked McLean.

"Oh, you—you are the doctor?" she cut in anxiously. "He—he doesn't know I sent for you. Please—please hurry! He is so—so ill."

She spoke with a very strong accent, and was evidently full of apprehension. McLean and Brook pushed past her, and then she appeared to notice that neither of them carried a bag such as a doctor might be expected to bring on an urgent summons.

"You—you are the doctor?" she asked.

"No," said McLean. "But I wish to see your—uncle."

"But he is ill. You cannot——"

McLean removed her restraining arm and moved forward down the narrow passage. There was a door on the right, and he opened it and entered a room that was almost bare of furniture. On a rough bed in the corner lay a dark, haggard man, writhing in agony. His features were fixed in a kind of horrible smile, and his body was arched—almost like a bow.

"Good God!" ejaculated McLean. "Tetanus!"

The girl came forward.

"What do you want? Why do you come here? Can't you—can't you see he is dying?"

"How long has he been like this?"

"Days—days. He would not let me get a doctor. He—he told me what to do. He has medicine—for he has been a doctor himself."

"Doctor Volsky, eh?"

"Yes—yes. But he changed his name—when we came to England. Oh, what shall I do? What shall I do?"

"Get a doctor—quick! There is not a moment to spare. Bring along the first medical man you can find. Hurry!"

She went off, and McLean leaned over the dying man. There was a festering sore on one of his hands, and McLean nodded as he noticed it. The eyes of the dying man came round. He was trying to speak, but his jaws were fixed.

"Listen!" said McLean. "You killed Count Ronke—didn't you?"

Again there was the slightest movement of the jaws.

"He means 'yes,'" said Brook.

" On a rough bed in the corner lay a dark, haggard man, writhing
in agony."

ON A ROUGH BED IN THE CORNER LAY THE SICK, EMACIATED MAN, WRITHING IN AGONY

" That might mean anything. But I am certain he did. Poor devil—he can't last more than a few minutes ! "

McLean paced up and down, waiting for the doctor, and before he could arrive, Volsky uttered a kind of gurgle, and lay perfectly still. McLean went to the bed.

" Dead ! "

" Now we shall never know the truth," said Brook.

" You're wrong. I know it already, but cannot prove it. Is that a medicine chest, over there ? "

" Looks like it."

McLean went to the black box and opened the lid. Inside were a great number of bottles and phials. Most of them were labelled, and at last McLean found what he expected to find. It was a culture labelled " Tetanus."

" Ghastly ! " he said.

" You mean he used —microbes ? "

" Yes. He took a novel sort of revenge, and killed himself in doing so. He broke that bathroom window with a definite object : to gain access to the room on the following day, by posing as a glazier. With this culture he must have doctored either the shaving soap or the brush, and in doing that fiendish work a germ got into a small wound in his finger."

Brook's eyes opened in horror.

" Then the Count had the germs in him when he came to see us ? "

" Yes, and Volsky probably knew it. He didn't utter his threat until he had seen Ronke face to face, and knew by certain signs that his scheme was working."

" But why didn't he die as quickly as his victim ? "

" Because he took steps to fight the disease. It must have been a ghastly fight."

" But it wasn't certain that Ronke would contract it, by using germ-laden soap, or an infected brush ? "

" Not certain, but in shaving a man may cause minute abrasions—almost invisible to the eye, but large enough to let a virulent germ enter his system. What do you think of that for revenge ? "

" Horrible ! But why did he do it ? "

McLean shook his head, as he covered the contorted face with a sheet.

" That we shall never know. Two men only possessed

that information, and the lips of both of them are now sealed.
Well, that is the end of the Volsky case ! "

"And the girl ? "

"Innocent—I think.   In any case I shall take no further
action.   Providence has returned a true bill and exacted the
penalty.   A rather sordid profession, ours—at times ! "

IAN HAY

Set to Partners

¶ Major "IAN HAY" BEITH, C.B.E.,
M.C., is possibly the best case of the
schoolmaster turned novelist. He
served in the Argyll and Sutherland
Highlanders during the War, and made
a world-wide reputation with *The First
Hundred Thousand*. He has written
successful plays in conjunction with
such collaborators as Seymour Hicks,
P. G. Wodehouse, Stephen King-Hall,
and Anthony Armstrong.

SET TO PARTNERS

I

THE simplest way to study the development of Margaret Dale is to follow her successive changes of style.

When she was a fat little girl in a bassinette she was called Baby. However, a large number of quite ordinary people are called that at the outset of their careers, so we will not labour the point. About the time that she learned to walk, her mother, who was subject to outbreaks of imagination, called her Toddles ; but this was sternly discouraged by Mr. Dale, who was a bluff, plain, straightforward Englishman, with no frills or nonsense about him—one of those men who have made the English race beloved throughout the world.

" Shut up ! " he said ; " and call the child Maggie. If the name my father called my mother for forty years isn't good enough for you—well, I'm a reasonable man ; tell me *why !* "

Mrs. Dale, however, preferred to call the child Maggie.

When Margaret was sent to a school for fat little girls at Wimbledon Park it was decided by the authorities to call her Daisy, there being a superfluity of Maggies on the strength of the establishment. So during the next three years she was known and addressed by the infant population of Wimbledon Park as Daisy Dale—which her papa said reminded him of a burlesque actress, but found himself powerless to prevent.

About the time that Daisy reached the age of fourteen, and had begun to develop a fondness for her own point of view—which her father attributed to lack of maternal discipline, and her mother (in an unpublished verdict) to heredity—she was sent to a large school for girls at Brighton. Here she contrived to imbue her preceptors with the belief that her name was Marguérite ; and as such, despite vociferous remonstrances from the usual quarter, she continued to exist until the age of seventeen, when she was sent to be " finished "—which usually means " begun "—in an expensive establishment situated in a suburb of Paris almost entirely given over to such establishments. She returned home at the end of a year with her hair bobbed and expressed a desire to be addressed in future as Margot.

After this she settled down to her foreordained calling of scalp-collectress.

She began upon second-lieutenants, undergraduates, and eighteen-year-old schoolboys home for the holidays. She smoked cigarettes with them, danced continuously, drank cocktails when invited, and was particularly gracious to such as were proprietors of two-seaters. She received sundry proposals of marriage, all of which she accepted in the spirit in which they were offered. At length, having rendered Wimbledon Park a devastated area incapable of further exploitation, she contracted the habit of slipping into the West End of London by the Underground Railway. You can get from Wimbledon Park Station to Charing Cross direct in about half an hour ; which means that you can lunch domestically and virtuously in Wimbledon Park at one o'clock, yet keep an appointment at a matinée in the Strand by half-past two. Margot kept quite a number of these. But they were seldom with the same person. She was quite heart-whole.

One afternoon, after one of these agreeable excursions, she was handed into the Wimbledon train at Charing Cross Underground Station by an adoring youth named Reggie Bingham, and sank down, pleasantly fatigued, in the only vacant seat in the car, beside a City gentleman in a tall hat, whom she recognised at once without any difficulty as her father. During the scene which immediately ensued Margot seized the opportunity—which she had awaited for some time—to press the entire question of parental interference to a definite and victorious issue.

The battle raged all the way home. The advantage inclined at first to the side of Mr. Dale, whose voice could easily be heard above the roar of trains, while Margot's could not. But after Putney Bridge Station, where the train emerged into upper air and cavernous noises ceased, Miss Dale was enabled to bring her lighter artillery to bear with telling effect. Finally, on the walk home from Wimbledon

Park Station to The Limes, Acacia Avenue, S.W.17, she launched a counter-attack of such a voluble and penetrating character that her slow-moving opponent was reduced first to inarticulate boomings and then to vindictive sulks.

"Had to take a pretty stiff line with her ladyship this afternoon," he reported to his wife when he emerged from his dressing-room arrayed for dinner. "Caught her gallivanting round town with some half-baked young pup or other. I don't think she'll forget the telling-off I gave her. Not *my* job, of course; but if her mother can't handle her I suppose I must ! Come along down."

At the foot of the staircase, cool, fresh, slim, and provokingly pretty, stood Margot, wearing an exiguous frock and smoking a Russian cigarette.

"Hallo, Pongo ! " she remarked cheerfully. "Out of your sulks, old man ? "

Mr. Dale, who disliked being addressed as Pongo, began to boom again.

"Now for goodness' sake pull yourself together ! " urged his daughter ; "and listen to me. I didn't hear all you said coming out in the train, though most of the passengers did ; but I heard enough to make it quite clear to me that it was time I put my foot down. I don't intend to go into the matter again, because I gave it to you pretty straight walking home ; and naturally you are like a bear with a sore head over it. I expect you have been taking it out of mother upstairs. She rather likes it, because she thinks being boomed at is one of her privileges as your wife. Well, I don't happen to regard it as one of mine as your daughter. So keep a hold on yourself, my dear old Early Victorian progenitor, and leave me to live my own life. I'm no fool, despite my parentage. Now, what about a bite of dinner ? "

That is all about Margot for the present. Let us turn to William Peck.

William Peck was roughly what his name implies. He did not know this, because he regarded himself exactly as Margot's papa regarded himself,—namely, as a bluff, plain, straightforward Englishman, with no frills or nonsense about him. As a matter of fact he was a serious-minded young man with a perfect passion for performing uncongenial duties. To him work was not worthy of the name if it was of a kind that could be enjoyed. So at the Bank which employed him they always allotted to him tasks of monotonous drudgery, because he was miserable doing anything which involved variety or initiative.

William Peck cherished two ambitions—one immediate, the other remote. The first was to maintain himself in the extreme of physical fitness. By characteristic methods, of course. At school he had been accustomed to sleep nightly wrapped in a sheet which he had previously soaked in cold water. This was to harden him. For exercise he preferred some pastime which would render him utterly exhausted, exceedingly muddy, and, if possible, a casualty from time to time—a broken collar-bone, or something of that kind. His passion for personal discomfort reached its apotheosis during the War. He was one of the few combatants on either side who honestly enjoyed trench-life. When home on leave he insisted upon sleeping on the floor of the smoking-room in his mother's house, in his " flea-bag," rather than avail himself of the greater comfort and privacy of the spare room. It was a pity, he considered, to sacrifice laboriously acquired physical fitness for the sake of a few nights' slothful ease.

As for his other and more remote ambition—it was this. At the right moment he intended to meet, woo, and marry the right girl. He did not propose to do this, though, until he was thirty-six. At present he was only twenty-eight— at which distance of time the enterprise appeared to him simpler of execution than it really was.

His ideas of the girl, and her functions as his wife, were quite clear in his mind. She would be beautiful, affectionate and endowed with perfect taste. She would be fond of home and an economical manager. Every morning she would give William Peck his breakfast at eight, while William read aloud to her all about the Australian Eleven. She would then hand him his hat, kiss him, and dispatch him in good time for the nine-seven. She would be waiting to kiss him again on his return by the six-fourteen. On fine evenings she would sometimes meet him at the station and walk back with him, thus enabling William to tell her the Bank Rate ten minutes earlier than would otherwise have been possible. William would then change into shorts and a sweater and go off for a brisk trot by the River Thames— they were going to live at Twickenham—for naturally he

would not permit domestic felicity to interfere with the gospel
of physical fitness. On his return he would find that his
wife had prepared a cold bath for him and put out his
Indian clubs.

They would dine together in intimate cosiness, with a red-
silk-shaded lamp over the table, and he would tell her some
more about the Bank Rate and how his chest measurement
was keeping up. Anon, they would proceed upstairs to
William Peck's " den "—of course his wife would have her
own dainty drawing-room, but that would be reserved for
the entertainment of her own friends in the afternoon—and
he would take down one of his trusty old pipes from the
trusty old rack over the trusty old fireplace and puff away,
while his wife sat on the other side of the hearth with her
embroidery ; and they would gossip about the Bank Rate
again, or the English Fifteen against Wales, or the time when
William Peck was kicked on the head when stopping a rush
of the opposing forwards in the match against the West Ham
Harriers. They would retire to bed early, because a man with
a hard day's work behind and ahead of him must maintain a
perfect standard of physical fitness. (Forgive me if I have
referred to this already.) On Saturday nights, however, they
would really kick up their heels a bit—dine somewhere, go to
the Coliseum, and, as likely as not, not get home until the
eleven-forty. It was right to unbend the bow occasionally.

By the way, on Saturday afternoons William Peck, once
married, would relinquish manly sports and play some form
of pat-ball game with his wife, or take her for a long country
ramble ; for of course William Peck's helpmeet must maintain a perfect standard of physical fitness too.

II

That is the sort of man William Peck was. Hence it was
only in consonance with the general irony of things that he
should fall helplessly in love with Margot Dale.

They met at a dinner-party given by one of the directors
of William Peck's bank. The director, whose name was
Jobling, lived in a large house near the top of Putney Hill,
while William occupied modest lodgings somewhere near the
bottom, near the river. (Have I mentioned that upon
Saturday afternoons in summer he excoriated himself on

a fixed seat for the honour of the Putney Bridge Rowing Club ?) William was invited to the party because a stockbroker disappointed Mrs. Jobling at the last moment, and there was no time to get anyone else. Mr. Dale was also there, and he brought Margot, who had volunteered, in a spirit of sheer irresponsibility, to deputise for her mother, who had influenza. (She had it twice a year.)

Margot looked distractingly pretty ; and although William Peck could not fail to note that her evening frock was not of a material or cut calculated to promote that comfortable circulation of the blood which is so essential to physical fitness, he felt gratified when bidden to take her in to dinner. He found her a quiet, well-mannered, almost diffident partner. During the soup and fish she said practically nothing at all, which enabled William Peck to start upon the Bank Rate at once. After that he proceeded to consider the depreciation of the rouble and mark. Margot, with wondering eyes and parted lips, appeared to hang upon his words. When William desisted in order to eat a sweetbread she said he was marvellous. Confirmed in his favourable opinion of her, William proceeded to the material and mechanical side of banking. He told her how he reduced dollars to pounds by means of a graph. Then he explained to her what a graph was.

Suddenly he noted that Margot's attention was wandering. In fact, she was flipping a portion of salted almond across the table at her friend, Miss Rita Jobling.

" In this manner," said William Peck, raising his voice reprovingly, " the daily fluctuations of international exchange—— "

Margot swung round upon him. Her former expression of adoration—what she herself was wont to term " the village-idiot stunt "—was gone.

" Do you ever do anything at all with yourself," she demanded, " except hop about behind a counter ? "

" The only members of the personnel of a bank," William explained with an indulgent smile, " who actually do their work behind the counter are the cashiers. Now, I—— "

" Never mind that," said Margot hastily. " What I mean is, what do you do when they open the door of the hutch at five o'clock, and put you out ? "

" You mean, what do I do for exercise ? Ah ! " . . .

When William Peck paused for his next mouthful he had told her all about the difference between fixed and sliding seats, and also about the time he had been kicked on the head.

" I was insensible for three-quarters of an hour," he said.

Once more Margot appeared impressed.

" It's unbelievable ! " she said—" absolutely ! "

" Oh, not at all ! " said William Peck, who really was a very modest fellow.

" It is unbelievable," reiterated Margot emphatically, " that any human being should go about doing such uncouth and stuffy things and actually *boast* of it ! "

William Peck, who for nearly twenty-eight years had cherished a belief that the one thing which a woman requires of a man is rugged strength (such as his own), merely gaped.

" Have you no recreations, my good Peck," continued Margot compassionately, " except those of a hobbledehoy ? "

Hobbledehoy ? William Peck gasped—then pulled himself together for a great and stern effort. He must cope with this heresy. He must controvert this pernicious doctrine. It might be difficult, he knew. He was only a strong, silent Englishman, master of his job and in perfect physical condition ; he was no dialectician. His strength lay in deeds, not words. How he wished Margot could see him casting up three columns of figures simultaneously, or taking a firm line with the office-boy, or being hacked off the ball on a wet Saturday afternoon. Still, he would do his best ; it was his duty.

He turned to Margot, and opened his mouth to begin. It stayed open quite a long time—hanging open, in fact. For Margot lifted her long lashes deliberately and of set purpose, and gave him a look. It was a fleeting look—a mere artless glance—but it was the first time that he had met her eyes fairly. Instead of delivering the homily he had contemplated, he floundered, reddened, and said feebly :

" Other recreations ? Oh yes, I have lots."

Which was a lie.

III

Margot drove home not altogether unimpressed with William Peck. He was a clean-run and broad-shouldered youth. True, his hair cried aloud for unguents and his evening tie required tying more tightly. His moustache,

which was red and entirely lacking in symmetry, must be
dispensed with altogether. His conversation was bucolic,
and his ideals were those of the Stone Age. Still, it would be
rather fun to civilise him—without prejudice, of course.
When his locks had been sheared and he had been trained to
toe the line with the rest of the youth of Philistia, Margot
could decide what she was going to do with him.

So William Peck was invited to a *Thé Dansant* at The
Limes, Wimbledon Park. He accepted, smiling loftily to
himself. With his masculinity and sturdy indifference to
boudoir ways he would feel, he knew, rather like a Dreadnought at an up-river Regatta. But William Peck rather
liked feeling like that ; and of course he often did, associat-
ing, as a man often must, with puny folk. So he accepted.
He was not conscious of being in love yet.

But he was wrong about feeling like a Dreadnought at a
Regatta. What he really felt like was a worm at a conven-
tion of boa-constrictors. He " did not " dance—which
means that he could not. Instead of sitting apart with his
young hostess, as he had expected, smiling indulgently upon
the antics of the pigmies around him, he found himself
drifting sheepishly from the tea-room to the drawing-room
and back again, with intervals of complete self-effacement
in the cloak-room. Once or twice he endeavoured to put
a bold face on things. He would dash out of his hiding-
place, walk briskly into the dancing-room, look masterfully
round as if for an appointed partner, glance at his wrist-
watch, nod his head, and stride masterfully out, as if remembering that she was in the tea-room after all. In the tea-
room he would repeat the performance, and stride out again,
ostensibly to the dancing-room. But where he really went
was to his old refuge among the coats and hats. Here
ultimately the housemaid found him. William Peck suddenly lost his head, became panic-stricken, broke from cover,
and interned himself on the stairs above the first-floor
landing for the duration.

He was dislodged about seven o'clock by damsels coming
up for their outer garments ; and descended in the hope of
finding Margot at last disengaged. He had previously had
speech with her upon arrival. She had offered to provide him
with a partner, but his spirit being as yet unbroken he had refused, saying sarcastically that he had no " monkey-tricks."

Consequently she had abandoned him to his wretched fate.
Now, relenting a little, she allowed him to pour out some
orangeade for her. By this time he was utterly broken.
Still, Margot was minded to make the lesson permanent.

" My good Peck," she said, " I had no idea that you were
as impossible as all this. I thought every human being with
two feet could dance the one-step ! "

" I don't dance," muttered William Peck doggedly.

" One-stepping isn't dancing. It's putting one foot before
the other. Surely you can do that ! Or is it that you're
afraid to hold on to a girl ? "

Dumb, driven, inarticulate, William Peck merely gaped
like a fish. He realised now that he could never make this
adorable—yes, she *was* adorable—but unreasonable being
understand that he did not dance because he considered
dancing effeminate, or that he objected to holding on to a
girl not because he was afraid, but because he had decided
not to do that sort of thing until he was thirty-six. Instead,
he deliberately jettisoned the accumulated ballast of more
than twenty years, and said :

" Won't you please teach me ? "

" Good gracious, no ! " replied Miss Dale frankly. " Why
should I ? "

In his complete abasement William Peck could think of
nothing but to apologise ; which he did.

" I only wanted to please you," he said humbly.

Margot lit a cigarette.

" Then go and learn, my child ! " she said.

IV

" After all," William Peck argued to himself as he trotted
home in the dark—he made a point of running a mile every
day, and the *Thé Dansant*, with its vitiated atmosphere, had
rendered this exercise even more indispensable than usual—
" she would not have told me to go and learn unless she had
taken some interest in my progress, *would* she ? . . . Besides, one must make allowances for women. They are "—
—*pant, pant, pant*—" wayward, and "—*pant*—" capricious.
One must indulge them to a certain extent ; come down to
their level, and so on. If Miss—if Margot and I get into the
habit of dancing together—the Side-Step, or whatever she

calls it—I shall get more opportunities of conversing with her intimately, and forming her mind." . . . He slowed down to a walk, for fear of rousing unworthy suspicions in the mind of the policeman at the cross-roads; then resumed. " I'm sorry she refused to come to the match on Saturday, though. It does help so to be seen in one's proper environment. . . . I don't think I shall play now. . . . I wonder if she will be at home at tea-time. No, I forgot : she said she was going to a matinée. What a way to spend a crisp autumn afternoon ! . . . I wonder if she would come to one with me ? I must find out about these things."

So the next step in the downward path of our apostle of physical fitness was a letter to his divinity, suggesting an expedition to the theatre. If he had had the sense to leave the selection of the play to the lady herself it is possible that William might have met with more success this time. But through an entirely unwarrantable over-estimate of Miss Dale's intellectuality, he proposed a visit to a Shakespearean revival at a local suburban theatre. The result was a horrified refusal. Recoiling abjectly to the opposite pole of error, William called at The Limes and suggested a certain musical comedy—the rage of the West End. Margot replied that she had seen it fourteen times, and inquired how William Peck's dancing was progressing. She also commanded him, as she showed him to the door, to remove his moustache, or for ever remain invisible.

Incredible as it may appear, William Peck succeeded in extracting certain crumbs of comfort—even encouragement —from this barren interview. It implied, he considered, a certain interest in his appearance and personality. The main result was that on the following Saturday the Putney Hill Gladiators took the field without their usual heavy forward. About the time that the match commenced, on a crisp autumn afternoon, a clean-shaven young man might have been observed knocking timidly upon the door of a modest villa in Fulham, bearing the legend :

MLLE ESTELLE
BALL-ROOM DANCING
FOX-TROT GUARANTEED IN SIX LESSONS

" Well," remarked Mademoiselle Estelle, at the end of a laborious and hard-breathing hour, " you may have brains, but they're not in your feet."

" Do you think if I work hard that I shall have a chance ? " inquired William Peck earnestly.

" A chance to do what ? " Mademoiselle turned off the gramophone and regarded her pupil quizzically. She was an alert little person with bright blue eyes and honey-coloured hair. Her cheeks and arms were too thin. The profession of Teacher of Ball-Room Dancing, especially when proficiency is guaranteed in six lessons, is more arduous than lucrative.

" A chance," replied William Peck hesitatingly, " to—to dance well enough to—to—— "

" To what ? "

" To satisfy myself."

" Yourself ? H'm ! They all say that ! " Mademoiselle smiled indulgently. " I think I know your trouble," she added. " When are you coming again ? "

William Peck suggested Monday afternoon at five-fifteen, and departed in the gloaming in search of open-air exercise. He was still feeling a little dizzy, and far more tired than if he had taken part in the football match.

His constitutional, oddly enough, took him across Putney Bridge, up the Hill, and toward Wimbledon Park, where he ultimately found himself striding down Acacia Avenue, in which it will be remembered The Limes was situated. He did not run. Instead, he occasionally changed feet and broke into a curious double-shuffle. He was practising the one-step—or thought he was.

The gate of The Limes stood hospitably open. William Peck hesitated in a painfully indecisive fashion—his moral fibre had crumbled during the past few days—then finally turned into the short drive and approached the house itself. But his feet lagged. He had reached the phase of love-sickness at which the lover's deadly fear is lest he should appear to be intruding.

Sounds of music greeted his ears ; active shadows on the blinds of a large room on the ground floor apprised him of the fact that a *Thé Dansant* was in progress—to which he had not been invited. Well, a time would come !

The Dales possessed a powerful gramophone. At present it was in full blast close to the open window outside which William stood. Had Miss Margot pulled aside the blind at any moment during the next half-hour and looked out upon the moonlit lawn, she might have observed a substantial phantom methodically dancing the fox-trot with itself, counting audibly the while.

VI

" Will you stay and take a cup of tea ? " inquired Mademoiselle after the next lesson. " I've no one else coming this evening, worse luck ; and you don't look as if you had too many people to talk to in your spare time, either."

Now that William Peck came to think of it, this was true, though no one had ever said it before. His colleagues at the Bank were too much occupied with recurrent and continuous affairs of the heart to have any particular leaning towards the society of an apostle of strenuous celibacy ; while the Putney Hill Gladiators, though stout fellows on the battle-field, were not socially entertaining. This discerning little creature was right. William *was* a lonely man ; and at the present moment he was more lonely than he had ever been before. In fact, he had reached the stage when a man simply has to tell someone about it—It.

So they took tea together ; and over the cigarette which followed he recited to Mademoiselle the idyll of Margot Dale.

" I'm afraid I'm rather too muscular and masculine for her," he said sorrowfully, when he had finished his recital. " Too big and blundering for a fragile little bit of Dresden china like that," he added, growing lyric.

" Fragile ? " commented his confidante. " To me she sounds the other way. Tough, I should call her."

" You don't know her ! " said loyal William warmly.

" Don't I ? " Mademoiselle nodded her shapely little head wisely. " I knew one once just like her. I had good cause to remember her, too."

" How ? "

" She took my husband from me—or tried to."

" Husband ? You are married, then ? "

" Widow," replied Mademoiselle briefly.

" Then your name——? " William Peck began to feel that this was rather irregular. He had a natural sense of propriety.

" Oh, my real name is Esther Green. You can cut out the Estelle stuff—that's only for the brass plate—and call me Esther if you like. It would do you a lot of good to be able to call a girl by her Christian name. Have you finished that cigarette ? Well, I bet you've got a pipe in your pocket. Light it, and put your feet on the fender, and I'll tell you," commanded this discerning young person.

William Peck, feeling strangely soothed and comfortable, obeyed.

" I was married all right," continued Esther presently. " All wrong, rather. It was one of those war weddings— me eighteen and Ted twenty-one. London was full of schoolboys dressed up as officers, all mad to have a good time dining and dancing before they went out and—and went west. You couldn't blame them, either. Mother and I started a dancing-school over a tea-shop in Regent Street. It was a little gold-mine to us for a year or so. Up to that time mother had kept rooms. She had always had to work hard, ever since father left her. She's dead now—two years ago. She was never strong ; and the raids, and the rationing, and things like that were too much for her. I met Ted at the dancing-school. I taught him : he paid for private lessons : he was that sort. He was a second-lieutenant in a split-new uniform, and I was about as green as grass ; and when we came out of the chloroform we found ourselves married. Just like that !

" It was more than a year before he went out, and I had my hands full most of that time, I can tell you. He wasn't a bad boy ; not vicious ; but weak—my word ! Putty was strong to him ! Anything in eyelashes could make him eat out of her hand. He was fond of me, though, and none of his little affairs ever looked like coming to anything until he ran into Babs Newberry. She was the same sort of girl as your Margot, I should say. Bobbed hair—liqueurs— despised her parents—and all that. Ted was in camp at Bramshott, and used to come up to me for week-ends. When he missed two week-ends running I began to think a bit. Finally another girl told me something, and I went to the

Savoy the next Saturday night. There was my lord dancing with his Babs." Esther Green's voice shook a little.

" Unutterable cad ! " said William Peck firmly.

" No, it wasn't that. It was just weakness. I spoke to them, and in ten minutes I had Miss Babs packing back to her people at Lewisham. As I suspected, *they* hadn't known anything about the affair ; and the moment I said a few words about seeing them about it I had her squealing Kamerad ! There was no real harm in her—just want of looking after and the freedom the War gave to silly girls. I took Ted home with me. He was very much ashamed of himself—and we had no open trouble after that. I dare say he saw his Babs again sometimes, but I kept my mouth shut. I didn't want to have a row so near the time of his going out. I was glad afterwards, because—because, when he did go, he never—never—— "

" Came back ? " said William gently.

" Yes." A tear ran down the girl's cheek. She wiped it away composedly, and continued :

" It was at the Second Battle of the Somme—a machine gun. He was Mentioned in Despatches, though. I'm glad he was Mentioned in Despatches."

There was a long pause. William was trying, without success, to picture himself married to Margot and being caught by her dancing with someone else at the Savoy. Presently his eyes turned again to the slim figure on the other side of the hearth.

" I expect you miss him," he said awkwardly.

" Yes, I do. Of course, I dare say I should have had trouble with him ; but he'd have been something to look after. Perhaps, he would have gotten more sense as he got older, too. I don't know, though. People don't change much. Perhaps he wasn't the sort of man I ought to have married."

" What sort of man ought you to have married ? " inquired William curiously. He was impartially interested in the question of affinities just now.

" A man who would like being taken care of," replied Esther with great vigour. " I used to wish the War was over, so that I could really take care of Ted. You know ? Look after his clothes, and see he got his meals properly, and get

him off in comfortable time for the morning train, and be
there when he came back in the evening——"

"And give him a kiss," said William Peck automatically.

"Yes ; that's right. Then we would dine together and
talk over all the gossip of the day. There's nothing so dull
in life as having a lot of interesting things to happen to you
all day and know that there'll be no one to tell them to in
the evening."

"That's very true," said William Peck with a sigh. Of
late he had contracted the habit of jotting down memoranda
of interesting things which happened to him, with the intention of retailing the same to Margot when an opportunity
should arise. He had a rather congested list in his pocket
now.

"Then," continued Esther, "we would have gone out
together sometimes—to the theatre, or the pictures." She
gave another little sigh. "I don't know, though. Perhaps
things are best as they are. Ted didn't like staying at home
much any evening, and if he had gone out I dare say he'd
have gone out without me. I may be one of the lucky ones,
really ! " She smiled and looked up briskly. "Finished
your pipe ? I don't want to turn you out ; but you know
what neighbours are. When'll suit you again ? "

William Peck suggested the following Saturday afternoon.

But he did not keep the appointment. Margot had returned a reply to a long-rehearsed invitation which exceeded
his wildest hopes, and they had attended a matinée together.
The excursion was not altogether as successful as it might
have been, because William's ideas on the subject of *chic*
restaurants and the best seats in theatres were on a considerably lower plane than his guest's ; but Margot, softened
probably by her cavalier's rapturous oblivion to all save her
presence, and the misguided pains which he had lavished
upon the details of the entertainment (down to the box of
uneatable chocolates which he produced from his hat as
soon as they sat down in the seventh row of the Dress
Circle), suffered for once in silence. On the way home she
reaped her reward, in the form of her seventeenth proposal.

William Peck accompanied his petition by a set speech of
considerable length, which he had composed and carefully
committed to memory against the moment when opportunity
should arise to deliver it. Knowing William Peck, we can

surmise its general trend. It included an outline of William's views on domestic routine which gave Margot chills down her spine ; and she said so. But there was another item, which she had not expected and which roused emotions of an entirely contrary nature—to wit, a financial statement. Hitherto Margot had regarded William Peck as a bank clerk —a small-time cavalier ; an escort of the Landsturm class. The fact that William Peck was sole relative and heir of the Chairman of the Board of the Bank, and had elected characteristically to ground himself in the rudiments of his profession by five years of monotonous routine before taking a seat on the Board itself, was a revelation to her. Though the halting proposal made but slight impression upon Margot's resilient little heart, it made an appeal to her business instincts which could not be ignored. William Peck was immediately promoted, mentally, to the rank of Business Proposition. However, she realised that she need not be in a hurry to take up her option. Firmly hooked fish can wait.

" Don't be a sentimental idiot," she said. " And don't go and blow out your brains or anything, because it isn't done. We're having a *Thé Dansant* on Saturday. Come, and let me see if you can dance a one-step without treading on my feet. We can always be friends, can't we ? " she concluded, a trifle mechanically.

" I believe you're right," said William Peck.

Margot stared at him.

VII

Two days later William Peck completed his course of six lessons, within the period of which, it will be remembered, proficiency had been guaranteed.

" Will I do ? " he asked, as Esther turned off the gramophone for the last time.

" Do for what ? "

" I mean, will I pass in a crowd ? "

" That isn't what you came here to learn to do—is it ? You wanted to make a real hit with a certain person, didn't you ? "

" I suppose we are always trying to make a hit with somebody," said William Peck, regarding her thoughtfully. " In fact "—his face broke into a cheerful smile, the first for weeks—" I should like some more lessons."

" All right. You needn't pay in advance this time. I can trust you."

" I'm glad of that," said William, " because I shall want a lot."

" Certainly. How much of my valuable time do you propose to engage ? " inquired Esther briskly.

William Peck told her.

He ultimately stayed to supper.

VIII

Margot, whose conscience told her that she had been perhaps a little too careless with her latest suitor, felt distinctly relieved when he duly appeared at the *Thé Dansant*. This time he boldly interrupted her in a dance and asked when he might have the pleasure.

" Come back in about five minutes," she said, " when I have got rid of this infant." The gentleman referred to was a Mr. Toby Deverill, a fair average specimen of the flower of modern chivalry.

William Peck withdrew, and Margot said :

" I think he's rather a lamb, Toby."

" Tripe ! " growled the flower.

" Little boys mustn't be jealous," replied Margot, entering with zest into the game which she loved best in all the world.

" Muck ! " rejoined Mr. Deverill.

Margot, with whom this brand of repartee was quite in order, gave him an affectionate pat.

" You're rather a lamb too, Toby dear," she said, and rising, signalled to William Peck to approach.

They took the floor together—with remarkable smoothness. (All the same, it was only by an effort that William Peck refrained from counting out loud.)

" You've made marvellous progress, Peck," announced Margot graciously. " Who has been teaching you ? "

" My wife," panted William Peck.

Reprinted with the Author's permission from *The Lucky Number*.

fact,"—his face broke into a cheerful smile, the first for weeks—" I should like some more lessons."

"All right. You needn't pay in advance this time. I can trust you."

"I'm glad of that," said William, " because I shall want a lot."

"Certainly. How much of my valuable time do you propose to engage?" inquired Esther briskly.

William Peck told her.

He ultimately stayed to supper.

VIII

Margot, whose conscience told her that she had been perhaps a little too careless with her latest suitor, felt distinctly relieved when he duly appeared at the Thé Dansant. This time he boldly interrupted her in a dance and asked when he might have the pleasure.

"Come back in about five minutes," she said, " when I have got rid of this infant." The gentleman referred to was Mr. Toby Deverill, a fair average specimen of the flower of modern chivalry.

William Peck withdrew, and Margot said:

"I think he's rather a lamb, Toby."

"Tripe!" growled the flower.

"Little boys mustn't be jealous," replied Margot, entering with zest into the game which she loved best in all the world.

"Much!" rejoined Mr. Deverill.

Margot, with whom this brand of repartee was quite in order, gave him an affectionate pat.

"You're rather a lamb too, Toby dear," she said, and hung, signalled to William Peck to approach.

They took the floor together—with remarkable smoothness. (All the same, it was only by an effort that William Peck refrained from counting out loud.)

"You've made marvellous progress, Peck," announced Margot graciously. "Who has been teaching you?"

"My wife," purred William Peck.

JAMES HILTON

He Hadn't the Nerve

Mr. JAMES HILTON'S first literary work appeared in a Northern daily newspaper while he was still a schoolboy, but his fame as a novelist began with the appearance of *And now, Goodbye* in 1931. In 1934 his position among English post-war novelists was assured by the award of the Hawthornden Prize, which he received for his novel *Lost Horizon*. His recreations are foreign travel and mountain-climbing.

HE HADN'T THE NERVE

THROUGH the slanting cabin-windows the sea glittered like blue diamanté, and one of the three passengers in the aeroplane gazed down exultantly as he caught sight of the Channel steamer plodding its way from Dover to Calais. He was an interesting-looking man, blue-eyed, fair-haired, and with a tanned complexion that accorded well with his physique and with the rough genuineness of his travelling tweeds.

Temple Jones was travelling by air for the first time in his life ; and he was to be met by a very charming and pretty woman at the end of the trip ; but that woman was not his wife. His wife, in fact, was in Cheltenham, and knew nothing at all about the somewhat curious affair.

From which, perhaps, it would be tempting to conclude . . . but most of the conclusions would be wrong. Temple Jones was not the sort of man who makes a habit of it. Until only the other day, so to speak, he had been all that could be expected of a husband, a father, a half-commission man in a stockbroker's office, and a season-ticket holder on the Southern Railway. He was thirty-eight years of age. (During the War, incidentally, he had won the Military Cross.) He was liked, respected, admired. He had a thousand or so a year, a detached villa at Chislehurst, two boys at a prep. school, a quite excellent wife, and a Morris-Oxford car. All of which would have been paradise to many a fellow.

Yet to Temple, after ten years of it, it had all become suddenly preposterous—yes, *all*—that crowded 9.35 to London Bridge each morning, and the pinky smoothness of the *Financial Times*, and the quarterly payments to the building society and old Robbins's chatter at the golf-club, and the Sunday motor-trips to Brighton, and—oh, especially —that crazy paving in the garden that was somehow neither more nor less crazy than everybody else's crazy paving.

It was all a groove, and in his soul he knew he was not made for grooves, and always in spring and early summer he knew it most of all.

Usually such moods passed over with no result save a fretfulness which his wife diagnosed as " wanting a change "; but this year two extra circumstances had arisen. The first was his wife's visit to friends at Cheltenham, leaving him on his own ; and the second was little Mitzi Felsenberg. She was an Austrian girl, charming and vivacious, who had been working in the office as foreign correspondent for several months before he had taken any notice of her. She liked him ; he was a gentleman. He liked her ; she was attractive and efficient. That was how it stood, as it so often stands in offices. Then, one morning in June, she had said : " I'm afraid I shan't be coming after to-day, Mr. Jones. I have to go back home."

" What ? To Austria ? "

" Yes."

" Why all the hurry ? "

" Your Ministry of Labour won't renew my permit. I have to leave at once."

" At once ? "

" Yes. Within a few days if I can arrange things."

" I say, that's bad. Do you want to go ? "

" Not particularly." And she had looked at him then and blushed. He had answered haltingly : " Well, I—we, I mean—the firm that is—don't want you to go, either. It really is *too* bad." And an hour or so later, with a growing sense of inward perturbation that surprised him, he had said : " Oh, well, if you really have to be off and away so soon, better lunch with me—must have a good old farewell talk together, eh ? "

Once before he had taken her to lunch, at a cheap teashop in Broad Street, but this time he hailed a taxi and said " Frascati's." Worth the expense, he felt ; it was a special occasion ; he would probably never meet her again ; he liked her ; they had got on well together.

That was on Monday morning, and by Wednesday Temple was in the midst of the most extraordinary adventure that had befallen him for a decade. He was having an " affair " ; his whole mind and being seemed suddenly to have diverted themselves into new and fascinating channels. It was absurd to talk of him as having fallen in love with Mitzi ; love was not the name, or not quite the name, for the fever of excitement that possessed him. She focussed all his vague and shadowy restlessness into a single direction, her own.

He was somehow in a strange dream, living the life of a strange and different man. He still caught the 9.35 as usual, but everything else was not as usual. Even the June sunlight seemed more brilliant than he had ever known it before ; all the world was tremulously alive ; and as he climbed the dark stairs to the fourth-floor office in Draper's Gardens he had to fight hard to remember where he was, and why, and what he was expected to do. . . .

But that same evening, dining with Mitzi and taking her to a theatre, he was all he knew himself to be—the hero, the adventurer, planning the joint adventure of man and woman with one whose eagerness seemed no less than his own.

And the plan was really quite simple and perfect. She left England on Thursday. On that same Thursday he made it known at the office that he was going away golfing from Friday to Tuesday. He wrote to his wife the usual sort of letter in answer to her last one ; he assured her that all was still as it should be at the house, that the man had called about the vacuum-cleaner, and that the sweet peas looked as if they were going to have a good year. He wrote also to his two youngsters at school, enclosing a ten-shilling note for them to spend at the tuck-shop. And he took care to inform the maid, the fellows at the golf-club and a few train acquaintances that he was off for a long week-end in the country.

Then on Thursday evening he called personally at the air-travel agency and made inquiries. All the seats on the Basle air-liner were already booked, they told him ; but later, they said, they would be sending a relief 'plane.

So now he looked down exultingly as he saw the silver Channel, and the steamer, like a small toy, moving across it half a mile below. He was—no need to deny it—absurdly, almost hysterically happy. Adventure ! Excitement ! LIFE—with every letter a momentous capital ! And Mitzi at Basle aerodrome, waiting for him when the 'plane swooped down ; they were to go on from Basle to some quiet place that she knew of, some little paradise by a Swiss lakeside. . . .

And he was to be back by Tuesday. That, rather oddly, only served to accentuate the marvellousness of it. It was, in a sense, no more than a gigantic spree. Nobody would ever know anything about it. He was very fond of his wife ; they had always " hit it " pretty well ; ridiculous to pretend that, in the long run, he could have been happier with anyone else. But you could not expect any woman to give a man absolutely all he craved for.

He was not sharing with Mitzi anything that his wife had ever had, or ever could have. She had always failed to understand that part of him—the mad, adventurous part of him. She would have had him a model of domestication in all things ; and yet, with woman's supreme illogicality and ignorance of men's affairs, she always wondered why he was not more dashingly adventurous in business.

" You're on the Stock Exchange," she used to say. " I can't see why it is you don't make more money—you must get all sorts of tips." And when he replied : " I do, but I'm wise enough not to take 'em," she would look at him half-pityingly, half-protectively, as if she were ashamed of having married such a weakling.

Their only real quarrel during ten years of married life had been on this point ; she had wanted him to buy some shares which, as it happened, did go up, and then, of course, she reproached him with not having taken her advice.

" I suppose you hadn't the nerve," she had said calmly, and then, for the first time, he had really lost his temper.

" I can't afford to have the nerve," he had answered savagely. " Perhaps if I hadn't school fees to pay, and a house mortgage, and the instalment on the car, and the maid's wages, and your dress bills——"

He smiled now when he thought of that stupid and quite transient little tiff—he smiled, and looked about him in the small cabin. It was rather lucky being in the relief 'plane—not so crowded—only two other passengers, in fact. Both were men. One was a short and very stout little man with a Jewish countenance ; the other, making a rather piquant contrast, was quite one of the biggest and most magnificently proportioned fellows Temple had ever seen.

There was a fourth occupant of the cabin—a uniformed

attendant—guard, conductor, perhaps. He was a thin, delicate-looking fellow with whom Temple had already exchanged a few commonplaces. Now, observing the latter's roving eye, he moved over to an adjacent seat and remarked that it looked like being a good trip.

Temple nodded.

" A good trip, eh ? You mean the weather ? "

" Yes, sir. Sometimes it can be pretty rough."

" That must be bad. Only two drawbacks to air-travel that I can see—first, the racket, and second, you can't smoke."

" Yes, sir. The later machines, though, aren't so noisy as this one."

" This is a bit old-fashioned, you mean, eh ? "

The man smiled.

" I wouldn't say that, sir, but it's—well, it isn't one of the latest. Just a straightforward, single-engined bus—perfectly sound and fast enough—that's what this one is. But no frills about it. Now, if this were one of the latest, sir, I could serve you with a cocktail or a cup of tea."

" I should choose the cocktail, I think."

" No doubt, sir. . . . However, as I said, it's quite a fast machine, and we ought to be in Basle by tea-time, especially with such a light load."

" Yes, I suppose we *are* light in point of numbers. But our two fellow-passengers do their best to make up for it, don't they ? "

The attendant smiled again.

" Yes, they certainly do. I suppose you know who they are, sir ? "

" No. Haven't the slightest idea."

" Cowboy Clarke and his manager, sir. Off to Rome to fight that Italian fellow."

" Really now. That's interesting."

But Temple didn't think it was particularly ; he wasn't a boxing " fan." That a professional pugilist should be flying across Europe to meet another professional pugilist did not seem to him half so sensational as that he himself should be flying across Europe to meet another woman.

He felt the droning rhythm of the engine rising into his head and making him drowsy. The fringe of sea and land crawled across the panorama below like a curtain drawn

14

slowly over a picture. He felt himself relapsing into the most tranquil and satisfying slumber.

He was awakened by an impression that he was slipping out of his chair and painfully barking his shins against something ; then, as he opened his eyes and achieved partial consciousness, he could see and feel that the machine had lost its steadiness. It was in fact, rocking rather violently. Momentarily, he glanced through the window, but to his surprise there was nothing at all to see ; no suggestion of sunlight or of the earth below—nothing but a dim and rather incomprehensible greyness. And even as he looked, a particularly violent lurch sent him half-skidding into the next seat and brought nearly into collision with him the face of the larger of his two fellow-passengers.

That face, shot suddenly to within a few inches of his own, was one which Temple just fancied that he recognised. Previously he had seen nothing but the man's powerful shoulders and strong, well-poised neck. Cowboy Clarke, yes—Temple faintly remembered a photograph in the picture-papers.

And now the great man was actually talking to him, though Temple could not catch all the words, partly because of the racket and partly because the other fellow's accent was so emphatically transatlantic. But the general meaning was that Cowboy was sorry for crashing across the cabin like that, but that he couldn't help it. . . . And Temple, still half-drowsy, shouted " Oh yes, that's all right."

A few seconds later he knew that he himself was lurching across the floor as if pulled by some giant and invisible magnet ; he fell over chairs, struck something soft and yielding, heard a smothered scream from beneath his feet. Heavens—the other passenger—that little fat man—was there. He was actually treading on him. He shouted " Sorry ! " at the top of his voice, but the only reply was a rather terrified whine. Then he found himself lurching back, and managed to cling to a stanchion in the middle of the cabin. That seemed a miracle ; he held on and looked about him again.

Something, quite evidently, was wrong. Yet the loud thrum-thrum of cylinder-explosions was still continuing normally. And then, down the little iron ladder that led to the pilot's cockpit from the front of the cabin, he saw the

attendant making slow and difficult progress. At the foot
of the ladder the man halted, then made a dash across the
swaying floor, and shouted almost in Temple's ear : " Are
you by any chance a doctor, sir ? "

Temple answered : " I'm afraid not. What's the
matter ? "

" The pilot, sir."

It was curious how the two men, Temple and the attendant, felt themselves instinctively drawn together as against
the other two, who were by this time crouching and yelling
in various parts of that dizzying cabin.

Temple shouted : " Yes ? What's been happening ?
I was asleep."

" Don't know exactly, sir. The pilot——"

" Yes, the pilot. All right. I'll——" The rest of his
words were lost as a plunge of the machine shot them both
across the floor again, fortunately near to the iron stairway.
" Up there, sir ! " shouted the attendant, and Temple
climbed. It was not easy, peering over the edge into that
confined space ; there were the gauges and instruments, all
apparently in order, but facing them, huddled into a curious
and rather shapeless attitude, was the pilot—not quite in
order. Temple shouted at him, shook him ; then made
what cursory inspection he could in the restricted space.
It was perhaps sixty seconds before he descended the ladder
and faced the waiting attendant.

" I've had a look," he said. " He's either very ill or dead.
Dead, I fear."

" Good God, sir ! "

" Yes. Awkward, isn't it ? Can you bring her down ? "

" I—I don't think I could, sir. I don't know anything
about them."

" Same here, worse luck. We ought to get the fellow
out, anyway. Help me with him."

Shouting further directions, Temple re-climbed the ladder,
and with his powerful arms and hands unstrapped the pilot's
body and hauled it through the hatchway into the attendant's waiting arms. This procedure, accompanied as it was
by an intensified plunging and bucking of the 'plane, drew
from the other two men a half-fascinated and half-horrified
attention. Both came pressing forward in wildest panic.

Temple shouted : " The pilot's ill. Do either of you

know anything about these contraptions? How to make a landing, I mean?"

The question was answered instantly and without words. The little fat man, white as chalk, staggered against the wall of the cabin and set up a shrieking that was just audible above the din of the engine. The other, the big fellow, lived up to his profession and reputation by giving the whiner a push that sent him sprawling to the floor.

"Curse your howling!" he bellowed fiercely, and turned to Temple as if on the point of felling him with one of those world-famous left hooks.

Temple recognised in both men the varying aspects of terror. He faced the big man as squarely as the rocking of the floor would permit, and shouted: "You can't help at all, then, eh?"

Cowboy Clarke, his huge arms still poised threateningly, moistened his lips to make some reply. Fear in him was translated into a mounting anger, a stupefied resentment that such an august being as a champion boxer, used to earning his hundreds of pounds a minute, should ever be faced with the ordinary hazards of life and death.

"Hell!" he screamed, almost inarticulate. "When we get to earth I'll have the law on this company! Gotta date on the 16th against Bimbo Bambino—Wop heavyweight— purse of fifty thousand dollars—guess if I'm hurt in this somebody'll have to chew dirt—you—*you*——" he swung round menacingly on the attendant—"you rep'sent the company—company contracted to fly me over—guess you'd better do something pretty quick——"

Temple pushed himself between the boxer and the pale but quite collected object of so much fear-begotten fury.

"Cut out all that!" he interrupted, with a sharpness which, though audible above the din, yet somehow still contrived to be quiet. "You don't seem to understand the position. This man knows nothing about 'planes. Neither do I. We're just flying blind at present—God knows how or where. I just wondered if you knew how to do anything, that's all. As you don't, you'd better keep quiet. See?"

He had his hand on the ladder and was about to climb again when the big man pulled him back. "Eh? Eh? What's the big idea? Where you goin'?"

" Up there. Leave go."

" Wha—what you goin' up there for ? "

" See what I can do."

" Can you—do you know how—how—— ? "

" No, unfortunately——"

" Why, then, you fool, you'll kill us all—you'll crash the whole damned thing——"

" The whole damned thing'll crash anyhow. Make your mind easy about that."

" But—but——"

" I'll stand down, though, if you think you'd have a better chance yourself."

" Chance ? You mean—you mean you gonner try—tc get us down ? "

" Can't do any harm, anyhow. Sure you won't have a try for it ? "

Cowboy Clarke's arms fell limply to his side. He had reached the point where fear, having run the complete gamut of rage, could no longer keep up even that surface disguise. It was fear now, naked and shameless, that stared from the quivering eyes and twitching lips—but a simple, honest fear, for all that—not the cringing panic of the little stout man who still lay whining on the floor. There was something in Cowboy Clarke that Temple did not altogether dislike, and when the boxer stammered thickly : " Not me, boss—not me ! " Temple answered : " Very well, I'll go. Pull yourself together, man, and hope for the best."

A few seconds later Temple sat in the cockpit of the 'plane and wondered if ever since the beginning of the world a man had been in just such a position. Four living human beings, thousands of feet above ground, crashing through the air at two miles a minute—and crashing blindly and uncontrollably ! Yet the secret of control was there, perfectly to hand—a cipher, as it were, with life depending on the discovery of a correct solution within a few moments.

Temple fixed himself squarely in the seat and for a few seconds actually closed his eyes. Not exactly to pray, yet when he opened them again both brain and nerves seemed to have stretched themselves taut. A curtain was rising on a new act ; he was icily cool. He felt as he had done years before, when sometimes in the darkness of early morning, he had set out " over the top " on a trench raid. Or, for that matter, as he had always felt when running down the rugger-field to take a place kick. Just icily cool, and—for some extraordinary and inexplicable reason—icily happy as well.

Even while he was adjusting and tightening the strap he was calm enough to think how puzzled people would be if, and when, amongst the wreckage, his body and not the pilot's were discovered with the strap round it !

Then he studied the gauges immediately in front of him. He had no more than the ordinary man's knowledge of such things, but he guessed the identity and function of the altimeter, and noticed that it registered six thousand. Over a mile high, that was ; it gave him a chance. And the petrol-gauge, too, indicated a tank still fairly full. Not too bad ; things might, anyhow, have been worse. His feet were firmly fixed on a sort of pedal-bar ; the control-lever (it must be that, though how and what it controlled were other matters) pushed up between his legs in the most convenient and reasonable way ; really, if one had had the time to enjoy it, things were dashed comfortable in that cockpit.

Then he looked at his watch ; five to four ; hadn't the fellow talked of reaching Basle by tea-time ? Basle, then, mightn't be so very far away. The map in the holder was a detailed one, but as he hadn't the slightest idea where he was, it was of little use for the time being ; nor could the utmost straining of his eyes, as he stared through the glass windscreen, reveal any break in that infinite greyness ahead. Flying through cloud, of course ; moisture was streaming down the glass ; and then he noticed a rubber screen-wiper obviously controlled by a near-at-hand switch.

He pressed the switch and was quite cheered by the instant response of that rotating arm ; to discover anything at all in common between a runaway 'plane and his own Morris-Oxford gave him a comfortable sensation of not being such an outsider after all.

He grasped the control-lever—yes, he had to begin somehow—and just pushed it very slightly forward until, with a rather sickening swing, he felt the pressure of the strap and realised that his forehead was doing its best to hit the windscreen. Ah, gently does it . . . so . . . so . . . and he brought the lever back—just in time, he felt (though he could not be certain) to avoid a most dreadful dive to death.

He saw the speed indicator mounting; the 'plane had gained momentum during that forward plunge. And then, before he could think of anything to do next, the greyness dissolved before his eyes, and he saw something that, for the moment, snatched the breath out of his lungs.

Far away, at the very limit of distance, lay range upon range of snow-capped mountains, with an advance guard of green and rounded foothills. The air blazed into livid sunshine. The whole effect of that horizon was unreal, stagy, like an impossible backcloth done by some futurist scene-painter. And yet—and his thrill came with the word —they must be the Alps. He had never seen them before, and had never in his wildest dreams guessed that he would see them first of all like this. . . .

And then he looked below and saw that the country was a distant, meaningless patchwork of browns and greens; he could discern nothing at such a height. He stared hard for a moment and then slowly, by way of experiment, depressed the pedal under his left foot.

The effect was disconcerting though not unexpected; he felt the side of the seat pressing against his ribs, and for an instant, during the swing, the control-lever fell forward out of his hands. He clutched it sharply, but not in time to prevent a terrifying downward swerve; then, almost automatically, he stepped on the right-hand pedal and brought the lever back with a jerk.

What happened next was sheerly stupendous. The entire horizon gave a heave and seemed to lift itself completely over his head. He dared not breathe; the strap tightened about his waist as if he were being swung aloft by some celestial crane. The blood rushed tinglingly into his head; he gasped, pushed the lever forward again, and waited, the earth rushed at him like a monster taking an upward spring; he was lost, he had done something tragically, irreparably wrong; he was plunging to destruction at two hundred, three hundred, any number of hundred miles an hour; nothing to do but wait, wait for the almighty climax . . . then, with a slow effort, he pushed back the lever with just the last flicker of hope.

Every strut and timber of the machine quivered and strained, but the pace was checked; the downward rush came to an end. But soon, instead of tranquillity, came another horizon, swooping over his head like a brown-green monster; he gasped again, and something small and hard really did hit him in the face, and when he looked he saw that it was his own fountain-pen.

Now how could his fountain-pen, which he always carried in his waistcoat-pocket, fall on him, by some astonishing freak of gravity, from above? He was puzzled, and rather dazed, but still ready to continue battle with those obstreperous horizons. Yet another of them was coming; he felt the warning sensation in his stomach, and then the drag of his body against the strap.

Lever forward again, then back, but this time not quite so far—steady now, don't give in—those horizons have to be stopped somehow . . . steady, old man, steady now . . . and, with sudden sweetness and unimaginable relief, he felt the swirl of the cosmos obedient to his will. He had done the trick! The machine, with an almost muscular clench of all its parts, was flying on even keel once more! He looked at the altimeter, and all at once the thought occurred to him: " Good God! Must have been looping the loop or some such devilment—look at the thing—it says only two thousand now! "

The earth, indeed, was much nearer, and that horizon of snowy peaks had receded before the nearer limit of green ridges. He looked down and could see a streak that was probably a river, a few puffs of white smoke that suggested a train, a patch of red that might have been either a large roof or a field of poppies. He felt: " By Jove, I'm doing this rather well. Now I must think about landing. How *do* you land? How do you stop the thing? Stop the engine, of course—one of those switches." He pressed one, and the roar of the engine ceased so suddenly that even his calmness hardly survived that startling silence. Then he pressed the switch again and the engine burst into renewed and comforting clamour.

He felt like a child in a train who has discovered the secret of a patent window-catch and must make the most of it before a harsh parent drags him away. He switched the engine off again. Silence. On. Off. On. . . . Then, during one of those uncanny intervals of silence, he heard, above the scream of the wind, his own voice—laughing. . . .

Come, come, that sounded dangerous ; mustn't laugh—not yet, anyhow.   Yet all his soul was laughing ; he felt as if this were the apex of all existence, as if all his life had been. leading nowhere but to this supreme moment.

And the earth was rising all the time to meet him— perceptibly, like the bosom of a breathing animal.   He was low enough now to see a winding road, with little dark rectangles on it that were probably motor-cars, and a few patches of deeper green that looked like woods.   Avoid trees, of course—likewise houses and telegraph poles. Look for nice stretch of open field.   Plane down gently. Shut engine off. . . . Touch ground, come to standstill. . . . How easy it seemed when one merely imagined it . . . and then, as he kept his eyes below, he saw a large stretch of wooded hillside sweeping towards him like a wave of the sea.

Push back the lever—marvellous—up again—now make the turn—soon cross those damned trees—try again—looks more promising over there. . . . And as he skimmed over the crest of the hill, not more than a few hundred feet above the tallest tree-tops, he thought : " By Jove, old man, if you're doing nothing else, you're learning to fly."

A minute later he saw just what he wanted—a big grassy field, hedgeless and looking reasonably flat.   No sense in hesitating.   Take the risk ; keep calm ; trust, in the very last resort, to luck. . . . He saw the field swelling towards him like a green sea ; he had shut off his engine ; all was tense, silent, expectant ; by God, as he came down to it, that field didn't look so flat after all—had the most devilish-looking ridges and hillocks—still, never mind—take the chance—too late to change plan—something now was going to happen in a minute or so, in half a minute, in a few seconds . . . there . . . there . . . there . . . damnation, what a hell of a bump ! . . .

But he had, despite a burst tyre, a damaged wing, and a completely shattered tail-skid, performed the miracle. He had brought the thing to earth, and neither he nor the three living occupants of the cabin behind had suffered anything worse than shocks and bruises.   But what shocks and what bruises !   When they hauled themselves out of the cabin and climbed unsteadily down to the field he was amazed at their streaked and haggard faces ; he wanted

14*

to laugh at them, they looked so terribly absurd ; he could not at first realise that the experience which had been so marvellous and exhilarating to him had not been so to them also.

It was the little fat man who first recovered himself sufficiently for speech. But he did not speak to Temple. All his thoughts were for Cowboy in that supreme moment of thankfulness.

" Gee ! " he exclaimed, almost tearfully, taking hold of the boxer's arm. " There's a t'ing to have happen to you ! And you're not hurt bad—no ? Oh, boy—what a story for the papers—won't that little dago just squeal with envy when he reads about it ! "

Cowboy Clarke took longer to recover, but when he did he walked over to Temple. With blood dripping from a cut on the forehead and with hands that still trembled violently, he gripped him by the arm. He did not speak for several seconds, but his lips moved as if he were trying to. Then he just said : " Gee, boss, but you did it ! "

The attendant, also cut and bruised, but otherwise unperturbed as ever, was busy inside the 'plane. Temple went over to him, away from the two others, and found him stooping over the pilot's body.

" Yes, he's quite dead, sir, as you thought. Perhaps we ought to leave him here for the doctor."

Deliberately, it seemed, they were both trying to pretend that this was quite an ordinary, everyday occasion.

Temple was still calm, though there was a look of gathering dazedness in his eyes, and he put his hand to his forehead as if to brush away confusing thoughts.

" Yes, I suppose so," he answered. " A doctor, yes. No doubt there'll be all kinds of fuss. Have you any idea where we are ? "

" In a field in either France or Switzerland, sir—that's all I can say. Probably somewhere near the frontier."

" I suppose we'd better walk off somewhere and find out definitely."

" Yes, sir. It looks rather lonely country—we may not have been seen coming down."

" Well, let's go."

" With the others ? "

" If they care to come too—I don't care what they do.

All the little Jew chap seems to be thinking of is how to get publicity for his man out of it."

The attendant whistled softly.

" Publicity, eh ? Well, yes, that's rather inevitable. But, if you'll pardon my saying so, sir, it isn't Cowboy Clarke who's going to get the star publicity out of all this."

" No ? You mean——"

" Yes, sir. Exactly. I daresay it won't please you to hear it, but I really must say that it seems to me one of the most remarkable things ever done—anywhere—by anybody. Excuse my enthusiasm, sir. You really can't blame people if they make rather a fuss over it."

And suddenly then, for the first time for at least two hours, he thought about Mitzi. Mitzi waiting for him at the Basle aerodrome. The thought did not give him a wholly ecstatic thrill, for it was so soon eclipsed by other more complicating thoughts. Publicity, yes—of course, there was bound to be a good deal of that. He pictured his exploit being headlined in all the English papers, pictured old Robbins at the club-house reading it, pictured his fellows at the office discussing it over their desks ; and the awful thing was, of course, that he had told them all a pack of lies about where he was going. They would all say—" What the devil was he doing flying to Basle, anyway ? " And then, perhaps, some fool who remembered that Mitzi was on her way home through Switzerland would link their names together—there had already been harmless chaff about the pair of them—harmless chaff that could, however, at any moment become retrospectively poisonous.

And his wife, in Cheltenham—he pictured her amazement, her stupefaction, at reading in the papers that her husband, whom she believed to be at home in Chislehurst, had been acting the giddy hero in mid-air and half-way across Europe. . . . And his two boys at school. . . . Good God, what an appalling thing to happen ! And for the moment he felt a touch of wild heart-shattering panic.

.   .   .   .   .   .

He began to set off across the field with the attendant, and hardly noticed whether or not the two others were following. They were, however, but a few paces behind. After traversing that field and several other fields, the procession reached at last a narrow lane, into which they turned.

Temple's heart was sinking with every step—partly from reaction after the exhilaration of that swoop to earth, and partly as he realised what might be in store for him in the way of notoriety and exposure. The boxer and his manager, however, were in increasingly high spirits—the former full of sheer animal delight at having escaped with his life, and the latter excited at the prospect of all the fuss that must ensue. Both were loud in their praises of Temple and his achievement, but from a standpoint which rather tacitly assumed that his chief title to fame was having saved such illustrious fellow-passengers.

" Gee ! " the little man kept saying. " There's going to be front-page news for you now, Cowboy ! Guess the actress's stolen jools aren't nothin' to what this'll be ! " And so on.

Temple, walking those few paces ahead with the attendant, was sombrely silent at first, till the continual chatter behind drove him to give some utterance to his feelings.

"You see," he muttered, with curt emphasis, "those chaps are just greedy for all the fuss ! It's all they care about."

" They live by it, sir. You can't blame them."

" I'm not blaming them. But it's hard luck on me. I don't live by it. I don't care about it. I hate it, in fact."

" But surely, sir, it's what you must expect."

Temple stifled an exclamation.

" Possibly. But it's all a confounded nuisance. I suppose there's no way of escaping it, though."

" I don't see any, sir. We shall have to report to the authorities and explain everything quite fully. You see, the pilot having died makes everything rather serious. There'll be an inquiry, no doubt—we shall have to give evidence, most likely. I don't see how we can keep anything in the dark."

Temple walked a further stretch in silence and then suddenly remarked : " Look here, I've thought of an idea. All I want, you see, is to avoid the fuss attaching to me personally—all the hero stuff, you know. Now supposing we said that the pilot himself brought the machine to earth —just in time before he died—what about that ? Perjury, I suppose, technically, but I don't see that it would do anyone a scrap of harm, and I'm pretty certain, in fact, that people would believe it much more readily than the truth."

The other pondered.

" Well, sir, it's an idea, as you say. Of course, if we all stuck to it, I don't see that anyone could doubt our word. But *should* we all stick to it, do you think ? "

" I don't see why not."

" I'm afraid, sir, there are many reasons. And one of them is that Cowboy and his manager probably wouldn't agree to it in the first place. They're not going to spoil the story, sir, to please you or me or anyone else. You see, sir, it's such a marvellous story—it's new—it's never happened before to any boxer, film star, jockey, tennis champion, or anyone of that kind. So naturally you can't expect Cowboy to agree to anything less than the truth. Of course, if it were a matter of something *more* than the truth——" He paused and flashed a curious glance out of his deep-set rather intelligent eyes.

" *More* than the truth, eh ? I'm not sure that I understand. What do you mean ? "

" Well, sir, just now you were suggesting that all the credit should go to the pilot. I told you I didn't think Cowboy would agree to such a variation of the truth, and quite frankly, I'm sure he wouldn't. But there is, perhaps, a variation that he and his manager *would* agree to—and it would let you out of the fuss equally well. . . . Supposing—supposing—we were all to agree that Cowboy had done the trick himself ? "

" Good heavens ! And you really expect——"

Temple stopped, speechless, but vaguely and tremendously indignant. It was one thing to give posthumous credit to a poor fellow who had died at his post, but quite another thing to bestow quantities of unearned kudos upon an already too-much-advertised professional bruiser. Temple's first instincts were to reject the idea absolutely and with scorn, but his second thoughts inclined to caution.

The attendant, watching him carefully, continued : " I know how you feel about it, sir, and I feel the same—but if you really are keen on escaping attention I can assure you it's altogether the best way. They'll turn the limelight on themselves so effectively that there'll be little left for anyone else. And also, if I might mention it, they would be willing to pay—to buy from you, as it were, sir, the complete publicity rights of the affair——"

" To *pay* me ? "

" Well, why not, sir ?   Why should you present them with such a valuable gift for nothing ?   Personally, sir, if I were you, I should make all I could out of it."

" How do you know they'd pay me anything at all ? " The other half-smiled.

" Because, sir, the little manager-chap has already approached me on the subject.   He guessed you were the sort that wouldn't care for all the fuss.   He offered a hundred pounds, but I'm pretty sure he'd come out with much more than that if you drove him to it.   Only—if you'll take my advice, sir—don't have anything to do with cheques.   Insist on cash down, and in banknotes."

Temple was becoming more and more astonished.

" But, my dear man, how on earth have you managed to discover all this ?   You haven't had a chance of a word with the fellow since we left the 'plane——"

" It was before then, sir.   It was inside, while you were unstrapping yourself and getting out of the cockpit.   As soon as we came to rest, the little fellow called me over and made the suggestion.   Green with terror, he was, but he wasn't too far gone to make a business proposition.   Fear's a queer thing, sir—it don't always take people as you think it will."

Temple shrugged his shoulders irritably.

" I'll take his money, then," he snapped, " if he'll offer enough of it."

" Perhaps, sir, you would allow me to negotiate on your behalf ? "

" Yes, by all means.   I was never any good at driving a bargain."

" Very good, sir."

The attendant dropped back a few paces and joined the other two, and Temple could hear a subdued but animated conversation proceeding from the rear.   It piqued him to reflect that, from the sound of things, the little Jew fellow was in a much more normal condition now than he was himself.   He felt, indeed, rather tired, rather sorry for himself, and—in a curious way—apprehensive and melancholy.

In a few minutes the attendant returned.

" I did pretty well for you, sir.   Five hundred pounds. In notes.   Here they are, sir."   He handed over a thick wad.   Temple took them dreamfully, without even looking at them, much less counting them, and put them in his pocket. The whole affair seemed by this time so fantastic, so incredible, that he was almost beyond being interested in it. As an afterthought, however, he said : " Oh, well, that's very satisfactory, I'm sure. And I think you yourself —some little remuneration——"

But the other again half-smiled.

" Not at all, sir. I have already drawn my commission— don't you worry about that. I know how to look after myself."

So it was all amicably arranged along that lane to the nearest village, which proved to be a small one just over the Swiss border, and not far from Basle itself.

He met Mitzi late that evening at Basle railway station, whither he had arrived by train. She had heard, of course, of the aeroplane adventure ; the evening papers were all full of it. " Boxing Champion's Superb Daring "—" Stupendous Drama in Mid-Air"—" Cowboy Clarke the Hero of Unprecedented Air-Thrill "—all that sort of thing. Cowboy's photograph, his boxing record, the photograph of his manager, his sparring partners and his training-ground at Palm Beach—all were featured in grand style, culminating with special interviews, in which Cowboy's manager said : " Cowboy has nerves like steel. I guess a little adventure like that was just nothing to him. He'll thrive on it—he's a living marvel, that boy. And don't you forget it—on the 16th he's just going to knock Bimbo Bambino to little pieces ! You bet he is ! "

Temple and Mitzi sat over coffee at the station buffet. For some reason he was very shy ; he hardly knew what to say to her ; he felt very much less of a hero than during those exciting hours in London restaurants. She was thrilled, of course, when he told her that he had been an occupant of the 'plane which Cowboy Clarke had brought safely to earth.

" I read in the paper," she said, " that a Mr. Jones of London, was one of the passengers, but Jones is such a common name in England—I didn't really think it could be you. But what an experience ! Were you very terrified ? "

" Pretty badly."

" Wasn't that boxing man marvellous ? Such coolness in an emergency—not one man in a million could have done a thing like that——"

" It was partly luck as well, you know, I mean, he might easily have had the coolness without the luck."

She looked at him rather reproachfully.

" I don't think you ought to disparage what he did, any-how. You owe your life to him."

" Oh, quite," he answered. " I'm really full of admiration, of course."

" And so am I, for if anything had happened to you——"
She added, softly : " Our train leaves at ten. Oh, Temple, aren't you thrilled ? "

And suddenly, then, he knew that he was not thrilled at all, but quite the contrary. He gave her an uncomfortable glance ; it had to be, after all ; there was no sense in post-poning it.

" The fact is," he began, " I—I'm afraid—we'd better—perhaps—you see. . . . Oh, I know it sounds pretty mean to back out of it at this stage—but—well, circumstances *have* been rather altered—haven't they ?—and—and——"

She faced him with a sudden coldness that rather relieved him—he had been afraid she would cry or make some sort of a scene.

" How, precisely, have they been altered ? " she asked quietly.

" Well, you see—this aeroplane business. Dashed un-fortunate—happening at such a time. Had to show my papers and things—all sorts of formalities—there's to be an official inquiry next week . . . see what I mean ? Wouldn't be very wise for us to follow out our original plan—somebody'd be sure to get on our tracks—and then—well, I'm sure you can see——"

" You mean that you don't want to come with me ? "

" It's—it's not quite a question of that. It's more a matter of—of prudence. After all, don't you see, if we went to this place, wherever it is, and some newspaper fellow hunted us out—as he very well might—they've been nuisance enough already——" He paused wearily and added : " Besides, there's that inquiry next week. I may be called on for evidence. If so, perhaps I'd better return to England and then come out again." He made a final despairing attempt to say what he wanted to say. " You see—all this was to have been *sub rosa*, don't you know—our little trip together, I mean—but this wretched affair has flashed the

limelight so confoundedly near that—well, playing for safety
—if you know what I mean——"

" Yes, yes," she interrupted frostily. " I know what you
mean. I think we had better say good-bye. I can take
the train on—and you—well, you can go where you like."

" I'm dashed sorry," he stammered. " I feel I'm behaving like a pretty awful cad——"

" Oh, not at all," she replied. " You can't help it.
Perhaps that air adventure has upset you. You just haven't
the nerve, that's all."

As it chanced, he didn't have to give personal evidence
at the inquiry. He returned to London by the next train
and boat, arriving at Victoria on a rainy morning when the
familiar streets ought to have looked at their worst, but
somehow didn't. The bare announcement in the papers
that a " Mr. Jones, of London," had been a passenger in
Cowboy Clarke's aeroplane had not attracted the slightest
attention either in Draper's Gardens or at Chislehurst. All
Temple's friends believed him to have been peacefully
golfing, and when he arrived at the office on Monday morning
instead of Tuesday, explaining that he had cut short his
holiday on account of bad weather, he could see that nothing
untoward was known or suspected.

And on Monday evening, smoking his pipe at home, he
sat down to answer a letter from his wife which had just
arrived. He wrote:

My Dear Isabel—I am so glad you are coming back
quite soon, and you must let me know your train, so that I
can have the old Morris along to Paddington to meet you.
Everything here is pretty much the same ; the sweet peas
are very good, and the man brought the vacuum-cleaner
back this morning. By the way, I've a bit of rather good
news for you—I made myself £500 on 'Change last week—
sheer gambling—the sort of thing you are always urging me
to do. But I shan't do it again—it was far too worrying,
and I feel I had far better luck than I could ever hope to
have again. Still, the money's made, and I'm glad you're
coming home to help me to spend it. Don't forget to let me
know your train.—Love. Tem.

Then, with a little sigh of relief, he went into the garden
and admired—yes, positively *admired*—the crazy paving.

GAVIN HOLT

Death at the Seventh Hole
The Man in the Boat
Láulee

⁋ Mr. GAVIN HOLT, the creator of
Professor Bastion, has been a great
traveller all his life, and lived both
in Australia and the United States
before settling in England. He is
passionately fond of music, and his
musical training often shows itself in the
working out of his thrillers. In one
of his stories a murder is committed
during the final act of " Carmen."

DEATH AT THE SEVENTH HOLE

DICK SANDERS never suspected that anything was wrong when Fenley waved his cleek from the rim of the seventh green. In the rough at the side of the bunker Dick grinned to himself good-naturedly. Fenley seemed to lose his balance. He wobbled in a comical fashion on the sky-line, then disappeared. Serve the beggar right if he had slipped in the sand and gone rolling down the slope to the green.

That wave of the cleek had been like a gesture of triumph. Of course Fenley was just the kind of creature to make a faultless approach. He had probably landed right on the lip of the ticklish crater hole. Dick grinned again. His lie was not so bad. A good mashie shot lifted the ball cleanly over the grass-fringed dune. He measured the trajectory. Fairly on the green, he judged, and Fenley was notoriously bad with the putter.

Dick hesitated a moment and looked around him. He stood in the trough of a sandy wave. There was not a soul in sight. Far down the little valley in the dunes he saw the sea sparkling under the sun. He picked up his bag of clubs and began to climb the ridge. His shoes slipped in the sand.

Funny beggar, Fenley! Big, awkward chap. The gesture with the cleek had been so characteristic. Proud of everything he did : proud of his business, proud of his golf, proud of his daughter. The last was a fitting subject for pride. Dick wondered if his employer were also proud of his private life. There had been ugly talk ; some of it true.

So far this game of golf had not been a friendly one. Dick resented Fenley's assumption that because he paid a man a good salary for expert service in his rubber business he had the right to command his appearance on the links. Besides, Dick was uneasy. There was Joan Fenley. Dick had been warned off, but Joan had been quite unfilial about the edict. The two had continued to meet. And now Fenley had commanded him to play golf, declaring that he had something to talk about and that the open air was as good as any place for the purpose.

Six holes had been divided, and Fenley had scarcely opened his mouth. There had been a flare-up at the club-house over some trivial thing, and the big man had started from the first tee in the devil of a temper. He had insisted that they dispense with caddies, obviously because of the promised talk. No doubt he would soon begin to roar about his daughter and his ducats. But why, in the name of goodness, had he wanted to play golf ?

Dick climbed slowly up the hill. When he was near the ridge he looked back over the course and signalled to Prentiss and Clayton, who were waiting to follow. He watched the lanky Prentiss take his stance and prepare to drive from the far-off tee. Then he topped the hill and glanced down into the crater. He blinked with amazement. It was a moment before he felt a sense of shock and anxiety.

Stretched prone on the green, with one arm extended towards the sloping flag-pin, lay Horst Fenley. From the eminence of the ridge, the appearance of the man was that of an utterly insignificant animal. One leg, the right, was bent at the knee and drawn up in frog fashion. Indeed, the whole burly figure, with coat wrinkled around the neck and plus-fours draped amply over the heavy limbs, bore a resemblance to a stricken frog.

Dick looked for the caddy-bag, though he did not know why. It had lodged in a bushy growth of grass half-way down the slope. Fenley had dropped the bag and plunged on, carrying his cleek with him. The club, still grasped in his hand, was drawn half under his chest. The metal head shone brightly in the strong light.

Dizziness, acute indigestion—the fellow had eaten too much, as usual—or a touch of sun ! Explanations occurred to Dick. He ran down the slope to give first aid.

" What's the matter, sir ? " he called as he approached. " Aren't you well ? "

Fenley did not move. Dick dropped his own bag, went down on his knees, lifted the man's head, turned him over. Some uncontrollable force thrust him back on to his feet. The face before him was contorted until it was almost un-recognisable. The skin seemed to have turned a strange blue colour. The heavy jaw hung down, the mouth was twisted; there was fixed terror in the staring, unseeing eyes.

A golf ball thudded on the green and rolled past the pin. Prentiss and Clayton were coming over. A figure appeared above the rim of the crater.

" Hey, Prentiss ! " Dick shouted. " Give a hand, will you ? "

Prentiss came half gliding, half running down the sandy slope.

" What's up ? " he demanded.

" I think he's dead," said Dick.

" Dead ! "

Prentiss turned to the caddy who had followed him.

" Run back to that foursome, boy ! " he ordered. " One of them's Dr. Sinclair. Know him ? Fetch him here as fast as you can. Mr. Fenley's had a stroke."

Five minutes later Dr. Sinclair and his party were on the green. In less than a minute thereafter Dr. Sinclair confirmed Dick's opinion. Horst Fenley was dead.

The doctor asked questions.

" It's curious," he said. " Nothing wrong with him for six holes, and at the seventh he crumples up." He looked up at the sky, as if a bolt from heaven were the explanation of the tragedy. He knelt down and began a more thorough examination of the dead man. Dick saw that Fenley's shirt had been torn open at the neck. Part of the man's powerful chest was exposed. The tough silk tie had been ripped in two ; a piece of it lay on the green. The doctor turned to one of his friends.

" Clark," he addressed him. " Be a good fellow and run back to the club-house. Get a message through to the police. This is a case for the coroner."

The disturbed golfer started on his errand at once. Dick was dazed. He stood there staring down at the body. More players and their caddies reached the green. They exclaimed. They talked a lot. They wanted to help. The police-station at Bannerlea was no more than two miles away. It was not long before two uniformed men appeared. One of them was a sergeant. He spoke earnestly to the doctor.

" Who discovered the body ? " he asked.

Sinclair named Dick. The sergeant was full of questions.

He made copious notes in a pocket-book. Now and then he looked at Dick with fierce little eyes that peered from under heavy brows.

" You say you were only a few yards away, sir," he remarked. " Didn't you hear any sounds of a struggle or a fight ? "

" Struggle ! " Dick exclaimed. " There was no struggle."

" But Mr. Fenley's shirt has been ripped open ; his tie is torn ! "

" Possibly in his own convulsive fight for breath," put in the doctor, but the suggestion was not welcomed.

" An official examination will show if there are any marks of violence," declared the sergeant. " And now, Mr. Sanders, I want you to think carefully. Could anyone have been in this—this crater, as you call it ? Remember there are dunes all around, and you were on the other side of them. Could anyone have assaulted Mr. Fenley and got away without your knowledge ? "

Something in the sergeant's voice aroused antagonism in Dick.

" Not unless the man could have made himself invisible," he answered.

The sergeant scribbled in his book, and finally turned to a bag of golf clubs that lay on the green. He assumed they were the property of the deceased. Dick corrected him, claimed the bag as his own, and pointed to Fenley's clubs half-way up the slope of the crater. The officer had no more questions. Dick picked up his bag. Some sticks had been cast from it as he threw it down. He collected these, thrust them into the bag, and started back to the club-house. He was thinking of Joan Fenley. Somehow he would have to tell her the news, and he was afraid of the task, knowing how grieved she would be.

Quite a crowd of members were discussing the sensation in the lounge. Dick went hurriedly to the locker-room. The secretary came to him.

" I hate to trouble you just now, Mr. Sanders," he said, " but I've been instructed to ask members if they've missed anything from their lockers."

" Missed anything ! " Dick ejaculated.

"There was a burglary last night," the secretary explained. " The shop was entered and a few trifles stolen. Judging from the things he took, the burglar must have been crazy. I wish you'd look in your locker."

Dick complied. There was nothing missing. The secretary was again apologetic. Dick went to the telephone and called up Poins-Ladrick, Fenley's London manager. Once more he had to go over the story. Ladrick seemed speechless with shock at first. When he recovered he said he would come straight to the golf-course.

"I shan't be here," said Dick. "I'm going to over see Joan at once."

The Fenley country house was the other side of Bannerlea. Dick reached it quickly in his car. He was afraid the police might anticipate him, but as soon as he saw Joan he knew that the blow had not yet fallen upon her. He did his best to prepare her for the devastating news. She seemed to realise at once that some terrible thing had happened, and the ordeal for him was made more dreadful because of his love for her. He saw her stricken by his words. She was tearless, frozen. Then she was weeping in his arms.

He stayed with her a long time, trying to comfort her, but at last she made him leave her. She wanted to be alone, and, understanding her grief, he acquiesced.

Again and again, as he drove back to town, he went over the details of the scene on the seventh green. It occurred to him that when he collected his clubs he must have picked up Fenley's cleek and placed it in his own caddy-bag. He wondered if he should drive back to the club-house, recover the cleek from his locker, and hand it over to the police. But the thing seemed to be too trivial. He dismissed it from his mind. There were more important things to consider.

Fenley must have had some sort of stroke. The notion that he might have been attacked on the hidden green was ridiculous, yet if it persisted in the official mind it might lead to probings into the private life of the dead man. Inevitably some scandal would be raked up, and Dick was anxious to spare Joan from such a sequel. It never entered his head that a charge could be formulated against him.

When he reached his rooms he was restless and worried about Joan. Later he went out to dinner, but could eat nothing, though he felt weak from hunger. He called at

Ladrick's flat. The manager had just returned from Bannerlea. He spoke of the sergeant's theory. Once more Dick denied that an assailant could have attacked Fenley and escaped from the crater.

" I don't know," insisted Ladrick. " The chief had enemies. He was a bit careless in his dealings with people. Apart from rubber, I mean."

" That's what I came to talk about," said Dick.

Ladrick frowned.

" I can't get that fellow Segrano out of my head," he confessed.

Dick started, for he, too, had been thinking of Segrano. The man was vividly before him, a dark, ferret-like little fellow with a vicious temper. Fenley had involved himself with Segrano's wife.

" Segrano swore he would shoot Fenley," added Ladrick.

" Yes," Dick agreed, " but there was no one in the crater. Fenley died alone. And he wasn't shot. He must have had some kind of seizure."

" One of the golfers has proposed another theory. He saw a snake near the seventh hole two days ago. He thinks Fenley slipped and fell and was bitten by a disturbed adder."

Dick disposed of this with a grimace and a shrug.

" The point that concerns us," he asserted, " is that the sergeant fellow suspects violence. If there are any inquiries about Fenley's private affairs, we must try to save a scandal—for Joan's sake. But the thing's not likely to go any further. I can't see that any coroner could possibly take it up."

" But the coroner is taking it up, my dear fellow," returned Ladrick. " The inquest is fixed for Wednesday morning."

Dismayed by this piece of news, Dick went home. Some vague premonition of disaster was implanted in his mind, and this kept him from sleep. The feeling of apprehensiveness grew upon him next day, though he did his best to put it away from him. He went down to the country to see Joan, and was relieved to find that she was bearing the bereavement bravely.

Inevitably, at some time during the day, he considered

his own position in relation to the changes that must follow in the Fenley business. Poins-Ladrick would now be the dominant figure in the firm, and he, Dick, would no doubt be second-in-command. Dick had not been in close touch with Ladrick, but their association had always been friendly. They both knew rubber from A to Z, from the plantations to the market-place ; they had both been through a phase of hard work in the tropics, where Fenley had built up great holdings of land. Ladrick was a taciturn, lonely type, but Dick believed that he would get along with him all right. There was nothing to fear for the future of the business. It was the thought of the coming inquest that raised uneasy forebodings.

And when the coroner sat at Bannerlea, Dick was called quite early to the witness-stand. His acquaintance, the sergeant, peered at him from under his bushy eyebrows, but the sergeant was now merely a respectful second to Superintendent Bancroft. It was the superintendent who asked questions, and Joan's name was quickly brought into the proceedings. Dick wanted to protest, but was carried along by a swift examination. What were his relations with the deceased ? With the deceased's daughter ? The attitude of the deceased ? Had they quarrelled ? Wasn't it true that they had quarrelled before leaving the club-house ?

Dick realised what was in the official mind. He was in danger. The thing seemed absurd, but they were actually trying to implicate him. He saw Joan, white-faced, where she sat in the corner of the room next to Poins-Ladrick. He saw the busy clerk taking down every word he uttered, but they had not warned him that what he said might be used in evidence against him.

" Will you be good enough to answer my last question, Mr. Sanders ? "

The superintendent was scrupulously polite.

" We did not quarrel in the club-house," Dick replied. " Mr. Fenley missed something from his caddy-bag. He seemed to think, unreasonably, that I was responsible for his loss."

" And what was the nature of this loss ? "

Dick tried to remember.

" I can't recall," he said at last. " It was nothing of consequence. Quite a small golfing accessory. Mr. Fenley went to the pro's shop and tried to replace it, but failed. That made him more angry."

" Oh ! " The superintendent examined his notes. " Can you recall whether either you or the deceased took a drink between the first and the seventh holes ? "

" Yes. At the sixth tee Mr. Fenley asked me if my flask was full. I gave it to him, and he took a drink."

" I must ask the clerk to make a careful note of that answer," said the superintendent. " ' I gave it to him, and he took a drink.' And now, Mr. Sanders, what became of the flask ? "

" I left it in my locker."

" You can produce it ? "

" At any time."

The next witness was the police-surgeon.

" Have you arrived at a definite conclusion as to the cause of death ? " asked the coroner.

" I have," the doctor answered. " The deceased came to his death from poison, administered in a way not yet determined."

" Is the theory of snake-bite tenable then ? "

" I would rather not answer that question. I am waiting for a report from a toxicologist."

The superintendent rose.

" Can you tell us, doctor, if any marks of violence were found on the deceased ? " he asked.

" None at all," came the answer. " There is, however, a slight abrasion near the top part of the second finger of the right hand, with a consequent inflammation and the clotting of a few drops of blood."

Dick was alert at once. So was the coroner. The latter spoke.

" Does that suggest snake-bite ? "

" Not at all," the doctor replied. " I've ascertained that the grip used by the deceased in handling his golf-clubs caused chafing. Repeated swings in driving had the effect of breaking the skin at the point I've described."

Now an adjournment was asked for. It seemed that the toxicologist's report had been expected that day, and the police did not wish to proceed without it. The coroner directed that the inquiry should be continued next morning, but Dick paid little attention to what was happening. He suddenly remembered the article that Fenley had missed from the pocket of his caddy-bag, the article the Bannerlea shop had been unable to replace. He had thought of it as a triviality. It was now of tremendous significance.

Amid a confusion of scraping chairs, moving feet, and conversational murmurs, he went to Joan's side.

" What does it all mean ? " she asked.

It meant, of course, that in a few hours he might be arrested on a charge of murder, but he made light of the obvious police suspicions before her. He had the rest of the day and all of the night to clear up the mystery. Not much time, but at least there was a chance of success.

" They're trying to make out that you quarrelled with dad ! " Joan was not to be taken from the point. " You couldn't have quarrelled. When he left for the links, he told me he had good news for you. Didn't he say anything to you ? "

" No." Dick shook his head. " I expected a lecture of some sort."

" But it wasn't a lecture," the girl explained. " Nothing was further from his mind. He seemed to have changed entirely towards you. He told me he'd been deceived about you—and others. He wanted to put himself straight. He had some plans for you in the business, but wouldn't tell me anything definite."

He subdued his amazement. Fenley's attitude was no doubt of great importance. It was, nevertheless, a puzzle that must wait, for he had a more promising clue to follow up.

" I've much to do, Joan," he said. " Get Ladrick to drive you home. I'll call on you later, if I can. If I don't show up, you mustn't mind. And don't worry ! "

Ladrick, who had been talking to Superintendent Bancroft, joined them.

" These insinuations are preposterous, Sanders," he declared. " The police are making a muddle of it. I think you'd better have a lawyer to represent you to-morrow. Hastings is the man. Will you see him, or shall I ? "

Dick thanked him for the suggestion, but did not stay to discuss it. His car was waiting outside. He drove to the golf links. The secretary was nowhere in the club-house, but, in the shop, Dick found the assistant who looked after the various accessories on sale. He questioned the man about the burglary that had taken place on the eve of Fenley's death. The thing appeared fantastic. By opening a show-case the marauder might have taken some valuable plate, but, instead, he had been content to help himself to a few golf balls, a putter, and some even more negligible articles. Dick was excited when he saw the list of stolen goods.

Next he went to his locker, took Fenley's cleek from his bag, wrapped it in an old piece of brown paper, and carried it off with him to his car. As he drove back to town, he observed that he was followed by a small saloon car that painstakingly kept its distance. It was a definite indication that he was under surveillance. Bancroft was taking no chances.

Dick reached the city late in the afternoon. He visited a laboratory that sometimes did analytical work for the Fenley firm. He asked to see the head chemist, a man he knew very well. There was a consultation. Fenley's cleek was produced. The chemist took Dick into the laboratory. It was dusk when they parted company. Dick called up Ladrick's flat. The manager was at home. Dick went along to see him.

" I don't want to go to trial for the murder of Fenley," he told Ladrick. " If we do have to give the police a clue about Segrano, I want it to be something definite. I know Segrano wrote threatening letters. Do you mind if I run through Fenley's desk ? "

" There's nothing there," answered Ladrick. " I've looked through everything myself. You can take the keys and satisfy yourself if you wish. But you don't want to worry about things, Sanders. I've spoken to Hastings. He's coming to Bannerlea with me to-morrow. He hasn't a chance to see you to-night, but he must speak to you first thing in the morning."

Dick scarcely listened. He took a ring of keys from Ladrick and hurried to the office. The cleaners had gone. The place was deserted. He made his way to the dead man's private room. If he could find one of Segrano's threatening letters, he felt he would have the details of a fairly good case. If other suspects should be disclosed, they must be limited to persons who had played golf with Fenley. Segrano had played golf with him.

Questions arose in his mind as he searched, but the drawers of Fenley's desk held nothing of consequence. First he made a hurried examination ; then he went over the papers more closely. The task was a formidable one, and it was nearly midnight before he admitted failure.

But there was still a chance that he would find what he wanted at Fenley's residence. He drove down to the country. He hated to disturb Joan in the middle of the night, but he saw no alternative. When he reached the house, there was some delay before he could arouse a servant. Then he must wait while a message was taken to Joan.

The girl came to him, and he told her of his search at the office. At once she assented when he declared he must go over whatever papers her father had left in the house. She remained at his side, helping him, as he went through the drawers of a library desk.

It was Joan who found a scribbled memorandum attached to an envelope. Dick read notes in Fenley's scrawl. An exclamation of triumph came from him. Joan's hands were trembling as she took the sheet of paper to read it again. Dick opened the envelope and examined the contents. A few minutes later he was on the way back to London.

When he drove down to Bannerlea next morning, his chemist friend accompanied him. They arrived late at the scene of the inquest. There was no time now for consultations with lawyers. Dick nodded to Ladrick, shook hands with Hastings, and excused himself at once so that he might have a word with Joan. She was nervous. Dick had written a note to the coroner. He handed it to the clerk. A moment later the inquest was resumed.

The toxicologist mentioned on the previous day had come to make his report in person. He declared that Fenley was killed by poison from a snake, a little-known reptile found on rare occasions in tropical jungles.

Tropical jungles. Rubber plantations. The unexpressed association must have been in everyone's mind. There was a murmur. Dick was unmoved, though eyes were turned upon him. It was known, of course, that he had served Fenley in the tropics.

" Is it possible that the reptile could have been on the golf links ? " asked the coroner.

" No ! Impossible ! " The toxicologist was emphatic.

" To my knowledge, a live specimen has never been brought to this country."

He would advance no opinion as to how the poison had been administered. That, he said, was not his task.

The coroner proposed to recall Mr. Richard Sanders, who had requested permission to add a statement to his evidence of yesterday.

Dick walked quickly to the witness-stand. He spoke quietly, deliberately. He began by telling how he had picked up Fenley's cleek on the seventh green and locked it up with his own clubs. Then he turned to Superintendent Bancroft.

" Yesterday," he said, " you asked me what it was that Fenley missed from his caddy-bag. I can now answer you. The article was a rubber thimble or finger-guard which Fenley wore to prevent the second finger of his right hand from splitting. He had always had trouble with that finger when playing golf. He usually wore a guard to prevent chafing. The man who caused his death knew of this habit. He knew also that Fenley had engaged to play me a round. The night before our match there was a burglary at the club-house. The man who broke into the place opened Fenley's locker and removed the finger-guard from his caddy-bag. Then he entered the pro's shop and took away a card of similar finger-guards. He took a few other articles as well, but that was just by way of camouflage. His purpose was to see that Fenley played without a protector on his finger."

The coroner stared at the witness. Superintendent Bancroft looked puzzled.

" The man was familiar with other golfing habits of Fenley's," Dick continued. " He knew, for instance, that his intended victim used the cleek more frequently than he used the other clubs. He knew that after a few strokes the skin of Fenley's finger, being without protection, would break. He impregnated the leather handle of the cleek with this snake venom. That was how Fenley came by his death."

There was a chorus of exclamations. A burly policeman at the door shouted for silence.

" How can you substantiate what you say ? " the coroner asked Dick.

" The handle of the cleek was tested by a chemist yesterday afternoon," came the answer. " I have brought this expert with me. He will give evidence if you wish to hear him."

Superintendent Bancroft, smitten by what he imagined to be the explanation, got upon his feet.

" I should like to ask the witness," he cried, " if his statement is to be taken as a confession ? "

" A confession ! " Dick echoed in astonishment. " Good heavens, no ! " He, also, was on his feet, staring into the corner where Joan sat. A police officer caught his arm and motioned him back to his seat, but Dick was staring, not at Joan, but at Poins-Ladrick, who sat next to her. He was looking for a sign, and he had it. The rufous face of the manager was drained of blood till the fellow looked like a corpse.

" I'm not the only member of the Fenley firm who has done duty on the plantations," said Dick quickly. " There's another in this room who might be able to tell you something about our venomous snake. He had reason for getting rid of his employer. He was a forger, threatened with exposure and dismissal. He killed to get himself out of a hole. If you want the man who murdered Horst Fenley, superintendent, there he is ! "

Ladrick lurched from his seat.

" It's a lie ! " he shouted. " It's an outrage ! "

The coroner's court, startled by this sudden development, stared at Ladrick.

" I have evidence in Fenley's own hand," said Dick. " Evidence of the forgery."

Then Ladrick lost his nerve. He started for the door, pushing a man violently from his path.

" Wait ! " commanded the coroner, but Ladrick flung himself at the constable who barred his way. He kicked and punched and tried to wrench himself from restraining hands. Then others seized him, and the struggle was soon over. The coroner again adjourned the inquest, but the police detained Ladrick, pending a fuller investigation. Dick, the chemist, the toxicologist, all gave their aid, and a final damning fact was established when a finger-print clue in the club-house affair was examined. Ladrick had betrayed himself by his action at the inquest. He tried hard

15

to recover himself, but the weight of evidence was too much for him. He never got his nerve back.

Late in the afternoon Dick drove again to the Fenley house outside Bannerlea. Joan was waiting for him.

"I've just come from the police," he told her. "It's all cleared up now. Ladrick has confessed."

THE MAN IN THE BOAT

It was the discovery of the derelict motor-boat that gave a new sensational twist to the disappearance of Fenndred Galter. Before this event the case looked like one of simple defalcation and flight, and it seemed that there would be little in it to engage the talents of Dr. Luther Bastion. If it had not been for something singular in the character of Arthur Ross, Professor Bastion would doubtless have referred him to Scotland Yard and dismissed the affair as out of his province.

Ross came to Fordis Place with the story of his troubles mainly because he was acquainted with the Professor's colleague, Major Bevis. Bevis was patently disturbed by the young man's plight. The Professor was not so sympathetic. His first reaction was that Arthur Ross had only himself to blame for his difficulties.

" Galter's gone, vanished ! " Ross explained in his abrupt, nervous way, and his hands waved helplessly. " He took everything, every penny. If he can't be brought back, it means the end of me. The end of the firm."

Major Bevis looked shocked. The probity and soundness of Ross and Ross, brokers, had never been questioned. But it was now some years since the elder Ross had died, and the title of the firm had been changed to Ross and Galter.

" Things were going from bad to worse five years ago," said Arthur. " I'm not much of a hand at business, you see. Not like the old man. I was a bit at sea after his death, and it seemed a godsend to me when Galter came along with some capital."

It had never occurred to him to doubt the integrity of Galter. His papers, his reputation had stamped him as an ideal man. And Galter had proved himself a wizard in the City. Arthur had been able to sit back at ease and let his partner make the money. It was true, the firm had departed somewhat from the rigid formulas of the past.

451

Hide-bound conservatism was out of date. One had to take chances. But the chances were always legitimate. Trust funds had been kept intact, inviolable. Now all was gone. . . .

" How much ? " demanded the Professor.

" It will take a hundred thousand to meet everything," answered Arthur, clenching his hands. " I can't raise ten thousand."

" When did the man disappear ? "

" Monday was the last I saw of him."

" This is Wednesday, and you've made no report to the police ? "

" I've been simply dazed—dazed one minute, investigating the next, going over the books, checking up."

" But, good heavens, Arthur ! " exclaimed the Major. " You've let him get two days' start. He might be at the other end of Europe by now."

" I know. I've been foolish. It's all so incredible. Galter was the best of fellows. If you'd known him, you'd realise it. There's his wife, too ! She can't credit it. They were married only a year ago, and he seemed to worship her."

" You mean he has left his wife ? "

" Yes. There's something terribly queer about it. I can't believe that he won't turn up and explain everything. And then there's the boat business."

" What boat business ? " asked the Professor.

" He'd just bought a motor-launch. But, look here, I wish you'd come along and see Mrs. Galter. She's just as worried and puzzled as I am."

Bastion hesitated. It seemed entirely a case for the police. By now a description of Galter should have been flashed to every city in Europe. The American ports should be watched, but there was still time for that.

The tall Bevis read something of the little Professor's mind.

" I think we might see the man's wife," he urged.

" All right," decided Bastion.

It was dusk when they set out from Fordis Place. A short taxi journey brought them to the flat that had been the home of the missing broker. Mrs. Galter, young, blonde, strikingly handsome, received them. She appeared calm enough, her emotions quite under control, as she admitted the callers, but when Ross informed her of their purpose, a flood of tears came to her eyes.

" My husband ! " she cried. " Is there news of him ? "

Ross shook his head. " We're here to help you if we can, Emily," he said.

" When did you last see your husband ? " asked Bastion.

" On Monday evening. We had dinner together in the restaurant below. Then he went out. He said he'd be back about eleven."

" Did it seem that he was prepared for a trip ? "

" No, of course not. There was nothing unusual in his manner. He took a light coat and an old hat. He told me he was going to the river to have a look at his motor-boat."

" Ah, the motor-boat," murmured the Professor. " Tell me about it."

" There's nothing to tell. He was very much interested in it. He bought it only a few weeks ago, and he was keen to have it fixed up for the summer. There was a man working on it at Aswell's yards. Fenn was just like a boy with a new toy."

" So he went to the river, and he didn't come home ! But surely, Mrs. Galter, the matter was obviously one for police inquiry without delay ! "

Once more there were tears.

" I didn't know what to do," she answered at last. " I called up Mr. Ross in the morning, and he told me to wait. He came here yesterday afternoon, and I knew from his manner that there was something wrong at the office."

Arthur was nervous and uncomfortable as the Professor turned to scrutinise him through gig-lamp spectacles.

" And, even then, neither of you thought of going to the police ? " Bastion inquired.

" We talked it over and decided to wait a while longer," said Arthur uneasily.

" It was my fault," asserted Mrs. Galter forlornly. " I begged him not to be hasty. I told him I was sure Fenn would come back. Don't you see there's some awful error somewhere ? Fenn couldn't have done it. He's not a thief ! He's not ! He's not ! "

Her voice rose hysterically. Bastion was unmoved. His pale eyes flashed censure at Arthur.

"We went to the river," asserted the young man. "To the boat-yard."

"Was the launch there?"

"No."

"What did they have to say at Aswell's?"

"Nothing. They knew only that Fenn had taken his boat away on Monday night. The watchman reported it, but the fellow wasn't there when we called."

"There's one course for you now, Mr. Ross," said the Professor. "This is a matter for something more than my limited resources. I advise you to go to Scotland Yard at once and tell them the whole story."

Emily Galter exclaimed in mingled horror and despair. She protested wildly that her husband would yet come back, but the Professor evinced no jot of sympathetic feeling. He peered curiously, meeting her glance. For all the display of hysteria, he perceived something cold in her eyes.

"I think I'll make a call at Aswell's," he said.

．　　．　　．　　．　　．　　．

A long low shed was dimly visible in the darkness of the riverside. Water lapped against the timbers of an abbreviated pier. The only light was a dull glow that came through the grimy window of the watchman's cabin. It faintly revealed a yard littered with iron scraps, pieces of timber, discarded paint tins, and other rubbish.

The night watchman was taciturn, but responded to the blatant persuasion of a crisp note. The Professor learned little of value. The motor-boat had not been built at Aswell's. It had been brought to the yard for sale, a cheap, battered craft that had passed through several hands. Galter had become its owner three weeks ago. He had commissioned Job Aswell to put it in order and give it a coat of paint.

A nice, affable, generous man was Mr. Galter. "A real gentleman, if ever there was one," said the watchman. "Not that I saw much of him. He was down here once or twice at night to look at his boat."

On Monday night the boat was all ready for him, and he told the watchman that he intended to take it down-stream to a more convenient mooring place.

"How were the conditions that night?" demanded the Professor.

" Very calm and clear, sir," answered the man.

" H'm ! Would you say the boat was sea-worthy ? "

" Well, it was built for smooth water, but it was quite a tidy tub in its way. Mr. Galter did say he was going to get a bit of sea-fishing during the summer."

A clear, calm night. The Professor meditated. A desperate adventurer might attempt the Channel or even the North Sea. Or he might have arranged to be picked up in the estuary.

It really seemed that the case was too simple. By now, if he had not come to grief, Galter was probably on the Continent, and there was nothing for it but an official hue and cry. But the Professor mistrusted simplicity. The recent scene at the flat of Mrs. Galter suggested a more complex rhythm than the plain-song of a marine-engine pushing a small craft out to sea.

Bastion was intrigued.

" That young woman was almost too convincing," he told the Major when they were back at Fordis Place. " Her tears, her accent, the break in her voice, the emphasis on the right phrase ! Emotional and moving, Bevis, but there was something hard and cold and calculating behind it. I wonder if Ross was also playing a scene. His nervousness was real, but nervousness might be ambiguous."

" It struck me that he was very concerned for the lovely Emily," asserted Bevis.

" And by that token he might be even more of a fool than he appears to be. The woman is undoubtedly pretty, attractive, and, I would venture, unscrupulous. But anyway, it looks as if we'll have to leave the absconding partner to Scotland Yard."

Nevertheless, the Professor was reluctant to give up the case before he had made a few more inquiries, and next morning he took Bevis along to the office of Ross and Galter.

There was confusion in the place. Ross and his accountant, Shrivett, had just endured a session with an officer from headquarters. Ross had indeed told the whole story to Scotland Yard, and Shrivett had, it seemed, been put through a considerable cross-examination.

The official detective had been very curious about the method adopted by Galter in securing control of the firm's funds. Professor Bastion was similarly curious. The accountant, a tall, thin man of cadaverous aspect, enlightened him. As Arthur Ross had taken little part in the details of administration, the operations of the thief had been made beautifully easy. Certainly the accountant, had he been wary, must have questioned some of these operations, but Shrivett maintained that he had been victimised.

It seemed that much use had been made of a man named Wallace in the course of systematic jugglery. Time and again cheques had been paid into the account of this Wallace. There had been a pretence of business, much correspondence, but his address had proved to be a fake, his letter-heads printed for the purpose of deception. The man who had opened a bank account in the name of Wallace was said to have been tall, dark, and clean-shaven. Therefore it could not have been Galter himself, who was of medium height and wore a close-clipped sandy moustache.

The Professor stared at Shrivett. It was incredible to him that an alert mind could have been unsuspicious of fraud, but men like Shrivett were often just book-keeping machines.

" How long have you been with the firm ? " asked Bastion.

" Two years," answered the accountant.

" Were you engaged by Mr. Ross ? "

" No, sir ! By Mr. Galter."

" Ah ! You knew him before you came to this office, perhaps ? "

" No. I never saw him before. I applied for the position through an advertisement."

" We were both agreed about Shrivett's appointment," interposed Ross. " His work has been more than satisfactory."

" So ! " ejaculated Bastion. " And his predecessor ? Did he resign or was he discharged by Mr. Galter ? "

" Galter found him a little old-fashioned. I got him a job with another firm."

" Oh, I see ! Well, I think Mr. Shrivett, as your accountant, might have inquired a little more closely into the affairs of this mysterious Wallace."

Shrivett flushed darkly.

" I'm not accustomed to suspecting the honesty of my employers," he protested. " I believe——"

But what Mr. Shrivett believed was not disclosed. The telephone bell rang. Ross jerked forward in his chair and picked up the receiver. His nerves were obviously on edge.

" Yes, yes," he answered the caller. " Scotland Yard ? Yes, this is Mr. Ross. What is it ? "

The Professor watched. The knuckles of the man at the 'phone showed in white spots as he tightened his grip on the receiver.

" Yes," he said, and again " yes." Then came a sharp exclamation, and the colour left his face. Bastion waited with no sign of excitement, but Shrivett leaned forward, staring, tense, as if he expected something.

Ross put down the receiver and rose unsteadily.

" They've found Galter," he announced in a shaky voice. " Found him in the bottom of his motor-boat, with a bullet in his head."

The derelict launch, left to the tide, had run ashore in Barking Reach, and there a police boat had salvaged it and brought it up stream. Detective-Inspector Burchell was in charge when Professor Bastion reached the waterside. In the well of the boat lay the dead man, staring up at the sky. His right arm was stretched out. The hand almost touched a revolver. It was found that the weapon had been fully loaded. One shot had been discharged.

Arthur Ross identified the body. There could be no doubt about it, he said. The man was Galter.

Everything bore out the suggestion of suicide except that there was no logical motive. If Galter had intended to kill himself when he took his motor-boat down stream, why had he first robbed his partner ? And what had become of the money ? He had carried out his big theft. Why, then, should he have shot himself in the moment of his success ?

The Professor stood by while Burchell completed his examination. The dead man was dressed in a brown tweed suit. Ross said that Galter had worn that same suit at the office on Monday. He also felt pretty sure that the tan shoes had not been changed.

Bastion made a suggestion to his friend the Inspector. The shoes were removed ; the socks also. Both Burchell and the Professor looked closely at the feet of the dead man. Then their glances met. The Inspector nodded

15*

slowly, as if he were agreeing to something understood between them.

" Looks like suicide all right, sir," commented Burchell's aid, Detective-Sergeant Fabian.

The Professor was kneeling in the well of the boat, bending over the body, intent, seemingly, on the fabric of the man's vest. He peered through a large magnifying-glass. He brushed something from the knotted silk of the tie, picked up a minute section of hair from the lapel of the coat, then turned his magnifying-glass on the lower half of the dead man's face. He got up, apparently satisfied. There was a suggestion of a grin on his elderly cherub's face as he again sought Burchell's eyes.

" Plenty of clues, maybe," he remarked. " Eight fingers and two thumbs ! "

" And you never know your luck in a big city," responded Burchell, in an equally cryptic mood.

" The intelligence of Scotland Yard is—h'm—impressive ! " Bastion began to roll himself a cigarette. " I think I'll run up and see you some time. You might telephone me when you have a spare minute."

He left the waterside with Bevis and Arthur Ross.

" By the way," he said to Ross, when the trio had found a taxi. " What do you know of Mrs. Galter ? "

" Not much," was the reply. " She was an actress before she married poor old Fenn."

" An actress ! In the West End ? "

" No. Provinces, mostly."

" What was her name ? "

" Gymel—Emily Gymel. But she used some other name on the stage."

" Ah ! Quite a good actress ! "

" What do you mean ? If you think she's implicated in this business, you're wrong. Why, I'd trust her with my life."

" The trouble with you, Mr. Ross," murmured the Professor, " is that you're too trusting altogether. I'll just step up to your office for a moment. There's a question or two I want to put to your excellent Mr. Shrivett."

But when they arrived at the office, the accountant was no longer on the premises. He had complained of feeling unwell and had gone home.

The Professor made a dash for the telephone before the stenographer had finished delivering this message. He spoke hastily to Scotland Yard about Shrivett. Ross stared in amazement as he heard the call for urgent action.

" You can't mean that Shrivett was in the swindle ! " he exclaimed, as Bastion put down the receiver.

" We'll see," answered the little Professor. " The play's a deep one, and it looks to me as if Shrivett was the amateur in the cast. You can't trust amateurs in an important production. They get stage fright at the wrong moment."

.   .   .   .   .   .

Soon after midday a summons came from Burchell. Bastion made all speed to Scotland Yard. " The finger-prints turned up a nice little exhibit," said the Inspector. " Cast your eyes over that classic profile. The full face isn't so good."

The Professor examined the police photographs that had been discovered in an old file.

" He came here from Hamburg a year ago," explained Burchell. " Officially described as Wilhelm Vielke, but better known in this country as Willy the Whelk. Missing since Sunday noon. Popularly supposed to have gone abroad."

" So that's why the moustache was trimmed ! " commented Bastion.

" What's more," said Burchell, " here's some of his foot-gear recovered from his little backroom. Size nine. Comfortable, easy-fitting."

The Professor changed the subject.

" How about Shrivett ? "

" Bolted all right. We'll pick him up."

Bastion hummed.

" I believe the woman's maiden name was Gymel. She used to be on the stage."

" Are you telling me ? " Burchell grinned. " Here's another camera study for you. Emily's own little brother. By way of being a bit of a swell mobsman. Tall and refined, Oxford accent. Already identified as the missing Wallace, with the single objection that Wallace had black hair and wore it rather long."

" A nice bit of emphasis in make-up," observed the Professor.

"What I can't see is why Emily was left behind to hold the fort." Burchell frowned.

"That's easy," asserted Bastion. "There's the estate to be wound up, and what suspicion could fall on a bereaved widow? She's capable of a most convincing performance. If she's left to herself, she'll gather up the odds and ends and slip quietly out of the country."

"So you suggest a waiting game?"

"My dear Burchell, there's a better card up your sleeve. Bring it out, and use it! Emily's banking on a verdict of suicide. A hint that the game is up will scare fits out of her. She'll run in panic and perhaps she'll lead you straight to the conspirators' nest."

Burchell agreed. Immediately he busied himself with instructions to a group of his subordinates. A half-hour later he called at the Galter flat. The Professor accompanied him.

Mrs. Galter was a figure of tortured grief. The face that she turned to her visitors was a mask of stark tragedy. Sobs caught her breath. She was scarcely able to speak. Neither Burchell nor the Professor could hope to achieve anything like such a standard of art in their counterfeit sympathy. Burchell looked decidedly ill at ease. Bastion became very paternal. For a moment it seemed that Emily might shift her stance and cry out her grief on his shoulder, but Burchell ruthlessly opened the attack.

"I understand, Mrs. Galter, you've paid a visit to the mortuary. You, of course, identify the . . ."

A quavering moan halted him. Mrs. Galter raised her shapely arms as if to defend herself from a thunderbolt. She shrank back and subsided gracefully into a chair.

"Yes," she whispered. "It was horrible—horrible."

"There, there, my dear," murmured the Professor soothingly. "You must pull yourself together."

"I can't believe it," she sobbed. "It's incredible that Fenn should have done such a thing. Suicide . . ."

Then came the thunderbolt.

"Suicide!" exclaimed Burchell. "Who told you it was suicide? The man in the boat was murdered!"

There was no doubting the shock she received. She sprang up from her chair, and her grief fell from her like discarded mourning.

"Murdered!" she screamed. "He wasn't murdered! He killed himself." Her eyes revealed an angry intensity of feeling as she faced the Inspector. Then, as he stared steadily at her as if he could read what was in her mind, her expression changed to one of fear. "But the revolver," she said, and her face was ghastly. "He . . . he . . . alone in the boat. It's all a mistake. Of course it's a mistake. You must see . . ."

"There's certain evidence." Burchell spoke quietly. "I thought I'd better warn you—before the inquest. I'm sorry if I've added to your distress."

But the Inspector seemed not at all contrite as he left the building with Bastion. He had sown panic in the woman's mind. He had placed his observers to watch for the result.

.   .   .   .   .

The expected move came after nightfall, and by that time Burchell himself had joined his party of watchers. Shortly before nine o'clock a closed car called for Mrs. Galter. When she drove off in it, a large limousine started from its position a little way down the street.

It was a long chase that followed. It ended in Greenwich when the quarry pulled up before a small house in a side street near the river. Burchell saw Mrs. Galter and her driver, a tall, thin man, enter the house. The Inspector waited only to station a guard at the rear door.

There was an attempt at flight when the occupants of the house were made aware of the position. Two of them ran for the back door and were immediately seized. One of them was the driver, and he turned out to be the man Gymel, alias Wallace. The other was the accountant, Shrivett.

Mrs. Galter was discovered in an upstairs room, and with her was a sandy-haired man with a close-clipped moustache. Detective-Sergeant Fabian gasped when he saw that man. It seemed to the detective that he gazed at a corpse or a ghost. But the corpse or ghost was decidedly active. He shouted to the frightened Emily, then rushed across the room and tried to fight his way through the little group of raiders. Fabian grabbed him. He grabbed solid flesh and held on while his superior pronounced the formula prescribed for the occasion.

"Fenndred Galter, I arrest you for the murder of Wilhelm

Vielke. I have to warn you that anything you may say . . ."

But Galter said nothing. He was suddenly in a state of collapse.

.　　.　　.　　.　　.　　.

Arthur Ross heard the news at Professor Bastion's flat. A considerable sum of the stolen money had been found in Galter's possession, and it was made clear that most of the rest would be recovered from the Continent, where Galter, with the aid of his brother-in-law, had opened accounts in several cities. The police action had come none too soon, for it seemed that the leader of the conspiracy had planned to get out of England that night.

Possibly, as the Professor explained to the bewildered Arthur, an accidental encounter with Wilhelm Vielke had first given Galter the idea of staging his callous alibi of death. " The police do not look any further for an absconder when they are presented with his dead body," observed Bastion. " Galter used his double to confound the investigation. The likeness was close enough to deceive you, and there was also his wife to identify the man in the boat. If he had not been dressed in the familiar clothes of Galter, you might have hesitated. Myself, I did not question your identification till I noticed that the shoes on the man were curiously tight."

" So that was why you asked to have them removed ? "

" Quite," agreed the Professor. " I've observed that the ' perfect crime ' is always betrayed by small errors. Inspector Burchell saw the point about the shoes at once. Galter obviously failed to notice that his victim took a larger size until it was too late to do anything about it. He crammed the man's feet into the shoes somehow, but not without abrading the skin. Then the moustache needed a little trimming. Evidently he was careful in his barbering, but not careful enough, for a few fragments of clipped hair lodged in the clothing. These were the minor errors. There was another factor that contributed more largely to his downfall. His victim was a man with a criminal record, a man whose finger-prints were filed at Scotland Yard. Once suspicion was aroused, true identification was a simple matter. A comparison of finger-prints proved that the man in the boat was not the missing Galter. He was Wilhelm

Vielke, of Hamburg. Probably Vielke was brought to the house in Greenwich by Gymel. When Galter took possession of his boat, he had only to slip down the river to Greenwich, and there the rest of the cold-blooded alibi was prepared. The house is conveniently near the water. A secluded lane. Darkness. The launch drifts on the tide."

" But Galter ! " ejaculated Ross. " He was always such an amiable, pleasant fellow ! "

The Professor rolled a cigarette.

" I've heard it remarked," he said, " that a man may smile and smile and be a villain. Be careful when you choose another partner, Mr. Ross ! "

LÁULEE

AFTER it was over, Baxter declared he had expected trouble. A hunch, he said. It had come to him the day Fleming's topsail schooner entered the lagoon. There could have been no thought of Láulee and Malifa in his mind ; it had simply been a matter of turning his nose to the wind.

" Wyn Johnson ! " he ejaculated in the time of his rage. " Wyn Johnson ! If we'd let him lie in the fo'c'sle of Fleming's tub with his broken leg, nothing would have happened."

Brent turned away. Baxter kept his head down, his eyes squinting because of the glare of the sand. The two stood on the beach in silence then, breathing heavily. Each was glad to avoid the glance of the other.

The sun was gold, the sea blue. Malifa, rock still by the water's edge, isolated, was a god in bronze. From huts of bamboo and pandanus logs came wailing. The palm tops shivered under the breath of the trades. The sea, drawing its plume-like line along the reef, sounded a deep, keening note—the insistent, monotonous organ-point of a dirge. And high, half-way up the cliff, caught on a twig and flaming against the velvet-green of thick vegetation, fluttered a shred of scarlet cloth, vivid as a flower of the hibiscus.

.   .   .   .   .   .

Láulee was a child when Baxter came to the island seven years before. She walked the woods and beach, slim and graceful and lithe. She was beautiful, and she placed a scarlet blossom in her black hair. Malifa was always at her side, and like brother and sister they played on the beach and climbed the tall, green-clad cliff in search of orchids. None marked when they ceased to be like brother and sister and first walked as lovers. It was as natural as a flower's unfolding. When the jasmine buds, it must surely bloom.

Malifa and Baxter became friends. Often they would

shoot the surf in a light outrigger, the round-figured Baxter in gleaming ducks, the superb Malifa naked except for a claret-coloured lava-lava about his waist. Brent, the owner of the largest plantation on the island, sometimes joined them in the fishing.

An old man who had travelled much about the Pacific, Brent loved the islands and the people of the islands. Because of a misadventure in which Malifa saved him from a shark, he came to think he ought to do something for the young native. One of his fads was education—the development of the island race by education. He got the idea of sending Malifa to Honolulu. Baxter argued and protested. Brent was obstinate, an old man with an idea.

" Malifa will be chief some day," he said. " Think what it will mean to him, and to this place, if he could go away for a bit and learn something of the world. There are good schools in Honolulu."

" You want to make him a subject for experiment," retorted Baxter. " You don't know what you're doing. I warn you, it's dangerous." The red point of his cigar glowed angrily in the dusk. " Besides," he added, " there's Láulee."

Malifa was adventurous. From the kanaka crews of copra-hunting schooners he had heard strange tales of lands far away ; lands of fabulous size and filled with wonders. If they laboured for all time, the sons of Lono could not raise such lands from the sea. Even when Láulee sang to him, he dreamed of these far-off wonders. Malifa was ripe for the suggestions of Brent.

The parting from Láulee was difficult, but Malifa bade her think of his return. From Honolulu he would bring her many beautiful presents, and, when he came back, they would be married. Láulee wept ; it was many days before she sang again.

Malifa had been gone a little more than five months when Fleming's schooner put in. Baxter and Brent were together, ready to talk copra, but Fleming was not in a business mood when he first came ashore.

" Bring your tool-kit on board, Baxter," he requested. " We've had a casualty. You're a better hand at setting a broken leg than I am."

" Kanaka ? " asked Baxter.

" No, Yankee ! And enough trouble he's given me ! For two pins I'd maroon him and let you put up with him. Came on with a jag and tried to start a mutiny before he was through with it. Now he seems to think I'm running a floating hospital. Got his leg smashed last night, blast him ! Fell off a ladder that's safe for a blind man."

They went on board to see the patient. They expected some ordinary bit of Pacific flotsam. They found Wyn Johnson.

Brent studied him while Baxter did his best for the injured limb. The skipper had cursed Wyn Johnson all the way from the shore ; now he was paternal, almost affectionate. " There was something about the youngster that got you from the jump," Baxter afterwards admitted.

Perhaps mild surprise left them unguarded. Anything less like a Pacific rouseabout than Wyn Johnson would be hard to imagine. He was more of a poet, by the cut of his face—dark, with a bit of the dago in him. Brent was a sentimentalist, given to what he called human sympathy.

The boy went chalky with pain under the ministrations of Baxter, but not a murmur came from him. The human sympathy fairly oozed from Brent. It was the eyes of the sufferer—something pathetic in them, like the expression, half-pleading, half-apologetic, in the eyes of a hurt dog.

" Can't you get me off this damn lugger for a bit ? " he asked when Baxter was done with his bush surgery. Brent fell for that ; said he'd have him over at his house for a spell.

" Who is he ? " he inquired, when Fleming took his guests to the cabin.

" Search me ! " answered the skipper. " He told Billings he'd been singing in a 'Frisco cabaret. Got slung out on his neck for punching one of the clientèle. Something about a girl. He stowed away on a tramp, and they kicked him off at Apia."

Two days later, from a cane lounge on the verandah of Brent's house, Wyn Johnson watched the schooner sail out of the lagoon. Brent had decided that he was to stay till he was well again.

Láulee first saw the patient one hot, lazy afternoon. She had come to Brent's place with a present of fruit from her mother, and Wyn was on the verandah, reading a magazine.

He looked up and returned the innocent smile she gave

him with a sophisticated grin of appraisal. The scarlet
flower in her dark hair seemed to fascinate him.

" Hello ! " he exclaimed. " Where do you come from ? "

" Come from ? I come to Brent."

" He's not around. Sit down and talk. Tell me your
name."

" Láulee," she said.

" Láulee," he repeated. " It's a name like a song. Do
you sing, Láulee ? "

With her lips shaped to a smile she answered him. They
were full lips, but not over-full in the native way. Her
bronze skin was fine and soft, splendid under the play of a
sun ray that struck through a tangle of wild vine. Her jet
hair, unbound except for a floral knot at the back of the
neck, fell to her waist. From a piece of patterned scarlet
stuff she had fashioned a graceful skirt in the island manner.
It was scant, and her limbs moved freely, unimpeded. The
colour of the cloth matched the red hibiscus in her hair.
She came from under the natural pergola on to the verandah.
The boy saw her small feet, traced the slender lines of her
lithe body, stared at the shoulder from which she shook back
a strand of hair.

Brent was absent, and Láulee forgot her mission. They
laughed and talked, and before long were singing to one
another. She sat close to the low chair on which he lay,
and, as he sang, he caught up in his hand the long string of
scarlet beads she wore. Scarlet and bronze, and the sun
struck light from the polished leaves of palms.

" Come again, Láulee," he said. " Come again, and teach
me some of your songs."

She came often as Wyn's hurt mended. She picked up
the dance melodies that Wyn had heard in the cabarets of
San Francisco, and he laughed gaily as she repeated them.

Baxter found them together one day. Their pleasure in
each other's company made him uneasy and he frowned.
He told the girl of a letter he had received from Malifa, but
she smiled and turned again to Wyn. Baxter, disturbed,
spoke to Brent. The host questioned the guest. The boy
was indignant.

" What do you think I am, anyway ? " he demanded.
" If you've anything against Láulee, I'm not going to stand
for it. She's just an innocent kid ! "

He stopped suddenly.

" I'm sorry, Mr. Brent," he said. " I didn't mean to lose my temper. It looks ungrateful, and I'm not that."

Láulee's visits continued, and presently Wyn was hobbling about with a stick. Then it was not long before he could take short walks. He still delighted to sing with Láulee, and often of an evening they would sit together watching the waves creaming on the reef. There were days when they would venture in an outrigger far beyond the break in the coral. She taught him the trick of the sail.

The fact that the two were constantly together worried Baxter, but he did not speak to Brent again. Instead he told Wyn about Malifa.

" Well ? " Wyn questioned him sharply.

" Well ! " echoed Baxter. " Seems to me you're making a nice mess of trouble. I wouldn't like to be the man to face Malifa, if anything happened to the girl."

" You've got me all wrong," answered Wyn. " Nothing's going to happen to Láulee except what's right and proper. We're going to be married."

Baxter stared for fully a minute.

" I'm here to stay," Wyn added, and the usual note of jaunty impudence left his voice.

They were married by the missionary from a neighbouring island ; Láulee's people gave them a native house. Brent was furious, and did not relent when Wyn almost broke down on leaving him.

" I'm going to be good to Láulee," said the boy. " She'd never be happy now if I went away, and . . . I can't go away."

Wyn avoided the two white men after that. He brooded under their condemnation, but presently forgot them, for he was happy with Láulee. They lived indolently together, going the island ways. Their ease lasted a few months ; then Malifa came home.

He went to Baxter on the night of his arrival, and Baxter saw that there was nothing for him to tell. Malifa had heard the story. The look of a slayer was in his eyes, and something else, too ; something soft and pitiable. Already he had thrown away the clothes he had learned to wear in Honolulu ; he was nude except for the lava-lava he had caught up in his father's house.

"Láulee has forgotten me," he said. "She has gone away, but she will return. I will set everything right."

"You can't do anything. She couldn't help it. You mustn't do anything to hurt her."

Malifa held himself stiffly.

"Láulee has not sinned," he declared. "Someone has sinned, but not Láulee. Her spirit is true to Malifa, but it is wandering and lost. I will help her to find what she has lost. I will kill."

"No," cried Baxter, but Malifa turned abruptly and strode away. Baxter panted after him, caught his arm. "No, Malifa," he urged. "Listen to me. It'll do no good. Let's talk it over. I'll help you."

Baxter wanted to give the man's anger time to cool, but the native wrenched away from him and went on. Baxter tried to keep up with him, vainly. In the darkness of the wood he tripped and came down heavily, wrenching his ankle. Intense pain forced him to pause against his will. Then, resting, he heard sounds that made him get up and limp on. He came to the hut of Wyn and Láulee. The stars were bright. He saw the girl crouching on the ground, her face hidden by her hands. He saw Wyn Johnson and Malifa struggling together, but it was the end of the struggle. Malifa lifted the boy and threw him against the trunk of a tree. He would have leaped upon him, but at that instant Láulee looked up and screamed.

Malifa turned and held out his arms to her. She climbed to her feet, grasping at the doorpost of the hut. Malifa advanced as if he had forgotten Wyn Johnson, as if there were nothing but joy for him in this meeting, but, with another shrill cry, the girl fled from him, running into the jungle by the path that led to the top of the cliff. Malifa stepped back as though she had struck him. Then he started after her. A figure pushed past the staring Baxter. He saw that it was Wyn. He called to him; no answer came back.

Baxter called to the hurrying, excited natives. He limped to Brent's house as fast as he could, and found the old man on the verandah. Brent said they must wait; they could do nothing. He sent a boy for news, but the boy did not return. They sat on the verandah drinking whisky, waiting. Like Baxter, Brent was afraid of something in the night.

Through the leaning coco-palms they could see the low stars, and the stars were bright.

A scream sounded, but Brent said it was the cry of a gull. Then, definitely, there was noise in the undergrowth. It must be the boy returning. Baxter looked at his watch. It was past two. They had been waiting for hours.

Wyn Johnson moved heavily into the light that came through the window; he clutched at the verandah railing for support. His face was bruised and marked with blood.

" Where's Láulee ? " he cried, and swayed, pausing for answer. " Where's Láulee, Brent ? Is she here ? "

Brent shook his head. Wyn Johnson half raised his arms, and the movement of his unbuttoned coat showed his white chest.

" I've searched the island," he shouted in a frenzy. " She started up the cliff with that damn kanaka after her. She didn't come down again, but he did. He's on the beach now, moaning and groaning with his tribe around him. Where's Láulee ? God ! can't you answer ? Can't you ? "

He fell against the steps, reaching towards them.

" Take it easy," Brent urged.

" If Malifa's done anything to her, I'll kill him ! By hell, I will ! "

" Easy, easy ! "

Wyn was on his feet again.

" I've got to find her," he said, half to himself. " Got to find her. Láulee."

He caught his breath on the name ; he repeated it again and again as he moved away. Brent and Baxter followed him through the tangled night of the woods.

They came out on the beach at last. There was no one in sight. The huts were deserted, and sounds and calls told that the natives were searching.

Through what remained of the night, the two men followed the boy. Up the path of the cliff they toiled, bruising their limbs against obstacles unseen in darkness.

" Láulee, Láulee ! "

The name went crying to the bright stars, but there was no answer for Wyn Johnson. He pressed on to the little plateau high above the sea.

" Láulee, Láulee ! "

Down the slope, away from the sea, they passed, forcing

a path through the thick wood. They stumbled in the bracken. The tendrils of wild vines caught at their feet. Liana ropes barred their way. Still they went on, and in the dawn they came back to the beach at the foot of the tall cliff. Baxter exclaimed at what he saw, plucked at Brent's coat-sleeve. The search was ended.

In the shadow of the cliff was Láulee. Her lips smiled, and a scarlet hibiscus flamed in her hair.

Wyn broke through the group of natives and stared down at her.

" She fell. She fell as she fled along the path of the cliff."

Voices joined in the murmured explanation. The group fell back as Malifa came across the sand. With head bowed he came, for they had told him the news. Motionless he stood by the body of Láulee, and the islanders waited, apprehensive, for they could not read what was in the heart of Malifa.

At last he raised his head and looked at Wyn. The boy had seemed paralysed by grief, but now he, too, lifted his head. Their eyes met, and in the eyes of the boy was the helpless, dumb pleading of the hurt dog.

For a moment they stood with their sorrow between them. Then Wyn turned and moved down the beach to the out-rigger in which he had sailed with Láulee. Malifa swung about suddenly as if he would follow, but Brent laid a hand on his arm.

" Let him go," he said. " It is best."

The watchers on the beach saw the boy launch the canoe and climb into it. He paddled swiftly, frantically, as though he feared pursuit and interference. When he was through the gap in the reef he raised the sail and went on, out into the great blue of the Pacific.

Malifa stood, isolated, rock still, staring at the sail of the outrigger until it was lost in the blue. He turned, and he bowed his head again.

The people of the island gathered about Láulee. Her eyes were closed, but still her lips smiled. The palm tops shivered, and the sea on the reef sounded the organ-point of a dirge. And half-way up the cliff, a flame against the green leafage, a shred of scarlet cloth fluttered in the wind like a flower of the hibiscus.

SYDNEY HORLER

Black Magic
The Curious Episode of the Swearing Ghost

¶ SYDNEY HORLER began life as a
journalist, but after gaining considerable experience in Bristol, Manchester,
and Fleet Street, decided to take up
novel writing, and has earned a
first-class reputation as a writer of
" thrillers," of which he is one of the
most prolific producers now working.

BLACK MAGIC

The Horror of " The Height "

" My friend and assistant, Mr. Martin Huish," announced Sebastian Quin.

I acknowledged the introduction by bowing to the girl who sat in the client's chair in Quin's consulting-room. She was about twenty-four, I judged, tastefully dressed and normally very pretty. I say normally, because Violet Loring's face was now tortured by a look of restrained horror, which went straight to my heart.

" Miss Loring has come to us in great—very great—trouble," explained Quin. " She was about to tell me her story when you came in."

He looked encouragingly at the girl, whose hands were locked. Quite obviously, she had to brace herself before she could start on her narrative.

" What I am going to tell you, Mr. Quin, may sound so fantastic, so utterly preposterous that you will have difficulty, perhaps, in believing I am sane." She stopped, unable for a minute to go on.

" I may say I have listened to many strange statements in my time, Miss Loring ; and my experience of life is that the fantastic is usually the likeliest thing to happen—given certain conditions."

The tone was grave but encouraging. Sebastian Quin, his thin, almost cadaverous, face thrust forward, was an impressive figure in that moment. His critics, whose scoffings were in every case occasioned by bitter jealousy, might say that he looked more like a jockey than a crime investigator, but the visitor evidently derived satisfaction from his manner.

" I live at Trevelyn, in Cornwall," she continued, gaining courage. " As you know, it is a popular seaside resort in the summer, but in the winter it is very lonely and desolate. Yet my father and I have been happy—he with his books

475

and I with my sport and out-of-doors life—until the last few months. All this trouble has happened since "—she shuddered—" that man came ! "

" What man ? " inquired Quin.

" The man Memory—Rathin Memory, he calls himself."

" A singular name," commented Quin. " And what —— ? "

" He's horrible, dreadful," cried the visitor. " Mr. Quin, help me to save my father from that devil's power ! "

Violet Loring's face had become convulsed. She was struggling for breath.

Sebastian Quin made me a sign, and I brought the brandy.

After a while the visitor became more controlled.

" I must tell you everything now," she said, " and I promise I shall not be so foolish again." Her hands locked tightly, she went on with her story.

" It was in late September last that this man, Rathin Memory, arrived in Trevelyn. He took the house called ' The Height,' on Pentire, which is a rocky headland jutting into the sea on the north side of the town. This house had been unoccupied for so long that the place was in a dreadful state of neglect. The iron entrance-gates were rusty and almost hidden by the weeds and coarse grass which had been allowed to grow.

" I should explain that this house, ' The Height,' has an evil reputation—the local story is that a dreadful murder and suicide took place there many years ago, that the bodies of the wretched people mysteriously disappeared in the night, and that the place—which is very old—is haunted. And it was to this house that the man who, for some mysterious reason, has constituted himself my enemy, came." The visitor's body was shaken by a fresh shudder before she continued :

" You can imagine, perhaps, what an interest was taken in the new resident. Everybody in Trevelyn knows everybody else, the town being so small, and the fact that Rathin Memory had taken a house which was generally believed to be haunted and which had never been let, even in the summer months, had increased the natural curiosity about the man."

Quin nodded.

" Will you describe him, Miss Loring ? "

Again the visitor shuddered. But the hesitation was only momentary.

" Please do not think it is my shattered nerves which make me describe him as a man one doesn't like to look at," she replied. " His age is something between forty and fifty, I should say ; he is very hairy—lets his hair grow and has a beard—and has remarkable eyes. Even when he has passed me in the street in broad daylight his eyes have filled me with fear. And I am not an imaginative person usually."

" A highly curious individual, I should imagine. But please go on, Miss Loring. Is anything known of the man —where he came from, for instance ? "

" Nothing very much. The local newspaper tried to interview him, but all he would say was that he had been a traveller all over the world, that he had lately arrived from Tibet, and that he wished to be undisturbed. He lives quite alone in that huge house, with only a foreign manservant."

" He has done no entertaining, then ? "

" None. As a matter of fact, there isn't a soul in Trevelyn who would venture into ' The Height.' And the man him-self—as I know to my cost—is mysterious, devilish. He has a power over people, as I shall convince you, I believe, Mr. Quin."

Quin almost imperceptibly stiffened in his chair.

" I shall do everything I can to help you, Miss Loring, but I must have your complete story."

" You shall—whatever it costs me to tell it. Perhaps you will be able to realise my position better if I say now that this—this monster is in love with me ! And I am already engaged to be married," she went on before either Sebastian Quin or I could interject a comment.

" It was about a month ago that I first met Memory alone," Miss Loring explained. " I was walking on Pentire when I heard a footstep behind me. Looking around, I saw that the mystery-man—as Memory is called at Trevelyn— was close upon me. Although it was early in the afternoon and quite light, I felt myself suddenly trembling. That may seem a very weak and cowardly confession to make, but I cannot hope to convey the devilish atmosphere with which the man seems to be surrounded ! I only know that it was very real to me when he looked at me with those awful staring eyes of his.

" I merely nodded when he raised his hat, and went to pass on. But he placed himself in my way.

" ' You are Miss Loring, are you not ? ' he asked, and I said ' Yes ! '

" ' I should like you to be friends with me,' he went on. ' I am a very lonely man. I do not want many friends, but I should like to know you.'

" You can imagine, Mr. Quin, what my feelings were when I heard those words. For a moment I could not find my voice. But then, realising my position, I replied : ' I am afraid that is impossible. I do not know you, and I do not want to know you. Consequently, any question of friendship between us is absurd.'

" Once again I made to move on, but he would not let me pass.

" ' That which I desire I always obtain,' he said in a voice that filled me with fresh fear. ' I have asked for your friendship and I shall have it. There is no one strong enough to prevent me.'

" At that I became indignant.

" ' My father will prevent it, for one,' I said.

" ' Your father ! ' He laughed contemptuously. ' I tell you that no one is strong enough to prevent me from enjoying your friendship now that I wish it. You will see ! '

" If he had not turned away then, I believe I should have struck him, for my rage had overcome my fear. The idea of this creature daring to dictate to me, presuming to force himself upon me, was so overwhelming that I scarcely knew what I was doing.

" I went straight back and told my father. Dad is usually a quiet man, whose only wish is to be left in peace to enjoy his beloved books, but when he heard my story he went straight away to consult his solicitor. Mr. Denning wrote a letter to Memory, warning him that his attentions were unwelcome to me, that I was already engaged to be married, and that any repetition of his conduct that afternoon would be communicated without delay to the local police. The local police," repeated the visitor in a hopeless voice. " Little did I realise at the time how helpless any police could be in dealing with a monster like Memory ! "

Her strange words filled me with a sense of foreboding. I

glanced at Quin, and saw that his eyes were unnaturally bright. Evidently this case was interesting him intensely.

Before she continued, Miss Loring took another sip of brandy.

" The following night the first terrible thing happened," she resumed. " My father had gone to bed early, but I had been sitting with my—the man to whom I am engaged, Mr. Harry Sinclair. Suddenly I heard a cry. I rushed upstairs, Harry by my side. I found my father——" Sobs now choked her so that she could not continue.

" If you are too distressed, Miss Loring——"

" No ! No ! I must tell it and get it over. I was saying that I found my father—*paralysed !* He could speak, but that was all. He said he had cried out because he felt a strange numbness creeping over him, robbing him of all strength and power.

" No "—answering my look ; " my father had not been stricken with any stealthy disease ; neither had he had a stroke. The local doctor was puzzled and sent for a specialist from Plymouth. The latter in turn wired for a big London man—Sir Timothy Brash——"

" I know him quite well," commented Quin. " He is a member of the same club as I. A thoroughly good man ; about as good as any in the world, I should say. What did Sir Timothy say, Miss Loring ? "

The girl's body was shaken by one of those convulsive shudders which were so distressing to see.

" It was Sir Timothy who referred me to you, Mr. Quin. After examining poor Daddy, he said that it was a case outside of medical science, because, as far as he could determine, there was no physical cause for father's condition. Although not a robust man—but then Daddy had never been that— he said my father was wonderfully healthy and well preserved for his age. When I first heard him mention your name I thought you were still another doctor——"

" Naturally," was the grave comment.

" And, to be frank, Mr. Quin, while of course I was anxious to do anything—*anything*—which could make Daddy better, I was so disappointed that I did not act at once upon his advice. You are not a doctor, Mr. Quin ? "

" No—only of the mind," replied my friend. " I can tell you why Sir Timothy Brash mentioned my name to you,

Miss Loring. He considered that your father's illness was due to another agency rather than disease."

" What agency, Mr. Quin ? "

" That I cannot say with certainty until I reach the spot. Huish, look up the next train to Trevelyn. We shall return with Miss Loring. There is not a moment to lose ! "

I consulted the Bradshaw and glanced at my watch.

" There is a train from Paddington in an hour's time."

" We will catch it," said Quin decisively.

In the train Miss Loring told the rest of her amazing story. The malignant influence which was at work in her life had manifested itself in another direction besides rendering her father a helpless cripple. Harry Sinclair, her devoted lover, the man to whom she was engaged, had suddenly seemed to become bereft of his senses, to lose his reason.

" Not that he has become actually mad," explained the girl, " but he regards me now more or less as a stranger, and he spends all his time mooning about on the sands. His manner has become so peculiar that he is the talk of the town, and people are saying that—that he ought to be taken away. Mr. Quin,"—stretching out a beautiful hand in anguished appeal—" do you think you will be able to help me ? "

" I shall do all I can," was the grave response. " I promise you not to leave Trevelyn until the mystery is solved, in any case."

" What is your view, Quin ? "

He turned on me impatiently.

" I have no view at present," he replied. " There may be a filmy thought at the back of my mind, but it is far too early to speak about that yet. All I can say now, Huish, is that we are faced with a problem that has so many terrors attached that we simply must not fail ! Even the thought of failure is so ghastly as to terrify me ! "

I knew better than to provoke him into further speech at that moment, although God knows how anxious I was. The story which had brought us post-haste from London to this dreary Cornish coast town would have seemed incredible had I not been mixed up sufficiently in Sebastian Quin's affairs to know from experience that, to quote the words he had himself said to the victim of this diabolical plot, " the fantastic is usually the likeliest thing to happen—given certain conditions."

I looked at the man who had solved more mysteries than any other person living. He was so deep in thought over his pipe that there was a deep furrow in his forehead.

Sebastian Quin was an enthusiast of the bizarre. He was as unlike the ordinary crime investigator as the real detective is unlike the fiction variety. Possessed of comfortable means, he devoted his life to the study of crime in its more exotic and weird manifestations. He was a repository of so much varied knowledge that I often marvelled how and by what means he could have accumulated so many facts, knowing that he was still under forty. Quin had learned Chinese well enough to pass for a native within a month, and could speak altogether eighteen languages. That in itself gives proof of his mental powers.

He was far more than a mere detective of crime : he was a dissector, an analyst, an anatomist of the mind of the criminal. He was never satisfied with merely stopping a crime ; he delved beneath and learned what had prompted the outrage. Altogether an amazing person, and my friendship with him was the greatest honour that I—or any other man—could have experienced. It pleased Quin to let me accompany him on certain of his investigations. The part I played was always an exceedingly humble one—I was merely a super on the stage ; but Quin, like many other great men, had his moments of pardonable vanity, and he liked to have someone near him to whom he could explain and expound after a " case " had come to a satisfactory conclusion.

We had decided upon The Grand because it was the hotel nearest to " The Height "—that mysterious house in which Rathin Memory lived ; and, late as it was after we had seen Violet Loring safely to her own door, Quin and I had walked the half-mile of desolate cliff-land which separated the Grand Hotel from " The Height."

I shall never forget that walk. The wind had sprung up and was howling like the spirits of tortured fiends ; every now and then the thundering of giant waters sounded, and we were drenched with spray as we walked along the zigzag path that ran between the golf course and the towering range of cliffs.

16

"This should be the place," Quin remarked, flashing the small electric torch he carried.

We climbed the mighty headland which Violet Loring had called Pentire, and a laborious business it was. A strange and erratic mind it must have been that conceived the idea of building a house on the top of that cliff which jutted straight out into the Atlantic Ocean. Like the nest of some gigantic eagle "The Height" looked as we stood before the iron gates which were rusty with disuse and almost hidden—as Violet Loring had said—by rank weeds and grasses as tall as a man's body.

The place was a monstrous blot of gloom. Not a light showed. There was no sign of any human habitation, and yet—I told myself it was fancy brought on by the story which had brought us to this spot at eleven o'clock of a winter's night—something seemed to grip me by the throat as I stood staring there in the darkness.

"Quin!" I called, and then was ashamed of myself.

My companion came up and looked at me fixedly.

"What is it?" he demanded.

I tried to laugh, but succeeded only in making a dismal croak.

"I—I can't explain it, Quin," I stammered, "but just then—when I called, I mean—something devilish seemed to be trying to choke the life out of me! It had me by the throat. I was afraid for myself and for you too—that was why I called. Don't laugh at me!" I went on angrily. "The sensation was real enough—too real for my liking."

Quin switched off his torch.

"I am not going to laugh," he replied seriously. "I had exactly the same feeling myself—and you would not call me an unduly imaginative man, Huish?"

"I should not!" I said emphatically.

Quin was silent as we walked away.

.   .   .   .   .

The whole affair was steeped in mystery—evil mystery. On the morning following our arrival we saw David Loring, the girl's father. He was a pitiable object. Apart from the fact that he could speak, he was a complete paralytic. But his mind was clear enough.

"I am under the spell of some devilish influence," he told

Quin. " That may seem an incomprehensible thing to you—
and, on the other hand, you may accept the statement
because I understand you have had many strange experiences
yourself, Mr. Quin. Dr. Logan will tell you the exact words
that Sir Timothy Brash, the great consultant, said when he
examined me."

Sebastian Quin, nodding gravely, took the grey-haired
local practitioner on one side.

" From a medical point of view," said Dr. Logan, " Mr.
Loring ought to be as well as you or I. He has been over-
hauled inside and out ; all sorts of tests were made by Sir
Timothy Brash, who said at the end : ' Well, the whole
thing is incomprehensible from a medical point of view.'
Poor Mr. Loring himself talks a lot about some malign
influence, but, of course, all that is nonsense. This is not
the Middle Ages."

" It may or it may not be nonsense," replied Sebastian
Quin.

A short time after this we met Harry Sinclair, Violet
Loring's fiancé, as he was about to enter the house. He
proved to be a good-looking, manly young fellow—at least,
I should perhaps say he would no doubt have given that
impression in ordinary circumstances.

Now he did not appear to be in possession of all his
faculties. His mind was wandering, and he was so careless
in his attire that I noticed a flash of pain come into Violet
Loring's face.

As for Sinclair, he stared blankly at her, and glared
around at the rest of us.

" Harry, this is Mr. Sebastian Quin, from London," the
girl announced.

Again she received a disconcerting, blank stare.

" Who are you ? Why do you keep on speaking to me ?
Leave me alone ! " the man said fretfully, and then a look of
loathsome cunning transfigured his face as he added : " But
I know who you are ! You're David Loring's daughter.
You're a bad lot, and I don't want anything to do with you !
It's your father I want—I'm very fond of your father ! "
He chuckled obscenely.

A sob sounded behind me.

" You can see for yourselves," said Violet Loring, her

distress racking her, " that this is not my Harry. This is some monster he has been changed into ! "

While I tried to comfort her, Sebastian Quin had stepped between Sinclair and the door of the Lorings' house.

" I shouldn't go in now," he said quietly to the stricken man.

The wave of madness which made Sinclair's eyes glare and his whole body stiffen died down as suddenly as it was born when he looked into Quin's face. With a snarl like that of an angry dog, he turned away without saying another word.

For the rest of that day Quin kept a close watch on the Lorings' home, and noticing how tense and strung-up he was, I ventured to ask him the reason.

" You may know to-night," was the only reply he would give me.

.   .   .   .   .   .

" Ah ! " cried Sebastian Quin softly, yet with intense satisfaction. " There it is ! "

He pointed upward. The left wing of " The Height " took the form of a short, squat tower, and it was from a window in this tower that a light—the first sign of human life or activity in the place that we had yet observed—now glowed like a star in a dark sky.

" Our vigil is ended," said Quin. " What we have to do now is to ascertain what is going on in that room with the light. The question is whether we shall achieve that purpose by entering the house, or whether we can sufficiently satisfy our curiosity by climbing up this incline, which is on a level with the window, and looking through by lying on our stomachs. I propose the latter method, for it will be quicker, and I feel pretty certain that time is valuable. Now for the climb. Be careful you don't fall ! "

We were already standing beneath the shadow of the house of mystery. My heart beat at twice its normal rate when I contemplated the task which Quin had set us.

The progress of that hazardous climb, one false step in which would have meant not only the ruination of our plans, but inevitable death, is a memory upon which I never afterward liked to look back. It seemed to last an eternity, but eventually I found myself lying side by side with Quin upon the small plateau, and looking into the room the light from which had attracted us from the ground. There were some curtains to the window, but the man inside had evidently felt so secure in his own mind about not being overseen, that he had not troubled to draw them.

" Stay perfectly still, and do not do anything until I give you the word, *whatever you may see !* " whispered my companion, stressing the last few words in a way that sent a cold chill down my spine.

Every separate nerve in my body seemed to be twitching as I saw a man enter the room. By the description which Violet Loring had given us, I recognised him at once as Rathin Memory.

She had not exaggerated the dread which this man would have inspired in the ordinary clean-living, clean-thinking, normal person. The man, even from a distance, seemed to be surrounded by an aura of evil.

" Watch ! " came the tense whisper from Quin.

Memory was carrying a bundle when he entered the room, which as far as I could see was quite bare of furniture. Placing the bundle on the floor, he first took out five brass lamps of a peculiar design. Then followed a stoppered vessel. After that the man produced a white cock, alive— for it struggled—but with its feet and beak tied in some fashion that I could not ascertain because I was too far away. Then followed a knife, the blade of which gleamed in the light.

" What——? " I whispered, but Quin ordered me to be quiet.

I followed the subsequent actions of the man in the lighted room with breathless attention, for I realised that I was the witness of something which was full of significance —otherwise why should Sebastian Quin have been so absorbed ?

I saw Rathin Memory measure out a space. Having counted off a number of feet—how many I could not reckon —he drew a circle of chalk. Then, taking the bottle, he pulled out the stopper and walked around inside the circle, sprinkling the chalk line with the liquid the bottle contained. At each step he stopped and made a peculiar gesture.

" The second sign of the unholy celebration," I heard Quin mutter.

The complete circle having been sprinkled, the man drew a five-pointed star with the chalk. Then, lighting the five small lamps which he had brought, he placed one at each of the five points. He seemed to be muttering some ritual as he did so, for I could see his lips move.

Placing himself in the centre of the pentacle, he commenced what must have been a chant, for his lips moved again and his hands swept upward and outward. Presently the uncanny thing which I had been expecting ever since I had first looked into the room happened—for from each of the five lamps guarding the points of the pentacle there suddenly sprang a reddish tongue of flame. These met and formed a solid barrier of fire around the man in the centre.

At this point Memory thrust out his hand and seized the white cock. Holding the knife aloft, as though first consecrating it to its task, he decapitated the bird with a single stroke, and I saw the blood splash on the floor inside the circle.

" Now that the blood is warm——" I heard Sebastian Quin mutter, but I was too fascinated by the horrible ritual I was witnessing to turn to him.

I saw the unholy celebrant lift up his hands as though saying a prayer. As he did so, the wall of flame with which he had been surrounded died down. Five tongues of flame issued out of the solid fire and returned to the lamps which burned at the five points of the pentacle. The light of the lamps now burned low, flickered just as though assailed by a gale of wind. They were trembling as though some unseen force were trying to put them out.

" My God ! " breathed Quin. " The real thing—the real thing ! "

Again I was too absorbed to take any notice of my companion.

Spellbound I saw—or fancied I saw—a grey cloud beat about the figure of the man in the circle of the pentacle. I saw Rathin Memory's lips move again.

" Quickly ! " A grip of steel was on my arm, and a voice that brooked no denial sounded in my ear. " Huish, get back to the Lorings' house at once ! Murder may be done there at any moment ! Go at once—I must stay here. Go, man ! "

So strong was his control over me at that moment that I did not hesitate. I moved like a man in a dream, for the dreadful images I had seen were vivid in my mind—but I

"At this point Memory thrust out his hand and seized the white cock."

must have been quick, for within a surprisingly short space of time I found myself in the garden and climbing over the high wall that separated it from the cliff-land.

Once on the other side, I took to my heels like a man pursued by fiends. But I was not frightened. My one idea was to get to the Lorings' house as quickly as possible.

Though it was long past midnight when I arrived there, I hammered at the door loudly enough to wake the dead.

But I was in the house long before the door could be opened. Going around to the side, I saw a ladder placed against a bedroom window. In a flash the realisation came to me that this led to David Loring's room.

Rushing up the ladder, I flung myself through the window —just in time to prevent a man from plunging a knife into the breast of the sleeping paralytic.

" Sinclair ! " I cried. " What the devil are you doing here ? "

I had hold of his wrist, and the knife clattered to the floor. And although he struggled like the madman he was, I was desperate myself and ruthless. Getting clear, I swung a right to the jaw that carried every ounce in my body, and he crumpled helpless across the bed of the man he had intended to murder.

" What's the matter ? Why—I can move ! I'm better ! I'm well ! "

This night of strangeness was to hold another mystery. Imagine my amazement when David Loring, a hopeless paralytic the short time I had known him, jumped out of bed and came across to me.

" I'm well ! I'm cured ! " he cried, tears running down his cheeks.

The next moment Violet Loring rushed into the room.

" Daddy ! "

She had been in his arms for several seconds before she seemed to realise that anyone else was in the room.

Then—

" Mr. Huish ! . . . *Harry !* " she cried.

As she spoke his name her lover sat up and rubbed his eyes.

" Vi ! I've had such a horrible dream ! What am I doing here ? " he said.

.   .   .   .   .   .

16*

It was not until Sebastian Quin and I were ensconced cosily before our sitting-room fire at the Grand Hotel that I regained my normality. The mysteries I had seen following so quickly one upon the other that night had been too much for me to grasp.

" For Heaven's sake, Quin, explain matters—everything ! " I snapped. This was 1930, and I was tired of trying to probe things to which there appeared to be no earthly explanation. Paralysed men suddenly jumping out of bed . . . madmen becoming sane through a blow on the jaw . . . tongues of flame . . . slaughtered cocks . . .

" I have already told you that Rathin Memory is dead," said Quin. " Exactly how he died is too horrible to relate, but briefly, the evil forces which he conjured up by means of the black magic you saw to-night, and which he had used to work evil upon two other men—to paralyse David Loring and to make Harry Sinclair mad—destroyed him. Once I had wrecked the five guarding lamps of the pentacle, which I did with my revolver shortly after you had left, he was no longer safe. And the spell which he had caused to be cast upon Loring and Sinclair was broken. The devils which he could control as long as those lamps served as protection seized him. I heard one short, strangled scream of dreadful horror, and I knew it was over."

While I stared at him in speechless amazement Quin continued : " If you told the ordinary person that Black Magic was practised in England to-day, you would be thought a lunatic ; but the fact is true, as you have yourself had the proof, Huish. I had my suspicions that this man Rathin Memory was an adept in the unholy art when I first heard Miss Loring's story, but it was too early for me to give any opinion on the matter until I had myself seen him at the actual practice."

" But that grey shape, Quin ? "

" Was one or more spirits of evil—devils, if you care for the usual superstitious term. It is too technical a matter for me to explain now at length, but there is no doubt that the rites of Black Magic have been carefully preserved and handed down. The Egyptians unquestionably had the power to raise evil spirits and use them for purposes of personal vengeance. And have you not read how Madame de Montespan consulted a witch and took part in a Black

Mass with the notorious Abbé Guibourg, so that she might
win back the love of Louis the Fourteenth of France ?
Indeed, there is evidence enough !

" In Tibet to-day spirit-raising is practised in its most
elaborate and secret forms. That was what first gave me
the idea that this man Memory was an adept—the news
that he had recently returned from that land of weird and
uncanny mystery. And now "—yawning—" I'm off to bed."
I too went to bed—but I could not sleep.

THE CURIOUS EPISODE OF THE SWEARING GHOST

THE man opposite Sir Herbert Mandeville, British Secret Service Chief, smiled and drew his own chair nearer.

" Yes, Sir Herbert," he said, " I've come all the way from the States to inquire into the thing for myself. The pity is that most of the real old-fashioned ghosts appear to have got disheartened and to have gone out of the business ; but this fellow, if all the accounts I've heard are true, can be guaranteed to deliver the goods ! He can make hair stand upright on the head of a bald man ! But perhaps you're not interested ? "

The Secretary of England's National Security Department opened his eyes.

" On the contrary," he replied convincingly, " I am very interested indeed. The fact that my eyes were closed is but evidence of that." Indeed, Sir Herbert Mandeville was absorbed in the turn of the conversation. When he was not engaged in laying snares for the criminals whose activities it was the duty of his department to checkmate, he spent his time investigating the claims of various spiritualistic mediums and in examining other evidence of life on the " other side of the wall." Particularly was he interested in alleged ghosts, and many nights' rests had he sacrificed in the pursuit of this strange but fascinating hobby.

The man who had accepted his invitation to luncheon at the Five Arts Club had written previously from the Fitzherbert Hotel, Piccadilly, enclosing a letter of recommendation from the Psychical Society of America. Anxious to talk to a fellow-enthusiast, Sir Herbert had arranged a meeting. The luncheon had been excellent, and his companion entertaining. With the first mention of the Rockleigh Hall ghost, Sir Herbert had given himself up to a real sense of enjoyment.

Mr. Benjamin Chadwick, the man who had travelled all

the way from America in order to meet an English ghost face to face, continued :

" Of course, you know the main features of the story, Sir Herbert ? The history of this particular apparition is included in the book *Famous British Ghosts*, I understand ? "

" That is so," replied his host. " As a matter of fact "— a note of pride in his voice—" I had a hand in the compilation of that volume myself."

" So I understand. That was one of the reasons why I looked forward with such pleasure to meeting you. Now, Sir Herbert "—speaking with evident relish—" just humour me by narrating exactly as much of the Rockleigh Hall ghost story as you know."

Sir Herbert flicked the ash off his cigar.

" On a night in October 1542, Sir Roger Freyne, a nobleman living in the Buckinghamshire village of Rockleigh, gave a dinner-party. It was a gay and gallant affair, and wine flowed freely. Too freely, as it chanced ; for Sir Roger, hearing the Earl of Rothersay speaking lightly of a woman's name, followed the Earl to his bedchamber, drew his sword, and plunged it into the heart of the Earl, killing him immediately.

" The fact that the lady whose chastity had been called into question was a relative of the murderer may have been some excuse for the ruthless deed, but the conscience of the killer would seem to have been disturbed, because many credible witnesses have testified that the spirit of Sir Roger haunts the scene of his violent deed. There would seem to be just one flaw in the evidence, however——"

" And that is ? " questioned the other.

" The ghost of Sir Roger Freyne, as seen by various witnesses, is wearing armour. Now that to me is incongruous. All the writers on the subject distinctly stated that, directly he heard the remark which the Earl of Rothersay was stated to have uttered, Sir Roger left the banqueting-hall and went straight to the Earl's bedroom. The Earl had been carried to his room some short time earlier, overcome by wine. Now it is extremely unlikely that his host would have been wearing armour during a drinking carouse."

Mr. Benjamin Chadwick's eyes glistened.

" That is just the point I was considering myself, Sir Herbert. Now, coming over, whom do you think I met ? "

" I'm sure I don't know."

" Sir Arthur Freyne, the present owner of Rockleigh Hall ! Naturally enough, when I found out who this pleasant young fellow was, I raised the question of the family ghost. He tried to put me off at first—told me he was sick of the subject ; owing to the yarns about the apparition the mansion has been lying derelict for years (his mother would never spend a night there), and he was tired of answering what he called ' damn fool questions.' But this he did promise— that I could spend a night in the place, and that I could take with me any friend interested in spirit phenomena I cared to choose. . . . What do you say, Sir Herbert ? "

" By Jove ! I believe I should like to come. That point about the armour ought certainly to be settled," Mandeville said. " When can you fix it up, Chadwick ? "

The other tried to hide his excitement by lighting a fresh cigar.

" I'll let you know, Sir Herbert. It will take a day or so's arranging, of course."

" Of course," supported the Secretary of the National Security Department.

.   .   .   .   .

Sir Bernard Bannister, C.M.G., Chief Commissioner of Scotland Yard, passed over the photographs with the air of a collector showing his most prized specimens.

" Yes," he said enthusiastically, " they're all beauties, every mother's son of 'em ! "

" H'm ! " commented Peter Repington, as he went through the lot, " they certainly look a hard-boiled crowd. Swift workers to a man, I should say. Who's the gentleman with the mole ? " He was looking at this moment at the keen, handsome, but unscrupulous face of a middle-aged man whose left cheek was decorated by a peculiarly-shaped mole.

The Chief Commissioner took the photograph.

" Mike Hennessy, otherwise known as ' Chicago Red,' on account of the colour of his hair. An American crook of genius. He specialises in the confidence trick, but will not stop at murder when there is sufficient at stake. He's got the most colossal nerve of any crook living. If ever you see him, Repington, run him along to me, and I shall be very much obliged. By the way, how's your uncle ? I tried to get him on the 'phone yesterday."

Peter smiled.   He was very fond of his uncle, but he had a mild contempt for certain of Sir Herbert Mandeville's characteristics.

" Oh, he's off on some fresh bogey hunt or other," he said ; " why he wants to chase ghosts when there are so many crooks about I can't conceive, but he will do it."

" Ah, well, we all have our little weaknesses," commented Sir Bernard.   " You won't forget to give me the tip if you see our friend ' Chicago Red ' hanging about ? It's just about his time for coming to Europe."

Leaving Scotland Yard, Repington took a taxi to his office.   As he passed through to his private room he saw Elsie Summers, his secretary, bending over a cabinet file. The temptation to kiss the back of the beautiful neck was almost overwhelming, but he overcame it.   He had to remember his promise :   that until he had captured Paul Vivanti he would not broach the subject of love to the girl he adored.   It was an exceedingly difficult problem—having to spend several hours each day in the company of a girl with the radiant personality and intoxicating charm of Elsie Summers and yet to maintain their relationship on a strictly business footing.   Only a fresh herculean effort each day enabled Peter to stand the strain.

Elsie Summers looked up.

" Lord Headbury has been 'phoning to know if you can put him in touch with Sir Herbert Mandeville," she announced.

" Come into the office," he returned, holding open the door of his private room.   " I am weary and want refreshment.   Do you think you could make some tea ? "

" I'm sure I could."   She set about the preparations at once.

Balancing the cup on his knee, Repington looked across at his companion.

" I am getting tired of that uncle of mine," he remarked ; " between ourselves, what can be said of a man who leaves his work at a time like this——? "

" But you know the department is very slack," put in his secretary, a stickler for truth.

Her principal frowned.

" Please do not interrupt," he said.   " I ask you again, what can be said of a man who leaves his work—jolly in-

teresting work, even if it does lead me some highly fantastic
dances and breaks into my beauty sleep of nights—to go
chasing ghosts ?   *Ghosts !* "   Peter snorted in contempt.

" There are such things, people say," replied Elsie Summers, who was sometimes dogmatic.

" Even if there are, what good can a man like my uncle
do chasing 'em ? "

" He is an earnest student of spiritualism—we had quite
a long chat about it the other night.   He is very sincere—
and we all have our pet foibles."

" I seem to have heard that remark, or something like it,
before.   A man occupying the exalted position of my uncle
should be above reproach : I take it that is what you mean ?
However, I'm tired of ghosts.   I want to see humanity—
preferably some exotic specimens—for a change.   Are you
doing anything to-night ? "

" Not a thing," admitted his secretary.

" Then hie thee, girl, to thy lodging and garb thyself in
the choicest and most saucy raiment available——"

" *Mr.* Repington ! "

" Oh, it's quite all right !   I was only going to suggest
that we should dine and dance at the Café Blue Moon to-
night.   Any good ? "

Elsie Summers wrinkled her adorable forehead in thought.

" I think I'll risk it," she said at length.

" *Bon !* "

.   .   .   .   .

Those of you who live quiet, orderly suburban lives probably do not know the Café Blue Moon.   You have read of
it, however, even if you have not actually seen it.   A visit
should be paid forthwith ; the Café Blue Moon, lying due
N.W. of Piccadilly Circus, is one of the sights of the
Metropolis.

The crowds that throng it night after night are picturesque,
picaresque, highly sophisticated, not to say exotic.   A good
proportion are also dangerous, for it is here that the big
fish of the criminal world make their *rendezvous*.   The
leeches of modern society complete their plans, and draw up
fresh engagements, over wine at the Café Blue Moon.
Benisty, the best-seller, says there's a novel a night there.

The management—suave, polite Italian men—do not
welcome the presence of known police officers, but Peter

Repington had a way with him, and consequently it was to one of the most sought-after tables on the balcony that Elsie Summers was led that evening.

The dinner was excellently chosen, superbly cooked, and admirably served. As he lit his companion's cigarette, Peter Repington decided that the world had not a great deal more to offer him at that moment.

" This place fascinates me," said Elsie Summers, drawing contentedly at her cigarette.

" You have the true enthusiast's zest," Repington assured her, pointing to the floor below, where dancing had started ; " in that crowd, I wouldn't mind betting, are some of the most dangerous crooks in the world."

Her smile was half a challenge.

" I'm not proud," she said ; " let's mix with them ! I have every confidence in your ability to look after me, Mr. Repington."

" When will it be ' Peter ' ? " he asked.

A look of regret passed into the girl's face.

" You know our compact," she reminded him ; " but I do not wish to be sad to-night—we will dance ! "

Amid that gay throng it was easy enough to forget carking care and dull responsibility. The orchestra was perfect. Elsie Summers danced like a butterfly. She was easily the loveliest woman in the room.

Peter Repington was as happy as any man in the world has any right to be.

Yet suddenly he turned to his very delightful companion. His expression changed.

" Are you game for an adventure ? "

There was a quality in his voice which made Elsie Summers look at him curiously.

" What sort of an adventure ? " she inquired.

" It would probably involve your being made love to. And the man would be dangerous. Also, I should have to keep out of the way."

Elsie Summers pressed the stub of her cigarette into the ash-tray.

" It is scarcely the thing I should have thought you would have suggested."

" Hang it ! Do you think that I should even mention such a thing if——? "

She faced him. " This is business then—Peter ? "

Repington flushed, and then drew his chair closer.

" Yes," he said ; " now, listen ! This afternoon I had a chat with Sir Bernard Bannister, the Chief Commissioner at Scotland Yard. He told me that if I ever met a man with a heart-shaped mole on the left cheek, to try to take him along to the Yard."

" There is a man over there with a heart-shaped mole on his left cheek. He has been looking in our direction. Is he the person you would like to see making love to me ? "

" I didn't mean to put it as crudely as that, dash it ! " Repington replied gloomily.

The girl laughed.

" When I entered into a working partnership with you, it involved taking the rough with the smooth," she remarked. " Every crook fascinates me, because I always have the hope that he will be the means of leading me to Paul Vivanti. If you want me to do this thing, I will."

" Hunting criminals has become a disease and a mania with me," Repington confessed ; " I never realised until now how low I had fallen. No, I can't let you take the risk, my dear ! "

Elsie Summers opened her vanity-bag.

" Look ! " she said.

Repington caught a glimpse of a tiny pearl-handled revolver, and nodded.

" You are a very wonderful girl ; otherwise I should not allow you to take the risk."

" We will leave that out of it. What is it exactly you wish me to do ? "

" I should like to know the present and future plans of the gentleman with the mole."

" If you leave me now, I will see what can be done," replied the girl. " I hope not to be late for business tomorrow."

" Say, sweetie, you and I could work well as a team ! "

Elsie Summers shrugged her beautiful shoulders with a gesture copied from Hollywood's most famous vamp.

" I'm not falling for any rough stuff," she replied, sipping wine.

" Rough stuff ! " Judging by the indignation in his voice, Michael Hennessy's pride was wounded vitally.

" Over on the other side they would tell you that ' Chicago Red ' never does any rough stuff," he said. " Why, I take their rolls away from 'em without so much as raising a squeal. Some day, kid, when I know you better, I'll tell you of some of the ' plays ' I've made."

" You're a good talker ! " commented his companion, with almost studied insolence.

" Talker ! I'll *show* you. Why, if you only knew the stunt I'm going to pull off in a day or so. . . ."

" Any room for me in it ? "

He looked at her intently. Elsie Summers's heart gave a jump. Had she played her part well enough to convince this King of the Underworld that she really was on the shady side of the law herself, or did this declared Master Bluffer suspect that she was trying to " squeeze " him ?

" No," he told her, " there's no room for you in it. It's not a job for a woman."

His companion yawned, showing a shapely hand and pearly teeth.

" I thought you were going to tell me something interesting," she complained. " Good-night ! I'll be getting along."

Mr. Michael Hennessy caught her hand.

" Don't go yet, kid ! " he pleaded. " Say, you're the loveliest thing I've seen this side of the Windy Burg. We'll have some more wine."

Elsie Summers slipped her hand inside her vanity-bag. What she touched was reassuring.

.   .   .   .   .

The wind howled dismally, and with an eerie note.

" I don't mind confessing that I was thankful for that dinner, Sir Herbert," said Mr. Benjamin Chadwick ; " to come to such a place, and on such an errand as ours, without having fed, would be rather too much of a good thing, don't you think ? "

" I quite agree," replied that inveterate ghost-stalker, the Secretary of the National Security Department, pulling at his cigar. " The present owner keeps a small staff always on the premises, then ? The food to-night was quite admirably cooked, I must say."

" Yes, on the off-chance of anyone—preferably an American like myself—being attracted by one of the advertisements which are continually being inserted in the more important papers, a small staff is retained by the owner. Gosh! I only wish I could afford to buy the place," the speaker added regretfully.

He drew his chair nearer the blazing fire.

" The ghost doesn't walk until twenty minutes past midnight, according to all the legends," Benjamin Chadwick continued, " so there's plenty of time. I really think we shall see something to write home about to-night, Sir Herbert."

" I sincerely trust we shall." The usually grave features of the Secretary of the National Security Department relaxed into a slight smile. " I suppose a good many people would consider our waiting here a somewhat mad proceeding ? " he went on.

His fellow-investigator turned.

" Since I had the pleasure of lunching with you, Sir Herbert, I've made the acquaintance of two men who have had personal experience of this ghost of Rockleigh Hall. The first was a priest. I was dining with some friends in Clarges Square the night before last, and this Father O'Reilly chanced to be present. During the course of conversation I happened to mention that I was taking the opportunity of investigating, whilst I am in England, the authenticity of various ghosts, amongst them the Rockleigh Hall apparition.

" The priest approached me in the smoking-room after dinner. He gave me a solemn warning."

" A warning ? " ejaculated Sir Herbert Mandeville.

" A solemn warning," repeated the other. " He said he was not able to forget the encounter he had had himself with this particular ghost. Would you like to hear the story, Sir Herbert ? "

" I most certainly would," replied his companion.

The American settled himself more comfortably in his chair.

" The incident occurred many years ago, but, none the less, it bears the imprint of truth. Certainly I did not doubt the worthy father's statement ; he was much too sincere. The way he gripped my arm when he was telling me . . . I have the marks still! Father O'Reilly, in spite of his religious beliefs, or perhaps because of them, was undoubtedly terrified. He warned me most solemnly and dramatically against ever putting foot inside this house. Of course, we have all heard the same kind of thing——"

" Of course," agreed his listener, " but tell me the priest's story, there's a good fellow ! "

Smiling sympathetically at the other's impatience, Chadwick said : " Well, according to O'Reilly, this happened about ten years ago. The hall had been let to a wealthy South American for a time, and Father O'Reilly was invited, amongst a number of other guests, to a big dinner-party. The priest did not know until the last moment whether he could turn up, and his arrival created a *contretemps*. There was only the haunted bedroom vacant, and his host did not like, he said, to offer him that.

" As Father O'Reilly said to me, it seemed at the time as though he were being challenged—not by his host, but by the unseen Powers of Darkness. He felt he could not, in justice to his calling, ignore this challenge ; and so he professed himself as not only willing, but eager, to spend the night in the haunted room.

" At first, none of the servants would consent to get the room ready, and eventually the butler himself, with the assistance of the chief footman, did what was necessary. I'm afraid I'm telling the story rather badly, Sir Herbert."

" On the contrary," replied Sir Herbert Mandeville somewhat testily, " I think you are telling it very well indeed—but please do get on ! "

Mr. Benjamin Chadwick acknowledged the mild rebuke by bowing his head.

" Father O'Reilly was very emphatic on the point that he was perfectly sober at the time he went to bed. Indeed, he stated that he had had only two glasses of wine—one of champagne and the other of port—throughout the evening.

" He stated, moreover, that he was perfectly calm and rational. He had sought help and solace in prayer, he said, and his nerves were quite controlled. He knew he had nothing to fear. I must say he convinced me on all these points, Sir Herbert."

The latter nodded.

" So composed was the priest that he dropped off to sleep almost immediately he got into bed. He was awakened——" The speaker stopped. Something like the scream of a human being in mortal terror sounded from close at hand.

" It is only the wind," said Sir Herbert Mandeville ; " go on with your story, Chadwick."

" I was saying," complied the American investigator, " that the priest was awakened at exactly twenty minutes past midnight. As he opened his eyes a sense of helpless terror seized him. To use his own words, he was ' aghast with fear.'

" And, according to his own statement, he had a very good reason for being afraid. Bending over the bed was a knightly figure in full armour. As he stared, this terrible apparition raised a mailed fist——"

" Oh, come ! " protested the listener.

" I am merely giving you the story word for word as it was given to me," replied Chadwick. " I agree it sounds preposterous that a ghost can inflict a physical blow, but the priest insisted that not only did he receive a blow from the mailed fist of the ghost which knocked him back with staggering force amongst the pillows, but that for days afterwards the marks of the blow were distinctly imprinted on his chest. It is hard to believe, I know."

" It *is* hard to believe," agreed Sir Herbert. " The fact that a ghost can inflict a physical blow is scarcely credible. However, we may have an opportunity of judging the truth of the worthy father's story for ourselves to-night."

Chadwick raised his eyes.

" I believe that to be quite likely, Sir Herbert." There was a curious expression on his face as he spoke which, if the Secretary of the National Security Department had chanced to notice it, would have caused him some grounds for speculation. Sir Herbert Mandeville, however, was looking into the fire at the time.

" One more story about this ghost—if it does not bore you," continued the man who called himself Benjamin Chadwick.

" If it is half as interesting as the last——"

And the American plunged into a second narrative.

" This incident does not go back so far as the priest's story," he said ; " it took place, I believe, not more than five years ago.

" The hall was deserted at the time. Not even a caretaker could be found to stay in the house.

" The man who tried to lay the ghost this time was named Matthew Durban. He was a solicitor by profession, but a most enthusiastic amateur criminologist in his spare time. Somehow or other he gained the idea that a gang of crooks were using this haunted house idea for purposes of their own —probably, it occurred to him, so that they could utilise the hall as a living-place for themselves as well as a storehouse for their swag.

" Quite a likely idea—or so it seemed to this Durban.

" What did he do but buy a couple of trained police dogs, and proceed with these to the hall !

" This young man was not above breaking the laws which it was his profession to observe," continued Chadwick ; " he contrived to effect an entrance to the house, dragging the dogs after him."

" Why ' dragging ' the dogs ? Did they evince any reluctance to enter the house ? " asked Sir Herbert Mandeville, turning in his chair.

" They certainly did ! I ran this man Durban down in his stuffy little office in the City yesterday, and he assured me that both the dogs commenced to whine and to hang back when within fifty yards of the lodge gates. He had the utmost difficulty in dragging them into the house, and when he tried to pull them up the staircase—it was his intention to spend the night in the haunted room with the two dogs, after roaming through the whole house—they moaned piteously. Finally, one of them, after trying to escape from the lead, fell at Durban's feet—*dead* ! "

" Dead ! " ejaculated the listener.

" Dead ! How do you account for that ? But here I'm doing all the talking. Let me offer you another drink, Sir Herbert ? "

" Not for me, thank you," was the reply.

A surprising change came over the face of Mr. Benjamin Chadwick.

" But surely——! " he persisted.

Sir Herbert Mandeville evidenced a surprising firmness.

" I have already refused to take anything else to-night, Mr. Chadwick," he said in a tone that admitted of no further argument.

" Oh, well, if you won't——" The other turned away.
" If you are quite ready, Sir Herbert," he added, " we will
adjourn to the—er—haunted room. I have had two beds
put in . . . what the devil's that ? "

The last words were uttered in a voice that held not only
surprise, but terror. Suddenly the light had flashed out,
leaving the room in darkness, except for the glow of the fire.

For a few seconds there was a tense silence.

Then, from the direction of the door, there came a sound
that brought Sir Herbert Mandeville's heart leaping into his
mouth. The noise came nearer, then suddenly ceased.

By this time his eyes had grown accustomed to the dim
light, and he was able to make out a form completely clad in
sombre armour.

The ghost of Rockleigh Hall !

" I've come for you, Mike Hennessy ! " said a hollow
voice. It came from behind the visor.

Instantly a stream of profanity poured from the lips of
the man Sir Herbert Mandeville had hitherto regarded as a
cultured gentleman.

The most astonishing events followed. While he stared
in amazement, the Secretary of the National Security Department saw the man he knew as Benjamin Chadwick whip
a revolver from a hip pocket and fire twice in rapid succession
at the apparition in armour.

Before he could fire a third shot, however, the Thing was
on him, dealing sledgehammer blows with its mailed fists.
While Sir Herbert Mandeville was still stricken with astonishment, Chadwick, with the horror on top of him, crashed to
the ground.

A second later a voice—an undoubtedly human voice—
said loudly and distinctly : " Damn and blast this old
iron ! "

Sir Herbert Mandeville awoke out of his reverie. He
knew that voice ; had heard it thousands of times.

" *Peter !* " he cried.

The apparition in armour retained his position on Benjamin Chadwick's chest.

" If you have a grain of sense left," came the voice from
behind the visor, " you'll take that gun away from this
swine ; after that, you'll fetch the handcuffs I've left on the
table in the hall."

" But——? " expostulated the astonished Mandeville.

" Hell !   This fellow is a crook—and he meant to murder you ! " came the startling reply.

After that Sir Herbert Mandeville hurried.

It was only when Peter Repington's cosy chambers in the Albany were reached a couple of hours later that a full explanation was given the bewildered Secretary of the National Security Department.

" I have to thank Miss Summers for putting me on the track," said Peter Repington.   " What the literary critics would call ' the long arm of coincidence ' came into the thing a bit, I suppose, for it happened that, on the night of the same day as Sir Bernard Bannister at the Yard had been showing me the photograph of a certain hard-boiled American crook he expected to be popping up in Europe fairly soon, I caught sight of the very fellow in the Café Blue Moon."

" *We* caught sight of him," corrected Elsie Summers ; " and what do you think he had the audacity to propose to me, Sir Herbert ? "

" Goodness knows," replied the official, who had not yet recovered from the shock.

" He suggested that I should allow that beastly man to make love to me ! "

" And did you ?   I mean, did he ?   Dear me, what am I saying ? "

" Sufficiently to allow me to get the information I required," smiled back the girl.

" But—— " started Sir Herbert Mandeville, still befogged.

" I'll tell you as simply as possible, uncle," replied Repington.   " This crook, who is known to the Yard as ' Chicago Red,' wanted to get you out of London and away from all help.   His purpose was to murder you—now, wait a minute and everything will be explained !   I repeat that his purpose was to murder you—although the verdict at the inquest would have been ' Death by natural causes,' or ' Misadventure,' or something equally pot-house.   With considerable subtlety he played upon your pet weakness—this ghost-hunting rubbish—to such an extent that he was able to lure you down to that supposed haunted house.   He knew very well that, absorbed by your pet obsession, you would be off your guard somewhat ; the shrewdest men have their stupid moments, as we both know from experience. It was a clever scheme—a devilishly clever scheme, in fact ! Look here, uncle, did you have anything to drink with this man ? "

" He suggested a night-cap of whisky, but I refused."

" Lucky for you ! I happen to know that that whisky and soda would have been drugged with one of the most fiendish poisons known—or, rather, unknown, because there aren't many chemists in this country, or, indeed, Europe, who know anything about it. To-morrow "—taking a bottle from his pocket—" I'm going to see Pryor about this ; he ought to be able to give me an inkling of what's in it."

" Poison ! " exclaimed Sir Herbert.

" Yes, sir. It would have affected your heart to such an extent that when the bogus ghost——"

" Bogus ghost ! " Sir Herbert Mandeville's usually disciplined brain was now completely out of control. " He told me the most astounding things—stories about priests being awakened in the night and dogs dying——"

" Simply artistic padding. The fellow had imagination, and he played you up. I'm afraid, uncle, you've been a bit of a fool over this job. Shall I push on ? "

" Please ! " replied Mandeville stiffly.

" Friend Hennessy had hired a brother thug to get inside this armour and impersonate the joker who's supposed to keep himself busy haunting this show. When I got the necessary idea of what was due to happen, I hopped down and beat the other crook to it—that's all. Only, as I wanted to get to work pretty badly, I made my appearance rather earlier than had been arranged."

" And the other man ? "

" Oh, I left him trussed up like a fowl, with a gag in his mouth to keep him quiet. He doesn't matter. Neither does ' Chicago Red,' if it comes to that. The man who planned the whole thing never appeared, more's the pity ! "

" The man who planned it—what man are you talking about ? "

" Paul Vivanti ! He wanted to get at me through you. Besides, you were too dangerous an adversary to allow to go on living. It was his brain at the back of the scheme—but I wonder if ' Chicago Red ' received his fee ! " replied Peter Repington grimly.

WILLIAM LE QUEUX

The Secret of a Hushed-up Affair

The Secret of the Missing Bride

¶ WILLIAM LE QUEUX studied art in the Quartier Latin, toured France and Italy on foot, and was for two years a special correspondent of *The Times* before he decided to devote his whole time to novel-writing. He was a qualified wireless engineer, and was the first to broadcast concerts over the British Isles in 1920–21. He was responsible for over 130 novels, as well as many films.

THE SECRET OF A HUSHED-UP AFFAIR

My meeting with the handsome, dark-haired Anastasia, or Stana, as she was called, was destined to bring me certain exciting adventures, and disclose a very strange and important secret.

When, one morning at the Gare du Nord, in Paris, I entered the express for London, I found ensconced opposite the seat reserved for me a smartly-dressed, dark-eyed young girl of perhaps twenty-two, rather *petite* and very dainty, who was busy looking at the pictures in *Excelsior*, and who raised her eyes with covert glance.

There were not so many passengers as usual that morning, and we were alone. I was on my way from Cairo to London, by way of Marseilles, and had indeed only arrived at the Gare de Lyon an hour before, just in time to take my coffee hastily and cross Paris in a taxi.

The morning was grey and cold after the bright warm sunshine of Egypt, and I rather envied my smart companion her warm furs.

Soon after the train had moved out on its rush to Calais we began to chat, first in French and then in English, which she spoke exceedingly well. She had come by the Sud Express from Madrid on the previous night, it seemed, and was going to London to join her brother. She was, however, not Spanish, but had been born at Wolmar, in Livonia, and her name, I afterwards learnt, was Anastasia Irmann.

While we were chatting, a man in a soft felt hat and travelling coat, passing along the corridor, recognised me, and, putting his head into the compartment, addressed me by name, inquiring how I was, and adding:

" See you on the boat, old chap ! "

It was Jack Woodward, naval attaché at our Embassy in Constantinople, on his way home on leave, no doubt.

When he had gone I saw that my pretty companion

became more interested than ever in myself, and at last she remarked :

" I heard your friend call you by name. Are you really the novelist ? "

I pleaded guilty to having written a few books, and with a laugh asked why my presence in that train should be in any way remarkable.

" Oh, no," she hastened to assure me. " Only—only— well, I—I was thinking—just thinking——"

" Thinking what, mademoiselle ? " I asked, much puzzled. In reply she merely shrugged her shapely shoulders, and laughed.

" Nothing, Monsieur Le Queux ! I was only thinking because—well, because I have read your books in Russian, in French, and in English. My brother will be so very interested when I tell him that I have met you."

" Ah, mademoiselle, you really pay me too many compliments," I declared in French. " I am one of many English writers."

" True. But you are the one who really knows things— who is cosmopolitan, lives the life of the world, and who writes it as he lives ! Ah, m'sieur, I could tell you some very strange things to put into one of your books, but——"

" Do, I beg of you ! " I said eagerly.

She shook her head, and her attitude instantly altered. She took up a French novel and turned over its pages reflectively.

At the moment, we stopped at Amiens and the conductor bustled us into the *wagon-restaurant* for lunch.

Woodward was there, and waved to me from a table at the other end. The conductor had given us a *table-à-deux*, as conductors of the restaurants of the Wagon-Lit Company always do when they see a man and a girl together. With them " The tip's the thing ! "

We ate our *déjeuner* together, and an excellent luncheon it was. As a cosmopolitan she took a glass of Château Lafitte with me, but she would not allow me to pay her bill. That showed her independence and her good breeding.

Back again in the compartment, as we passed the sharp curve outside Boulogne, and were on our way to Calais, I tried to extract from her something more concerning herself, but she would admit nothing.

Naturally I suspected some little love-affair. Girls who are pretty are certainly abnormal if they have no male acquaintances on the tender-heart side. The serving-maid, if she is pretty and has fuzzy hair, has her inevitable " boy," much to the despair of her mistress.

Having boarded the boat, I settled her in the best deck-chair I could get by means of a tip, and though the sky and sea were grey, I knew by my experience of the Channel that the passage would be good.

In her furs she sat thinking, while I paced the deck with my old friend Woodward, excited over his two-months' leave. Then, when we came into Dover, I rejoined my dark-eyed little friend, and we travelled again in a compartment alone to Charing Cross, both of us having tea-baskets. Tea-basket ! Those are the first words in English which welcome the home-coming traveller, perhaps after long years of foreign tongues.

Before we arrived in London we had become increasingly friendly, and she told me that I could send a letter to her to the poste restante at Charing Cross.

Though she was travelling first-class, I was rather surprised, judging by her exterior, when she told me that she had been in service as French governess to a noble Spanish family at Villalba, outside Madrid.

" Really, mademoiselle," I said as the train dashed past Tonbridge, " it is very clever of you to teach French when Russian is your native language."

" No, m'sieur ! Is it not the same with you, when you spoke Italian first, and now you speak English ? "

Her knowledge of my birth and of my past struck me as distinctly curious.

As the train at last ran over the bridge at Charing Cross into the station, I exclaimed :

" Now give me an appointment. Will you not lunch or dine with me somewhere ? You are interested in me, mademoiselle ; hence I am interested in you."

She reflected for a moment.

" Very well," she replied. " The Marguerite Café in Oxford Street."

" When ? "

" Next Friday at seven."

" I shall be delighted to be there, mademoiselle," I said.

" Very well," was her reply. " But we are arriving," she said, looking out apprehensively as the train was drawing slowly along the platform. " Please do not appear to know me, I beg of you. My brother will be awaiting me—well, there are reasons why I do not wish him to know of our acquaintance. I have reflected. I shall not tell him."

" Certainly," I said, but in wonder. " Very well, we will now be strangers."

And springing to the other side of the compartment, I pretended a complete disinterest in my fellow-traveller.

She alighted, and I saw that she was met by a curiously ill-conditioned man of low type, tall and shabby, with a cropped brown beard—evidently a foreigner.

The instant they met, he put to her some sudden and serious question. She replied, and at once he was evidently satisfied.

I saw her go off with him to a taxi, he carrying her dressing-case. Curious that a governess should possess a dressing-case !

We cosmopolitans who travel up and down Europe in slow trains or in the *wagons-lits* have always our eyes open upon the personal baggage of our fellow-travellers, for it teaches us much concerning them.

On the following Friday, just before seven, having engaged a table and ordered a little dinner at the Marguerite, I arrived, and was idling about the entrance. She was punctual, but dressed differently—more neatly and more becoming a governess, I thought.

She greeted me merrily, and very soon we were sitting together, discussing the *hors-d'œuvre*.

I asked her what she had been doing, and she replied :

" Oh, I've been down in Essex with my brother."

" On pleasure ? "

" No, on business. He had some business there," and she moved uneasily.

She did not name the town, for she seemed strangely reticent about herself and her doings. I tried to ascertain where she was living in London, and she simply replied :

" Oh, what does it really matter to you, Monsieur Le Queux ? I live in—well, in the West End."

I recollected that strange, gaunt brother of hers, that dark, narrow-eyed, shabby man who had emerged from the waiting crowd at Charing Cross and had pounced upon her like a bird of prey upon its victim, those quick questions and the rapid replies. Yes, my pretty fellow-traveller was a mystery. Mysteries are always attractive to the novelist as a student of human nature, and the wiles and woes of his fellow men and women.

She seemed in excellent spirits, but when I asked her point-blank where she was living, she closely evaded my question by replying :

" Really, I would prefer not to say."

" Why ? "

She shrugged her shoulders, smiling, and, after a pause, said :

" That is my own business. Pardon me for being so frank. A letter to the poste restante will always reach me in due course."

" Always ! Then you are remaining in London ? " I asked.

" For a week or two," she answered. " Afterwards, I shall go away, and we shall never meet again," she added in a strange tone, as though of regret.

We ate our meal, but I confess she was to me a complete enigma. In the course of my cosmopolitan life, a wanderer in every capital of Europe, I have met many women of varying ages who have endeavoured to surround themselves by an atmosphere of romance, which an old hand like myself can easily penetrate. To the man who has lived the life of the capitals, and who has become shell-backed by experience —often dearly bought—the wiles of the romantic of both sides are amusing.

But in this case I felt that Stana was holding back from me certain information because she dared not confide in me.

She wished to do so, but she feared.

That is why I found myself so much attracted by her.

After dinner I took her to a theatre, hoping that afterwards she would betray herself as to her abode. But no such thing ! When we came out upon the pavement in St. Martin's Lane, she halted and said :

" Well, m'sieur, so many thanks for a delightful evening. I'm sure it's awfully good of you to have been so kind to me."

17

" But I'll get you a taxi," I urged.

" Oh, no, I'll walk," she said firmly. " I live here—in the West End."

" May I not see you as far as your home ? " I begged.

" No," was her sharp reply. " I have certain reasons, but please do not ask. Good night ! " and she held out her gloved hand in the half-light.

" But you will meet me again ? " I urged.

" Perhaps," she laughed. " If you write to me at the poste restante I will answer you. Now that's a promise."

So with that I had to be content, and while she passed through into Long Acre, I went along Coventry Street to my rooms in Ryder Street, St. James's. Truly, Stana Irmann was a mysterious person.

As I walked home, I could not put away from me thoughts of that tall, low-bred, ruffianly fellow, the brother, who on meeting her at Charing Cross had put those questions so roughly.

Why did she shroud herself in such an air of mystery ? Why also had she been so intensely interested when in the train she had discovered my identity by reason of Jack Woodward's indiscretion ? The more I thought it over, the more complicated and romantic became the problem.

In the course of our conversation over dinner that night, she had revealed herself as unusually intelligent and well-informed. The governess is, of course, ever an intelligent young person, but in her I saw a young woman of deep thought and earnest convictions.

We had spoken of Russia, her native country, whereupon she said :

" Ah ! you here in England are so ignorant of our Russia. Yet I might except m'sieur, who knows my country well." And she smiled as, with her elbows on the table, she looked into my eyes. " There will be a great upheaval ere long. Russia will free herself by great sacrifices and by plots far greater than any hitherto imagined in the world."

" But you are a revolutionist ! " I said, looking back into her pretty face.

" Ah, no ! That is a rather ugly word, m'sieur ! I only look for the freedom of my country." And she added, " I know you are not now in accord with my view. Yet did you not once write a book in which you disagreed with the autocratic policy of our poor, weak Emperor and his sycophant advisers ? "

I laughed. But it still struck me that she knew more of my life and my writings than the casual train-acquaintance might know.

" Well, I expressed certain views," I replied. " Views which were, at the time, impressed upon me. But, to tell you the truth, mademoiselle, I have no patience with extremists, either in the ' advanced ' thought of yesterday, or the ' spooks ' of to-day. If one desires to live to old age one has to preserve the level of one's mental capacity—with those of unbalanced brain or distorted ideas I have nothing in common."

At those words my companion's attitude struck me as extremely curious.

Next day I wrote to her to the poste restante at Charing Cross. She must have called daily for letters because, on the following day, I received a scribbled letter-card—one of those gummed-down abominations which postal officialdom has foisted upon the British public. On tearing off three-quarters of its edge I could read the scribbled words :

" I shall be outside the Criterion at three o'clock to-morrow. *Do* be there. So sorry to worry you.— STANA."

Of course I was there. I stood in the entrance to the restaurant, gazing up and down the busy pavement, but very punctually, as always, she came, dressed again differently—richly, so that I hardly knew her.

We met merrily, and I took her into the café on the right-hand side of the entrance. She had lunched early, she said. She would, however, take a cup of *café noir*.

" Well ? " I asked, as she daintily took a cigarette from my case. " What has happened ? Why do you want to see me ? "

" A lot has happened ! There will, before long, be startling developments. Be careful of yourself," she answered, in a startled whisper.

" Of myself ? What do you mean ? " I asked, much surprised.

" My dear Monsieur Le Queux, I only tell you this in order to warn you of certain things being arranged," she replied.

" You have wondered why I have enveloped myself in mystery. Well, it is because I have been compelled, in your own interests, as well as my own ! Ah, if I dared tell you all—but I cannot ! "

" Really, mademoiselle, I don't follow you," I said. " I cannot see why our chance meeting should have placed me in any peril."

" It has—in personal peril," she declared. Then, looking straight into my face across the marble-topped table as we sat in the corner, she said, " Ah, you do not know. How could you possibly suspect ? "

" Suspect what ? " I asked my pretty *vis-à-vis*. " Really, do be more explicit ! I am in complete ignorance of all this enigmatical talk ! " This girl, who had been a French governess in Madrid, was certainly an unusually intellectual person, yet the sight I had had at Charing Cross of the low-bred foreigner who had met her, and who was of criminal type, was ever uppermost in my mind.

" It is fortunate for me that I met you in the train, m'sieur, but perhaps unfortunate for yourself."

" Why ? " I demanded, increasingly mystified.

But she refused to tell me anything further, and at four o'clock declared that she must go. " I have to get back to my brother's," she said.

" In Essex ? "

She nodded.

She had hinted that I was in personal peril. Surely that was strange. I knew of no enemies. Besides, why should our meeting be fortunate for her, yet unfortunate for myself ? The enigma became greater each hour.

I looked steadily into those mysterious, fathomless dark eyes, and wondered.

She was persistent and determined to go.

Before doing so she promised, at my request, to write me very soon, for she had the address of my chambers in Ryder Street.

" Yes," she said, " we will meet again. Then perhaps I shall be compelled to ask a favour of you. If I do, I wonder whether you would be generous enough to grant it ? "

" Of course, mademoiselle," I said eagerly. " Please command me in any way you wish. I am entirely at your disposal."

She smiled again mysteriously, and drew a breath of relief. Then she replied slowly, her eyes again fixed upon me :

" No. Do not make any such rash promise, m'sieur. Wait until you know the truth."

" I am anxious and eager to know it," I said.

" Well, perhaps you may—if I find it necessary, and then——"

" Yes, and what then ? "

" Even then, perhaps, you could not keep a secret—one that, if disclosed, would mean death to me ! "

I started. She was so deeply in earnest, so intense, and her voice so altered, that instantly I saw that she was full of trouble and serious apprehension.

" I can keep a secret, mademoiselle," I assured her, " especially if the secret concerns one of my friends."

" Ah, but I am only an acquaintance, not a friend," she sighed.

We were almost alone in the great gilded café, which at that hour is usually deserted, save for the waiters.

" But, mademoiselle, are we not already friends ? Be frank with me on that account. Do."

" To-day I cannot. But I may be if—if it becomes necessary. Yet——" and she paused. " Yet I fear you will think ill of me if I revealed to you the truth," she added bitterly.

" Why should I ? "

" Because you would not—you would not believe me ! " she said, in a strange, faltering voice, and then, rising, she drew a long breath, repeating that she must really go.

I hailed a taxi outside for her, and she told the man to drive to Liverpool Street Station.

" Don't be surprised if you hear from me soon. That is, if I dare write to you," she whispered as she took my hand.

" Dare ! Why ? "

" Ah ! There are reasons—reasons you do not suspect," was her reply, and, entering the taxi, she waved her hand, and with a sad smile drove off.

As soon as she had gone, I stepped into another taxi that was at the kerb, and told the man to drive also to Liverpool Street. Stana's cab was already lost in the maze of traffic at Piccadilly Circus. My hope was to watch my mysterious little friend, and ascertain to what station she booked on the Great Eastern line.

My driver hastened, and got to the station quickly. I had resolved that, if she recognised me, my excuse for my presence there was that I had forgotten to ask her something. But though I looked through the booking-offices and departure platforms I failed to find her.

For a full quarter of an hour I searched. Then at last, to my surprise, I saw her smartly-dressed little figure standing on the arrival platform awaiting an incoming train.

I watched. Ten minutes later a train slowly drew in, whereupon she searched eagerly in the crowd of arrivals and presently discovered her tall, gaunt brother with another man of short stature, old, and white-bearded. The three held a hurried conversation, and then leisurely crossed to a taxi and drove away.

Once again I was on the alert and in a taxi, giving orders to my driver to follow the three at double fare, and endeavour to evade observation. They reached Maida Vale and, branching suddenly to the left, went up Shirland Road to Malvern Road, where they drew up before a high block of red-brick flats. There Stana's brother paid the man, and all three entered.

My driver very discreetly took me slowly past the door after they had entered, so that I might note it. Afterwards, at the corner of Canterbury Road, he pulled up.

" You saw where they went, sir, eh ? Into the last of those flats."

" Yes, thanks," I said, paying and dismissing him.

Then I sought a place of concealment, and kept observation upon their coming forth.

Till nearly six o'clock I waited, when the two men reappeared.

Neither knew me by sight, therefore I followed them without difficulty to a small French restaurant in Old Compton Street, where they met another younger man, no doubt a foreigner, whose lank, dark hair and clean-cut countenance gave him the appearance of an artist. Later they all three sat down to dinner.

That flat off Maida Vale was evidently Stana's dwelling-place. The story of Essex was, of course, merely a fiction in order to mislead me.

Nevertheless, her brother and his elderly companion had arrived from Essex by train.

Personally, I here confess that, though I had never spoken to him, I greatly disliked this brother. He was distinctly of criminal type.

With his friends at that obscure little café he seemed to enjoy himself immensely. I ate a frugal meal of tinned prawns and rice—which costs little in that cosmopolitan quarter of London—and watched how, ever and anon, he snapped his fingers in the faces of his two companions. They were evidently dubious. He was confident. And his confidence at last led him into hilarity as they drained a rush-covered *fiasco* of Italian wine.

After the dinner they took a long walk and I followed. The three went northward up Regent Street and across Regent's Park, back in the direction of the house from which they had come.

In Portland Place I hurried, overtaking them, in a dark spot in the road near the Turkish Embassy. They were speaking in Spanish—a language with which I am a little acquainted.

" Yes," exclaimed the brother as I passed. " The girl thinks it all plain-sailing. But I chance to be a little dubious."

" If anyone is to take the risk, then let the girl take it," said the white-bearded old man who had arrived at Liverpool Street. " She is ready and willing. Let her do it."

" Ah, true," replied the younger man, who had met them in the little restaurant, " but is it really fair to leave it all to a woman ? "

" Why not ? " I heard Stana's brother ask quickly. " All is fair in this great stroke of ours, is it not ? Surely, neither of us are growing chicken-hearted ? "

" I am not, for one," laughed the young man. " But I consider that we ought not to allow Stana to take the risk," he declared. " I would rather take it—if it falls to me."

What risk ? I wondered. To follow them further would, I foresaw, court suspicion, therefore I turned the next corner and left them.

The young man struck me as of a very superior and refined type. I liked his appearance. By his dark eyes and rather sallow complexion I judged him to be either Spanish or Italian—probably Spanish, because he had spoken that language. Yet Stana's brother I instinctively disliked, and more especially after what I had overheard.

I feared to go near those flats in Malvern Road lest she should suspect me of spying. So, as the many days passed, I could only reflect upon those curiously apprehensive words of hers. All was mysterious.

Why should I be placed in personal peril merely because we had met casually on the journey between Paris and London ?

Time after time I wondered who were those three men who spoke so glibly about the " risk " which Stana was prepared to run. The fact that she had been so well and expensively dressed on her journey from Madrid, while she confessed to me that she was only a governess, combined with the fact that though she had been born in Livonia she spoke French so well that she could carry out her duties as French governess, were in themselves requiring much explication.

Yes, Anastasia Irmann was certainly a girl of no ordinary type.

I had many affairs, both family and business, to attend to in the next few days. Much of my business concerned my forthcoming books, for I had been abroad many months and matters had accumulated in the hands of my agents. Therefore my time was fully occupied, and I was seldom in my chambers, save to dress for dinner, to sleep, and to take my breakfast.

A fortnight passed, yet no word had come from Stana. I could only suppose that she dared not write, as she had so frankly confessed to me.

I had been away to spend a week-end golfing at Cromer, when, upon my return, the man who looked after my rooms told me that a young foreign lady had called and inquired for me on two occasions, apparently much disappointed on finding me away. She left neither name nor message, but said she would call again.

That night I returned from the club about eleven and sat reading till past one o'clock, when suddenly my telephone rang.

" Ah ! " exclaimed a female voice, " so you are back at

last ! I'm Stana ! May I come and see you now ? I know it's awfully late, but I will explain."

" Of course," I said. " But where are you ? "

" Oh, at a call office not far away. Will you open your front door, and—and I do hope you will forgive me for disturbing you, won't you ? "

I laughed merrily, and then went down and unbolted the door.

A quarter of an hour later she arrived—pale, even haggard, but very demurely, almost shabbily, dressed.

" It is awfully good of you ! " she faltered, as I shook her hand. " I know I ought not to come here to your rooms, and especially at this hour ! " Then she asked apprehensively, " Is anyone here ? "

" Not a soul," I assured her, as I led the way into my little den.

" Well," she exclaimed, as soon as she was seated, " I feared to come this evening, as they are ever watching me. So I had to wait until they went to bed."

" They ? " I echoed. " Who are they ? "

" Louis and Xavier. My friends," she said. " If they knew I had come here it would go hardly with me. But I have risked it because—because of Eugène."

" And who is Eugène ? " I inquired, looking straight across at her, for it was evident that she was greatly perturbed.

" The man I hope very soon to marry. I followed him here from Madrid."

I wondered whether Eugène was that handsome, artistic-looking young man who had met her brother and the elder man in that restaurant in Old Compton Street. Yet to question her would have been to have revealed the fact that I had been spying.

" Well, mademoiselle, it seems you are in distress. How can I assist you ? " I asked.

She seemed longing to tell me, yet again she hesitated. At last she said :

" I—I do not care for myself in the least, but—but I want you to save him, because—because I love him ! "

" Save him from what ? "

" From committing a terrible deed—from death ! " was her answer. " Ah, you cannot know what position I am

17*

in ! And not only myself, but you also, m'sieur ! They have their suspicions, and hence you are a marked man. They are plotting to kill you ! "

" What ! These men Louis and Xavier ? " I asked in surprise. " I certainly haven't done anything against the interests of either of those two unknown persons. Why should they conspire against me ? " I demanded in dismay.

" But they have, I tell you. They suspect that on our journey from Paris I told you something ; they believe that I may have betrayed their secret ! "

" You certainly have not," I said. " But tell me at once about these two men who are plotting my death."

Again she was silent, but at last she said :

" Louis Fontan and Xavier Ferraz."

" And your lover's name ? "

" Eugène Romero."

" Thanks. In what manner do you suggest that I should act ? " I asked, greatly puzzled.

" At the moment, I am too confused to say anything," she replied, in a strangely reflective tone. " If by any means they learn that I have been here to-night, then I can hope for nothing further—only death ! They would kill me, and you also, m'sieur. But," she went on, " I want you to help me, if you will," and she produced from her handbag a sealed envelope. " To-day is Tuesday," she went on breathlessly. " If you hear no word from me by Friday at midnight, then you will know that something evil has befallen me, and that your life too is in serious jeopardy. If you hear nothing at midnight, open this—not before— and I beg of you to give me your word of honour ! "

" I will, mademoiselle," I replied.

" Good ! I can trust you to help Eugène and myself," she said. " Be careful to conceal that envelope, for it contains a great secret. I know I have done wrong, but—but I hope for your forgiveness, and to make atonement ! "

I took the white envelope and before her eyes locked it in my heavy steel dispatch-box.

Then she grasped my hand convulsively, and, accepting the glass of wine I offered her—for her nerves were unstrung —she later on slipped out into Ryder Street, where she was lost in the darkness, having absolutely refused to allow me to accompany her, as being too " dangerous."

The days went on. Friday dawned. I remained at home all day, awaiting a ring on the telephone, but each time I received a summons it was on business from a publisher or a newspaper editor. Night came, and instead of going out to dinner my man brought me in a cold meal. Each moment that evening my anxiety increased. What could have happened to my dainty little companion? Further, was my life really in jeopardy, as she had alleged?

I confess to a " creepy " feeling that night as I sat alone, watching my clock, the hands of which had passed eleven, and were well on the way towards midnight.

At last the old clock struck its musical chimes of Westminster. I glanced at my watch to see that it was correct. It was. Then the deep-toned bell slowly struck the hour of midnight.

She had given no sign!

I rose, unlocked the dispatch-box, and with frantic fingers tore open the envelope. The words I read were as follows :

" Eugène and I are in deadly peril! Go at once to Scotland Yard and tell them to send detectives to No. 11 Markinfield Mansions, Malvern Road. Tell them to exercise every precaution, because in one of the rooms— the first on the left—are high explosives which Louis and Xavier will, if the police do not prevent it, themselves detonate, and blow us all up. I rely upon you, Monsieur Le Queux, to secure our liberty, because I will stand as King's evidence. Be most careful of your own life. When the police have made the raid, you will then know of the plot which has been in progress. If I am already dead—as I may be—then I ask forgiveness for disturbing you.—STANA."

I re-read the letter, and then, hurrying on my coat, went out, found a taxi, and was soon seated with my friend Chief Inspector Pearson, of the Criminal Investigation Department at Scotland Yard.

" Really, that's most curious! " he exclaimed when, in a few brief sentences, I told him what had occurred, and he had read the strange letter. " I wonder what can be in progress? " he asked.

" Something desperate, without a doubt," I said. " The

girl has warned me that she believes me to be in personal danger, because they suspect that I know their secret. But I don't ! "

" Then it is for us to investigate the clever game these people are evidently playing, and at once ! " he said.

" Whatever it is, recollect that mademoiselle has made the disclosure to us, therefore neither she nor the young fellow Eugène must be arrested—that is, if they are still alive. I make that a condition," I added very seriously.

" Certainly. But we can't arrest anybody until we know that we can bring an absolute charge against them," he said. " Nevertheless, we will go at once and make a call."

Five detective-sergeants, with an inspector, were at once summoned into the room, and were told the object of our midnight adventure.

It was, then, nearly half-past one in the morning when we arrived, all being quiet. In the great block of flats, lights still showed in several windows.

The door leading to the stone stairs was unlocked, with a glimmering gas-jet, there being no hall-porter. Cautiously all eight of us crept slowly upstairs, each recollecting that the first room on the left was said to be filled with explosives. That room, we had arranged, should be first secured.

As we approached the door of the flat in question noise-lessly we could hear men's voices within !

Pearson suddenly gave a loud double-knock at the door, in imitation of a night telegraph messenger. Instantly all was quiet, when presently there came to the door an old woman with tousled grey hair. As she opened it, we all made a rush within.

Next moment there reigned a perfect pandemonium of shouts and cries ; of shrieks and fierce imprecations in Spanish ; for while the room on the left had been seized by two of our party the others had gained the apartment beyond, in which stood Stana's brother, his elderly friend, and three other men of swarthy complexion—Spaniards, all of them.

The moment the tall, evil-faced man who had met Stana at Charing Cross realised that we were there, he made a dash towards the room of danger. Ere he could reach the door, however, he was secured, but, drawing a revolver, he fired.

:" Next moment there reigned a perfect pandemonium."

"Next moment there reigned a perfect pandemonium."

For a full five minutes there was a " rough and tumble." Without doubt something desperate had been afoot in the place, therefore all were arrested.

On searching the flat we found a room the door of which was strongly barred, which, on being opened, revealed Stana in a state of collapse upon an old sofa, and near her stood the good-looking young fellow who was her lover. Both were so weak that they could make no statement. They had, no doubt, been incarcerated there for some time, and it seemed to us as though they were drugged.

Those arrested were hurried at once to the nearest police-station, while Stana and her lover were taken under Inspector Pearson's personal care.

What I learnt later was amazing, for next day, when I sat with Pearson at Scotland Yard, he exclaimed :

" By Jove ! Mr. Le Queux, you've come across, by mere chance, a most dastardly plot ! That girl Stana relented because her lover Eugène had been chosen by lot to blow up a certain railway-bridge in the Peak District to-night at ten-fifty ! "

" Why ? " I inquired eagerly.

" Well, the men under arrest are delegates from the Anarchist Group of Barcelona, the most dangerous of all, and have followed their King here ! He is coming from Manchester to London to-night, and the bridge has been prepared for demolition as the special train passes over it. I have just been on the telephone with the railway police. The nitro-glycerine we found in rubber hot-water bottles in Malvern Road is part of the stuff they brought over with them. It seems that the charges were to be fired electrically, but that the person doing it would no doubt lose his life, as the train would be hurled into the ravine."

Later that day I saw Stana, who had then sufficiently recovered to tell us the truth.

" They somehow knew that I had called upon you that night, therefore they suspected us ! " she told me. " Eugène had been chosen to blow up the bridge, but I knew that the man who passed as my brother intended that he should lose his life. Therefore I would not allow him to make the attempt. Because of that they drugged our food and then shut us both in that room awaiting the success of their coup, which was, nevertheless, to be attempted. If it failed, then we were to die, and your life probably would not have been spared, for they knew you were in touch with the police."

" You did quite right in exposing the plot and saving your King's life, mademoiselle," I said.

"Ah ! m'sieur, I confess that I came to London as an anarchist prepared to do my share in the assassination of any crowned head. Both Eugène and I, however, have relented. I love Eugène, and I could not bear to see him sacrifice his life while the others—who were plotting against him as well as against our King—escaped. And if the plot had failed, you yourself would certainly have been killed on the following day, because of their suspicion that I had disclosed something to you ! "

Pearson, who was present at the interview, and was accompanied by the young Spaniard Eugène, remarked :

" The warning given by mademoiselle was certainly only in the nick of time. Last night I spoke to the King's private secretary over the telephone to Manchester, informing him of our discovery, and to-night he is travelling by another route. His Majesty has already exercised his clemency towards mademoiselle and her fiancé, but he presses for the extradition of the others for trial in Spain. I find from our records that all are wanted by the Barcelona police, therefore they will, no doubt, be extradited by the magistrate at Bow Street."

This, indeed, was done, hence the secret of the dastardly attempt never appeared in the English newspapers.

Stana and Eugène have married, and now live in Paris, where I visited them about a year ago.

THE SECRET OF THE MISSING BRIDE

The secret of Joan Wharncliffe, aged twenty-two, who had not been married a week, was perhaps one of the most jealously guarded that I have ever known.

My own connection with the affair—of which I know that many different versions have been told, all of them wrong—came about in a rather curious way.

I happened to be staying with an elderly aunt who lives just outside the pleasant little town of Helmsley, in Yorkshire, between Pilmoor and Malton, and who, having lived there for twenty years, had naturally many friends in the neighbourhood. One of the most intimate was a widow named Calvert, who lived with her daughter Joan at Heddon Manor, about a mile and a half away. When on visits to my aunt I frequently called upon Mrs. Calvert, but only on two occasions I met her daughter—a young and extremely attractive fair-haired girl.

The young lady in question fell in love with a man named Charles Wharncliffe, who was well off, though somewhat her senior. He was engaged in the cotton trade in Manchester, but, for some unaccountable reason, Joan's mother objected to the marriage, and it was quite six months before she reluctantly gave her consent.

These facts were told me by my aunt on the night of my arrival. I was the only guest, and we sat together after dinner in the old-fashioned drawing-room which smelt sweetly of the pot-pourri in the blue-and-white Chinese jars.

" I can't think why Mrs. Calvert should have raised such objection to Joan's marriage. Wharncliffe is a very nice fellow. I like him immensely—hard-headed, as are all the Lancashire folk, but he'll make her a very good husband," she said.

" Has Mrs. Calvert told you the reason ? " I asked.

" No. She won't. She says that she instinctively dislikes him. Why, she can't say."

" That's curious," I remarked. " But a mother usually knows best, doesn't she ? "

" Joan does not look at it in that light," laughed my aunt. " In fact, to tell you the truth, she came here a month ago and told me in confidence that if her mother continued to object she intended to run away and marry Charles."

" A wonder she didn't do so."

" Well, I advised her not to be foolish and pain her mother. Runaway matches seldom turn out well. Nevertheless, it's all over now. They were married at Malton the day before yesterday, and are now on their honeymoon. I had an invitation, but I dared not go to the church on account of my cold. I was at the breakfast, and Joan looked a most delightful bride."

" Where have they gone for their honeymoon ? "

" First to London, and then on the Continent. Joan loves France. She was at school there for some years."

And our conversation drifted on to other topics.

A week later, on the day before I was due to conclude my visit, Mrs. Calvert drove up in her car and was ushered in to where I was taking tea with my aunt.

" Oh, my dear ! " she gasped, her countenance pale and her hands trembling in great excitement. " I've had such awful news. Joan is missing. She can't be found anywhere ! "

" Missing ! " we both echoed.

" What have you heard, Mrs. Calvert ? " I asked.

" Only this," and she took a telegram from her bag, which she handed to me.

It was from Charles Wharncliffe at the Carlton Hotel, London, and read : " Joan is missing. Is she with you ? "

" Ah ! Perhaps they have quarrelled ! " remarked my aunt. It was the natural supposition.

" Perhaps so," said Joan's mother. " But I felt certain that something would happen if my daughter married him."

" Why ? " I asked quickly.

" I can't tell you. That's just the curious part of it."

" What will you do, my dear ? " asked my aunt.

" Do ? What can I do ? It is useless for me to go to London. If they have quarrelled she will surely return home."

" No," I said, " I don't think so. She would be too proud

to return home so soon. She will more likely write to you, and go into retirement for a while."

"I have replied to Charles that Joan is not here, and asked for further details," explained Mrs. Calvert.

"Well, my dear, I shouldn't worry if I were you," my aunt urged. "She's safe enough somewhere. Joan is quite able to take care of herself."

"Ah, but you hear of such awful things nowadays, don't you?"

"True. But I don't think there is any cause for alarm. We must first find out if there has been a quarrel," I said.

"You will be in London to-morrow night, William," remarked my aunt. "Why not go to the Carlton, and see Wharncliffe on Mrs. Calvert's behalf?"

"Well, to tell the truth," I replied, "I hardly like putting my nose into the matrimonial affairs of other people. I've seen so much of the evil of it in the case of others."

"Oh, won't you do so for me?" urged Mrs. Calvert. "I'd be so grateful to you if you would try and find out what really has happened."

I hesitated. I have often found that in trying to do a favour for a friend I have made myself highly unpopular.

"I see you do not feel inclined to interfere," Joan's mother remarked. "But I do beg of you to see Wharncliffe to-morrow and try to discover what has occurred."

"Well, Mrs. Calvert," I replied. "Wharncliffe may resent my intrusion upon his private affairs. If I were in his place I should probably object to the inquisitiveness of an outsider. Of course, he has to answer to you, his wife's mother, and to nobody else."

"Yes. And he shall answer to me," said the well-preserved widow, in a tone of great determination. "But you will do me this favour, won't you? What time shall you be in London?"

"I arrive at King's Cross about dinner-time."

"Then let me wire to Charles saying that you will call on him on my behalf—say, at nine o'clock to-morrow night. Do, I beg of you."

"I think you ought to do this for Mrs. Calvert, William," my aunt said.

So that decided me, and I consented. My aunt had been as a second mother to me, and she was very dear to me.

Whatever she wished I tried to carry out. In this case I often wonder if I did right by acceding to Mrs. Calvert's request, but I will leave my readers to judge after learning the whole of the tangled circumstances.

Next day I left Helmsley, Mrs. Calvert having already sent word to the bridegroom that I was calling upon him at the Carlton.

When at nine o'clock I called, I found him awaiting me in the hall. I saw that he was pale and nervous. I had only met him once before, and then only for half an hour at a tennis-party at Heddon Manor.

" Come up to my room," he said in a low, hard voice. " We can talk better up there."

And so we entered the lift and went to his bedroom on the third floor.

When inside, he closed the door and said :

" Look here ! There's some infernal mystery that I can't understand. I'm glad you've come to see me, and I only hope to Heaven you will be able to find poor Joan."

His words were not those of a man who had quarrelled with his newly-wed wife.

" Well," I said, standing with him before the dressing-table, " be frank with me, Wharncliffe, and tell me exactly what has happened."

" I'll tell you all that I know."

" First," I said, " have you quarrelled ? "

" Quarrelled ? Why, of course not ; we love each other far too well for that," he declared. " We've never had a cross word. And yet, she's left me ! This is all I've had."

And he showed me a telegram which had been handed in at Maidstone, in Kent, and which read :

" Do not worry. Shall return soon.—JOAN."

Certainly it was curious that a bride of a week should leave her husband suddenly without explanation and send him that reassuring message.

" What do you think of it, eh ? "

" How long has she been gone ? " I asked.

" Three days. I intended to go to the police to-night, but I thought the papers might get hold of it, and I don't want that under any circumstances."

" Well, first tell me what has happened ever since you arrived from Malton," I said.

" Nothing much. We've been about a good deal, shopping and to the theatres. We had to stay in London in order to get my passport viséd for France. She had hers six months ago. We intended to go to Biarritz for three weeks, and should have left yesterday. She was looking forward to it very eagerly, as she was there directly after she left school. She had a schoolgirl friend there—a Mademoiselle Vinel. Shall we go to Scotland Yard and report that my wife is missing ? What do you advise ? "

I reflected.

" At present, I think I should refrain from raising the hue-and-cry. Better advertise in half a dozen of the daily papers, and see whether we have any result. It is evident that your wife has gone off of her own free will. If she sees that you are really distressed she will, no doubt, communicate with you."

" Yes, you're right," he said. " I don't want it all in the papers. All the people in Manchester would laugh at me. Besides, it wouldn't be fair to Joan. I've bought a comfortable house out at Eccles, and she's very pleased with it. The neighbourhood is not all that might be desired, yet it will suit us for a year or so—while I'm on 'Change."

We went across to the writing-table, where we drafted an advertisement, brief, but to the point, and which read :

" To JOAN.—It is unfair ! Come back or write. Have forgiven you.—CHARLES."

This appeared in the papers two days later, but as day after day I called upon him—having, of course, reported to Joan's mother—no answer came.

It became quite clear to me that there had been no quarrel between the pair. Each time I saw Wharncliffe he seemed to be increasingly anxious, and yet there was one small fact which I discovered and which set me thinking deeply.

About a week after the advertisement had appeared, I happened to go with a man who had invited me to dinner at a small restaurant in Soho, and there, as I entered the door, I saw Wharncliffe seated at a table with a rather good-looking girl, somewhat flashily dressed.

For an instant I drew back, so that he should not see me. It was, to say the least, curious that if he were so infatuated with his young wife, who was missing, he should be found in a little foreign restaurant, where he might not be recognised, with a girl whom I took to be a chorus lady.

I made an excuse to my friend, and we dined elsewhere. But the circumstance set me thinking.

Next day I called again at the Carlton.

" I fear I'll have to be back in Manchester," he said. " My business is going on anyhow. At the office they are asking me to return. I've some big deals on just now."

" Surely you won't give up all hope of tracing your wife ? " I said, not without suspicion. What I had discovered on the previous night had caused me much reflection. Did he know of her whereabouts ? I wondered. Had he himself sent that telegram from Maidstone ? Besides, why should he be averse to the affair getting into the papers ? Further, by marrying Joan he had become possessed of certain funds which would help him considerably in his business.

I longed to demand of him point-blank the identity of the girl with whom he had dined on the previous night, but I resolved to wait and watch.

" Don't you think it is now time that we went to Scotland Yard ? If we gave a photograph of your wife to the newspapers they would publish it, and, no doubt, she would soon be found."

" No," he promptly replied. " I'm beginning to think that she changed her mind after we married, and that she had discovered we are unsuited to each other. So she has simply disappeared."

" What causes you to imagine that ? " I asked with curiosity.

" Well, everything points to it. Why should she get up in the morning and wait about the hotel while I went into the City on business ? Then, on my return, I found that she had taken her two dressing-bags and gone away."

" What money did she have ? " I inquired.

" Oh, she had about seventy pounds, I think. Not more."

" That would not last her for ever," I said. I knew she had a banking account, but up to the present no cheque had been drawn since her disappearance.

" You see, she had an important engagement on the afternoon of her disappearance. She had seen a French maid two days before, and had made an appointment with her in order to engage her, it being proposed that she should enter my wife's service after her return from France. The maid, a girl named Georgette Jacquard, called, and I saw her. She expressed surprise that madame had not kept her appointment, and went away in apparent disgust."

" How did you find this maid ? "

" Joan advertised."

" Where did she come from ? "

" She was from Dinard. She had come to London to seek an engagement, she told me. I gave the girl ten shillings for her trouble, and asked her to write to madame. I never thought, of course, that Joan had left me."

" And did the maid write ? "

" No. I've heard nothing," he replied.

The whole affair was a complete mystery. I could not discern the motive of Wharncliffe's reluctance to inform the police. To me there seemed to be something curious behind it all—some secret which I failed to fathom.

Next day the desolate bridegroom left the Carlton and returned to Manchester to conduct his business, while the same day I went up to Helmsley, and there saw the mother of the missing girl, to whom I told the exact facts, omitting, of course, the incident of the Soho restaurant.

" There's something wrong, radically wrong, somewhere ! " declared Mrs. Calvert, as we sat together in the big drawing-room at Heddon Manor. " Fancy ! He has gone back to his money-making in Manchester, instead of going to the police and getting Joan's portrait into the papers."

The widow was furious, and, after all, I did not wonder at it.

" Your daughter was at school in France, was she not ? " I asked, when her anger had subsided, for, though at first I had refrained from entering into the affair, my curiosity had now been thoroughly aroused.

" Yes. She was at Madame Binet's, at Versailles, for four years. It is a most excellent school. I went there several times."

" And that is why she wanted to go to France for her honeymoon perhaps ? "

" Probably," said her mother.

" And because of it she wanted to engage a French maid? "

" I know nothing of that. Joan did not mention it to me. I suppose she had arranged it with her husband," replied the mother of the missing girl. " But why did she telegraph from Maidstone ? " she added.

That was just the point which sorely puzzled me. I could suggest no explanation, save that she had done it for a blind. Truth to tell, however, I was wondering whether Wharncliffe had been to Maidstone and sent the message to himself.

I still recollected what I had seen in that obscure restaurant in Soho when the deserted bridegroom was actually merrily chatting with the dark-eyed girl over a bottle of Pommery. At that moment he did not present the figure of the husband perturbed concerning his wife's whereabouts.

" The whole affair is exceedingly strange, Mrs. Calvert," I said. " I have done my best, but I fail to see how we can proceed further. No doubt your daughter is safe somewhere, and will either come home or write to you in due course."

" But have they quarrelled ? "

" I certainly don't think so," was my reply.

As a matter of fact, I had had a chat with the head porter of the Carlton, whom I knew quite well. He had noticed young Mrs. Wharncliffe, and had described to me how very happy the pair had appeared.

On the day of her disappearance the porter had called him a taxi from the rank at ten o'clock, and the bridegroom, who was standing in the hall with his wife, had bade her good-bye, promising to return to lunch. He had then driven off to the City.

An hour later the young wife had ordered her two dressing-bags to be brought down and soon afterwards a hired touring-car had driven up. This she had entered, and had driven away.

And that had been the last seen of her.

The head porter had, unfortunately, not taken the number of the car. So there we were, absolutely at a dead end. Her bags, however, were morocco ones, with green waterproof cases, and bore the initials " J. F. W." in gilt.

It struck me as very peculiar that Wharncliffe should give up the search for his wife in such a hopeless manner and return to his speculation on the cotton market. True, he was making a vast pile of money, with his shrewdness and his knowledge of the markets, but that was hardly what a man would do if his bride had disappeared after a week of marriage.

Was there some secret which he had not told ?

Mrs. Calvert became frantic. She bombarded me with letters and telegrams until, at last, in order to pacify her, I went to Scotland Yard—without the husband's knowledge, be it said.

The police were ready, as they always are, to raise the hue-and-cry and to circulate the photograph of the lady— one taken by a York photographer a month before her marriage.

But to this I could not give consent. Of course the missing girl's mother was most eager that due inquiry should be made, but Wharncliffe had set his face against it, a fact which further increased my suspicion. He had not behaved as one would have expected a distressed husband to behave. True, the new house at Eccles was awaiting its mistress, and he himself was living at the Midland Grand Hotel at Manchester.

At Mrs. Calvert's request I went up there and saw him again.

His manner was that of one annoyed by my reappearance.

" I don't see what we can do if Joan refuses to answer my appeal," he said. " It was repeated in the papers twice last week, and yet we receive no reply. She's all right, otherwise I should not have received that telegram from Maidstone."

Had he himself sent that telegram ? That was the question which obsessed me. I had endeavoured to account for his whereabouts on that day. But all I had discovered from the hotel porter was that he went to the City at ten o'clock in a taxi, and returned to the hotel in the afternoon. Further than that I could gather nothing.

I returned to London more puzzled than ever. I had spent two days with Charles Wharncliffe, and had found him so engrossed in making money in cotton that he seemed already to have forgotten his young wife's unaccountable absence.

And I must here declare that my suspicions had become greatly increased. That he was aware of some important fact which he was concealing I now felt quite confident. Gradually, by degrees, I had been drawn into that tangle of mystery, and now, even against my will, I found myself impelled towards a strenuous effort to solve the mystery.

As I sat alone in my rooms on my return from Manchester that night, I took a piece of paper and worked out the exact situation. It was a complete puzzle. When I had concluded I saw plainly that if what Wharncliffe had said was true, namely, that no difference had arisen between them, there was no reason whatever why Joan should have deliberately left her husband.

Had she been enticed away ? Perhaps. That reassuring telegram might have been forged. That mysterious motor-car—a hired one, for it had borne the plate " Hackney Carriage " upon it—might have passed through Maidstone, where the telegram was dispatched. If so, the car was travelling south. Why ? Perhaps to Dover or to Folke-stone !

Was it possible that Joan Wharncliffe had crossed to the Continent alone ? And if she had done so, what could have been the motive ? If she had gone to France, it was within the bounds of probability that she had not seen the English newspapers.

But would she go abroad alone when her husband was to take her in a day or two ? Besides, she would not have left England without her passport. Had she taken it with her ?

An hour later I got on to Wharncliffe by telephone and his reply was :

" She had her passport in her maiden name, so it is quite possible that she's taken it with her."

Then, after exchanging a few more words, we were cut off.

Next day I drew up an advertisement asking the maid Georgette Jacquard to communicate with Mrs. Wharncliffe, and gave my own address. This I thought would attract her, as she would believe that the lady who wished to engage her had returned. This advertisement was placed by an advertising agency in Fleet Street in three London morning papers, and three of the principal papers in Paris.

Then I waited—and very anxiously.

About a week later I received a letter addressed to " Madame Wharncliffe." It was in a thin, angular hand, and bore a French stamp. The writer gave her address as 78 Rue

Royale, Nevers, and the note, which was in French, read as
follows :

" DEAR MADAME,—At last I have news of you ! *Dieu !*
I have been much worried and frightened.   Where have you
been ?   At the Cheval Blanc they lied to me, and said you
had never arrived there.   I knew they lied, for did I not
arrive with you ?   Do, I beg of you, tell me what has
happened.   The police of Marseilles did nothing.   They
did not believe what I told them.   Shall I join you in
London ?   I thank Heaven, madame, that you are safe.
                              " Your obedient servant.
                                   " GEORGETTE JACQUARD."

This, indeed, was a curious response.   The Cheval Blanc
was evidently an hotel, and the mention of the police showed
that it was in Marseilles.

On the day following the receipt of the letter I left London
for Paris, and travelled straight through to Nevers, where I
arrived at the old Hôtel de France late in the evening.
Next morning I called at the address in the Rue Royale.   It
was a small modiste's kept by the sister of the girl Georgette
Jacquard, a good-looking young person of the usual type
of French maid.

When I inquired for her and she came forward, she
regarded me with distinct suspicion.

" You have written to Madame Wharncliffe in London,
mademoiselle," I said in French.   " I have come here to
inquire what you know of her."

Her face changed, and I saw that she was much agitated.

" I know nothing, m'sieur."

" But pardon, your letter to her shows that you know a
great deal."

" I repeat that I know nothing," the girl declared.

" May we go into that room yonder ? " I asked, indicating
a small room at the back of the obscure little shop.   " I
have some questions to put to you."

Her face went as pale as death, but she consented.

" Now, mademoiselle," I commenced seriously, " I want
you to answer my questions frankly, for much depends upon
you.   What do you know concerning madame ?   You saw
her at the Carlton Hotel in London, did you not ? "

" Yes, and madame engaged me as her maid."

" But you called at the Carlton and saw Monsieur Wharn-cliffe after his wife had disappeared ? "

" She sent me," was the reply.

" Why ? "

" I do not know madame's reasons," was her rather sullen answer. " How can I ? "

" But you were in madame's confidence," I said. " Why did she leave her husband ? "

" I do not know. She told me hardly anything."

" What did she tell you ? "

" She imposed secrecy upon me, and I do not mean to divulge it."

" But you may be compelled," I remarked. " Please recollect, mademoiselle, that madame is missing, and you were the last to see her, so——"

" Madame is not missing now. I wrote to her in London in response to her advertisement in the *Petit Journal* ! "

" Madame is still missing," I said gravely. " I put that advertisement in the paper ! "

The girl was silent for some moments. Then she ex-claimed :

" I see. You are an English police-officer, eh ? "

To this I gave denial, assuring her I was not there with any hostile intent, but merely to solve the mystery of the bride's disappearance.

" I am afraid, m'sieur, that I cannot help you," she replied, shaking her head. " Madame's disappearance is just as great a mystery to me as it is to you."

" In your letter to her you mention the Cheval Blanc, at Marseilles," I remarked.

Again her face blanched.

" Yes," she faltered.

" Will you explain why you went to Marseilles ? "

" I don't know. Madame simply went there."

" Alone ? "

" No. I was with her."

" Where did you meet her after you called upon Monsieur Wharncliffe ? "

" I took train to Folkestone, where madame waited for me. She had gone down by car by way of Maidstone, and had sent monsieur a telegram from there. I joined her at

Folkestone, and we crossed to Boulogne together, and on to Paris."

" Did she keep any appointment with any person ? "

" Not to my knowledge, m'sieur."

" But she had engaged you on the previous day, unknown to her husband, eh ? "

" Yes. She told me to call after she had gone and pretend that she had not engaged me."

" She had a motive in that—in order to put her husband off the scent, no doubt."

" I think so, m'sieur. In Paris we remained at the Ritz Hotel for three days. Madame had telegraphed to someone in the South of France, and awaited a reply."

" Did you discover to whom she had telegraphed ? "

" No, m'sieur. Madame told me practically nothing."

" But what conclusions did you form ? " I asked. " Come, you have some idea of why she left her husband so suddenly and took precautions to engage you as her maid and travelling companion ? "

The girl again hesitated. It was quite evident that she knew something of her mistress's secret, but was determined not to divulge it. She had given her word of honour not to do so.

" I formed no conclusions, m'sieur," she murmured.

" Where did you last see your mistress ? "

" In her room at the hotel in Marseilles."

" Now, why did she go to Marseilles ? "

The girl shrugged her shoulders, but made no reply.

" Was it not to meet a man in secret—a man who had gone to Marseilles to see her ? Am I correct ? "

" I don't know," was her reply.

" Have I guessed the truth ? " I asked with a smile.

But she still preserved silence.

I, however, felt convinced that such was the fact. What hold could the man—whoever he might be—have upon her which could compel her to leave her husband's side and meet him on the other side of France ? Was it fear that had driven her to make the journey ?

More than ever I felt confident that the dainty Georgette knew the truth, and could tell much if she chose.

" Now, look here, mademoiselle," I said at last, looking straight into her face, " I must ask you to travel with me down to Marseilles. I mean to clear up this mystery!"

She started. In an instant I saw reluctance written upon her features.

" I'm afraid I cannot do that," she answered.

" But you must. Your mistress is missing, and you must assist me in tracing her," I said determinedly.

She made many excuses, and it was not before I had pointed out the responsibility, and her half-admissions that she knew more than she had told me, that she consented to accompany me to Marseilles on the following morning.

We met at the station, and through the long, tedious journey to the Mediterranean I tried in vain to get from her what she knew concerning madame's mysterious friend whom she was to meet in Marseilles.

But I dragged from her the story of what had occurred at Marseilles.

Georgette had, on arrival, suggested that they should go to the Hôtel Louvre et Paix, one of the most famous hotels in Europe, so well known to travellers going East, but madame had been persistent that they should go to the Cheval Blanc.

" I know Marseilles," I said, " but I have never heard of the place."

" And I also, m'sieur," she said. " I did not like the idea. But madame insisted. She thought she would be recognised at the Louvre et Paix. Her brother-in-law was on his way home from India and was due in Marseilles. She feared to meet him there. So on arrival we took a taxi to the Cheval Blanc. I don't like the place, and I am sorry I am returning there."

" Why ? "

" Well, m'sieur, I shall say nothing. Judge for yourself."

" But what happened there ? " I asked.

" Simply this," she said, in a strangely changed voice. " We arrived at the Cheval Blanc very late at night, and found it an obscure place in a side-street off the Cannebière— a third-class hotel. Madame was not very well—overtired after the journey from Paris—otherwise she would have gone elsewhere. I saw her to bed and left her, but next morning, when I went to her room, No. 42, the door was unlocked. I went in, but found it empty. The bed had not been slept in ! "

" Madame's bags were there ? "

" No, m'sieur. The room was empty, with clean towels prepared for the reception of visitors," declared the girl. " I went to the manager, a beetle-browed little Italian, and asked where madame was, but to my amazement he denied all knowledge of her. He told me laughingly that I had arrived alone on the previous night, and that madame only existed in my imagination ! I was naturally indignant, and demanded to know where madame's bags were, but he simply dismissed me, telling me to go to the police if I had any complaint."

" And you went ? "

" I went to the Prefecture of Police and made a statement. I was told to return in six hours. When I did so, the *sous-chef* saw me and told me that the most searching inquiries had been made, and that madame had never arrived in Marseilles. I remained a week at another hotel, trying to identify the cabman who had driven us to the Cheval Blanc, but, being unsuccessful, I went to my sister at Nevers. I dared not write to Monsieur Wharncliffe, because I feared that some accusation might be made against me. And besides, I had given my word of honour to madame."

Her story was, indeed, a strange one. The more I reflected, the more curious the whole affair appeared.

Three hours after she had related it to me, we ascended the steps of the rather unwholesome Cheval Blanc, and I demanded of the beetle-browed manager to know the whereabouts of the young English lady. He, however, denied all knowledge of her.

Later I went to the Prefecture of Police, and there saw Monsieur Jules Guerin, the Director of Police, whom I happened to know.

He greeted me pleasantly, but when I told him the object of my errand he pursed his lips, and his manner changed.

A silence fell between us in that cold, bare official room. At last he spoke.

" I suppose, Monsieur Le Queux, it is useless for us to further preserve the truth concerning your poor lady friend. Now, can you keep a secret if I tell you the truth ? "

" I cannot keep the secret from her husband," I replied.

" Certainly not. It is only right that he should know. Poor fellow, he must be greatly distressed. We know all the circumstances. His wife came here in secret to meet a young Frenchman named Monier, who had been blackmailing her—a young blackguard whom we have since arrested on another charge. He had some letters of hers which she came here to purchase."

" Ah, then it was fear that caused her to leave her husband so mysteriously, and she intended to return."

" Yes, fear," replied the Director of Police. " But her disappearance came about in this way. On the day of her arrival the Exhibition was opened, and Marseilles was full of visitors from France, Spain, and Italy. In the night madame rang her bell, and complained to the night-porter of being very ill. He summoned a doctor, when it was found that she was suffering from bubonic plague, and at five o'clock in the morning she died. We were informed, and at once took precautions to suppress the news that plague had broken out in Marseilles. So we ordered the body to be buried in secret, and imposed the strictest silence upon the hotel-keeper and the servants. That is why all knowledge of madame was denied at the hotel."

I sat aghast. The mystery was solved.

Four days later I was in Manchester, where I revealed to the bereaved husband the bitter truth. And if to-day you go to the high-up cemetery of Notre Dame de la Garde you will find a great white marble cross which Charles Wharncliffe erected to the memory of his wife.

DENIS MACKAIL

Mr. (and Mrs.) Mystery
The Chink in Miss Flamborough's Armour

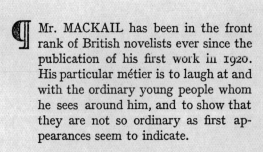 Mr. MACKAIL has been in the front rank of British novelists ever since the publication of his first work in 1920. His particular métier is to laugh at and with the ordinary young people whom he sees around him, and to show that they are not so ordinary as first appearances seem to indicate.

MR. (AND MRS.) MYSTERY

In the issue of *Snappy Snips* to which Mr. Mystery contributed his one thousandth Kurious Konundrum—and as he contributed three of these problems every week, you will realise after a little trouble that he had been associated with the periodical in question for nearly six and a half years—a corner of the veil which had hitherto hidden him from his readers was suddenly twitched aside.

" No," the editor had said. " I don't think we want to give your real name away, because that would be rather reversing our policy." (And also, he was thinking, we don't want to overdo the thing, so that you think you're worth more than you're getting.) " But I'll tell you what I will do," he went on. " I'll shift you on to the front page—just for this once, I mean—and I'll print your photograph, and—— Oh, I say ! "

" Yes ? " said Harold Flapton, at the other end of the line.

" It's just struck me. I suppose you haven't got a photograph in a mask ? No, no ; not a comic one. Just a plain mask, like a highwayman."

" I'm afraid not," said Harold Flapton. " Would you like me to——"

" No, no. It doesn't matter. We can easily fake it here in the office. But this is what I was trying to say. Can you hear me ? "

" Yes," said Harold Flapton.

" Well, look here, will you just jot down a few notes for Miss Peckwater—anything that comes into your head—and post it off to-night, and she'll turn it into an interview. Eh ? "

" Oh, certainly," said Harold Flapton, blushing and blinking. " What sort of——"

" Oh, anything, anything," said the editor breezily. " She'll want to make it into about five hundred words. Right. That's all, Flapton. G'bye."

547

" Shall I——" began Harold Flapton. But the line was dead.

He had been on the point of inquiring whether he, or only Miss Peckwater, might expect to be paid for those five hundred words, but on second thoughts this seemed immaterial compared with the unexpected publicity which was to be his in next week's *Snips*. " Of course," he thought, as he returned to the desk in his little study, " it would have been nice, in a way, if they *had* printed my real name. I mean, I think mother would have liked it. And I don't really see why they want to put me in a mask—though of course their blocks are all smudges and speckles anyhow. But it was decent of the old boy to be so decent, and I must say it was very decent of him."

So he unscrewed the cap of his fountain-pen, and covered a page and a half of foolscap with a description of his birthplace in Beckenham, and of his late father's success as a house-agent, and of how one of his uncles had once gone up in a balloon, and of how he himself had been educated at such-and-such a school, and had won a prize for scripture and a certificate for wood-carving. And warming to his subject, he went on to relate how, after one or two shots at various professions, in which he had not seemed to be doing himself justice, he had found himself with a certain amount of spare time on his hands, and how he had taken to inventing little puzzles and sending them up to newspapers. And how, after a bit, he had found that he was doing well enough in this line to make it a whole-time job. And that for five years he had been on the regular staff of *Snappy Snips*, and was very glad if his little efforts had amused anyone. And that he wasn't married, but lived alone with his mother. And—with a sudden memory of *Who's Who*—that his favourite recreation was walking on Clapham Common.

" There," said Harold Flapton, as he laid down his pen. " I think they ought to like that. It's dignified, I mean. It gives all the facts, but you couldn't call it conceited." And he posted it off to Miss Peckwater, who read it through, and smiled pityingly, and shrugged her shoulders, and dropped it into the waste-paper basket, and wrote five hundred words entirely out of her own head which represented Mr. Mystery as a cross between Cagliostro and Capablanca, and would have been worth another five guineas a week to anyone with the sense to see it.

" But *he* won't see it," said Miss Peckwater, when the editor pointed this out. And she was quite right. What she didn't realise, though, was that the only reason why Mr. Flapton never complained about this extraordinary article was that he thought Miss Peckwater had made some kind of mistake, and he didn't want to get her into trouble.

So now you understand why we were so careful at the beginning to say that only a corner of the veil covering Mr. Mystery had been twitched aside. For the general public, indeed, he still remained a sufficiently enigmatical figure ; but there is nothing on earth to prevent our having another look through that veil for ourselves.

On a fine summer day, then, Mr. Flapton was sitting in his little study at *Sunnybrae*, with his work spread out before him, and his whole mind concentrated on completing his weekly contribution to *Snappy Snips*. Already two Kurious Konundrums lay finished on the corner of his desk, and the third was merely awaiting another burst of inspiration to join them and to enter the long envelope which must be posted not later than half-past ten to-night. But inspiration flagged, and Mr. Flapton—as other authors have done before him—sought it by glancing again at these earlier efforts.

" An old farmer," he read thoughtfully to himself, " had a house in the middle of a square field. In each corner of this field there was one tree and one pond—as shown in the accompanying diagram. When he died, his four sons found that he had left the farmhouse as their joint property, but that each one was to have one tree and the pond in the opposite corner. How was the field divided so that the provisions of the old farmer's will could be carried out, and each son could also have direct access to the house in the centre of the field ? Solution next week."

In real life, of course—and assuming that such a queer field could exist—it should have been child's play for the four sons to have convinced the proper authorities that their father was off his head, and to have re-divided the property in a more sensible manner. Alternatively, they might have put the matter in the hands of their lawyers, in which case there would very shortly have been no property to divide.

But in Harold Flapton's solution—which it would delight so many thousand readers to discover for themselves—the sons had actually built a series of long, serpentine fences which wound about among the ponds and trees ; and their ingenious piety was presumably its own reward, since the field was now rendered definitely useless as anything except a memorial to their father's eccentricity. What would happen if they started having children of their own, one simply trembled to think.

But Harold Flapton gave a satisfied nod, and passed on to the second sheet of paper which he had just picked up.

" Two cyclists," this announced, " named James and Charles, decided to ride their machines from London to Brighton, a distance of fifty-two and a half miles. It was agreed that James should start at ten o'clock in the morning and ride half as fast as Charles, and that Charles should start at one o'clock in the afternoon and decrease his speed by one third after covering forty miles. Which of the two cyclists reached his destination first ? "

Neither, we should say, because we all know what the Brighton road is like—and especially if you start doing arithmetic instead of dodging the traffic. But again Harold Flapton had provided a solution for next week, and again he gave a satisfied nod as he laid the sheet of paper down.

" Now then," he muttered, as he hunched his shoulders and seized his pen. Inspiration seemed very near at this moment, after that refreshing draught of recent accomplishment. " Kurious Konundrum," he wrote, " Number——"

" Harold ! " said a voice outside the door.

Mr. Flapton dropped his pen, and sighed.

" Yes, mother ? " he answered.

The door opened.

" I don't want to interrupt you," said the majestic widow of the successful house-agent. " But the sun's off that side bed now."

" Is it, mother ? "

" So I thought it would be a good thing if you watered it," said Mrs. Flapton. " You can finish your writing afterwards, can't you ? "

" Would it matter if——"

" Now, Harold, you know quite well what will happen if that bed isn't watered."

" But couldn't——"

Mrs. Flapton closed her eyes.

" Very well, mother," said her gifted son. " I'll do it now."

" Ah," said Mrs. Flapton, and she came across and had a good look at her gifted son's desk—just to make certain that he hadn't been writing to anyone without telling her—and she took his half-finished pipe away and put it on the mantel-piece, and she stood and watched him while he replaced the cap of his fountain-pen, and then she smiled a calm, maternal smile, and Harold slunk out through the french window into the garden.

" Do it thoroughly now," she called after him.

" Yes, mother," said Harold Flapton.

So Mr. Mystery's mother went back to her novel in the drawing-room, and Mr. Mystery himself ducked his head carefully and crept into the tool-shed. But he didn't dare even to look mutinous until he was quite sure that he was out of sight. As for actual disobedience, such an idea had never entered his talented head. Slowly and painstakingly he began disentangling the coils of the garden hose.

As we watch his Laocoon-like struggles through the cob-webby window of the *Sunnybrae* tool-shed, we can hardly fail to be struck by the vast difference between practice and theory. If there were one man in England, you would say, capable of realising at a glance the swiftest means of remov-ing several sections of hose from the handle of a garden roller, or of determining the correct number of sections required to reach the side bed, then surely that man should be the author of the Kurious Konundrums. One instant, you would have thought, for algebraical calculation, and the thing should be as good as done. But you are wrong. It is the old story of the physician attempting to heal himself, and of the lawyer trying to make his own will. Let Mr. Flapton but get back into his study, and put Charles or James or an old farmer in the tool-shed, and the problem will have been solved for them like lightning. Leave him where he is, and after about twenty minutes he will emerge in the last stage of heated exhaustion, and trailing behind him a series of imperfectly united lengths of rubber tubing which forthwith begin spouting and bubbling at every joint. Moreover, as he discovered on this occasion—after making a number of laborious adjustments—he had over-estimated the quantity of hose required by about twenty-five feet.

However much this may surprise us, though, it was no surprise to Mr. Flapton. He kicked the superfluous convolutions out of the way to the best of his ability, and proceeded to direct a stream of water on to the side bed with the utmost generosity. The soothing sound of drops pattering against dry leaves restored some of the calm which he had lost in the tool-shed, and he began thinking about that third problem again. The more he thought, the further his interrupted ideas seemed to recede from him, and the less attention he paid to the irrigation of the side bed. Sometimes he watered his own feet, sometimes the gravel path, occasionally the geraniums, and frequently the wooden fence behind them ; and all the while he was struggling to recapture those mental fumblings which Mrs. Flapton's entrance had driven clean out of his head.

He had a vague recollection that he had been on the track of some novel method of turning a hexagon into an isosceles triangle ; but that wasn't the important part. The important part, as always, had lain in the little story which was to gild the geometrical pill. Had it been something to do with a speculative builder, or a master mariner, or a skating instructor, or——? No ; those were the characters that he had employed last week.

" Bother ! " said Harold Flapton, raising his hand in a weak gesture of annoyance. " I'd practically got it half an hour ago ; and now——"

" Help ! " cried a fresh soprano voice about four yards away. " Oh, please don't do that ! Oh, what *are* you doing ! "

The hose fell from Mr. Flapton's grasp, and he plunged on to the flower-bed.

" I'm most awfully sorry," he said. " I say—did I wet you ? "

" Look out ! " said the fresh soprano voice. " It's going all over your legs now."

" Oh, dear ! " said Harold Flapton. " Oh, so it is. Oh, do let me apologise."

" I'm not stopping you," said the young woman on the other side of the fence. " But just look at my hair now. And it isn't even Friday night."

" I cannot tell you," said Harold, standing firmly on a geranium, " how distressed I am that—ah—er . . ."

" That what ?   Go on."

" Um—er—oo . . ."

" What did you say ?   I can't hear you."

" Erm.   Oop . . ."

The young woman came a little nearer, and leant on the wooden fence.

" Are you ill ? " she asked sympathetically.

" No, no," said Harold.   " But I've just noticed. . . . I mean, your hair. . . .   That's to say, you said just look at it, and I hadn't noticed it till then, but—I mean, it's perfectly wonderful ! "

" How sweet of you," said the young woman next door. " You're forgiven."

Mr. Flapton blushed all over.

" I don't mean," he explained, " that it's your hair alone. But—I say, why have I never noticed you before ? "

" I can't think," said the young woman.   " I've been here six months."

" Extraordinary," said Mr. Flapton.   " And yet I'm out here almost every evening."

" I know you are," said the young woman.   " You're an author, aren't you ?   I mean, the milkman said you were. I think that sounds perfectly thrilling ! "

" Erp . . ."

" What do you write, Mr. Flapton ? "

Mr. Flapton blushed again as he heard his own name from those lips.   He was wondering if he dared ask the milkman a few questions himself.

" What do I write ? " he repeated foolishly.   " Oh— just stuff for a weekly."

" I think you're awfully modest," said the young woman. " I've always wanted to meet an author, you know.   I once had a friend who saw Ian Hay at a bazaar.   She said he was fascinating."

Mr. Flapton had hardly recovered from his second blush, but his third one was almost a super-blush.

" I wonder," he said—and he was astonished at his own courage—" I wonder if you'd let me send you some of my work.   You needn't read it, of course," he added hastily.

18*

" But of course I'd read it," said the young woman. " Unless—I mean . . ."

" What ? "

" Well, it's not like Michael Arlen, is it ? Father doesn't approve of him."

" Nor do I," said Mr. Flapton firmly. " I've never read a word he's written."

" How awfully interesting. I say—you won't forget, will you ? "

" Forget ? Rather not. Only . . ."

" What ? "

" Well, would you mind telling me your name ? That is, if you don't mind."

The young woman laughed, and Mr. Flapton's blush definitely beat the geraniums.

" Oh," she said, " we're called Blankett. And my name's Dorothy. Dorothy Blankett, you see."

Harold thought it the most exquisite name that he had ever heard in his life. He would have sacrificed a month's salary for the pluck to repeat it aloud, but such a bargain was clearly impracticable.

" All right," was what he actually said. " I'll send some back numbers round to-night. I don't use my own name professionally, but I'll mark the stuff with a blue pencil. I only hope you'll like it."

" I'm sure I shall," said Miss Blankett. " And now I mustn't keep you any longer."

" Oh, but——"

" Good night, Mr. Flapton."

" Good night, Miss—erm—oop—Blankett. I—ah——"

But she was gone. He stood watching the empty space above the wooden fence, until an uncomfortable feeling drew his attention to the fact that he was also standing in a large puddle. " Wonderful ! " he murmured, as he turned off the tap. " Marvellous ! " he added, as he lugged the hose into the tool-shed. " Amazing ! " he muttered, as he re-entered his little study.

He sat down at his desk, and drew a blank sheet of paper towards him. He unscrewed the cap of his fountain-pen.

" A man and a girl," he wrote, without blot or pause, " resided on adjoining properties, as shown in the accom-

panying diagram.   The man fell in love with the girl, and
proposed to her as follows. ' If,' he said, ' you accept me
and we make an opening in the fence AB, at what point
should it be made so as to provide the shortest path between
our two houses C and D ?   I will remind you that E, F and
G are flower-beds which must not be disturbed, and that the
landlord will not allow us to cut down any of the trees I, K,
L, M and N.'   What did the girl reply ? "

What, indeed ?

" Harold ! " shouted Mrs. Flapton from the passage.
" Didn't you hear the gong ? "

" Just coming, mother."

" You watered that side bed ? "

" Yes, mother."

" Look at your feet, dear !   What have you been doing ? "

" I'm afraid I got them a little wet, mother."

" Wet ! " cried Mrs. Flapton.   " You must go and change
at once ! "

So Harold went and changed at once ; but after dinner,
as well as taking his weekly contribution to the pillar-box,
he also took a large pile of back numbers of *Snappy Snips*
round to the house next door.   To D, in fact ; though it was
more generally known as *Bongaloo*—after the spot where
Mr. Blankett had once served as District Commissioner.

" Would you," said Harold to the neat maid who opened
the door, " be so good as to let Miss—oop—Blankett have
these ? "

" Righto," said the neat maid.

" Thank you," said Harold ; and left her ; and sighed ;
and gazed at the crescent moon ; and bolted the front door ;
and did his breathing-exercises ; and went to bed.

Now, whether it be the case—as many philosophers hold—
that no woman can detect the difference between literature
and trash, let alone between fact and fiction, or whether
Miss Blankett's finer judgment was blunted by the interest
which she took in the writer, the fact remains that you were
quite wrong when you said to yourself (as you undoubtedly
did) : " Ah ! Just wait till she finds out what sort of an
author this Mr. Mystery is, and then see how she turns up
that pretty nose at him."

Not a bit of it.   Once a woman feels towards a man as

Dorothy Blankett felt towards Harold Flapton, she will be equally proud of him and his work whether he is a politician or a pork-butcher, a haberdasher or a hangman. And though it is true that Mr. Flapton had one or two qualms when he feared that his writings might be a little over the head of even so delightful and intelligent a girl, his suspense was as short as his suspicions were unfounded. Strolling in his garden the very next morning, he was hailed by a cry from beyond the fence AB ; and having looked round to make certain that his mother was still indoors, he rushed on to the geranium-bed.

" Oh, Mr. Flapton," said the vision next door, " I *must* thank you for sending me those papers. I'd no *idea* you were so clever."

" Oh, well . . ." said Harold, beginning to blush again.

" And how on earth you think of it all, I simply can't imagine. I simply loved them ! "

" Er."

" And it's so thrilling to think that you're so famous, and that I know who you really are."

" Erp."

" And father thought them most awfully clever, too. He got quite excited trying to guess that one about the two monkeys eating the nuts. How *do* you get such wonderful ideas ? "

" They—they just come," said Harold modestly.

" I'm going straight off," said Dorothy, " to order *Snappy Snips* at once. I couldn't possibly miss anything you wrote."

" Oop," said Harold, suddenly remembering the third Konundrum which he had sent off last night.

" Father's simply longing to meet you," added Miss Blankett. " Do you think you could possibly come and dine with us one night ? When you're not too busy, I mean ? "

Mr. Flapton looked nervously back at the house C.

" I—I'd be delighted," he said longingly. " Only my mother . . ."

" Oh, but couldn't she come too ? I'd make father write to her, of course. And, after all, we are neighbours. And the grocer's always sending us your things by mistake, and the other way round, so that it isn't as if we were quite strangers. Is it ? "

" Gug."

" Then you will come ? "

" Gug-gug."

" How splendid ! One night quite soon ? That *is* good of you. Father'll be delighted, and I'm longing to hear more about your writing. Good-bye, Mr. Flapton, and don't forget, will you ? "

She had gone again, but of course Mr. Flapton didn't forget. The only diagram which he succeeded in completing that morning was of a face with large eyes and wavy hair, which—although it bore no sort of resemblance to Miss Blankett, or, indeed, to any human being—he hid most carefully before leaving his little study for lunch.

" You look pale, dear," said his mother. " What about a nice walk on the Common this afternoon ? "

He may have looked pale, but there was no doubt that he also looked extraordinarily guilty. For what on earth would Mrs. Flapton say if she knew that he was dreaming of deserting her ?

But he went on dreaming, and never had the garden been so well watered as it was during the days that followed.

The dinner-party was over. Old Mr. Blankett had proved a genial and talkative host, even if a little over-fond of anecdotes about his career as a District Commissioner. But it was easy to forgive him this when he invited Mrs. Flapton to come into what he called his den to inspect what he described as his curios.

" You young people," he said, " had better amuse yourselves. Dorothy's heard enough of her old father's stories. Eh ? What ? Ha, ha ! "

So Dorothy and Harold went out into the garden—so incredibly romantic to the latter as the spot on which he had gazed and gazed ever since the adventure with the hose—and the moon was full now, and the shadows were mysterious, and the scent of the flowers was heavy and intoxicating, and the distant sound of the electric trams was curiously sad and soothing.

" This," said Dorothy, pausing suddenly, " is where you turned the water on me. Do you remember ? "

" I shall never forget," said Harold, who was finding it much easier to speak in the darkness. " I have been a different man since then."

" So have I," said Dorothy softly. " If you see what I mean."

" How strange it all is," said Harold.

" Oh, Mr. Flapton," said Dorothy, " I have just been reading this week's *Snappy Snips*."

" An excellent number," said Harold, trembling all over.

" I loved the puzzle about the old farmer," said Dorothy.

" Did you ? "

" And the one about the two cyclists."

" You did ? "

" And the third one—— Oh, Mr. Flapton——"

" Oh, Dorothy ! " said Mr. Flapton, trembling now so that only the darkness prevented his appearing in two places at once. " Could you—would you—I mean, do you—— Oh, gosh, I haven't slept for a week, but you're the most wonderful girl in the world ! "

" So are you," said Miss Blankett, very gently. " If you see what I mean."

And she melted into his arms, and he kissed her with increasing accuracy and skill at each shot, not to mention enjoyment and satisfaction, and she clung to him, and they murmured the most awful piffle, and their hearts beat to all intents and purposes as one, and they were very, very happy; and they were engaged.

There was no question of that, because Harold asked her.

" We're engaged, aren't we ? " he said.

" You silly darling," said Dorothy. " Of course we are."

Congratulations, then. Well done *Sunnybrae* and *Bongaloo*. As neat a piece of work as we have come across for some time, and let no critic complain that the hero has been backward or the heroine unmaidenly. In nine other cases out of ten the same qualities would have been infinitely more exaggerated, and what on earth does it matter so long as two hearts are beating to all intents and purposes as one ?

The answer is that it doesn't matter a pin. Only—and this identical thought has just arisen to torment the prospective bridegroom—they've still got to deal with Mr. Blankett and Mrs. Flapton.

How often does the difficulty which we foresee turn out to be no difficulty at all. How still oftener is our relief at this fact swept aside by the totally unexpected difficulty which instantly supervenes. There can be no copyright in these commonplaces, which have often been far better expressed ; but can any amount of familiar philosophy prepare us for the surprises of everyday existence ?

Mr. Blankett was delighted at the great news. " An excellent fellow," he said. " Both clever and modest. I took to him the moment we met." And Mrs. Flapton, though it is true that she wept copiously, was no less encouraging. " A sweet girl," she said. " How happy this has made me. May Heaven bless you both."

So far, in fact, so good. But then came the surprise.

" If I have the spare room done up," added Mrs. Flapton, " then we can all go on living here. Won't that be delightful ? "

" What ! " said Harold, in spite of himself.

" But, my dear boy, what's wrong with the spare room ? "

" Nothing," said Harold faintly. " But——"

" Speak up," said Mrs. Flapton, smiling through her tears.

" Ug," said Harold.

For it seemed to him that the arrangement was the most unspeakable arrangement that had ever been suggested ; but he could no more say so than he could see how to avoid it. He had obeyed his mother all his life, and no amount of experience in propounding and solving the Kurious Konundrums was the least help in escaping from the habit now.

" But it's impossible," said Dorothy, when he told her.

" I know," he said gloomily.

" It wouldn't work for five minutes."

" Not for one."

" Is it money, then ? "

" No, of course it isn't. Don't you know my father was a house-agent ? "

" What are we to do ? "

" I can't very well break her heart," said Harold regretfully.

" It's an insane idea," said Dorothy.

" Quite," said Harold, looking nervously over his shoulder.

" Do you think she'll change her mind ? "

" Not she."

" But what if we took another house somewhere else ? "

" She'd come too," said Harold.

" Um," said Dorothy.

" I beg your pardon ? "

" I'm thinking. There ought to be a way out of this, you know. We must both think."

They both thought. They went on thinking for days, and then for weeks. The engagement was announced, and the editor of *Snappy Snips* and Miss Peckwater—whom you have probably forgotten, but who never forgot anything herself— both sent letters of congratulation and wedding-presents. So did others. But the date for the wedding itself still remained unfixed.

" Couldn't you risk it ? " Mr. Flapton would beg. " I've thought you were getting on so well together lately. She's always going in to see you."

" That's different," said Dorothy inflexibly. " You know it is."

He knew it was.

" But I still can't see any way out," he groaned.

" Can't you ? "

" No. I say—can you ? "

" Wait," said Dorothy.

" But I'm sick of waiting. It's upsetting all my work."

" Your work ! "

" What do you mean ? "

" If you're so jolly good at puzzles," said Dorothy—and you may have noticed that women soon start talking to authors like this after they are engaged to them—" why don't you solve this one ? I should have thought it would have been just in your line."

" Dorothy ! "

" All right, darling. I'm sorry."

And she kissed him, and flitted away.

It was true, though, that his anxiety was upsetting all his work. Ideas were slow in coming, and useless when they arrived. He found himself writing the most extraordinary things.

" A contributor to a popular weekly," he wrote, one morning, " was faced with the choice of breaking (*a*) his engagement, or (*b*) his mother's heart. How did he avoid doing either, and yet continue to keep up his ordinary output ? "

How, indeed ? Mr. Mystery stared at this sheet of paper,

and moaned aloud. Then he suddenly snatched it up, for
there was a rattle at the door-handle of his little study.

" Yes, mother ? " he croaked.

But it wasn't Mrs. Flapton. It was Miss Blankett.

" Hullo, darling."

" Working ? "

" No—I mean, yes—I mean——"

" Let me see."

" Oh, it's nothing. I was just——"

She took the paper from his reluctant grasp.

" Oh, my poor boy ! "

" Eh ? "

" It has been awful, hasn't it ? But, you know, the
contributor never solved it at all ? "

" What ? "

" Someone else did."

" Who ? "

" Do you know where your mother is ? "

" No. Do you want her ? "

" Not in the least. She's next door."

" What do you mean ? At *Bongaloo* ? "

" No. In the garden."

" What are you talking about ? "

" Come here," said Dorothy. " This way. And for
heaven's sake don't make that noise with your feet. Now,
then."

She led him out of the french window, and across the lawn,
and to the spot where he had first turned the hose on her.

" Look ! " she whispered, pointing over the fence CD.
" That's my solution."

Mr. Blankett and Mrs. Flapton were standing locked in a
close, though elderly, embrace. Harold was at once disgusted and fascinated. Dorothy was smiling like the goddess, and the very hard-working and ingenious goddess, that
she was.

" I didn't like to tell you till I'd brought it off," she said.
" But it's all right. They were married half an hour ago."

There is no record that the present Mrs. Harold Flapton,
who lives so happily and domestically at *Sunnybrae*, ever
repeated her incursion into that field of industry where her
husband is still so successful. But he published his two

thousandth Kurious Konundrum the other day—and Miss
Peckwater did another first-rate write-up—and shows no
sign whatever of exhausting himself. And when authors
show no sign whatever of exhausting themselves, almost any
editor could tell you where to look for the source of their
inspiration.

Reprinted with the Author's permission from *Having Fun.*

THE CHINK IN MISS FLAMBOROUGH'S ARMOUR

SHE—meaning that interesting and entertaining character, Woman—has, as you may have noticed, done a whole lot of things in recent years to throw off the chains and shackles and swaddling-bands and so forth in which Man (the Tyrant) had for so long confined her. Or in which she had confined herself. Or in which Providence or Evolution or Nature or something of that sort had gone and shoved her. Or——

Well, you know what we mean, anyhow. There she was, only the other day, one mass of hairpins, hatpins, helplessness and headaches, all petted and patronised, all coddled and kept apart, all frills, fluff, flannel, flightiness and folly. And then just look at the creature now.

Unrecognisable. She has removed almost all her hair and about eighty per cent. of her clothes. She shoots and skis, she burgles and broadcasts, she votes and is voted for, she plays polo and she joins the police. There isn't a man in these days, whatever his job, who doesn't live in daily dread of being replaced by a member of the opposite or alternative sex ; while the last trace of open competition has been banished by the fact that he is outnumbered, at any rate in the United Kingdom, by two million vigorous and pitiless souls. Yes, Providence or Evolution or Nature, or something of that sort, has indeed effected a remarkable change during the present remarkable century. You have noticed it yourself, of course, and it may even have occurred to you that the world is turning upside down.

Perhaps you're right. Yet somehow it continues to revolve, and we all know what makes it do that. For Woman, in spite of everything, is still wooed and occasionally won. Man, notwithstanding his increasing inferiority, still aspires and occasionally achieves. It seems that in the last resort they still need each other, and have got to have what they need. And in the last resort, also, though you never know how, when or where it is going to show itself and a lot of people might doubt this statement altogether, there is a certain difference even between men and women of the very latest and most up-to-date description. It takes a bit of spotting, you may go a long way before you find it ; but in the end——

However, we haven't reached the end yet, and if we go on like this we shall never get past the beginning. No more profundity, please. We're going to tell you a story.

There was an average-adjuster called Archibald Applethwaite ; young, healthy, clean, personable, punctual and pleasant ; altogether an average average-adjuster, and as free from intellectual brilliance as from moral turpitude. He worked in an office, shared a flat with a bill-broker called George Wilkes, ate, drank, slept, took a reasonable amount of exercise, and generally speaking was a credit to his mysterious profession. Though he had no sisters, he was neither shy nor shambling when he had to speak to a woman, nor on the other hand bumptious and bouncing. He accepted them, and was content to accept them, as human beings with high heels whom one sat next to at dinner-parties and who were indispensable at dances. He had a vague idea that they were credited with other qualities by novelists and foreigners, but he was no great reader and he hardly ever went abroad. He quite liked them, but then he quite liked everybody. It had not yet occurred to him that they had been placed in this world either for the purpose of being wooed or won.

Protected by this serene and somewhat stupid attitude, young Archibald had also so far eluded all attempts to ensnare him in the meshes of any sentimental entanglement. Miss Buckingham had given him her photograph, and he had put it away in the bottom drawer of his desk. Miss Lancaster had invited him to remove a small fly from her eye, and he had done so without even glancing at her mouth. Miss Shrewsbury had offered to tell his fortune by the so-called science of palmistry, but though she had held his hand for ten minutes and predicted the most passionate passages with a fair-haired female—Miss Shrewsbury, by the way, was a blonde—young Archibald hadn't even momentarily held hers. Mocking laughter had been tried on young Archibald, and soulful sighs, and flattery, and tantrums, and even tears. But to all these manifestations he had presented the same easy-going insensitiveness. He had supposed that the creatures were a bit upset about something, and as it was clearly no affair of his, he had left them as soon as possible so as to avoid embarrassing them. On the occasion when Miss Windermere had wept, he had certainly stayed a little longer—but this was only so as to give her his advice about the best treatment for a cold.

A big stiff, you might say, or a silly ass, or a mutt—or conceivably a very sane and sensible young man.

It doesn't matter, however, what line of criticism you choose to take, for as you know perfectly well and there is no sort of need to tell you, it is just this kind of gentleman at whom an undersized god with wings will sooner or later aim one of his sharpest and most penetrating darts ; after which, of course, the gentleman will become a very different kind of gentleman altogether. Young Archibald didn't know this, but it is a sure bet almost amounting to a dead cinch. It follows practically as the night follows the day.

So that the night came when young Archibald, having adjusted a number of averages, further adjusted his white tie, his crimson buttonhole and the angle of his shiny black hat, and went out to dine with the Murgatroyds in the neighbourhood of Knightsbridge. And there he entered the drawing-room, and Mrs. Murgatroyd said : " I want to introduce you to Miss Flamborough." Whereupon and in the twinkling of an eye and in far less time than it takes to relate, Archie Applethwaite kicked his left ankle with the point of his right shoe, shook at the knees, lost his breath, gaped, gulped and gasped, and simultaneously became possessed of an almost ungovernable desire to seize Miss Flamborough in both his arms, to crush her towards him, and to imprint a series of extremely violent kisses as near to her slightly parted lips as he could possibly manage without either previous experience or the full use of his faculties.

" How do you do ? " he said.

" How do you do ? " said Miss Flamborough, apparently but not really floating about the drawing-room on a small pink cloud.

This concluded their conversation for the time being, since there were other introductions to be made and other salutations to be offered and exchanged. Archie Applethwaite went downstairs to the dining-room, because everybody else seemed to be going downstairs to the dining-room, and sat where he was told, and used a number of knives, forks and spoons more or less in the manner to which he was accustomed, and poured a certain quantity of champagne into his person, and even spoke to the women on either side of him with idiomatic accuracy and many signs of intelligence. Also after these and the other women had left him, he smoked one of Mr. Murgatroyd's cigars without once placing the lighted end in his mouth or the whole thing in his waistcoat pocket.

Nevertheless it was more luck than cunning which preserved him from these solecisms and enabled him to take a certain share in the dialogue, for he was still by no means positive whether he were on his head or his heels, while so far as he was capable of identifying his own thoughts, they consisted entirely of one stupefied realisation that the life of a bachelor was the life of an outcast and a worm.

Young Archibald, in fact, imagined himself to be in love ; and, since there is no difference which anyone has yet been able to define between imagining oneself to be in love and being in love, one may as well go the whole hog and assert that young Archibald *was* in love. Sitting there in Mr. Murgatroyd's dining-room and twiddling Mr. Murgatroyd's nutcrackers and even talking to Mr. Murgatroyd's guests, he was filled with an intense and intolerable longing to detach Miss Flamborough from all her friends and relations, to become responsible for her debts, to feed, clothe and house her, and, above all, to guard and protect her. Though he was still unaware of her Christian name, and had so far only heard her utter four simple words, he positively yearned to spend the rest of his career in her company, and to place his strong right arm and masculine intellect exclusively at her service. He wanted to care for her, to remove obstacles from her path, to help her in all her difficulties, to guide her footsteps and offer her perpetual support. All this had now become the sole aim and object of his existence, and no other aim or object counted for so much as two pins.

Well, in the bad old days it might have taken quite a little time to carry even the preliminary stages of this ambition into effect. In the bad old days young Archibald would probably have had to suggest calling on Miss Flamborough's parents on a Sunday afternoon, and only after he had done this several times and at considerable intervals could he have hoped to have perhaps two minutes alone with her while she showed him the cactuses in the conservatory ; and even after this it might well have been many months before the formal interview could reasonably take place at which he might ask her father for permission to pay his addresses. In those bad old days a job like this could often and easily take two or three years in coming to a head, and no gentleman, however passionate, could have remained a gentleman if he had tried to cut it any shorter.

Now, however, it is all rather different. Mr. Applethwaite made straight for Miss Flamborough as soon as he returned to the drawing-room, discovered that she was called Cicely by the simple method of asking her, talked to her without stopping until a quarter past eleven, drove her home in his little car, invited her to dine with him on the following night at the Bow-wow—an invitation which she appeared delighted to accept—and so left her, feeling that he hadn't done so badly in the time at his disposal, but determined to do a great deal better before very long.

So far, in fact, it had all been extraordinarily simple, as it generally is in these days—up to a certain point—when we all do exactly what we like and say exactly what we think and go exactly where we choose. If young Archibald had troubled to tell George Wilkes that he was dining alone with a girl at the Bow-wow, or if Miss Flamborough had bothered to make a similar confession to her mother, neither confidant would have thought anything particular of the news. " All right," George Wilkes might have said ; " see you in the morning, I dare say." And : " Have a good time," Mrs. Flamborough might have remarked ; " and try not to forget your latchkey this time." For this is the era of freedom and good-fellowship, and we're all the same age as each other, and we have no intention of doing anything which might show that we're not. Once it was enough to start everyone talking if you were seen looking across the aisle at a young woman in church. Now you actually have to lead her down it before most people will believe that either of you mean anything.

Simplicity, in short, if you do mean anything, has become

a remarkably complicated affair. Not once during the five hours or so which they spent at the Bow-wow did Miss Flamborough fail to look Mr. Applethwaite straight in the eyes, or appear to notice his somewhat laboured compliments, or do anything which he could interpret as a sign of encouragement or even interest. She was perfectly polite, she answered when he spoke to her, and seemed ready to discuss almost any general subject with ease and intelligence. She danced exquisitely, but without a hint that she regarded her partner as anything but a concomitant of the music. She certainly appreciated the food which he ordered ; but only as food, not as a tribute to her own charm and beauty. Besides, she knew so much too much about it. You couldn't hope to surprise or impress a girl who read a menu like that, and could obviously have ordered just as good a dinner herself. She even had a palate for champagne.

And she knew and nodded at the head-waiter and the band-leader and far too many of the other diners and dancers, and told Mr. Applethwaite the names of all the tunes without a pause or an effort. If he hadn't been so madly in love with her, she might, in fact, have been an ideal companion for an evening at the Bow-wow ; so pleasant and friendly, so frank and natural, so neat and well-dressed, so full of enjoyment and so prompt with expressions of gratitude when it was all over.

But when it was all over, when Mr. Applethwaite had driven her home and returned to his flat and put on his pyjamas and gone to bed, he tossed and turned, and muttered and groaned. For it seemed to him that though he now called her Cicely and she called him Archie—which of course was little or nothing in these days—he had made no sort of progress during his long and extremely expensive evening. She had been as cool and collected at the end as at the beginning, and he had been as little of an ostensible suitor. Not once had he been able to protect her or support her or guard her, because not once had she given him the flimsiest shadow of a pretext. The world, as it now seemed, was so arranged that men and women were indeed equal, and what the dickens was the use of deathless devotion or a strong right arm when a girl was so efficient and independent without either ?

If only some fellow had insulted her, if only she had even

lost her bag or dropped her handkerchief ! But not one of these things had happened, and not one of them, so it seemed to Mr. Applethwaite as he tossed and turned, ever would.

Was there no chink in her extraordinarily up-to-date armour ? Was she never going to *be* a woman, as well as looking like one ?

Young Archibald, so we understand, appeared distinctly pale and haggard the next morning as he set off for the City, and distinctly glum and gloomy as he sat adjusting his averages. But presently it occurred to him that in the first place faint heart never won fair lady, and that in the second place the Bow-wow had perhaps been the wrong spot in which to exhibit his own masculine strength and reliability. Possibly Miss Flamborough had thought him a mere trifler, gigolo or roué, the kind of self-indulgent weakling whom a girl would hardly consider a man at all. But if he could get her into the open air next time—well, that ought to make a difference, oughtn't it ? That, surely, ought to show her a little more of the depth and breadth of his ardent soul.

So young Archibald reached for his telephone, and twiddled the dial until he heard the voice of Miss Flamborough's maid. And then he heard Miss Flamborough's own voice—and what an enchanting voice it was—and he invited her to play golf with him on Sunday at Sandy Heath, at the same time offering to call for her in his little car.

" Thanks awfully," said Miss Flamborough. " Yes, I'd love to do that."

" Would you really ? " said young Archibald.

" Rather," said Miss Flamborough. " What's your handicap ? "

" Two," said young Archibald. " But——"

" Good," said Miss Flamborough. " That's all right. Only look here."

" Yes ? "

" Would you mind if I drove you down instead ? I mean, I've just had my engine hotted up and I want a chance to try it properly. I'll come round for you about half-past ten, shall I ? "

" Oh," said young Archibald. " Very well. I mean, thanks very much."

" Right you are," said Miss Flamborough, ringing off.

And of course this all rather altered it again, so far as the relationship between the sexes was concerned ; because you couldn't call it the same thing to sit idly on the front seat of a car, probably trying not to look frightened, when you might have been very dashing and dangerous at the wheel of your own. Besides, the more that Mr. Applethwaite thought about the tone in which Miss Flamborough had said " Good," the less confidence he felt in his ability to justify that rather flattering handicap. His original idea had been to offer his opponent something like a stroke a hole, to play well within his game, and finally to beat her by about three and two. That, he had imagined, would establish his athletic superiority without spoiling her day in the country or letting her feel that she was spoiling his. But what if she beat him ?

Well, she did. She beat him fairly and squarely, without any assistance or allowance, by a three-yard putt on the eighteenth green. And young Archibald, who had never battled more desperately in his life, was extremely exhausted, while Miss Flamborough was considerably fresher than paint.

" Come on," she said. " I'll race you to the car."

And she raced him to the car, and beat him again, though she was carrying her clubs now and he had left his with the caddie to be cleaned.

" This is ghastly," thought young Archibald. " How on earth does she do it, when she's only about half my weight and half my size ? I haven't done a dashed thing for her yet, except pay a couple of bills which she could easily have paid herself. How the blazes can one make love to a girl like this when she never seems to have heard of such a thing ? Isn't there anything that could make her realise I'm a man ? Is there nothing that she can't do for herself ? "

He had a moment of hope on the way back ; for suddenly, as they were darting in and out of the traffic, and as Miss Flamborough was giving him some very knowledgeable advice about the stock-markets, her hotted-up engine began to race and roar, while the car itself began to slow down.

" Bother ! " said Miss Flamborough. " That's the clutch slipping again. What a nuisance ! "

They drew up by the side of the road, and here, thought the passenger, was his chance.

" Don't you move——" he began.

But Miss Flamborough had uttered exactly the same words.

" Don't you move," she said. " At least, just shift your feet a second, and I'll fix it."

" But can't I——"

" No, you stay where you are. I know just what to do."

" Yes, but——"

She was out of the car, though. She had got hold of the tool-kit. She was taking up the floor-boards. She was burrowing among the entrails. Mr. Applethwaite had a superb view of the nape of her neck—and what an enchanting nape it was—but he could hardly have been more out of the subsequent procedure if he had been a centenarian taking his first ride. For you couldn't force a girl to let you tinker with her clutch, if she had definitely refused your aid. You couldn't even pass her the wrench or the screwdriver, if she kept them both well out of your reach.

Moreover, as young Archibald observed with a sinking heart, it wasn't one of those clutches which can be taken up with a single screw. On the contrary it was the kind of job which would have taken him an hour, and an ordinary garage the best part of a day ; and it took Miss Flamborough exactly fifteen minutes.

" There ! " she said, standing up again and looking as cool and clean as ever. " That's done it. On we go."

" Won't you——" stammered young Archibald, faintly and feebly ; " I mean, wouldn't you like to borrow my handkerchief ? "

" What for ? "

" Aren't your hands dirty ? "

" No, thanks," said Miss Flamborough. " I always carry this pair of old gloves."

She pulled them off as she spoke, and flung them into the tool-box. As she replaced her original spotless pair, Mr. Applethwaite was left to reflect that as well as breaking all records for an adjustment like that, and as well as making him look a helpless ignoramus, she had also shown more forethought and general competence than he had ever yet beheld. Not only, therefore, had he to deal with someone as good as any man, but with someone a dashed sight better.

And as Mr. Applethwaite came to this realisation—which, if you are a woman, you will doubtless say that he should have reached a long time ago—he also became plunged in bottomless despair. For gosh, how he loved this creature, and gosh, how he adored her, and gosh, how he worshipped the ground on which she trod. But gosh, how in the wide world could he ever tell her all this, or get her to take the slightest interest in it, when everything that she did showed him more and more clearly that she hadn't one weak point in her defences ? He had tried the stuffy dance-floor, he had tried the breezy golf-course, and he had tried the open road. Was she never, never going to lean on him and need him ?

So glum and gloomy, so pale and haggard, did young Archie Applethwaite appear on his return from this disastrous expedition, that even George Wilkes, who was not ordinarily renowned for his powers of observation, actually noticed that something was up.

" Archie," he said, in his outspoken way ; " you're looking blue, old man. By Jove, you're looking green. It's my belief you're sickening for something."

" No, I'm not," said his fellow-tenant, with a slight blink.

" Well," said George Wilkes, in his outspoken way, " all I can say is that you're looking positively putrid. Worried about your work or something ? "

" No," said his fellow-tenant.

" Well," said George Wilkes, in his outspoken way, " what are you worried about ? Come on, old man. Spill it."

Mr. Applethwaite had no intention of spilling it. No one but a cad would dream of spilling anything so secret and sacred. Let the canker gnaw at his vitals, let his nights be sleepless, let his days be interminable and intolerable, let his heart ache and his reason totter ; but in no circumstances——

" Well, as a matter of fact," he said. " There's a girl. She's—she's—I mean, she's——"

" After you ? " suggested George Wilkes, in his outspoken way.

" No," said young Archibald, a trifle coldly. " On the contrary, I worship the ground on which she treads. It is my hope, my prayer, my ambition——"

" Quite," said George Wilkes.

" To me," said young Archibald, " she is like some——"

" Absolutely," said George Wilkes.

" Her voice——"

" I'll bet it is."

" Her eyes——"

" Oh, every time," said George Wilkes ; and he hit his fellow-tenant suddenly between the shoulder-blades. " When," he inquired, " is it all coming off ? "

" When," retorted young Archibald, " is all what coming off ? "

" The wedding, old boy," said George Wilkes. " When do we forgather at the altar steps ? "

At this pertinent and painful question, Mr. Applethwaite gave vent to a hollow groan, yet having now spilt practically everything, he was fain to spill the rest. He informed his old friend that the date of the ceremony bore a fatal resemblance to the Greek Kalends, that so far from being engaged to Miss Flamborough he hadn't even proposed to her, and proceeded to give the reasons why, in his opinion, no such proposal could ever be made. For how, he demanded, could a fellow offer to look after a girl, to shield her and shelter her and defend her from the rough world, when she was perfectly capable of doing all these things for herself ? Where, with a girl like Miss Flamborough, could a fellow even begin ?

" Do you mean," asked George Wilkes, in his outspoken way, " that she's one of those masculine ones ? Wears a man's tie and a monocle, what ? Because if so——"

And Mr. Applethwaite rejected this description with disgust. Miss Flamborough, he insisted, to all outward appearance was femininity personified.

" To look at——" he continued.

" Quite," said George Wilkes. " I get you. But, my dear boy, all women are the same underneath. She's bound to have a soft spot somewhere, and once—— By Jove, I've got it. Mice ! "

" Mice ? "

" Yes. Why don't you call on her with a couple of brace in your pocket, and let 'em loose ? Then she's bound to scream, and——"

" No," said young Archibald. " As it happens, Miss Flamborough is devoted to mice. She told me the first time I met her that she adores all animals, and particularly mentioned mice and snakes."

" Well, beetles," said George Wilkes.

" She has a passion for beetles. She said so at the Bow-wow."

" Well, guns, then," said George Wilkes. " Supposing you borrowed a revolver and let it off by accident——"

" No," said young Archibald regretfully. " Miss Flamborough happens to be a very good shot herself. She told me so."

" Um," said George Wilkes. And then suddenly he snapped his fingers and smote his forehead. " Look here," he burst out ; " I suppose she doesn't go about with a pistol or anything, in the ordinary way, does she ? "

" No, of course not," said Archibald. " What on earth ——"

" Well," said George Wilkes, " if you're quite certain she doesn't, here's another idea—and a dashed good one. You take her down to Richmond Park or some quiet spot like that —any day you like, after I get away from the office. And then you get out of the car and go for a little stroll. Have you got that ? "

" Well ? "

" Well," said George Wilkes, " I'll be there—we'll fix the place and time, you see—and I'll turn up my collar and rumple my hair a bit ; and then I'll jump out on you with a stick ; and then you'll rush at me and we'll have a bit of a fight—only mind you don't get too rough. And then I'll fall down, as if you'd knocked me out. And then——"

" By Jiminy ! " cried young Archibald, with his eyes glistening. " That *is* an idea, if you like. George, old man, I'm most terribly obliged to you. You'd better wear a beard or something, in case she recognises you afterwards, but— yes, I believe it's going to do the trick. We'll rehearse a bit first, you see, and perhaps we'd better run over the ground and find a good place. But we could do that to-morrow, and then on Tuesday——"

" Wednesday," said George Wilkes, " would suit me better."

" All right. Wednesday, then. And I'll use my car this time, whatever happens. No more of that passenger business. And I'll ring her up to-morrow evening and get it all settled—or I might go and see her—or I might take her out to a play. But anyhow . . ."

In the depth of his emotion and gratitude Mr. Applethwaite wrung his old friend warmly by the hand and returned the blow which he had recently received between the shoulder-blades.   Moreover they rehearsed the struggle there and then with such vehemence and vigour that they not only broke two chairs, a small table and a number of gramophone records, but also received no less than three letters of complaint in the morning from the tenants underneath, overhead and across the landing.

In the afternoon, when they had both finished their work, they drove down to Richmond Park and selected a remote spot with a large tree behind which George Wilkes was to lurk ; and when they returned, Mr. Applethwaite telephoned to Miss Flamborough—and oh, what an enchanting voice she had !—and asked her if she could accompany him to a musical comedy on the following night.

And she would.   And she did.   And he was more madly in love with her than ever, even though she still looked him straight in the eyes and continued to treat him exactly as though he were her brother.   And he was still full of hope and confidence about his old friend's very ingenious and kind-hearted plan, even though Miss Flamborough still further established her equality or ascendancy by telling him that she had been spending the afternoon piloting a light aeroplane.

" By the way," he said later on, as they danced at the Jim-jam ; " are you doing anything particular to-morrow afternoon ?   Between tea and dinner, I mean ? "

" No," said Miss Flamborough.   " I'm riding in the morning, and swimming after lunch, but I'll be clear about five, I expect.   Why ? "

" I wondered," said young Archibald, " if you'd care to come out for a breath of fresh air.   I thought of going down to Richmond Park, and if you'd let me call for you—well, I mean, we might have a bit of a walk."

Did she suspect his casual airiness ?   She didn't.

" All right," said Miss Flamborough.   " Yes, let's."

" Fine," said young Archibald, more airily and casually than ever.   But his heart beat so violently that he had to pretend his shoelace had come undone, lest she should feel its wild fluttering.   Shortly after this he took her home again, and she thanked him, and they separated, and he went back to bed.

At half-past five on Wednesday afternoon, having in the meantime adjusted quite a quantity of averages, Mr. Applethwaite drove his little car and Miss Flamborough in at the Sheen Gate of Richmond Park, proceeded to a point within easy reach of the rendezvous with George Wilkes, saw that George's car was already waiting, switched off his engine, disembarked and began strolling across the greensward with the light of his soul in close attendance by his side.

"I do hope," he was now thinking, as he discussed the beauty of the surroundings ; "I do hope this isn't going to give her too much of a shock. It'll be awkward if she faints when she sees us going for each other. It'll be awkward if we overdo it and really frighten her out of her wits. I wish to goodness I could have another word with old George before we start, just to warn him not to yell the way he did last time, but—— Gosh, there he is ! "

And there, without any doubt, he was. You couldn't miss him, in fact. For not only was he naturally something of an outsize figure, but at the present moment he had carried his disguise to such lengths that he stood out as almost the most conspicuous object in the park. Few tramp-cyclists can have worn a more unusual collection of ancient garments, while the beard which masked two-thirds of his face should have secured a first prize in almost any exhibition of tropical plants. Really, thought young Archibald, it was very decent of old George to have taken so much trouble, and he very nearly said so.

But not quite ; for old George had just given him his first cue—a menacing growl—and it behoved him to take it up quickly.

"Look out," he said—though Miss Flamborough was already staring at the apparition. "I'm afraid that man means mischief."

"Nonsense," said Miss Flamborough, making a rather unhelpful interpolation in the script. "He's only clearing his throat."

"I don't like the look of this," said Archibald, sticking doggedly to his lines. "You'd better get behind me, Cicely."

Here, according to the plan, George Wilkes was to have made a grab at Miss Flamborough's arm, at which point the fight was to have begun in real earnest. But what actually happened was quite different. That is to say that George Wilkes did, with a still more threatening snarl, attempt the preliminary grab ; but it was a complete failure. Also, so far from getting behind her would-be protector, Miss Flamborough side-stepped right in front of him. And the next thing that the would-be protector beheld was Miss Flamborough collaring his old friend remarkably low, after which he appeared to shoot through the air in a prodigious arc, and landed on the back of his neck among a quantity of ferns, where he lay very much as if dead.

" That'll teach him," said Miss Flamborough, turning aside without a trace of excitement. " Come along, Archie."

It says much for Mr. Applethwaite's generous nature that he didn't leave his old friend lying there without first rushing and bending over him—and being saluted with a volley of extremely outspoken language. But having gathered that no bones were broken and that George Wilkes was entirely opposed to another trial of strength, he was more or less compelled to leave him there, since Miss Flamborough was already walking rapidly away. During the rest of this unlucky outing he underwent considerable mental agony, for now it seemed to him that his last chance was gone, that his love must remain for ever undeclared and unrequited, and that he could hardly hope ever to be on the old terms with his fellow-tenant again.

So perhaps you can imagine how glum and gloomy, and pale and haggard, he was when at last—having nearly walked him off his legs—Miss Flamborough took her seat for the return journey. As he drove out of the Sheen Gate again, it seemed to him that his cup was full and that no more unfortunate average-adjuster existed on the whole face of the globe. " I'm finished," he thought. " I've tried everything, and I've failed. Can anyone kindly tell me any possible thing that could make it all more utterly unbearable ? "

The mocking Fates heard him, and took up the challenge. In Hammersmith Broadway—and of course it would not have happened if he hadn't been so miserable that he never heard the warning shouts—a large lorry swerved violently into his little car. Too late Mr. Applethwaite stamped on his foot-brake and tugged at his hand-brake. There was a crash, a crunch, a volley of tinkling glass. The little car subsided in a mangled heap, and Miss Flamborough was pulling him out of the wreckage.

" Hurt ? " she asked, brightly.

" No," said young Archibald. " Are you ? "

" Not in the least," said Miss Flamborough. " I saw it coming."

" Oh," said young Archibald. He could add no further comment at the moment, for, as you can also imagine, there was a good deal of interest being shown by a couple of policemen, and by the lorry-driver and his mate, and by a number of eye-witnesses, and by a number of other people who all wanted to discuss the accident with him. But who dealt with them all ? Who got the policeman on her side, and silenced the lorry-driver and his mate, and cleared away the rest of the crowd, and made arrangements with the representative of a neighbouring garage to take charge of the debris ? It was Miss Flamborough who did all this, while her companion stood helplessly by her side, and when she had done it all—and hadn't even reproached him so that he could lose his temper—it was Miss Flamborough who tried to hail a taxi.

But here young Archibald's degradation reached its lowest depths. For it was borne in upon him with irresistible force that if he entered any kind of motor-vehicle until his nerves had recovered from their recent shock, he would almost certainly scream and very likely be sick.

" Do you—do you mind awfully," he suggested, " if we go back by tube ? It's just—I mean, I can't——"

" Rattled ? " said Miss Flamborough, sympathetically. " That's all right, Archie. Certainly."

They went into the Underground station, where Mr. Applethwaite dropped all his money while attempting to book the tickets, and Miss Flamborough still further humiliated him by picking most of it up. And then they took their seats in a train, and the train passed into a cutting, and from the cutting into the bowels of the earth, and Mr. Applethwaite sat in it cursing the day on which he had been born and looking forward with some impatience to the day on which he should leave this unspeakable existence. So they passed through South Kensington and Knightsbridge and Dover Street, and at Piccadilly Circus Mr. Applethwaite suddenly realised that they had gone far past their station—

which happened to be Brompton Road—and that again he had made an abject fool of himself.

" I'm most awfully sorry," he said, " but I've taken you too far without thinking. Come on, Cicely, I'll take you back in a taxi. I—I think I'm feeling better now."

He wasn't really, but at least she shouldn't know it, and at least he could shut his eyes if the taxi went too fast. Out they got, and along the platform they walked, and into another catacomb they turned, and up some steps. And then, suddenly, Miss Flamborough stopped.

" Oh ! " she exclaimed, pointing at the escalator. " One of those things ! "

" What ? " said Mr. Applethwaite.

Miss Flamborough put out one exquisite foot, and drew it back again.

" I can't," she said—and to her companion's astonishment she seemed to be shuddering.

" Can't what ? " asked Mr. Applethwaite, as the crowds swept past them and went gliding aloft.

" Oh, dear," said Miss Flamborough. " I can't bear those things. Isn't there any other way up ? "

" Come, come," said Mr. Applethwaite, kindly. " It's perfectly safe. You've only got to step on it, and—— Here, let me take your arm."

" No ! " cried Miss Flamborough, stiffening in his grasp. " I can't do it. I can't, I tell you. I shall fall down."

" Nonsense. You'll be all right."

" I won't. I've always hated these awful moving stair-cases. Oh, Archie, what am I to do ? "

An extraordinary sensation filled Mr. Applethwaite's bosom, causing it almost visibly to swell. Poor little girl, he thought, how he had misunderstood her all this time. How pitiful she was, how frail, how weak. How desperately she needed a man's loving care and protection.

" Hold my hand," he said ; and she held it.

" Look at me," he added ; and, blushing and trembling, she looked at him.

" Don't think of anything," he continued, encircling her with his other arm, " except that I've got you, and you're safe with me, and——"

The escalator bore them steadily upward.

" Cicely—darling ! "

" Oh, Archie ! "

" I adore you," said Mr. Applethwaite.

" My hero ! " said Miss Flamborough.

In these unusual circumstances their troth was plighted, without a thought of the season-ticket holders whom they were obstructing or of the official who kept shouting to them to keep to one side.   By the time that they had surmounted the second flight they had agreed that their engagement should be one of the shortest on record, and as they drove happily away in a nice new taxi it was Miss Flamborough, and not Mr. Applethwaite, whose eyes were shut.   For Mr. Applethwaite's nerves were in perfect order again ; but Miss Flamborough was being steadfastly kissed.

Have hope, therefore, young gentlemen of the present generation, and remember—as we said at the beginning—that when most you doubt it and least you expect it Woman, that interesting and entertaining character, is still and always a woman.

Reprinted with the Author's permission from *Having Fun*.

A. E. W. MASON

The House of Terror
The Affair at the Semiramis Hotel

Mr. S. P. B. Mais has called Mr.
MASON " the prince of Romantics of
our time." His popularity as a novelist
has been continually on the increase
since his *Courtship of Morrice Buckler*
was issued in 1896. His love for the
theatre has remained with him since
his Oxford days ; and when not writing,
he is frequently mountain-climbing or
boat-sailing—as befits a member of
the Royal Yacht Squadron at Cowes.

THE HOUSE OF TERROR

THERE are eager spirits who enter upon each morning like adventurers upon an unknown sea. Mr. Rupert Glynn, however, was not of that company. He had been christened " Rupert " in an ironical moment, for he preferred the day to be humdrum. Possessed of an easy independence, which he had never done a stroke of work to enlarge, he remained a bachelor, not from lack of opportunity to become a husband, but in order that his comfort might not be disarranged.

" A hunting-box in the Midlands," he used to say, " a set of chambers in the Albany, the season in town, a cure in the autumn at some French spa where a modest game of baccarat can be enjoyed, and a five-pound note in my pocket at the service of a friend—these conditions satisfy my simple wants, and I can rub along."

Contentment had rounded his figure, and he was a little thicker in the jaw and redder in the face than he used to be. But his eye was clear, and he had many friends, a fact for which it was easy to account. For there was a pleasant earthliness about him which made him restful company. It seemed impossible that strange, startling things could happen in his presence ; he had so stolid and comfortable a look, his life was so customary and sane. " When I am frightened by queer shuffling sounds in the dead of night," said a nervous friend of his, " I think of Rupert Glynn and I am comforted." Yet just because of this atmosphere of security which he diffused about him, Mr. Glynn was dragged into mysteries, and made acquainted with terrors.

In the first days of February Mr. Glynn found upon his breakfast-table at Melton a letter which he read through with an increasing gravity. Mr. Glynn being a man of method, kept a file of the *Morning Post*. He rang the bell for his servant, and fetched to the table his pocket diary. He turned back the pages until he read in the space reserved for November 15th, " My first run of the year."

Then he spoke to his servant, who was now waiting in the room :

" Thompson, bring me the *Morning Post* of November 16th."

Mr. Glynn remembered that he had read a particular announcement in the paper on the morning after his first run, when he was very stiff. Thompson brought him the copy for which he had asked, and, turning over the pages, he soon lighted upon the paragraph.

" Mr. James Thresk has recovered from his recent breakdown, and left London yesterday with Mrs. Thresk for North Uist."

Glynn laid down his newspaper and contemplated the immediate future with gloom. It was a very long way to the Outer Hebrides, and, moreover, he had eight horses in his stable. Yet he could hardly refuse to take the journey in the face of that paragraph. It was not, indeed, in his nature to refuse. For the letter written by Linda Thresk claimed his presence urgently. He took it up again. There was no reason expressed as to why he was needed. And there were instructions, besides, which puzzled him, very explicit instructions. He was to bring his guns, he was to send a telegram from Loch Boisdale, the last harbour into which the steamer from Oban put before it reached North Uist, and from no other place. He was, in a word, to pretend that he had been shooting in a neighbouring island to North Uist, and that, since he was so near, he ventured to trespass for a night or two on Mrs. Thresk's hospitality. All these precautions seemed to Glynn ominous, but still more ominous was the style of the letter. A word here, a sentence there—nay, the very agitation of the handwriting, filled Glynn with uneasiness. The appeal was almost pitiful. He seemed to see Linda Thresk bending over the pages of the letter which he now held in his hand, writing hurriedly, with a twitching, terrified face, and every now and then looking up, and to this side and to that, with the eyes of a hunted animal. He remembered Linda's appearance very well as he held her letter in his hand, although three years had passed since he had seen her—a fragile, slender woman with a pale, delicate face, big dark eyes, and masses of dark hair—a woman with the look of a girl and an almost hothouse air of refinement.

Mr. Glynn laid the letter down again, and again rang for his servant.

" Pack for a fortnight," he said. " And get my guns out. I am going away."

Thompson was as surprised as his self-respect allowed him to be.

" Your guns, sir ? " he asked. " I think they are in town, but we have not used them for so long."

" I know," said Mr. Glynn impatiently. " But we are going to use them now."

Thompson knew very well that Mr. Glynn could not hit a haystack twenty yards away, and had altogether abandoned a sport in which he was so lamentably deficient. But a still greater shock was to be inflicted upon him.

" Thompson," said Mr. Glynn, " I shall not take you with me. I shall go alone."

And go alone he did. Here was the five-pound note, in a word, at the service of a friend. But he was not without perplexities, to keep his thoughts busy upon his journey.

Why had Linda Thresk sent for him out of all her friends ?

For since her marriage three years before, he had clean lost sight of her, and even before her marriage he had, after all, been only one of many. He found no answer to that question. On the other hand, he faithfully fulfilled Mrs. Thresk's instructions. He took his guns with him, and when the steamer stopped beside the little quay at Loch Boisdale he went ashore and sent off his telegram. Two hours later he disembarked at Lochmaddy in North Uist, and, hiring a trap at the inn, set off on his long drive across that flat and melancholy island. The sun set, the swift darkness followed, and the moon had risen before he heard the murmurous thunder of the sea upon the western shore. It was about ten minutes later when, beyond a turn of the road, he saw the house and lights shining brightly in its windows. It was a small white house with a few out-buildings at the back, set in a flat peat country on the edge of a great marsh. Ten yards from the house a great brake of reeds marked the beginning of the marsh, and beyond the reeds the bog stretched away glistening with pools to the low sand-hills. Beyond the sand-hills the Atlantic ran out to meet the darkness, a shimmering plain of silver. One sapling stood up from the middle of the marsh, and laid a finger across the

19*

moon. But except that sapling, there were not any trees.

To Glynn, fresh from the meadowlands of Leicestershire with their neat patterns of hedges, white gates and trees, this corner of the Outer Hebrides upon the edge of the Atlantic had the wildest and most desolate look. The sea-gulls and curlews cried perpetually above the marsh, and the quiet sea broke upon the sand with a haunting and mournful sound. Glynn looked at the little house set so far away in solitude, and was glad that he had come. To his southern way of thinking, trouble was best met and terrors most easily endured in the lighted ways of cities, where companionship was to be had by the mere stepping across the threshold.

When the trap drove up to the door, there was some delay in answering Glynn's summons. A middle-aged man-servant came at last to the door, and peered out from the doorway in surprise.

" I sent a telegram," said Glynn, " from Loch Boisdale. I am Mr. Glynn."

" A telegram ? " said the man. " It will not come up until the morning, sir."

Then the voice of the driver broke in.

" I brought up a telegram from Lochmaddy. It's from a gentleman who is coming to visit Mrs. Thresk from South Uist."

In the outer islands, where all are curious, news is not always to be had, and the privacy of the telegraph system is not recognised. Glynn laughed, and the same moment the man-servant opened an inner door of the tiny hall. Glynn stepped into a low-roofed parlour which was obviously the one living-room of the house. On his right hand there was a great fireplace with a peat fire burning in the grate, and a high-backed horsehair sofa in front of it. On his left at a small round table Thresk and his wife were dining.

Both Thresk and his wife sprang up as he entered. Linda advanced to him with every mark of surprise upon her face.

" You ! " she cried, holding out her hand. " Where have you sprung from ? "

" South Uist," said Glynn, repeating his lesson.

" And you have come on to us ! That is kind of you ! Martin, you must take Mr. Glynn's bag up to the guest-room. I expect you will be wanting your dinner."

" I sent you a telegram asking you whether you would mind if I trespassed upon your hospitality for a night or so."

He saw Linda's eyes fixed upon him with some anxiety, and he continued at once :

" I sent it from Loch Boisdale."

A wave of relief passed over Linda's face.

" It will not come up until the morning," she said with a smile.

" As a matter of fact, the driver brought it up with him," said Glynn. And Martin handed to Mrs. Thresk the telegram. Over his shoulder, Glynn saw Thresk raise his head. He had been standing by the table listening to what was said. Now he advanced. He was a tall man, powerfully built, with a strongly-marked, broad face, which was only saved from coarseness by its look of power. They made a strange contrast, the husband and wife, as they stood side by side—she slight and exquisitely delicate in her colour, dainty in her movements, he clumsy and big and masterful. Glynn suddenly recalled gossip which had run through the town about the time of their marriage. Linda had been engaged to another—a man whose name Glynn did not remember, but on whom, so the story ran, her heart was set.

" Of course you are very welcome," said Thresk, as he held out his hand, and Glynn noticed with something of a shock that his throat was bandaged. He looked towards Linda. Her eyes were resting upon him with a look of agonised appeal. He was not to remark upon that wounded throat. He took Thresk's hand.

" We shall be delighted if you will stay with us as long as you can," said Thresk. " We have been up here for more than three months. You come to us from another world, and visitors from another world are always interesting, aren't they, Linda ? "

He spoke his question with a quiet smile, like a man secretly amused. But on Linda's face fear flashed out suddenly and was gone. It seemed to Glynn that she was at pains to repress a shiver.

" Martin will show you your room," said Thresk. " What's the matter ? "

Glynn was staring at the table in consternation. Where had been the use of all the pretence that he had come unexpectedly on an unpremeditated visit ? His telegram had only this minute arrived—and yet there was the table laid for three people. Thresk followed the direction of his visitor's eyes.

" Oh, I see," he said with a laugh.

Glynn flushed. No wonder Thresk was amused. He had been sitting at the table ; and between himself and his wife the third place was laid.

" I will go up and change," said Glynn awkwardly.

" Well, don't be long ! " replied Thresk.

Glynn followed Martin to the guest-room. But he was annoyed. He did not, under any circumstances, like to look a fool. But he had the strongest possible objection to travelling three hundred miles in order to look it. If he wanted to look a fool, he grumbled, he could have managed it just as well in the Midlands.

But he was to be more deeply offended. For when he came down into the dining-room he walked to the table and drew out the vacant chair. At once Thresk shot out his hand and stopped him.

" You mustn't sit there ! " he cried violently. Then his face changed. Slowly the smile of amusement reappeared upon it. " After all, why not ? " he said. " Try, yes, try," and he watched Glynn with a strange intentness.

Glynn sat down slowly. A trick was being played upon him—of that he was sure. He was still more sure when Thresk's face relaxed and he broke into a laugh.

" Well, that's funny ! " he cried, and Glynn, in exasperation, asked indignantly :

" What's funny ? "

But Thresk was no longer listening. He was staring across the room towards the front door, as though he heard outside yet another visitor. Glynn turned angrily towards Linda. At once his anger died away. Her face was white as paper, and her eyes full of fear. Her need was real, whatever it might be. Thresk turned sharply back again.

" It's a long journey from London to North Uist," he said pleasantly.

" No doubt," replied Glynn, as he set himself to his dinner. " But I have come from South Uist. However, I am just as hungry as if I had come from London."

He laughed, and Thresk joined in the laugh.

" I am glad of that," he said, " for it's quite a long time since we have seen you."

" Yes, it is," replied Glynn carelessly. " A year, I should think."

" Three years," said Thresk. " For I don't think that you have ever come to see us in London."

" We are so seldom there," interrupted Linda.

" Three months a year, my dear," said Thresk. " But I know very well that a man will take a day's journey in the Outer Islands to see his friends, whereas he wouldn't cross the street in London. And, in any case, we are very glad to see you. By the way," and he reached out his hand carelessly for the salt, " isn't this rather a new departure for you, Glynn ? You were always a sociable fellow. A hunting-box in the Midlands, and all the lighted candles in the season. The Outer Islands were hardly in your line." And he turned quickly towards him. " You have brought your guns ? "

" Of course," said Glynn, laughing as easily as he could under a cross-examination which he began to find anything but comfortable. " But I won't guarantee that I can shoot any better than I used to."

" Never mind," said Thresk. " We'll shoot the bog to-morrow, and it will be strange if you don't bring down something. It's full of duck. You don't mind getting wet, I suppose ? There was once a man named Channing——" he broke off upon the name, and laughed again with that air of secret amusement. " Did you ever hear of him ? " he asked of Glynn.

" Yes," replied Glynn slowly. " I knew him."

At the mention of the name he had seen Linda flinch, and he knew why she flinched.

" Did you ? " exclaimed Thresk, with a keen interest. " Then you will appreciate the story. He came up here on a visit."

Glynn started.

" He came here ! " he cried, and could have bitten out his tongue for uttering the cry.

" Oh, yes," said Thresk easily, " I asked him," and Glynn looked from Thresk to Thresk's wife in amazement. Linda for once did not meet Glynn's eyes. Her own were fixed upon the tablecloth. She was sitting in her chair rather rigidly. One hand rested upon the tablecloth, and it was tightly clenched. Alone of the three James Thresk appeared at ease.

" I took him out to shoot that bog," he continued with a laugh. " He loathed getting wet. He was always so very well dressed, wasn't he, Linda ? The reeds begin twenty yards from the front door, and within the first five minutes he was up to the waist ! " Thresk suddenly checked his laughter. " However, it ceased to be a laughing matter. Channing got a little too near the sapling in the middle."

" Is it dangerous there ? " asked Glynn.

" Yes, it's dangerous." Thresk rose from his chair and walked across the room to the window. He pulled up the blind and, curving his hands about his eyes to shut out the light of the room, leaned his face against the window-frame and looked out. " It's more than dangerous," he said in a low voice. " Just round that sapling, it's swift and certain death. You would sink to the waist," and he spoke still more slowly, as though he were measuring by the utterance of the syllables the time it would take for the disaster to be complete—" from the waist to the shoulders, from the shoulders clean out of sight, before any help could reach you."

He stopped abruptly, and Glynn, watching him from the table, saw his attitude change. He dropped his head, he hunched his back, and made a strange hissing sound with his breath.

" Linda ! " he cried, in a low, startling voice, " Linda ! "

Glynn, unimpressionable man that he was, started to his feet. The long journey, the loneliness of the little house set in this wild, flat country, the terror which hung over it and was heavy in the very atmosphere of the rooms, were working already upon his nerves.

" Who is it ? " he cried.

Linda laid a hand upon his arm.

" There's no one," she said in a whisper. " Take no notice."

And, looking at her quivering face, Glynn was inspired to ask a question, was wrought up to believe that the answer would explain to him why Thresk leaned his forehead against the window-pane and called upon his wife in so strange a voice.

" Did Channing sink—by the sapling ? "

" No," said Linda hurriedly, and as hurriedly she drew away in her chair. Glynn turned and saw Thresk himself standing just behind his shoulder. He had crept down noiselessly behind them.

" No," Thresk repeated. " But he is dead. Didn't you know that ? Oh, yes, he is dead," and suddenly he broke out with a passionate violence. " A clever fellow—an infernally clever fellow. You are surprised to hear me say that, Glynn. You underrated him like the rest of us. We thought him a milksop, a tame cat, a poor, weak, interloping, unprofitable creature who would sidle obsequiously into your house, and make his home there. But we were wrong —all except Linda there."

Linda sat with her head bowed, and said not a word. She was sitting so that Glynn could see her profile, and though she said nothing, her lips were trembling.

" Linda was right," and Thresk turned carelessly to Glynn. " Did you know that Linda was at one time engaged to Channing ? "

" Yes, I knew," said Glynn awkwardly.

" It was difficult for most of us to understand," said Thresk. " There seemed no sort of reason why a girl like Linda should select a man like Channing to fix her heart upon. But she was right. Channing was a clever fellow— oh, a very clever fellow," and he leaned over and touched Glynn upon the sleeve, " for he died."

Glynn started back.

" What are you saying ? " he cried.

Thresk burst into a laugh.

" That my throat hurts me to-night," he said.

Glynn recovered himself with an effort. " Oh, yes," he said, as though now for the first time he had noticed the bandage. " Yes, I see you have hurt your throat. How did you do it ? "

Thresk chuckled.

" Not very well done, Glynn. Will you smoke ? "

The plates had been cleared from the table, and the coffee brought in. Thresk rose from his seat and crossed to the mantelshelf on which a box of cigars was laid. As he took up the box and turned again towards the table, a parchment scroll which hung on a nail at the side of the fireplace caught his eye.

"Do you see this ? " he said, and he unrolled it. " It's my landlord's family tree. All the ancestors of Mr. Robert Donald McCullough right back to the days of Bruce. McCullough's prouder of that scroll than of anything else in the world. He is more interested in it than in anything else in the world."

For a moment he fingered it, and in the tone of a man communing with himself, he added :

" Now, isn't that curious ? "

Glynn rose from his chair, and moved down the table so that he could see the scroll unimpeded by Thresk's bulky figure. Thresk, however, was not speaking any longer to his guest. Glynn sat down again. But he sat down now in the chair which Thresk had used ; the chair in which he himself had been sitting between Thresk and Linda was empty.

" What interests me," Thresk continued, like a man in a dream, " is what is happening now—and very strange, queer, interesting things are happening now—for those who have eyes to see. Yes, through centuries and centuries, McCulloughs have succeeded McCulloughs, and lived in this distant, little corner of the Outer Islands through forays and wars and rebellions, and the over-setting of kings, and yet, nothing has ever happened in this house to any one of them half so interesting and half so strange as what is happening now to us, the shooting tenants of a year."

Thresk dropped the scroll, and, coming out of his dream, brought the cigar-box to the table.

" You have changed your seat ! " he said with a smile, as he offered the box to Glynn. Glynn took out of it a cigar, and leaning back, cut off the end. As he stooped forward to light it, he saw the cigar-box still held out to him. Thresk had not moved. He seemed to have forgotten Glynn's presence in the room. His eyes were fixed upon the empty chair. He stood strangely rigid, and then he suddenly cried out :

" Take care, Linda ! "

There was so sharp a note of warning in his voice that Linda sprang to her feet, with her hand pressed upon her heart. Glynn was startled too, and because he was startled he turned angrily to Thresk.

" Of what should Mrs. Thresk take care ? "

Thresk took his eyes for a moment, and only for a moment, from the empty chair.

" Do you see nothing ? " he asked, in a whisper, and his glance went back again. " Not a shadow which leans across the table there towards Linda, darkening the candle-light ? "

" No ; for there's nothing to cast a shadow."

" Is there not ? " said Thresk, with a queer smile. " That's where you make your mistake. Aren't you conscious of something very strange, very insidious, close by us in this room ? "

" I am aware that you are frightening Mrs. Thresk," said Glynn roughly ; and, indeed, standing by the table with her white face and her bosom heaving under her hand, she looked the very embodiment of terror. Thresk turned at once to her. A look of solicitude made his gross face quite tender. He took her by the arm, and in a chiding, affectionate tone he said very gently :

" You are not frightened, Linda, are you ? Interested— yes, just as I am. But not frightened. There's nothing to be frightened at. We are not children."

" Oh, Jim," she said, and she leaned upon his arm. He led her across to the sofa, and sat down beside her.

" That's right. Now we are comfortable." But the last word was not completed. It seemed that it froze upon his lips. He stopped, looked for a second into space, and then, dropping his arm from about his wife's waist, he deliberately moved aside from her, and made a space between them.

" Now we are in our proper places—the four of us," he said bitterly.

" The three of us," Glynn corrected, as he walked round the table. " Where's the fourth ? "

And then there came to him this extraordinary answer, given in the quietest voice imaginable.

" Between my wife and me. Where should he be ? "

Glynn stared. There was no one in the room but Linda, Thresk, and himself—no one. But—but—it was the lone-liness of the spot, and its silence, and its great distance from his world, no doubt, which troubled him. Thresk's manner, too, and his words were having their effect. That was all, Glynn declared stoutly to himself. But—but—he did not wonder that Linda had written so urgently for him to come to her. His back went cold, and the hair stirred upon his scalp.

" Who is it, then ? " he cried violently.

Linda rose from the sofa, and took a quick step towards him. Her eyes implored him to silence.

" There is no one," she protested in a low voice.

" No," cried Glynn loudly. " Let us understand what wild fancy he has ! Who is the fourth ? "

Upon Thresk's face came a look of sullenness.

" Who should he be ? "

" Who is he ? " Glynn insisted.

" Channing," said Thresk. " Mildmay Channing." He sat for a while, brooding with his head sunk upon his breast. And Glynn started back. Some vague recollection was stirring in his memory. There had been a story current amongst Linda's friends at the time of her marriage. She had been in love with Channing, desperately in love with him. The marriage with Thresk had been forced on her by her parents—yes, and by Thresk's persistency. It had been a civilised imitation of the Rape of the Sabine Women. That was how the story ran, Glynn remembered. He waited to hear more from James Thresk, and in a moment the words came, but in a thoroughly injured tone.

" It's strange that you can't see either."

" There is someone else, then, as blind as I am ? " said Glynn.

" There was. Yes, yes, the dog," replied Thresk, gazing into the fire. " You and the dog," he repeated uneasily, " you and the dog. But the dog saw in the end, Glynn, and so will you—even you."

Linda turned quickly, but before she could speak, Glynn made a sign to her. He went over to her side. A glance at Thresk showed him that he was lost in his thoughts.

" If you want me to help you, you must leave us alone," he said.

She hesitated for a moment, and then swiftly crossed the room and went out at the door. Glynn, who had let his cigar go out, lit it again at the flame of one of the candles on the dining-table. Then he planted himself in front of Thresk.

" You are terrifying your wife," he said. " You are frightening her to death."

Thresk did not reply to the accusation directly. He smiled quietly at Glynn.

" She sent for you."

Glynn looked uncomfortable, and Thresk went on :

" You haven't come from South Uist. You have come from London."

" No," said Glynn.

" From Melton, then. You came because Linda sent for you."

" If it were so," stammered Glynn, " it would only be another proof that you are frightening her."

Thresk shook his head.

" It wasn't because Linda was afraid that she sent for you," he said stubbornly. " I know Linda. I'll tell you the truth," and he fixed his burning eyes on Glynn's face. " She sent for you because she hates being here with me."

" Hates being with you ! " cried Glynn, and Thresk nodded his head. Glynn could hardly even so believe that he had heard aright. " Why, you must be mad ! " he protested. " Mad or blind. There's just one person of whom your wife is thinking, for whom she is caring, for whose health she is troubled. It has been evident to me ever since I have been in this house—in spite of her fears. Every time she looks at you her eyes are tender with solicitude. That one person is yourself."

" No," said Thresk. " It's Channing."

" But he's dead, man ! " cried Glynn in exasperation. " You told me so yourself not half an hour ago. He is dead."

" Yes," answered Thresk. " He's dead. That's where he beat me. You don't understand that ? "

" No, I don't," replied Glynn.

He was speaking aggressively ; he stood with his legs apart in an aggressive attitude. Thresk looked him over from head to foot and agreed.

" No," he said, " and I don't see why you should. You are rather like me, comfortable and commonplace, and of the earth earthy. Before men of our gross stamp could believe and understand what I am going to tell you, they would have to reach—do you mind if I say a refinement ?— by passing through the same fires which have tempered me."

Glynn made no reply. He shifted his position so that the firelight might fall upon Thresk's face with its full strength.

Thresk leaned forward with his hands upon his knees, and very quietly, though now and then a note of scorn rang in his voice, he told his story.

"You tell me my wife cares for me. I reply that she would have cared, if Channing had not died. When I first met Linda she was engaged to him. You know that. She was devoted to him. You know that too. I knew it and I didn't mind. I wasn't afraid of Channing. A poor, feeble creature—heaps of opportunities, not one of them foreseen, not one of them grasped when it came his way. A grumbler, a bag of envy, a beggar for sympathy at any woman's lap! Why should I have worried my head about Channing? And I didn't. Linda's people were all for breaking off their engagement. After all, I was some good. I had made my way. I had roughed it in South America ; and I had come home a rich man—not such a very easy thing, as the superior people who haven't the heart even to try to be rich men are inclined to think. Well the engagement was broken off, Channing hadn't a penny to marry on, and nobody would give him a job. Look here!" And he suddenly swung round upon Glynn.

"I gave Channing his chance. I knew he couldn't make any use of it. I wanted to prove he wasn't any good. So I put a bit of a railway in Chili into his hands, and he brought the thing to the edge of bankruptcy within twelve months. So the engagement was broken off. Linda clung to the fellow. I knew it, and I didn't mind. She didn't want to marry me. I knew it, and I didn't mind. Her parents broke her down to it. She sobbed through the night before we were married. I knew it, and I didn't mind. You think me a beast, of course," he added, with a look at Glynn. "But just consider the case from my point of view. Channing was no match for Linda. I was. I wanted time, that was all. Give me only time, and I knew that I could win her."

Boastful as the words sounded, there was nothing aggressive in Thresk's voice. He was speaking with a quiet simplicity which robbed them quite of offence. He was unassumingly certain.

"Why?" asked Glynn. "Why, given time, were you sure that you could win her?"

"Because I wanted enough. That's my creed, Glynn.

If you want enough, want with every thought, and nerve, and pulse, the thing you want comes along all right. There was the difference between Channing and me. He hadn't the heart to want enough. I wanted enough to go to school again. I set myself to learn the small attentions which mean so much to women. They weren't in my line naturally. I pay so little heed to things of that kind myself that it did not easily occur to me that women might think differently. But I learnt my lesson, and I got my reward. Just simple little precautions, like having a cloak ready for her, almost before she was aware that she was cold. And I would see a look of surprise on her face, and the surprise flush into a smile of pleasure. Oh, I was holding her, Glynn, I can tell you. I went about it so very warily," and Thresk laughed with a knowing air. " I didn't shut my door on Channing either. Not I ! I wasn't going to make a martyr of him. I let him sidle in and out of the house, and I laughed. For I was holding her. Every day she came a step or two nearer to me."

He broke off suddenly, and his voice, which had taken on a tender and wistful note, incongruous in so big a creature, rose in a gust of anger.

" But he died ! He died and caught her back again."

Glynn raised his hands in despair.

" That memory has long since faded," he argued, and Thresk burst out in a bitter laugh.

" Memory," he cried, flinging himself into a chair. " You are one of the imaginative people after all, Glynn." And Glynn stared in round-eyed surprise. Here to him was conclusive proof that there was something seriously wrong with Thresk's mind. Never had Mr. Glynn been called imaginative before, and his soul revolted against the aspersion. " Yes," said Thresk, pointing an accusing finger. " Imaginative ! I am one of the practical people. I don't worry about memories. Actual real things interest me— such as Channing's presence now—in this house." And he spoke suddenly, leaning forward with so burning a fire in his eyes and voice that Glynn, in spite of himself, looked nervously across his shoulder. He rose hastily from the sofa, and rather in order to speak than with any thought of what he was saying, he asked :

" When did he die ? "

"Four months ago. I was ill at the time."

"Ah!"

The exclamation sprang from Glynn's lips before he could check it. Here to him was the explanation of Thresk's illusions. But he was sorry that he had not kept silent. For he saw Thresk staring angrily at him.

"What did you mean by your ' Ah ' ? " Thresk asked roughly.

"Merely that I had seen a line about your illness in a newspaper," Glynn explained hastily.

Thresk leaned back satisfied.

"Yes," he resumed. "I broke down. I had had a hard life, you see, and I was paying for it. I am right enough now, however," and his voice rose in a challenge to Glynn to contradict him.

Nothing was further from Glynn's thoughts.

"Of course," he said quickly.

"I saw Channing's death in the obituary column whilst I was lying in bed, and, to tell you the truth, I was relieved by it."

"But I thought you said you didn't mind about Channing ? " Glynn interrupted, and Thresk laughed with a little discomfort.

"Well, perhaps I did mind a little more than I care to admit," Thresk confessed. "At all events, I felt relieved at his death. What a fool I was ! " And he stopped for a moment as though he wondered, now that his mind was so clear, at the delusion which had beset him.

"I thought that it was all over with Channing. Oh, what a fool I was ! Even after he came back and would sidle up to my bedside in his old fawning style, I couldn't bring myself to take him seriously, and I was only amused."

"He came to your bedside ! " exclaimed Glynn.

"Yes," replied Thresk, and he laughed at the recollection. "He came with his humble smirk, and pottered about the room as if he were my nurse. I put out my tongue at him, and told him he was dead and done for, and that he had better not meddle with the bottles on my table. Yes, he amused me. What a fool I was ! I thought no one else saw him. That was my first mistake. I thought he was helpless. . . . That was my second."

Thresk got up from his chair, and, standing over the fireplace, knocked the ash off his cigar.

" Do you remember a great Danish boar-hound I used to have ? " he asked.

" Yes," replied Glynn, puzzled by the sudden change of subject. " But what has the boar-hound to do with your story ? "

" A good deal," said Thresk. " I was very fond of that dog."

" The dog was fond of you," said Glynn.

" Yes. Remember that ! " Thresk cried suddenly. " For it's true." Then he relapsed again into a quiet, level voice. " It took me some time to get well. I was moved up here. It was the one place where I wanted to be. But I wasn't used to sitting round and doing nothing. So the time of my convalescence hung pretty heavily, and, casting about for some way of amusing myself, I wondered whether I could teach the dog to see Channing as I saw him. I tried. Whenever I saw Channing come in at the door, I used to call the dog to my side and point Channing out to him with my finger as Channing moved about the room."

Thresk sat down in a chair opposite to Glynn, and with a singular alertness began to act over again the scenes which had taken place in his sick-room upstairs.

" I used to say, ' Hst ! Hst ! ' ' There ! Do you see ? By the window ! ' or if Channing moved towards Linda I would turn the dog's head and make his eyes follow him across the room. At first the dog saw nothing. Then he began to avoid me, to slink away with his tail between his legs, to growl. He was frightened. Yes, he was frightened ! " And Thresk nodded his head in a quick, interested way.

" He was frightened of you," cried Glynn, " and I don't wonder."

For even to him there was something uncanny and impish in Thresk's quick movements and vivid gestures.

" Wait a bit," said Thresk. " He was frightened, but not of me. He saw Channing. His hair bristled under my fingers as I pointed the fellow out. I had to keep one hand on his neck, you see, to keep him by me. He began to yelp in a queer, panicky way, and tremble—a man in a fever couldn't tremble and shake any more than that dog did.

And then one day, when we were alone together, the dog and I and Channing—the dog sprang at my throat."

" That's how you were wounded ! " cried Glynn, leaping from his sofa. He stood staring in horror at Thresk. " I wonder the dog didn't kill you."

" He very nearly did," said Thresk. " Oh, very nearly."

" You had frightened him out of his wits."

Thresk laughed contemptuously.

" That's the obvious explanation, of course," he said. " But it's not the true one. I have been living amongst the subtleties of life. I know about things now. The dog sprang at me because——" He stopped and glanced uneasily about the room. When he raised his face again, there was a look upon it which Glynn had not seen there before— a look of sudden terror. He leaned forward that he might be the nearer to Glynn, and his voice sank to a whisper— " well, because Channing set him on to me."

It was no doubt less the statement itself than the crafty look which accompanied it, and the whisper which uttered it, that shocked Glynn. But he *was* shocked. There came upon him—yes, even upon him, the sane, prosaic Glynn— a sudden doubt whether, after all, Thresk was mad. It occurred to him as a possibility that Thresk was speaking the mere, bare truth. Suppose that it were the truth ! Suppose that Channing were here ! In this room ! Glynn felt the flesh creep upon his bones.

" Ah, you are beginning to understand," said Thresk, watching his companion. " You are beginning to get frightened, too." And he nodded his head in comprehension. " I used not to know what fear meant. But I knew the meaning well enough as soon as I had guessed why the dog sprang at my throat. For I realised my helplessness."

Throughout their conversation Glynn had been perpetually puzzled by something unexpected in Thresk's conclusions. He followed his reasoning up to a point, and then came a word which left him at a loss. Thresk's fear he understood. But why the sense of helplessness ? And he asked for an explanation.

" Because I had no weapons to fight Channing with," Thresk replied. " I could cope with the living man and win every time. But against the dead man I was helpless. I couldn't hurt him. I couldn't even come to grips with him. I had just to sit by and make room. And that's what I have been doing ever since. I have been sitting by and watching—without a single resource, without a single opportunity of a counterstroke. Oh, I had my time—when Channing was alive. But upon my word, he has the best of it. Here I sit without raising a hand while he recaptures Linda."

" There you are wrong," cried Glynn, seizing gladly, in the midst of these subtleties, upon some fact of which he felt sure. " Your wife is yours. There has been no recapture. Besides, she doesn't believe that Channing is here."

Thresk laughed.

" Do you think she would tell me if she did ? " he asked. " No."

He rose from his chair, and walking to the window, thrust back the curtains and looked out. So he stood for the space of a minute. Then he came back, and looking fixedly at Glynn, said with an air of extraordinary cunning :

" But I have a plan. Yes, I have a plan. I shall get on level terms with Mr. Channing again one of these fine days, and then I'll prove to him for a second time which of us two is the better man."

He made a sign to Glynn, and looked towards the door. It was already opening. He advanced to it as Linda came into the room.

" You have come back, Linda ! I have been talking to Glynn at such a rate that he hasn't been able to get a word in edgeways," he said, with a swift change to a gaiety of voice and manner. " However, I'll show him a good day's sport to-morrow, Linda. We will shoot the bog, and perhaps you'll come out with the luncheon to the sand-hills ? "

Linda Thresk smiled.

" Of course I will," she said. She showed to Glynn a face of gratitude. " It has done you good, Jim, to have a man to talk to," and she laid a hand upon her husband's arm and laughed quite happily. Glynn turned his back upon them and walked up to the window, leaving them standing side by side in the firelight. Outside, the moon shone from a clear sky upon the pools and the reeds of the marsh and the low white sand-hills, chequered with their tufts of grass. But upon the sea beyond, a white mist lay thick and low.

" There's a sea-fog," said Glynn ; and Thresk, at the fire,

suddenly lifted his head, and looked towards the window with a strange intensity. One might have thought that a sea-fog was a strange, unusual thing among the Outer Islands.

" Watch it ! " he said, and there was a vibration in his voice which matched the intensity of his look. " You will see it suddenly creep through the gaps in the sand-hills and pass over the marsh like an army that obeys a command. I have watched it by the hour, time and time again. It gathers on the level of the sea and waits and waits until it seems that the word is given. Then it comes swirling through the gaps of the sand-hills and eats up the marsh in a minute."

Even as he spoke Glynn cried out :

" That's extraordinary ! "

The fog had crept out through the gaps. Only the summits of the sand-hills rose in the moonlight like little peaks above clouds ; and over the marsh the fog burst like cannon smoke and lay curling and writhing up to the very reeds twenty yards from the house. The sapling alone stood high above it, like the mast of a wreck in the sea.

" How high is it ? " asked Thresk.

" Breast high," replied Glynn.

" Only breast high," said Thresk, and there seemed to be a note of disappointment in his voice. However, in the next moment he shook it off. " The fog will be gone before morning," he said. " I'll go and tell Donald to bring the dogs round at nine to-morrow, and have your guns ready. Nine is not too early for you, I suppose ? "

" Not a bit," said Glynn ; and Thresk, going up to the door which led from the house, opened it, went out, and closed it again behind him.

Glynn turned at once toward Linda Thresk. But she held up a warning hand, and waited for the outer door to slam. No sound, however, broke the silence. Glynn went to the inner door and opened it. A bank of white fog, upon which he saw his own shadow most brightly limned by the light behind him, filled the outer passage and crept by him into the room. Glynn closed the latch quickly.

" He has left the outer door open," he said, and, coming back into the room he stood beside the fire looking down into Linda's face.

" He has been talking to me," said Glynn.

Linda looked at him curiously.

" How much did he tell you ? "

" There can be little he left unsaid.   He told me of the dog, of Channing's death——"

" Yes ? "

" Of Channing's return."

" Yes ? "

" And of you."

With each sentence Glynn's embarrassment had increased. Linda, however, held him to his story.

" What did he say of me ? "

" That but for Channing's death he would have held you. That since Channing died—and came back—he had lost you."

Linda nodded her head.   Nothing in Glynn's words surprised her—that was clear.   It was a story already familiar to her which he was repeating.

" Is that all ? " she said.

" I think so.   Yes," replied Glynn, glad to get the business over.   Yet he had omitted the most important part of Thresk's confession—the one part which Linda did not already know.   He omitted it because he had forgotten it.   There was something else which he had in his mind to say.

" When Thresk told me that Channing had won you back, I ventured to say that no one watching you and Thresk, even with the most indifferent eyes, could doubt that it was always and only of him that you were thinking."

" Thank you," said Linda, quietly.   " That is true."

" And now," said Glynn, " I want, in my turn, to ask you a question.   I have been a little curious.   I want, too, to do what I can.   Therefore, I ask you, why did you send for me ? What is it that you think I can do ?   That other friends of yours can't ? "

A slight colour came into Linda's cheeks ; and for a moment she lowered her eyes   She spoke with an accent of apology.

" It is quite true that there are friends whom I see more constantly than you, Mr. Glynn, and upon whom I have, perhaps, greater claims."

" Oh, I did not mean you to think that I was reluctant

to come," Glynn exclaimed, and Linda smiled, lifting her eyes to his.

"No," she said. "I remembered your kindness. It was that recollection which helped me to appeal to you," and she resumed her explanation as though he had never interrupted her.

"Nor was there any particular thing which I thought you could do. But—well, here's the truth—I have been living in terror. This house has become a house of terror. I am frightened, and I have come almost to believe——" and she looked about her with a shiver of her shoulders, sinking her voice to a whisper as she spoke—"that Jim was right—that *he is* here after all."

And Glynn recoiled. Just for a moment the same fancy had occurred to him.

"You don't believe that—really!" he cried.

"No—no," she answered. "Once I think calmly. But it is so difficult to think calmly and reasonably here. Oh——" and she threw up her arms suddenly, and her whole face and eyes were alight with terror—"the very air is to me heavy with fear in this house. It is Jim's quiet certainty."

"Yes, that's it!" exclaimed Glynn, catching eagerly at that explanation because it absolved him to his own common sense for the inexplicable fear which he had felt invade himself. "Yes, Jim's quiet, certain, commonplace way in which he speaks of Channing's presence here. That's what makes his illusion so convincing."

"Well, I thought that if I could get you here, you who——" and she hesitated in order to make her description polite—"are not afflicted by fancies, who are pleasantly sensible"—thus did Linda express her faith that Mr. Glynn was of the earth earthy—"I myself should lose my terror, and Jim, too, might lose his illusion. But now," she looked at him keenly, "I think that Jim is affecting you—that you, too—yes"—she sprang up suddenly and stood before him, with her dark, terror-haunted eyes fixed upon him—"that you, too, believe Mildmay Channing is here."

"No," he protested violently—too violently unless the accusation were true.

"Yes," she repeated, nodding her head quietly. "You, too, believe that Mildmay Channing is here."

And before her horror-stricken face the protest which was on the tip of his tongue remained unuttered. His eyes sought the floor. With a sudden movement of despair Linda turned aside. Even the earthliness of Mr. Glynn had brought her no comfort or security. He had fallen under the spell, as she had done. It seemed that they had no more words to speak to one another. They stood and waited helplessly until Thresk should return.

But that return was delayed.

" He has been a long time speaking to the keeper," said Linda listlessly, and rather to break a silence which was becoming intolerable, than with any intention in the words. But they struck a chord of terror in Glynn's thoughts. He walked quickly to the window, and hastily tore the curtain aside.

The flurry of his movements aroused Linda's attention. She followed him with her eyes. She saw him curve his hands about his forehead and press his face against the pane, even as Thresk had done an hour before. She started forward from the fireplace and Glynn swung round with his arms extended, barring the window. His face was white, his lips shook. The one important statement of Thresk's he now recalled.

" Don't look ! " he cried, and as he spoke, Linda pushed past him. She flung up the window. Outside the fog curled and smoked upon the marsh breast high. The moonlight played upon it ; above it the air was clear and pure, and in the sky stars shone faintly. Above the mist the bare sapling stood like a pointing finger, and halfway between the sapling and the house Thresk's head and shoulders showed plain to see. But they were turned away from the house.

" Jim ! Jim ! " cried Linda, shaking the window-frame with her hand. Her voice rang loudly out on the still air. But Thresk never so much as turned his head. He moved slowly towards the sapling, feeling the unstable ground beneath him with his feet.

" Jim ! Jim ! " again she cried. And behind her she heard a strange, unsteady whispering voice.

" ' On equal terms ! ' That's what he said—I did not understand. He said, ' On equal terms.' "

And even as Glynn spoke, both Linda and he saw Thresk

throw up his arms and sink suddenly beneath the bog. Linda ran to the door, stumbling as she ran, and with a queer, sobbing noise in her throat.

Glynn caught her by the arm.

" It is of no use. You know. Round the sapling—there is no chance of rescue. It is my fault, I should have understood. He had no fear of Channing—if only he could meet him on equal terms."

Linda stared at Glynn. For a little while the meaning of the words did not sink into her mind.

" He said that ! " she cried. " And you did not tell me." She crept back to the fireplace and cowered in front of it, shivering.

" But he said he would come back to me," she said in the voice of a child who has been deceived. " Yes, Jim said he would come back to me."

Of course it was a chance, accident, coincidence, a breath of wind—call it what you will, except what Linda Thresk and Glynn called it. But even as she uttered her complaint, " He said he would come back to me," the latch of the door clicked loudly. There was a rush of cold air into the room. The door swung slowly inwards and stood wide open.

Linda sprang to her feet. Both she and Glynn turned to the open door. The white fog billowed into the room. Glynn felt the hair stir and move upon his scalp. He stood transfixed. Was it possible ? he asked himself. Had Thresk indeed come back to fight for Linda once more, and to fight now as he had fought the first time—on equal terms ? He stood expecting the white fog to shape itself into the likeness of a man. And then he heard a wild scream of laughter behind him. He turned in time to catch Linda as she fell.

Reprinted with the Author's permission from *The Four Corners of the World*.

THE AFFAIR AT THE SEMIRAMIS HOTEL

I

MR. RICARDO, when the excitements of the Villa Rose were done with, returned to Grosvenor Square and resumed the busy, unnecessary life of an amateur. But the studios had lost their savour, artists their attractiveness, and even the Russian opera seemed a trifle flat. Life was altogether a disappointment ; Fate, like an actress at a restaurant, had taken the wooden pestle in her hand and stirred all the sparkle out of the champagne ; Mr. Ricardo languished—until one unforgettable morning.

He was sitting disconsolately at his breakfast-table when the door was burst open and a square, stout man, with the blue shaven face of a French comedian, flung himself into the room. Ricardo sprang towards the new-comer with a cry of delight.

" My dear Hanaud ! "

He seized his visitor by the arm, feeling it to make sure that here, in flesh and blood, stood the man who had introduced him to the acutest sensations of his life. He turned towards his butler, who was still bleating expostulations in the doorway at the unceremonious irruption of the French detective.

" Another place, Burton, at once," he cried, and as soon as he and Hanaud were alone : " What good wind blows you to London ? "

" Business, my friend. The disappearance of bullion somewhere on the line between Paris and London. But it is finished. Yes, I take a holiday."

A light had suddenly flashed in Mr. Ricardo's eyes, and was now no less suddenly extinguished. Hanaud paid no attention whatever to his friend's disappointment. He pounced upon a piece of silver which adorned the tablecloth and took it over to the window.

" Everything is as it should be, my friend," he exclaimed,

with a grin. " Grosvenor Square, *The Times* open at the money column, and a false antique upon the table. Thus I have dreamed of you. All Mr. Ricardo is in that sentence."

Ricardo laughed nervously. Recollection made him wary of Hanaud's sarcasms. He was shy even to protest the genuineness of his silver. But, indeed, he had not the time. For the door opened again and once more the butler appeared. On this occasion, however, he was alone.

" Mr. Calladine would like to speak to you, sir," he said.

" Calladine ! " cried Ricardo in an extreme surprise. " That is the most extraordinary thing." He looked at the clock upon his mantelpiece. It was barely half-past eight. " At this hour, too ? "

" Mr. Calladine is still wearing evening dress," the butler remarked.

Ricardo started in his chair. He began to dream of possibilities ; and here was Hanaud miraculously at his side.

" Where is Mr. Calladine ? " he asked.

" I have shown him into the library."

" Good," said Mr. Ricardo. " I will come to him."

But he was in no hurry. He sat and let his thoughts play with this incident of Calladine's early visit.

" It is very odd," he said. " I have not seen Calladine for months—no, nor has anyone. Yet, a little while ago, no one was more often seen."

He fell apparently into a muse, but he was merely seeking to provoke Hanaud's curiosity. In this attempt, however, he failed. Hanaud continued placidly to eat his breakfast, so that Mr. Ricardo was compelled to volunteer the story which he was burning to tell.

" Drink your coffee, Hanaud, and you shall hear about Calladine."

Hanaud grunted with resignation, and Mr. Ricardo flowed on :

" Calladine was one of England's young men. Everybody said so. He was going to do very wonderful things as soon as he had made up his mind exactly what sort of wonderful things he was going to do. Meanwhile, you met him in Scotland, at Newmarket, at Ascot, at Cowes, in the box of some great lady at the Opera—not before half-past ten in the evening *there*—in any fine house where the candles that night happened to be lit. He went everywhere, and then a day came and he went nowhere. There was no scandal, no trouble, not a whisper against his good name. He simply vanished. For a little while a few people asked : ' What has become of Calladine ? ' But there never was any answer, and London has no time for unanswered questions. Other promising young men dined in his place. Calladine had joined the huge legion of the Come-to-nothings. No one even seemed to pass him in the street. Now unexpectedly, at half-past eight in the morning, and in evening dress, he calls upon me. ' Why ? ' I ask myself."

Mr. Ricardo sank once more into a reverie. Hanaud watched him with a broadening smile of pure enjoyment.

" And in time, I suppose," he remarked casually, " you will perhaps ask him ? "

Mr. Ricardo sprang out of his pose to his feet.

" Before I discuss serious things with an acquaintance," he said with a scathing dignity, " I make it a rule to revive my impressions of his personality. The cigarettes are in the crystal box."

" They would be," said Hanaud unabashed, as Ricardo stalked from the room. But in five minutes Mr. Ricardo came running back, all his composure gone.

" It is the greatest good fortune that you, my friend, should have chosen this morning to visit me," he cried, and Hanaud nodded with a little grimace of resignation.

" There goes my holiday. You shall command me now and always. I will make the acquaintance of your young friend."

He rose up and followed Ricardo into his study, where a young man was nervously pacing the floor.

" Mr. Calladine," said Ricardo. " This is Mr. Hanaud."

The young man turned eagerly. He was tall with a noticeable elegance and distinction, and the face which he showed to Hanaud was, in spite of its agitation, remarkably handsome.

" I am very glad," he said. " You are not an official of this country. You can advise—without yourself taking action, if you'll be so good."

Hanaud frowned. He bent his eyes uncompromisingly upon Calladine.

" What does that mean ? " he asked, with a note of sternness in his voice.

20

" It means, that I must tell someone," Calladine burst out in quivering tones. " That I don't know what to do. I am in a difficulty too big for me. That's the truth."

Hanaud looked at the young man keenly. It seemed to Ricardo that he took in every excited gesture, every twitching feature in one comprehensive glance. Then he said in a friendlier voice :

" Sit down and tell me "—and he himself drew up a chair to the table.

" I was at the Semiramis last night," said Calladine, naming one of the great hotels upon the Embankment. " There was a fancy-dress ball."

All this happened, by the way, in those far-off days before the war—nearly, in fact, four years ago to-day—when London, flinging aside its reticence, its shy self-consciousness, had become a city of carnivals and masquerades, rivalling its neighbours on the Continent in the spirit of its gaiety, and exceeding them by its stupendous luxury.

" I went by the merest chance. My rooms are in the Adelphi Terrace."

" There ! " cried Mr. Ricardo in surprise, and Hanaud lifted a hand to check his interruptions.

" Yes," continued Calladine. " The night was warm, the music floated through my open windows and stirred old memories. I happened to have a ticket. I went."

Calladine drew up a chair opposite to Hanaud, and seating himself, told, with many nervous starts and in troubled tones, a story which, to Mr. Ricardo's thinking, was as fabulous as any out of the " Arabian Nights."

" I had a ticket," he began, " but no domino. I was consequently stopped by an attendant in the lounge at the top of the staircase leading down to the ball-room.

"' You can hire a domino in the cloak-room, Mr. Calladine,' he said to me. I had already begun to regret the impulse which had brought me, and I welcomed the excuse with which the absence of a costume provided me. I was, indeed, turning back to the door, when a girl who had at that moment run down from the stairs of the hotel into the lounge, cried gaily : ' That's not necessary ' ; and at the same moment she flung to me a long scarlet cloak which she had been wearing over her own dress. She was young, fair, rather tall, slim, and very pretty ; her hair was drawn back from her face with a ribbon, and rippled down her shoulders in heavy curls ; and she was dressed in a satin coat and knee-breeches of pale green and gold, with a white waistcoat and silk stockings and scarlet heels to her satin shoes. She was as straight-limbed as a boy, and exquisite like a figure in Dresden china. I caught the cloak and turned to thank her. But she did not wait. With a laugh she ran down the stairs, a supple and shining figure, and was lost in the throng at the doorway of the ball-room. I was stirred by the prospect of an adventure. I ran down after her. She was standing just inside the room alone, and she was gazing at the scene with parted lips and dancing eyes. She laughed again as she saw the cloak about my shoulders, a delicious gurgle of amusement, and I said to her :

" ' May I dance with you ? '

" ' Oh, do ! ' she cried, with a little jump, and clasping her hands. She was of a high and joyous spirit and not difficult in the matter of an introduction. ' This gentleman will do very well to present us,' she said, leading me in front of a bust of the God Pan, which stood in a niche of the wall. ' I am, as you see, straight out of an opera. My name is Celymène or anything with an eighteenth-century sound to it. You are—what you will. For this evening we are friends.'

" ' And for to-morrow ? ' I asked.

" ' I will tell you about that later on,' she replied, and she began to dance with a light step and a passion in her dancing which earned me many an envious glance from the other men. I was in luck, for Celymène knew no one, and though, of course, I saw the faces of a great many people whom I remembered, I kept them all at a distance. We had been dancing for about half an hour when the first queerish thing happened. She stopped suddenly in the midst of a sentence with a little gasp. I spoke to her, but she did not hear. She was gazing past me, her eyes wide open, and such a rapt look upon her face as I had never seen. She was lost in a miraculous vision. I followed the direction of her eyes and, to my astonishment, I saw nothing more than a stout, short, middle-aged woman, egregiously overdressed as Marie Antoinette.

" ' So you do know someone here ? ' I said, and I had to repeat the words sharply before my friend withdrew her eyes.

But even then she was not aware of me. It was as if a voice had spoken to her whilst she was asleep and had disturbed, but not wakened her. Then she came to—there's really no other word I can think of which describes her at that moment—she came to with a deep sigh.

" ' No,' she answered. ' She is a Mrs. Blumenstein from Chicago, a widow with ambitions and a great deal of money. But I don't know her.'

" ' Yet you know all about her,' I remarked.

" ' She crossed in the same boat with me,' Celymène replied. ' Did I tell you that I landed at Liverpool this morning ? She is staying at the Semiramis too. Oh, let us dance ! '

" She twitched my sleeve impatiently, and danced with a kind of violence and wildness as if she wished to banish some sinister thought. And she did undoubtedly banish it. We supped together and grew confidential, as under such conditions people will. She told me her real name. It was Joan Carew.

" ' I have come over to get an engagement if I can at Covent Garden. I am supposed to sing all right. But I don't know anyone. I have been brought up in Italy.'

" ' You have some letters of introduction, I suppose ? ' I asked.

" ' Oh, yes. One from my teacher in Milan. One from an American manager.'

" In my turn I told her my name and where I lived, and I gave her my card. I thought, you see, that since I used to know a good many operatic people, I might be able to help her.

" ' Thank you,' she said, and at that moment Mrs. Blumenstein, followed by a party, chiefly those lapdog young men who always seem to gather about that kind of person, came into the supper-room and took a table close to us. There was at once an end of all confidences—indeed, of all conversation. Joan Carew lost all the lightness of her spirit ; she talked at random, and her eyes were drawn again and again to the grotesque slander on Marie Antoinette. Finally I became annoyed.

" ' Shall we go ? ' I suggested impatiently, and to my surprise she whispered passionately :

" ' Yes. Please ! Let us go.'

" Her voice was actually shaking, her small hands clenched. We went back to the ball-room, but Joan Carew did not recover her gaiety, and half-way through a dance, when we were near to the door, she stopped abruptly—extraordinarily abruptly.

" ' I shall go,' she said abruptly. ' I am tired. I have grown dull.'

" I protested, but she made a little grimace.

" ' You'll hate me in half an hour. Let's be wise and stop now whilst we are friends,' she said, and as I removed the domino from my shoulders she stooped very quickly. It seemed to me that she picked up something which had lain hidden beneath the sole of her slipper. She certainly moved her foot, and I certainly saw something small and bright flash in the palm of her glove as she raised herself again. But I imagined merely that it was some object which she had dropped.

" ' Yes, we'll go,' she said, and we went up the stairs into the lobby. Undoubtedly all the sparkle had gone out of our adventure. I recognised her wisdom.

" ' But I shall meet you again ? ' I asked.

" ' Yes. I have your address. I'll write and fix a time when you will be sure to find me in. Good-night, and a thousand thanks. I should have been bored to tears if you hadn't come without a domino.'

" She was speaking lightly as she held out her hand, but her grip tightened a little and—clung. Her eyes darkened and grew troubled, her mouth trembled. The shadow of a great trouble had suddenly closed about her. She shivered.

" ' I am half inclined to ask you to stay, however dull I am ; and dance with me till daylight—the safe daylight,' she said.

" It was an extraordinary phrase for her to use, and it moved me.

" ' Let us go back then ! ' I urged. She gave me an impression suddenly of someone quite forlorn. But Joan Carew recovered her courage. ' No, no,' she answered quickly. She snatched her hand away and ran lightly up the staircase, turning at the corner to wave her hand and smile. It was then half-past one in the morning."

So far Calladine had spoken without an interruption. Mr. Ricardo, it is true, was bursting to break in with the most important questions, but a salutary fear of Hanaud restrained him. Now, however, he had an opportunity, for Calladine paused.

" Half-past one," he said sagely. " Ah ! "

" And when did you go home ? " Hanaud asked of Calladine.

" True," said Mr. Ricardo. " It is of the greatest consequence."

Calladine was not sure. His partner had left behind her the strangest medley of sensations in his breast. He was puzzled, haunted and charmed. He had to think about her ; he was a trifle uplifted ; sleep was impossible. He wandered for a while about the ball-room. Then he walked to his chambers along the echoing streets and sat at his window ; and some time afterwards the hoot of a motor-horn broke the silence and a car stopped and whirred in the street below. A moment later his bell rang.

He ran down the stairs in a queer excitement, unlocked the street door and opened it. Joan Carew, still in her masquerade dress with her scarlet cloak about her shoulders, slipped through the opening.

" Shut the door," she whispered, drawing herself apart in a corner.

" Your cab ? " asked Calladine.

" It has gone."

Calladine latched the door. Above, in the well of the stairs, the light spread out from the open door of his flat. Down here all was dark. He could just see the glimmer of her white face, the glitter of her dress, but she drew her breath like one who has run far. They mounted the stairs cautiously. He did not say a word until they were both safely in his parlour ; and even then it was in a low voice.

" What has happened ? "

" You remember the woman I stared at ? You didn't know why I stared, but any girl would have understood. She was wearing the loveliest pearls I ever saw in my life."

Joan was standing by the edge of the table. She was tracing with her finger a pattern on the cloth as she spoke. Calladine started with a horrible presentiment.

" Yes," she said. " I worship pearls. I always have done. For one thing, they improve on me. I haven't got any, of course. I have no money. But friends of mine

who do own pearls have sometimes given theirs to me to wear
when they were going sick, and they have always got back
their lustre. I think that has had a little to do with my love
of them. Oh, I have always longed for them—just a little
string. Sometimes I have felt that I would have given my
soul for them."

She was speaking in a dull, monotonous voice. But
Calladine recalled the ecstasy which had shone in her face
when her eyes first had fallen on the pearls, the longing which
had swept her quite into another world, the passion with
which she had danced to throw the obsession off.

"And I never noticed them at all," he said.

"Yet they were wonderful. The colour! The lustre!
All the evening they tempted me. I was furious that a fat,
coarse creature like that should have such exquisite things.
Oh, I was mad!"

She covered her face suddenly with her hands and swayed.
Calladine sprang towards her. But she held out her hand.

"No, I am all right." And though he asked her to sit
down she would not. "You remember when I stopped
dancing suddenly?"

"Yes. You had something hidden under your foot?"

The girl nodded.

"Her key!" And under his breath Calladine uttered a
startled cry.

For the first time since she had entered the room Joan
Carew raised her head and looked at him. Her eyes were
full of terror, and with the terror was mixed an incredulity
as though she could not possibly believe that that had happened which she knew had happened.

"A little Yale key," the girl continued. "I saw Mrs.
Blumenstein looking on the floor for something, and then I
saw it shining on the very spot. Mrs. Blumenstein's suite
was on the same floor as mine, and her maid slept above.
All the maids do. I knew that. Oh, it seemed to me as if
I had sold my soul and was being paid."

Now Calladine understood what she had meant by her
strange phrase—"the safe daylight."

"I went up to my little suite," Joan Carew continued.
"I sat there with the key burning through my glove until I
had given her time enough to fall asleep"—and though she
hesitated before she spoke the words, she did speak them,

not looking at Calladine, and with a shudder of remorse making her confession complete. " Then I crept out. The corridor was dimly lit. Far away below the music was throbbing. Up here it was as silent as the grave. I opened the door—her door. I found myself in a lobby. Her rooms, though bigger, were arranged like mine. I slipped in and closed the door behind me. I listened in the darkness. I couldn't hear a sound. I crept forward to the door in front of me. I stood with my fingers on the handle and my heart beating fast enough to choke me. I had still time to turn back. But I couldn't. There were those pearls in front of my eyes, lustrous and wonderful. I opened the door gently an inch or so—and then—it all happened in a second."

Joan Carew faltered. The night was too near to her, its memory too poignant with terror. She shut her eyes tightly and cowered down in a chair. With the movement her cloak slipped from her shoulders and dropped on to the ground. Calladine leaned forward with an exclamation of horror ; Joan Carew started up.

" What is it ? " she asked.

" Nothing. Go on."

" I found myself inside the room with the door shut behind me. I had shut it myself in a spasm of terror. And I dared not turn round to open it. I was helpless."

" What do you mean ? She was awake ? "

Joan Carew shook her head.

" There were others in the room before me, and on the same errand—men ! "

Calladine drew back, his eyes searching the girl's face.

" Yes ? " he said slowly.

" I didn't see them at first. I didn't hear them. The room was quite dark except for one jet of fierce white light which beat upon the door of a safe. And as I shut the door the jet moved swiftly and the light reached me and stopped. I was blinded. I stood in the full glare of it, drawn up against the panels of the door, shivering, sick with fear. Then I heard a quiet laugh, and someone moved softly towards me. Oh, it was terrible ! I recovered the use of my limbs ; in a panic I turned to the door, but I was too late. Whilst I fumbled with the handle I was seized ; a hand covered my mouth. I was lifted to the centre of the room. The jet went out, the electric lights were turned on. There were two men dressed as apaches in velvet trousers and red scarves, like a hundred others in the ball-room below, and both were masked. I struggled furiously ; but, of course, I was like a child in their grasp. ' Tie her legs,' the man whispered who was holding me ; ' she's making too much noise.' I kicked and fought, but the other man stooped and tied my ankles, and I fainted."

Calladine nodded his head.

" Yes ? " he said.

" When I came to, the lights were still burning, the door of the safe was open, the room empty ; I had been flung on to a couch at the foot of the bed. I was lying there quite free."

" Was the safe empty ? " asked Calladine suddenly.

" I didn't look," she answered. " Oh ! "—and she covered her face spasmodically with her hands. " I looked at the bed. Someone was lying there—under a sheet and quite still. There was a clock ticking in the room ; it was the only sound. I was terrified. I was going mad with fear. If I didn't get out of the room at once I felt that I should go mad, that I should scream and bring everyone to find me alone with—what was under the sheet in the bed. I ran to the door and looked out through a slit into the corridor. It was still quite empty, and below the music still throbbed in the ball-room. I crept down the stairs, meeting no one until I reached the hall. I looked into the ball-room as if I was searching for someone. I stayed long enough to show myself. Then I got a cab and came to you."

A short silence followed. Joan Carew looked at her companion in appeal. " You are the only one I could come to," she added. " I know no one else."

Calladine sat watching the girl in silence. Then he asked, and his voice was hard :

" And is that all you have to tell me ? "

" Yes."

" You are quite sure ? "

Joan Carew looked at him perplexed by the urgency of his question. She reflected for a moment or two.

" Quite."

Calladine rose to his feet and stood beside her.

" Then how do you come to be wearing this ? " he asked, and he lifted a chain of platinum and diamonds which she

20*

was wearing about her shoulders. " You weren't wearing it when you danced with me."

Joan Carew stared at the chain.

" No. It's not mine. I have never seen it before." Then a light came into her eyes. " The two men—they must have thrown it over my head when I was on the couch —before they went." She looked at it more closely. " That's it. The chain's not very valuable. They could spare it, and—it would accuse me—of what they did."

" Yes, that's very good reasoning," said Calladine coldly.

Joan Carew looked quickly up into his face.

" Oh, you don't believe me ! " she cried. " You think— oh, it's impossible ! " And, holding him by the edge of his coat, she burst into a storm of passionate denials.

" But you went to steal, you know," he said gently, and she answered him at once :

" Yes, I did, but not this." And she held up the neck-lace. " Should I have stolen this, should I have come to you wearing it, if I had stolen the pearls, if I had "—and she stopped—" if my story were not true ? "

Calladine weighed her argument, and it affected him.

" No, I think you wouldn't," he said frankly.

Most crimes, no doubt, were brought home because the criminal had made some incomprehensibly stupid mistake ; incomprehensibly stupid, that is, by the standards of normal life. Nevertheless, Calladine was inclined to believe her. He looked at her. That she should have murdered was absurd. Moreover, she was not making a parade of remorse, she was not playing the unctuous penitent ; she had yielded to a temptation, had got herself into desperate straits, and was at her wits' ends how to escape from them. She was frank about herself.

Calladine looked at the clock. It was nearly five o'clock in the morning, and though the music could still be heard from the ball-room in the Semiramis the night had begun to wane upon the river.

" You must go back," he said. " I'll walk with you."

They crept silently down the stairs and into the street. It was only a step to the Semiramis. They met no one until they reached the Strand. There many, like Joan Carew, in masquerade, were standing about, or walking hither and thither in search of carriages and cabs. The whole street was in a bustle, what with drivers shouting and people coming away.

" You can slip in unnoticed," said Calladine as he looked into the thronged courtyard. " I'll telephone to you in the morning."

" You will ? " she cried eagerly, clinging for a moment to his arm.

" Yes, for certain," he replied. " Wait in until you hear from me. I'll think it over. I'll do what I can."

" Thank you," she said fervently.

He watched her scarlet cloak flitting here and there in the crowd until it vanished through the doorway. Then, for the second time, he walked back to his chambers, while the morning crept up the river from the sea.

.   .   .   .   .

This was the story which Calladine told in Mr. Ricardo's library. Mr. Ricardo heard it out with varying emotions. He began with a thrill of expectation like a man on a dark threshold of great excitements. The setting of the story appealed to him, too, by a sort of brilliant bizarrerie which he found in it. But, as it went on, he grew puzzled and a trifle disheartened. There were flaws and chinks ; he began to bubble with unspoken criticisms, with swift and clever thrusts which he dared not deliver. He looked upon the young man with disfavour, as upon one who had half-opened a door upon a theatre of great promise and shown him a spectacle not up to the mark. Hanaud, on the other hand, listened imperturbably, without an expression upon his face, until the end. Then he pointed a finger at Calladine and asked him what to Ricardo's mind was a most irrelevant question.

" You got back to your rooms, then, before five, Mr. Calladine, and it is now nine o'clock less a few minutes."

" Yes."

" Yet you have not changed your clothes. Explain to me that. What did you do between five and half-past eight ? "

Calladine looked down at his rumpled shirt front.

" Upon my word, I never thought of it," he cried. " I was worried out of my mind. I couldn't decide what to do. Finally, I determined to talk to Mr. Ricardo, and after I had come to that conclusion I just waited impatiently until I could come round with decency."

Hanaud rose from his chair. His manner was grave, but conveyed no single hint of an opinion. He turned to Ricardo.

" Let us go round to your young friend's rooms in the Adelphi," he said ; and the three men drove thither at once.

II

Calladine lodged in a corner house and upon the first floor. His rooms, large and square and lofty, with Adam mantelpieces and a delicate tracery upon the ceilings, breathed the grace of the eighteenth century. Broad high windows, embrasured in thick walls, overlooked the river and took in all the sunshine and the air which the river had to give. And they were furnished fittingly. When the three men entered the parlour, Mr. Ricardo was astounded. He had expected the untidy litter of a man run to seed, the neglect and the dust of the recluse. But the room was as clean as the deck of a yacht ; an Aubusson carpet made the floor luxurious underfoot ; a few coloured prints of real value decorated the walls ; and the mahogany furniture was polished so that a lady could have used it as a mirror. There was even by the newspapers upon the round table a china bowl full of fresh red roses. If Calladine had turned hermit, he was a hermit of an unusually fastidious type. Indeed, as he stood with his two companions in his dishevelled dress he seemed quite out of keeping with his rooms.

" So you live here, Mr. Calladine ? " said Hanaud, taking off his hat and laying it down.

" Yes."

" With your servants, of course ? "

" They come in during the day," said Calladine, and Hanaud looked at him curiously.

" Do you mean that you sleep here alone ? "

" Yes."

" But your valet ? "

" I don't keep a valet," said Calladine ; and again the curious look came into Hanaud's eyes.

" Yet," he suggested gently, " there are rooms enough in your set of chambers to house a family."

Calladine coloured and shifted uncomfortably from one foot to the other.

" I prefer at night not to be disturbed," he said, stumbling a little over the words. " I mean, I have a liking for quiet."

Gabriel Hanaud nodded his head with sympathy.

" Yes, yes. And it is a difficult thing to get—as difficult as my holiday," he said ruefully, with a smile for Mr. Ricardo. " However "—he turned towards Calladine— " no doubt, now that you are at home, you would like a bath and a change of clothes. And when you are dressed, perhaps you will telephone to the Semiramis and ask Miss Carew to come round here. Meanwhile, we will read your newspapers and smoke your cigarettes."

Hanaud shut the door upon Calladine, but he turned neither to the papers nor the cigarettes. He crossed the room to Mr. Ricardo, who, seated at the open window, was plunged deep in reflections.

" You have an idea, my friend," cried Hanaud. " It demands to express itself. That sees itself in your face. Let me hear it, I pray."

Mr. Ricardo started out of an absorption which was altogether assumed.

" I was thinking," he said with a far-away smile, " that you might disappear in the forests of Africa, and at once everyone would be very busy about your disappearance. You might leave your village in Leicestershire and live in the fogs of Glasgow, and within a week the whole village would know your postal address. But London—what a city ! How different ! How indifferent ! Turn out of St. James's into the Adelphi Terrace and not a soul will say to you : ' Dr. Livingstone, I presume ? ' "

" But why should they," asked Hanaud, " if your name isn't Dr. Livingstone ? "

Mr. Ricardo smiled indulgently.

" Scoffer ! " he said. " You understand me very well," and he sought to turn the tables on his companion. " And you—does this room suggest nothing to you ? Have you no ideas ? " But he knew very well that Hanaud had. Ever since Hanaud had crossed the threshold he had been like a man stimulated by a drug. His eyes were bright and active, his body alert.

" Yes," he said, " I have."

He was standing now by Ricardo's side with his hands in

his pockets, looking out at the trees on the Embankment and the barges swinging down the river.

" You are thinking of the strange scene which took place in this room such a very few hours ago," said Ricardo. " The girl in her masquerade dress making her confession with the stolen chain about her throat——"

Hanaud looked backwards carelessly. " No, I wasn't giving it a thought," he said, and in a moment or two he began to walk about the room with that curiously light step which Ricardo was never able to reconcile with his cumbersome figure. With the heaviness of a bear he still padded. He went from corner to corner, opened a cupboard here, a drawer of the bureau there, and—stopped suddenly. He stood erect again with a small box of morocco leather in his hand. His body from head to foot seemed to Ricardo to be expressing the question, " Have I found it ? " He pressed a spring and the lid of the box flew open. Hanaud emptied its contents into the palm of his hand. There were two or three sticks of sealing-wax and a seal. With a shrug of the shoulders he replaced them and shut the box.

" You are looking for something," Ricardo announced with sagacity.

" I am," replied Hanaud ; and it seemed that in a second or two he found it. Yet—yet—he found it with his hands in his pockets, if he had found it. Mr. Ricardo saw him stop in that attitude in front of the mantelshelf, and heard him utter a long, low whistle. Upon the mantelshelf some photographs were arranged, a box of cigars stood at one end, a book or two lay between some delicate ornaments of china, and a small engraving in a thin gilt frame was propped at the back against the wall. Ricardo surveyed the shelf from his seat in the window, but he could not imagine which it was of these objects that so drew and held Hanaud's eyes.

Hanaud, however, stepped forward. He looked into a vase and turned it upside down. Then he removed the lid of a porcelain cup, and from the very look of his great shoulders Ricardo knew that he had discovered what he sought. He was holding something in his hands, turning it over, examining it. When he was satisfied he moved swiftly to the door and opened it cautiously. Both men could hear the splashing of water in a bath. Hanaud closed the door

"He moved swiftly to the door and opened it cautiously."

" He moved swiftly to the door and opened it suddenly.

again with a nod of contentment and crossed once more to the window.

" Yes, it is all very strange and curious," he said, " and I do not regret that you dragged me into the affair. You were quite right, my friend, this morning. It is the personality of your young Mr. Calladine which is the interesting thing. For instance, here we are in London in the early summer. The trees out, freshly green, lilac and flowers in the gardens, and I don't know what tingle of hope and expectation in the sunlight and the air. I am middle-aged—yet there's a riot in my blood, a recapture of youth, a belief that just round the corner, beyond the reach of my eyes, wonders wait for me. Don't you, too, feel something like that ? Well, then——" and he heaved his shoulders in astonishment.

" Can you understand a young man with money, with fastidious tastes, good-looking, hiding himself in a corner at such a time—except for some overpowering reason ? No. Nor can I. There is another thing—I put a question or two to Calladine."

" Yes," said Ricardo.

" He has no servants here at night. He is quite alone and—here is what I find interesting—he has no valet. That seems a small thing to you ? " Hanaud asked at a movement from Ricardo. " Well, it is no doubt a trifle, but it's a significant trifle in the case of a young rich man. It is generally a sign that there is something strange, perhaps even something sinister in his life. Mr. Calladine, some months ago, turned out of St. James's into the Adelphi. Can you tell me why ? "

" No," replied Mr. Ricardo. " Can you ? "

Hanaud stretched out a hand. In his open palm lay a small round hairy bulb about the size of a big button and of a colour between green and brown.

" Look ! " he said. " What is that ? "

Mr. Ricardo took the bulb wonderingly.

" It looks to me like the fruit of some kind of cactus."

Hanaud nodded.

" It is. You will see some pots of it in the hot-houses of any really good botanical gardens. Kew has them, I have no doubt. Paris certainly has. They are labelled ' Anhalonium Luinii.' But amongst the Indians of Yucatan the plant has a simpler name."

" What name ? " asked Ricardo.

" Mescal."

Mr. Ricardo repeated the name. It conveyed nothing to him whatever.

" There are a good many bulbs just like that in the cup upon the mantelshelf," said Hanaud.

Ricardo looked quickly up.

" Why ? " he asked.

" Mescal is a drug."

Ricardo started.

" Yes, you are beginning to understand now," Hanaud continued, " why your young friend Calladine turned out of St. James's into the Adelphi Terrace."

Ricardo turned the little bulb over in his fingers.

" You make a decoction of it, I suppose ? " he said.

" Or you can use it as the Indians do in Yucatan," replied Hanaud. " Mescal enters into their religious ceremonies. They sit at night in a circle about a fire built in the forest and chew it, whilst one of their number beats perpetually upon a drum."

Hanaud looked round the room and took notes of its luxurious carpet, its delicate appointments. Outside the window there was a thunder in the streets, a clamour of voices. Boats went swiftly down the river on the ebb. Beyond the mass of the Semiramis rose the great grey-white dome of St. Paul's. Opposite, upon the Southwark bank, the giant sky-signs, the big Highlander drinking whisky, and the rest of them waited, gaunt skeletons, for the night to dress them in fire and give them life. Below the trees in the gardens rustled and waved. In the air were the uplift and the sparkle of the young summer.

" It's a long way from the forests of Yucatan to the Adelphi Terrace of London," said Hanaud. " Yet here, I think in these rooms, when the servants are all gone and the house is very quiet, there is a little corner of wild Mexico."

A look of pity came into Mr. Ricardo's face. He had seen more than one young man of great promise slacken his hold and let go, just for this reason. Calladine, it seemed, was another.

" It's like bhang and kieff and the rest of the devilish things, I suppose," he said, indignantly tossing the button upon the table.

Hanaud picked it up.

" No," he replied. " It's not quite like any other drug. It has a quality of its own which just now is of particular importance to you and me. Yes, my friend "—and he nodded his head very seriously—"we must watch that we do not make the big fools of ourselves in this affair."

" There," Mr. Ricardo agreed with an ineffable air of wisdom, " I am entirely with you."

" Now, why ? " Hanaud asked. Mr. Ricardo was at a loss for a reason, but Hanaud did not wait. " I will tell you Mescal intoxicates, yes—but it does more—it gives to the man who eats of it colour-dreams."

" Colour-dreams ? " Mr. Ricardo repeated in a wondering voice.

" Yes, strange heated dreams, in which violent things happen vividly amongst bright colours. Colour is the gift of this little prosaic brown button." He spun the bulb in the air like a coin, and catching it again, took it over to the mantelpiece and dropped it into the porcelain cup.

" Are you sure of this ? " Ricardo cried excitedly, and Hanaud raised his hand in warning. He went to the door, opened it for an inch or so, and closed it again.

" I am quite sure," he returned. " I have for a friend a very learned chemist in the Collège de France. He is one of those enthusiasts who must experiment upon themselves. He tried this drug."

" Yes," Ricardo said in a quieter voice. " And what did he see ? "

" He had a vision of a wonderful garden bathed in sunlight, an old garden of gorgeous flowers, and emerald lawns, ponds with golden lilies and thick yew hedges—a garden where peacocks stepped indolently and groups of gay people fantastically dressed quarrelled and fought with swords. That is what he saw. And he saw it so vividly that when the vapours of the drug passed from his brain and he waked, he seemed to be coming out of the real world into a world of shifting illusions."

Hanaud's strong, quiet voice stopped, and for a while there was a complete silence in the room. Neither of the two men stirred so much as a finger. Mr. Ricardo once more was conscious of the thrill of strange sensations. He looked round the room. He could hardly believe that a room which had been—nay, was—the home and shrine of mysteries in the dark hours could wear so bright and innocent a freshness in the sunlight of the morning. There should be something sinister which leapt to the eyes as you crossed the threshold.

" Out of the real world," Mr. Ricardo quoted. " I begin to see."

" Yes, you begin to see, my friend, that we must be very careful not to make the big fools of ourselves. My friend of the Collège de France saw a garden. But had he been sitting alone in the window-seat where you are, listening through a summer night to the music of the masquerade at the Semiramis, might he not have seen the ball-room, the dancers, the scarlet cloak, and the rest of this story ? "

" You mean," cried Ricardo, now fairly started, " that Calladine came to us with the fumes of mescal still working in his brain, that the false world was the real one still for him."

" I do not know," said Hanaud. " At present I only put questions. I ask them of you. I wish to hear how they sound. Let us reason this problem out. Calladine, let us say, takes a great deal more of the drug than my professor. It will have on him a more powerful effect while it lasts, and it will last longer. Fancy dress balls are familiar things to Calladine. The music floating from the Semiramis will revive old memories. He sits here, the pageant takes shape before him, he sees himself taking his part in it. Oh, he is happier here sitting quietly in his window-seat than if he were really at the Semiramis. For he *is* there more intensely, more vividly, more really than if he had actually descended this staircase. He lives his story through, the story of a heated brain, the scene of it changes in the way dreams have, it becomes tragic and sinister, it oppresses him with horror, and in the morning, so possessed by it that he does not think to change his clothes, he is knocking at your door."

Mr. Ricardo raised his eyebrows and moved.

" Ah ! You see a flaw in my argument," said Hanaud. But Mr. Ricardo was wary. Too often in other days he had been leaped upon and trounced for a careless remark.

" Let me hear the end of your argument," he said. " There was, then, to your thinking, no temptation of jewels, no theft, no murder, in a word no Celymène ? She was born of recollections and the music of the Semiramis."

" No," cried Hanaud. " Come with me, my friend. I am not so sure that there was no Celymène."

With a smile upon his face, Hanaud led the way across the room. He had the dramatic instinct, and rejoiced in it. He was going to produce a surprise for his companion and savouring the moment in advance, he managed his effects. He walked towards the mantelpiece and stopped a few paces away from it.

" Look ! "

Mr. Ricardo looked and saw a broad Adam mantelpiece. He turned a bewildered face to his friend.

" You see nothing ? " Hanaud asked.

" Nothing ! "

" Look again ! I am not sure—but is it not that Celymène is posing before you ? "

Mr. Ricardo looked again. There was nothing to fix his eyes. He saw a book or two, a cup, a vase or two, and nothing else really except a very pretty and apparently valuable piece of—and suddenly Mr. Ricardo understood. Straight in front of him, in the very centre of the mantelpiece a figure in painted china was leaning against a china stile. It was the figure of a perfectly impossible courtier, feminine and exquisite as could be, and apparelled also even to the scarlet heels exactly as Calladine had described Joan Carew.

Hanaud chuckled with satisfaction when he saw the expression upon Mr. Ricardo's face.

" Ah, you understand," he said. " Do you dream, my friend ? At times—yes, like the rest of us. Then recollect your dreams ? Things, people, which you have seen perhaps that day, perhaps months ago, pop in and out of them without making themselves prayed for. You cannot understand why. Yet sometimes they cut their strange capers there logically too, through subtle associations which the dreamer, once awake, does not apprehend. Thus, our friend here sits in the window, intoxicated by his drug, the music plays in the Semiramis, the curtain goes up in the heated theatre of his brain. He sees himself step upon the stage, and who else meets him but the china figure from his mantelpiece ? "'

Mr. Ricardo for a moment was all enthusiasm. Then his doubt returned to him.

"What you say, my dear Hanaud, is very ingenious. The figure upon the mantelpiece is also extremely convincing. And I should be absolutely convinced but for one thing."

"Yes?" said Hanaud, watching his friend closely.

"I am—I may say it, I think—a man of the world. And I ask myself"—Mr. Ricardo never could ask himself anything without assuming a manner of extreme pomposity—"I ask myself, whether a young man who has given up his social ties, who has become a hermit, and still more, who has become the slave of a drug, would retain that scrupulous carefulness of his body which is indicated by dressing for dinner when alone?"

Hanaud struck the table with the palm of his hand and sat down in a chair.

"Yes. That is the weak point in my theory. You have hit it. I knew it was there—that weak point, and I wondered whether you would seize it. Yes, the consumers of drugs are careless, untidy—even unclean as a rule. But not always. We must be careful. We must wait."

"For what?" asked Ricardo, beaming with pride.

"For the answer to a telephone message," replied Hanaud, with a nod towards the door.

Both men waited impatiently until Calladine came into the room. He wore now a suit of blue serge, he had a clearer eye, his skin a healthier look; he was altogether a more reputable person. But he was plainly very ill at ease. He offered his visitors cigarettes, he proposed refreshments, he avoided entirely and awkwardly the object of their visit. Hanaud smiled. His theory was working out. Sobered by his bath, Calladine had realised the foolishness of which he had been guilty.

"You telephoned to the Semiramis, of course?" said Hanaud cheerfully.

Calladine grew red.

"Yes," he stammered.

"Yet I did not hear that volume of 'Hallos' which precedes telephonic connection in your country of leisure," Hanaud continued.

"I telephoned from my bedroom. You would not hear anything in this room."

" Yes, yes ; the walls of these old houses are solid."
Hanaud was playing with his victim. " And when may we
expect Miss Carew ? "

" I can't say," replied Calladine. " It's very strange.
She is not in the hotel. I am afraid that she has gone
away, fled."

Mr. Ricardo and Hanaud exchanged a look. They were
both satisfied now. There was no word of truth in Calladine's story.

" Then there is no reason for us to wait," said Hanaud.
" I shall have my holiday after all." And while he was yet
speaking the voice of a newsboy calling out the first edition
of an evening paper became distantly audible. Hanaud
broke off his farewell. For a moment he listened, with his
head bent. Then the voice was heard again, confused,
indistinct ; Hanaud picked up his hat and cane, and without
another word to Calladine, raced down the stairs. Mr.
Ricardo followed him, but when he reached the pavement,
Hanaud was half down the little street. At the corner,
however, he stopped, and Ricardo joined him, coughing and
out of breath.

" What's the matter ? " he gasped.

" Listen," said Hanaud.

At the bottom of Duke Street, by Charing Cross Station,
the newsboy was shouting his wares. Both men listened,
and now the words came to them mispronounced but
decipherable.

" Mysterious crime at the Semiramis Hotel."

Ricardo stared at his companion.

" You were wrong then," he cried. " Calladine's story
was true."

For once in a way Hanaud was quite disconcerted.

" I don't know yet," he said. " We will buy a paper."

But before he could move a step a taxi-cab turned into the
Adelphi from the Strand, and wheeling in front of their faces,
stopped at Calladine's door. From the cab a girl descended.

" Let us go back," said Hanaud.

III

Mr. Ricardo could no longer complain. It was half-past
eight when Calladine had first disturbed the formalities of

his house in Grosvenor Square. It was barely ten now, and during that short time he had been flung from surprise to surprise, he had looked underground on a morning of fresh summer, and had been thrilled by the contrast between the queer sinister life below and within and the open call to joy of the green world above. He had passed from incredulity to belief, from belief to incredulity, and when at last incredulity was firmly established, and the story to which he had listened proved the emanation of a drugged and heated brain, lo ! the facts buffeted him in the face, and the story was shown to be true.

" I am alive once more," Mr. Ricardo thought as he turned back with Hanaud, and in his excitement he cried his thought aloud.

" Are you ? " said Hanaud. " And what is life without a newspaper ? If you will buy one from that remarkably raucous boy at the bottom of the street I will keep an eye upon Calladine's house till you come back."

Mr. Ricardo sped down to Charing Cross and brought back a copy of the fourth edition of the *Star*. He handed it to Hanaud, who stared at it doubtfully, folded as it was.

" Shall we see what it says ? " Ricardo asked impatiently.

" By no means," Hanaud answered, waking from his reverie and tucking briskly away the paper into the tail pocket of his coat. " We will hear what Miss Joan Carew has to say, with our minds undisturbed by any discoveries. I was wondering about something totally different."

" Yes ? " Mr. Ricardo encouraged him. " What was it ? "

" I was wondering, since it is only ten o'clock, at what hour the first editions of the evening papers appear."

" It is a question," Mr. Ricardo replied sententiously, " which the greatest minds have failed to answer."

And they walked along the street to the house. The front door stood open during the day like the front door of any other house which is let off in sets of rooms. Hanaud and Ricardo went up the staircase and rang the bell of Calladine's door. A middle-aged woman opened it.

" Mr. Calladine is in ? " said Hanaud.

" I will ask," replied the woman. " What name shall I say ? "

" It does not matter. I will go straight in," said Hanaud quietly. " I was here with my friend but a minute ago."

He went straight forward and into Calladine's parlour. Mr. Ricardo looked over his shoulder as he opened the door and saw a girl turn to them suddenly a white face of terror, and flinch as though already she felt the hand of a constable upon her shoulder. Calladine, on the other hand, uttered a cry of relief.

" These are my friends," he exclaimed to the girl, " the friends of whom I spoke to you " ; and to Hanaud he said : " This is Miss Carew."

Hanaud bowed.

" You shall tell me your story, mademoiselle," he said very gently, and a little colour returned to the girl's cheeks, a little courage revived in her.

" But you have heard it," she answered.

" Not from you," said Hanaud.

So for a second time in that room she told the history of that night. Only this time the sunlight was warm upon the world, the comfortable sounds of life's routine were borne through the windows, and the girl herself wore the inconspicuous blue serge of a thousand other girls afoot that morning. These trifles of circumstance took the edge of sheer horror off her narrative, so that, to tell the truth, Mr. Ricardo was a trifle disappointed. He wanted a crescendo motive in his music, whereas it had begun at its fortissimo. Hanaud, however, was the perfect listener. He listened without stirring and with most compassionate eyes, so that Joan Carew spoke only to him, and to him, each moment that passed, with greater confidence. The life and sparkle of her had gone altogether. There was nothing in her manner now to suggest the waywardness, the gay irresponsibility, the radiance which had attracted Calladine the night before. She was just a very young and very pretty girl, telling in a low and remorseful voice of the tragic dilemma to which she had brought herself. Of Celymène all that remained was something exquisite and fragile in her beauty, in the slimness of her figure, in her daintiness of hand and foot—something almost of the hot-house. But the story she told was, detail for detail, the same which Calladine had already related.

" Thank you," said Hanaud when she had done. " Now I must ask you two questions."

" I will answer them."

Mr. Ricardo sat up. He began to think of a third question which he might put himself, something uncommonly subtle and searching, which Hanaud would never have thought of. But Hanaud put his questions, and Ricardo almost jumped out of his chair.

"You will forgive me, Miss Carew. But have you ever stolen before ? "

Joan Carew turned upon Hanaud with spirit. Then a change swept over her face.

"You have a right to ask," she answered. "Never." She looked into his eyes as she answered. Hanaud did not move. He sat with a hand upon each knee and led to his second question.

"Early this morning, when you left this room, you told Mr. Calladine that you would wait at the Semiramis until he telephoned to you ? "

"Yes."

"Yet when he telephoned, you had gone out ? "

"Yes."

"Why ? "

"I will tell you," said Joan Carew. "I could not bear to keep the little diamond chain in my room."

For a moment even Hanaud was surprised. He had lost sight of that complication. Now he leaned forward anxiously ; indeed, with a greater anxiety than he had yet shown in all this affair.

"I was terrified," continued Joan Carew. "I kept thinking : ' They must have found out by now. They will search everywhere.' I didn't reason. I lay in bed expecting to hear every moment a loud knocking on the door. Besides— the chain itself being there in my bedroom—her chain—the dead woman's chain—no, I couldn't endure it. I felt as if I had stolen it. Then my maid brought in my tea."

"You had locked it away ? " cried Hanaud.

"Yes. My maid did not see it."

Joan Carew explained how she had risen, dressed, wrapped the chain in a pad of cotton-wool and enclosed it in an envelope. The envelope had not the stamp of the hotel upon it. It was a rather large envelope, one of a packet which she had bought in a crowded shop in Oxford Street on her way from Euston to the Semiramis. She had bought the envelopes of that particular size in order that when she sent her letter of introduction to the Director of the Opera at Covent Garden she might enclose with it a photograph.

" And to whom did you send it ? " asked Mr. Ricardo.

" To Mrs. Blumenstein at the Semiramis. I printed the address carefully. Then I went out and posted it."

" Where ? " Hanaud inquired.

" In the big letter-box of the Post Office at the corner of Trafalgar Square."

Hanaud looked at the girl sharply.

" You had your wits about you, I see," he said.

" What if the envelope gets lost ? " said Ricardo.

Hanaud laughed grimly.

" If one envelope is delivered at its address in London to-day, it will be that one," he said. " The news of the crime is published, you see," and he swung round to Joan.

" Did you know that, Miss Carew ? "

" No," she answered in an awe-stricken voice.

" Well, then, it is. Let us see what the special investigator has to say about it." And Hanaud, with a deliberation which Mr. Ricardo found quite excruciating, spread out the newspaper on the table in front of him.

IV

There was only one new fact in the couple of columns devoted to the mystery. Mrs. Blumenstein had died from chloroform poisoning. She was of a stout habit, and the thieves were not skilled in the administration of the anæsthetic.

" It's murder none the less," said Hanaud, and he gazed straight at Joan, asking her by the direct summons of his eyes what she was going to do.

" I must tell my story to the police," she replied painfully and slowly. But she did not hesitate ; she was announcing a meditated plan.

Hanaud neither agreed nor differed. His face was blank, and when he spoke there was no cordiality in his voice.

" Well," he asked, " and what is it that you have to say to the police, miss ? That you went into the room to steal, and that you were attacked by two strangers, dressed as apaches, and masked ? That is all ? "

" Yes."

" And how many men at the Semiramis ball were dressed as apaches and wore masks ? Come ! Make a guess. A hundred at the least ? "

" I should think so."

" Then what will your confession do beyond—I quote your English idiom—putting you in the coach ? "

Mr. Ricardo now smiled, with relief. Hanaud was taking a definite line. His knowledge of idiomatic English might be incomplete, but his heart was in the right place. The girl traced a vague pattern on the tablecloth with her finger.

" Yet I think I must tell the police," she repeated, looking up and dropping her eyes again. Mr. Ricardo noticed that her eyelashes were very long. For the first time Hanaud's face relaxed.

" And I think you are right quite," he cried heartily, to Mr. Ricardo's surprise. " Tell them the truth before they suspect it, and they will help you out of the affair if they can. Not a doubt of it. Come, I will go with you myself to Scotland Yard."

" Thank you," said Joan, and the pair drove away in a cab together.

Hanaud returned to Grosvenor Square alone and lunched with Ricardo.

" It was all right," he said. " The police were very kind. Miss Joan Carew told her story to them as she had told it to us. Fortunately, the envelope with the platinum chain had already been delivered, and was in their hands. They were much mystified about it, but Miss Joan's story gave them a reasonable explanation. I think they are inclined to believe her ; and, if she is speaking the truth, they will keep her out of the witness-box if they can."

" She is to stay here in London, then ? " asked Ricardo.

" Oh, yes ; she is not to go. She will present her letters at the Opera House and secure an engagement, if she can. The criminals might be lulled thereby into a belief that the girl had kept the whole strange incident to herself, and that there was nowhere even a knowledge of the disguise which they had used." Hanaud spoke as carelessly as if the matter was not very important ; and Ricardo, with an unusual flash of shrewdness, said :

" It is clear, my friend, that you do not think those two men will ever be caught at all."

Hanaud shrugged his shoulders.

"There is always a chance. But, listen. There is a room with a hundred guns, one of which is loaded. Outside the room there are a hundred pigeons, one of which is white. You are taken into the room blindfolded. You choose the loaded gun and you shoot the one white pigeon. That is the value of the chance."

"But," exclaimed Ricardo, "those pearls were of great value and I have heard at a trial expert evidence given by pearl merchants. All agree that the pearls of great value are known ; so, when they come upon the market——"

"That is true," Hanaud interrupted imperturbably. "But how are they known ? "

"By their weight," said Mr. Ricardo.

"Exactly," replied Hanaud. "But did you not also hear at this trial of yours that pearls can be peeled like an onion ? No ? It is true. Remove a skin, two skins, the weight is altered, the pearl is a trifle smaller. It has lost a little of its value, yes—but you can no longer identify it as the so-and-so pearl which belonged to this or that sultan, was stolen by the vizier, bought by Messrs. Lustre and Steinopolis, of Hatton Garden, and subsequently sold to the wealthy Mrs. Blumenstein. No, your pearl has vanished altogether. There is a new pearl which can be traded." He looked at Ricardo. "Who shall say that those pearls are not already in one of the queer little back streets of Amsterdam, undergoing their transformation ? "

Mr. Ricardo was not persuaded because he would not be. "I have some experience in these matters," he said loftily to Hanaud. "I am sure that we shall lay our hands upon the criminals. We have never failed."

Hanaud grinned from ear to ear. The only experience which Mr. Ricardo had ever had was gained on the shores of Geneva and at Aix under Hanaud's tuition. But Hanaud did not argue, and there the matter rested.

The days flew by. It was London's play-time. The green and gold of early summer deepened and darkened ; wondrous warm nights under England's pale blue sky, when the streets rang with the joyous feet of youth, led in clear dawns and lovely glowing days. Hanaud made acquaintance with the wooded reaches of the Thames ; Joan Carew sang "Louise" at Covent Garden with notable success ; and the affair of the Semiramis Hotel, in the minds of the few who remembered it, was already added to the long list of un-fathomed mysteries.

But towards the end of May there occurred a startling development. Joan Carew wrote to Mr. Ricardo that she would call upon him in the afternoon, and she begged him to secure the presence of Hanaud. She came as the clock struck; she was pale and agitated; and in the room where Calladine had first told the story of her visit she told another story which, to Mr. Ricardo's thinking, was yet more strange and—yes—yet more suspicious.

" It has been going on for some time," she began. " I thought of coming to you at once. Then I wondered whether, if I waited—oh, you'll never believe me ! "

" Let us hear ! " said Hanaud patiently.

" I began to dream of that room, the two men disguised and masked, the still figure in the bed. Night after night ! I was terrified to go to sleep. I felt the hand upon my mouth. I used to catch myself falling asleep, and walk about the room with all the lights up to keep myself awake."

" But you couldn't," said Hanaud with a smile. " Only the old can do that."

" No, I couldn't," she admitted; " and—oh, my nights were horrible until "—she paused and looked at her com-panions doubtfully—" until one night the mask slipped."

" What——? " cried Hanaud, and a note of sternness rang suddenly in his voice. " What are you saying ? "

With a desperate rush of words, and the colour staining her forehead and cheeks, Joan Carew continued :

" It is true. The mask slipped on the face of one of the men—of the man who held me. Only a little way; it just left his forehead visible—no more."

" Well ? " asked Hanaud, and Mr. Ricardo leaned forward, swaying between the austerity of criticism and the desire to believe so thrilling a revelation.

" I waked up," the girl continued, " in the darkness, and for a moment the whole scene remained vividly with me— for just long enough for me to fix clearly in my mind the figure of the apache with the white forehead showing above the mask."

" When was that ? " asked Ricardo.

" A fortnight ago."

" Why didn't you come with your story then ? "

" I waited," said Joan. " What I had to tell wasn't yet helpful. I thought that another night the mask might slip lower still. Besides I—it is difficult to describe just what I felt. I felt it important just to keep that photograph in my mind, not to think about it, not to talk about it, not even to look at it too often lest I should begin to imagine the rest of the face and find something familiar in the man's carriage and shape when there was nothing really familiar to me at all. Do you understand that ? " she asked, with her eyes fixed in appeal on Hanaud's face.

" Yes," replied Hanaud. " I follow your thought."

" I thought there was a chance now—the strangest chance —that the truth might be reached. I did not wish to spoil it," and she turned eagerly to Ricardo, as if, having persuaded Hanaud, she would now turn her batteries on his companion. " My whole point of view was changed. I was no longer afraid of falling asleep lest I should dream. I wished to dream, but——"

" But you could not," suggested Hanaud.

" No, that is the truth," replied Joan Carew. " Whereas before I was anxious to keep awake and yet must sleep from sheer fatigue, now that I tried consciously to put myself to sleep I remained awake all through the night, and only towards morning, when the light was coming through the blinds, dropped off into a heavy, dreamless slumber."

Hanaud nodded.

" It is a very perverse world, Miss Carew, and things go by contraries."

Ricardo listened for some note of irony in Hanaud's voice, some look of disbelief in his face. But there was neither the one nor the other. Hanaud was listening patiently.

" Then came my rehearsals," Joan Carew continued, " and that wonderful opera drove everything else out of my head. I had such a chance, if only I could make use of it. When I went to bed now, I went with that haunting music in my ears—the call of Paris—oh, you must remember it. But can you realise what it must mean to a girl who is going to sing it for the first time in Covent Garden ? "

Mr. Ricardo saw his opportunity. He, the connoisseur, to whom the psychology of the green room was as an open book, could answer that question.

"It is true, my friend," he informed Hanaud with quiet authority. "The great march of events leaves the artist cold. He lives aloof. While the tumbrils thunder in the streets he adds a delicate tint to the picture he is engaged upon or recalls his triumph in his last great part."

"Thank you," said Hanaud gravely. "And now Miss Carew may perhaps resume her story."

"It was the very night of my début," she continued. "I had supper with some friends. A great artist, Carmen Valeri,"—and as Joan Carew uttered the name, almost imperceptibly Hanaud started—"honoured me also with her presence. I went home excited, and that night I dreamed again."

"Yes?"

"This time the chin, the lips, the eyes were visible. There was only a black strip across the middle of the face. And I thought—nay, I was sure—that if that strip vanished I should know the man."

"And it did vanish?"

"Three nights afterwards."

"And you did know the man?"

The girl's face became troubled. She frowned.

"I knew the face, that was all," she answered. "I was disappointed. I had never spoken to the man. I am sure of that still. But somewhere I have seen him."

"You don't even remember when?" asked Hanaud.

"No." Joan Carew reflected for a moment with her eyes upon the carpet, and then flung up her head with a gesture of despair. "No. I try all the time to remember. But it is no good."

Mr. Ricardo could not restrain a movement of indignation. He was being played with. The girl with her fantastic story had worked him up to a real pitch of excitement only to make a fool of him. All his earlier suspicions flowed back into his mind. What if, after all, she was implicated in the murder and the theft? What if, with a perverse cunning, she had told Hanaud and himself just enough of what she knew, just enough of the truth, to persuade them to protect her? What if her frank confession of her own overpowering impulse to steal the necklace was nothing more than a subtle appeal to the sentimental pity of men, an appeal based upon a wider knowledge of men's weaknesses than a girl of nineteen or twenty ought to have ? Mr. Ricardo cleared his throat and sat forward in his chair. He was girding himself for a singularly searching interrogatory when Hanaud asked the most irrelevant of questions :

" How did you pass the evening of that night when you first dreamed complete the face of your assailant ? "

Joan Carew reflected. Then her face cleared.

" I know," she exclaimed. " I was at the opera."

" And what was being given ? "

" ' The Jewels of the Madonna.' "

Hanaud nodded his head. To Ricardo it seemed that he had expected precisely that answer.

" Now," he continued, " you are sure that you have seen this man ? "

" Yes."

" Very well," said Hanaud. " There is a game you play at children's parties—is there not ?—animal, vegetable or mineral, and always you get the answer. Let us play that game for a few minutes, you and I."

Joan Carew drew up her chair to the table and sat with her chin propped upon her hands and her eyes fixed on Hanaud's face. As he put each question she pondered on it and answered. If she answered doubtfully he pressed it.

" You crossed on the *Lucania* from New York ? "

" Yes."

" Picture to yourself the dining-room, the tables. You have the picture quite clear ? "

" Yes."

" Was it at breakfast that you saw him ? "

" No."

" At luncheon ? "

" No."

" At dinner ? "

She paused for a moment, summoning before her eyes the travellers at the tables.

" No."

" Not in the dining-room at all, then ? "

" No."

" In the library, when you were writing letters, did you not one day lift your head and see him ? "

" No."

" On the promenade deck ? Did he pass you when you

21

sat in your deck-chair, or did you pass him when he sat in his chair ? "

" No."

Step by step Hanaud took her back to New York, to her hotel, to journeys in the train. Then he carried her to Milan, where she had studied. It was extraordinary to Ricardo to realise how much Hanaud knew of the curriculum of a student aspiring to grand opera. From Milan he brought her again to New York, and at the last, with a start of joy, she cried : " Yes, it was there."

Hanaud took his handkerchief from his pocket and wiped his forehead.

" Ouf ! " he grunted. " To concentrate the mind on a day like this, it makes one hot, I can tell you. Now, Miss Carew, let us hear."

It was at a concert at the house of a Mrs. Starling in Fifth Avenue and in the afternoon. Joan Carew sang. She was a stranger to New York and very nervous. She saw nothing but a mist of faces whilst she sang, but when she had finished the mist cleared, and as she left the improvised stage she saw the man. He was standing against the wall in a line of men. There was no particular reason why her eyes should single him out, except that he was paying no attention to her singing, and, indeed, she forgot him altogether afterwards.

" I just happened to see him clearly and distinctly," she said. " He was tall, clean-shaven, rather dark, not par- ticularly young—thirty-five or so, I should say—a man with a heavy face and beginning to grow stout. He moved away whilst I was bowing to the audience, and I noticed him after- wards walking about, talking to people."

" Do you remember to whom ? "

" No."

" Did he notice you, do you think ? "

" I am sure he didn't," the girl replied emphatically. " He never looked at the stage where I was singing, and he never looked towards me afterwards."

She gave, so far as she could remember, the names of such guests and singers as she knew at that party. Carmen Valeri was amongst them. " And that is all," she said.

" Thank you," said Hanaud. " It is perhaps a good deal. But it is perhaps nothing at all."

" You will let me hear from you ? " she cried, as she rose to her feet.

" Miss Carew, I am at your service," he returned. She gave him her hand timidly and he took it cordially. For Mr. Ricardo she had merely a bow, a bow which recognised that he distrusted her and that she had no right to be offended. Then she went, and Hanaud smiled across the table at Ricardo.

" Yes," he said, " all that you are thinking is true enough. A man who slips out of society to indulge a passion for a drug in greater peace, a girl who, on her own confession, tried to steal, and, to crown all, this fantastic story. It is natural to disbelieve every word of it. But we disbelieved before, when we left Calladine's lodging in the Adelphi, and we were wrong. Let us be warned."

" You have an idea ? " exclaimed Ricardo.

" Perhaps ! " said Hanaud. And he looked down the theatre column of *The Times*. " Let us distract ourselves by going to the theatre."

" You are the most irritating man ! " Mr. Ricardo broke out impulsively. " If I had to paint your portrait, I should paint you with your finger against the side of your nose, saying mysteriously : ' *I* know,' when you know nothing at all."

Hanaud made a schoolboy's grimace. " We will go and sit in your box at the opera to-night," he said, " and you shall explain to me all through the beautiful music the theory of the tonic sol-fa."

They reached Covent Garden before the curtain rose. Mr. Ricardo's box was on the lowest tier and next to the omnibus box.

" We are near the stage," said Hanaud, as he took his seat in the corner and so arranged the curtain that he could see and yet was hidden from view. " I like that."

The theatre was full ; stalls and boxes shimmered with jewels and satin, and all that was famous that season for beauty and distinction had made its tryst there that night.

" Yes, this is wonderful," said Hanaud. " What opera do they play ? " He glanced at his programme and cried, with a little start of surprise : " We are in luck. It is ' The Jewels of the Madonna.' "

" Do you believe in omens ? " Mr. Ricardo asked coldly. He had not yet recovered from his rebuff of the afternoon.

" No, but I believe that Carmen Valeri is at her best in this part," said Hanaud.

Mr. Ricardo belonged to that body of critics which must needs spoil your enjoyment by comparisons and recollections of other great artists. He was at a disadvantage certainly to-night, for the opera was new. But he did his best. He imagined others in the part, and when the great scene came at the end of the second act, and Carmen Valeri, on obtaining from her lover the jewels stolen from the sacred image, gave such a display of passion as fairly enthralled that audience, Mr. Ricardo sighed quietly and patiently.

" How Calvé would have brought out the psychological value of that scene ! " he murmured ; and he was quite vexed with Hanaud, who sat with his opera glasses held to his eyes, and every sense apparently concentrated on the stage. The curtains rose and rose again when the act was concluded, and still Hanaud sat motionless as the Sphinx, staring through his glasses.

" That is all," said Ricardo when the curtains fell for the fifth time.

" They will come out," said Hanaud. " Wait ! " And from between the curtains Carmen Valeri was led out into the full glare of the footlights with the panoply of jewels flashing on her breast. Then at last Hanaud put down his glasses and turned to Ricardo with a look of exultation and genuine delight upon his face which filled that season-worn dilettante with envy.

" What a night ! " said Hanaud. " What a wonderful night ! " And he applauded until he split his gloves. At the end of the opera he cried : " We will go and take supper at the Semiramis. Yes, my friend, we will finish our evening like gallant gentlemen. Come ! Let us not think of the morning." And boisterously he slapped Ricardo in the small of the back.

In spite of his boast, however, Hanaud hardly touched his supper, and he played with, rather than drank, his brandy and soda. He had a little table to which he was accustomed beside a glass screen in the depths of the room, and he sat with his back to the wall watching the groups which poured in. Suddenly his face lighted up.

" Here is Carmen Valeri ! " he cried. " Once more we
are in luck. Is it not that she is beautiful ? "

Mr. Ricardo turned languidly about in his chair and put
up his eyeglass.

" So, so," he said.

" Ah ! " returned Hanaud. " Then her companion will
interest you still more. For he is the man who murdered
Mrs. Blumenstein."

Mr. Ricardo jumped so that his eyeglass fell down and
tinkled on its cord against the buttons of his waistcoat.

" What ? " he exclaimed. " It's impossible ! " He looked
again. " Certainly the man fits Joan Carew's description.
But——" He turned back to Hanaud utterly astounded.
And as he looked at the Frenchman all his earlier recollections of him, of his swift deductions, of the subtle imagination which his heavy body so well concealed crowded in
upon Ricardo and convinced him.

" How long have you known ? " he asked in a whisper of
awe.

" Since ten o'clock to-night."

" But you will have to find the necklace before you can
prove it."

" The necklace ! " said Hanaud carelessly. " That is
already found."

Mr. Ricardo had been longing for a thrill. He had it now.
He felt it in his very spine.

" It's found ? " he said in a startled whisper.

" Yes."

Ricardo turned again, with as much indifference as he
could assume, towards the couple who were settling down at
their table, the man with a surly indifference, Carmen Valeri
with the radiance of a woman who has just achieved a
triumph and is now free to enjoy the fruits of it. Confusedly,
recollections returned to Ricardo of questions put that
afternoon by Hanaud to Joan Carew—subtle questions into
which the name of Carmen Valeri was continually entering.
She was a woman of thirty, certainly beautiful, with a clear,
pale face and eyes like the night.

" Then she is implicated too ! " he said. What a change
for her, he thought, from the stage of Covent Garden to the
felon's cell, from the gay supper-room of the Semiramis,
with its bright frocks and its babel of laughter, to the silence

and the ignominious garb of the work-rooms in Aylesbury Prison.

" She ? " exclaimed Hanaud ; and in his passion for the contrasts of drama, Ricardo was almost disappointed. " She has nothing whatever to do with it. She knows nothing. André Favart there—yes. But Carmen Valeri ! She's as stupid as an owl, and loves him beyond words. Do you want to know how stupid she is ? You shall know. I asked Mr. Clements, the director of the opera house, to take supper with us, and here he is."

Hanaud stood up and shook hands with the director. He was of the world of business rather than of art, and long experience of the ways of tenors and prima-donnas had given him a good-humoured cynicism.

" They are spoilt children, all tantrums and vanity," he said, " and they would ruin you to keep a rival out of the theatre."

He told them anecdote upon anecdote.

" And Carmen Valeri," Hanaud asked in a pause ; " is she troublesome this season ? "

" Has been," replied Clements dryly. " At present she is playing at being good. But she gave me a turn some weeks ago." He turned to Ricardo. " Superstition's her trouble, and André Favart knows it. She left him behind in America this spring."

" America ! " suddenly cried Ricardo ; so suddenly that Clements looked at him in surprise.

" She was singing in New York, of course, during the winter," he returned. " Well, she left him behind, and I was shaking hands with myself when he began to deal the cards over there. She came to me in a panic. She had just had a cable. She couldn't sing on Friday night. There was a black knave next to the nine of diamonds. She wouldn't sing for worlds. And it was the first night of ' The Jewels of the Madonna ' ! Imagine the fix I was in ! "

" What did you do ? " asked Ricardo.

" The only thing there was to do," replied Clements with a shrug of the shoulders. " I cabled Favart some money and he dealt the cards again. She came to me beaming. Oh, she had been so distressed to put me in the cart. But what could she do ? Now there was a red queen next to the ace of hearts, so she could sing without a scruple so long, of course, as she didn't pass a funeral on the way down to the Opera House. Luckily she didn't. But my money brought Favart over here, and now I'm living on a volcano. For he's the greatest scoundrel unhung. He never has a farthing, however much she gives him ; he's a blackmailer, he's a swindler, he has no manners and no graces, he looks like a butcher and treats her as if she were dirt, he never goes near the Opera except when she is singing in this part, and she worships the ground he walks on. Well, I suppose it's time to go."

The lights had been turned off, the great room was emptying. Mr. Ricardo and his friends rose to go, but at the door Hanaud detained Mr. Clements, and they talked together alone for some little while, greatly to Mr. Ricardo's annoyance. Hanaud's good humour, however, when he rejoined his friend, was enough for two.

" I apologise, my friend, with my hand on my heart. But it was for your sake that I stayed behind. You have a meretricious taste for melodrama which I deeply deplore, but which I mean to gratify. I ought to leave for Paris to-morrow, but I shall not. I shall stay until Thursday." And he skipped upon the pavement as they walked home to Grosvenor Square.

Mr. Ricardo bubbled with questions, but he knew his man. He would get no answer to any one of them to-night. So he worked out the problem for himself as he lay awake in his bed, and he came down to breakfast next morning fatigued but triumphant. Hanaud was already chipping off the top of his egg at the table.

" So I see you have found it all out, my friend," he said.

" Not all," replied Ricardo modestly, " and you will not mind, I am sure, if I follow the usual custom and wish you a good-morning."

" Not at all," said Hanaud. " I am all for good manners myself."

He dipped his spoon into his egg.

" But I am longing to hear the line of your reasoning."

Mr. Ricardo did not need much pressing.

" Joan Carew saw André Favart at Mrs. Starling's party, and saw him with Carmen Valeri. For Carmen Valeri was there. I remember that you asked Joan for the names of the artistes who sang, and Carmen Valeri was amongst them."

Hanaud nodded his head.

" Exactly."

" No doubt Joan Carew noticed Carmen Valeri particularly, and so took unconsciously into her mind an impression of the man who was with her, André Favart—of his build, of his walk, of his type."

Again Hanaud agreed.

" She forgets the man altogether, but the picture remains latent in her mind—an undeveloped film."

Hanaud looked up in surprise, and the surprise flattered Mr. Ricardo. Not for nothing had he tossed about in his bed for the greater part of the night.

" Then came the tragic night at the Semiramis. She does not consciously recognise her assailant, but she dreams the scene again and again, and by a process of unconscious cerebration the figure of the man becomes familiar. Finally she makes her début, is entertained at supper afterwards, and meets once more Carmen Valeri."

" Yes, for the first time since Mrs. Starling's party," interjected Hanaud.

" She dreams again, she remembers asleep more than she remembers when awake. The presence of Carmen Valeri at her supper-party has its effect. By a process of association, she recalls Favart, and the mask slips on the face of her assailant. Some days later she goes to the Opera. She hears Carmen Valeri sing in ' The Jewels of the Madonna.' No doubt the passion of her acting, which I am more prepared to acknowledge this morning than I was last night, affects Joan Carew powerfully, emotionally. She goes to bed with her head full of Carmen Valeri, and she dreams not of Carmen Valeri, but of the man who is unconsciously associated with Carmen Valeri in her thoughts. The mask vanishes altogether. She sees her assailant now, has his portrait limned in her mind, would know him if she met him in the street, though she does not know by what means she identified him."

" Yes," said Hanaud. " It is curious the brain working while the body sleeps, the dream revealing what thought cannot recall."

Mr. Ricardo was delighted. He was taken seriously.

" But, of course," he said, " I could not have worked the problem out but for you. You knew of André Favart and the kind of man he was."

Hanaud laughed.

" Yes. That is always my one little advantage. I know all the cosmopolitan blackguards of Europe." His laughter ceased suddenly, and he brought his clenched fist heavily down upon the table. " Here is one of them who will be very well out of the world, my friend," he said very quietly, but there was a look of force in his face and a hard light in his eyes, which made Mr. Ricardo shiver.

For a few moments there was silence. Then Ricardo asked : " But have you evidence enough ? "

" Yes."

" Your two chief witnesses, Calladine and Joan Carew— you said it yourself—there are facts to discredit them. Will they be believed ? "

" But they won't appear in the case at all," Hanaud said. " Wait, wait ! " and once more he smiled. " By the way, what is the number of Calladine's house ? "

Ricardo gave it, and Hanaud therefore wrote a letter. " It is all for your sake, my friend," he said with a chuckle.

" Nonsense," said Ricardo. " You have the spirit of the theatre in your bones."

" Well, I shall not deny it," said Hanaud, and he sent out the letter to the nearest pillar-box.

Mr. Ricardo waited in a fever of impatience until Thursday came. At breakfast Hanaud would talk of nothing but the news of the day. At luncheon he was no better. The affair of the Semiramis Hotel seemed a thousand miles from any of his thoughts. But at five o'clock he said as he drank his tea :

" You know, of course, that we go to the Opera to-night ? "

" Yes ? Do we ? "

" Yes. Your young friend Calladine, by the way, will join us in your box."

" That is very kind of him, I am sure," said Mr. Ricardo.

The two men arrived before the rising of the curtain, and in the crowded lobby a stranger spoke a few words to Hanaud, but what he said Ricardo could not hear. They took their seats in the box, and Hanaud looked at his programme.

" Ah ! It is ' Il Ballo di Maschera ' to-night. We always seem to hit upon something appropriate, don't we ? "

Then he raised his eyebrows.,

21*

" Oh-o ! Do you see that our pretty young friend, Joan Carew, is singing in the rôle of the page ? It is a showy part. There is a particular melody with a long-sustained trill in it, as far as I remember."

Mr. Ricardo was not deceived by Hanaud's apparent ignorance of the opera to be given that night and of the part Joan Carew was to take. He was, therefore, not surprised when Hanaud added :

" By the way, I should let Calladine find it all out for himself."

Mr. Ricardo nodded sagely.

" Yes. That is wise. I had thought of it myself." But he had done nothing of the kind. He was only aware that the elaborate stage-management in which Hanaud delighted was working out to the desired climax, whatever that climax might be. Calladine entered the box a few minutes later and shook hands with them awkwardly.

" It was kind of you to invite me," he said, and very ill at ease, he took a seat between them and concentrated his attention on the house as it filled up.

" There's the overture," said Hanaud. The curtains divided and were festooned on either side of the stage. The singers came on in their turn ; the page appeared to a burst of delicate applause (Joan Carew had made a small name for herself that season), and with a stifled cry Calladine shot back in the box as if he had been struck. Even then Mr. Ricardo did not understand. He only realised that Joan Carew was looking extraordinarily trim and smart in her boy's dress. He had to look from his programme to the stage and back again several times before the reason of Calladine's exclamation dawned on him. When it did, he was horrified. Hanaud, in his craving for dramatic effects, must have lost his head altogether. Joan Carew was wearing the same dress which she had worn on the tragic night at the Semiramis Hotel. He leaned forward in his agitation to Hanaud.

" You must be mad. Suppose Favart is in the theatre and sees her. He'll be over on the Continent by one in the morning."

" No, he won't," replied Hanaud. " For one thing, he never comes to Covent Garden unless one opera, with Carmen Valeri in the chief part, is being played, as you heard the other night at supper. For a second thing, he isn't in the house. I know where he is. He is gambling in Dean Street, Soho. For a third thing, my friend, he couldn't leave by the nine o'clock train for the Continent if he wanted to. Arrangements have been made. For a fourth thing, he wouldn't wish to. He has really remarkable reasons for desiring to stay in London. But he will come to the theatre later. Clements will send him an urgent message, with the result that he will go straight to Clements' office. Meanwhile, we can enjoy ourselves, eh ? "

Never was the difference between the amateur dilettante and the genuine professional more clearly exhibited than by the behaviour of the two men during the rest of the performance. Mr. Ricardo might have been sitting on a coal fire from his jumps and twistings ; Hanaud stolidly enjoyed the music, and when Joan Carew sang her famous solo his hands clamoured for an encore louder than anyone's in the boxes. Certainly, whether excitement was keeping her up or no, Joan Carew had never sung better in her life. Her voice was clear and fresh as a bird's—a bird with a soul inspiring its song. Even Calladine drew his chair forward again and sat with his eyes fixed upon the stage and quite carried out of himself. He drew a deep breath at the end.

" She is wonderful," he said, like a man waking up.

" She is very good," replied Mr. Ricardo, correcting Calladine's transports.

" We will go round to the back of the stage," said Hanaud.

They passed through the iron door and across the stage to a long corridor with a row of doors on one side. There were two or three men standing about in evening dress, as if waiting for friends in the dressing-rooms. At the third door Hanaud stopped and knocked. The door was opened by Joan Carew, still dressed in her green and gold. Her face was troubled, her eyes afraid.

" Courage, little one," said Hanaud, and he slipped past her into the room. " It is as well that my ugly, familiar face should not be seen too soon."

The door closed and one of the strangers loitered along the corridor and spoke to a call-boy. The call-boy ran off. For five minutes more Mr. Ricardo waited with a beating heart. He had the joy of a man in the centre of things. All those people driving homewards in their motor-cars along the Strand—how he pitied them ! Then, at the end of the corridor, he saw Clements and André Favart. They approached, discussing the possibility of Carmen Valeri's appearance in London opera during the next season.

" We have to look ahead, my dear friend," said Clements, " and though I should be extremely sorry——"

At that moment they were exactly opposite Joan Carew's door. It opened, she came out ; with a nervous movement she shut the door behind her. At the sound André Favart turned, and he saw drawn up against the panels of the door, with a look of terror in her face, the same gay figure which had interrupted him in Mrs. Blumenstein's bedroom. There was no need for Joan to act. In the presence of this man her fear was as real as it had been on the night of the Semiramis ball. She trembled from head to foot. Her eyes closed ; she seemed about to swoon.

Favart stared and uttered an oath. His face turned white ; he staggered back as if he had seen a ghost. Then he made a wild dash along the corridor, and was seized and held by two of the men in evening dress. Favart recovered his wits. He ceased to struggle.

" What does this outrage mean ? " he asked, and one of the men drew a warrant and notebook from his pocket.

" You are arrested for the murder of Mrs. Blumenstein in the Semiramis Hotel," he said, " and I have to warn you that anything you may say will be taken down and may be used in evidence against you."

" Preposterous ! " exclaimed Favart. " There's a mistake. We will go along to the police and put it right. Where's your evidence against me ? "

Hanaud stepped out of the doorway of the dressing-room.

" In the property-room of the theatre," he said.

At the sight of him Favart uttered a violent cry of rage. " You are here, too, are you ? " he screamed, and he sprang at Hanaud's throat. Hanaud stepped lightly aside. Favart was borne down to the ground and when he stood up again the handcuffs were on his wrists.

Favart was led away, and Hanaud turned to Mr. Ricardo and Clements.

" Let us go to the property-room," he said. They passed along the corridor, and Ricardo noticed that Calladine was no longer with them. He turned and saw him standing outside Joan Carew's dressing-room.

" He would like to come, of course," said Ricardo.

" Would he ? " asked Hanaud. " Then why doesn't he ? He's quite grown up, you know," and he slipped his arm through Ricardo's and led him back across the stage. In the property-room there was already a detective in plain clothes. Mr. Ricardo had still not as yet guessed the truth.

" What is it you really want, sir ? " the property-master asked of the director.

" Only the jewels of the Madonna," Hanaud answered.

The property-master unlocked a cupboard and took from it the sparkling cuirass. Hanaud pointed to it, and there, lost amongst the huge glittering stones of paste and false pearls, Mrs. Blumenstein's necklace was entwined.

" Then that is why Favart came always to Covent Garden when ' The Jewels of the Madonna ' was being performed ! " exclaimed Ricardo.

Hanaud nodded :

" He came to watch over his treasure."

Ricardo was piecing together the sections of the puzzle.

" No doubt he knew of the necklace in America. No doubt he followed it to England."

Hanaud agreed.

" Mrs. Blumenstein's jewels were quite famous in New York."

" But to hide them here ! " cried Mr. Clements. " He must have been mad."

" Why ? " asked Hanaud. " Can you imagine a safer hiding-place ? Who is going to burgle the property-room of Covent Garden ? Who is going to look for a priceless string of pearls amongst the stage jewels of an opera house ? "

" You did," said Mr. Ricardo.

" I ? " replied Hanaud, shrugging his shoulders. " Joan Carew's dreams led me to André Favart. The first time we came here and saw the pearls of the Madonna, I was on the look-out, naturally. I noticed Favart at the back of the stalls. But it was a stroke of luck that I noticed those pearls through my opera-glasses."

" At the end of the second act ? " cried Ricardo suddenly. " I remember now."

" Yes," replied Hanaud. " But for that second act the

pearls would have stayed comfortably here all through the season. Carmen Valeri—a fool as I told you—would have tossed them about in her dressing-room without a notion of their value, and at the end of July, when the murder at the Semiramis Hotel had been forgotten, Favart would have taken them to Amsterdam and made his bargain."

" Shall we go ? "

They left the theatre together and walked down to the grill-room of the Semiramis. But as Hanaud looked through the glass door he drew back.

" We will not go in, I think, eh ? "

" Why ? " asked Ricardo.

Hanaud pointed to a table. Calladine and Joan Carew were seated at it taking their supper.

" Perhaps," said Hanaud with a smile, " perhaps, my friend—what ? Who shall say that the rooms in the Adelphi will not be given up ? "

They turned away from the hotel. But Hanaud was right, and before the season was over Mr. Ricardo had to put his hand in his pocket for a wedding present.

Reprinted with the Author's permission from *The Four Corners of the World.*

E. PHILLIPS OPPENHEIM

The Indiscretion of Letty Shaw
The Little Marquis
Neap-tide Madness

¶ Mr. E. PHILLIPS OPPENHEIM
is known throughout England and
America as the Prince of Storytellers.
He has written every type of book
about every type of person ; but
although his imagination has carried
him to every corner of the world, the
scene of perhaps his most famous novels
is that South of France which he loves
so well. Among his recreations are
yachting, shooting, and golf.

THE INDISCRETION OF LETTY SHAW

AMIDST a storm of whispered criticisms the general opinion was that Letty Shaw was a silly little fool, who ought to have known better. When she had entered the restaurant a few minutes before midnight, followed by Austen Abbott, everyone looked to see a third person following them. No third person, however, appeared. Gustav himself conducted them to a small table laid for two, covered with pink roses, and handed his fair client the menu of a specially ordered supper. There was no gainsaying the fact that Letty and her escort proposed supping alone !

The café at the Milan was, without doubt, the fashionable rendezvous of the moment for those ladies connected with the theatrical profession who, after their performance, had not the time or the inclination to make the conventional toilette demanded of the larger restaurants. Letty Shaw, being one of the principal ornaments of the musical comedy stage, was well known to everyone in the room. There was scarcely a person there who within the last fortnight had not found an opportunity of congratulating her upon her engagement to Captain the Honourable Brian Sotherst. Sotherst was rich, and one of the most popular young men about town. Letty Shaw, although she had had one or two harmless flirtations, was well known as a self-respecting and hard-working young actress who loved her work, and against whom no one had ever found a word to say. Consequently, the shock was all the greater when, within a fortnight of her engagement, she was thus to be seen openly supping alone with the most notorious woman-hunter about town—a man of bad reputation, a man, too, towards whom Sotherst was known to have a special aversion. Nothing but a break with Sotherst or a fit of temporary insanity seemed to explain, even inadequately, the situation.

Her best friend—the friend who knew Letty and believed in her—rose to her feet and came sailing down the room.

She nodded gaily to Abbott, whom she hated, and whom she had not recognised for years, and laid her hand upon Letty's arm.

" Where's Brian ? " she asked.

Letty shrugged her shoulders—it was not altogether a natural gesture.

" On duty to-night," she answered.

Her best friend paused for a moment.

" Come over and join our party, both of you," she said. " Dicky Pennell's here and Gracie Marsh—just landed. They'd love to meet you."

Letty shook her head slowly. There was a look in her face which even her best friend did not understand.

" I'm afraid that we can't do that," she said. " I am Mr. Abbott's guest."

" And to-night," Austen Abbott intervened, looking up at the woman who stood between them, " I am not disposed to share Miss Shaw with anybody."

Her best friend could do no more than shake her head and go away. The two were left alone for the rest of the supper-hour. When they departed together, people who knew felt that a whiff of tragedy had passed through the room. Nobody understood—or pretended to understand. Even before her engagement Letty had never been known to sup alone with a man. That she should do so now, and with this particular man, was preposterous !

" Something will come of it," her best friend murmured sadly, as she watched Austen Abbott help his companion on with her cloak.

Something did !

Peter Ruff rose at his accustomed hour the following morning, and attired himself, if possible, with more than his usual care. He wore the grey suit which he had carefully put out the night before, but he hesitated long between the rival appeals of a red tie with white spots and a plain mauve one. He finally chose the latter, finding that it harmonised more satisfactorily with his socks, and, after a final survey of himself in the looking-glass, he entered the next room, where his coffee was set out upon a small round table near the fire together with his letters and newspapers.

Peter Ruff was, after all, like the rest of us, a creature of habit. He made an invariable rule of glancing through the newspapers before he paid any regard at all to his letters or his breakfast. In the absence of anything of a particularly sensational character he then opened the former in leisurely fashion and went back afterwards to the newspaper as he finished his meal. This morning, however, both his breakfast and letters remained for some time untouched. The first paragraph which caught his eye as he shook open the *Daily Telegraph* was sufficiently absorbing. There it was in great black type :

TERRIBLE TRAGEDY IN THE FLAT OF A
WELL-KNOWN ACTRESS
AUSTEN ABBOTT SHOT DEAD !
ARREST OF CAPTAIN SOTHERST

Beyond the inevitable shock which is always associated with the taking of life, and the unusual position of the people concerned in it, there was little in the brief account of the incident to excite the imagination.

A policeman on the pavement outside the flat in which Miss Shaw and her mother lived, fancied that he heard, about two o'clock in the morning, the report of a revolver shot. As nothing further transpired, and as the sound was very indistinct, he did not at once enter the building, but kept it, as far as possible, under observation. About twenty minutes later a young gentleman in evening dress came out into the street, and the policeman noticed that he was carrying a small revolver, which he attempted to conceal. The constable thereupon whistled for his sergeant, and accompanied by the young gentleman—who made no attempt to escape—ascended to Miss Shaw's rooms, where the body of Austen Abbott was discovered lying upon the threshold of the sitting-room, with a small bullet mark through the forehead. The inmates of the house were aroused and a doctor sent for. The deceased was identified as Austen Abbott—a well-known actor—and the man under arrest gave his name at once as Captain the Honourable Brian Sotherst.

Peter Ruff sighed as he laid down the paper. The case seemed to him perfectly clear, and his sympathies were altogether with the young officer who had taken the law into his own hands. He knew nothing of Miss Letty Shaw, and, consequently, did her, perhaps, less than justice in his thoughts. Of Austen Abbott, on the other hand, he knew a great deal—and nothing of good. It was absurd, after all, that anyone should be punished for killing such a brute !

He descended, a few minutes later, to his office, and found Miss Brown busy arranging a bowl of violets upon his desk.

" Isn't it horrible ? " she cried, as he entered, carrying a bundle of papers under his arm. " I never have had such a shock ! "

" Do you know any of them, then ? " Peter Ruff asked, straightening his tie in the mirror.

" Of course ! " she answered. " Why, I've been in the same company as Letty Shaw for a year. I was at the Milan, too, last night. Letty was there having supper alone with Austen Abbott. We all said that there'd be trouble, but, of course, we never dreamed of this ! Isn't there any chance for him, Peter ? Can't he get off ? "

Peter Ruff shook his head.

" I'm afraid not," he said. " They may be able to bring evidence of a quarrel and reduce it to manslaughter, but what you've just told me about this supper-party makes it all the worse. It will come out in the evidence, of course."

" Captain Sotherst is such a dear," Miss Brown declared, " and so good-looking ! And as for that brute Austen Abbott, he ought to have been shot long ago ! "

Peter Ruff seated himself before his desk and hitched up his trousers at the knees.

" No doubt you are right, Violet," he pronounced, " but people go about these things so foolishly. To me it is simply exasperating to reflect how little use is made of persons such as myself, whose profession in life it is to arrange these matters. Take the present case, for example. Captain Sotherst had only to lay the facts before me, and Austen Abbott was a ruined man. I could have managed the affair for him in half a dozen different ways. Whereas now it must be a life for a life—the life of an honest young English gentleman for the life of a creature who should have been kicked out of the world as vermin ! . . . I have some letters to give you, Violet, if you please."

She swung round in her chair reluctantly.

"I can't help thinking of that poor young fellow," she said with a sigh.

"Sentiment after office hours, if you please!" Mr. Peter Ruff ordered.

Then there came a knock at the door.

His visitor lifted her veil and Peter Ruff recognised her immediately. Once again the breath was short in his throat, and the smell of the fog was in his nostrils. She wore no jewels now—a plain tailor-made gown and toque. But the fear was there, deeper engraven this time.

Peter Ruff bowed.

"What can I do for you, Lady Mary?" he asked.

She saw the recognition in his eyes even before he spoke, and wondered at it.

"You know me?" she exclaimed.

"I know most people," he answered drily—"it is part of my profession."

"Tell me—you are Mr. Peter Ruff," she said, "the famous specialist in the detection of crime. You know that Brian Sotherst is my brother?"

"Yes," he answered, "I know it! I am sorry, very sorry indeed."

He handed her a chair. She seated herself with a little tightening of the lips.

"I want more than sympathy from you, Mr. Ruff," she warned him. "I want your help."

"It is my business," he admitted, "but your brother's case makes intervention difficult, does it not?"

"You mean——" she began.

"Your brother himself does not deny his guilt, I understand," Peter Ruff said.

"He has not denied it," she answered. "Very likely he will not do so before the magistrate; but neither has he admitted it. Mr. Ruff, you are such a clever man. Can't you see the truth?"

Peter Ruff looked at her steadily for several moments.

"Lady Mary," he said, "I can see what you are going to suggest. You are going on the assumption that Austen Abbott was shot by Letty Shaw, and that your brother is taking the thing on his shoulders."

"I am sure of it!" she declared. "The girl did it herself ! Brian would never have shot anyone. He might have horsewhipped him, perhaps—even beaten him to death—but shoot him in cold blood—never ! "

" The provocation——" Ruff began.

" There was no provocation," Lady Mary interrupted. " He was engaged to the girl, and of course we hated it, but she was an honest little thing, and devoted to him."

" Doubtless," Ruff admitted. " But all the same, as you will hear before the magistrates, or at the inquest, she was having supper alone with Austen Abbott that night at the Milan."

Lady Mary's eyes flashed.

" I don't believe it ! " she declared.

" It is nevertheless true," Peter Ruff assured her. " There is no shadow of doubt about it."

Lady Mary was staggered. For a few moments she seemed struggling to rearrange her thoughts.

" You see," Ruff continued, " the fact that Miss Shaw was willing to sup with Austen Abbott *tête-à-tête* renders it all the more improbable that she should shoot him in her sitting-room, an hour or so later, and then go calmly into her mother's sleeping-chamber as though nothing had happened."

Lady Mary had lost some of her confidence, but she was not daunted.

" Even if we have been deceived in the girl," she said thoughtfully, " even if she were disposed to flirt with other men, even then there might be a stronger motive than ever for her wishing to get rid of Abbott. He may have become jealous and threatened her."

" It is, of course, possible," Ruff assented politely. " Your theory would, at any rate, account for your brother's present attitude."

She looked at him steadfastly.

" You believe, then," she said, " that my brother shot Austen Abbott ? "

" I do," he admitted frankly. " So does every man or woman in London of common sense to-day. On the facts as they are stated in the newspapers, with the additional one of which I have told you, no other conclusion is possible."

Lady Mary rose.

" Then I may as well go," she said tearfully.

" Not at all," Peter Ruff declared. " Listen. This is a matter of business with me. I say that on the facts as they are known, your brother's guilt appears indubitable. I do not say that there may not be other facts in the background which alter the state of affairs. If you wish me to search for them, engage me, and I will do my best."

" Isn't that what I am here for ? " the girl exclaimed.

" Very well," Peter Ruff said. " My services arc at your disposal."

" You will do your best—more than your best, won't you ? " she begged. " Remember that he is my brother— my favourite brother ! "

" I will do what can be done," Peter Ruff promised. " Please sit down at that desk and write me two letters of introduction."

She drew off her gloves and prepared to obey him.

" To whom ? " she asked.

" To the solicitors who are defending your brother," he said, " and to Miss Letty Shaw."

" You mean to go and see her ? " Lady Mary asked doubtfully.

" Naturally," Peter Ruff answered. " If your supposition is correct, she might easily give herself away under a little subtle cross-examination. It is my business to know how to ask people questions in such a way that if they do not speak the truth their words give some indication of it. If she is innocent I shall know that I have to make my effort in another direction."

" What other direction can there be ? " Lady Mary asked dismally.

Peter Ruff said nothing. He was too kind-hearted to kindle false hopes.

" It's a hopeless case, of course," Miss Brown remarked after Lady Mary had departed.

" I'm afraid so," Peter Ruff admitted. " Still, I must earn my money. Please get someone to take you to supper to-night at the Milan, and see if you can pick up any scandal."

" About Letty ? " she asked.

" About either of them," he answered. " Particularly I

should like to know if any explanation has cropped up of her supping alone with Austen Abbott."

"I don't see why you can't take me yourself," she remarked. "You are on the side of the law this time, at any rate."

"I will," he agreed, after a moment's hesitation. "I will call for you at eleven o'clock to-night."

He rose and closed his desk emphatically.

"You are going out?" she asked.

"I am going to call on Miss Letty Shaw," he answered.

He took a taxicab to the flats, and found a handful of curious people still gazing up at the third floor. The parlour-maid, who obeyed his summons, was absolutely certain that Miss Shaw would not receive him. He persuaded her, however, after some difficulty, to take in his letter, whilst he waited in the hall. When she returned she showed him into a small dining-room and pulled down the blinds.

"Miss Shaw will see you, sir, for a few minutes," she announced in a subdued tone. "Poor, dear young lady," she continued, "she's been crying her eyes out all the morning."

"No wonder," Peter Ruff said sympathetically. "It's a terrible business, this."

"One of the nicest young men as ever walked," the girl declared firmly. "As for that other brute, he deserved all he's got, and more!"

Peter Ruff was left alone for nearly a quarter of an hour. Then the door was softly opened, and Letty Shaw entered. There was no doubt whatever about her suffering. Ruff, who had seen her only lately at the theatre, was shocked. Under her eyes were blacker lines than her pencil had ever traced. Not only was she ghastly pale, but her features seemed wan and shrunken. She spoke to him the moment she entered, leaning with one hand upon the sideboard.

"Lady Mary writes that you want to help us," she said. "How can you? How is it possible?"

Even her voice had gone. She spoke hoarsely, and as though short of breath. Her eyes searched his feverishly. It seemed cruelty not to answer her at once, and Peter Ruff was not a cruel man. Nevertheless he remained silent, and it seemed to her that his eyes were like points of fire upon her face.

" What is the matter ? " she cried with breaking voice.
" What have you come for ? Why don't you speak to
me ? "

" Madam," Peter Ruff said, " I should like to help you,
and I will do what I can. But in order that I may do so,
it is necessary that you should answer me two questions—
truthfully ! "

Her eyes opened wider—became almost distended. It
was the state of a terrified child.

" Why not ? " she exclaimed. " What have I to
conceal ? "

Peter Ruff's expression never changed. There was
nothing about him, as he stood there with his hands behind
him, his head bent a little forward, in the least inspiring—
nothing calculated to alarm the most timid person. Yet
the girl looked at him with the eyes of a frightened bird.

" Remember, then," he continued smoothly, " that what
you say to me is sacred. You and I are alone, without
witnesses or eavesdroppers. Was it Brian Sotherst who
shot Abbott—or was it you ? "

She gave a low cry. Her hands clasped the sides of her
head in horror.

" I ! " she exclaimed. " I ! God help me ! "

He waited. In a moment she looked up.

" You cannot believe that," she said with a calmness
for which he was scarcely prepared. " It is absurd. I left
the room by the inner door as he took up his hat to stroll
out into the hall."

" Incidentally," he asked—" this is not my other question, mind—why did you not let him out yourself ? "

" We had disagreed," she answered curtly.

Peter Ruff bent his head in assent.

" I see," he remarked. " You had disagreed. Abbott
probably hoped that you would relent, so he waited for a
few minutes. Brian Sotherst, who had escaped from his
engagement in time, he thought, to come and wish you
good-night, must have walked in and found him there. By
the by, how would Captain Sotherst get in ? "

" He had a key," the girl answered. " My mother lives
here with me, and we have only one maid. It was more
convenient. I gave him one washed in gold for a birthday
present only a few days ago."

"Thank you," Peter Ruff said. "The revolver, I understand, was your property?"

She nodded.

"It was a present from Brian," she said. "He gave it me in a joke, and I had it on the table with some other curiosities."

"The first question," Peter Ruff said, "is disposed of. May I proceed to the second?"

The girl moistened her lips.

"Yes," she answered.

"Why did you sup alone with Austen Abbott last night?"

She shrank away.

"Why should I not?" she asked.

"You have been on the stage, my dear Miss Shaw," Peter Ruff continued, "for between four and five years. During the whole of that time it has been your very wise habit to join supper-parties, of course, when the company was agreeable to you, but to sup alone with no man. Am I not right?"

"You seem to know a great deal about me," she faltered.

"Am I not right?" he repeated.

"Yes," she answered.

"You break your rule for the first time," Peter Ruff continued, "in favour of a man of notoriously bad character a few weeks after the announcement of your engagement to an honourable young English gentleman. You knew very well the construction likely to be put upon your behaviour; you, of all people, would be the most likely to appreciate the risk you ran. Why did you run it? In other words, I repeat my question. Why did you sup alone with Austen Abbott last night?"

All this time she had been standing. She came a few steps forward now, and threw herself into an easy chair.

"It doesn't help!" she exclaimed. "All this doesn't help!"

"Nor can I help you, then," Peter Ruff said, stretching out his hand for his hat.

She waved him to put it down.

"I will tell you," she said. "It has nothing to do with the case, but, since you ask, you shall know. There is a dear little girl in our company—Fluffy Dean we all call her—

only eighteen years old. We all love her, she is so sweet, and just like I was when I first went on the stage, only much nicer. She is very pretty, she has no money, and she is such an affectionate dear that, although she is as good as gold, we are all terrified for her sake whenever she makes acquaintances. Several of us who are most interested made a sort of covenant. We all took it in turns to look after her and try to see that she did not meet anyone she shouldn't. Yet for all our precautions Austen Abbott got hold of her and turned her silly little head. He was a man of experience, and she was only a child. She wouldn't listen to us—she wouldn't hear a word against him. I took what seemed to me to be the only chance. I went to him myself. I begged for mercy, I begged him to spare the child. I swore that if anything happened to her I would start a crusade against him. I would pledge my word that he should be cut by every decent man and woman on the stage. He listened to what I had to say, and at first he only smiled. When I had finished he made me an offer. He said that if I would sup with him alone at the Milan, and permit him to escort me home afterwards, he would spare the child. One further condition he made—that I was to tell no one why I did it. It was the man's brutal vanity ! I made the promise, but I break it now. You have asked me, and I have told you. I went through with the supper, although I hated it. I let him come in for a drink as though he had been a friend. Then he tried to make love to me. I took the opportunity of telling him exactly what I thought of him. Then I showed him the door and left him. After-wards—afterwards—Brian came in ! They must have met upon the very threshold ! "

Peter Ruff took up his hat.

" Thank you," he said.

" You see," she continued drearily, " that it all has very little to do with the case. I meant to keep it to myself, because, of course, apart from anything else—apart from Brian's meeting him coming out of my rooms—it supplies an additional cause for anger on Brian's part."

" I see," he answered. " I am much obliged to you, Miss Shaw. Believe me that you have my sincere sympathy."

Peter Ruff's farewell words were unheard. Letty

had fallen forward in her chair, her head buried in her hands. . . .

Peter Ruff went to Berkeley Square, and found Lady Mary waiting for him. Sir William Trencham, the great solicitor, was with her. Lady Mary introduced the two men. All the time she was anxiously watching Ruff's face.

" Mr. Ruff has been to see Miss Shaw," she explained to Sir William. " Mr. Ruff, tell me quickly," she continued, with her hand upon his shoulder, " did she say anything ? Did you find anything out ? "

He shook his head.

" No," he said ; " I found nothing out."

" You don't think, then," Lady Mary gasped, " that there is any chance—of getting her to confess—that she did it herself ? "

" Why should she have done it herself ? " Peter Ruff asked. " She admits that the man tried to make love to her. She simply left him. She was in her own home, with her mother and servant within call. There was no struggle in the room—we know that. There was no necessity for any."

" Have you made any other inquiries ? " Lady Mary asked.

" The few which I have made," Peter Ruff answered gravely, " point all in the same direction. I ascertained at the Milan that your brother called there late last night, and that he heard Miss Shaw had been supping alone with Austen Abbott. He followed them home. I have ascertained, too, that he had a key to Miss Shaw's flat. He apparently met Austen Abbott upon the threshold."

Lady Mary covered her face with her hands. She seemed to read in Ruff's words the verdict of the two men —the verdict of common sense. Nevertheless, he made one more request before leaving.

" I should like to see Captain Sotherst, if you can get me an order," he said to Sir William.

" You can go with me to-morrow morning," the lawyer answered. " The proceedings this morning, of course, were merely formal. Until after the inquest it will be easy to arrange an interview."

Lady Mary looked up quickly.

" There is still something in your mind, then ? " she asked. " You think that there is a bare chance ? "

" There is always the hundredth chance ! " Peter Ruff replied.

Peter Ruff and Miss Brown supped at the Milan that night, as they had arranged, but it was not a cheerful evening. Brian Sotherst had been very popular amongst Letty Shaw's circle of friends, and the general feeling was one of horror and consternation at this thing which had befallen him. Austen Abbott, too, was known to all of them, and although a good many of the men—and even the women—were outspoken enough to declare at once that it served him right, nevertheless the shock of death—death without a second's warning—had a paralysing effect even upon those who were his severest critics. Violet Brown spoke to a few of her friends—introduced Peter Ruff here and there—but nothing was said which could throw in any way even the glimmering of a new light upon the tragedy. It all seemed too hopelessly and fatally apparent.

About twenty minutes before closing time the *habitués* of the place were provided with something in the nature of a sensation. A little party entered who seemed altogether free from the general air of gloom. Foremost amongst them was a very young and exceedingly pretty girl, with light golden hair waved in front of her forehead, deep blue eyes, and the slight, airy figure of a child. She was accompanied by another young woman, whose appearance was a trifle too obvious to be prepossessing, and three or four young men—dark, clean-shaven, dressed with the irritating exactness of their class—young stockbrokers or boys about town. Miss Brown's eyes grew very wide-open.

" What a little beast ! " she exclaimed.

" Who ? " Peter Ruff asked.

" That pretty girl there," she answered—" Fluffy Dean her name is. She is Letty Shaw's *protégée*, and she wouldn't have dreamed of allowing the child to come out with such a crowd ; to-night of all nights," she continued indignantly, " when Letty is away ! "

Peter Ruff was interested.

" So that is Miss Fluffy Dean," he remarked, looking at her curiously. " She seems rather excited."

" She's a horrid little wretch ! " Miss Brown declared. " I hope that someone will tell Letty, and that she will drop her now. A girl who would even dream of coming here with such a party to-night isn't worth taking care of ! Just listen to them all ! "

They were certainly becoming somewhat boisterous. A magnum of champagne had been opened. Fluffy Dean's cheeks were already flushed, and her eyes glittering. Every-one at the table was talking a great deal and drinking toasts.

" This is the end of Fluffy Dean," Violet said severely. " I hate to be uncharitable, but it serves her right."

Peter Ruff paid his bill.

" Let us go," he said.

In the taxi-cab, on their way back to Miss Brown's rooms, Ruff was unusually silent ; but just before he said good-bye to her, outside her front door, he asked a question.

" Violet," he said, " would you like to play detective for an hour or two ? "

She looked at him in some surprise.

" You know I always like to help in anything that's going," she answered.

" Letty Shaw was an Australian, wasn't she ? " he asked.

" Yes ! "

" She was born there, and lived there till she was nearly eighteen—is that true ? " he asked again.

" Quite true," Miss Brown answered.

" You know the offices of the P. & O. line of steamers in Pall Mall ? " he asked.

She nodded.

" Well ? "

" Get a sailing list to Australia—there should be a boat going Thursday. Present yourself as a prospective pas-senger. See how many young women alone there are going out, and ask their names. Incidentally, put in any spare time you may have watching the office."

She looked at him with parted lips and wide-open eyes.

" Do you think——" she began.

He shook her hand warmly, and stepped back into the taxi.

" Good night," he said. " No questions, please. I shan't expect you at the office at the usual time to-morrow, at any rate. Telephone or run round if you have anything to tell me."

The taxi-cab disappeared round the corner of the street.

Miss Brown was standing still upon the pavement with the latchkey in her hand.

It was the afternoon before the inquest on the body of Austen Abbott, and there were gathered together in Letty Shaw's parlour a curiously assorted little group of people. There was Miss Shaw herself—or rather what seemed to be the ghost of herself—and her mother ; Lady Mary and Sir William Trencham ; Peter Ruff and Violet Brown—and Mr. John Dory, of Scotland Yard. The eyes of all of them were fixed upon Peter Ruff, who was the latest arrival. He stood in the middle of the room, calmly taking off his gloves, and glancing complacently down at his well-creased trousers.

" Lady Mary," he said, " and Miss Shaw, I know that you are both anxious for me to explain why I asked you to meet me here this afternoon, and why I also requested my friend Mr. Dory from Scotland Yard, who has charge of the case against Captain Sotherst, to be present. I will tell you."

Mr. Dory nodded, a little impatiently.

" Unless you have something very definite to say," he remarked, " I think it would be as well to postpone any general discussion of this matter until after the inquest. I must warn you that so far as I, personally, am concerned, I must absolutely decline to allude to the subject at all. It would be most unprofessional."

" I have something definite to say," Peter Ruff declared mildly.

Lady Mary's eyes flashed with hope. Letty Shaw leaned forward in her chair with tense, drawn face.

" Let it be understood," Peter Ruff said, with a slight note of gravity creeping into his tone, " that I am here solely as the agent of Lady Mary Sotherst. I am paid and employed by her. My sole object is, therefore, to discover, on her behalf, proof of the innocence of Captain Sotherst. I take it, however," he added, turning towards the drooping figure in the easy chair, " that Miss Shaw is equally anxious to have the truth known."

" Of course ! Of course ! " she murmured feverishly. " How can there be any question about it ? It is the truth we want—nothing else ! "

Peter Ruff bowed his head.

" In France," he continued quietly, " there is a somewhat curious custom, which, despite a certain theatricality, yet has its points. The scene of a crime is visited, and its events, so far as may be, reconstructed. Let us, if you please, suppose for a moment that we are now engaged upon something of the sort."

Letty Shaw shrank back in her chair. Her thin, white fingers were gripping its sides. Her eyes seemed to look upon terrible things.

" It is too—awful ! " she faltered.

" Madam," Peter Ruff said firmly, " we seek the truth. Be so good as to humour me in this. Dory, will you go to the front door, stand upon the mat—so ! You are Captain Sotherst—you have just entered. I am Austen Abbott. You, Miss Shaw, have just ordered me from the room. You see, I move toward the door. I open it—so. Miss Shaw," he added, turning swiftly towards her, " once more will you assure me that everyone who was in the flat that night, with the exception of your domestic servant, is present now ? "

" Yes ! " she murmured.

" Good ! Then who," he asked, suddenly pointing to a door on the left—" who is in that room ? "

They had all crowded after him to the threshold—thronging around him as he stood face to face with John Dory. His finger never wavered—it was pointing steadily towards that closed door a few feet to the left. Suddenly Letty Shaw rushed past them with a loud shriek.

" You shall not go in ! " she cried. " What business is it of yours ? "

She stood with her back to the door, her arms outstretched like a cross. Her cheeks were livid. Her eyes seemed starting from her head. Opposite to her was Lady Mary, also trembling with excitement, obviously struggling with a fierce desire to tear the girl from her post.

" Will you men move her, please ? " she asked, with an effort at calmness.

Peter Ruff and John Dory laid their hands upon the girl's wrists. She clung to her place frantically. She was dragged from it, screaming. Peter Ruff, as was his right, entered first. Almost immediately he turned round, and his face was very grave.

" Something has happened in here, I am afraid," he said.
" Please come in quietly."

On the bed lay Fluffy Dean, fully dressed—motionless.
One hand hung down towards the floor—from the lifeless
fingers a little phial had slipped. In the room were several
trunks, addressed to :

MISS SMITH,
PASSENGER TO MELBOURNE.
S.S. *Caroline*.

Peter Ruff moved over towards the bed, and took up a
piece of paper, upon which were scribbled a few lines
in pencil.

" I think," he said, " that I must read these aloud.
You all have a right to hear them."

No one spoke. He continued :

" Forgive me, Letty, but I cannot go to Australia. They
would only bring me back. When I remember that awful
moment, my brain burns—I feel that I am going mad !
Some day I should do this—better now. Give my love to
the girls.

" FLUFFY."

They sent for a doctor, and John Dory rang up Scotland
Yard. Letty Shaw had fainted, and been carried to her
room. Whilst they waited about in strange, half-benumbed
excitement, Peter Ruff once more spoke to them.

" The reconstruction is easy enough now," he remarked.
" The partition between this sitting-room and that bedroom is only an artificial one—something almost as flimsy
as a screen. You see," he continued, tapping with his
knuckles, " you can almost put your hand through it. If
you look a little lower down, you will see where an opening
has been made. Fluffy Dean was being taken care of by
Miss Shaw—staying with her here, even. Miss Dean hears
her lover's voice in this room—hears him pleading with
Miss Shaw on the night of the murder. She has been sent
home early from the theatre, and it is just possible that she
saw or had been told that Austen Abbott had fetched Miss
Shaw after the performance and had taken her to supper.

" She is mad with anger and jealousy. The revolver

22

was there upon the table, with a silver box of cartridges. She possesses herself of it, and waits in her room. What she hears proves, at least, her lover's infidelity. She stands there at her door, waiting. When Austen Abbott comes out, she shoots, throws the revolver at him, closes her door, and goes off into a faint. Perhaps she hears footsteps—a key in the door. At any rate, Captain Sotherst arrives a few minutes later. He finds, half in the hall, half on the threshold of the sitting-room, Austen Abbott dead, and Miss Shaw's revolver by the side of him. If he had been a wise young man, he would have aroused the household. Why he did not do so, we can perhaps guess. He put two and two together a trifle too quickly. It is certain that he believed that the dead man had been shot by his *fiancée*. His first thought was to get rid of the revolver. At any rate, he walked down to the street with it in his hand, and was promptly arrested by the policeman who had heard the shot. Naturally he refused to plead because he thought that Miss Shaw had killed the man probably in self-defence. She, at first, believed her lover guilty, and when afterwards Fluffy Dean confessed, she, with feminine lack of common sense, was trying to get the girl out of the country before telling the truth. A visit of hers to the office of the Steamship Company gave me the clue I required."

Lady Mary grasped both his hands.

" And Scotland Yard," she exclaimed, with a withering glance at John Dory, " have done their best to hang my brother ! "

Peter Ruff raised his eyebrows.

" Dear Lady Mary," he said, " remember that it is the business of Scotland Yard to find a man guilty. It is mine, when I am employed for that purpose, to find him innocent. You must not be too hard upon my friend Mr. Dory. He and I seem to come up against each other a little too often, as it is."

" A little too often ! " John Dory repeated softly. " But one cannot tell. Don't believe, Lady Mary," he added, " that we ever want to kill an innocent man."

" It is your profession, though," she answered, " to find criminals—and his," touching Peter Ruff on the shoulder, " to look for the truth."

Peter Ruff bowed low, the compliment pleased him.

THE LITTLE MARQUIS

THE quaint invasion of his otherwise empty carriage at one of the small stations between Cromer and Melton Constable, at first a mildly annoying episode, became to Jasper Slane, a few minutes later, a matter for benign and tolerant curiosity. It was evident that his prospective fellow-passengers were people of local consequence. First of all, a porter opened the door and, glancing around, surreptitiously dusted one of the seats. Then a chauffeur in black livery deposited two dressing-cases and a kit-bag upon one of the vacant places. As soon as he stood away, the station-master appeared, hat in hand. Following him, a solemn, pale-faced, clean-shaven functionary in black cut-away coat, grey trousers, and black bow tie stepped into the carriage, and, turning round, extended his hand to the very diminutive person lingering in the background.

" If you will permit me, my lord," he murmured, in a deep, sonorous voice.

His lordship, helped by the station-master from behind and this obvious manservant in front, stepped into the carriage without any manifest need of such assistance. He was very small indeed—scarcely more than five feet high, with the sort of skin which looks as though hair had never grown upon it, a sensitive mouth, and the eyes of a child. He was dressed in an old-fashioned tweed suit of pepper-and-salt design, with broad-toed shoes, a black satin four-in-hand tie of such dimensions that it seemed almost like a stock, and his hat was a flat-topped bowler of a fashion long since discarded. He wore heavy dog-skin gloves, and he might very well have stepped out from one of *Punch's* cartoons of between 1850 and 1860. He sank into his corner seat, and turned towards the station-master. Jasper Slane almost started at the sound of his voice—unnaturally high pitched, the thin treble of a child.

" Thank you very much, Mr. Station-master," he said.

" We shall be very comfortable, I am sure. My trunk is safely in the van ? . . . Good ! Mason," he added, turning to his companion, " you have remunerated the porter ? "

" Certainly, my lord."

The little man raised his hat pleasantly, the servant winked at the station-master, and the train glided off. Jasper Slane resumed his reading, but found it almost impossible to keep his eyes from straying towards this strange couple. The master drew from his pocket a Christie's catalogue, in which, after the first few moments, he seemed completely absorbed. The servant respectfully unfolded the morning paper and began to read. So the journey commenced, placidly enough. Its end was to be otherwise.

It was not until nearly midday that Jasper Slane rose and stretched himself. His diagonally placed *vis-à-vis* was still deep in a perusal of the catalogue, whilst his manservant had closed his eyes in slumber. Slane, disturbed by the frantic whistling of the engine, leaned out of the window and thereby probably saved his life. There was a final screech of the locomotive, a violent succession of jolts, and a sensation of delirium, as though that quiet, well-behaved country train had suddenly gone mad. Then the compartment seemed slowly to break up around them. A portion of the luggage rack behind the pompous-looking domestic was smashed in half by some obtruding force, and the man, with a groan, collapsed on to the floor. Then the train ceased to move. The carriage was inclined at a perilous angle towards the ground, and looked as though it might turn over at any moment. There was a terrific babel of shouting and groaning outside, and the hissing of escaping steam mingled with the slow crunching-up of the woodwork. The accident, however, so far as they were concerned, seemed to be over. Jasper Slane, holding on to his end of the luggage rack, stared around him in dazed fashion. The manservant upon the floor was bleeding from the forehead and unconscious. His master was doubled up in a most extraordinary attitude upon the crumpled remains of the seat which he had occupied, his legs in the air, his knees almost touching his chin. He had apparently escaped being crushed to death by a trifle. He turned his head and looked at Jasper Slane.

" Please help me down," he begged, in his funny, piping voice, without the slightest trace of emotion or distress.

Slane did as he was bidden. He took the little man almost in his arms, and deposited him upon the one seat which remained intact. Then he turned towards the door.

" I'll see if I can open it," he suggested.

The rescued man took no notice. His eyes were fixed upon the figure on the floor.

" Is he badly hurt, do you think ? " he asked.

" I shouldn't think so," was the consoling reply. " He only seems to have that head wound."

" Do you think he will have to go to hospital ? "

" Very likely, for a few days."

Then a curious thing happened. His neighbour looked across at Slane and smiled happily.

" That will be very pleasant," he said. " I hope they look after him well there, but it will be very pleasant. In the meantime I had better have the keys."

He went down on his knees upon the floor, felt in the injured man's pockets, and drew out a bunch of keys. He placed them carefully in his own pocket, and, without even a second glance at the unconscious servant, turned towards Slane with the smile still lingering upon his lips.

" Do you think we shall be kept here long ? " he inquired.

Further speech just then was not possible, for someone had wrenched open the door, and they descended on to the track. The accident, after all, proved to be only a minor affair, but there was the usual miserable period of waiting around, and Slane, being something of a surgeon, busied himself in attending to several of the less severely injured. Presently a relief train appeared, in which he found an empty carriage and seated himself once more in the corner. Just as the whistle had blown, he heard an agitated little voice from the footboard.

" Can I get in, please ? Please, can I come in ? Please open the door."

Just in time a guard came running up with two dressing-cases, and, with Jasper Slane's assistance, the little man climbed into the compartment. He was still wearing his beatific smile.

" They have taken Mason off on the ambulance train," he

confided. " He is still unconscious, and the doctor said he
thought he might be in hospital for at least a week."

" Where are you going ? " Slane asked.

" London," the squeaky voice piped out. " I am going
to the great china sale to-morrow. Do you collect china,
sir ? "

" Well, I'm afraid I'm not a collector," Slane confessed,
" but I have one or two rather good pieces of Ming."

His companion's eyes shone.

" Ming," he repeated. " I can tell you all about Ming."

" Have a sandwich first," Slane invited, drawing a package from his pocket.

" Thank you very much indeed. I will eat a sandwich
with pleasure. I do not know what arrangements Mason
had made about luncheon. Will you tell me your name,
please ? Mine is Aberway—the Marquis of Aberway."

" Mine is Jasper Slane."

The Marquis stopped eating his sandwich. He looked
hard at his *vis-à-vis.*

" Jasper Slane," he reflected. " Now that is very curious.
Someone has told me something about you, Sir Jasper. I
cannot remember exactly what it was, but I made up my
mind once to write to you, only I could never find your
address. You are not a doctor ? "

" No, I am not a doctor," Slane acknowledged. " I am
really nothing very much professionally. Occasionally, if
there is a case in which I am interested, or if any of my
friends are in trouble through no fault of their own, I try
to help them, if I can do so without interfering with the
law."

" A private detective ! " the Marquis exclaimed exultantly. " That was it. I remember thinking how
strange it was—a baronet, but a private detective."

" Have another sandwich," Slane suggested.

His companion accepted the offering almost mechanically.

" Jasper Slane," he repeated once more. " When we get
to London, may I call on you ? "

Slane handed him a card.

" Delighted to see you at any time. I have a little house
in Hampstead. It's rather out of the way, so you'd better
telephone before you come."

" Hampstead is not far," the Marquis observed. " You

must allow me—you must really allow me—one moment, please."

He fumbled with the fastenings of one of his flat dressing-cases, opened it, and triumphantly produced a bottle of white wine and some glasses.

" You will drink a glass of wine with me," he begged.

" Rather ! " Slane accepted. " I was just wishing that I had brought my flask."

The Marquis produced two glasses and filled them. Jasper Slane stared at the label on the bottle, which was brown with age and almost illegible, sipped his wine appreciatively, and studied the label once again.

" This is a very marvellous wine to be drinking in a railway carriage," he remarked.

" I am glad that you find it so," was the gratified reply. " It is Château Yquem of a very old vintage. I know very little about wines—only that I am fond of them. If Mason were here, I should have had to drink mine with water. I am glad that Mason is not here. I hope that he will be ill for a long time. It would not distress me if he were to die."

Slane looked curiously at his companion. He was obviously entirely in earnest.

" If you don't like him," he inquired, " why don't you get rid of him ? "

The Marquis laughed—a queer, metallic little sound it was, like a child's titter.

" Get rid of Mason," he repeated. " Why, it was her ladyship who engaged him. She sent away Craske, who had been with the family for thirty-five years. If I told Mason to go——"

He paused, took another mouthful of sandwich, and drank some more wine.

" This is all so exciting," he confided, " that I forgot myself. You must excuse me, Sir Jasper."

" Supposing you tell me all about Ming china ? " the latter suggested good-naturedly.

The Marquis finished his sandwich, wiped his fingers with his handkerchief, replenished his companion's glass and his own, and began. The words tumbled from his lips like a cascade—periods, dynasties, private marks, texture, colour, design—all like the waters of Lodore—speech which seemed to become shriller with eloquence, never deeper than the treble of a child of eight. He was still in full swing when they ran into King's Cross Station.

" What a pity ! " he sighed, looking around him. " I must come and see you and tell you some more. You should understand all about china, Sir Jasper. I will come and see you, and we will go together to the museums."

" In the meantime, can I be of any assistance to you now ? " Slane offered, as he glanced out at the crowded platform. " I imagine you are not used to travelling without a servant."

The Marquis chuckled.

" I have not been a yard without Mason since he came to me," he confided. " I hope very much that he dies. Good-afternoon, Sir Jasper."

He removed his strangely shaped hat with courtesy, superintended the disposal of his bags, and disappeared. Slane watched him step into a taxicab. That was the last the world saw of Henry James Marmaduke, Marquis of Aberway, for some weeks to come.

" Will the gentleman who travelled in the relief train to London with the Marquis of Aberway, after the railway accident near Massingham on the 17th instant, communicate with the Marchioness at Aberway House, Berkeley Square."

A tired but very beautiful lady of foreign appearance roused herself languidly from her environment of silk sheets, lace-edged pillows, and perfumed coverlet to swear softly at the sombre, apologetic figure leaning towards her.

" Marie ! " she exclaimed. " But this is unforgivable ! It is not yet eleven o'clock, and you disturb me like this ! "

" Milady," the maid apologised, " there is a gentleman below who has already been waiting some time. He offers a card, but his errand with you concerns, he says, an advertisement which appeared in *The Times* this morning."

The Marchioness became suddenly wide awake. She raised herself in bed.

" Is he the man, do you think, Marie, who travelled with my husband to London ? "

" One imagines so."

" Draw the curtains," the Marchioness ordered. " Turn on my bath. Be polite to monsieur. Beg him to wait for a few minutes only. Say that I was a trifle *malade* and resting, but will hasten now. Give him papers, magazines ; make him comfortable. Then fly back. A négligé will be sufficient."

Confusion reigned throughout that very beautiful bed-room, bathroom, and boudoir for the next three-quarters of an hour. At the end of that time, Sir Jasper Slane rose with an irritated frown to be greeted by the outstretched hands and the apologetic smile of one of the most beautiful women in London.

"But, Sir Jasper," she exclaimed, "how ashamed I am ! For myself, I was at that terrible party at Bledistow Palace last night, and afterwards—well, what does it matter ? I was asleep when you came, but I have hurried—believe me, I have hurried. Now tell me. After the accident you travelled up to London with that strange husband of mine ? "

"I certainly did," Slane admitted.

She sank on to a divan a few feet away from him.

"Tell me—tell me quickly," she begged. "Did he talk to you ? Did he tell you what he was going to do ? "

"I understood," Slane replied, "that he was going to buy china at Christie's most of the next day."

Up went her eyebrows. She extended her hands.

"Never did he go near Christie's ! " she cried. "Neither, when he arrived in London, did he come here—his own house. No one has heard of him. Yesterday I put an advertisement in *The Times*, and I telephoned to Scotland Yard. Sir Jasper, my husband has disappeared."

Slane smiled sympathetically.

"Do you know," he confided, " it rather occurred to me, from the way he was behaving, that he was contemplating something of the sort."

"But how extraordinary ! " she murmured. "Tell me, Sir Jasper, you had some conversation with him. How did my husband impress you ? "

"Like an elderly schoolboy who had escaped from his schoolmaster and meant to play truant for a time," was the prompt reply. "I know nothing definite about the matter, of course. Your husband talked more about china than anything else, but from the remarks he made when he saw his servant unconscious with a wound in his head, and knew

22*

that he had to be transported to a hospital, I gathered that his attitude towards him was not altogether friendly."

" Henry is so foolish," she faltered, with a tender little uplifting of the eyebrows ; " there is no one in the world so devoted to him as Mason."

" And how is Mason getting on ? "

" He is still in hospital. It may be weeks before he is about again. He was the only one in the train who seems to have received serious injuries. But what does it matter about him ? My great concern is for my husband. You are sure, Sir Jasper, that he gave you no idea whatsoever as to what he meant to do ? "

" Not the ghost of a one."

The Marchioness extended her beautifully shaped hands.

" Here is his house," she said. " His rooms are all prepared for him. The car was waiting at the station. You are sure that he had no injury in the accident which could cause forgetfulness ? "

" None at all," Slane declared confidently. " So far as we were both concerned, the accident was more comic than anything else. Your husband was sitting with his knees up to his chin like a trussed fowl when it was over, and I was standing with the seat under me destroyed."

She sighed in disappointment.

" You do not seem able to help me very much," she complained.

" How can I help you further ? " he rejoined. " You advertised in the agony column of *The Times* for the man who travelled up from the scene of the accident to King's Cross with the Marquis of Aberway. I hurried round, and what I had to tell I have told."

She looked at his card again.

" Sir Jasper Slane," she meditated. " The name seems somehow familiar to me."

His gesture was entirely non-committal. She reflected for a moment.

" Tell me, have you not a profession ? " she asked.

" I am a private detective when I find a case which interests me," he admitted.

" I knew it ! " she exclaimed excitedly. " You were a witness in the Le Bretton case. I shall offer you a thousand pounds reward to find my husband."

Jasper Slane rose to his feet.

" I will hurry," he announced, " or Scotland Yard may get ahead of me. One thousand pounds, dead or alive, eh ? "

" Dead or alive," she repeated.

He left her with a disagreeable impression—a queer instinct of repulsion against the callousness with which she had despatched him upon his errand.

. . . . . .

Henry James Marmaduke, Marquis of Aberway, was at no time a person of particularly dignified appearance, but his attitude in the small parlour, seated upon his haunches and endeavouring to spin a refractory top for the benefit of three shouting children, possessed elements of the ridiculous. His absence of self-consciousness, however, redeemed the situation. At his visitor's entrance, he laid the top on its side, patted the nearest child on her head, and rose to his feet.

" Sir Jasper Slane ! " he exclaimed, in that strange, piping squeak. " Now, how did you find me, I should like to know ? "

" Well, I was offered a thousand pounds, for one thing," was the good-humoured reply. " That quickens the wits."

" Come with me," the Marquis invited, leading the way across the passage and opening another door. " You see, I have a little parlour to myself here. Not much room for a big man like you, but very snug for me."

A neatly dressed woman was bending down attending to the fire. She curtsied as the two approached.

" Craske wished to know if there was anything he could do about this gentleman, my lord," she asked, looking at Jasper in belligerent fashion. " He slipped in before I could say a word."

" Nothing at all," the Marquis assured her pleasantly. " He is my friend, Emma. I shall enjoy a few minutes' conversation with him."

The woman curtsied once more and left the room.

" Old servants of mine," the Marquis explained. " Craske was the family butler, and the best in the world. He left at her ladyship's wish—not mine. He may return—who knows ? I feel that things are going to be different. . . . So you have seen my wife, Sir Jasper. Did she seem very worried at my disappearance ? "

" So much so that she offered a thousand pounds reward if I could find you."

The little man smiled knowingly.

" The thousand pounds reward was not for finding me, Sir Jasper," he declared. " It was to find out whether I had the keys."

" The keys ? " Slane repeated, mystified.

" Yes, the keys. You have not forgotten that when Mason was lying there groaning I went through his trousers' pockets and found a bunch of keys ? Here they are."

He produced them, attached by a chain to his trousers' button.

" Her ladyship would give a thousand pounds for these, I believe," he went on. " You didn't happen to mention that I had them, did you, Sir Jasper ? " he added anxiously.

" I certainly did not."

" You showed an amazing discretion," the Marquis acknowledged, in a tone of relief. " It is what I should have expected from you, Sir Jasper. You're a very shrewd man, I am sure."

" Look here," Slane inquired, " how long are you going to stay here ? "

" I am very happy with my friends, Mr. and Mrs. Craske," the Marquis confided. " I am studying Chinese at the museum opposite. Already I have been able to decipher several inscriptions which I have never properly understood. That takes quite a great deal of my time. Still, everything must come to an end, especially now that you have discovered me. But, Sir Jasper—Sir Jasper, please grant me a great favour. Before you go back to my wife to claim that thousand pounds, will you accept a small commission from me ? "

Slane smiled encouragingly.

" I will, if I can, of course," he promised. " What is it ? "

" I am going down to Norfolk this morning—starting at once—back this evening. One half-hour in the house alone. That is all I want. We come back together. You shall return in triumph. I will go with you to Berkeley Square."

" Well, that sounds simple enough," Slane agreed, " but why do you want to go all the way down there for such a short time ? "

The Marquis swung his bunch of keys and laughed his shrill little laugh.

" Some day you shall understand," he promised. " Very soon, too. I may need your help. You see. We start at once."

He pointed out of the window. A large Daimler car was drawn up by the kerb.

" We can lunch at Newmarket," he went on ; " have a cup of tea at home, and be back for dinner."

Slane reflected for a moment. As it happened, he had nothing particular to do that day.

" All right. I'll come," he decided.

The Marquis rang the bell. An elderly man, who had the unmistakable air of a butler, answered it, brought him a coat and hat, and escorted them respectfully to the car. The Marquis leaned back in his place with a shrill giggle.

" This is going to be very funny," he declared. " This is an expedition I shall enjoy. And let me tell you something, Sir Jasper. In Norfolk I was ill. Here I am feeling better every hour. . . ."

It was an early spring day with a cold wind but occasional bursts of sunshine. The Great North Road, with its magnificently prepared surface, was free of dust, and the long stretch from Royston bend northwards almost empty of traffic. They lunched at Newmarket according to arrangement, and were on the road again in three-quarters of an hour. At half-past three they entered the first of the series of lodge gates which led to the house. The outer part was really nothing but meadow-land, across which wound a road that followed the curving progress of a clear and beautiful trout-steam. Afterwards they passed into a domain of greater dignity studded with magnificent trees, and finally emerged in front of a great mansion, beautiful in outline, but a little depressing with its long rows of drawn blinds. A surprised servant answered their summons. The Marquis tripped across the hall like a schoolboy.

" Bring me a knife, Robins," he ordered the footman.

The man obeyed in stupefied silence. The Marquis calmly hacked in two the main telephone cord.

" Tell Mrs. Simmons or somebody to send tea to my small study as soon as possible," the master of the house ordered. " I am going to the butler's pantry."

" Certainly, my lord," the man replied. " I am afraid you will find the door of the butler's pantry locked, though. Mr. Mason took the keys away with him."

The Marquis produced the keys, and indulged in one of his peculiar staccato chuckles.

" Might I inquire how Mr. Mason is, my lord ? " the man ventured.

" Mason is getting on very well," the Marquis announced. " He will probably recover. It will be some time, however, before he is able to get about. You needn't wait, Robins. The little business I have in the butler's pantry I shall do alone. Show this gentleman into the small library. Just five minutes, that is all. . . ."

In less than that time the Marquis, with the keys once more attached to his chain, entered the room, where a footman and maid were arranging tea.

" Let the chauffeur have anything he wants," their master directed. " Bring cigars and whisky for Sir Jasper here, and tell Mrs. Simmons that I wish to speak to her. . . ."

In ten minutes Mrs. Simmons, the housekeeper, who showed signs of having changed her dress in a hurry, made her appearance. Her august master greeted her in friendly fashion, but his tone when he spoke was, for him, exceptionally grave.

" Mrs. Simmons," he announced, " I have disconnected the telephone. I have done so for reasons of my own. I do not wish any mention to be made to any single person of my visit here. I do not wish even her ladyship to be informed—or anyone. You understand me ? "

" I understand, my lord," the woman assented, a little diffidently, " but you will forgive me if I point out that all the papers are speaking of your disappearance since the railway accident. Surely it would be a great relief to her ladyship——"

" I dine with her ladyship to-night," the Marquis interrupted. " My orders—and I have seldom given orders here lately, as you know, Mrs. Simmons—are to be obeyed literally. Any person who telegraphs, or speaks now or at any future time, of my visit here to-day, will leave the house within an hour. That, I hope, is understood."

The housekeeper, trying in vain to conceal her bewilderment, curtsied and backed away.

" Your lordship's wishes will be obeyed, of course," she promised. " I will communicate them to each one of the servants myself. Your lordship is remaining to-night ? "

" We depart within five minutes. . . ."

The journey back to London was accomplished without a pause. As they neared the outskirts, however, Slane broke a rather lengthy silence.

" What about announcing your return to life, Marquis ? " he asked.

The latter smiled.

" I myself will proclaim your triumph," he decided. " You shall put me down at Berkeley Square. You admired my wife, I trust, Sir Jasper ? I met her in Bucharest years ago. She is a Roumanian, as I dare say you have heard."

" I fancy that I have heard something of the sort," Slane acknowledged.

" I have met some Roumanians whom I have liked," the Marquis reflected, " but I am not sure about the men. My wife's cousin, now—Prince Pitescue—is a great deal with us, but I fear that he does not appeal to me. You shall judge for yourself. You shall tell me what you think of him. You are free for this week-end, I hope. I need your services. I insist upon having them."

Slane, who had an idea of a week-end at Rye, hesitated.

" Well, I am not sure," he demurred. " What for ? "

" You have earned a thousand pounds from her ladyship for finding me," the Marquis chuckled. " How she will hate paying it ! I shall give you a thousand pounds now to be my companion and protector for five days. We shall spend the week-end at Aberway Court, and you will come down on Friday. Your duties will not be strenuous, but, do you know, Sir Jasper, just for a day or two I would rather not be in the house alone with her ladyship and the Prince. Something might happen. I might need support. I should like a friend near. You are a strong man, you know, Sir Jasper. I am a very small one, and sometimes very timid. Craske used to look after me, but her ladyship sent Craske away, and Mason—I do not think that Mason ever liked me. I think that he favours her ladyship. Until Friday, Sir Jasper. You will catch the three o'clock train from King's Cross, and I shall meet you. It will be a professional visit, of course. You will not find me ungrateful."

The car pulled up in front of Aberway House in Berkeley Square. Its master descended briskly. He held out his hand to Slane.

" I thank you very much for your company to-day, Sir Jasper," he said. " You will not fail me on Friday ? "

" No, I'll come," Slane promised.

The doors were opened. A major-domo appeared upon the top step. There was a vista in the background of bowing servants. The Marquis had returned home.

. . . . . .

Jasper Slane duly travelled down to Norfolk by the three o'clock train on the following Friday afternoon. He was met at the wayside station by the Marquis, who piped out the shrillest but most hospitable of greetings. He trotted by Slane's side along the platform, obviously pleased and contented with his visitor.

" We are a very small party," he announced, as they took their places in the car—" my wife, her cousin Prince Pitescue, of whom I spoke to you, yourself and myself—a *partie carrée*. You play billiards ? "

" Rather fond of it," Slane admitted. " I'm only average form, though."

The Marquis beamed with pleasure.

" My favourite recreation," he confided. " After dinner we will have a game."

" What about your man Mason ? "

" He's hanging on still," was the cheerful reply. " That wound must have been deeper than it seemed. I called at the hospital, but he won't be allowed to see anyone for a fortnight. Really most providential, his little accident ! Did you get your thousand pounds, Slane ? "

" I did," the latter acknowledged, " but I returned the cheque to your wife. The thing was ridiculous. I shall send her in a bill for fifty guineas. That will more than pay for my two men's time."

" We'll see," the Marquis chirped. " There may be a few other little things to straighten out, eh ? We'll see. This is the part of my estate I like best," he went on, as the car turned in through the first gate. " Ever fish ? "

" I'm not an expert."

" Full of trout, that stream. I try a cast sometimes myself. That's a good wood—the one on the right. Too high birds for me. A twenty bore is as much as I can manage. . . . Here we are. You'll just have time for a comfortable bath before dinner. You haven't brought a servant, I see. Robins will look after you excellently. He is almost as good as Craske used to be."

The Marquis, in high good humour, ushered his guest across the hall, and, preceded by an august major-domo, conducted Slane to his very delightful suite of rooms. He glanced at the clock.

" Short coat to-night, please," he begged. " We are quite alone. A little old-fashioned in our hours, I am afraid. Dinner at eight. I hope you don't mind. Cocktails at a quarter to eight in the library. Robins," he added, turning to the footman who was in attendance, " see that Sir Jasper lacks nothing."

" Very good, my lord."

The man began to unpack. Slane drew an easy-chair up to the window of the sitting-room, lit a cigarette, and helped himself to a whisky-and-soda from the bounteously supplied sideboard.

* * * * * *

The Marchioness was, without a doubt, a wonderfully beautiful woman. She wore black that night, a marvellous setting for her priceless pearls and her light, almost golden, hair. She came forward to meet Slane, and shook hands with him as with an honoured guest.

" And you sent back my thousand pounds, you bad man !" she exclaimed. " It was not kind of you. It was quite worth that to get my dear husband back again."

" I am afraid it was a little too easy a task," Slane replied. " You see, I happen to know one of your husband's hobbies, and I felt sure that he would be somewhere round the Museum."

" I am keeping up my Chinese," the Marquis confided, smiling. " I find it most interesting. Anita, my dear, do not forget to present Sir Jasper to your cousin."

" Of course not. Sir Jasper, this is Prince Pitescue. He has just left our legation in London, and is hoping to be sent to New York. You have perhaps met."

" I think that I have not had the pleasure," the young man murmured regretfully.

Slane shook hands, and disliked his new acquaintance on

sight. The Prince had the sallow complexion, dark eyes, and rather too full red lips of his country. His attire was elegant, almost foppish. He was evidently a frequent visitor, and had the air of being very much at home—so much so that he seemed to regard his fellow-guest almost as an intruder. The conversation had scarcely passed the monosyllabic stage when it was interrupted by the arrival of cocktails. Two of these stood together upon a corner of the tray, the other two a little way apart. The Marquis smiled as his wife took one of the former.

" In Mason's absence," he explained, " it is my wife who prepares the cocktails. Very good we find them, too. You observe that our glasses are not scanty in size. That is because we never serve more than one. That is yours. I hope you approve."

" Excellent ! One of the best Martinis I have had for a long time. Why is it, however, that mine is quite clear, and yours a little cloudy ? "

" Mine," the Marquis confided, " contains just a pinch of bicarbonate of soda. In fact, we three have all the same idiosyncrasy—just a touch of indigestion now and then— nothing serious. You, Sir Jasper, look far too healthy to need anything of that sort."

" Oh, I sometimes take a dose of bicarbonate of soda," Slane admitted, " but I must confess that I never heard of taking it in cocktails."

" My wife's idea," the Marquis chuckled. " I used to shy at it. Now we none of us mind—even our young friend here, who at his age—how old are you, Rudolph ? Twenty-nine ?—should know nothing of illness. It is, however, a habit," he went on, his voice seeming to reach even a higher altitude, " in which I am not sure that I shall persevere. Sometimes I fancy—especially since Mason left—that I feel a slight pain—nothing to speak of. No reflection upon your skill, my dear. Still, my digestion is better. Why interfere with it ? "

" So is mine," the Marchioness agreed. " I think we might leave off dosing our cocktails for a time. We'll see— after to-morrow. . . ."

Dinner was announced—a very wonderful banquet, served, as it transpired later, by accident, in the large dining-room, generally called the banqueting-hall. As the meal progressed and the daylight faded, candles in wonderful silver candelabra of great height were lit upon the table. The only other illumination was from the electric lamp above the great pictures with which the room was hung. A mediæval silver bowl, filled with red roses, occupied the centre of the table, and there was scarcely an appurtenance of the service which was not in itself an *objet d'art*. The food was wonderful, and Jasper Slane, who was a constant "diner out," found himself drinking wines of which he had heard but which he had never tasted. The service was noiseless and perfect—the men in their somewhat worn but picturesque livery passed like shadows to and from the dim recesses of the room. Conversation alone was now and then a little difficult. The Marchioness at times seemed vaguely uneasy. She watched Slane half curiously, half suspiciously—more than once she and the young man exchanged a rapid glance of mutual comprehension. All the time the Marquis, in his high-pitched, childish treble, talked nonsense, yet nonsense which seemed as though it might have some underlying purpose. The meal moved with a sort of effortless grace of service and luxury to its appointed end. Fruit, hothouse peaches and muscatel grapes, port in amazing decanters, and old madeira, were placed upon the table.

"The last of my '68," the Marquis indicated shrilly. "For you alone, I fear, Sir Jasper. One glass, perhaps, for me. The Marchioness knows nothing of port, nor, I am afraid, does Pitescue. '68 Cockburn—never been touched since it was laid down."

"It is marvellous," Slane truthfully admitted, as he sipped his wine.

The Marchioness and her cousin drank madeira. The latter lit a cigarette. His host made a grimace, but forbore from comment. He raised himself higher upon the cushion which was always placed in his chair.

"Listen," he enjoined, "I am going to tell you something which seems to me very strange—you, particularly, Anita —you and Rudolph."

He looked around. The servants had departed. For long afterwards that scene was to remain in Slane's memory, chiefly on account of its dramatic setting—the cathedral-like room, with its cloistered ceiling ; the small, round table a little pool of shaded illumination in the midst of a gloom almost mysterious ; three white faces, two of them growing paler with every spoken word.

" Before I went to London," the Marquis began, leaning forward, " I was not well. For four days I had been taking this bicarbonate of soda mixed for me with my cock-tail by Mason, and I had pains which I could not understand, and a weakness which seemed to be increasing hour by hour. Yet all the time, you two," he went on—" you, Anita, and my young friend Rudolph—you thrived on it. Young and blooming, both of you, of course, whilst I am elderly, still the difference puzzled me—so now I have played a trick upon you," he chuckled. " Tell me, Anita—tell me, Rudolph— how have you been feeling since we came down here, these last five days ? "

There was a brief but tense silence. The expression of somewhat bored indifference with which the Marchioness had been listening passed from her face. She stared at her husband. The Prince laid down his cigarette. He, too, leaned forward.

" What do you mean ? " the Marchioness asked shrilly. " I have not felt well. I never feel well in the country— but what of it ? "

" I have suffered from headaches," the Prince confessed. " Early though we have retired, I have awakened the last two mornings with a *mal de tête incroyable.*"

" On Thursday morning," his cousin added, " I nearly sent for the doctor. I had a pain over my heart, and a giddiness which was incomprehensible. What do you mean, Henry ? "

The Marquis rocked from side to side of his cushioned chair with silent laughter.

" Last week," he confided, " when I was lost, I came down here. I went to Mason's cupboard."

" You had not the keys," his wife broke in swiftly.

" Ah, but I did have the keys," he went on, smiling. " I took them from Mason's pocket when he was unconscious. Do not interrupt me, my dear. Let me have my little joke. I opened his cupboard and I saw that there were two bottles there—one blue and one white—both filled with white powder. Both were labelled ' *bicarbonate of soda,*' but one was also labelled—' For Lord Aberway only.' I—listen, Slane, for this is funny—I changed the contents. These

two have been taking my bicarbonate of soda for five days.
I have been taking theirs, and I feel well. Really I have
never felt better. I could walk for miles. I was longing to
play tennis this afternoon when I passed the Vicarage and
saw all the young—Anita ! Anita ! What is wrong ? "

The Marchioness's scream rang through the room. She
half rose to her feet, pointing to her husband, but words
seemed to fail her, and she collapsed across the table.

" Rudolph ! " she moaned.

The young man, who had already left his place, took no
notice of her. There were drops of sweat upon his forehead.
He rushed madly towards the door, shouting. Half-way
there, however, he stopped and staggered back again.

" Where is there a doctor ? " he cried. " Where is one
to be found ? Why don't you do something, Anita ? This
is your fault. It is you who are responsible. Why do you
not send someone for a doctor ? Oh, my God ! "

His knees were shaking. His voice died away into a
whimper. He collapsed into a chair. The Marquis touched
Slane upon the shoulder.

" Come with me," he invited. " They are better left
alone. They must have much to say to one another. We
will have our game of billiards."

.   .   .   .   .

Slane, somewhat dazed, still lacking full comprehension
of the inner meaning of the drama at which he had assisted,
followed his host across the hall. The latter threw open the
door of the billiard-room, turned on the lights, and began
carefully to chalk a cue.

" Any one of those is good," he said, indicating a row of
cases which hung upon the wall. " You should give me
something, but I will try you level."

Slane pulled himself together.

" Marquis," he demanded, " do you suspect that one of
those bottles really contained poison ? "

" Of course it did," was the shrill reply. " Shall I break,
or will you ? "

" But you can't leave them like this if they are really
poisoned," Slane expostulated. " You must find doctors."

The Marquis dragged out a stool from under the table,
and touched Slane upon the shoulder.

" My friend," he said, " they would have given me months

of agony, and a place in the family vault. I shall give them an hour in which to suffer, and no more. See—I play."

He mounted on to the low stool, which was specially made with squat, flat legs, and gave an accurate miss in baulk.

" You mean——" Slane began.

" Trust me," the Marquis begged. " I am a quaint little man. I have my ways. Trust me."

.   .   .   .   .   .

There was commotion throughout the house, but they played their game of billiards without interruption. At the end, when the Marquis had won by over forty points, he regretfully laid down his cue.

" My friend," he said, " I see that you are upset. Now, come with me."

He led the way back to the dining-room. The Marchioness —the central figure in that little pool of shaded light—sat still in her place, white as death, her hand pressed to her heart, breathing convulsively. The young man was sprawling over the table, apparently drinking everything within reach.

" The doctor ! " he shrieked. " Will he never come ? Is there no antidote for this accursed stuff ? "

" Antidote for sodina ! " the Marquis exclaimed, closing the door. " Sodina is a poison invented by the Medicis, they say, still found in Italy—can be bought, too, I think, in Bucharest. A harmless-looking white powder, though six doses will suffice to kill the strongest man and leave no trace behind. But it is not sodina that you have drunk, you —nor you, Anita. It is not the poison of which I have had four doses, and of which six would have killed me. For all your fancied pains, what you took to-night is bicarbonate of soda. You will not be much the worse unless you frighten yourselves to death. He-he ! "

Anita looked strangely up. A light suddenly flashed into the glazed eyes of the young man, though he was still shaking from head to foot. Neither of them was capable of speech.

" You poor fools ! " the Marquis scoffed. " I guessed the truth. I went to London to save my life, not to buy china. When the accident happened to Mason, the chance to teach you a lesson was too tempting. The poison is in a safe place, but you have taken none of it. I filled both bottles when I got back here with bicarbonate of soda. You have had your hour of fright—many would say that you deserved a sterner lesson. The car, which was supposed to fetch a doctor, waits, by my orders, still at the door. You can take it as far as you like, Pitescue. There are night trains running from Peterborough."

The young man stumbled from the room. He was tall, elegant, and of military carriage, yet as he passed the little Marquis he seemed insignificant. The latter looked towards his wife.

" Your cousin is, I fear, somewhat disturbed," he said. " He forgot to invite you to accompany him."

The passion flamed from her eyes.

" He is a coward ! " she cried. " Oh, God, how I hate cowards ! Henry, if I go—and I deserve that you should send me away—it will not be with him."

The Marquis rang the bell. Almost immediately a footman appeared.

" Robins," he directed, " will you tell her ladyship's maid that her ladyship is fatigued and will retire at once ? "

The man bowed and departed on his errand. The Marchioness rose trembling to her feet and moved towards the door, and again, as she passed the man who held it open for her, he seemed to gain in stature and dignity. She stooped down and kissed his hand. He bent his head gracefully, and closed the door behind her.

" And now, my dear Sir Jasper," he proposed, in his highest, shrillest tones, " we will have a serious game. We will play two hundred up, and I shall give you thirty, but you must allow me my stool and the rest. Robins," he added, as the man reappeared, " serve refreshments in the billiard-room. Do not forget the Napoleon brandy."

NEAP-TIDE MADNESS

SLANE saw tragedy coming to him through the bank of white mist which had fallen suddenly over the marshes. A breath of wind unscreened those ghostly arms, he saw the dim figure of a man, saw the blinding flash of a gun, heard the shrill whistle of a bullet. Once more the wall of floating vapours closed up, and there was silence.

" What the hell do you mean by that ? " Slane shouted.

His voice seemed the most ineffectual thing in this wilderness of silence. There was no reply. High overhead, a flight of geese went honking along the shore. From the side of the road came the sibilant, soft suction of the tidal waters, but of human sound there was none. Slane, who had courage enough, felt only one sensation—anger. He plunged forward blindly, left the road, made breathless passage over the mossy, sea-riven land, only to put his foot deep into a morass and fall headlong before he had gone a dozen paces. He picked himself up, and listened. Again there was that queer, brooding silence, which at this hour of the evening always seemed to come down from the skies. The cold water chilled him. He stumbled on his way—an undignified object, his clothes soaking, his anger finding no form of expression. The mist was denser now—so dense that as he struggled towards the rough lane he walked into a startled pony, which galloped off at his touch. With a sense of bewilderment, he strode on until he reached the first gate, grasped the white timber bars and raised his voice again—in vain. A dog was barking somewhere in the far distance. There was the eternal swish and suction of the waters, the breathing of a cow close at hand—so close that, as he pushed the gate open, he set the beast stampeding into the mist. The furtive lights of the Dormy House now shone dimly through the hanging gloom. He unlatched the gate and stepped, dripping, into the hall. Harrison, the butler, hastened forward to meet him.

" Harrison," he demanded, " who the hell wanders over these marshes in the mists with a gun, trying to commit murder ? "

" A gun, Sir Jasper ?　One of the duck shooters, lost his way, I expect. You don't mean to say he came nigh hitting you ? "

" Blast him, he tried to murder me ! " Slane cried, the fury still hot in his veins. " It was no shot gun. It was an automatic, or a rifle. Fired a bullet at me through the mist. He couldn't have missed me by more than a yard. What maniacs are there loose in the neighbourhood ? "

Harrison's expression was a little grave as he took Slane's wringing wet coat.

" If you'll come straight upstairs, sir," he proposed, " I'll get you a bath quick. As to whom you might come across on them marshes, God only knows, but there be queer tales at times."

" I'll have the queer tales out of someone," Slane muttered. " I'm no more careful of my life than most men, but I've no fancy to be a target for a lunatic."

" There's few of the gentlemen, sir," Harrison ventured, " who stay out quite so late."

" And why the hell not ? " Slane demanded. " I had a late tea, and a whisky in the bar, and a chat with Tom Ryder afterwards in his workshop. Then I saw the mists come down, and I made for home. Why shouldn't I stay as long as I want to ? I'll get to the bottom of this, Harrison."

They had reached the bathroom. The man turned on the tap, and the room was soon full of hissing steam.

" If you'll take your bath, Sir Jasper," he suggested, " you'll find your clothes all laid out for you. I'll bring a cocktail up, if I may, to keep the cold out, and what there may be to tell, I'll just tell you, if the other gentlemen don't, sir."

.　　　.　　　.　　　.　　　.

The evening meal in the long, low dining-room of the Dormy House was always a simple but pleasant function. It was served by Harrison, a maid, and a rather clumsy boy, and consisted usually of soup, fish, and a joint. Whisky-and-soda, followed by a bottle of port, was the staple drink, and golf the invariable subject of conversation. To-night, however, Slane introduced what was evidently a disturbing note. He turned to Major Lyall, the secretary, who sat at the head of the table, and asked him a portentous question.

" Why do you allow madmen to go about on the links, Lyall ? "

" Can't help it so long as they're not certified and have paid their subscriptions," was the cheerful reply. " Some-one has to lose. Was it the old Colonel you were thinking of ? I saw him break two clubs this afternoon."

" I am not referring to the usual type of golfing lunatic," Slane continued. " Do you know, coming back to-night, I was shot at, at point-blank range, by some beast of a fellow with a gun."

There was a moment's silence, and the secretary—a broad-shouldered man of fine physique, with healthily tanned cheeks, loud voice, and breezy manner—seemed unaccount-ably embarrassed. The other three men showed their interest in various ways. Ferguson, a barrister, clean-shaven, a little worn and grizzled, was clearly taken by surprise. The other two men—Paul Fenton, a stockbroker, and Walter Seymour, a lawyer, who came from somewhere in the Midlands—seemed to share the secretary's discom-fiture.

" What made you come home by the marsh road ? " Major Lyall asked, rather with the air of an unsympathetic magistrate cross-examining a witness.

" Well, I suppose I can if I want to, can't I ? " was the impatient rejoinder. " As a matter of fact, I lost my way. There was one of those beastly sea fogs about, and I didn't realise that I had missed the turning until I was half-way here."

The secretary sipped his wine.

" You haven't been down for a month or so, Slane," he said. " Otherwise you'd know that that road isn't safe now for anyone staying at the Dormy House."

" Why on earth not ? "

Lyall shrugged his shoulders.

" Well, I should have thought you'd have found out," he vouchsafed dryly.

Slane was puzzled, and a little indignant.

" Do you know who the fellow was ? " he asked.

" I can guess," Lyall acknowledged. " It was Mark Rennett."

" Then I shall take a policeman and have a talk with Mr. Mark Rennett in the morning," Slane declared. " He'd better choose some other form of amusement than mistaking human beings for ducks."

The secretary moved uneasily in his chair.

" The fellow's a damned nuisance, of course," he admitted, " but he doesn't seem to do any mischief unless anyone goes near his cottage. I should leave him alone, I think."

" Why should I ? " Slane demanded. " The fellow fired at me deliberately. I'm not going to give him the chance of doing it a second time."

" You'll be all right," Major Lyall assured him, " so long as you stick to the main road. The fellow's a difficult proposition. He built that cottage of old timbers and beach stones on a piece of reclaimed land twenty years ago, and I don't think anyone could turn him out if they tried. He's made a living somehow or other. He has a boat on one of the reaches, and can bring fish out of the water and duck from the skies like no ordinary man. He was a civil enough chap, too, until a year ago—used to caddy sometimes when the weather was bad, and knew the game as well as any of us."

" What's happened to him since a year ago ? " Slane asked bluntly.

There was a moment's silence. Seymour seemed about to speak, but thought better of it. Lyall stretched out his hand for the decanter and filled his glass.

" The fact is," he confided, " that Rennett, although he's a man past middle age, has a wife who in her way is really beautiful. I won't even qualify it. She is an amazingly beautiful human being. One or two of the visitors down here used to go out of their way to stroll home by Rennett's cottage—one especially—a man you know, I think, Slane. If ever he comes back—which he hasn't done for the last eight months—I think Rennett will shoot him. Not that he's really to blame. I don't believe anyone who's stayed here has even spoken more than a dozen words to the woman. As a matter of fact, Rennett himself—a sour, sullen dog he is—has never made any serious complaint, and I shouldn't imagine he's had any cause to. The trouble is, the man's half a gipsy, and at times he's mad. He's sworn to shoot anyone from the Dormy House who goes near the cottage, and there you are."

"And you put up with it ? " Slane asked in amazement. The secretary laughed a little apologetically.

" I suppose, upon the face of it," he said, " it does seem rather ridiculous, but what are we to do ? The man's his own landlord. He can't be turned out, even if one wanted to do it. The grievance against us may have some foundation, or it may not—no one really knows—but so long as he's left alone, he does no harm. He's never raised his gun that I've heard of, or attempted any form of violence against anyone, except—except against one man. Supposing you take your story to the police. He'll just say that he was duck shooting, and didn't notice anyone coming, and all the police can do is to warn him to be more careful in the future."

" They can take his gun licence away," Slane pointed out.

" I doubt whether they could. In this part of the world it's like drawing a man's teeth."

Slane abandoned the subject. It seemed to him a curious thing that the fact of his doing so was a matter for obvious relief to everyone.

⁕⁕⁕⁕⁕⁕

" Playing with us to-day, Slane ? " Fenton asked at breakfast-time the next morning.

Slane looked over his shoulder from the sideboard from which he was helping himself.

" After lunch," he assented. " This morning I am going to pay a call upon Mr. Mark Rennett."

There was a brief silence. Major Lyall looked up from behind the local paper.

" I wouldn't do that if I were you, Slane," he advised.

" I'd let the fellow alone," Seymour echoed.

Slane looked at them both curiously.

" Well," he said, as he seated himself, " I have my own ideas of what to do when a fellow takes a pot shot at you from twenty yards away, because you happen to be passing near his cottage. If I didn't go to see him, I should go to the police. Perhaps that would be better, anyway."

" It wouldn't do any good," Seymour confided. " I know the sergeant here, and I know the policeman. I bet you a fiver that neither of them would go near."

" Well, let's hope it won't be necessary," Slane remarked, settling down to his breakfast. " I shall try the effect of a little gentle persuasion first."

Major Lyall crumpled up his paper angrily.

" You're asking for trouble, Slane," he remonstrated. " The man's as strong as an ox, and he'd kill anyone as soon as look at them."

" Quite time he was talked to, then," Slane observed imperturbably. . . .

Nevertheless, when he set out for his excursion, he was fully conscious that in a way it was a rash one. He had gone so far as to arm himself with a short, thick stick, but he had no intention of being driven to use it. The morning was fine, though a little cold, and the marshes seemed alive with insects and twittering birds. There was a scent of wild thyme in the air, and in the distance patches of wild lavender. Mark Rennett's abode was easily to be seen—a strange, rough-looking erection, standing absolutely by itself near one of the arms of the sea—a muddy ditch now, but transformed into a glittering waterway with the turn of the tide. There was no sign of human life about the place as Slane approached, and he had time to take note of his surroundings. There were several things that surprised him. In the first place, everything was spotlessly neat. In one of the front windows was a great bowl of wild lavender ; in another a pot of primroses. A long fishing-net, reeking with odours of the sea, was laid out to dry. There had been no attempt to enclose any space for a garden—the door opened on to the soft, spongy turf—but in a sheltered corner, where one might catch the sunlight, there was a wicker chair upon which were some articles of woman's clothing. Slane was in the act of tapping at the door with his stick when it suddenly opened, and he received a shock which bereft him for a moment of speech. Mark Rennett's wife stood upon the threshold looking out at him.

Afterwards, for his own pleasure, he tried to collect those first impressions of her, and though he never failed to weave them into a wonderful picture, he always felt that in certain mysterious ways memory failed him. To his first surprised fancy she resembled nothing so much as Fra Lippo Lippi's Florentine " Madonna "—her face, its features chiselled with all the painter's flawless delicacy, her nose

with its quaint, piquant outline, her richly human mouth,
the deep-set blue eyes, now a little startled as they looked
upon this unexpected stranger.   She wore a queer blue
garment, which covered her from head to foot, but which,
shapeless though it was, seemed here and there to reveal
the grace of her slim limbs.   She stood with one hand upon
her hip, leaning a little forward, and, as she looked at Slane,
that first gentle smile of inquiry seemed to become to him
something subtly different, something which stirred him as
he had seldom before been stirred in his life.

" What might you be wanting ? " she asked.

Her voice was soft enough, but it had more than a touch
of the East Anglian accent.

" I wanted a word with Mark Rennett," he announced.

" My husband," the woman said, a little uneasily.   " He
is out along the dyke side.   There was a call of snipe this
morning—or maybe he fancied it.   What do you want
with him, may I ask, sir ? "

She crossed the threshold towards him, and shaded her
eyes with her hand, looking down the curving waterway.
Slane was speechless.   In a dim sort of way, he understood
the reticence of the men at the Dormy House.   No words
could deal adequately with the subject of this woman.

" He's not partial to strangers, Mark isn't," she confided,
turning towards him with a faint deprecatory gesture.   " I
don't know that I'd stay, if I were you, unless the business
is serious.   He be a violent man, and suspicious beyond all
things."

Her delicate mouth—heavens to find such a mouth in such
a place !—broke into a smile, her eyes seemed to be asking
him for understanding.

" Well, the fact of it is," Slane told her, pulling himself
together, " I came to complain.   I lost my way and passed
along the path there last night, and he shot at me—missed
me by no more than a foot or two."

She seemed to treat the incident lightly.

" Mark's peculiar," she admitted.   " He has strange ideas
in his head—mostly about me.   I'd let it be, sir.   I wouldn't
wait for him now.   Don't come this way again by night, if
Mark's about."

" That's all very well," Slane protested, with an effort at
good humour, " but one doesn't expect to be shot at just

because a madman doesn't like one near his cottage. I very nearly went to the police instead of coming here."

She laughed gaily.

" And what did you think they'd do ? " she mocked him. " There's old Sergeant Pardowe. He'd tighten his belt, and cough and wheeze, but he'd never step this far across the marshes. He'd wait until he found Mark in a public-house, and then have a solemn word with him. Young Clooney would come fast enough if he'd send him, but young Clooney is afraid of Mark. They mostly are," she went on, looking at him with wistful, wide-open eyes, seeking for sympathy. " Mark's so queer about me. The sight of a man near the cottage drives him crazy. Some day there will be trouble."

" It must make life lonely for you," he ventured.

Again she laughed, and Slane fought against the stealthy conviction of what that call in her eyes might mean.

" There come times," she confided, and there was a magic in her tone which seemed to be telling him that it was for him alone she spoke, " when the wind sets fair, and the boats go out, and Mark must fish. That's in the full spring-time, too. He's away for weeks—the spring-time when the nights here are soft and velvety, and the stars shine, and one can see the sea and the lights of the boats without moving from my window. I am thankful for those fishing days and nights sometimes, for Mark's a gloomy man."

In the distance they heard the report of a gun. Once more she leaned forward and gazed down the waterway.

" He's coming back," she whispered. " If I were you, mister, I wouldn't wait. I shan't tell him you've been."

" If you don't mind," Slane insisted, " I should like to stay and see him. I do not wish my visit to be a secret. I came here to warn him."

" He'll take no notice," she assured him. " He's a fearsomely determined man. Do you come from the Dormy House, by chance, mister ? "

" I do," Slane admitted. " I'm staying there."

" Then he'll hate you just like the rest of them," she predicted. " He can't abide the sight of a gentleman. I'd rather you went," she begged, moving back a little. " If he sees me here talking to you, there may be trouble, mister. He can't help it. He's like that."

" I'll take my chance," Slane decided. " Or—wait !

It's safe going by the side of your creek, I suppose ? I can reach the links that way. I'll go and meet him, and then there's no chance of getting you into trouble."

She looked upwards, her eyes searching for a lark, singing unusually high. At that moment her face was like the face of an angel. She was listening to, her eyes were seeking for, something beautiful.

"Go and meet him, then," she sighed, "if you must. For myself, I would rather everyone left him alone. There's the spring fishing, and the winter fishing, and when he's away I can breathe. When he's here there's always terror in the air."

"I think," Slane remonstrated, "that you get a little over-nervous living here alone and without neighbours. I'll have my talk with him, anyway."

He lifted his hat. She had drawn back into the shelter of the cottage, out of sight of the distant but approaching figure. She made no reply to his farewell, but, with her hand straying back once more to her hip, she stood looking at him, and there was something in the flicker of her eyelids, the promise of her eyes, the faint curve of her lips, which a less experienced man than Slane might have recognised as something akin to the witchery which has set men's hearts trembling and crumbled to dust their wills since the days of Delilah. Slane went tramping across the marshes, with a singing in his ears, but without a backward glance. . . .

Mark Rennett, at close quarters, had at least personality. In costume and appearance he seemed to be a composite picture of the gipsy and the fisherman. His complexion was swarthy and his hair black. He had a distinctly hooked nose, and harsh, angry mouth. He wore a fisherman's jersey, seaboots over his trousers, and a red handkerchief around his neck. He was a fine, upstanding figure of a man, with a slight stoop of the neck. His pockets were bulging with the snipe he had shot, and as Slane approached he brought another one down from the skies, picked up the fluttering little mass of feathers, chucked it into his pocket, and reloaded his gun. Then he changed his course so as to meet Slane.

"What does you want with me, mister ? " he inquired truculently. "I don't allow visitors at my cottage."

"You'll have visitors you won't want if you're not careful,

my man," Slane replied. " You'll have the police. I nearly went for them this morning."

" Fat lot of good that would do you," the man snarled. " Say your business with me and be off."

" I shall be off when I choose," was the calm rejoinder. " The marshes don't belong to you, my man, and you'll quit them for prison if you go about letting off firearms as you did last night."

Mark Rennett laughed unpleasantly.

" So the marshes are yours, and the sea and the air as well, I reckon, mister," he jeered. " Will you fight me for them ? "

" We can neither of us fight for what does not belong to either of us," Slane replied. " They are free for me as they are for you, so long as you behave yourself. Last night in the fog you fired off a gun which barely missed me."

" Well, if there was a fog, mister, how could I see ? " the man demanded insolently.

" You saw me right enough."

" Then what were you doing nigh to my cottage ? "

" You don't deserve a civil answer," Slane said, " but you shall have one. I missed my way walking from the golf club house to the Dormy House."

" I guessed you was one of those lazy, ball-playing pigs," Mark Rennett gibed. " Nothing to do but eat and drink and knock a little ball about, and skulk after other men's belongings. Sorry I missed you the other night, guv'nor. I could always have said I thought I 'eered duck. You listen to me," he went on, coming half a yard nearer. " It isn't often I get a chance to talk to one of you blokes, except Major Lyall. He's the only gentleman of the lot of you. Minds his own business, he does. Now I've got you here I'm going to tell you summat. You can bawl about the police until your throat aches. I don't care. The police won't touch me. They dursn't. But as for you chaps up at the Dormy House there, I hate the lot of you. D'you hear that ? You're a lot of mucking, idling hogs. I beat up one on 'em, come a year ago, and I did my two months for it. I'll swing maybe for the next. So now you know. Get on your ways, mister. You're the first one I've seen as can look a man in the eyes, anyway. Keep t'other side of Rennett's dyke, and you'll keep out of mischief.' "

23

The man strode away. Jasper Slane filled his pipe and turned towards the golf house. Somehow or other he was not utterly convinced that he had had the best of the interview. The memory of that singing bullet still filled him with a curious sort of irritation when he thought of it. He sat on the beach, deliberating what to do, and then fate solved the problem for him. A boy from the Dormy House arrived on a bicycle with a telegram. He was wanted in Town, and wanted urgently. He caught the three o'clock train, and for the time being his acutely vivid impressions of the last few hours passed into the background of his mind.

. . . . . .

It was May before Slane found himself able to take another few days' holiday. He packed his golf clubs and fishing rods, wrote for his usual room, and travelled down to Norfolk. In the hall of the Dormy House, Lyall met him.

" Come down alone ? " the latter asked eagerly, as they shook hands.

" Didn't seem to be anyone at the junction for here," Slane replied. " I kept the car waiting five minutes or so in case anyone turned up."

Lyall drew a little breath of relief. Slane looked at him curiously.

" You don't look very fit, old chap," he remarked.

The secretary took his arm and led him to the little smoke-room. He made signs to the steward, and they were served with whiskies-and-sodas. Slane glanced at the man again. There were deeper lines in his long, narrow face, from which the healthy sunburn seemed to have vanished, and his grizzled hair was more grey than ever. About his eyes, too, there was that look of trouble which grows when men live under the shadow of some fear.

" I want a change," he confessed. " The solitude and quietness of this place through the winter get on one's nerves. One magnifies little things, and one can't sleep."

" Is that murderous fellow Rennett still tramping the marshes with his gun ? " Slane asked.

Lyall's face was like a mask.

" That fellow, Slane," he confessed, " is the curse of my life. He'll do someone a mischief some day or other. By-the-by, I think you know Ebben—Julius Ebben ? "

" Very slightly. I'm really not sure that I have ever met

him. He's a banker, isn't he—one of the famous Jew family ? A tidy golfer, I believe."

" Yes, he's a scratch player. To tell you the truth he's one of my troubles just now. He wanted to come down here. I wired that every room was full, and that it was quite impossible. I'm afraid, all the same, he'll turn up. He's one of these persistent devils. You never can get a millionaire to understand that there are things he can't buy. If I had my way," Lyall continued, filling a pipe with long, yellow-stained, nervous fingers, " I'd blow the roof off this place before he slept under it."

" What's the trouble ? "

Lyall smoked gloomily.

" Nothing that men of common sense—healthy men, like you and me—could understand. It is these romanticists— Jews, artists, chaps of that sort—who get the poison into their veins sometimes. Don't let's talk about it. Ebben mayn't come, and," he added, looking out of the window at the storm which had suddenly blown up, " the fishing boats mayn't go out."

" So that's it," Slane murmured softly.

They finished their whiskies-and-sodas, and Slane rose and stretched himself.

" You've got your same room," Lyall told him, " the big corner one. Who the devil's this ? "

A car drove up to the front door, and a soberly dressed manservant descended from the box. A tall man in a huge ulster climbed out and entered the hall.

" It's Ebben ! " Lyall exclaimed hoarsely. " Damn the fellow ! I wired him that we were full up."

The door of the smoking-room was thrown open. Julius Ebben entered—a tall, good-looking man, slim and athletic, with bright, dark eyes, just then filled with laughter.

" It's no good, Lyall, old man," he said. " You can't rob a man of his week's golf like that. Any old crib will do for me."

" I wired you we hadn't a room, Ebben," Lyall protested. " There isn't a hole or corner for you. You had better have a drink and go on to Hunstanton."

Ebben smiled.

" Now, Lyall," he begged, " don't be unreasonable. This is Slane, isn't it ? " he added, turning to the latter.

" Glad to see you. Lyall, you've plenty of rooms, and you know you have, and you can't keep me out of the place. Why, damn it all, I'm a director ! Don't be stupid. We'll have a drink together, and you shall tell my servant where to put my things. I warn you, though, arguments are no use with me. I shall open the door of every bedroom in the place and select the first empty one I come to."

" There are a lot of fellows coming to-morrow," Lyall muttered ungraciously.

" Then perhaps there may be one of them," Ebben declared, " for whom there won't be a room, but first come, first served, you know. *J'y suis, j'y reste.* Three whiskies-and-sodas, Harrison. Now come along ! Slane, I'm looking forward to playing golf with you. I saw you win the big pot at Cromer last year. Lyall, old man, get rid of that melancholy expression. Life isn't worth it."

Lyall was beaten, and he knew it. His whisky-and-soda remained untasted, however, and he left the room to give some orders. Ebben watched his great, shambling figure with a smile of amusement.

" Poor old Lyall ! " he murmured. " He takes everything so damned seriously. Looks upon us all when we come here as being under his parental eye, or something of the sort— as though we couldn't take care of ourselves."

. . . . . .

Four times that evening, between the service of dinner and bedtime, Lyall, on some excuse or another, walked out into the night and stood on the wall, his hands outstretched, his head thrown back, scenting for the wind. The last time he came back, Ebben looked up from the bridge-table.

" What about the weather, Lyall ? "

" The wind has gone down," was the grumpy reply. " You'll get your golf to-morrow."

But both men knew that it wasn't the golf Lyall was thinking about. They knew it then, and they knew it when, from the ninth green on the following morning, they turned to see the little procession of boats coming down from the harbour along the widening estuary. Along a narrow creek, running at right-angles, a single sail was visible, gliding between the two banks of marshy land down to join the others. The little company of golfers stood and watched it. Not one of them spoke a word. They stood there gazing until the small boat reached the broader waters. After they had driven from the tenth tee, they turned round again. The sail of the little dinghy had been furled. Its solitary occupant had clambered into one of the larger boats. The smaller one was made fast behind. Lyall watched it curiously.

" I wonder," Julius Ebben murmured, " why our friend Rennett is taking his dinghy ? "

No one answered, but three other men also wondered. The cottage on the marshes seemed dead and lifeless. Not even a wisp of smoke came from the chimney. . . .

That evening the wind had dropped, and the lights of the fishing fleet were dimly visible on the horizon. At night they had disappeared. At the Dormy House, the time passed apparently in the usual fashion. There were some new arrivals, and three tables of bridge. When Slane retired to bed, Julius Ebben was still playing. Lyall, in a distant corner, was seated with his arms folded and with the air of a watchdog.

. . . . . .

Slane awoke the next morning to find the room full of sunlight and Lyall's tall form bending over him. Some instinct of apprehension caused him to become suddenly alert. He swung himself out of bed.

" What's wrong, Lyall ? " he asked.

" The inevitable," Lyall groaned. " I thought you'd better see the body before it was moved. These local police are no use, although, of course, I've sent for them and a doctor. Come along, man ! Into some clothes, quick ! "

All the usual matutinal instincts were forgotten. In a pair of trousers, a shirt and a pull-over, Slane was prepared in a matter of seconds.

" Tell me about it ? " he begged, as the two men left the room.

" Everyone went to bed about twelve last night," Lyall recounted. " I locked up myself. This morning Ebben wasn't in his room. They came and told me. I got up. I knew where to go. He's outside the door of the cottage, dead. Mark Rennett sitting a few yards away, smoking and looking at him."

" And the woman ? "

" I haven't seen her."

It was a few minutes before seven o'clock when they reached the hall.   Lyall hesitated.

" I wonder whether you'd better take a gun ? " he said.

There were four or five in a corner.   Slane handled them thoughtfully.

" It wouldn't be a bad idea," he agreed.   " What about this one ? "

" Take the next one," Lyall suggested hastily.   " Here are some cartridges."

" And you ? "

" Oh, he wouldn't touch me, even if he were crazy ! "

They crossed the lawn, stepped out on to the marsh, turned a little to the right, and walked in single file along the top of the dyke.   There were clouds coming up from behind the crest of hills landwards, though for the moment the sun shone.   The water in the dyke was like a streak of silver, and the shallow pools dotted about here and there like burnished shields.   The place seemed alive with larks and singing birds, and there, stark before them, was the strangely fashioned cottage with the wisp of blue smoke curling upwards.   Slane saw with a shudder that the dinghy was back, moored in its place.   Where the dyke turned seaward they had to jump it, and pick their way around the sedgy places to where the turf again became hard and unyielding.   In the distance they could see Mark Rennett seated apparently on a kitchen chair outside, and something a few feet away from him lying stretched upon the ground.

" Where is the woman, I wonder ? " Slane muttered.

" Inside, I suppose," Lyall answered.   " I can't think why the sergeant hasn't come by this time," he added uneasily.

They were about fifty yards off now, and he paused.

" I don't know why the mischief I should drag you into this, Slane," he continued.   " There's nothing to be done, nothing can be done.   Ebben's dead.   A whole shell of number four shot plugged into his heart at not more than a dozen paces away, I should say."

" What about Rennett ?   Did he speak to you ? "

" Not a word."

" We might have waited for the police and the doctor," Slane meditated, " but now we're here we'd better go on. He might try to get away."

They stepped across the last little creek, and drew near to the cottage. Ebben lay, as Lyall had left him, with the latter's coat over his face, one leg doubled up. He seemed to have changed since evening into a suit of rough golfing clothes, with rubber shoes. Opposite to him, Rennett remained seated in his hard-backed chair. He glowered at the two arrivals, but made no movement. Slane bent for a moment over Ebben's prostrate body, raised the coat reverently and replaced it. Lyall was gazing all the time at the cottage. Every one of the windows was framed with coquettish-looking dimity curtains, but there was no sign of life behind. Slane crossed the few yards of turf to where Rennett was seated, and stooping down, picked up his gun and looked at it.

" Where's your wife, Rennett ? " he asked.

The man, although his eyes had been wide open, started as though he had been awakened from sleep.

" I were watching he," he said. " He's dead."

" I can see that he is," Slane assented gravely. " Where's your wife, Rennett ? "

The man glanced towards the sun and back to the windows of the cottage.

" She do sleep steady," he replied, " but it's past seven o'clock in the morning. Give her a call, mister."

Slane knocked on the door. When he tried to call out, he was surprised to find his voice tremulous.

" Mrs. Rennett—Mrs. Rennett ! "

There was no reply. The man on the chair moved nervously.

" She do be a sound sleeper at times," he repeated.

This time Slane thundered upon the door. His first blow had scarcely fallen when it was thrown open. The woman stood for a moment framed upon the threshold. She was wrapped in a strangely fashioned dressing-gown, which she clutched tightly round her slim body. Her feet were bare. A breath of wind disclosed her throat. Her hair, unbraided and loose, was in wild disorder. The sun touched it, bringing out red glints of fire. Her large eyes seemed weary with sleep.

" Why, what's amiss ? " she asked, in her soft, disturbing voice. " Mark, thou't back ? I dreamed I heard the dinghy in the creek."

No one spoke for a moment. Her eyes lit as they looked into Slane's. Then, behind him, she saw the body, stretched upon the ground, and shrank a little backwards.

" Up to thy killing games, Mark ? " she cried. " They'll bring thee to the gallows. Who lies there ? "

Still no one spoke for a moment. Then Lyall stepped forward. He had seen over his shoulder the approach of the little company of men from the village.

" You'd better go inside, Mrs. Rennett," he advised.

She stepped out, and walked swiftly across to the prostrate body. She had the wanton's trait of being unable to conceal her nakedness. There was no one there who did not realise that, save for the flimsy dressing-gown, she was naked. She stooped down, and before Lyall could stop her, raised the coat and glanced underneath at Ebben's face. Then she turned round, and looked at them all one after the other. There was no problem picture of modern days, or ancient history, which failed to answer its own riddle so completely as did her expression. For a moment it seemed almost triumphant. Certainly there was in it nothing of pity— very little of horror. Her bare feet flashed over the turf as she turned back towards the door. From there she faced them all. She looked first at her husband, still sitting in his chair.

" Thee had better have stayed with the fleet and caught thy fish, Mark Rennett," she said. " Is this for what you came stealing home on the tide ? It sings in your blood, too, though to a different tune, the neap-tide madness."

Her eyes travelled round the little group once more, but met Slane's fairly with the witches' challenge flashing from their depths. She closed the door with something almost like a laugh. The sun was growing warmer every moment, and exactly overhead, dropping slowly towards them, a lark was singing. A few yards away now, a scattered crowd of the villagers was approaching. A doctor sunk on his knees by the side of Julius Ebben's body and opened his case, which a rough-looking youth had been carrying. A police sergeant whispered on one side with Lyall. The village constable sidled up to Rennett and possessed himself of his gun, a feat of which he bragged many a time afterwards. The sergeant turned away and approached the man, who was still seated upon his chair.

"Mark Rennett," he said, "I've a few questions to ask you. You needn't answer them unless you choose—may be used in evidence against you afterwards. Keep your mouth closed if you will."

Rennett threw back his head and laughed.

"What's all the palavering about, sergeant?" he asked. "There lies one of them Dormy House muck rats, dead, and in hell by this time, and there's my cottage ten yards away."

"Hold out your hands, Rennett," the sergeant ordered.

The man obeyed. The sergeant fastened the handcuffs with a click. It was perhaps the proudest moment of his life.

"You're a wise man, Rennett, to keep a still tongue in your head and to give no trouble," he said. "There's a trap on the road. We'll be making for the station."

Rennett had suddenly the appearance of a man who is waking up. He looked at the sergeant with a dazed light in his eyes.

"You be taking me for killing he?" he demanded.

"A still tongue in your head is the greatest wisdom," the sergeant reiterated. "There's many a man has hanged himself with his own lips. We'll be making a move. Bob," he went on, turning to his subordinate, "you stay here and see that nothing's touched until I return. These gentlemen will walk along with me."

Slane brought up the rear of the little procession. Twice he deliberately turned and looked at those empty windows. There was no sign of life from behind them, nothing to tell him whether the woman was combing her hair, or sobbing her heart out on the bed, or shaking with terror in her chair.

.   .   .   .   .   .

The garden at the Dormy House was fragrant with spring flowers as Slane and Lyall pushed open the gate. Down the lane they could hear the sergeant's mare trotting off towards the police station. Some of the curious had wandered back on to the marshes. The whole of the little place was in a fever. It seemed to Slane that his companion, too, had something of the dazed expression of the hand-cuffed man as he had been driven off to the police station. Slane passed an arm through his as they entered the passage, and stopped to whisper a word or two to Harrison, the steward.

23*

" Just one minute, Lyall," Slane begged. " Come in here."

They entered the bar. The Dormy House was a very well-ordered establishment, and all signs of the last night's festivities had disappeared. The tables were bright and shining. There were no glasses anywhere about. The window was open, letting in the fresh, hyacinth-scented air.

" Lyall," Slane asked, " what are you going to do about this ? "

His companion looked at him with burning eyes.

" What do you mean ? " he demanded.

Slane hesitated.

" You shot Julius Ebben," he said. " Mark Rennett came back when it was all over."

Lyall sank into a chair. His little groan was horrible in a way, and yet Slane fancied that there was a note almost of relief in it.

" It must come out," Slane continued. " When you asked me to take a gun, I felt yours. The muzzle was warm. One cartridge was still in it. Your shoes, reeking wet, were just by the side. I told Harrison not to move them for a moment. Rennett's gun, on the other hand, was fully loaded, and as cold as ice. I heard you leave the house last night, Lyall. It's no business of mine, but I heard you. I am sorry. I can't say more. Rennett would have done it right enough if he'd been there. I wish he had."

Lyall rose to his feet. For a moment he leaned out of the window, and half closed his eyes. The breeze was becoming a little stronger, and its fragrance seemed to fill the room. His lips twitched once or twice. Then he moved back to the bar, stretched across the counter, took a bottle of brandy, half filled a tumbler, and drank it as though it were water.

" We always blame the woman, Slane," he said, " but if ever one was born without soul or heart, and with a call to evil singing in her blood and out of her eyes, and quivering in her limbs—well, let it go ! I suppose it was the solitude here, and it's a strange, lone place through the grey months. You'll give me five minutes upstairs, Slane ? I'll leave everything straight. It's the best way."

" I'm damned sorry, old chap," Slane sighed, as he held out his hand.

Lyall left the room, and in less than five minutes, Slane,

who had walked out into the garden, heard the sound for which he had been listening. A man stepped through the French windows of the dining-room, his napkin in his hand.

" Did you hear that shot ? " he asked.

Harrison, too, was standing in an attitude of startled attention, and, looking into the man's pale face, Slane realised that he, too, knew.

" It seemed to me to come from the Major's room," Slane said. " You'd better step up there, Harrison."

BARONESS ORCZY

The Fenchurch Street Mystery
An Unparalleled Outrage

The BARONESS ORCZY was born in
Hungary, and studied in Brussels and
Paris before she began writing in 1900.
Five years later came the publication
of *The Scarlet Pimpernel*, and the
production of the play of the same name
which made its author world-famous.
The latest story was added to the
Scarlet Pimpernel saga in 1933. It
has been said that children read about
the French Revolution in preference
to any other historical period because
it was in those colourful days that
Sir Percy Blakeney lived.

THE FENCHURCH STREET MYSTERY

I

THE FENCHURCH STREET MYSTERY

THE man in the corner pushed aside his glass, and leant across the table.

"Mysteries!" he commented. "There is no such thing as a mystery in connection with any crime, provided intelligence is brought to bear upon its investigation."

Very much astonished Polly Burton looked over the top of her newspaper, and fixed a pair of very severe, coldly inquiring brown eyes upon him.

She had disapproved of the man from the instant when he shuffled across the shop and sat down opposite to her, at the same marble-topped table which already held her large coffee (3*d*.), her roll and butter (2*d*.), and plate of tongue (6*d*.).

Now this particular corner, this very same table, that special view of the magnificent marble hall—known as the Norfolk Street branch of the Aerated Bread Company's depots—were Polly's own corner, table, and view. Here she had partaken of eleven pennyworth of luncheon and one pennyworth of daily information ever since that glorious never-to-be-forgotten day when she was enrolled on the staff of the *Evening Observer* (we'll call it that, if you please), and became a member of that illustrious and world-famed organisation known as the British Press.

She was a personality, was Miss Burton, of the *Evening Observer*. Her cards were printed thus:

MISS MARY J. BURTON

Evening Observer.

She had interviewed Miss Ellen Terry and the Bishop of Madagascar, Mr. Seymour Hicks and the Chief Commissioner of Police. She had been present at the last Marlborough House garden party—in the cloak-room, that is to say, where she caught sight of Lady Thingummy's hat, Miss What-you-may-call's sunshade, and of various other things modistical or fashionable, all of which were duly described under the heading " Royalty and Dress " in the early afternoon edition of the *Evening Observer*.

(The article itself is signed M. J. B., and is to be found in the files of that leading halfpennyworth.)

For these reasons—and for various others, too—Polly felt irate with the man in the corner, and told him so with her eyes, as plainly as any pair of brown eyes can speak.

She had been reading an article in the *Daily Telegraph*. The article was palpitatingly interesting. Had Polly been commenting audibly upon it ? Certain it is that the man over there had spoken in direct answer to her thoughts.

She looked at him and frowned ; the next moment she smiled. Miss Burton (of the *Evening Observer*) had a keen sense of humour, which two years' association with the British Press had not succeeded in destroying, and the appearance of the man was sufficient to tickle the most ultra-morose fancy. Polly thought to herself that she had never seen anyone so pale, so thin, with such funny light-coloured hair, brushed very smoothly across the top of a very obviously bald crown. He looked so timid and nervous as he fidgeted incessantly with a piece of string ; his long, lean, and trembling fingers tying and untying it into knots of wonderful and complicated proportions.

Having carefully studied every detail of the quaint personality Polly felt more amiable.

" And yet," she remarked kindly but authoritatively, " this article, in an otherwise well-informed journal, will tell you that, even within the last year, no fewer than six crimes have completely baffled the police, and the perpetrators of them are still at large."

" Pardon me," he said gently, " I never for a moment ventured to suggest that there were no mysteries to the *police* ; I merely remarked that there were none where intelligence was brought to bear upon the investigation of crime."

" Not even in the Fenchurch Street *mystery*, I suppose,"
she asked sarcastically.

" Least of all in the so-called Fenchurch Street *mystery*,"
he replied quietly.

Now the Fenchurch Street mystery, as that extraordinary
crime had popularly been called, had puzzled—as Polly well
knew—the brains of every thinking man and woman for the
last twelve months. It had puzzled her not inconsiderably ;
she had been interested, fascinated; she had studied the case,
formed her own theories, thought about it all often and
often, had even written one or two letters to the Press on the
subject—suggesting, arguing, hinting at possibilities and
probabilities, adducing proofs which other amateur detectives were equally ready to refute. The attitude of that
timid man in the corner, therefore, was peculiarly exasperating, and she retorted with sarcasm destined to completely
annihilate her self-complacent interlocutor.

" What a pity it is, in that case, that you do not offer your
priceless services to our misguided though well-meaning
police ! "

" Isn't it ? " he replied with perfect good-humour.
" Well, you know, for one thing I doubt if they would accept
them ; and in the second place my inclinations and my duty
would—were I to become an active member of the detective
force—nearly always be in direct conflict. As often as not
my sympathies go to the criminal who is clever and astute
enough to lead our entire police force by the nose.

" I don't know how much of the case you remember," he
went on quietly. " It certainly, at first, began even to
puzzle me. On the 12th of last December, a woman, poorly
dressed, but with an unmistakable air of having seen better
days, gave information at Scotland Yard of the disappearance
of her husband, William Kershaw, of no occupation, and
apparently of no fixed abode. She was accompanied by a
friend—a fat, oily-looking German—and between them they
told a tale which set the police immediately on the move.

" It appears that on the 10th of December, at about three
o'clock in the afternoon, Karl Müller, the German, called on
his friend, William Kershaw, for the purpose of collecting a
small debt—some ten pounds or so—which the latter owed
him. On arriving at the squalid lodging in Charlotte Street,
Fitzroy Square, he found William Kershaw in a wild state of

excitement, and his wife in tears. Müller attempted to state the object of his visit, but Kershaw, with wild gestures, waved him aside, and—in his own words—flabbergasted him by asking him point-blank for another loan of two pounds, which sum, he declared, would be the means of a speedy fortune for himself and the friend who would help him in his need."

"After a quarter of an hour spent in obscure hints, Kershaw, finding the cautious German obdurate, decided to let him into the secret plan, which, he averred, would place thousands into their hands."

Instinctively Polly had put down her paper ; the mild stranger, with his nervous air and timid, watery eyes, had a peculiar way of telling his tale, which somehow fascinated her.

" I don't know," he resumed, " if you remember the story which the German told to the police, and which was corroborated in every detail by the wife or widow. Briefly it was this : Some thirty years previously, Kershaw, then twenty years of age, and a medical student at one of the London hospitals, had a chum named Barker, with whom he roomed together with another.

" The latter, so it appears, brought home one evening a very considerable sum of money, which he had won on the Turf, and the following morning he was found murdered in his bed. Kershaw, fortunately for himself, was able to prove a conclusive *alibi* ; he had spent the night on duty at the hospital ; as for Barker, he had disappeared, that is to say, as far as the police were concerned, but not as far as the watchful eyes of his friend Kershaw were able to spy—at least, so the latter said. Barker very cleverly contrived to get away out of the country, and, after sundry vicissitudes, finally settled down at Vladivostok, in Eastern Siberia, where, under the assumed name of Smethurst, he built up an enormous fortune by trading in furs.

" Now, mind you, everyone knows Smethurst, the Siberian millionaire. Kershaw's story that he had once been called Barker, and had committed a murder thirty years ago, was never proved, was it ? I am merely telling you what Kershaw said to his friend the German and to his wife on that memorable afternoon of December the 10th.

" According to him Smethurst had made one gigantic

mistake in his clever career—he had on four occasions written to his late friend, William Kershaw. Two of these letters had no bearing on the case, since they were written more than twenty-five years ago, and Kershaw, moreover, had lost them—so he said—long ago. According to him, however, the first of these letters was written when Smethurst, *alias* Barker, had spent all the money he had obtained from the crime, and found himself destitute in New York.

" Kershaw, then in fairly prosperous circumstances, sent him a £10 note for the sake of old times. The second, when the tables had turned, and Kershaw had begun to go downhill, Smethurst, as he then already called himself, sent his whilom friend £50. After that, as Müller gathered, Kershaw had made sundry demands on Smethurst's ever-increasing purse, and had accompanied these demands by various threats, which, considering the distant country in which the millionaire lived, were worse than futile.

" But now the climax had come, and Kershaw, after a final moment of hesitation, handed over to his German friend the last two letters purporting to have been written by Smethurst, and which, if you remember, played such an important part in the mysterious story of this extraordinary crime. I have a copy of both these letters here," added the man in the corner, as he took out a piece of paper from a very worn-out pocket-book, and, unfolding it very deliberately, he began to read :

" ' SIR,—Your preposterous demands for money are wholly unwarrantable. I have already helped you quite as much as you deserve. However, for the sake of old times, and because you once helped me when I was in a terrible difficulty, I am willing once more to let you impose upon my good nature. A friend of mine here, a Russian merchant, to whom I have sold my business, starts in a few days for an extended tour to many European and Asiatic ports in his yacht, and has invited me to accompany him as far as England. Being tired of foreign parts, and desirous of seeing the old country once again after thirty years' absence, I have decided to accept his invitation. I don't know when we may actually be in Europe, but I promise you that as soon as we touch a suitable port I will write to you again, making an appointment for you to see me in London. But remember that if your demands are too preposterous I will not for a moment listen to them, and that I am the last man in the world to submit to persistent and unwarrantable blackmail.

"'I am, sir,
"'Yours truly,
"'FRANCIS SMETHURST.'

"The second letter was dated from Southampton," continued the old man in the corner calmly, "and, curiously enough, was the only letter which Kershaw professed to have received from Smethurst of which he had kept the envelope, and which was dated. It was quite brief," he added, referring once more to his piece of paper.

"'DEAR SIR,—Referring to my letter of a few weeks ago, I wish to inform you that the *Tsarskoe Selo* will touch at Tilbury on Tuesday next, the 10th. I shall land there, and immediately go up to London by the first train I can get. If you like, you may meet me at Fenchurch Street Station, in the first-class waiting-room, in the late afternoon. Since I surmise that after thirty years' absence my face may not be familiar to you, I may as well tell you that you will recognise me by a heavy Astrakhan fur coat, which I shall wear, together with a cap of the same. You may then introduce yourself to me, and I will personally listen to what you may have to say.

"'Yours faithfully,
"'FRANCIS SMETHURST.'

"It was this last letter which had caused William Kershaw's excitement and his wife's tears. In the German's own words, he was walking up and down the room like a wild beast, gesticulating wildly, and muttering sundry exclamations. Mrs. Kershaw, however, was full of apprehension. She mistrusted the man from foreign parts—who, according to her husband's story, had already one crime upon his conscience—who might, she feared, risk another, in order to be rid of a dangerous enemy. Womanlike, she thought the scheme a dishonourable one, for the law, she knew, is severe on the blackmailer.

"The assignation might be a cunning trap, in any case it was a curious one ; why, she argued, did not Smethurst elect to see Kershaw at his hotel the following day ? A thousand

whys and wherefores made her anxious, but the fat German
had been won over by Kershaw's visions of untold gold held
tantalisingly before his eyes. He had lent the necessary £2,
with which his friend intended to tidy himself up a bit before
he went to meet his friend the millionaire. Half an hour
afterwards Kershaw had left his lodgings, and that was the
last the unfortunate woman saw of her husband, or Müller,
the German, of his friend.

" Anxiously his wife waited that night, but he did not
return : the next day she seems to have spent in making
purposeless and futile inquiries about the neighbourhood of
Fenchurch Street ; and on the 12th she went to Scotland
Yard, gave what particulars she knew, and placed in the
hands of the police the two letters written by Smethurst."

II

A MILLIONAIRE IN THE DOCK

THE man in the corner had finished his glass of milk. His
watery blue eyes looked across at Miss Polly Burton's eager
little face, from which all traces of severity had now been
chased away by an obvious and intense excitement.

" It was only on the 31st," he resumed after a while,
" that a body, decomposed past all recognition, was found
by two lightermen in the bottom of a disused barge. She
had been moored at one time at the foot of one of those dark
flights of steps which lead down between tall warehouses to
the river in the East End of London. I have a photograph
of the place here," he added, selecting one out of his pocket,
and placing it before Polly.

" The actual barge, you see, had already been removed
when I took this snapshot, but you will realise what a perfect
place this alley is for the purpose of one man cutting another's
throat in comfort, and without fear of detection. The body,
as I said, was decomposed beyond all recognition ; it had
probably been there eleven days, but sundry articles, such
as a silver ring and a tie pin, were recognisable, and were
identified by Mrs. Kershaw as belonging to her husband.

" She, of course, was loud in denouncing Smethurst, and
the police had no doubt a very strong case against him, for
two days after the discovery of the body in the barge, the

Siberian millionaire, as he was already popularly called by
enterprising interviewers, was arrested in his luxurious suite
of rooms at the Hotel Cecil.

" To confess the truth, at this point I was not a little
puzzled.   Mrs. Kershaw's story and Smethurst's letters had
both found their way into the papers, and following my
usual method—mind you, I am only an amateur, I try to
reason out a case for the love of the thing—I sought about
for a motive for the crime which the police declared Smethurst had committed.   To effectually get rid of a dangerous
blackmailer was the generally accepted theory.   Well! did
it ever strike you how paltry that motive really was ? "

Miss Polly had to confess, however, that it had never
struck her in that light.

" Surely a man who had succeeded in building up an
immense fortune by his own individual efforts was not the
sort of fool to believe that he had anything to fear from a man
like Kershaw.   He must have *known* that Kershaw held no
damning proofs against him—not enough to hang him,
anyway.   Have you ever seen Smethurst ? " he added, as
he once more fumbled in his pocket-book.

Polly replied that she had seen Smethurst's picture in the
illustrated papers at the time.   Then he added, placing a
small photograph before her :

" What strikes you most about the face ? "

" Well, I think its strange, astonished expression, due to
the total absence of eyebrows, and the funny foreign cut of
the hair."

" So close that it almost looks as if it had been shaved.
Exactly.   That is what struck me most when I elbowed my
way into the court that morning and first caught sight of the
millionaire in the dock.   He was a tall, soldierly-looking
man, upright in stature, his face very bronzed and tanned.
He wore neither moustache nor beard, his hair was cropped
quite close to his head, like a Frenchman's ; but, of course,
what was so very remarkable about him was that total
absence of eyebrows and even eyelashes, which gave the face
such a peculiar appearance—as you say, a perpetually
astonished look.

" He seemed, however, wonderfully calm ; he had been
accommodated with a chair in the dock—being a millionaire
—and chatted pleasantly with his lawyer, Sir Arthur Ingle-

wood, in the intervals between the calling of the several
witnesses for the prosecution ; whilst during the examination of these witnesses he sat quite placidly, with his head
shaded by his hand.

" Müller and Mrs. Kershaw repeated the story which they
had already told to the police. I think you said that you
were not able, owing to pressure of work, to go to the court
that day, and hear the case, so perhaps you have no recollection of Mrs. Kershaw. No ? Ah, well ! Here is a snapshot I managed to get of her once. That is she. Exactly as
she stood in the box—overdressed—in elaborate crape, with
a bonnet which once had contained pink roses, and to which a
remnant of pink petals still clung obtrusively amidst the
deep black.

" She would not look at the prisoner, and turned her head
resolutely towards the magistrate. I fancy she had been
fond of that vagabond husband of hers : an enormous
wedding-ring encircled her finger, and that, too, was
swathed in black. She firmly believed that Kershaw's
murderer sat there in the dock, and she literally flaunted her
grief before him.

" I was indescribably sorry for her. As for Müller, he
was just fat, oily, pompous, conscious of his own importance
as a witness ; his fat fingers, covered with brass rings,
gripped the two incriminating letters, which he had identified. They were his passports, as it were, to a delightful land
of importance and notoriety. Sir Arthur Inglewood, I think,
disappointed him by stating that he had no questions to ask
of him. Müller had been brimful of answers, ready with the
most perfect indictment, the most elaborate accusations
against the bloated millionaire who had decoyed his dear
friend Kershaw, and murdered him in Heaven knows what
an out-of-the-way corner of the East End.

" After this, however, the excitement grew apace. Müller
had been dismissed, and had retired from the court altogether, leading away Mrs. Kershaw, who had completely
broken down.

" Constable D21 was giving evidence as to the arrest in the
meanwhile. The prisoner, he said, had seemed completely
taken by surprise, not understanding the cause or history of
the accusation against him ; however, when put in full
possession of the facts, and realising, no doubt, the absolute

futility of any resistance, he had quietly enough followed the constable into the cab. No one at the fashionable and crowded Hotel Cecil had even suspected that anything unusual had occurred.

" Then a gigantic sigh of expectancy came from everyone of the spectators. The ' fun ' was about to begin. James Buckland, a porter at Fenchurch Street railway station, had just sworn to tell all the truth, etc. After all, it did not amount to much. He said that at six o'clock in the afternoon of December the 10th, in the midst of one of the densest fogs he ever remembers, the 5.5 from Tilbury steamed into the station, being just about an hour late. He was on the arrival platform, and was hailed by a passenger in a first-class carriage. He could see very little of him beyond an enormous black fur coat and a travelling cap of fur also.

" The passenger had a quantity of luggage, all marked F. S., and he directed James Buckland to place it all upon a four-wheel cab, with the exception of a small hand-bag, which he carried himself. Having seen that all his luggage was safely bestowed, the stranger in the fur coat paid the porter, and, telling the cabman to wait until he returned, he walked away in the direction of the waiting-rooms, still carrying his small hand-bag.

" ' I stayed for a bit,' added James Buckland, ' talking to the driver about the fog and that ; then I went about my business, seein' that the local from Southend 'ad been signalled.'

" The prosecution insisted most strongly upon the hour when the stranger in the fur coat, having seen to his luggage, walked away towards the waiting-rooms. The porter was emphatic. ' It was not a minute later than 6.15,' he averred.

" Sir Arthur Inglewood still had no questions to ask, and the driver of the cab was called.

" He corroborated the evidence of James Buckland as to the hour when the gentleman in the fur coat had engaged him, and having filled his cab in and out with luggage, had told him to wait. And cabby did wait. He waited in the dense fog—until he was tired, until he seriously thought of depositing all the luggage in the lost property office, and of looking out for another fare—waited until at last, at a quarter before nine, whom should he see walking hurriedly towards his cab but the gentleman in the fur coat and cap, who got in quickly and told the driver to take him at once to the Hotel Cecil. This, cabby declared, had occurred at a quarter before nine. Still Sir Arthur Inglewood made no comment, and Mr. Francis Smethurst, in the crowded, stuffy court, had calmly dropped to sleep.

" The next witness, Constable Thomas Taylor, had noticed a shabbily dressed individual, with shaggy hair and beard, loafing about the station and waiting-rooms in the afternoon of December the 10th. He seemed to be watching the arrival platform of the Tilbury and Southend trains.

" Two separate and independent witnesses, cleverly unearthed by the police, had seen this same shabbily dressed individual stroll into the first-class waiting-room at about 6.15 on Wednesday, December the 10th, and go straight up to a gentleman in a heavy fur coat and cap, who had also just come into the room. The two talked together for a while ; no one heard what they said, but presently they walked off together. No one seemed to know in which direction.

" Francis Smethurst was rousing himself from his apathy ; he whispered to his lawyer, who nodded with a bland smile of encouragement. The employés of the Hotel Cecil gave evidence as to the arrival of Mr. Smethurst at about 9.30 p.m. on Wednesday, December the 10th, in a cab, with a quantity of luggage ; and this closed the case for the prosecution.

" Everybody in that court already *saw* Smethurst mounting the gallows. It was uninterested curiosity which caused the elegant audience to wait and hear what Sir Arthur Inglewood had to say. He, of course, is the most fashionable man in the law at the present moment. His lolling attitudes, his drawling speech, are quite the rage, and imitated by the gilded youth of society.

" Even at this moment, when the Siberian millionaire's neck literally and metaphorically hung in the balance, an expectant titter went round the fair spectators as Sir Arthur stretched out his long loose limbs and lounged across the table. He waited to make his effect—Sir Arthur is a born actor—and there is no doubt that he made it, when in his slowest, most drawly tones he said quietly :

" ' With regard to this alleged murder of one William Kershaw, on Wednesday, December the 10th, between 6.15

and 8.45 p.m., your Honour, I now propose to call two witnesses, who saw this same William Kershaw alive on Tuesday
afternoon, December the 16th, that is to say, six days after
the supposed murder.'

" It was as if a bombshell had exploded in the court.
Even his Honour was aghast, and I am sure the lady next to
me only recovered from the shock of the surprise in order to
wonder whether she need put off her dinner party after all.

" As for me," added the man in the corner, with that
strange mixture of nervousness and self-complacency which
had set Miss Polly Burton wondering, " well, you see, *I* had
made up my mind long ago where the hitch lay in this
particular case, and I was not so surprised as some of the
others.

" Perhaps you remember the wonderful development of
the case, which so completely mystified the police—and in
fact everybody except myself. Torriani and a waiter at his
hotel in the Commercial Road both deposed that at about
3.30 p.m. on December the 10th a shabbily dressed individual
lolled into the coffee-room and ordered some tea. He was
pleasant enough and talkative, told the waiter that his name
was William Kershaw, that very soon all London would be
talking about him, as he was about, through an unexpected
stroke of good fortune, to become a very rich man, and so on,
and so on, nonsense without end.

" When he had finished his tea he lolled out again, but no
sooner had he disappeared down a turning of the road than
the waiter discovered an old umbrella, left behind accidentally by the shabby, talkative individual. As is the custom
in his highly respectable restaurant, Signor Torriani put the
umbrella carefully away in his office, on the chance of his
customer calling to claim it when he had discovered his loss.
And sure enough, nearly a week later, on Tuesday, the 16th,
at about 1 p.m., the same shabbily dressed individual called
and asked for his umbrella. He had some lunch, and chatted
once again to the waiter. Signor Torriani and the waiter
gave a description of William Kershaw, which coincided
exactly with that given by Mrs. Kershaw of her husband.

" Oddly enough, he seemed to be a very absent-minded
sort of person, for on this second occasion, no sooner had he
left than the waiter found a pocket-book in the coffee-room,
underneath the table. It contained sundry letters and bills,

all addressed to William Kershaw. This pocket-book was produced, and Karl Müller, who had returned to the court, easily identified it as having belonged to his dear and lamented friend ' Villiam.'

" This was the first blow to the case against the accused. It was a pretty stiff one, you will admit. Already it had begun to collapse like a house of cards. Still, there was the assignation, and the undisputed meeting between Smethurst and Kershaw, and those two and a half hours of a foggy evening to satisfactorily account for."

The man in the corner made a long pause, keeping the girl on tenterhooks. He had fidgeted with his bit of string till there was not an inch of it free from the most complicated and elaborate knots.

" I assure you," he resumed at last, " that at that very moment the whole mystery was, to me, as clear as daylight. I only marvelled how his Honour could waste his time and mine by putting what he thought were searching questions to the accused relating to his past. Francis Smethurst, who had quite shaken off his somnolence, spoke with a curious nasal twang, and with an almost imperceptible soupçon of foreign accent. He calmly denied Kershaw's version of his past ; declared that he had never been called Barker, and had certainly never been mixed up in any murder case thirty years ago.

" ' But you knew this man Kershaw,' persisted his Honour, ' since you wrote to him ? '

" ' Pardon me, your Honour,' said the accused quietly, ' I have never, to my knowledge, seen this man Kershaw, and I can swear that I never wrote to him.'

" ' Never wrote to him ? ' retorted his Honour warningly. ' That is a strange assertion to make when I have two of your letters to him in my hands at the present moment.'

" ' I never wrote those letters, your Honour,' persisted the accused quietly, ' they are not in my handwriting.'

" ' Which we can easily prove,' came in Sir Arthur Inglewood's drawly tones, as he handed up a packet to his Honour ; ' here are a number of letters written by my client since he has landed in this country, and some of which were written under my very eyes.'

" As Sir Arthur Inglewood had said, this could be easily proved, and the prisoner, at his Honour's request, scribbled a

few lines, together with his signature, several times upon a
sheet of note-paper. It was easy to read upon the magistrate's astounded countenance that there was not the
slightest similarity in the two handwritings.

"A fresh mystery had cropped up. Who, then, had
made the assignation with William Kershaw at Fenchurch
Street railway station ? The prisoner gave a fairly satisfactory account of the employment of his time since his
landing in England.

"'I came over on the *Tsarskoe Selo*,' he said, 'a yacht
belonging to a friend of mine. When we arrived at the
mouth of the Thames there was such a dense fog that it was
twenty-four hours before it was thought safe for me to land.
My friend, who is a Russian, would not land at all ; he was
regularly frightened at this land of fogs. He was going on
to Madeira immediately.

"'I actually landed on Tuesday, the 10th, and took a
train at once for town. I did see to my luggage and a cab,
as the porter and driver told your Honour ; then I tried to
find my way to a refreshment-room, where I could get a glass
of wine. I drifted into the waiting-room, and there I was
accosted by a shabbily dressed individual, who began telling
me a piteous tale. Who he was I do not know. He *said* he
was an old soldier who had served his country faithfully, and
then been left to starve. He begged of me to accompany
him to his lodgings, where I could see his wife and starving
children, and verify the truth and piteousness of his tale.

"'Well, your Honour,' added the prisoner with noble
frankness, 'it was my first day in the old country. I had
come back after thirty years with my pockets full of gold,
and this was the first sad tale I had heard ; but I am a business man, and did not want to be exactly "done in the eye."
I followed my man through the fog, out into the streets.
He walked silently by my side for a time. I had not a
notion where I was.

"'Suddenly I turned to him with some question, and
realised in a moment that my gentleman had given me the
slip. Finding, probably, that I would not part with my
money till I *had* seen the starving wife and children, he left
me to my fate, and went in search of more willing bait.

"'The place where I found myself was dismal and deserted. I could see no trace of cab or omnibus. I retraced

my steps and tried to find my way back to the station, only to find myself in worse and more deserted neighbourhoods. I became hopelessly lost and fogged. I don't wonder that two and a half hours elapsed while I thus wandered on in the dark and deserted streets ; my sole astonishment is that I ever found the station at all that night, or rather close to it a policeman, who showed me the way.'

" ' But how do you account for Kershaw knowing all your movements ? ' still persisted his Honour, ' and his knowing the exact date of your arrival in England ? How do you account for these two letters, in fact ? '

" ' I cannot account for it or them, your Honour,' replied the prisoner quietly. ' I have proved to you, have I not, that I never wrote those letters, and that the man—er— Kershaw is his name ?—was not murdered by me ? '

" 'Can you tell me of anyone here or abroad who might have heard of your movements, and of the date of your arrival ? '

" ' My late employés at Vladivostok, of course, knew of my departure, but none of them could have written these letters, since none of them know a word of English.'

" ' Then you can throw no light upon these mysterious letters ? You cannot help the police in any way towards the clearing up of this strange affair ? '

" ' The affair is as mysterious to me as to your Honour, and to the police of this country.'

" Francis Smethurst was discharged, of course ; there was no semblance of evidence against him sufficient to commit him for trial. The two overwhelming points of his defence which had completely routed the prosecution were, firstly, the proof that he had never written the letters making the assignation, and secondly, the fact that the man supposed to have been murdered on the 10th was seen to be alive and well on the 16th. But then, who in the world was the mysterious individual who had apprised Kershaw of the movements of Smethurst, the millionaire ? "

III

HIS DEDUCTION

THE man in the corner cocked his funny thin head on one side and looked at Polly ; then he took up his beloved bit of string and deliberately untied every knot he had made in it. When it was quite smooth he laid it out upon the table.

" I will take you, if you like, point by point along the line of reasoning which I followed myself, and which will inevitably lead you, as it led me, to the only possible solution of the mystery.

" First take this point," he said with nervous restlessness, once more taking up his bit of string, and forming with each point raised a series of knots, which would have shamed a navigating instructor, " obviously it was *impossible* for Kershaw not to have been acquainted with Smethurst, since he was fully apprised of the latter's arrival in England by two letters. Now it was clear to me from the first that *no one* could have written those two letters except Smethurst. You will argue that those letters were proved not to have been written by the man in the dock. Exactly. Remember, Kershaw was a careless man—he had lost both envelopes. To him they were insignificant. Now it was never *disproved* that those letters were written by Smethurst."

" But——" suggested Polly.

" Wait a minute," he interrupted, while knot number two appeared upon the scene ; " it was proved that six days after the murder, William Kershaw was alive, and visited the Torriani Hotel, where already he was known, and where he conveniently left a pocket-book behind, so that there should be no mistake as to his identity ; but it was never questioned where Mr. Francis Smethurst, the millionaire, happened to spend that very same afternoon."

" Surely you don't mean——? " gasped the girl.

" One moment, please," he added triumphantly. " How did it come about that the landlord of the Torriani Hotel was brought into court at all ? How did Sir Arthur Inglewood, or rather his client, know that William Kershaw had on those two memorable occasions visited the hotel, and that its landlord could bring such convincing evidence forward that would for ever exonerate the millionaire from the imputation of murder ? "

" Surely," she argued, " the usual means, the police——"

" The police had kept the whole affair very dark until the arrest at the Hotel Cecil. They did not put into the papers the usual : ' If anyone happens to know of the whereabouts, etc., etc.' Had the landlord of that hotel heard of the disappearance of Kershaw through the usual channels, he would have put himself in communication with the police. Sir Arthur Inglewood produced him. How did Sir Arthur Inglewood come on his track ? "

" Surely, you don't mean——? "

" Point number four," he resumed imperturbably, " Mrs. Kershaw was never requested to produce a specimen of her husband's handwriting. Why ? Because the police, clever as you say they are, never started on the right track. They believed William Kershaw to have been murdered ; they looked for William Kershaw.

" On December the 31st, what was presumed to be the body of William Kershaw was found by two lightermen : I have shown you a photograph of the place where it was found. Dark and deserted it is in all conscience, is it not ? Just the place where a bully and a coward would decoy an unsuspecting stranger, murder him first, then rob him of his valuables, his papers, his very identity, and leave him there to rot. The body was found in a disused barge which had been moored some time against the wall, at the foot of these steps. It was in the last stages of decomposition, and, of course, could not be identified ; but the police would have it that it was the body of William Kershaw.

" It never entered their heads that it was the body of *Francis Smethurst, and that William Kershaw was his murderer.*

" Ah ! it was cleverly, artistically conceived ! Kershaw is a genius. Think of it all ! His disguise ! Kershaw had a shaggy beard, hair, and moustache. He shaved up to his very eyebrows ! No wonder that even his wife did not recognise him across the court ; and remember she never saw much of his face while he stood in the dock. Kershaw was shabby, slouchy ; he stooped. Smethurst, the millionaire, might have served in the Prussian army.

" Then that lovely trait about going to revisit the Torriani Hotel. Just a few days' grace, in order to purchase moustache and beard and wig, exactly similar to what he had himself shaved off. Making up to look like himself ! Splendid ! Then leaving the pocket-book behind ! He ! he ! he ! Kershaw was not murdered ! Of course not. He called at the Torriani Hotel six days after the murder, whilst Mr. Smethurst, the millionaire, hobnobbed in the Park with duchesses ! Hang such a man ! Fie ! "

He fumbled for his hat. With nervous, trembling fingers he held it deferentially in his hand whilst he rose from the table. Polly watched him as he strode up to the desk, and paid twopence for his glass of milk and his bun. Soon he disappeared through the shop, whilst she still found herself hopelessly bewildered, with a number of snapshot photographs before her, still staring at a long piece of string, smothered from end to end in a series of knots, as bewildering, as irritating, as puzzling as the man who had lately sat in the corner.

Reprinted with the Author's permission from *The Old Man in the Corner.*

AN UNPARALLELED OUTRAGE

I

AN UNPARALLELED OUTRAGE

" Do you care for the seaside ? " asked the man in the corner when he had finished his lunch. " I don't mean the seaside at Ostend or Trouville, but honest English seaside with nigger minstrels, three-shilling excursionists, and dirty, expensive furnished apartments, where they charge you a shilling for lighting the hall gas on Sundays and sixpence on other evenings. Do you care for that ? "

" I prefer the country."

" Ah ! perhaps it is preferable. Personally I only liked one of our English seaside resorts once, and that was for a week, when Edward Skinner was up before the magistrate, charged with what was known as the ' Brighton Outrage.' I don't know if you remember the memorable day in Brighton, memorable for that elegant town, which deals more in amusements than mysteries, when Mr. Francis Morton, one of its most noted residents, disappeared. Yes ! disappeared as completely as any vanishing lady in a music-hall. He was wealthy, had a fine house, servants, a wife and children, and he disappeared. There was no getting away from that.

" Mr. Francis Morton lived with his wife in one of the large houses in Sussex Square at the Kemp Town end of Brighton. Mrs. Morton was well known for her American-isms, her swagger dinner-parties, and beautiful Paris gowns. She was the daughter of one of the many American million-aires (I think her father was a Chicago pork-butcher) who conveniently provide wealthy wives for English gentlemen ; and she had married Mr. Francis Morton a few years ago and brought him her quarter of a million, for no other reason but that she fell in love with him. He was neither good-looking nor distinguished, in fact, he was one of those

men who seem to have CITY stamped all over their
person.

" He was a gentleman of very regular habits, going up to
London every morning on business and returning every
afternoon by the ' husbands' train.' So regular was he in
these habits that all the servants at the Sussex Square house
were betrayed into actual gossip over the fact that on
Wednesday, March 17th, the master was not home for dinner.
Hales, the butler, remarked that the mistress seemed a bit
anxious and didn't eat much food. The evening wore on
and Mr. Morton did not appear. At nine o'clock the young
footman was dispatched to the station to make inquiries
whether his master had been seen there in the afternoon, or
whether—which Heaven forbid—there had been an accident
on the line. The young man interviewed two or three
porters, the bookstall boy, and ticket clerk ; all were agreed
that Mr. Morton did not go up to London during the day ;
no one had seen him within the precincts of the station.
There certainly had been no accident reported either on the
up or down line.

" But the morning of the 18th came, with its usual post-
man's knock, but neither Mr. Morton nor any sign or news
from him. Mrs. Morton, who evidently had spent a sleepless night, for she looked sadly changed and haggard, sent a
wire to the hall porter at the large building in Cannon Street,
where her husband had his office. An hour later she had the
reply : ' Not seen Mr. Morton all day yesterday, not here
to-day.' By the afternoon everyone in Brighton knew that
a fellow-resident had mysteriously disappeared from or in
the city.

" A couple of days, then another, elapsed, and still no sign
of Mr. Morton. The police were doing their best. The
gentleman was so well known in Brighton—as he had been a
resident two years—that it was not difficult to firmly
establish the one fact that he had not left the city, since no
one saw him in the station on the morning of the 17th, nor at
any time since then. Mild excitement prevailed throughout
the town. At first the newspapers took the matter somewhat jocosely. ' Where is Mr. Morton ? ' was the usual
placard on the evening's contents bills, but after three days
had gone by and the worthy Brighton resident was still
missing, while Mrs. Morton was seen to look more haggard

and careworn every day, mild excitement gave place to anxiety.

" There were vague hints now as to foul play. The news had leaked out that the missing gentleman was carrying a large sum of money on the day of his disappearance. There were also vague rumours of a scandal not unconnected with Mrs. Morton herself and her own past history, which in her anxiety for her husband she had been forced to reveal to the detective-inspector in charge of the case.

" Then on Saturday the news which the late evening papers contained was this :

" ' Acting on certain information received, the police to-day forced an entrance into one of the rooms of Russell House, a high-class furnished apartment on the King's Parade, and there they discovered our missing distinguished townsman, Mr. Francis Morton, who had been robbed and subsequently locked up in that room since Wednesday, the 17th. When discovered he was in the last stages of inanition ; he was tied into an arm-chair with ropes, a thick wool shawl had been wound round his mouth, and it is a positive marvel that, left thus without food and very little air, the unfortunate gentleman survived the horrors of these four days of incarceration.

" ' He has been conveyed to his residence in Sussex Square, and we are pleased to say that Doctor Mellish, who is in attendance, has declared his patient to be out of serious danger, and that with care and rest he will be soon quite himself again.

" ' At the same time our readers will learn with unmixed satisfaction that the police of our city, with their usual acuteness and activity, have already discovered the identity and whereabouts of the cowardly ruffian who committed this unparalleled outrage.' "

II

THE PRISONER

" I REALLY don't know," continued the man in the corner blandly, " what it was that interested me in the case from the very first. Certainly it had nothing very out of the way or mysterious about it, but I journeyed down to Brighton nevertheless, as I felt that something deeper and more subtle lay behind that extraordinary assault, following a robbery, no doubt.

" I must tell you that the police had allowed it to be freely circulated abroad that they held a clue. It had been easy enough to ascertain who the lodger was who had rented the furnished room in Russell House. His name was supposed to be Edward Skinner, and he had taken the room about a fortnight ago, but had gone away ostensibly for two or three days on the very day of Mr. Morton's mysterious disappearance. It was on the 20th that Mr. Morton was found, and thirty-six hours later the public were gratified to hear that Mr. Edward Skinner had been traced to London and arrested on the charge of assault upon the person of Mr. Francis Morton and of robbing him of the sum of £10,000.

" Then a further sensation was added to the already bewildering case by the startling announcement that Mr. Francis Morton refused to prosecute.

" Of course, the Treasury took up the case and subpœnaed Mr. Morton as a witness, so that gentleman—if he wished to hush the matter up, or had been in any way terrorised into a promise of doing so—gained nothing by his refusal, except an additional amount of curiosity in the public mind and further sensation around the mysterious case.

" It was all this, you see, which had interested me and brought me down to Brighton on March 23rd to see the prisoner Edward Skinner arraigned before the beak. I must say that he was a very ordinary-looking individual. Fair, of ruddy complexion, with snub nose and the beginning of a bald place on the top of his head, he, too, looked the embodiment of a prosperous, stodgy ' City gent.'

" I took a quick survey of the witnesses present, and guessed that the handsome, stylish woman sitting next to Mr. Reginald Pepys, the noted lawyer for the Crown, was Mrs. Morton.

" There was a large crowd in court, and I heard whispered comments among the feminine portion thereof as to the beauty of Mrs. Morton's gown, the value of her large picture hat, and the magnificence of her diamond rings.

" The police gave all the evidence required with regard to the finding of Mr. Morton in the room at Russell House and also to the arrest of Skinner at the Langham Hotel in London.

It appears that the prisoner seemed completely taken aback at the charge preferred against him, and declared that though he knew Mr. Francis Morton slightly in business he knew nothing as to his private life.

" ' Prisoner stated,' continued Inspector Buckle, ' that he was not even aware Mr. Morton lived in Brighton, but I have evidence here, which I will place before your Honour, to prove that the prisoner was seen in the company of Mr. Morton at 9.30 o'clock on the morning of the assault.'

" Cross-examined by Mr. Matthew Quiller, the detective-inspector admitted that prisoner merely said that he did not know that Mr. Morton was *a resident* of Brighton—he never denied having met him there.

" The witness, or rather witnesses, referred to by the police were two Brighton tradesmen who knew Mr. Morton by sight and had seen him on the morning of the 17th walking with the accused.

" In this instance Mr. Quiller had no question to ask of the witnesses, and it was generally understood that the prisoner did not wish to contradict their statement.

" Constable Hartrick told the story of the finding of the unfortunate Mr. Morton after his four days' incarceration. The constable had been sent round by the chief inspector, after certain information given by Mrs. Chapman, the landlady of Russell House. He had found the door locked and forced it open. Mr. Morton was in an arm-chair, with several yards of rope wound loosely round him ; he was almost unconscious, and there was a thick wool shawl tied round his mouth which must have deadened any cry or groan the poor gentleman might have uttered. But, as a matter of fact, the constable was under the impression that Mr. Morton had been either drugged or stunned in some way at first, which had left him weak and faint and prevented him from making himself heard or extricating himself from his bonds, which were very clumsily, evidently very hastily, wound round his body.

" The medical officer who was called in, and also Dr. Mellish, who attended Mr. Morton, both said that he seemed dazed by some stupefying drug, and also, of course, terribly weak and faint with the want of food.

" The first witness of real importance was Mrs. Chapman, the proprietress of Russell House, whose original information to the police led to the discovery of Mr. Morton. In answer to Mr. Pepys, she said that on March 1st the accused called at her house and gave his name as Mr. Edward Skinner.

" ' He required, he said, a furnished room at a moderate rental, for a permanency, with full attendance when he was in, but he added that he would often be away for two or three days, or even longer, at a time.

" ' He told me that he was a traveller for a tea-house,' continued Mrs. Chapman, ' and I showed him the front room on the third floor, as he did not want to pay more than twelve shillings a week. I asked him for a reference, but he put three sovereigns in my hand, and said with a laugh that he supposed paying for his room a month in advance was sufficient reference ; if I didn't like him after that, I could give him a week's notice to quit.'

" ' You did not think of asking him the name of the firm for which he travelled ? ' asked Mr. Pepys.

" ' No, I was quite satisfied as he paid me for the room. The next day he sent in his luggage and took possession of the room. He went out most mornings on business, but was always in Brighton for Saturday and Sunday. On the 16th he told me that he was going to Liverpool for a couple of days ; he slept in the house that night, and went off early on the 17th, taking his portmanteau with him.'

" ' At what time did he leave ? ' asked Mr. Pepys.

" ' I couldn't say exactly,' replied Mrs. Chapman with some hesitation. ' You see, this is the off season here. None of my rooms are let, except the one to Mr. Skinner, and I only have one servant. I keep four during the summer, autumn, and winter season,' she added with conscious pride, fearing that her former statement might prejudice the reputation of Russell House. ' I thought I had heard Mr. Skinner go out about nine o'clock, but about an hour later the girl and I were both in the basement, and we heard the front door open and shut with a bang, and then a step in the hall.

" ' " That's Mr. Skinner," said Mary. " So it is," I said, " why, I thought he had gone an hour ago." " He did go out then," said Mary, " for he left his bedroom door open and I went in to do his bed and tidy his room." " Just go and see if that's him, Mary," I said, and Mary ran up to the hall and up the stairs, and came back to tell me that that was Mr. Skinner all right enough ; he had gone straight up to his room. Mary didn't see him, but he had another gentleman with him, as she could hear them talking in Mr. Skinner's room.'

" ' Then you can't tell us at what time the prisoner left the house finally ? '

" ' No, that I can't. I went out shopping soon after that. When I came in it was twelve o'clock. I went up to the third floor and found that Mr. Skinner had locked his door and taken the key with him. As I knew Mary had already done the room I did not trouble more about it, though I did think it strange for a gentleman to lock up his room and not leave the key with me.'

" ' And, of course, you heard no noise of any kind in the room then ? '

" ' No. Not that day or the next, but on the third day Mary and I both thought we heard a funny sound. I said that Mr. Skinner had left his window open, and it was the blind flapping against the window-pane ; but when we heard that funny noise again I put my ear to the keyhole and I thought I could hear a groan. I was very frightened, and sent Mary for the police.'

" Mrs. Chapman had nothing more of interest to say. The prisoner certainly was her lodger. She had last seen him on the evening of the 16th going up to his room with his candle. Mary the servant had much the same story to relate as her mistress.

" ' I think it was 'im, right enough,' said Mary guardedly. ' I didn't see 'im, but I went up to 'is landing and stopped a moment outside 'is door. I could 'ear loud voices in the room—gentlemen talking.'

" ' I suppose you would not do such a thing as to listen, Mary ? ' queried Mr. Pepys, with a smile.

" ' No, sir,' said Mary, with a bland smile, ' I didn't catch what the gentlemen said, but one of them spoke so loud I thought they must be quarrelling.'

" ' Mr. Skinner was the only person in possession of a latch-key, I presume. No one else could have come in without ringing at the door ? '

" ' Oh, no, sir.'

" That was all. So far, you see, the case was progressing splendidly for the Crown against the prisoner. The contention, of course, was that Skinner had met Mr. Morton, brought him home with him, assaulted, drugged, then gagged and bound him, and finally robbed him of whatever money he had in his possession, which, according to certain affidavits which presently would be placed before the magistrate, amounted to £10,000 in notes.

"But in all this there still remained the great element of mystery for which the public and the magistrate would demand an explanation: namely, what were the relationships between Mr. Morton and Skinner, which had induced the former to refuse the prosecution of the man who had not only robbed him, but had so nearly succeeded in leaving him to die a terrible and lingering death?

"Mr. Morton was too ill as yet to appear in person. Dr. Mellish had absolutely forbidden his patient to undergo the fatigue and excitement of giving evidence himself in court that day. But his depositions had been taken at his bedside, were sworn to by him, and were now placed before the magistrate by the prosecuting counsel, and the facts they revealed were certainly as remarkable as they were brief and enigmatical.

"As they were read by Mr. Pepys, an awed and expectant hush seemed to descend over the large crowd gathered there, and all necks were strained eagerly forward to catch a glimpse of a tall, elegant woman, faultlessly dressed and wearing exquisite jewellery, but whose handsome face wore, as the prosecuting counsel read her husband's deposition, a more and more ashen hue.

" ' This, your Honour, is the statement made upon oath by Mr. Francis Morton,' commenced Mr. Pepys in that loud, sonorous voice of his which sounds so impressive in a crowded and hushed court. ' " I was obliged, for certain reasons which I refuse to disclose, to make a payment of a large sum of money to a man whom I did not know and have never seen. It was in a matter of which my wife was cognisant and which had entirely to do with her own affairs. I was merely the go-between, as I thought it was not fit that she should see to this matter herself. The individual in question had made certain demands, of which she kept me in ignorance as long as she could, not wishing to unnecessarily worry me. At last she decided to place the whole matter before me, and I agreed with her that it would be best to satisfy the man's demands.

" ' " I then wrote to that individual whose name I do not wish to disclose, addressing the letter, as my wife directed me to do, to the Brighton post office, saying that I was ready to pay the £10,000 to him, at any place or time and in what manner he might appoint. I received a reply which bore the Brighton postmark, and which desired me to be outside Furnival's, the drapers, in West Street, at 9.30 on the morning of March 17th, and to bring the money (£10,000) in Bank of England notes.

" ' " On the 16th my wife gave me a cheque for the amount and I cashed it at her bank—Bird's in Fleet Street. At half-past nine the following morning I was at the appointed place. An individual wearing a grey overcoat, bowler hat, and red tie accosted me by name and requested me to walk as far as his lodgings in the King's Parade. I followed him. Neither of us spoke. He stopped at a house which bore the name ' Russell House,' and which I shall be able to swear to as soon as I am able to go out. He let himself in with a latch-key, and asked me to follow him up to his room on the third floor. I thought I noticed when we were in the room that he locked the door ; however, I had nothing of any value about me except the £10,000 which I was ready to give him. We had not exchanged the slightest word.

" ' " I gave him the notes, and he folded them and put them in his pocket-book. Then I turned towards the door, and, without the slightest warning, I felt myself suddenly gripped by the shoulder, while a handkerchief was pressed to my nose and mouth. I struggled as best I could, but the handkerchief was saturated with chloroform, and I soon lost consciousness. I hazily remember the man saying to me in short, jerky sentences, spoken at intervals while I was still weakly struggling :

" ' " ' What a fool you must think me, my dear sir ! Did you really think that I was going to let you quietly walk out of here, straight to the police-station, eh ? Such dodges have been done before, I know, when a man's silence has to be bought for money. Find out who he is, see where he lives, give him the money, then inform against him. No, you don't ! not this time. I am off to the Continong with this £10,000, and I can get to Newhaven in time for the midday

24*

boat, so you'll have to keep quiet until I am the other side of the Channel, my friend. You won't be much inconvenienced ; my landlady will hear your groans presently and release you, so you'll be all right. There, now, drink this— that's better.' He forced something bitter down my throat, then I remember nothing more.

" ' " When I regained consciousness I was sitting on an arm-chair with some rope tied round me and a wool shawl round my mouth. I hadn't the strength to make the slightest effort to disentangle myself or to utter a scream. I felt terribly sick and faint." '

" Mr. Reginald Pepys had finished reading, and no one in that crowded court had thought of uttering a sound ; the magistrate's eyes were fixed upon the handsome lady in the magnificent gown, who was mopping her eyes with a dainty lace handkerchief.

" The extraordinary narrative of the victim of so daring an outrage had kept everyone in suspense ; one thing was still expected to make the measure of sensation as full as it had ever been over any criminal case, and that was Mrs. Morton's evidence. She was called by the prosecuting counsel, and slowly, gracefully, she entered the witness-box. There was no doubt that she had felt keenly the tortures which her husband had undergone, and also the humiliation of seeing her name dragged forcibly into this ugly, blackmailing scandal.

" Closely questioned by Mr. Reginald Pepys, she was forced to admit that the man who blackmailed her was connected with her early life in a way which would have brought terrible disgrace upon her and upon her children. The story she told, amidst many tears and sobs, and much use of her beautiful lace handkerchief and beringed hands, was exceedingly pathetic.

" It appears that when she was barely seventeen she was inveigled into a secret marriage with one of those foreign adventurers who swarm in every country, and who styled himself Comte Armand de la Tremouille. He seems to have been a blackguard of unusually low pattern, for, after he had extracted from her some £200 of her pin money and a few diamond brooches, he left her one fine day with a laconic word to say that he was sailing for Europe by the *Argentina*, and would not be back for some time. She was in love with

"I felt terribly sick and faint."

"I THINK THAT I HAVE BEEN TOLD."

the brute, poor young soul, for when, a week later, she read
that the *Argentina* was wrecked, and presumably every soul
on board had perished, she wept very many bitter tears over
her early widowhood.

" Fortunately her father, a very wealthy pork-butcher of
Chicago, had known nothing of his daughter's culpable
foolishness. Four years later he took her to London, where
she met Mr. Francis Morton and married him. She led six
or seven years of very happy married life when one day, like
a thunderbolt from a clear, blue sky, she received a typewritten letter, signed ' Armand de la Tremouille,' full of
protestations of undying love, telling a long and pathetic
tale of years of suffering in a foreign land, whither he had
drifted after having been rescued almost miraculously from
the wreck of the *Argentina*, and where he never had been
able to scrape a sufficient amount of money to pay for his
passage home. At last fate had favoured him. He had,
after many vicissitudes, found the whereabouts of his dear
wife, and was now ready to forgive all that was past and take
her to his loving arms once again.

" What followed was the usual course of events when there
is a blackguard and a fool of a woman. She was terrorised
and did not dare to tell her husband for some time ; she
corresponded with the Comte de la Tremouille, begging him
for her sake and in memory of the past not to attempt to see
her. She found him amenable to reason in the shape of
several hundred pounds which passed through the Brighton
post office into his hands. At last one day, by accident,
Mr. Morton came across one of the Comte de la Tremouille's
interesting letters. She confessed everything, throwing
herself upon her husband's mercy.

" Now Mr. Francis Morton was a business man, who
viewed life practically and soberly. He liked his wife, who
kept him in luxury, and wished to keep her, whereas the
Comte de la Tremouille seemed willing enough to give her
up for a consideration. Mrs. Morton, who had the sole and
absolute control of her fortune, on the other hand, was willing
enough to pay the price and hush up the scandal, which she
believed—since she was a bit of a fool—would land her in
prison for bigamy. Mr. Francis Morton wrote to the
Comte de la Tremouille that his wife was ready to pay him
the sum of £10,000 which he demanded in payment for her

absolute liberty and his own complete disappearance out of her life now and for ever. The appointment was made, and Mr. Morton left his house at 9 a.m. on March 17th with the £10,000 in his pocket.

" The public and the magistrate had hung breathless upon her words. There was nothing but sympathy felt for this handsome woman, who throughout had been more sinned against than sinning, and whose gravest fault seems to have been a total lack of intelligence in dealing with her own life. But I can assure you of one thing, that in no case within my recollection was there ever such a sensation in a court as when the magistrate, after a few minutes' silence, said gently to Mrs. Morton :

" ' And now, Mrs. Morton, will you kindly look at the prisoner, and tell me if in him you recognise your former husband ? '

" And she, without even turning to look at the accused, said quietly :

" ' Oh, no ! your Honour ! of course that man is *not* the Comte de la Tremouille.' "

III

A SENSATION

" I CAN assure you that the situation was quite dramatic," continued the man in the corner, whilst his funny, claw-like hands took up a bit of string with renewed feverishness.

" In answer to further questions from the magistrate, she declared that she had never seen the accused ; he might have been the go-between, however, that she could not say. The letters she received were all typewritten, but signed ' Armand de la Tremouille,' and certainly the signature was identical with that on the letters she used to receive from him years ago, all of which she had kept.

" ' And did it *never* strike you,' asked the magistrate with a smile, ' that the letters you received might be forgeries ? '

" ' How could they be ? ' she replied decisively, ' no one knew of my marriage to the Comte de la Tremouille, no one in England certainly. And, besides, if someone did know the Comte intimately enough to forge his handwriting and to blackmail me, why should that someone have waited all these years ? I have been married seven years, your Honour.'

" That was true enough, and there the matter rested as far as she was concerned. But the identity of Mr. Francis Morton's assailant had to be finally established, of course, before the prisoner was committed for trial. Dr. Mellish promised that Mr. Morton would be allowed to come to court for half an hour and identify the accused on the following day, and the case was adjourned until then. The accused was led away between two constables, bail being refused, and Brighton had perforce to moderate its impatience until the Wednesday.

" On that day the court was crowded to overflowing ; actors, playwrights, literary men of all sorts had fought for admission to study for themselves the various phases and faces in connection with the case. Mrs. Morton was not present when the prisoner, quiet and self-possessed, was brought in and placed in the dock. His solicitor was with him, and a sensational defence was expected.

" Presently there was a stir in the court, and that certain sound, half rustle, half sigh, which preludes an expected palpitating event. Mr. Morton, pale, thin, wearing in his hollow eyes the stamp of those five days of suffering, walked into court leaning on the arm of his doctor—Mrs. Morton was not with him.

" He was at once accommodated with a chair in the witness-box, and the magistrate, after a few words of kindly sympathy, asked him if he had anything to add to his written statement. On Mr. Morton replying in the negative, the magistrate added :

" ' And now, Mr. Morton, will you kindly look at the accused in the dock and tell me whether you recognise the person who took you to the room in Russell House and then assaulted you ? '

" Slowly the sick man turned towards the prisoner and looked at him ; then he shook his head and replied quietly :

" ' No, sir, that certainly was not the man.'

" ' You are quite sure ? ' asked the magistrate in amazement, while the crowd literally gasped with wonder.

" ' I swear it,' asserted Mr. Morton.

" ' Can you describe the man who assaulted you ? '

" ' Certainly. He was dark, of swarthy complexion, tall,

thin, with bushy eyebrows and thick black hair and short beard. He spoke English with just the faintest suspicion of a foreign accent.'

" The prisoner, as I told you before, was English in every feature. English in his ruddy complexion, and absolutely English in his speech.

" After that the case for the prosecution began to collapse. Everyone had expected a sensational defence, and Mr. Matthew Quiller, counsel for Skinner, fully justified all these expectations. He had no fewer than four witnesses present who swore positively that at 9.45 a.m. on the morning of Wednesday, March 17th, the prisoner was in the express train leaving Brighton for Victoria.

" Not being endowed with the gift of being in two places at once, and Mr. Morton having added the whole weight of his own evidence in Mr. Edward Skinner's favour, that gentleman was once more remanded by the magistrate, pending further investigation by the police, bail being allowed this time in two sureties of £50 each."

IV

TWO BLACKGUARDS

" Tell me what you think of it," said the man in the corner, seeing that Polly remained silent and puzzled.

" Well," she replied dubiously, " I suppose that the so-called Armand de la Tremouille's story was true in substance. That he did not perish on the *Argentina*, but drifted home, and blackmailed his former wife."

" Doesn't it strike you that there are at least two very strong points against that theory ? " he asked, making two gigantic knots in his piece of string.

" Two ? "

" Yes. In the first place, if the blackmailer was the ' Comte de la Tremouille ' returned to life, why should he have been content to take £10,000 from a lady who was his lawful wife, and who could keep him in luxury for the rest of his natural life upon her large fortune, which was close upon a quarter of a million ? The real Comte de la Tremouille, remember, had never found it difficult to get money out of his wife during their brief married life, whatever Mr. Morton's subsequent experience in the same direction might have been. And secondly, why should he have typewritten his letters to his wife ? ''

" Because——''

" That was a point which, to my mind, the police never made the most of. Now, my experience in criminal cases has invariably been that when a typewritten letter figures in one, that letter is a forgery. It is not very difficult to imitate a signature, but it is a jolly sight more difficult to imitate a handwriting throughout an entire letter."

" Then, do you think——''

" I think, if you will allow me," he interrupted excitedly, " that we will go through the points—the sensible, tangible points of the case. Firstly : Mr. Morton disappears with £10,000 in his pocket for four entire days ; at the end of that time he is discovered loosely tied to an arm-chair, and a wool shawl round his mouth. Secondly : A man named Skinner is accused of the outrage. Mr. Morton, although he himself is able, mind you, to furnish the best defence possible for Skinner, by denying his identity with the man who assaulted him, refuses to prosecute. Why ? ''

" He did not wish to drag his wife's name into the case."

" He must have known that the Crown would take up the case. Then, again, how is it no one saw him in the company of the swarthy foreigner he described ? ''

" Two witnesses did see Mr. Morton in company with Skinner," argued Polly.

" Yes, at 9.20 in West Street ; that would give Edward Skinner time to catch the 9.45 at the station, and to entrust Mr. Morton with the latch-key of Russell House," remarked the man in the corner dryly.

" What nonsense ! '' Polly ejaculated.

" Nonsense, is it ? '' he said, tugging wildly at his bit of string ; " is it nonsense to affirm that if a man wants to make sure that his victim shall not escape, he does not usually wind rope ' loosely ' round his figure, nor does he throw a wool shawl lightly round his mouth. The police were idiotic beyond words ; they themselves discovered that Morton was so ' loosely ' fastened to his chair that very little movement would have disentangled him, and yet it never struck them that nothing was easier for that particular type of scoundrel than to sit down in an arm-chair and wind a few yards of rope round himself, then, having wrapped a wool shawl round his throat, to slip his two arms inside the ropes."

" But what object would a man in Mr. Morton's position have for playing such extraordinary pranks ? "

" Ah, the motive ! There you are ! What do I always tell you ? Seek the motive ! Now, what was Mr. Morton's position ? He was the husband of a lady who owned a quarter of a million of money, not one penny of which he could touch without her consent, as it was settled on herself, and who, after the terrible way in which she had been plundered and then abandoned in her early youth, no doubt kept a very tight hold upon the purse-strings. Mr. Morton's subsequent life has proved that he had certain expensive, not altogether avowable, tastes. One day he discovers the old love-letters of the ' Comte Armand de la Tremouille.'

" Then he lays his plans. He typewrites a letter, forges the signature of the erstwhile Count, and awaits events. The fish does rise to the bait. He gets sundry bits of money, and his success makes him daring. He looks round him for an accomplice—clever, unscrupulous, greedy—and selects Mr. Edward Skinner, probably some former pal of his wild oats days.

" The plan was very neat, you must confess. Mr. Skinner takes the room in Russell House, and studies all the manners and customs of his landlady and her servant. He then draws the full attention of the police upon himself. He meets Morton in West Street, then disappears ostensibly after the ' assault.' In the meanwhile Morton goes to Russell House. He walks upstairs, talks loudly in the room, then makes elaborate preparations for his comedy."

" Why ! he nearly died of starvation ! "

" That, I dare say, was not a part of his reckoning. He thought, no doubt, that Mrs. Chapman or the servant would discover and rescue him pretty soon. He meant to appear just a little faint, and endured quietly the first twenty-four hours of inanition. But the excitement and want of food told on him more than he expected. After twenty-four hours he turned very giddy and sick, and, falling from one fainting fit into another, was unable to give the alarm.

" However, he is all right again now, and concludes his part of a downright blackguard to perfection. Under the plea that his conscience does not allow him to live with a lady whose first husband is still alive, he has taken a bachelor flat in London, and only pays afternoon calls on his wife in Brighton. But presently he will tire of his bachelor life, and will return to his wife. And I'll guarantee that the Comte de la Tremouille will never be heard of again."

And that afternoon the man in the corner left Miss Polly Burton alone with a couple of photos of two uninteresting, stodgy, quiet-looking men—Morton and Skinner—who, if the old scarecrow was right in his theories, were a pair of the finest blackguards unhung.

Reprinted with the Author's permission from *The Old Man in the Corner*.

MARGARET PEDLER

The Retirement of Mr. Gregory

Mrs. PEDLER made her first great success as a novelist with *The Splendid Folly* in 1918. Before she became a writer, she studied music at the Royal Academy of Music, and she has written and composed several songs.

THE RETIREMENT OF MR. GREGORY

HE was a little old grey man, flitting noiselessly through the showrooms of Isaac Mosenthal & Co., dealers in antiques, like a vague shadow of times gone by.

Perhaps he was not so very old in reality, but the bowed shoulders, the straggling grey beard, and the careworn wrinkles round the peering hazel eyes combined to give an impression of age, and " old Gregory " he had been called by the heads of the firm and by the staff from time immemorial.

Most of his days were spent in making long and often fruitless journeys in the endless search for antiques—old silver, china, tapestries—of which a whisper that they were for sale had reached the ever-open ears of Isaac Mosenthal. When he was not thus occupied he was generally to be found wandering, with dreaming eyes, about the shop, handling the rare curios with frail hands whose touch was as tender and as loving as a violinist's when he sets his instrument beneath his chin. And as skilled—for no modern replica, fashioned by no matter how dexterous and trained a hand, could deceive those sensitive fingers, nor any forgery slip past the scrutiny of the gentle dreamy eyes.

No one paid much attention to old Gregory as he padded quietly about the showrooms. Occasionally a man or woman, pressed for money, would come in and diffidently offer some treasured curio for sale, and then, if there were any doubt about its genuineness or any difficulty in assessing its value, the matter was referred to the old man and his opinion taken.

" Fake," he would say, or briefly : " Buy it," naming the price. And without further question the bargain was concluded.

Invariably, should any antique jewellery be brought into the shop and offered across the counter for sale, whether or no his judgment were in requisition, old Gregory was at hand, watching with eager wistful eyes as though it had some special interest for him. But always he would turn away with a sigh and a patient little shrug of his bowed shoulders, seemingly disappointed.

The youngsters on the staff, seeing him rambling idly round the rooms crowded with priceless treasures, were apt at times to think he hardly earned his salary, but Mosenthal and his junior partner, Goldmark, knew that not one of their employees was better worth his wage.

Never once, in all the years that he had been their principal buyer, had he made a mistake, whether the newly-acquired treasure had been purchased at the dispersal of some vast collection into which it was surmised a few clever forgeries might have crept, or from an old county family fallen upon evil times, or had been sought for in some country farm-stead where a piece of priceless slipware might be found cheek by jowl with a gilt-emblazoned mug bearing the legend : *A Present from Margate.*

" The thing that surprises me," remarked Mosenthal in the seclusion of the partners' room, " is why old Gregory hangs on. Putting his screw and commission together, he must have made a tidy bit. I wonder he doesn't chuck the job and retire."

" Pray heaven he won't," returned Goldmark piously. " There isn't another buyer to equal him either in or out of London."

" True enough. But since his expenses must be very few and his savings pretty big, it's a marvel to me that he sticks to it."

" Not got an expensive wife by any chance ? "

" No. Wife died years ago—before he came to us."

" And certainly no other woman would have a claim upon his purse at this time of day," observed the junior partner frivolously. " He must have sown his wild oats long before I was born—if ever."

" Never, I should imagine. I'm sure old Gregory never had any eye for a chorus girl."

" No. But he's got unimpeachable vision when it comes to a tapestry or an old print."

Mosenthal nodded acquiescence.

" By the way," he said. " Just run your eye over this. Is it any good, do you think ? "

And he held out a letter written upon cheap note-paper

in an unformed girlish hand. The address in the right-hand top corner was " Rosetree Cottage, Langaton, Devon."

" Dear Sir " (ran the letter), " I have been told that you are always willing to buy antiques. I have some jewellery, all of which is old and very valuable, and which I am anxious to sell immediately.

" Yours truly,
" Mary le Neve Dormer."

" Humph," grunted Goldmark. " Le Neve Dormer. It's a good name—might have some old family stuff attached. But ' Rosetree Cottage ' ! Doesn't sound quite like the family estate, does it ? "

" Send for Gregory and see what he says about it."

The old man came in noiselessly in answer to the summons. All his movements were very quiet and gentle.

" You wanted to see me, sir ? " he asked.

" Yes. Just take a look at that and say whether you think it's worth while. Devon's a devil of a long way to go on chance."

Gregory's hand shook a little as he returned the letter to the senior partner and there was an unwonted sparkle in his eyes—a look of almost boyish eagerness.

" As though he'd just caught sight of his best girl across the road," as Mr. Goldmark facetiously observed when the two partners were once more alone.

" Yes, sir," said old Gregory. " I think it might be worth looking into. And it wouldn't be at all out of my way to go to Langaton, as my next journey is to Plymouth. Langaton is a little village just off the edge of Dartmoor, so I shall be passing it, as you may say."

" Very well, then, Gregory. We'll leave it to you to write and make an appointment."

Two days later saw Mr. Gregory and the very small amount of baggage with which he invariably travelled safely bestowed on board the Plymouth express, bound for Okehampton. The little man whiled away the greater part of the journey alternately dozing and reading a treatise on the rearing of canaries—a subject in which his interest was only second to his ardour for antiques. But towards its end, when the train was swinging along between the rich green

Devon pastures that billowed up on either side of the track, he let the treatise slip unheeded to the floor, and, suddenly very wide awake, kept muttering to himself as his eyes swept the flying landscape :

" It might be. Devon . . . Devon. . . . Perhaps I may come across it here."

There was a note of intense eagerness in his voice. Presently he closed his eyes for a moment and whispered :

" I never forget, Jennie girl. Don't think I ever forget."

Arrived at Okehampton, he found he would be compelled to drive thence to Langaton, since the little hamlet nestling on the fringe of the moor lay quite away from the beaten track. Accordingly, he hired a trap, and an hour and a half's drive through lanes that wound steeply uphill towards the moor brought him in sight of the few scattered cottages of which the village was composed.

Leaving the driver to put up his horse and trap at a tiny hostelry which boasted the imposing name of " The Langaton Arms," Mr. Gregory inquired which of the handful of thatched cottages was the one he sought and forthwith made his way there on foot.

A solitary standard rose tree, which had long ago given up the unequal contest with the bleak moorland winds, stood guard at the gateway, and as old Gregory approached the little dwelling he wondered what of value he might find hidden beneath its yellow-thatched roof.

There was no bell, so he evidenced his arrival by tapping diffidently on the wooden door. It flew open with such promptitude as to suggest that his knock had been eagerly anticipated.

" Oh, are you the antique man ? "

The voice held a note of almost passionate anxiety, and Gregory peered at the speaker in surprise. But in the dusk of the narrow passage-way he could discern little else than that it was a woman who had addressed him in those urgent tones and that she was quite young.

" Yes," he replied gently. " I am Mr. Mosenthal's representative. You wrote to him about some antique jewellery you wished to dispose of."

" Yes. Come in, please." And she led the way into a room which evidently served both as kitchen and living-room combined.

An oil-lamp burned on the table, and as the light fell on her face Gregory could see that she was even younger than he had thought. Not more than seventeen at the outside. Her face was drawn and pale-looking, and there were curiously dark shadows beneath the hyacinth-blue eyes. She looked as though recently she had lacked sufficiency of both food and sleep.

"Please sit down," she said, "and I will fetch the jewellery. I—I should not sell it only that my husband has been very ill——"

"Your husband!" Old Gregory was so startled that the exclamation escaped him before he could check it. She looked such a slip of a girl—hardly more than a child—that it seemed incredible she should be married.

She smiled at him wistfully. The brave little smile struck him as one of the saddest things he had ever seen and he felt the muscles of his throat suddenly contract.

"Yes," she said. "I've been married nearly a year, but my husband's been ill for the last six months. That's why I want to sell the jewellery. When he's well he writes for the papers and makes a lot of money by his articles, but since he's been so ill he hasn't been able to write. And now we've used up all the money which he had put by. It's very expensive being ill, you see," she added simply.

Mr. Gregory sat down abruptly on one of the plain deal chairs. For the moment he had forgotten all about Isaac Mosenthal & Co. and the primary object of his visit to Rosetree Cottage.

"Dear, dear," he said. "To be sure, it's a very expensive thing being ill. Haven't you anyone who could—could finance you until your husband is better? His people, now—why don't you write to them?"

She shook her head.

"That wouldn't help any. You see, I was on the stage and I—I wasn't good enough for the Le Neve Dormers, so when Dick married me his people refused to have anything more to do with him. If he hadn't been so ill we should have managed all right. But the London doctors ordered him down here, and—and invalid's food seems to cost such a lot that if I hadn't thought of the jewellery I don't know what we should have done."

Once more she smiled at him, the appealing, plucky little

smile which plays such tricks with a man's throat. Gregory cleared his.

" Oh, yes, the jewellery," he said, all at once recalled to his errand.

" I'll fetch it for you to see," she replied eagerly. " It's some old paste that belonged to Dick's grandmother. She gave it him years ago for his wife "—and here a faint colour crept into her thin cheeks—" when he should have one. So when we were married he gave it to me. Old paste is very valuable, isn't it ? "

" Some of it—some of it. Not all, of course," replied Mr. Gregory, with a swift belated recollection of his duty towards Isaac Mosenthal & Co.

She sped away on her errand, and the old man looked round the spotless little kitchen with troubled eyes.

" Poor child, poor child," he muttered. Then with a sigh : " Only old paste. No chance of finding it here, I'm afraid."

What " it " was he did not specify, but judging from the sudden yearning in his eyes it was something that lay very near his heart.

Presently the girl returned with several battered old jeweller's cases in her hands. These she spread out on the table, snapping them open one by one. There were some necklaces, a pair of ear-rings, several buckles and a quaint old thumb-ring. They made a brave show under the yellow lamplight.

Gregory summed them up at a glance.

" Modern," he said. " Quite worthless."

And then he could have bitten his tongue out, for all at once the young face opposite him seemed to grow small and pinched-looking and a curious blue shade spread itself round the nostrils and mouth.

" What—what did you say ? " she asked, her lip quivering. " That they are modern ? . . . Oh, I think "—with a sudden little touch of dignity—" you must be mistaken. Dick's grandmother wouldn't have had anything modern. Will you please look again ? "

There was no need to look a second time. Old Gregory's practised eye had at once detected the meretricious appearance of the pseudo-paste. Either grandmother must have been badly deceived or—more probably—Dick, in the course of a lurid and expensive youth, had disposed of the original antique paste ornaments and had caused some cheap replicas to be supplied in their place.

On many occasions had old Gregory seen that same blank expression of disappointment overspread a would-be vendor's face as the word " modern " fell inexorably from his lips, but never before had he shared so fully in the dismay of the owner of the property.   He felt physically incapable of repeating the abominable word with those frightened child's eyes gazing into his.

" Will you please look again ? " she asked wistfully.

He fidgeted with the glassy-looking gems, and then, catching sight of the thumb-ring, he seemed to be suddenly reminded of something, for there leaped into his face the boyishly eager expression that it had worn when Mosenthal had first shown him the letter from Rosetree Cottage.

" Haven't you anything else ? " he asked.   " Any other rings, for instance ? "

She gave him a wintry little smile.

" No, I've nothing else I can sell."

" Supposing you go and look in your jewel-case," he suggested gently, " while I examine this—this paste a little more carefully.   We are all liable to make mistakes, you know," he added, lying bravely, " and perhaps it is better than I at first thought."

She nodded.

" Yes, do look at it again.   I can't help thinking "— diffidently—" that you may find you were mistaken.   It's —it's such a poor light, you see," she added, fearful of hurting his feelings.

When she returned, a shabby leather jewel-case in her hand, he had taken his decision.

" I can offer you fifty pounds for these," he said, indicating the sham paste ornaments.

Instantly the tense, strained expression went out of her young face, and in spite of its thinness Gregory could see how extraordinarily pretty happiness and health would make it.   Already she looked a different being and he experienced a thrill of personal pride in the fact that he had been instrumental in effecting such a change—even though at a cost of fifty pounds.   Incidentally, he felt no

surprise that Dickie le Neve Dormer had defied his family
when making his choice of a wife.

" And now, what is there in the jewel-case ? " he asked.

" Nothing of any value, I'm afraid," she answered,
tumbling the things out pell-mell on to the table.

Suddenly old Gregory's eyes, darting hither and thither
amongst the odds and ends, fixed themselves with painful
intensity on a small object that had rolled a trifle to one side.
It was an intaglio, mounted as a ring, very finely cut in
onyx, its surface mellowed as only the fingering of centuries
could make it.

Drawing in his breath with a curious little sucking noise,
he pointed to it with a trembling finger.

" That ring," he said, and his voice shook.　" Where did
you get it ? "

She picked it up and laid it in his outstretched hand.

" It belonged to my mother.　It was her engagement
ring.　She had set her heart on an intaglio rather than
any gem ring, and I believe my father hunted high and
low before he found this one.　It's very old, I believe."

Lingeringly, delicately, as though it were something
most precious, old Gregory handled the onyx ring.

Once he brushed his sleeve across his eyes ; there were
tears in them—the slow, painful tears which memory wrings
from the old.

At last he spoke.

" I will give you another fifty pounds for this ring."

" Oh, I can't sell it," she replied hastily.

" A hundred pounds," he said steadily.

" I can't sell it," she repeated.　" It was my mother's."

The old eyes looked piteously across into the young ones.

" And it was—my wife's," he said.

Rather totteringly he sat down, still clasping the ring.

" She lay dying with that ring on her finger—forty years
ago."

Mary Dormer leaned her elbows on the table, propping
her chin on her clasped hands.

" Tell me," she said simply, sensing the little man's ache
to share his burden—the long burden of forty years.

It was quite a commonplace story—one that is told every
day amid the grim strife of big cities—the tale of a boy and
girl who had married on nothing a year except the lad's

wages. Presently there came ill-luck, loss of work and a consequent dearth of money, and finally, just when the perpetual miracle of birth should have shed a fresh radiance round the young pair, there was neither food nor firing to be found in the room where, with a tiny Third beside her, lay the frail form that meant everything in the world to old Gregory—young Gregory as he had been in those far-away days.

" She knew she couldn't live," he said, " and she gave me this ring—it was one she had always worn—to keep in remembrance. There was nothing to eat in the house and she and the child needed both warmth and food. I went straight out with the ring and pawned it—pawned it for money to buy what might keep the breath in her body. But when I returned with the food and wine that might have saved her, she had slipped out of the world, she and the child together. . . . And I had bartered away her last gift uselessly."

He was silent for a space, pushing the ring to and fro as it lay on his palm. Then he spoke again.

" Afterwards the luck turned and money began to flow in. With the first money that I saved I went to the pawn-shop to redeem the ring. But it was too late. It had been sold, they told me, to a gentleman who wanted it for an engagement ring."

" My father," said Mary Dormer softly.

" I advertised for it. I offered a big sum for its return, but it was all no use. Since then, for forty years, I've been searching—searching for the little ring, Jennie's ring, always thinking that some time I might come across it in the course of my work. I've made money and I could have retired from business long ago, but always I've been hoping—hoping that I should find the little ring."

Mary Dormer leaned forward and laid her young hand on his old wrinkled one.

" I'm so glad," she whispered, " so glad you've found it."

He did not seem to hear her, for he continued exactly as though she had not spoken.

" What do you want for the ring ? I will pay you just whatever price you ask."

She shook her head dumbly, seeking for words, and a look of mingled fear and cunning leaped into his eyes.

"I'll give you any price you name," he repeated doggedly.
She leaned forward and closed his fingers gently round the ring.

"Keep it," she said very softly. "But I can't sell it to you. It was yours before it was mine, and now it must be yours again. I have no right to it."

For a moment he seemed hardly to understand. Then, with a sudden quick motion, he slipped the ring into his breast-pocket.

He smiled, a contented, tired little smile, and his lips moved. Presently Mary Dormer caught the words:

"You see, Jennie girl, I didn't forget—I didn't forget."

．　．　．　．　．　．　．

"Well, Gregory, what luck? Did anything good come out of Rosetree Cottage?" And Isaac Mosenthal slapped the old man jocosely on the back. The brief interview in the partners' room when, after his return from a treasure-hunt, old Gregory invariably presented himself to make his report, was generally eminently satisfactory with its evidence of judicious purchases that would ultimately ensure large profits to the firm, and both the partners came to it, as a rule, in a genially expansive frame of mind.

In his hand Gregory carried a smallish package which he placed quietly upon the table, laying beside it the book of signed blank cheques with which Isaac Mosenthal had entrusted him. Only one cheque had been torn from the book and the counterfoil showed that the sum of £50 had been drawn to Mary le Neve Dormer.

Goldmark picked up the parcel and swept it with a humorous eye.

"Not a very large purchase, I see, Gregory. But little and good, I suppose, hey? Little and good."

"It's the jewellery Mrs. Dormer had for sale, sir."

"You bought, then? Let's see it."

Rapidly the junior partner undid the packet and spread out the opened cases under the glare of the electric light, Mosenthal leaning forward the better to view the new acquisition.

Suddenly the latter pursed his lips and gave vent to a low whistle. Then, stretching out a claw-like hand, he snatched up one of the necklaces and regarded it closely.

" How much did you say you paid for this, Gregory ? "
he asked, at last, in a queer voice.

" Fifty pounds, sir.   There's the counterfoil," replied the
old man, pointing to the cheque-book.

Mosenthal picked up the glittering ornaments one by one
and spun them across the table to the junior partner.

" Fifty pounds !   Fifty pounds for that—*rubbish !* " he
exclaimed.   " Heavens above, Gregory !   Have you taken
leave of your senses ?   Why, a child could detect that the
stuff is sham."

Goldmark surveyed the buyer curiously.

" It's very unlike you to be taken in, Gregory," he observed.

" It's the first time since I've been in your employ, sir,"
said the little man quietly.   " And I think it had better be
the last.   I came this morning to ask you and Mr. Mosenthal
to accept my resignation—and these."   He laid ten five-
pound notes on the table.   " I shouldn't like the firm to
lose by my—mistake."

The two partners cried out in hasty protest against his
resigning, for the fifty pounds loss he had incurred weighed
lightly enough in comparison with the immense gains he
had won for the firm during the years he had worked for
them.   But old Gregory shook his head obstinately.

" No, sir," he said.   " I've made my bit and there's nothing
—now "—he smiled to himself dreamily—" to prevent me
from retiring.   And if I can make such a mistake as—as
this, it looks like a hint that it's time I gave up."

He began to put the paste ornaments back into their cases.

" What are you going to do with them ? " asked Goldmark with some curiosity.

Mr. Gregory looked down at them reflectively.

" Well, I thought maybe I'd keep them.   They'd be—a
reminder."

" A reminder of your solitary mistake? " queried the junior
partner, laughing.   Then he added speculatively : " I believe
you're keeping them for some sentimental reason, Gregory."

Old Gregory busied himself stuffing the various cases with
their contents into his pockets.   For an instant an odd little
smile flickered across his face.

" Perhaps so, sir," was all he said.

Reprinted with the Author's permission from *Many Ways.*

25

EDEN PHILLPOTTS

Peacock House

Mr. EDEN PHILLPOTTS, who was born in India, began life as clerk in an Insurance office, and subsequently studied for the stage before he decided to write. In his longer works he has given Dartmoor a literary fame resembling that of Hardy's Wessex. Besides his short stories and novels he has written numerous poems and plays, among the latter *The Farmer's Wife*.

PEACOCK HOUSE

JANE CAMPBELL'S long journey was ended, and in August
sunset light, a dogcart, which conveyed her upon the last
stage, drove up an avenue of old elms, left the trees, skirted
a little lake, and presently brought the visitor before the face
of Pole Manor, a minor mansion lying at the foothills of
Dartmoor. Two storeys high and built of granite rose this
Georgian house, but the porch and its pillars were of red,
conglomerate stone. They broke the unbending gravity
of the grey front with a touch of colour. Behind rolled blue
hills, now melting into the splendour of gold and orange
above them ; while southward, beyond a little park, extended meadow lands, wooded ridges, and fields of corn
yellowing to harvest.

The dogcart brought up, and a footman descended from
the porch. He assisted the traveller, who was a pleasant-
looking, red-haired woman of robust build ; then he turned
his attention to her luggage, untied a bicycle fastened to
the back seat, set it against the steps, and picked up Miss
Campbell's plain, leathern trunk and suit-case. These he
took into the hall and handed to another man. The cart
drove away down a road to the left of the house, and presently a stable boy came up this path and trundled off the
bicycle. He waited until beyond observation, then mounted
it for his private amusement.

Jane had come to visit her godfather. She was a schoolmistress at Glasgow, and when in doubt as to where the latter
part of her summer holiday might be spent, to her amazement received a letter from a friend of her dead father, the
old soldier who had been her man gossip. From him she
had never heard until now, and only once had she seen him,
when he came, three-and-thirty years before, to Colonel
Campbell's funeral. Then she was but two years old, and
had, therefore, no recollection of him. Indeed, if she ever
thought of him, it was with impatience, for she had been

saddled with his surname and regarded it as rather stupid so to be. Jane Goodenough Campbell she was called, but few knew it save herself. Since her mother's death she was exceedingly alone in the world. She had been an only child, and of her father's people none remained; of her mother's, but an old aunt and some distant cousins whom she never saw.

She lived a monotonous, independent life, enjoyed the business of teaching, harboured no dreams, and was of a practical and stolid temperament. With men she was cold, and no romance added shadow or lustre to her recollections. She had once liked a man, and even sought to let him know it ; but she understood not how to do so, and the schoolmaster in question soon found out her temperamental lack and turned away.

Now came something of an adventure, and after fearing that such a visit as General George Goodenough proposed was quite out of her province, Jane, greatly daring, determined to accept the invitation, and did so. She had regretted it half a dozen times on the journey, and wished more than once that her destination was one of the whitewashed, thatched cottages that peered from nook and dingle upon her five-mile drive. Some weeks in one of them had better suited her modest ideas of rest and pleasure than a formal visit. But it was too late. She had glimpsed the unpromising front of Pole Manor ; she had passed through the lifeless hall and was waiting in an equally lifeless drawing-room for her host.

A housekeeper welcomed her—a cheerful old woman in black, with a little black cap on her few white hairs. The footman who took her luggage upstairs was also old and grey. A sense of age clung to everything, and the drawing-room seemed naked and archaic to Jane's eye. The furniture was tired-looking, faded, of little worth. Only a magnificent mantelshelf of the Adam period attracted her, and from it she lifted her eyes to the roof and saw that the ceiling was also distinguished.

Then came somebody on a stick. She heard the stick tapping, but no sound of feet. The door opened and a lame, bent figure appeared. Here indeed was eld, and her heart sank. She knew that a contemporary of her father, who had married at forty-five, must be stricken in years, but Time's self stood personified before her, and General

Goodenough, by reason of indifference to appearances, looked even more ancient than he was. He had been tall, but was now withered and shrunken. He wore a black skull-cap on his bald head, and a great, white beard and whiskers still thick and flowing. His face was thin and his cheeks hollow ; his eyes were dim behind their glasses, and a network of wrinkles extended from his high, narrow brow over his temples to his cheek-bones. His expression belied him and belonged, as it seemed, to his soldier days ; for it was still stern. But his voice was not. Though dimmed by the throttle of eighty-five years, it had good, deep notes yet, and it sounded kindly on the ear of all who ever heard it. His clothes seemed ridiculous to Jane. Such a venerable figure, she thought, should have worn Victorian garments at the least ; but the General was clad in a very shabby Norfolk jacket, a waistcoat of fawn-coloured leather, and knickerbockers, from which appeared legs still fairly sturdy, in homespun stockings. On one foot was a red slipper ; the other had been tied up in a shawl.

He bowed, shook Jane's hand with gnarled fingers distorted by chalk stones, and sank into a chair.

" Welcome," he said. " I take this visit kindly, young lady. But don't be discouraged. A touch of gout—quite unexpected, probably brought on by the excitement of entertaining you. Deal gently with me ; distract my mind, and it will be gone in twenty-four hours. Have you made a comfortable journey ? "

" Very much so, General Goodenough."

" Do you know Devon ? "

" I do not. I visited Cornwall once and found the air almost too strong."

" Did you ? Here the air is soft, or bracing, at will. The valleys are as good as a Turkish bath this summer ; but Dartmoor, five miles up above us, is always bracing."

" You're not in pain ? " she asked.

" Thank you, no. Mere discomfort. Gout won't kill me. A man is as old as his arteries, Jane Campbell ; and though I'm in my eighty-fifth year, my arteries happen to be only seventy or thereabout. So the doctor tells me. Don't think you've come to an invalid. Your good mother —I was so sorry to find she had gone. I hoped to have entertained you both,"

" She died ten years ago."

" Well, well. And you don't remember your father, my dear old companion in arms ? "

" Not very well, General. Just a shadow. I was a tiny thing when he died. But I dream about him sometimes—strange to say."

" So do I. It is said, you know, that we never see the faces of the dead in dream. For that matter, I have no other faces to see now. Your father possessed one or two gifts of the Scots and lacked some of their reputed failings. He had second sight—couldn't explain it, even disavowed it; but things happened to him only to be so understood. And he was a Scot in his love of metaphysics. What a man to split straws and prove black was white ! I should have hated it in anybody else ; but nothing was wrong that he did. A great man, and loved a joke, and couldn't keep money in his purse. Dear, dear me ! Really great ; and so he was passed over, and the show puppets, for whom he pulled the strings in such masterly fashion, got the honours. A common thing in India half a century ago. A mad world, Jane, and it always was—it always was. I read little but history nowadays, and I see the only thing that changes not is human nature."

" Psychology is in the air so much," she said. " I suppose there is something in what you speak of as second sight. But it isn't called that now."

" Inherited, they say," answered the old man. " Are you interested in it ? "

" In psychology and second-self, rather than second sight. I've read Freud. He's a pathologist, but seems to be more useful to the artists than the doctors. So far as I understand it, our unconscious minds seem to be very primitive and earthly and inferior, and impervious to conscience—most disappointing, in fact."

" You never found yourself possessed of any clairvoyant gift ? "

" No, indeed. I'm a schoolmistress, and the most matter of fact person in the world. I'm afraid you'll find me very dull, General Goodenough."

" Call me ' Godfather,' " he said. " I expect you think it strange that I should claim such a spiritual relationship after so many years. There's a respectable gap between the silver porringer and spoon I gave you when you were baptised and to-day. Still, bear no grudge. I'm lonely, and I must go soon, and there's no one in the wide world linked to me, even as slightly as you are. The natural fate of all old bachelors, if they refuse to send in their papers at three score and ten. So I thought, if you were willing, that we might have a look at each other. A schoolmistress, eh ?"

" It was very good of you to ask me."

" And rather good of you to come—also rather brave. But your father's daughter was sure to be brave. I counted on that. It took me some months to hunt you down. I thought you might be married and have a husband and perhaps half a dozen young people."

She shook her head, smiling.

" I shall never marry, Godfather," she said.

" Don't prophesy."

A gong sounded, and the faint rumble reached them.

" You're ready for your dinner, I hope ? Would you like a cup of tea, or anything, now ? "

" No, thank you. I had some tea at Exeter."

They met again at dinner, when Jane, in a new but unromantic gown, faced the General, who had donned evening dress.

He treated her as though he had known her all his life, and was vivacious, humorous, and cheerful. She admired his tact, for finding that they had nothing of taste or experience in common, he sought to learn what interested her and made her talk about it.

" I catch your father," he said. " It is wonderful to note how young people are often the unconscious echoes of those responsible for them. Not in what they say, or even think, for education has lifted them forward, and their values are changed ; but in the manner of thought and the angle of vision. That is what is handed down—temperament ; here cautious and reserved and self-contained, as you are ; here dashing and reckless ; here cold and calculating ; here big-hearted ; here small. An unconscious inflexion of voice, little mannerisms. . . . You have your father's accent, and you lift your chin when you're going to speak, just as he used to do."

" Mother always said I grew up to remind her of him. Have you, by any chance, a picture of my father ? I, to

25*

my sorrow, have none. He never would be photographed."
He shook his head.

" I much fear not, save in my old heart ; but we will see.
It is barely possible."

A curious emotion made Jane smile to herself that night,
though little that happened ever amused her. Her host
made her retire early, and, when she had done so, she
reflected that he was treating her exactly as she habitually
treated her pupils. To them she was old ; to General
Goodenough she appeared exceedingly young. She was
accustomed to the companionships of immature intellects,
as all teachers perforce must be ; but now she perceived that
to this venerable man she was immature herself ; and indeed
she knew it, for though clever and learned, her knowledge of
life outside her scholastic circle was but small.

She asked concerning his health next morning, and he
declared his gout to be better. She was touched by his
solicitude, and a thousand little attentions that it seemed
impossible that a man should have considered.

He took no breakfast himself, but drank a glass of hot
water and ate a thin slice of toast only. For her, however,
he had planned a generous meal : porridge, a grouse, scones
and marmalade.

" Don't forget the Devonshire cream," he said. " I love
to see young people eat."

" But I'm not young, Godfather ; I'm five-and-thirty."

" To be five-and-thirty is to retain all the possibilities of
youth, even if the bloom has been rubbed off," he said.
" One is generally younger at that age than ten years earlier.
To-day you are free of my company, to do as you please ;
to-morrow I shall be well enough to drive you to the Moor."

" May I take a long bicycle ride ? It's cool and fresh and
delicious. I've been in your garden an hour."

" Alas ! We are not gardeners."

" There are splendid possibilities about it."

" Most old Indians make gardens," he said. " I have
known old fellows who, if they could not have gardens,
amused themselves by growing seeds of date and palm
in little pots and watching them spring up. But I am an
exception. Horticulture never attracted me."

" You must tell me your hobbies."

" They are easily told : reading and driving. This year

I've had an excitement. A regiment, long resident in India, was sent to Dartmoor, to be braced and hardened. With that exquisite foresight so characteristic of our War Office these unfortunate Third Devons were brought straight from the Plains to the side of Cosdon Beacon, and there, under canvas in a harsh April, reminded of the glories of an English Spring. The weather, unhappily, could not have been worse; the ambulance was busy taking poor Tommies to the hospital at Okehampton. A man or two died of pneumonia. The officers welcomed my modest hospitality—good fellows."

" I'll take a long ride ; but I promise not to go up to the Moor. You have to show me that."

" Disregard all hours save that for dinner," he said. " At eight o'clock I shall expect you to dine. Until then you are free of me."

But this she would not have.

" No, no ; I'm coming back for lunch, please. Perhaps I'll take it with me sometimes—with you on your drives."

" I have no motor-car. You must be resigned to that ; but I love horses and drive myself very creditably."

They pleased one another, and Jane pleased herself also, to find that she could be so cheerful and at her ease with a strange man. But she understood why. This gracious and kind-hearted old figure was not a man. He had passed beyond manhood into the neuter state of the aged. She liked his physical weakness. It inspired instincts that belonged to her ; for had she not been a schoolmistress, she must have been a nurse.

She thought kindly about him as she rode away, but her imagination was not equal to picturing her future spent at Pole Manor, though her reason told her that such a purpose might lurk in the General's mind. She guessed that he would soon empty her and weary of the content ; while, for her part, she knew that a life plunged into such silence, even with this amiable old spirit for company, must quickly desolate and distract a being devoted to the stir and bustle of a girls' school.

She wondered as to General Goodenough's acquaintance, and suspected he had but few friends. His house did not suggest hospitality, though he himself did.

The cool grey of the morning broke to pearl when Jane

had ridden five miles, and she regretted her promise, for the valley lanes were hot and the hills beckoned. Climb indeed she did presently, and won to a little knap crowned with shade of beeches. Then an expanse of country was flung beneath her, and she rejoiced in beholding gentle and distinguished scenery of a sort unfamiliar to her. For she was something of a connoisseur of natural beauty, and protested at those who were learned in art and understood pictures, but cared nothing for the scenes of inspiration where a man had sweated, or frozen, for his achievement. She blamed those who only valued a work itself, but found no pleasure in its sources. She knew the meaning of scenery, distrusted the obvious and rhetorical, but found by experience much that promised least was like a fugue, whose fullness and significance could often only be won after many hours of patient service.

The quiet lands undulating in the diffused light of thin clouds pleased her, and she knew that this manifestation, albeit lumpy and over-green with the heaviness of English foliage, must be fairer at spring and autumn time. For it was built on a large pattern, finely knit together and broken by great passages of level earth where a river twinkled through the haze.

She thirsted presently, looked for a roof tree, and longed to be on the banks of the distant stream far below. Then, half a mile beneath her, she thought that she saw the gables and twisted chimneys of an old house ; and since inviting meadows sloped towards it, she left her bicycle hidden under a holly and descended for something to drink. Jane remembered at a later date that the hour was just after noon when she took her way.

Descending over a shorn hayfield and passing through a belt of trees, the wanderer entered suddenly upon a different world, and in the glen through which she was now proceeding, the very air seemed charged and charmed with a different quality. It was lustrous, burnished and radiant with light. The sun, that had created but a bright and misty zone behind the clouds all day, here emerged and rained into a woodland whereon no proleptic shadow of autumn had yet appeared. It seemed as though the valley still lay in the lap of early summer ; the very flowers were not the ragworts and hawkweeds of a later time ; but woodbine scented the thickets, the dogrose had not yet dropped her petals, the wayfaring-tree still blossomed.

Jane, emerging from the forest and passing into a meadow, came suddenly to a low bank where the grassland broke, and above which extended a garden to the front of a beautiful dwelling-house. Upon its wall hung a great magnolia with ivory cups glittering in the sunshine, and the lawn of the formal garden was such as the stranger had never seen. To the right and left stood wonders of topiary in the shape of yew trees, clipped to the shape of peacocks with tails outspread, and between them a round pond lay ; while above the water, in the midst of it, stood a marble urchin holding a great fish, from whose mouth leapt up a fountain. It flashed aloft and fell purring upon the water-lilies below.

Two living peacocks strutted on the gravel terrace before the house, and when Jane ascended to the garden by a flight of steps and felt the velvet of the lawn under her feet, one bird lifted the glittering mass of bronze and purple he dragged behind him and opened his tail fanwise, till it arched and quivered like a dark rainbow above his head.

Other sign of life there was none, and seeing no entrance at the front of the house, Jane was about to pass round and follow the path that curved to the right. But the sight of a great magnolia cup low on the tree tempted her to smell the fragrance ; and from that, moved by an impulse that seemed natural at the time, yet made her wonder afterwards, she found herself peeping into the window beyond it.

The room was occupied, but those within did not regard her, and she perceived that their own affairs shut out any thought or sight of another face. The sun beat down, and through the windows of the chamber cast its radiance on the oaken floor. The walls were of dark crimson and upon them hung old portraits in golden frames, while at the centre was a table of polished mahogany spread with a meal. Silver glittered upon the rich wood ; and a bowl of strawberries stood between two tall vases of Bohemian glass, from which sprayed down dark, Tuscan roses and the snowy stars of syringas.

Three people sat at the table, and while the obvious details of the room were unconsciously impressed on the watcher's memory, the living beings she more directly regarded and remembered for ever.

All sense of her own impropriety deserted Jane ; she forgot the glamorous garden and its adornments ; her purpose in being there fled from her ; as still as a statue she stood and stared upon the remarkable trio assembled so near and yet so far removed from her by their own present passions.

A young man and a young woman were seated at each end of the oval table ; while between them sat a man of middle age, who directly faced the eavesdropper. The girl was fair and seemed to have sprung out of some picture by Reynolds or Gainsborough. Her flaxen hair had been drawn to her crown, yet little curls, amber bright, hid her ears. She was in summer muslin sprigged with blue lavender, with a bunch of lavender ribbon at her throat for sole adornment. Her face was pale and pure—a beautiful, but fragile, Greuze face, with red, small lips, and large, lovely blue eyes. The younger man wore a black tail coat and riding-breeches. He was clean shorn, of good height and well-knit, with a fierce intent expression on his countenance. Brown, curly hair clustered low on his forehead. The natural expression of neither did Jane see, for the woman was evidently trembling with terror and the youth strained to some great indignation at what he heard. His attitude echoed his emotion, for he leant over the table with a large, white fist clenched upon it, and he had upset and broken a wine-glass at his elbow, from which purple wine trickled over the table edge to the floor.

The elder of the men was speaking vehemently, and fury contorted his features. He had shaven lips and chin, black, curly whiskers and black hair streaked with grey. He wore a dull, russet-coloured coat, very high in the neck, and a black stock with a diamond pin in it. His heavy jowl was as red as a peony, and his round, brown eyes bulged like a fish's from under stormy eyebrows and a wrinkled forehead. Jane had never seen such passion blaze on any human countenance ; she did not know that a face could writhe with such contortions of malice and hate. The stout, middle-aged sufferer shot his lips and spewed moisture, like a gargoyle that she had seen leer down from a mediæval rain-shoot. It seemed that he roared at the others, for the girl shrank back in her chair and put her little white hands over her ears. She wore a wedding ring, Jane noted ; then the watcher, echoing some of this tremendous surge of passion and almost sharing the other woman's terror, turned

her eyes again quickly to the raging creature who faced her.
She could not hear what he said, but saw the table shiver
as he struck, the silver leap, and roses fall from a glass.
Then she witnessed death, sudden and terrible, for as the
younger man leapt up, with the intention of silencing his
tormentor, the elder tore a heavy pistol from his breast,
pointed it and fired point-blank at the head of the girl upon
his left hand. There was a stab of flame, and the woman,
shot through her fair head, fell forward, then slipped
out of her chair and dropped to the ground. The murderer had only time to fire once, for as he turned upon the
other man, his weapon was torn from his hand and exploded
into the air. Then, snatching a great silver knife from the
table, the younger drove it with all his strength into the
other's breast and left it there. His victim fell and lay
without movement, while the man who had slain him
hastened to the girl, bent over her, perceived that she was
dead, then turned and strode to the window where Jane
watched, flung it open and emerged. He almost brushed her
elbow, but was apparently unconscious of her presence, for
his blazing eyes saw nothing. He passed her and vanished
so quickly that she had but a glimpse of the unspeakable
agony on his face. It seemed rather an incarnation of all
human woe than a living man who swept out of her sight ;
and now, looking into the room again, Jane saw the door
open and two liveried servants enter.

Then she shrank back, and, alarmed for herself, turned
into a shrubbery, where she could not be seen, and so regained the meadows beneath the garden. Still hastening,
not without personal fear, she ran, passed the belt of trees
and breasted the hayfield as swiftly as she might. Not
until she was at the summit of the knoll did she stay her
progress, sink down beside her bicycle and slowly regain her
breath.

Horror and thankfulness shared Jane's mind. She was
appalled at what she had seen, but unspeakably glad that
into this tragedy she could not be drawn and need not enter.
Neither the murdered man nor woman had seen her, while for
the youth, who had so terribly slain the slayer, she could only
hope that he might escape. Her sympathies were with him
—she knew not why. For an hour she lay retracing every
incident of the scene and marvelling that all had happened

in so brief a space of time. She looked at her watch and perceived that she had not been half an hour from the hill-top. Then she brooded on the story of these unfortunate people and what must have preceded this grim climax in their lives.

She rose presently, mounted and returned home, conscious that the outer world was changed, that autumn's stealthy signs were now again on field and hedge ; that the sun had retreated behind the clouds. Very poignant emotions filled Jane's heart and head, yet a feeling of gratitude that she had played no part in this awful scene also persisted, and a nature prone to reserve and caution determined her to keep silence before General Goodenough. To tell him was to endanger her own privacy, for it might be that he would demand she should make public what she had accidentally seen, for the benefit of those who must be concerned with the crime. But Jane's conscience did not prompt confession. She was of a practical mind. She knew that she could not bring the dead to life, and had no desire to say one word that might help to bring the living to death. Her instinct indeed forbade it. Therefore she held her peace and waited with profound but secret interest to learn what the morrow would bring and who were the unhappy ones involved.

But the morning came, and neither General Goodenough, the housekeeper, nor any other exclaimed at the contents of the local newspaper. It arrived after breakfast and con-tained no sensation ; neither, apparently, was any evil thing on the lips of tradesmen, the grooms, or the gardener. Jane marvelled, but still kept silence. Doubtless news travelled slowly upon the country-side, and she guessed it possible that the police, for their own ends, might be keeping the tragedy a secret.

To-day the General found himself well, and drove her in a wagonette to the moor, where she wondered at stone-crowned heights and admired the fabric of autumn furze and heather mingled in a tapestry of purple and gold upon the granite hills.

She called Dartmoor " a little pocket Highlands," and General Goodenough pretended to be greatly annoyed at such patronage.

" A ' pocket Highlands,' indeed ! " he said. " Was ever such a slight put upon our venerable tors ? No, no, Jane,

this wilderness echoes no other region on earth, believe me.
The mountains are molehills, I grant you : the rivers mere
filaments and threads of gold and silver twinkling over their
granite aprons and stickles ; but for all its smallness, there
is a quality here of greatness, too, a spirit of distinction,
austerity, and even grandeur that, once received and
accepted, soon wins from the heart to the head, and makes
you Dartmoor's willing slave. You must confess, before you
leave me, that there is nothing like this in Scotland. Better
knowledge will show you the weakness of your parallel."

She hoped they might approach the knoll of her adventure,
so that an opportunity would offer to ask concerning the
house beneath, but they did not go that way, and though the
General met a man or two, who saluted him, and one on
horseback, who stopped and was introduced to her, nobody
brought any startling intelligence ; none appeared aware of
the dark events accomplished so near at hand on the previous
morning.

For three days Jane Campbell waited in vain expectation
of some news, then, to her own amazement, she found the
memory already fading under stress of new impressions.
Of a stolid temperament, little happened to cause her
excitation at any time ; but this event had naturally done
so, and she would not let it fade. She shook off the shadow
of indifference and grew into an obstinate determination to
learn more. It was preposterous that such a thing could
occur and make no ripple in a civilised community. Finally,
Jane found her mind balanced in uncertain fashion between
a choice of actions. First she determined to tell General
Goodenough her story in every particular ; then she hesitated before a temptation to visit the house in the vale again.
She thought to revisit it upon the old pretext, find the door
and ask for a glass of water. Then, surely, something must
reach her comprehension concerning the awful sights of the
week before. Dead people must be buried ; such tragedies
must wing above the scene of their commission. It was
contrary to reason that things so horrible and extravagant
could happen and utter no reverberation beyond the spot of
their occurrence.

The latter idea more attracted Jane, and, after some few
days, she begged again for a bicycle ride of exploration, took
luncheon with her, and set out for a long day alone. Upon

certain landmarks she depended to find the former way, and
for a time she failed to do so ; then, by chance, she came to
a meeting of two roads that crossed at right angles, and she
remembered the curious name of the spot lifted up on a
sign-post. " Beggar's Bush," it was called, and thence she
took the left hand track, and presently found herself once
more upon the knoll. There was no mistake, for the holly
bushes reminded her where she had left her bicycle, and she
found the spot where she had sat to reflect after her former
adventure.

She now prepared to revisit the scene of the tragedy. It
was a lonely glen, and none met her on the road, or meadow,
as she descended into it. Nor did the sun break forth and
shine as on her first visit. Morning, indeed, had opened in
clear splendour ; but the day grew oppressively hot before
noon, and already a thin web of brown and sulky cloud stole
up against the little wind that blew. There was a heavy,
sickly feeling in the air, and every sign of electric changes
near at hand. Jane looked for the gabled roof and twisted
chimneys beneath her, but she could not discern them.
Neither were the white pigeons on the wing. The valley
seemed to have receded somewhat and the trees towered
higher, denser, more numerous than she remembered them.
Then she went down over the shorn hayfield as before, passed
the belt of wood, and presently, entering the glade beneath,
started to cross the meadow, and lifted her eyes to the dwelling as she did so. It had vanished, and the sudden sense of
this disappearance terrified Jane as though she had seen a
ghost. But the thrill of fear arose from what she did not
see, rather from anything she did. A sensation, strange,
and altogether beyond experience, crept into her consciousness, and she believed that she was moving in the spirit
rather than the flesh, and standing in some corridor of long,
vanished years, before the grey house rose, or the garden
spread before it. Time, it seemed, had winged backward to
the days when the glen was a wilderness and man had not
built a home therein, spread his garden and set his fountain
flashing. And into that far, anterior day she, too, had been
caught up and whirled back, to behold a scene that existed
thus before she was born. She rubbed her eyes and pinched
her hand to waken out of this mysterious plunge into the
past ; and then she discovered that stark reality awaited

her, while what she had before imagined real was the true
dream and figment.

The jungles and thickets before her resolved themselves,
and beneath them, like a palimpsest of dead writing, that
peered ghostly through a later script, she came upon decayed
traces and shadows of what she had seen so vividly the week
before. Here rose the fragments of steps in the bank up
which she had climbed to the garden. They were weed-
covered and broken, but again she ascended—to find, amid
coarse brakes of thistle, briar and eagle-fern, the shattered
circle of the fountain, its marbles green with moss, its statue
vanished, and its waters dry. One of the yew trees clipped
to the likeness of a peacock had disappeared, while the other
still rose above the scrub round it ; and on its now mature
and lofty limbs, Jane fancied that she could make out a
gesture of the old design. The tree had broken away and
taken a natural shape ; yet, to eyes familiar with the earlier
form, it still retained some cloudy semblance of a bird grown
gigantic. But the house had altogether departed, and in its
place, hemmed by a cincture of heavy woods with undergrowth of laurel and Pontic rhododendron, lay only an undulating litter of great and small stones—a heap largely concealed under seedling trees that rose above nettle and bur-
dock, darnel and dock. Overhead, where the white pigeons
had warped together, a buzzard hung high above the
woods ; then it uttered a complaining cry and glided on its
way.

No sound or sight of any human being marked the spot ;
but a fox, that had been sleeping on the stones, leapt up at
Jane's footfall and trotted swiftly into the trees. She
marked the white tip of his brush flash through the spinney,
and then he was gone. Far distant still, the first murmur
of thunder reached her ear, and she saw, amid the weeds,
that the yellow goat's-beard had already shut its golden eye
for the day.

Here was truth, and despite the loneliness and the melancholy of all human ruins, this seemed a better and purer
scene than that her vision had wakened from the past. She
feared no longer, but rebuilt the old house, imagined the
green lawn, the fountain with its little boy holding a big fish,
the magnolia lifting great chalices, that brimmed with scent
and sunshine, against the fabric behind it. Only for a few

moments she remained ; then followed the way of the fox, climbed the woods and so returned upwards, until once more she reached the hayfield and the summit of the knoll above it.

And there she made no stay, for the thunderstorm was lumbering up with wisps and snakes of fulvous cloud round its head, and diamonds of lightning intermittently flickering in its heart. Her way took her directly from the bad weather, and Jane set off to race this threat of the sky and reach home if possible before it overtook her.

But the thunder was rattling overhead and great splashes of rain spattered the dust before she had ridden half an hour, though she minded little, for she did not dread lightning, nor wince even when it seemed to drop a dazzling ribbon of blue flame a hundred yards ahead of her. Indeed, she rather enjoyed the storm and laughed at General Goodenough, who stood under his porch in anxiety, when she rode up the avenue very bedraggled and wet to the skin.

And while she changed her clothes, Jane considered the significance of all that she had experienced. Her father's reputed gift was hers without a doubt. To him also it had been given, once or twice, to peer through the curtain and survey the past, or future. And yet it was no gift, but rather a peculiarity—part of a psychical diathesis which gave this possessor little pride. She could not control it ; she had never before in her life been subjected to it ; she heartily disliked it. Nothing but a disagreeable impression was left, and Jane perceived no reason in the nature of things why this peculiar and terrible vision had been re-created and re-enacted for her eye and brain alone—why a palingenesis from this decay and ruin had flung off the mantle of years and restored it at the most terrific moment of its past. Presently, indeed, she began to doubt whether any significance whatever attached to the apparition—whether it was, indeed, an echo of things that had really happened, or more probably an hallucination of her own mind, built out of sleeping brain cells, charged, perhaps, with pages from forgotten novels. She even doubted if all were not a dream flashed through her thoughts at some drowsy moment.

Upon this point it was possible to satisfy herself, and after usual cautious deliberation, Jane determined to mention her adventure of that day, while still keeping silence concerning the earlier experience.

She told the General of the incident, and how she had left her bicycle on a little hilltop and then descended into the glen beneath, to find a ruin and frighten a fox. He was interested and able not only to tell her much that belonged to the scene, but narrated more than she knew ; and also less. There was a trace of cynicism in his way of telling the story, which Jane explained to herself as lying in her ears rather than in the tongue of the narrator. For she was so much nearer to these events than he. To him, the musty record meant nothing but an old-time tale ; to her it was a living mystery of yesterday. She had seen what he had only heard from ancient intelligencers ; and she had seen a great deal more than he had heard.

" Why, Jane, you've found the ruin of Peacock House ! " said General Goodenough. " What an explorer you are ! There's a story about the ruin, rather famous in these parts, and possibly truer than some stories."

The General thus played most amiably into her hands.

" It looked as though there ought to be a story," said Jane.

" Yes—I learned it from a farmer, nearly as old as myself, who had actually known the puppets, or vowed he had. It's not a particularly novel narrative and the agonists belonged to another age than this. One victim, however, by all accounts, was never content to stop in her grave, but visited the scene of her taking off so frequently that it became uninhabitable for the living, and was finally pulled down.

" A girl and her elderly spouse dwelt there. But I'll begin at the beginning. In those days, nearer a hundred than fifty years ago now, the Poles still reigned here at Pole Manor, though their stock was already near run out. Sir Walter Pole, the seventh baronet, his wife and their only child, a son, lived at Pole Manor, and upon the youth the parents' hopes were set ; for he was the last of his line. Eustace Pole was a name often mentioned at that time apparently, but never for any good. A spoiled boy, hard-hearted, selfish and vicious he appears to have been ; and while his father and mother made the best of him and condoned his adventures, yet, when there came a gleam and possibility of salvation for him, parent-like they failed to perceive its significance and withstood him at the turning-point of his career. Not that we can blame them over-much. Times were different then, and a misalliance—an event within the experience of most noble families nowadays—was then held somewhat more appalling. Apparently the only decent thing Eustace Pole ever did was to fall in love with the daughter of a small tradesman ; and since she appears to have been a girl of good education and refinement, had he married her the story of Peacock House had never been told. Perhaps tragedy was born with him and must in some shape have crowned his career. But what happened was this. His parents intrigued against him, after refusing definitely to sanction the engagement. They found a pretext for sending him to London on his father's affairs, which appear to have been very involved, and, while he was away, Sir Walter lied to the girl's father and explained that Eustace was disillusioned, much to that worthy man's satisfaction. There were no railroads in those days that embraced these regions, and the girl certainly heard nothing to contradict her father's information. Or his letters, if he wrote any, may have been intercepted. Who can say ? Probably young Pole, busy about saving what he might from his father's dwindling fortunes, proceeded with his affairs and felt no suspicion of the things being done behind his back.

" It happened May Ellis—that was her name—had an eligible but elderly suitor—a hotel-keeper. He, too, was superior to her in station, but desired her above all things ; and to this widower, being convinced that Eustace Pole was, indeed, a dream of the past, the girl at her father's entreaty affianced herself. Doubtless she was driven into it after the fashion of the times ; but she wedded him on the day that young Pole returned home ; and about the first thing he heard was that she had done so. Mr. Jonathan Foster had traded at Plymouth ; but now he was retired, and ignorant of, or indifferent to, the romance he had shattered, took his treasure to dwell at his Elizabethan dwelling of Peacock House—a case he held worthy of such a jewel. Here and there a very old body can yet remember it, with its fountains and lawns and fantastic, clipped trees, its little park and the fallow deer that roamed there.

" Jonathan Foster—a man of fifty, I imagine—had his

own circle of friends and, of course, did not exist for the
county. He was very well content apparently, and quite
ignorant of the hungry, young, robbed tiger who lived not
twenty miles away.

" History is silent as to what happened then ; but experience of life can fill the gap. Young Pole took his defeat ill,
no doubt, and a disposition such as his was certainly concerned to be level, not only with his supplanter, but the
woman also. He must, however, have hidden his heart for
many days, and what followed can only have resulted, it is
supposed, from one cause. I hesitate to go on with the story
in your ears, Jane ; but no doubt you are a student of human
nature and read the newspapers and modern novels. The
probability is that Pole must have met May Foster and
learned from her the particulars of the trick put upon them
both. She would tell him that her father had learned from
Sir Walter he was gone, and that believing it, broken-hearted
and indifferent, she had obeyed her parent. That much is
almost certain to have happened ; but beyond there lies a
measure of guesswork, the truth or falsehood of which can
never be certainly known. The sequel, however, upon which
this theory was founded, seems to substantiate it solidly
enough.

" We are to suppose that for his own reasons Eustace Pole
scraped acquaintance with the husband—in the hunting field
possibly, for both Foster and his wife rode to hounds. It is
then assumed that Pole either attempted to run away with
the young wife and failed, or endeavoured to seduce her and
was repulsed. Be that as it may, before the end it appears
that he hated the woman as much as the man. Clearly they
were not aware of it, for Pole came and went from Peacock
House and obviously had no recorded quarrel with Jonathan
Foster. He was actually lunching there, in a day in June,
when he committed his famous crime.

" The meal was over and the servants had withdrawn,
when they were suddenly alarmed by two reports of a pistol
following each other from the dining-room. They had
retired to their own quarters and a full minute probably
elapsed when they returned to find their master and mistress
murdered and the assassin disappeared. The unhappy girl
had been shot through the head ; the man was stabbed in
the heart with a heavy silver knife from the table. A double-

barrelled pistol was found with both barrels discharged ; but the murderer had missed with his second shot and the bullet was ultimately discovered in the panelling of the chamber.

" Mounted men rode to this house ; but none at Pole Manor knew anything, save that the last hope of his race had ridden from home early that morning and not returned. Nor did he ever return. The countryside was scoured, and Eustace Pole's horse was discovered the day afterwards, dead lame, in a meadow near Exeter. But the villain vanished off the face of the earth from that hour. It is supposed that he committed suicide, and that may well have happened.

" The hiatus in the story is, you see, fairly filled by the theory. If May Foster would neither desert her husband, nor become his mistress in secret, to this lawless young dog might well have come the temptation for such a revenge as he planned ; and as he had never fought temptation in his life, it conquered him.

" A grim tale for your young ears, yet that is how it runs. The house was taken again, but May Foster's unhappy spirit was seen so often in the dining-room at the precise hour when her life must have left her, that the tenants could not enjoy their mid-day meal, or find domestics to stay there. A time therefore came when it was dismantled, and all the material of value removed—some fifty years ago, I believe. Now let us talk of things more cheerful."

" And the Poles vanished, too ? " asked his listener. Already inherent caution was fighting with desire ; and though it had seemed the most natural thing in the world, for anybody but Jane Campbell, to confess to her vision, now lifted into a matter of intense interest by its variance from the accepted truth ; none the less she put off her story until she had thought about it, in her canny way, and decided whether to speak or be silent.

" Yes," answered the old man. " The Poles vanished, too. Sir Walter died ten years later and Lady Pole went to live at Torquay, a sanatorium the doctors had just discovered. There are plenty of stories about them, also. The Poles were always rather fond of the knife, apparently— a weakness won, perhaps, from Latin blood, that entered the family with Sir Walter's grandmother. When I came here, a cousin of these dead people was selling the Manor, and I

spent a few days with him before deciding whether the place
would suit me. I remember a family picture and a story
concerning Sir Walter and his wife. I remarked on the
beauty of a woman's portrait, and he told me that she was
the mother of the murderer. He showed me how the white
throat of the woman had been gashed open in the portrait
and afterwards restored. He recollected the story, too.
At dinner on one occasion—possibly Eustace Pole was
of the party—his parents fell out and his mother's tongue
loosed his father's temper. He leapt up, doubtless glared
at his wife, like the demon he was, and then, taking a knife,
turned upon Lady Pole's portrait, hanging behind him, and
cut its throat. A new way of committing murder without
disturbance to the victim, or danger to the assassin. But
consider the woman's emotions ! Surely he murdered her
soul when he struck, together with such love as she may still
have preserved for him. Let us hope the servants were not
in the room. Perhaps the bad-tempered ruffian had a
brighter side, made piacular overtures, and was forgiven
afterwards. Who can say ? "

But Jane had supped her fill of horrors, and felt not sorry
to bid her godfather " good night " and leave him. Her
first impulse was obvious ; yet the cautious lady seldom
gratified first impulses. She had thought to tell him her
story on the completion of his ; but she changed her mind
and went to bed with the two stories—his and her own.
She could not dismiss her vision as inferior in probability to
the regulation tale. She recognised that the legend made
Eustace Pole a fiend ; but in her version it seemed that he
was human enough and that, whatever his errors, he had,
at least while she watched him, done little more than became a man. She accepted the shadow play and the frenzy
of the scene returned to her for a while. Yet, what did it
matter, now ? she asked herself, impatiently ; and why
should she, on the strength of a fantastic and futile psychical experience, think twice about the incident ? But
she could not thus dismiss the matter. General Goodenough's narrative effectually destroyed her first suspicion,
that she had endured a purely subjective and personal
illusion ; for her vision, objectively real in every particular, actually served to correct the received opinion of
living people. Yet again, what did it matter, since no jus-

tice could be served, no name restored to reverence, no wrong righted ? The grave had long since swallowed these figures, and there was none to breathe easier for her story ; while she would certainly breathe less easily if she told her godfather of her experience and he laughed at her. She reduced the situation to one of mild psychologic interest, and no more. General Goodenough had mentioned how her father possessed the gift of second sight, and it was possible that he would be attracted to learn the endowment had been handed down. On second thoughts she felt sure that he would not laugh at her. For herself she took no pleasure in the incident, but rather felt pain, and she trusted that no such adventures would ever again befall her.

She told the General her story on the following evening.

"I don't think you've got the tragedy of Peacock House quite right, Godfather," she said after dinner, when she spent an hour with him and he smoked his trichinopoly.

"Don't you, Jane ? That's interesting. Perhaps I have not ; but I'm afraid the facts, if they differ from the chronicle, will be hidden until all things are revealed."

"I saw Peacock House before it was pulled down. I saw it on the very day those poor people died," she said simply, and he stared at her.

"My dear child, what on earth are you talking about ? "

"I have been there twice, and never mentioned the first visit to you. It seemed so mad, because nothing happened afterwards. And yet it was really like this—unless I dreamed it."

She told him everything, and his cigar went out as he listened with closest attention. Not once he interrupted her, nor did he speak when she had finished. Indeed, his silence was so lengthy that Jane grew uncomfortable and began to regret her confession.

"I believe you think I've invented this rigmarole to amuse you, Godfather," she said presently.

"No, indeed. A great entertainment—a wonderful entertainment, indeed, but not amusing ; much more than that. There's much to consider here, Jane. You probe the depths. For what springs from your experience ? A dozen things. It means, first, that the mysterious property of mind which your father possessed has been transmitted. That this can happen is possibly a familiar fact to science, but it is new to me. And secondly, it means, if these things really fell out as you saw them, that the old, accepted legend is false, and you have unearthed a new and very different story from under the dust of more than half a century."

" I suppose I have. And yet I'm rather annoyed with myself, Godfather, for it is annoying to find something hidden inside you that can play such weird tricks. I hope no such phenomena will ever fall to my lot again ; while, at the same time, I almost feel that I should like just one more peep into the past—to round off the adventure. But I know such a last peep would be painful. The end of that unhappy survivor must surely have been tragic."

" Only too probable, Jane."

" I've been trying to reconstruct the real truth ever since I heard your version. Perhaps it lies between the two—a third story that would more or less reconcile the others."

" No, that could not be," he said. " What you witnessed is the only basis to argue upon. You must build upon that ; but do you know enough about human nature to see a plausible prelude to your vision ? "

" I've tried, only there are difficulties I can't clear up. If my ears had heard while my eyes were seeing—then perhaps I should know. The old story comes in my way, I think. Your tale seems to argue people with rather different characters from those that I saw."

He nodded.

" Good. The accepted theory probably gave rise to the assumed qualities of the three actors in the scene. That's where history so often goes wrong. We have only actions to guide us ; and we assume that the actions arose from certain mental properties in those who did, or suffered. The result of action decides us as to character, rather than the motives for action, wherein character really resides. Achievement does not hang on motive. A thousand accidents may determine it. Perhaps these three people were radically different from the old interpretation of them—indeed, they must have been vastly different, and all their values for us are altered now."

" Except the woman's. She was surely deserving of death. And Eustace Pole may, after all, have been as much her murderer as if he had shot her himself. That leaves him a villain still. Everything seems to turn on Jonathan Fos-

ter. If he, indeed, destroyed his wife, and meant to destroy
her lover too——"

" Wait—wait ! You go too fast, Jane. You have opened
the door—not to an alternative, but to a dozen possible
variations. We may be as far from the truth as ever, and
can only reconstruct on human experience. We lack the
touch of poetic vision and inspiration needful to find the
truth, I fear. You, for example, are already weaving parts
of the apocryphal story into your own. You use the word
' lover ' as a matter of course. But why ? Why should
that be taken for granted ? "

" Because it was clearly the opinion of Jonathan Foster.
Surely nothing less than that would have made him try to
kill them both," argued Jane.

" Is it beyond peradventure that even Jonathan was mistaken ? "

" He is more likely to have been right than wrong, I'm
afraid. We have got to argue back from effect to cause,
Godfather. We see an elderly man attempt to kill his wife
and a young man—her former betrothed. Nothing but
jealousy explains that ; and he is a sane, successful business
man, who would hardly be led away by a delusion on the
subject. After all, he only did what plenty of other jealous
men have done."

" True," admitted the General. " But other jealous men
have been mistaken, and why not he ? He may have had
less ground for his jealousy than we suppose."

" There is Eustace Pole's notorious character."

" Of which, again, we only have oral traditions—largely
built on the assumption of a crime that we now know,
through your second-sight, he never committed. Perhaps
he was not as evil as we imagine. Then, again, another
possibility—Foster may have been deluded as Othello was.
Perhaps there existed an Iago, who does not come into our
story. Suppose, for the sake of argument, that Pole,
worthless and probably wicked as he appears to have been,
yet entertained respect for that particular woman, knew that
she had been taken from him through no fault of her own,
and still loved her too well to dishonour her."

But Jane shook her head.

" That is the least likely variation, not the most likely,
Godfather. It's very charitable of you, but I'm afraid too

much like a Sunday School story. At any rate, very improbable. No, be sure Eustace Pole wasn't that sort of
man ; and as to the woman—possibly she had been found
out and didn't know she had been. That's well inside human
nature, isn't it ? "

" It is, Jane ; but many innocent people have been ' found
out ' and paid the price of the guilty. Desdemona was
' found out.' I don't argue for the man, or the woman.
I'm only trying to show the obvious is not necessarily the
true. Once you dive into problems of character, you drown
in a case like this. Take even the suggested Iago, who
comes to poison the middle-aged husband's ear. Perhaps
he was no enemy—no Iago at all—but a well-meaning
friend, who dropped a word of caution, ignorant that he was
setting a match to a train already laid."

" You want to whitewash them all, I believe ! " said Jane.

" Modern history is largely a matter of whitewashing. We
tend to reconstruct the old giants on the new science
of sociology. We psycho-analyse them. We reduce them
to human dimensions from the fantastic stature of the dead,
and find them neither so black nor white as their contemporaries found them. But we shall never know enough
to reach the truth of this trio. There's nothing good or
evil but thinking makes it so ; and what did they think ?
We can hope for no answer to that. The interesting thing
is how are our own feelings now affected by them ? Do we
find ourselves nearer to forgiving Eustace Pole, or a little
farther from sympathising with Jonathan Foster ? "

" I can't feel they are real people at all, even though I have
seen them," answered Jane. " If you know men and women
have been dead for sixty years, you can't take more interest
in them than you do in characters of fiction—often not so
much. The puppets in a good story are more alive—while
you are reading it."

" I understand that. From your youthful standpoint the
ghosts at Peacock House must be shadows at best, and may
all have been sinners, too ; but I love a forlorn cause ; therefore, this revelation of yours has made me take the weaker
side. Quixote that I am, I cling to the frail possibility that
the young pair were innocent victims. It is rather a quality
of old age to flout reason and experience, Jane. So I bring
to your second-sight my second childhood."

" It's like you to think well of everybody ; but if you imagine the young people were innocent, then you make a demon of the poor, retired hotel-keeper."

" Not if he were *non compos*—driven out of his reason by fancied disasters to his honour. Suppose that Eustace Pole were really too convinced of his own integrity to imagine anybody could doubt it ; while the girl was too innocent to dream that she had wakened the passion of jealousy in the husband's hidden heart ? They were both very young and inexperienced, remember."

" You are on the side of the angels," said Jane, " and I should be a worldly, cynical wretch to take the other side." He smiled at that, and lit his cigar again.

" Yes, indeed. The cases ought to be reversed ; yet I, after eighty-five years in this wicked world, take up the cudgels for these ghosts, and you—out of a girls' school— snub my senile charity. And so we win a laugh. And there remains one certainty—your amazing endowment. Be sure to let me know if any further revelation overtakes you. I should like to conduct you to some other of our celebrated houses over which strange stories brood, and see what happened. Why, you may electrify the world yet, Jane, and re-write many pages of doubtful history."

" What a dreadful picture ! It would make me good for nothing, Godfather, and distrustful of my own shadow, if such a thing happened again," she assured him.

And then Jane went to bed, while the old man declared that he was not done with the problem, but intended to work out new answers, based on a surer interpretation of character and probability.

" We'll allow ourselves no more fairy stories to-morrow," he promised.

But he did not mention the subject on the following day, nor did she. Other interests filled the remaining week of Jane's visit, and in her honour General Goodenough gave a luncheon party. The guests were middle-aged and old. He regretfully confessed that he knew nobody save Jane herself, to be described as still of the rising generation.

Their friendship grew swiftly during the concluding days of her visit ; and yet, though he lived for five years longer, Jane never saw her godfather again after she bade him " good night " on her last evening at Pole Manor. For

strange things fell out in the final hour of their companionship, and, after dinner, a trivial accident created vast mental
changes in their relations from which the veteran found
himself unable to recover.

He had promised to give her mementoes, and ordered to
his study a large tin cabin box of a vanished type, which he
told her was filled with Indian relics.

" I haven't opened it for forty years," he said, " and yours
shall be the hand that does. I flung a thousand things into
it when I was packing to come home—gifts from native
friends, curios, and odds and ends of every description. It
will amuse us, Jane, and if there is anything among these
treasures that you admire, it shall be yours."

The box indeed offered excellent entertainment and
proved to contain trinkets of value among much that was
valueless ; but everything had a history for General Goodenough : everything reminded him of some Eastern incident ;
he blamed himself heartily that he had never been at the
trouble to open the box before, and censured the bygone
native servant who had finished his packing.

" I have wondered about that tiger-skin for a generation
and never dreamed it was here," he said. " But it's not done
for. These metal-boxes are vermin-proof, as Indian boxes
need to be."

They rummaged together, and he presently presented
Jane with a bizarre, but valuable ornament—a golden
Buddha with ruby eyes. Then dipping again, he exclaimed
in triumph and dragged to the light a roll of faded papers.

" Now, with a shadow of good fortune," he said, " I
shall find you something you will value above rubies,
Jane."

The roll contained photographs, and he handed to her old,
wet-plate pictures of scenery—the Taj, Benares, and familiar
wonders. There were groups of natives, too, and elephants
and photographs of the chase ; but he came at last upon
what he sought and, having looked upon it, handed to Jane
a picture of a group of officers in mufti. They wore Early
Victorian peg-top trousers and black coats. They were,
for the most part, hirsute men, with big beards, long whiskers
and moustaches, after the fashion of the time. Some sat,
some stood round their colonel—a handsome, grey-whiskered
soldier in a white sun-helmet.

" The third from the left is your father, Jane," said General Goodenough, and she thanked him very gratefully.

" That, indeed, will be precious above anything in the world, Godfather ! " she cried. Then she took it ; and though hungry to see the vanished face, her eyes never reached it. They were arrested by another—one never to be seen again, yet intensely familiar to her. Jane's wish was gratified ; she had the " one more peep " into the past that she desired.

Fortified by her own character and with a tremendous effort she controlled herself and spoke before her voice had time to waver.

" Who is the second from the left ? " she asked, and the General laughed, as yet not conscious of her profound agitation.

" You mustn't fall in love with him, child ! He doesn't look like that now, though still in the land of the living. That was how your god-parent appeared in his green youth —not a bad-looking——"

He broke off at sight of her face.

" My God ! My God ! I forgot," he whispered, stumbling over the words ; and then he seemed to crumple in his chair and shrink under her stare. He fell back and put his hand over his eyes, as though to hide Jane's face, or his own. She too, was terribly moved ; her countenance grew scarlet, then turned very pale. Her beating heart made her pant.

They were silent for some moments and she breathed hard, grew calmer and wondered what to do or say. She tried to speak and could not ; for it seemed that speech was denied her, or any immediate power of uttering the deep sympathy and compassion that alone filled her mind.

It was her godfather who broke the silence.

" Leave me," he said. " Go to your room now. Retire quickly—quickly, please, Jane."

Something quite unlike her unemotional self hovered over Jane's mind and prompted her to get up and kiss the old man. It seemed that such a caress—a thing she had never offered or imagined until now—might better tell him what was in her heart than words. But her womanly impulse clashed with her inherent quality and character. She felt what any woman might have felt ; but it was something that this woman could not translate into action.

She merely obeyed, went hurriedly, stupidly from the room and, glancing back, saw that his face was still hidden. Her last recollection of him centred about two gout-worn hands and the long, crippled fingers spread over his forehead.

She did not sleep that night, and planned, hour after hour, what she should say next morning ; but when day came and she descended to breakfast, Jane heard that the General was indisposed and much regretted his inability to take a farewell. He would write. And in a week, after she was home again and a new term beginning, Jane Campbell received a parcel containing a letter, the jewelled Buddha and a flat envelope with the group which embraced her father. The owner had left it just as she set it down in his study, without erasure or defacement.

" DEAR GODDAUGHTER," he wrote, " here are your father's picture and your toy. It is no fault of yours that you should have stumbled on agonies that I believed long hidden from any possibility of human knowledge. Even to your father, my best friend on earth, I never imparted the truth. Only an old man's treacherous memory is to be blamed for your shock. But since you know so much, hear all ; and then forget all.

" A sort of men are often purer and nobler at one-and-twenty than twenty years afterward. Into adolescence such men take something sweet from childhood, and some it never leaves ; while for the majority it fades and they forget their earlier ideals.

" For May Ellis I entertained a worship and reverence that would have scorned anything base or evil ; and, while no paragon, the legend that has grown round my youth owes its colour more to the false story of Peacock House than the true story of my life. If you can remember my arguments in our last conversation you may discount the special pleading ; and further, you may for ever believe that the girl was as pure in soul and flesh as any saint of God. We were a pair of fools, but our actions never exceeded folly.

" I knew all manner of people in my harum-scarum country life, and on the hunting field had no difficulty in finding common acquaintance who introduced me to Jonathan Foster. He hoped, through me, to enlarge his own

26

circle, and offered me hospitality, ignorant of the past. He liked me and had no reason not to do so. But he was morbidly jealous of his wife from the first, and when, unknown to her or me, our past relations came to his ears, he allowed himself to read evil into my continued friendship, and quickly created out of a poisoned spirit the conventional disaster for himself. It possessed him, but he concealed it so carefully that his wife did not guess it. She valued him and respected him, for he was a kind and amiable man until the well-springs of his nature were fouled by his imaginary wrongs.

"On the day of his crime and death—all, if expanded, so natural and inevitably springing from our ignorance and his infatuation—I came, at the man's invitation, to dine with him and his wife on a day in June. And I brought news that I had obtained a commission in the Army, and was about to go abroad. We had finished our meal when the storm broke upon us and he denounced us with horrible bitterness, pouring forth a volume of words that led to the final declaration of his purpose. He would not hear me or his wife ; he would not suffer the tissue of imaginary evil he had woven to be broken down. He was a raving maniac for five minutes, and then, drawing a pistol from his breast, he destroyed May.

"And to the Army I went, indeed, enlisting at Exeter, as 'George Goodenough' on the morning after I had seen the girl murdered and slain her assassin.

"Men did not rise from the ranks in those days, but I was favoured and given the choice between the new Victoria Cross, won in the Mutiny, and a commission. I chose the latter, and when I retired, finding it possible to end my days where I began them, for reasons beyond reason, did so, and spent most of my means in the repurchase of Pole Manor.

"We must not meet again, Jane, because neither of us can be asked to endure any such ordeal now ; but I shall think with affection of you, as you will live to know ; and you, of your charity, must hold me in Christian remembrance if you can.

"Your affectionate Godfather,
"GEORGE GOODENOUGH."

Jane pondered long upon this letter and wondered, in her

matter-of-fact way, why he had not even asked her to keep silence. He had taken that for granted, and it pleased her he should do so. Henceforward, once a year, she sent him a Christmas card, and devoted much trouble to appropriate words that should go with the picture. And he always wrote and thanked her—in caligraphy that grew more shaky year by year.

When he died, the little he had to leave came to Jane, and she sold Pole Manor for seven thousand pounds. All her life she wondered why the old man had found himself unable to endure the sight of her, or the sound of her voice. Her imagination extended to no solution. And yet imagination seemed to lift a sort of dim question in her head, or heart, sometimes.

" If I had kissed him on that awful night—I wonder——? " she would muse.

SAPPER

The Green Death
The Haunting of Jack Burnham

¶ Lieutenant-Colonel CYRIL McNEILE, who writes under the pseudonym " Sapper," retired from the Royal Engineers in 1919. He first became famous as the author of the War story *Sergeant Michael Cassidy*, but his greatest success has been achieved with the character of Bulldog Drummond, which has brought him fame in the theatre and the cinema as well as in novel form. His adventure stories are the model of all that adventure stories should be.

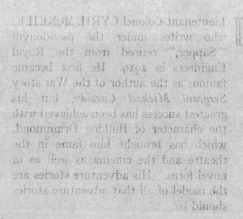

THE GREEN DEATH

PART I

I

" AND why, Major Seymour, do they call you ' Old Point of Detail ' ? "

The tall, spare man, with a face tanned by years in the tropics, turned at the question, and glanced at the girl beside him. At the time when most boys are still at school, force of circumstances had sent him far afield into strange corners of the earth—a wanderer, and picker-up of odd jobs. He had done police work in India—he had been on a rubber plantation in Sumatra. The Amazon knew him and so did the Yukon, while his knowledge of the customs of tribes in Darkest Africa—the very names of which were unknown to most people—was greater than the average Londoner has of his native city. In fact, before the war it would have been difficult to sit for an evening in one of those clubs which spring into being in all corners where Englishmen guard their far-flung inheritance without Bob Seymour's name cropping up.

Then had come the war, and in the van of the great army from the mountains and the swamps which trekked home as the first shot rang out, he came. As his reward he got a D.S.O. and one leg permanently shortened by two inches. He also met a girl—the girl who had just asked him the question.

He'd met her just a year after the Armistice, when he was wondering whether there was any place for a cripple in the lands that he knew. And from that day everything had changed. Even to himself he wouldn't admit it ; the thought of asking such a glorious bit of loveliness to tie herself to a useless has-been like himself was out of the question. But he let the days slip by, content to meet her occasionally at dinner—to see her, in the distance, at a theatre. And now, for the first time, he found himself staying under the same roof. When he'd arrived the preceding day and had seen her in the hall, just for a moment his heart had stopped beating, and then had given a great bound forward. She, of course, knew nothing of his feelings ; of that he felt sure. And she must never know ; of that he was determined. The whole thing was out of the question. Of course—naturally. And the only comment which a mere narrator of facts can offer on the state of affairs is to record the remark made by Ruth Brabazon to a very dear friend of hers after Bob Seymour had limped upstairs to his room.

" That's the man, Delia," she said, with a little smile. " And if he doesn't say something soon, I shall have to."

" He looks a perfect darling," remarked the other.

" He is," sighed Ruth. " But he *won't* give me the chance of telling him so. He thinks he's a cripple."

With which brief insight into things as they really were, we can now return to things as Bob Seymour thought they were. Beside him, on a sofa in the hall, sat the girl who had kept him in England through long months, and she had just asked him a question.

" The Old, I trust, is a term of endearment," he answered, with a smile, " and not a brutal reflection on my tale of years. The Point of Detail refers to a favourite saying of mine with which my reprobate subalterns—of whom your brother was quite the worst—used to mock me."

" Bill is the limit," murmured the girl. " What was the saying ? "

" I used to preach the importance of Points of Detail to 'em," he grinned. " One is nothing ; two are a coincidence ; three are a moral certainty. And they're very easy to see if you have eyes to see them with."

" I suppose they are, Old Point of Detail," she replied softly.

Was it his imagination or did she lay a faint stress on the Old ?

" It was certainly a term of endearment," she continued deliberately, " if what Bill says is to be believed."

" Oh ! Bill's an ass," said Seymour, sheepishly.

" Thank you," she remarked, and he noticed her eyes were twinkling. " I've always been told I'm exactly like

Bill. I know we used always to like the same things when we were children." She rose and crossed the hall. "Time to dress for dinner, I think."

In the dim light he could not see her face clearly ; he only knew his heart was thumping wildly. Did she mean——? And then from half-way up the stairs she spoke again.

"Two are certainly a coincidence," she agreed, thought-fully. "But the third would have to be pretty conclusive before you could take it as a certainty."

II

"Well, Major Seymour, hitting 'em in the beak ? " The Celebrated Actor mixed himself a cocktail with that delicate grace for which he was famed on both sides of the Atlantic.

"So—so, Mr. Trayne," returned the other. "All the easy ones came my way."

The house-party were in the hall waiting for dinner to be announced, but the one member of it who mattered to Bob had not yet appeared.

"Rot, my dear fellow," said his host, who had come up in time to hear his last remark. "Your shooting was magnificent—absolutely magnificent. You had four birds in the air once from your guns."

"Personally," murmured the Celebrated Actor, "it fails to appeal to me. Apart from my intense fright at letting off lethal weapons, I have never yet succeeded in hitting any-thing except a keeper or—more frequently—a guest. I abhor violence—except at rehearsals." He broke off as a heavy, bull-necked man came slowly down the stairs. "And who is the latest addition to our number, Sir Robert?"

"A man who did me a good turn a few weeks ago," said the owner of the house, shortly. "Name of Denton. Arrived only half an hour ago."

He moved away to introduce the newcomer, and the Actor turned to Bob Seymour.

"One wonders," he remarked, "whether it would be indis-creet to offer Mr. Denton a part in my new play. Nothing much to say. He merely drinks and eats. In effect, a publican of unprepossessing aspect. One wonders—so suitable."

26*

He placed his empty glass on the table and drifted charmingly away towards his hostess, leaving Bob Seymour smiling gently. Undoubtedly a most suitable part for Mr. Denton.

And then, quite suddenly, the smile died away. Bill Brabazon, who was standing near the fireplace, had turned round and come face to face with the new-comer. For a moment or two they stared at one another—a deadly loathing on their faces; then with ostentatious rudeness Denton turned his back and walked away.

" My God ! Bob," muttered Bill, coming up to Seymour. " How on earth did that swine-emperor get here ? "

His jaw was grim and set, his eyes gleaming with rage ; and the hand that poured out the cocktail shook a little.

" What's the matter, Bill ? " said Seymour, quietly. " For heaven's sake, don't make a scene, old man ! "

" Matter ! " choked Bill Brabazon. " Matter ! Why——"

But any further revelations were checked by the announcement of dinner, and the party went in informally. To his delight, Bob Seymour found himself next to Ruth, and the little scene he had just witnessed passed from his mind. It was not until they were half-way through the meal that it was recalled to him by Ruth herself.

" Who is that dreadful-looking man talking to Delia Morrison ? " she whispered.

" Denton is his name," replied Seymour, and every vestige of colour left her face.

" Denton," she muttered. " Good Heavens ! it can't be the same." She glanced round the table till she found her brother, who was answering the animated remarks of his partner with morose monosyllables. " Has Bill——"

" Bill has," returned Seymour, grimly. " And he's whispered to me on the subject. What's the trouble ? "

" They had the most fearful row—over a girl," she explained, a little breathlessly. " Two or three months ago. I know they had a fight, and Bill got a black eye. But he broke that other brute's jaw."

" Holy smoke ! " muttered Seymour. " The meeting strikes the casual observer as being, to put it mildly, embarrassing. Do you know how the row started ? "

" Only vaguely," she answered. " That man Denton got some girl into trouble, and then left her in the lurch—refused to help her at all. A poor girl—daughter of someone who had been in Bill's platoon. And he came to Bill."

" I see," said Seymour, grimly. " I see. Bill would."

" Of course he would ! " she cried. " Why, of course. Just the same as you would."

" I suppose that isn't pretty conclusive ? " he said, with a grin. " As a third point, I mean."

But Ruth Brabazon had turned to the Celebrated Actor on her other side. He had already said, " My dear young lady," five times without avail, and he was Very Celebrated.

Neglected for the moment by both his neighbours, Bob proceeded to study the gentleman whose sudden arrival seemed so inopportune. He was a coarse-looking specimen, and already his face was flushed with the amount of wine he had drunk. Every now and then his eyes sought Bill Brabazon vindictively, and Seymour frowned as he saw it. Denton belonged to a type he had met before, and it struck him there was every promise of trouble before the evening was out. When men of Denton's calibre get into the condition of " drink-taken," such trifles as the presence of other guests in the house do not deter them from being offensive. And Bill Brabazon, though far too well-bred to seek a quarrel in such surroundings, was also far too hot-tempered to take any deliberate insult lying down.

Suddenly a coarse, overloud laugh from Denton sounded above the general conversation, and Ruth Brabazon looked round quickly.

" Ugh ! what a horrible man ! " she whispered to Bob. " How I hate him ! "

" I don't believe a word of it," he was saying, harshly. " Fraud by knaves for fools. For those manifestations that have been seen there is some material cause. Generally transparent trickery." He laughed—again, sneeringly.

For a second or two there was an uncomfortable silence. It was not so much what the man had said, as the vulgar, ill-bred manner in which he had said it, and Sir Robert hastily intervened to relieve the tension.

" Ghosts ? " he remarked. " As impossible a subject to argue about as religion or politics. Incidentally, you know," he continued, addressing the table at large, " there's a room in this house round which a novelist might weave quite a good ghost story."

" Tell us, Sir Robert." A general chorus assailed him, and he smiled.

" I'm not a novelist," he said, " though for what it's worth I'll tell you about it. The room is one in the new wing which I used to use as a smoking-room. It was the part built on to the house by my predecessor—a gentleman, from all accounts, of peculiar temperament. He had spent all his life travelling to obscure places of the world ; and I don't know if it was liver or what, but his chief claim to notoriety when he did finally settle down appears to have been an intense hatred of his fellow-men. There are some very strange stories of the things which used to go on in this house, where he lived the life of an absolute recluse, with one old man to look after him. He died about forty years ago."

Sir Robert paused and sipped his champagne.

" However, to continue. In this smoking-room in the new wing, there is an inscription written in the most amazing jumble of letters by the window. It is written on the wall, and every form of hieroglyphic is used. You get a letter in Arabic, then one in Chinese, then an ordinary English one, and perhaps a German. Well, to cut a long story short, I took the trouble one day to copy it out, and replaced the foreign letters—there are one or two Greek letters as well—by their corresponding English ones. I had to get somebody else to help me over the Chinese and Arabic, but the result was, at any rate, sense. It proved to be a little jingling rhyme, and it ran as follows :—

' When 'tis hot, shun this spot.
When 'tis rain, come again.
When 'tis day, all serene.
When 'tis night, death is green.' "

Sir Robert glanced round the table with a smile.

" There was no doubt who had written this bit of doggerel, as the wing was actually built by my predecessor—and I certainly didn't. That's a pretty good foundation to build a ghost story on, isn't it ? "

" But have you ever seen anything ? " inquired one of the guests.

" Not a thing," laughed his host. " But "—he paused

mysteriously—" I've smelt something. And that's the reason why I don't use the room any more.

" It was a very hot night—hotter even than this evening. There was thunder about—incidentally, I shouldn't be surprised if we had a storm before to-morrow—and I was sitting in the room after dinner reading the paper. All of a sudden I became aware of a strange and most unpleasant smell : a sort of fetid, musty, rank smell, like you get sometimes when you open up an old vault. And at the same moment I noticed that the paper I held in my hand had gone a most peculiar green colour and I could no longer see the print clearly. It seemed to have got darker suddenly, and the smell became so bad that it made me feel quite faint.

" I walked over to the door and left the room, meaning to get a lamp. Then something detained me, and I didn't go back for an hour or so. When I did the smell was still there, though so faint that one could hardly notice it. Also the paper was quite white again." He laughed genially. " And that's the family ghost ; a poor thing, but our own. I'll have to get someone to take it in hand and bring it up-to-date."

" But surely you don't think there is any connection between this smell and the inscription ? " cried Denton.

" I advance no theory at all." Sir Robert smiled genially. " All I can tell you is that there is an inscription, and that the colour green is mentioned in it. It seemed to me most certainly that my paper went green, though it is even more certain that I did not die. Also there is at times in this room this rather unpleasant smell. I told you it was a poor thing in the ghost line."

The conversation became general, and Ruth Brabazon turned to Bob, who was thoughtfully staring at his plate.

" Why so pre-occupied, Major Seymour ? "

" A most interesting yarn," he remarked, coming out of his reverie. " Have a salted almond, before I finish the lot."

III

To have two hot-tempered men who loathe one another with a bitter loathing in a house-party is not conducive to its happiness. And when one of them is an outsider of the first water, slightly under the influence of alcohol, the situation becomes even more precarious. For some time after dinner was over Bill Brabazon avoided Denton as unostentatiously as he could, though it was plain to Bob Seymour and Ruth that he was finding it increasingly difficult to control his temper. By ten o'clock it was obvious, even to those guests who knew nothing about the men's previous relations, that there was trouble brewing ; and Sir Robert, who had been told the facts of the case by Bob, was at his wit's end.

"If only I'd known," he said irritably. "If only someone had told me. I know Denton is a sweep, but he did me a very good turn in the City the other day, and, without thinking, I asked him to come and shoot some time. And when he suggested coming now, I couldn't in all decency get out of it. I hope to Heaven there won't be a row."

"If there's going to be, Sir Robert, you can't prevent it," said Seymour. "I'm sure Bill will do all he can to avoid one."

"I know he will," answered his host. "But there are limits, and that man Denton is one of 'em. I wish I'd never met the blighter."

"Come and have a game of billiards, anyway," said the other. "It's no use worrying about it. If it comes, it comes."

When they had been playing about twenty minutes, Ruth Brabazon and Delia Morrison joined them, the billiard-room being, as they affirmed, the coolest room in the house.

"We'll have rain soon," said Sir Robert, bringing off a fine losing hazard off the red. "That'll clear the air."

And shortly afterwards his prophecy proved true. Heavy drops began to patter down on the glass skylight, and the girls heaved a sigh of relief.

"Thank goodness," gasped Ruth. "I couldn't have stood——" She broke off abruptly and stared at the door, which had just opened to admit her brother. "Bill," she cried, "what's the matter ? "

Bob Seymour looked up quickly at her words ; then he rested his cue against the table. Something very obviously was the matter. Bill Brabazon, his tie undone, with a crumpled shirt, and a cut under his eye on the cheek-bone, came into the room and closed the door.

" I must apologise, Sir Robert," he said quietly, " for what has happened. It's a rotten thing to have to admit in another man's house, but the fault was not entirely mine. I've had the most damnable row with that fellow Denton—incidentally he was half-drunk—and I've laid him out. An unpardonable thing to do to one of your guests, but—well—I'm not particularly slow-tempered, and I couldn't help it. He went on and on and on—asking for trouble : and finally he got it."

" Damnation ! " Sir Robert replaced his cue in the rack. " When did it happen, Bill ? "

" About half an hour ago. I've been outside since. Meaning to avoid him, I went to the smoking-room in the new wing, and I found him there examining that inscription by the window. I couldn't get away—without running away. I suppose I ought to have."

An uncomfortable silence settled on the room, which was broken at length by Sir Robert.

" Where is the fellow now, Bill ? "

" I haven't seen him—not since I socked him one on the jaw. I'm deucedly sorry about it," he continued, miserably, " and I feel the most awful sweep, but——"

He stopped suddenly as the door was flung open and the Celebrated Actor rushed in. The magnificent repose which usually stamped his features was gone : it was an agitated and frightened man who stood by the billiard table, pouring out his somewhat incoherent story. And as his meaning became clear Bill Brabazon grew white and leaned against the mantelpiece for support.

Dead—Denton dead ! That was the salient fact that stood out from the Actor's disjointed sentences.

" To examine the inscription," he was saying. " I went in to examine it—and there—by the window . . ."

" He can't be dead," said Bill, harshly. " He's laid out, that's all."

" Quick ! Which is the room ? " Bob Seymour's steady voice served to pull everyone together. " There's no good standing here talking——"

In silence they crossed the hall, and went along the passage to the new wing.

" Here we are," said Sir Robert, nervously. " This is the door."

The room was in darkness and in the air there hung a rank, fetid smell. The window was open, and outside the rain was lashing down with tropical violence. Bob Seymour fumbled in his pocket for a match ; then he turned up the lamp and lit it. Just for a moment he stared at it in surprise, then Ruth, from the doorway, gave a little stifled scream.

" Look," she whispered. " By the window——"

A man was lying across the window-sill, with his legs inside the room and his head and shoulders outside.

" Good Heavens," muttered Sir Robert, touching the body with a shaking hand, " I suppose—I suppose—he *is* dead ? "

But Seymour apparently failed to hear the remark.

" Do you notice this extraordinary smell ? " he said at length.

" Damn the smell," said his host, irritably. " Give me a hand with this poor fellow."

Seymour pulled himself together and stepped forward as the other bent down to take hold of the sagging legs.

" Leave him alone, Sir Robert," he said, quickly. " You must leave the body till the police come. We'll just see that he's dead, and then——"

He picked up an electric torch from the table and leant out of the window. And after a while he straightened up again with a little shudder.

It was not a pretty sight. In the light of the torch the face seemed almost black, and the two arms, limp and twisted, sprawled in the sodden earth of the flower-bed. The man was quite dead, and they both stepped back into the middle of the smoking-room with obvious relief.

" Well," said Brabazon, " is he——? "

" Yes—he's dead," said Seymour, gravely.

" But it's impossible," cried the boy, wildly. " Why, that blow I gave him couldn't have—have killed the man."

" Nevertheless he's dead," said Seymour, staring at the motionless body, thoughtfully. Then his eyes narrowed, and he bent once more over the dead man. Ruth, sobbing hysterically, was trying to comfort her brother, while the rest of the house-party had collected near the door, talking in low, agitated whispers.

" Bob—Bob," cried Bill Brabazon, suddenly, " I've just

remembered. I couldn't have done it when I laid him out. I told you I was walking up and down the lawn. Well, the light from this room was streaming out, and I remember seeing his shadow in the middle of the window. He must have been standing up. The mark of the window-sash was clear on the lawn."

Seymour glanced at him thoughtfully. " But the light was out, Bill. How do you account for that ? "

" It wasn't," said the other, positively. " Not then. It must have gone out later."

" We'll have to send for the police, Sir Robert," said Seymour, laying a reassuring hand on the boy's arm. " Tell them everything when they come."

" I've got nothing to hide," said the youngster, hoarsely. " I swear to Heaven I didn't do that."

" We'd better go," cried Sir Robert. " Leave everything as it is. I'll ring the police up."

With quick, nervous steps he left the room, followed by his guests, until only Seymour was left standing by the window with its dreadful occupant. For a full minute he stood there, while the rain still lashed down outside, sniffing as he had done when he first entered. And, at length, with a slight frown on his face, as if some elusive memory escaped him, he followed the others from the room, first turning out the light and then locking the door.

IV

It was half an hour before the police came, in the shape of Inspector Grayson and a constable. During that time the rain had stopped for a period of about twenty minutes ; only to come on again just before a ring announced their arrival.

The house-party were moving aimlessly about in little scattered groups, obsessed with the dreadful tragedy. In the billiard-room Ruth sat with her brother in a sort of stunned silence ; only Bob Seymour seemed unaffected by the general strain. Perhaps it was because in a life such as his death by violence was no new spectacle ; perhaps it was that there was something he could not understand.

Who had blown the light out ? That was the crux. Blown—not turned. The Celebrated Actor was very positive that the light had not been on when he first entered the room. It might have been the wind, but there was no wind. A point of detail—one. And then the smell—that strange, fetid smell. It touched a chord of memory, but try as he would he could not place it.

His mind started on another line. If the boy, in his rage, had struck the dead man a fatal blow, how had the body got into such a position ? It would have been lying on the floor.

" Weak heart," he argued. " Hot night—gasping for breath—rushed to window—collapsed. That's what they'd say."

He frowned thoughtfully ; on the face of it quite plausible. Not only plausible—quite possible.

" Major Seymour ! " Ruth's voice beside him made him look up. " What can we do ? Poor old Bill's nearly off his head."

" There's nothing to do, Miss Brabazon—but tell the truth," said Seymour, gravely. " What I mean is," he explained, hurriedly, " you've got to impress on Bill the vital necessity of being absolutely frank with the police."

" I know he didn't do it, Bob," she cried, desperately. " I know it."

Bob ! She'd called him Bob. And such is human nature that for a moment the dead man was forgotten.

" So do I, Ruth," he whispered, impulsively. " So do I."

" And you'll prove it ? " she cried.

" I'll prove it," he promised her. Which was no rasher than many promises made under similar conditions.

" Thank goodness you've come, Inspector." Sir Robert had met the police at the door. " A dreadful tragedy."

" So I gather, Sir Robert," answered the other. " One of your guests been murdered ? "

" I didn't say so on the 'phone," said Sir Robert. " I said—killed."

The inspector grunted, " Where's the body ? "

" In the smoking-room." He led the way towards the door.

" I've got the key in my pocket," said Seymour ; and the inspector looked at him quickly.

" May I ask your name, sir ? " he remarked.

" Seymour—Major Seymour," returned the other. " I turned out the light and locked the door while Sir Robert was telephoning for you, to ensure that nothing would be moved."

The inspector grunted again, as Seymour opened the door and struck a light.

" Over in that window, Inspector——" began Sir Robert, only to stop and gape foolishly across the room.

" I don't quite understand, gentlemen," said Inspector Grayson, testily.

" No more do I," muttered Bob Seymour, with a puzzled frown.

" I left him lying, as we found him, half in and half out of the window," said Seymour. " His legs were inside, his head and shoulders from the waist upwards were outside."

It was the constable who interrupted him. While the others were standing by the door he had crossed to the window and leaned out.

" Here's the body, sir," he cried. " Outside in the flower-bed."

PART II

I

The inspector went quickly to the window and peered out ; then he turned and confronted Sir Robert and Seymour.

" He's dead right enough *now*," he said, gravely. " It seems a pity that you gentlemen didn't take a little more trouble to find out if he was in the first place. You might have saved his life."

" Hang it, man ! " exploded Seymour, angrily, " do you suppose I don't know a dead man when I see one ? "

" I don't know whether you do or don't," answered the other, shortly. " But I've never yet heard of a dead man getting up and moving to an adjacent flower-bed. And you say yourself that you left him lying over the window-sill."

For a moment an angry flush mounted on the soldier's face, then with an effort he controlled himself. On the face of it, the inspector was perfectly justified in his remark : dead men do not move. The trouble was that Bob Seymour had felt the dead man's heart and his pulse ; had turned the light of his torch from close range into his eyes. And he *knew* that he had made no mistake ; he *knew* that the man was dead when he turned out the light and left the room. He *knew* it ; but—dead men do not move. What had happened in the room during the time they were waiting for the police ? The key had been in his pocket : who had moved the body ? And why ? Not Bill Brabazon : that he knew. With a puzzled frown he crossed slowly towards the two policemen, who were hauling the limp form through the open window. And once again he paused and sniffed.

" That smell again, Sir Robert," he remarked.

" What smell ? " demanded the inspector, as they laid the dead man on the floor.

" Don't you notice it ? A strange, fetid, rank smell."

The inspector sniffed perfunctorily. " I smell the ordinary smell of rain on dead leaves," he remarked. " What about it ? "

" Nothing, except that there are no dead leaves in June," returned Seymour, shortly.

" Well, sir," snorted the inspector, " whether there are dead leaves or not, we've got a dead man on the floor. And I take it he wasn't killed by a smell, anyway."

In the full light of the room Denton was an even more unpleasant sight than when he had lain sprawling over the window-sill. The water dripped from his sodden clothing, and ran in little pools on the floor ; the dark, puffy face was smeared with a layer of wet earth. But it was not at these details that Bob Seymour was staring : it was an angry-looking red weal round the neck just above the collar that riveted his attention. The inspector, taking no further notice of the two spectators, was proceeding methodically with his examination. First he turned out all the pockets, laying the contents neatly on the table ; then, with the help of the constable, he turned the body over on its face. A little fainter, but still perfectly discernible, the red weal could be traced continuously round the neck ; and after a while the inspector straightened up and turned to Sir Robert.

" It looks as if he had been strangled, sir," he remarked, professionally. " I should imagine from the size of the mark that a fairly thin rope was used. Have you any idea whether anyone had a grudge against him ? The motive was obviously not robbery."

" Strangled ! " cried Sir Robert, joining the other three. " But I don't understand." He turned perplexedly to Bob Seymour, who was standing near the window absorbed in thought. Then, a little haltingly, he continued : " Unfortunately there was a very severe row between him and another of my guests earlier in the evening."

" Where did the row take place ? "

" Er—in this room."

" Was anyone else present ? "

" No. No one heard them quarrelling. But Mr. Brabazon, the guest in question, made no secret about it—afterwards. He told us in the billiard-room that—that they had come to blows in here."

" I would like to see Mr. Brabazon, Sir Robert," said the inspector. " Perhaps you would be good enough to send for him."

" I will go and get him myself," returned the other, leaving the room.

" A very remarkable affair," murmured Seymour, as the door closed behind his host. " Don't you agree with me, Inspector ? "

" In what way ? " asked the officer, guardedly.

But the soldier was lighting a cigarette, and made no immediate answer. " May I ask," he remarked at length, " if you've ever tried to strangle a man with a rope ? Because," he continued, when the other merely snorted indignantly, " I have. During the war—in German East Africa. And it took me a long while. You see, if you put a slip-knot round a man's neck and pull, he comes towards you. You've got to get very close to him and kneel on him, or wedge him in some way so that he can't move, before you can do much good in the strangling line."

" Quite an amateur detective, Major Seymour," said the inspector condescendingly. " If you will forgive my saying so, however, it might have been better had you concentrated on seeing whether the poor fellow was dead."

He turned as the door opened, and Bill Brabazon came in, followed by Sir Robert.

" This is Mr. Brabazon, Inspector," said the latter.

The officer eyed the youngster keenly for a moment before

he spoke. Then he pointed to a chair, so placed that the light of the lamp would fall on the face of anyone sitting in it.

" Will you tell me everything you know, Mr. Brabazon ? And I should advise you not to attempt to conceal anything."

" I've got nothing to conceal," answered the boy, doggedly. " I found Denton in here about half-past ten, and we started quarrelling. I'd been trying to avoid him the whole evening, but there was no getting away from him this time. After a while we began to fight, and he hit me in the face. Then I saw red, and really went for him. And I laid him out. That's all I know about it."

" And what did you do after you laid him out ? "

" I went out into the garden to cool down. Then, when the rain came on, I went to the billiard-room and told Sir Robert. And the first thing I knew about this," with a shudder he looked at the dead body, " was when Mr. Trayne came into the billiard-room and told us."

" Mr. Trayne ? Who is he, Sir Robert ? "

" Another guest stopping in the house. Do you wish to see him ? "

" Please." The inspector paced thoughtfully up and down the room.

" The light was on, wasn't it, Bill, when you left the room ? " said Seymour.

" It was. Why, I saw his shadow on the lawn, as I told you."

" Did you ? ", said the inspector, watching him narrowly. " Would you be surprised to hear, Mr. Brabazon, that this unfortunate man was strangled ? "

" Strangled ! " Bill Brabazon started up from his chair. " Strangled ! Good God ! Who by ? "

" That is precisely what we want to find out," said the inspector.

" But, good heavens ! man," cried the boy, excitedly, " don't you see that that exonerates me. I didn't strangle him : I only hit him on the jaw. And that shadow I saw," he swung round on Seymour, " must have been the murderer."

" You wish to see me, Inspector ? " Trayne's voice from the doorway interrupted him, and he sat back in his chair again. And Seymour, watching the joyful look on Bill's face, knew that he spoke the truth. His amazement at hearing the cause of death had been too spontaneous not to be genuine. In his own mind Bill Brabazon regarded himself as cleared : the trouble was that other people might not. The majority of murderers have died, still protesting their innocence.

" I understand that it was you, Mr. Trayne, who first discovered the body," said the inspector.

" It was. I came in and found the room in darkness. I wished to study an inscription by the window to which Sir Robert had alluded at dinner. I struck a match, and then—I saw the body lying half in half out over the sill. It gave me a dreadful shock—quite dreadful. And I at once went to the billiard-room for assistance."

" So whoever did it turned out the light," said the inspector, musingly. " What time was it, Mr. Trayne, when you made the discovery ? "

" About half-past eleven, I should think."

" An hour after the quarrel. And in that hour someone entered this room, either by the window or the door, and committed the deed. He, further, left either by the window or the door. How did you leave, Mr. Brabazon ? "

" By the door," said the youngster. " The flower-bed outside the window is too wide to jump."

" Then if the murderer entered by the window, he will have left footmarks. If he entered by the door and left by it the presumption is that he is a member of the house-party. No one who was not would risk leaving by the door after committing such an act."

" Most ably reasoned," murmured Seymour, mildly.

But the inspector was far too engrossed with his theory to notice the slight sarcasm in the other's tone. With a powerful electric torch he was searching the ground outside the window for any trace of footprints. The mark in the ground where the body had lain was clearly defined ; save for that, however, the flower-bed revealed nothing. It was at least fifteen feet wide ; to cross it, leaving no trace, appeared a physical impossibliity. And after a while the inspector turned back into the room and looked gravely at Sir Robert Deering.

" I should like to have every member of the house-party

and all your servants in here, Sir Robert, one by one," he
remarked.

" Then you think it was done by someone in the house,
Inspector ? " Sir Robert was looking worried.

" I prefer not to say anything definite at present,"
answered the official, guardedly. " Perhaps we can start
with the house-party."

With a shrug of his shoulder, Sir Robert left the room,
and the inspector turned to the constable.

" Lend a hand here, Murphy ; we'll put the body behind
the screen before any of the ladies come in."

" Great Scott ! man," cried Seymour. " What do you
want the ladies for ? You don't suggest that a woman could
have strangled him ? "

" You will please allow me to know my own business
best," said the other, coldly. " Shut and bolt the windows,
Murphy."

The rain had stopped as the policeman crossed the room
to carry out his orders. And it was as he stood by the open
window, with his hands upraised to the sash, that he suddenly stepped back with a startled exclamation.

" Something 'it me in the face, sir," he muttered. Then
he spat disgustedly. " Gaw ! What a filthy taste ! "

But the inspector was not interested—he was covering
the dead man's face with a pocket handkerchief, and after
a moment's hesitation, the constable again reached up for
the sash, and pulled it down. Only the soldier had noticed
the little incident, and he was staring like a man bereft of
his senses at a point just above the policeman's head.

" Don't move," he ordered, harshly. " Stand still,
constable."

With a startled look the policeman obeyed, and Seymour
stepped over to him. And then he did a peculiar thing.
He lit a match and turned to the inspector.

" Just look at this match, Inspector," he murmured.
" Burning brightly, isn't it ? " He moved it a little, and
suddenly the flame turned to a smoky orange colour. For a
moment or two it spluttered ; then it went out altogether.

" You can move now, constable," he said. " I didn't
want any draught for a moment." He looked at Inspector
Grayson with a smile. " Interesting little experiment that
—wasn't it ? "

Grayson snorted. " If you've quite finished your conjuring tricks, I'll get on with the business," he remarked.
" Come along over here, Murphy."

" What is it, Bob ? " Bill Brabazon cried, excitedly.

" The third point, Bill," answered the other. " Great
Scott ! what a fool I've been. Though it's the most
extraordinary case I've ever come across."

" Think you can reconstruct the crime ? " sneered the
inspector.

" I don't think—I know," returned the other quietly.
" But not to-night. There's the rain again."

" And might I ask what clues you possess ? "

" Only one more than you, and that you can get from Sir
Robert. I blush to admit it, but until a moment ago I
attached no importance to it. It struck me as being merely
the foolish jest of a stupid man. Now it does not strike me
quite in that light. Ask him," he continued, and his voice
was grim, " for the translation of that inscription under the
window. And when you've got that, concentrate for a
moment on the other end of the dead man—his trousers just
above the ankles."

" They're covered with dirt," said the inspector, impressed, in spite of himself, by the other's tones.

" Yes—but what sort of dirt ? Dry, dusty, cob-webbed
dirt—not caked mud on his knees. Immense amount of
importance in dirt, Inspector."

But Mr. Grayson was recovering his dignity. " Any other
advice ? " he sneered.

" Yes. Hire a man and practise strangling him. Then
buy a really good encyclopædia and study it. You'll find
a wealth of interesting information in it." He strolled
towards the door. " If you want me I shall be in the billiard-
room. And, by the way, with regard to what I say about
strangling, don't forget that the victim cannot come
towards you if his feet are off the ground."

" Perhaps you'll have the murderer for me in the billiard-
room," remarked the inspector, sarcastically.

" I'm afraid not," answered the other. " The real
murderer, unfortunately, is already dead. I'll look for his
accomplice in the morning."

With a slight smile he closed the door and strolled into
the hall. The house-party were being marshalled by Sir

Robert preparatory to their inquisition ; the servants stood huddled together in sheepish groups under the stern eye of the butler.

"Have you found out anything, Major Seymour ? " With entreaty in her eyes, Ruth Brabazon came up to him. "Yes, Miss Brabazon, I have," answered the man, reassuringly. "You can set your mind absolutely at rest." "You know who did it ? " she cried, breathlessly.

"I do," he answered. "But unfortunately I can't prove it to-night. And you mustn't be alarmed at the attitude taken up by the inspector. He's not in a very good temper, and I'm afraid I'm the cause."

"But does he think——"

"I should hesitate to say what great thoughts were passing through his brain," said Seymour. "But I have a shrewd suspicion that he has already made up his mind that Bill did it."

"And who did do it, Bob ? " She laid her hand beseechingly on his arm as she spoke.

"I think it's better to say nothing at the moment," he answered, gently. "There are one or two points I've got to make absolutely certain of first. Until then—won't you trust me, Ruth ? "

"Trust you ! Why, my dear——" She turned away as she spoke, and Bob Seymour barely heard the last two words. But he did *just* hear them. And once again the dead man was forgotten.

II

"May I borrow your car, Sir Robert ? I want to go to London and bring back a friend of mine—Sir Gilbert Strangways." Bob Seymour approached his host after breakfast, the following morning. "I'll have to be back by three, in time for the inquest, and it's very important."

"Strangways—the explorer ! Certainly, Seymour ; though I'm not keen on adding to the house-party at present."

"It's essential, I'm afraid. They can only bring in one verdict this afternoon—Murder. That ass Grayson was nosing round this morning, and he, at any rate, is convinced of it."

" What—that Bill did it ? " muttered the other.

" He's outside there now, making notes."

" You don't think the boy did it, do you, Seymour ? "

" I *know* he didn't, Sir Robert. But to prove it is a different matter. May I order the car ? "

" Yes, yes, of course. Anything you like. Why on earth did I ever ask the poor fellow down here ? " Sir Robert walked agitatedly up and down the hall. " And anyway, who did do it ? " He threw out his hands in despair. " He can't have done it himself."

" All in good time, Sir Robert," said the other gravely. " The lucky thing for you is that you have practically never used that room."

" What do you mean ? " muttered his host, going a little white.

" If you had, the chances are that this house-party would never have taken place," answered Seymour. " At least, not with you as the host."

" My God ! " cried the other. " You don't mean to say that there's anything in that inscription ! "

" It's the key to everything," returned the other, shortly. " To put it mildly, your predecessor had a peculiar sense of humour."

Ten minutes later he was getting into the car, when Inspector Grayson appeared round the corner.

" You won't forget the inquest is at three, Major Seymour ? " he said, a trifle sharply.

" I shan't miss it," answered the soldier.

" Found the murderer yet ? " asked the detective.

" Yes—this morning," returned the other. " Haven't you ? "

And the officer was still staring thoughtfully down the drive long after the car had disappeared round a bend. This confounded soldier seemed so very positive, and Grayson, who was no fool, had been compelled to admit to himself that there were several strange features about the case. The inscription on the wall he had dismissed as childish ; from inquiries made in the neighbourhood, Sir Robert Deering's predecessor had obviously been a most peculiar specimen. Not quite all there, if reports were to be believed. To return to the case, however, a complete *alibi* had been proved by every single member of the household,

save one kitchen-maid, Mr. Trayne, and—Bill Brabazon.
The kitchen-maid and Mr. Trayne could be dismissed—the
former for obvious reasons, the latter owing to the impossi-
bility of having done the deed in the time between leaving
the drawing-room and arriving in the billiard-room with the
news. And that left—Bill Brabazon. Every single line of
thought led ultimately to—Bill Brabazon. Motive, opportunity, capability from a physical point of view—all pointed
to him. A further exhaustive search that morning of the
flower-bed outside the window had revealed no trace of any
footprint ; it was impossible that the murderer should have
entered by the window. Therefore—he shrugged his
shoulders. The house-party again—and Bill Brabazon.
Blind with fury, as he admitted himself, he had first knocked
the dead man down and then strangled him, turning out the
light lest anyone should see. Then, taking off the rope, he
had left him, almost, but not quite, dead on the floor. In
a last despairing gasp for air, Denton had staggered to the
window and collapsed—still not quite dead. Finally, he
had made one more convulsive effort, floundered on the
flower-bed, and had there died.

Such was the scene as Inspector Grayson reconstructed
it, and yet he was far from satisfied. Why strangle ? An
un-English method of killing a man. Still—facts were facts
—the man *had* been strangled. Un-English or not, that was
the manner in which he had met his death ; and since suicide
could be ruled out, only murder remained. If the soldier
could prove it was not young Brabazon—well and good.
Until he did, Mr. Grayson preferred to bank on facts which
were capable of proof.

The result of the coroner's inquest was a foregone conclusion. Death after strangulation, with a rider to the
effect that, had prompt assistance been given on the first
discovery of the body, life might have been saved.

Bob Seymour, seated beside another lean, sun-tanned
man, heard the verdict with an impassive face. He had
given his evidence, confining it to the barest statement of
fact ; he had advanced no theory ; he had not attempted
to dispute Inspector Grayson's deductions. Once he had
caught Ruth's eyes fixed on him beseechingly, and he had
given her a reassuring smile. And she—because she
trusted him—knew that all was well ; knew that the net

which seemed to be closing so grimly round her brother would not be fastened. But why—why didn't he tell them now how it was done ? That's what she couldn't understand.

And then, when it was all over, Bob and his friend disappeared in the car again.

" There's no doubt about it, Bob," said Strangways. " What a diabolical old blackguard the man must have been."

" I agree," answered Seymour, grimly. " One wishes one could get at him now. As it is, the most we can do is to convince our mutton-headed friend Grayson. I owe the gentleman one for that rider to the verdict."

The car stopped first at a chemist's, and the two men entered the shop. It was an unusual request they made—cylinders of oxygen are generally required only for sick rooms. But after a certain amount of argument the chemist produced one, and they placed it in the back of the car. Their next errand was even stranger, and consisted of the purchase of a rabbit. Finally, a visit to an iron-monger produced a rose such as is used on the end of a hose-pipe for watering.

Then, their purchases complete, they returned to the house, stopping at the police-station on the way. Grayson came out to see them, a tolerant smile on his face. Yes, he would be pleased to come up that evening after dinner.

" Do you want to introduce me to the murderer, Major ? " he asked, maliciously.

" Something of the sort, Inspector," said Seymour. " Studied that encyclopædia yet ? "

" I've been too busy on other matters—a little more important," answered the other, shortly.

" Good," cried Seymour, genially. " By the way, when you want to blow out a lamp what is the first thing you do ? "

" Turn down the wick," said Grayson.

" Wise man. I wonder why the murderer didn't."

And for the second time that day, Inspector Grayson was left staring thoughtfully at a retreating motor-car.

It was not till after dinner that Bob Seymour reverted to the matter which was obsessing everyone's mind. Most of the house-party had left ; only Mr. Trayne and Ruth and her brother remained. And even the Celebrated Actor had been comparatively silent throughout the meal, while Bill had remained sunk in profound gloom. Everything at the inquest had pointed to him as the culprit ; every ring at the bell and he had imagined someone arriving with a warrant for his arrest. And Bob had said nothing to clear him—not a word, in spite of his apparent confidence last night. Only Ruth still seemed certain that he would do something ; but what *could* he do, exploded the boy miserably, when she tried to cheer him up. The evidence on the face of it was damning.

" About time our friend arrived, Gilbert." Bob Seymour glanced at his watch, and at that moment there came a ring at the bell.

" Who's that ? " said Bill, nervously.

" The egregious Grayson, old boy," said Bob. " The experiment is about to begin."

" You mean——" cried Ruth, breathlessly.

" I mean that Sir Gilbert has kindly consented to take the place of Denton last night," said Bob, cheerfully. " He'll have one or two little props to help him, and I shall be stage-manager."

" But why have you put it off so long ? " cried Bill, as the inspector came into the room.

" ' When 'tis day, all serene,' " quoted Bob. " Good evening, Mr. Grayson. Now that we are all here, we might as well begin."

" Just as well," agreed the inspector, shortly. " What do we begin with ? "

" First of all a visit to the smoking-room," answered Seymour. " Then, except for Sir Gilbert Strangways, we shall all go outside into the garden."

In silence they followed him to the scene of the tragedy.

" I trust you will exonerate me from any charge of being theatrical," he began, closing the door. " But in this particular case the cause of Mr. Denton's death is so extraordinary that only an actual reconstruction of what happened would convince such a pronounced sceptic as the inspector. Facts are facts, aren't they, Mr. Grayson ? "

The inspector grunted non-committally. " What's that on the floor ? " he demanded.

" A cylinder of oxygen, and a rabbit in a cage," explained

Seymour, pleasantly. " Now first to re-arrange the room.
The lamp was on this table—very possibly placed there by
the dead man to get a better view of the inscription under
the window ; so that we may proceed to what happened.

" First, Inspector, Mr. Brabazon entered the room, and,
as he has already described, he and Mr. Denton came to
blows, with the result that he laid Denton out. Then Mr.
Brabazon left the room, as I propose we shall do shortly.
And, after a while, Mr. Denton came to his senses again,
and went to the window for air, just as Sir Gilbert has done
at the present moment."

" You can't prove it," snapped Grayson.

" True," murmured Seymour. " Just logical surmise—
so far ; from now onwards—irrefutable proof. The murderer is admirably trained, I assure you. Are you ready,
Gilbert ? "

" Quite," said Strangways, bending down and picking
up the rabbit-cage, which he placed on the table by the lamp.

" Perhaps, Inspector, you would like to examine the
rabbit ? " remarked Seymour. " No ! Well, if not, I
would just ask you to notice Sir Gilbert's other preparations.
A clip on his nose ; the tube from the oxygen cylinder in his
mouth."

" I don't understand all this, Major Seymour," cried
Grayson, testily. " What's the rabbit for, and all this other
tommy-rot ? "

" I thought I'd explained to you that Sir Gilbert is taking
the place of the murdered man last night. The tommy-rot
is to prevent him sharing the same fate."

" Good God ! " The inspector turned a little pale.

" Shall we adjourn to the garden ? " continued Seymour,
imperturbably. He led the way from the room. " I
think we'll stand facing the window, so that we can see
everything. Of course, I can't guarantee that the performance will be *exactly* the same ; but it will be near
enough, I think. Nor can I guarantee exactly when it will
start." As he spoke they reached a point facing the window.
The lamp was burning brightly in the room, outlining Sir
Gilbert's figure as he stood facing them, and with a little
shudder Ruth clutched her brother's arm.

" Even so did Denton stand last night." Seymour's even
voice came out of the darkness. " You see his shadow on

the grass, and the shadow of the sash ; just as Mr. Brabazon
saw the shadow last night, Inspector."

Silence settled on the group ; even the phlegmatic inspector seemed impressed. And then suddenly, when the
tension was becoming almost unbearable, Sir Gilbert's voice
came from the window.

"It's coming, Bob."

They saw him adjust his nose-clip and turn on the oxygen ;
then he stood up as before, motionless, in the window.

" Watch carefully, Inspector," said Seymour. " Do you
see those dark, thin, sinuous feelers coming down outside
the window ? Like strands of rope. They're curling
underneath the sash towards Sir Gilbert's head. The lamp
—look at the lamp—watch the colour of the flame. Orange
—where before it was yellow. Look—it's smoking ; thick
black smoke ; and the room is turning green. Do you see ?
Now the lamp again. It's going out—even as it went out
last night. And, by this time last night, Inspector, Denton
I think, was dead ; even as the rabbit on the table is dead
now. Now watch Sir Gilbert's shirt front."

"Great Heavens ! " shouted Sir Robert. " It's going
up."

" Precisely," said Bob. " At the present moment he is
being lifted off his legs—as Denton was last night ; and if
at this period Denton was not already dead, he could not
have lasted long. He would have been hanged."

" Oh, Bill, it's awful ! " cried Ruth, hysterically.

" Then came the rain," continued Seymour. " I have
here the hosepipe fitted with a rose." He dragged it nearer
the window, and let it play on the side of the house as far
up as the water would reach. Almost at once the body
of Sir Gilbert ceased rising ; it paused as if hesitating ; then
with a little thud, fell downwards half in half out of the
window, head and arms sprawling in the flower-bed.

" And thus we found Mr. Denton last night, when it was
still raining," said Seymour. " All right, Gilbert ? "

" All right, old boy ! " came from the other.

" But if he's all right," said the inspector, wonderingly,
" why wasn't the other ? "

" Because Sir Gilbert, being in full possession of his senses
when the hanging process started, used his hands to prevent
strangulation. To continue—the rain ceased. We were out

of the room waiting for your arrival, Mr. Grayson, and while we were out—— Look! Look!"

Before their eyes the top part of Sir Gilbert's body was being raised till once again he stood straight up. Then steadily he was drawn upwards till his knees came about level with the sill, when, with a sudden lurch, the whole body swung out and then back again, while the calves of his legs drummed against the outside of the house. " Do you remember the marks on the trousers, Inspector ? And then the rain came again." Seymour turned on the hose. Once more the body paused, hesitated, and then crashed downwards into the flower-bed.

" All right, Gilbert ? "

" All right," answered the other. " Merely uncomfortably wet." He rose and came towards them.

" And now, Inspector," murmured Seymour, mildly, " you know exactly how Mr. Denton was killed."

" But, good Lord ! gentlemen," said Grayson, feebly, " what was it that killed him ? "

" A species of liana," said Sir Gilbert. " In my experience absolutely unique in strength and size—though I have heard stories from the Upper Amazon of similar cases. It's known amongst the natives as the Green Death."

" But is it an animal ? "

" You've asked me a question, Inspector," said Sir Gilbert, " that I find it very difficult to answer. To look at—it's a plant—a climbing plant, with long, powerful tendrils. But in habits—it's carnivorous, like the insect-eating variety in England. It's found in the tropical undergrowth, and is incidentally worshipped by some of the tribes. They give it human sacrifices, so the story goes. And now I can quite believe it."

" But hang it, sir," exploded the inspector, " we aren't on the Upper Amazon. Do you mean to say that one of these things is here ? "

" Of course. Didn't you see it ? It's spread from the wall to the branches of that old oak."

" If you remember, Inspector, I pointed it out to you this morning," murmured Seymour, mildly. " But you were so engrossed with the flower-bed."

" But why did the lamp go out ? " asked Ruth breathlessly.

27

" For the same reason that the rabbit died," said Bob.
" For the same reason that the match went out last night,
and gave me the third clue. From each of the tendrils a
green cloud is ejected, the principal ingredient of which is
carbon-dioxide—which is the gas that suffocates. The
plant holds the victim, and they suffocate him. Hence the
oxygen and the nose-clip ; otherwise Sir Gilbert would have
been killed to-night. By the way, would you like to see
the rabbit, Inspector ? "

" I'll take your word for it, sir," he grunted, shortly.
" Only, why the devil you didn't tell me this last night I
can't understand."

" I'd have shown you—only the rain had come on again.
And you must admit I advised you to get an encyclopædia."

III

" Bob, I don't understand how you did it," cried Ruth.

It was after breakfast the following morning, and the
sound of axes came through the open window from the men
who were already at work cutting down the old oak tree.

The other laughed. " Points of detail," he said, quietly.
" At first, before the police arrived, I thought it possible
that Bill had been responsible for his death. I thought he'd
hit him so hard that the man's heart had given out, and that
in a final spasm he'd staggered to the window and died.
It struck me as just conceivable that Denton had himself
blown out the lamp, thinking it made it hotter. But why
not turn it out ? And would he have had time if he was at
his last gasp ? Then the police came, and the body had
moved. I *knew* the man was dead when he was lying over
the sill, though I hadn't seen the mark round his neck. I
therefore knew that some agency had moved the body.
That agency must have been the murderer—anyone else
would have mentioned the fact. Therefore it couldn't have
been Bill, because he was in the billiard-room the whole
time, and I'd locked the door of the smoking-room. Then
I saw the mark round his neck—strangled. But you can't
strangle a powerful man without a desperate struggle.
And why should the strangler return after the deed was
committed ? Also there were no footmarks on the flower-
bed. Then I noticed the grey dust on his trousers just

below the knee, and underneath the window outside, kept
dry by the sill, which stuck out, was ivy—dusty and cob-
webby as ivy always is. How had his legs touched it ? If
they had—and there was nowhere else the dirt could have
come from—he must have been lifted off the ground.
Strangulation, certainly, of a type—hung. The dirt had
not been there when we first found the body lying over the
sill. And if he'd been hung—who did it ? And why hang
a dead man ? What had happened between the time Bill
left the room and the police found the body ? A heavy
shower of rain, during which we found the body ; then clear
again, while we were out of the room ; then another shower,
when the police found the body. And then I thought of
the rhyme :—

> ' When 'tis hot, shun this spot ;
> When 'tis rain, come again.'

" Could it be possible that there was some diabolical agent
at work, who stopped, or was frustrated, by rain ? It was
then I saw the green cloud itself over the constable's head—
the cloud which extinguished my match.

" Incredible as it seemed, I saw at once that it was the
only solution which fitted everything—the marks on the back
of his trousers below the knee—everything. He'd been hung,
and the thing that had hanged him had blown out the lamp
—or extinguished it is a more accurate way of expressing
it—even as it extinguished my match. The smell—I'd
been searching my memory for that smell the whole evening,
and it came to me when I saw that green gas—it's some rank
discharge from the plant, mixed with the carbon-dioxide.
And I last saw it, and smelt it, on the Upper Amazon ten
years ago. My native bearers dragged me away in their
terror. There was a small animal, I remember, hanging from
a red tendril, quite dead. The tendril was round its neck,
exuding little puffs of green vapour. So I got Gilbert to
make sure. That's all."

" But what a wicked old man he must have been who
planted it ! " cried the girl, indignantly.

" A distorted sense of humour, as I told our host," said
Bob, briefly, starting to fill his pipe.

" Bill and I can never thank you enough, Major Seymour,"

said the girl, slowly, after a long silence. " If it hadn't been for you——" She gave a little shudder, and stared out of the window.

" Some advantages in wandering," he answered lightly. " One does pick up odd facts. Suppose I'll have to push off again soon."

" Why ? " she demanded.

" Oh, I dunno. Can't sit in England doing nothing."

" Going alone ? " she asked, softly.

" Do you think anybody would be mug enough to accompany me ? " he inquired, with an attempt at a grin. Dear Heavens ! If only he wasn't a cripple——"

" I don't know, I'm sure," she murmured. " You'd want your three points of detail to make it a certainty, wouldn't you ? We only reached the coincidence stage two nights ago."

" What do you mean, Ruth ? " he whispered, staring at her.

" That for a clever man—you're an utter fool. With a woman one is a certainty. However, if you'll close your eyes, I'll pander to your feeble intellect. Tight, please."

And it was as the tree fell with a rending crash outside that Ruth Brabazon found that, at any rate as far as his arms were concerned, Bob Seymour was no cripple. And Bob—well, a kiss is pretty conclusive. At least, some kisses are.

Reprinted with the Author's permission from *The Finger of Fate*.

THE HAUNTING OF JACK BURNHAM

" IT's an amazing story," said the doctor, " and I don't profess to account for it. Just one of those experiences which come out of the unexplored realms, and leave one utterly at a loss for any explanation. You remember Kipling's story of the man who was haunted by the ghost of the woman he'd lived with and chucked, and who went mad and died with the horror of it. Well, this might have ended the same way.

" We were at Rugby together—Jack Burnham and I. Went there the same term ; were put into the same form ; and were both at ʰhe same house. And there we laid the foundation of a friendship which has lasted till to-day. It was built somewhat on the law of opposites, for our characters and attainments are totally different. And the divergence was perhaps more noticeable at school than in later years. He was a magnificent athlete—a boy who stood out as a games player above the average ; whereas I was always a mediocre performer. He was in the eleven and the fifteen before he was sixteen, and his physical strength was phenomenal for a boy of his age. Moreover, he was intensely matter-of-fact, with the temperament that enabled him to go in to bat at a crucial stage in a cricket match with the same sang-froid as he would have when batting at the nets. It's important—that point ; it makes what is to come the more inexplicable.

" His father died when he was up at Oxford, leaving him quite comfortably off. I suppose Jack had four thousand a year, which relieved him of the necessity of earning his own living. It was just as well perhaps, because I don't think the old chap would ever have set the Thames on fire by his intellectual attainments. Moreover, it enabled him to become what he'd always been at heart—a wanderer.

" If ever a man had the *wanderlust* developed in him, it was Jack Burnham. He would disappear for years at a

time, leaving no address behind him—only to pop up again
in London as suddenly as he'd gone. And he was one of
those fellows with whom one could pick up the threads just
as if they had never been broken.

"I'd been installed in Harley Street about three years
when the story I'm going to tell you began. Jack had been
away for eighteen months, in the North of Africa somewhere,
and strangely enough I was thinking of him and wondering
where he was when the door opened and in he walked.

"My consulting hours were over, and I got up joyfully
to greet him.

" ' My dear old man,' I cried, ' this is great.'

"And then I saw his face clearly, and stopped short.
There was a strained, haggard look in his eyes which I'd
never seen before, and I realised at once that something was
the matter.

" ' Bill,' he said abruptly, as he shook hands, ' I want
you to dine with me to-night. I think I'm going mad.'

" ' Is that the reason of the invitation, old boy ? ' I said
lightly. ' You're looking a bit fine-drawn. What about
dining quietly with me here ? '

" ' Excellent. I'd love to.'

" I went over and rang the bell, and I was watching him
all the time. He kept glancing into different corners of
the room, and once he swung round suddenly and stared
over his shoulder. Nerves evidently like fiddle strings, I
reflected, and wondered what the devil had happened to
reduce Jack Burnham, of all people, to such a condition.

"All through dinner it was the same thing. When he
spoke at all his words were jerky and almost incoherent, and
by the time the port was on the table I realised that something pretty serious was the matter. In fact, if I hadn't
known him to be thoroughly abstemious, I should have
attributed it to drink or drugs. He had to use both hands
to lift his port glass, which was a bad sign.

" I didn't hurry him ; it was better to let him take his
fences his own way. And it wasn't until he'd lit a cigar
that he took the first with a rush.

" ' Do you know anything about the occult, Bill,' he said
suddenly.

" ' Just enough to leave it alone,' I answered. ' Why ? '

" ' I wish to God I'd known as much as that,' he cried

despairingly. ' Bill—you've seen the condition I'm in. My hands shaking like a man with the palsy ; my nerves screaming ; my reason tottering. I tell you, I *am* going mad—unless you can help me.'

" ' Steady, Jack,' I said. ' There's generally a cure for most things. Tell me the yarn, old man, and take your time over it.'

" He didn't answer for some time, and I could see he was taking a pull at himself.

" ' See here, Bill,' he said at length, ' what I'm going to tell you is God's truth. It's no hallucination—all the beginning part of it ; it's a cold, sober fact that I saw with my own eyes and heard with my own ears. Whether or not the result of what I saw and heard is hallucination ; whether or not what I'm tormented with now is a hideous delusion—or cold sober fact—I'll leave you to judge. I know what I think myself.

" ' It was a year ago that the thing began. You know I've wandered a good deal, and in the course of my wanderings I've seen some pretty strange things—things, that if you told 'em in a club smoking-room would be received with smiles of derision. I've seen black magic celebrated in age-old temples, where it was death to stir one step outside the circle of safety ; where the blood in the great bowl placed on the floor outside the circle swirled and heaved and monstrous shapes rose out of it and hovered round us— waiting. I have seen things which no man would believe secondhand ; but until a year ago I had never seen the most dreadful thing of all—the dead restored to life.

" ' I had heard rumours of it, but I had never actually witnessed it. So that when I found myself in the back of beyond in Morocco, as the guest of a chieftain for whom I had been able to do a service, and he asked me whether I would care to see it done, I accepted eagerly. I won't bore you with a detailed description of what happened : anyway, no spoken word could adequately paint the horror of the scene.

" ' Picture to yourself an Arab burial-ground—just a clearing in the scrub. Around us barked the jackals, and in answer the dogs from the village a few hundred yards away gave tongue. The smoke of the camel-dung fires came acrid to the nostrils, and the cemetery looked ghoulish in the greenish light of the flares carried by some of the men.

" ' It was a woman who was going to do the thing, and while some of the men removed the earth from a recent grave, she started singing some strange incantation.

" ' At last the men uncovered the corpse, and carried it in a piece of sheeting towards the central stone of the burial-ground. Then they withdrew, leaving the woman alone. Now, mark you, Bill, that man had been dead over a fortnight. . . .'

" He passed his hand over his forehead, and it was wet with perspiration.

" ' The woman, by now, was in a state of frenzy, and the harsh wailing from the other women who were seated in a circle around her seemed to madden her still more. And suddenly she began to shine with a faint radiance ; I suppose she'd rubbed phosphorus on herself. A few seconds passed and she seemed to be on fire, while the chant grew louder and louder, and then abruptly stopped as the woman advanced to the corpse.'

" Once again he paused and shook himself like a dog.

" ' I'll spare you the revolting details of the next few minutes—you wouldn't believe them if I told you ; but five minutes later she withdrew and the dead man was sitting up—alive. I don't profess to explain it ; I can only tell you what I saw. What power had entered that corpse to endow it with the capability of speech and movement I know not ; whether it came from the woman or whether it was some disembodied spirit—possibly that of the man himself—I can't say. All I do know is, that in the ordinary accepted meaning of words, the dead lived.

" ' Now he had been an ordinary peasant in life—a man of no account ; but the instant he sat up the whole circle prostrated itself around him. Grave, dread questions were asked him as to the life to come, and in every case the answer was coherent and sensible. And then my host intimated that I might ask him a question. Without thinking I said the first thing that came into my head.

" ' What does the future hold for me ? '

" ' For a while there was no reply, and, glancing up, I saw that the corpse was shaking uncontrollably. Then it spoke :

" ' Sleeping and waking you will be haunted by horror. Day and night it will be with you until the end. Then it will pass away.'

" ' That was all, and shortly after the ceremony ended. The corpse relaxed and was placed back in its grave, and I accompanied my host back to the village. He was silent and distrait, occasionally looking at me with an expression almost of fear in his deep-set eyes. But he said nothing, and as for me, my mind was far too occupied with what I had seen to want to talk. Of the answer to my question I barely thought ; it seemed such an insignificant part of such an amazing whole.

" ' I left the next day, and all the leading men of the village assembled to bid me good-bye. With the morning had come an amused scepticism, though I was careful not to show it. Ventriloquism undoubtedly : my eyes tricked by the smoky light. And as for the answer to my question, I forced myself to think of that ridiculous story of Oscar Wilde's—" Lord Arthur Savile's Crime."

" ' But there was no levity on the part of the Arabs : only a grave and dignified concern. I felt that they looked on me already as doomed and as such I was entitled to their commiseration and respect. And two months later I had forgotten all about it except as a strange and interesting experience.'

" He paused to relight his cigar, and I made no comment. In my own mind I felt tolerably certain that his morning reflections were correct and that he had been tricked, but the point was immaterial. The important part was still to come.

" ' So much is fact,' he went on after a while—' cold, hard fact. How it was done matters not. All that concerns us is that I saw and heard what I have told you. Now we come to the second chapter. I was in Biskra when it started—the thing that has gone on ever since. Never a night passes without it, Bill—so that I fight against sleep ; and now hardly a day passes without it too. It's a dream at night, always the same in every detail ; by day, God knows what it is.

" ' It starts with a kind of luminous cloud which swirls and dances as it retreats before me. Every moment I think I am going to catch it up—only for it to elude me always.

27*

But I know what's coming, and I wait—longing for it to happen. Out of the cloud there forms gradually a woman's face—lovely beyond the powers of description. And she beckons me to come to her. I strive madly to reach her, only to be eluded once more. I want to take her in my arms : and I swear she wants me to take her. But—never have I done so. Always just out of reach : always just beyond me. And then—sometimes very soon, sometimes after what seems hours—the horror comes. I know it's coming because I can see the look of frozen terror in her eyes, and I'm powerless to prevent it. And the horror—how shall I describe it ? Something comes flapping round my head buffeting me in the face : something that beats at me like the wing of some hideous bird till I feel smothered and choking ; something that leaves behind it still the awful smell of carrion. I tell you, Bill,' he shouted, ' I smell that smell : it's still lingering with me when I wake up sweating and dripping with fear.'

" Then he pulled himself together, and went on calmly.

" ' The first time it happened I put it down as an ordinary nightmare and thought no more about it. And then two or three nights later I had precisely the same dream. That was a year ago, Bill ; for the last six months I've had that dream every night. The details may vary a little, but it's always the same woman, and it's always the same ghastly horror at the end. I'm fighting for my life against that smothering, fetid terror.'

" ' Do you know the woman, Jack ? ' I said. ' Is she anyone you've ever seen ? '

" He shook his head.

" ' No, I've never seen her : I'm certain of that.'

" And even as he spoke his face turned grey, and he stared over my head into the shadows of the room.

" ' My God ! ' he whispered, ' she's just behind you.'

" I swung round in my chair : there was no one there.

" ' You thought you saw her, did you ? ' I said quietly.

" He shook himself, and the grey look slowly left his face.

" ' That's the second part of the terror, Bill,' he muttered. ' She's gone now, but three months ago she started to come to me by day as well. I've seen her on board ship, in restaurants, in the street—always beckoning and imploring me to come to her. The first few times, so vivid was the

hallucination that I thought she was really flesh and blood.
I followed her—madly ; to find she'd disappeared. She'd
never been there at all. " Day and night it will be with you
to the end." That's what that foul corpse said, and, dear
heavens ! it's true. It's true, Bill—I tell you : true. It's
with me day and night, for even when it isn't actually there
the thought that it may come at any moment haunts me.
Do you wonder I said I was going mad ? '

" He leaned forward, resting his head on his hands, and
I did some pretty powerful thinking. Remember, I knew
Jack's character, and his almost aggressive stolidity. He
was the last man in the world to give way to hysterical
fears : this thing that he had told me was as real to him
as I was. You might call it a delusion, an hallucination—
what you liked : there's no virtue in a name. To him it
was reality, and as such it had to be treated. And it
seemed to me that the cure would have to come largely from
himself. And it would have to come soon. Otherwise, in
very truth he might go mad.

" ' Well, Bill ? ' he said, looking at me with haggard eyes.
' What think you ? '

" ' It's difficult to say, Jack,' I answered. ' I would like
a little longer to think it over. But there are a few things
that seem to me to stick out as obvious. In the first place,
take what you see by day. Now you *know*, you've *proved*
that what you see is non-existent. *The woman is not there.*
Therefore you know that she is merely a figment of your
imagination. Don't misunderstand me : she seems very
real. But she isn't—and with one side of your mind you
know it. Now, have you tried fighting with that side of
your mind ? Have you tried throwing a loaf of bread at
this vision : kicking it hard : telling it to go to hell : forcing
yourself to believe that you see nothing. Or have you been
content to acquiesce in what you imagine you see, and not
help the rational side of your mind to fight ? Salvation,
Jack, has got to come from you yourself. I'll help to the
limit of my weight : but it's you, and you alone, who have
got to come to final grips with this thing ! '

" ' I get you,' he said quietly. ' But what about the
dream ? What about that ghastly end when she has
vanished ? '

" ' I believe, Jack, that the first thing to tackle is the daylight manifestation. If you can get rid of that, it will strengthen your subconscious mind to fight the dream. And I think '—it was a sudden inspiration that came to me—' that I can give you an explanation of the terror at the end. The clue lies in the fetid smell you imagine. Now, in that atrocious experiment you saw carried out, didn't the same smell of carrion hang round the graveyard ? '

" ' Why, yes ! ' he cried eagerly, ' it did.'

" ' Precisely,' I answered. ' Now, nothing will make me believe that what you described to me *really* happened that night. But you were in a state of partial hypnosis, induced by the chanting and the lighting effect, and you imagined it. And I know enough about such matters to realise your intense danger in being in such a condition in the circumstances. Your mind was a partial blank, ready to sop up impressions like blotting-paper sops up liquid. And one of the most vivid impressions that it absorbed was the fundamental one of the foul smell around you. And that impression comes back to you now each night. What the connection between it and the woman is, I don't profess to say. Don't forget that in the subconscious mind we have a jumble of disconnected thoughts, unlinked by any reason or argument. And for some strange reason the vision of this woman, and this beating, suffocating stench are joined together. Get rid of one, and you'll get rid of the other.'

" He was impressed, I could see, by my purposely materialistic arguments. And when two hours later he went to bed—I insisted on his stopping with me that night —he seemed a good deal calmer. I gave him a sleeping draught and waited until he'd gone off : then I got a book and settled myself down in his room for an all-night vigil.

" It was three-thirty when it began, and I woke with a start from a doze. And by the light of my reading-lamp I watched the terror come. Jack was sitting up in bed, his face convulsed with horror, beating with his hands at the empty air in front of him. He was croaking at it hoarsely, and his great fists were dealing savage blows at—nothing. I went over and stood beside him, and then there happened the thing which to this day I can't recall without a pricking at the back of my scalp. As distinctly as I can smell this cigar, did I smell the sickly stench of putrid carrion by his bed. And then it was gone, and Jack, wild-eyed and desperate, was staring up at me from the pillows.

" ' Again,' he said in a shaking voice—' I've just been through it again, Bill.'

" ' I know you have, old man,' I answered quietly. ' I've been with you the whole time.'

" He got up unsteadily and peeled off his pyjamas, and you could have wrung the sweat out of them on to the floor. Without a word he rubbed himself down with a bath-towel; then, putting on a dressing-gown, he lit a cigarette.

" ' Every night, Bill. I can't go on. For God's sake, man, do something.'

" And that was the devil of it—what to do. I didn't tell him so, of course, but that one staggering thing—the fact that I had noticed the smell—had knocked every idea of mine to smithereens. I realised that I was up against something beyond ordinary medical skill. And—what to do. . . .

" Gad! how he fought during the next week. I kept him with me, and one night he nearly caused my butler to give notice. He bunged a glass full of whisky and soda straight at him, and then cried triumphantly, ' It went clean through her, Bill.' Unfortunately the butler was not equally transparent, and objected to receiving heavy cut glasses full of liquid in the chest.

" But the dreams went on, and at length I insisted on him seeing a brain specialist. But it was no use, and ultimately I began to despair. So did he.

" ' To the end, Bill,' he said one day. ' To the end. Pray God it comes soon.'

" ' Then it will pass away,' I reminded him. ' Don't forget that, Jack.'

" But he only shrugged his shoulders : I think he had very nearly given up hope.

" And then one night came the staggering *dénouement*. We were dining at Claridge's—just the two of us alone. I used to make him go to restaurants and theatres in the hope of taking his mind off it, and as we were finishing our fish I happened to look up. A man and a woman had just come in, and the woman was quite one of the most lovely things I've ever seen. She was dressed in pale green, and

my eyes followed her as she went to the table reserved for
them. Head waiters were bowing obsequiously, so they
were evidently not unknown. And I began wondering who
they were.

"'Devilish good-looking woman just come in, Jack,' I
said idly. 'Three tables away on your right, in pale green.
Don't turn round for a moment : she's looking this way.'

"I saw him glance at her a few moments later, and the
next instant I thought he'd gone mad. He was staring at
me with his eyes blazing and his face a chalky white.

"'You see her, Bill ? ' he gasped. 'She's real ? You
saw her come in ? '

"'Of course I saw her come in,' I cried in amazement.

"'She is the woman of my dream,' he said stupidly.
'The woman who haunts me.'

"'Steady, old man,' I stammered urgently, while I tried
to grasp this vast, essential fact. 'People are looking at
you. You say that woman is the woman of your dream.
You're sure ? '

"He laughed shortly.

"'Don't be a damned fool. Do you think I could make
a mistake over *that* ? '

"'And you've never seen her before ? '

"'Never in my life. But one thing I'm certain of :
I'm never going to lose sight of her again. To the end,
Bill—to the end. And she and I have got to go there
together.'

"It was useless to argue, and anyway the situation had
gone beyond me. Half-dazedly I heard him send for a head
waiter, and ask who they were.

"'Kreseltein,' he said to me slowly, after the waiter had
gone. 'One of the South African diamond kings. Returning in the *Arundel Castle* next Friday week. To-
morrow, Bill, I go to the Union Castle office in Fenchurch
Street. I also travel by the *Arundel Castle* next Friday
week.'

"He was like a man bereft of his senses for the next ten
days. The Kreseltels were staying at the Ritz, and Jack
haunted the place like a detective. He lunched there, he
dined there, he very nearly breakfasted there, and as the
date of sailing drew nearer he grew more and more excited.
And there was another strange development : from the

night when he saw her first at Claridge's the dream and the daylight hallucinations completely ceased.

"I dined with him at the Ritz on the night before he sailed, and the Kreselteins were a few tables away. And he was his old self again.

"'It's flesh and blood, Bill, now,' he said, 'and flesh and blood I can cope with.'

"'Tell me, Jack,' I asked, 'as a matter of interest, has Mrs. Kreseltein ever seemed as if your face was familiar to her.'

"'Never,' he answered decisively. 'On the occasions when I've happened to catch her eye, she has always given me the blank look of a perfect stranger.'

"'I wonder who she was?' I remarked.

"'Well, I've been making a few inquiries, if you want to know,' he said. 'She's English, and she married Kreseltein when she was quite a girl. He's a German Jew, and I gather from what I've heard a pretty foul swine. He flies into the most maniacal rages if she even looks at another man. There's some story apparently about his having plugged someone in Kimberley with a revolver, who, he thought, was making love to his wife.'

"'You'd better watch it, Jack,' I said gravely.

"'My dear old Bill,' he answered, 'I'm no particular slouch with a gun myself. But even if I couldn't hit a haystack at five yards it would make no difference. That woman is all that stands between me and insanity, and so I've got to go through with it. If I didn't go in the *Arundel Castle* to-morrow, as sure as I am sitting here now the dream would start again. For some strange inscrutable reason Mrs. Kreseltein is going to be mixed up in my life. Her destiny and mine are going to meet—at the end. After that—God alone knows. But it will pass away ; the horror will be gone.'

"He stared at me gravely.

"'I'm under no delusion, Bill. I've got to go through the horror in reality, and I've got to come out on the other side. Only then will its power be dead!'

"The next day I saw him off in the boat train at Waterloo. He wrung my hand hard as he thanked me for the little I'd been able to do, and from my heart I wished him good luck. Then the train steamed out, and in almost the last carriage I saw the Kreselteins. He was deep in the morning paper ; she was staring out of the window at the people on the platform. And her face was the face of a woman who was tired unto death. But lovely—Lord ! how lovely—in spite of its weariness."

The Doctor paused and mixed himself a whisky and soda.

" And with that ended the first part of the story of Jack Burnham," he continued after a while. " Weeks turned into months, and I heard nothing more. Jack was always a bad letter-writer, and even this time he proved no exception. He had vanished into the blue as usual, and I had nothing for it but to bottle up my intense curiosity as well as I could.

" And then, one day came the first news, and, knowing what I did, it was grave enough in all conscience. It was in the morning paper with head-lines all complete :

" MYSTERIOUS DISAPPEARANCE OF SOUTH AFRICAN
DIAMOND KING
STILL NO TRACE OF MR. OTTO
KRESELTEIN

" ' The disappearance of Mr. Otto Kreseltein, the well-known owner of race-horses, and one of South Africa's wealthiest millionaires, grows more mysterious daily. It will be recalled that he left his house in Johannesburg somewhat suddenly about a fortnight ago, stating that he was going north into Rhodesia. From that day no further news has been heard of him. The station-master at Bulawayo states that he believes a gentleman answering to Mr. Kreseltein's description was on board the train bound for the Victoria Falls, but there were so many tourists travelling that he is unable to be certain. In the meantime an active search is being organised. It is thought possible that Mr. Kreseltein may be suffering from temporary loss of memory.'

" Three weeks later came another announcement.

" ' The gravest fears must now, we regret to state, be entertained concerning Mr. Otto Kreseltein. No trace has been found of him ; no word has been received for over five

weeks, and in view of the fact that he was in the middle
of a big scheme of amalgamation when he left Johannesburg,
and told his managing director that he only proposed to be
absent for four days, it is impossible to avoid fearing that
something very serious has happened.'

" Once again weeks passed by, and at last it was generally assumed that he was dead. Legally, of course, the
assumption could not be entertained as yet ; but from every
other point of view his death was regarded as certain. And
still I had no line from Jack to assuage my curiosity. For,
inwardly, I was convinced that he could throw some light
on the matter, though no mention of his name had ever been
made in the papers connecting him with Kreseltein in
any way.

" And then, six months later, he walked into my consulting-room. He looked a bit pale, and fine-drawn, but
his eye was clear and his smile was the smile of the Jack
Burnham of old.

" ' I've been to the end, Bill,' he cried. ' I've come out
on the other side. And it has passed away.'

" ' Why the devil haven't you dropped me a line, Jack,'
I demanded.

" ' Because, old man,' he said gravely, ' there are certain
things it is better not to put in writing. Have you seen the
papers this morning ? '

" He held out a copy of *The Times* to me, and indicated
a paragraph.

" ' The mystery of the disappearance of Mr. Otto Kreseltein has at last been solved. Two Englishmen, while
shooting in the district north of Bulawayo, discovered the
remnants of a skeleton lying behind a big rock. Vultures and
other beasts of prey had long since rendered any chance of
identification impossible, but some fragments of cloth and
part of an envelope supplied the necessary clues. There is
no doubt that the skeleton is all that remains of the unfortunate diamond magnate, whose sudden disappearance
caused such a stir some months ago. What Mr. Kreseltein
was doing there will probably remain an unsolved problem.'

" I put down the paper and glanced at Jack.

" ' An unsolved problem,' he said with a faint smile.

'Except to me, Bill, and one other. And now to you. I shot him.'

" ' The devil you did ! ' I said. ' Is it indiscreet to ask why ? '

" ' Largely because of the fact that of all the devils in human form I have ever met, Otto Kreseltein was the worst,' he answered grimly. ' He lived like a swine, and he died like one, and you can take it from me that he's no loss.'

" He flung himself into a chair and lit a cigarette.

" ' I'll tell you the yarn, Bill,' he said. ' I guess you've a right to know. It was after we left Madeira that I made Joan's acquaintance—his wife, I mean. He was mad keen on bridge, and with three others of the same kidney he spent the whole day in the smoking-room. And I talked to her. It was a case of love right from the very beginning—with both of us, I think. Even if it hadn't been for the special reason which actuated me ; even if I'd never been haunted by the horror, things would have come to a head. I'm going to marry her, you know. . . . She's in London. . . .

" ' However—to get back to it. After I'd known her for a few days I told her everything. I felt absolutely certain that something was going to happen some time, and I wanted her to be prepared. At first she hardly took it seriously, but after a while I convinced her that I wasn't fooling. And I think the thing that impressed her most was when I told her how I'd hit your butler in the chest with a whisky and soda.

" ' Towards the end of the voyage we grew a bit careless, I suppose. Not to put too fine a point on it, I was with her from after breakfast until we went to bed. And we danced a good deal together. Off and on in the intervals of bridge her husband had joined us, and I saw enough of him to fill in the gaps left by Joan. A thin-lipped, domineering swine, Bill ; a man of the most colossal conceit—and a cad. A clever cad, and an able cad ; but once or twice when he spoke to his wife my hands tingled to get at him. She might have been a junior clerk getting told off.

" ' He'd said nothing to me about being so much with his wife, and he'd said nothing to her. So it came as rather a surprise when, the night before we arrived in Cape Town, he came up to me as I was strolling up and down the deck waiting for the dinner bugle.

" ' " I have just been—ah—speaking to my wife, Mr. Burnham," he said softly. "And she quite understands that her acquaintanceship with you must cease forthwith. Should you take any steps to renew it, I shall have to deal with you in a way you may not like ! "

" ' And it was the way he said it, Bill, that finished me. Foolish perhaps, but I lost my temper—badly.

" ' " When your wife tells me the same thing, Mr. Kreseltein, I shall obey immediately. Until then I would be vastly obliged if you would go to hell and remain there. Your general appearance is not conducive to an appetite for dinner."

" ' And then, Bill, the primitive man came out in him. His face was red with passion, and he shot out a great hairy hand and caught me by the wrist. He was strong—but I was stronger. I removed his hand, and I held him powerless for a few seconds.

" ' " No, Mr. Kreseltein, I win on those lines," I said. " You'd better treat your wife better in future or I may have to give you a caning."

" ' Foolish, I frankly admit—but I was seeing red, old man. And the next morning as we got off the boat it wasn't red—it was scarlet. For on Joan's arms I saw two bruises, and I realised how he had spoken to her the night before. And for a moment or two I went mad.

" ' I went straight up to him in the Customs, and I got his arm in a grip I knew of old. I swung him round, and he faced me livid with fury.

" ' " If I see another bruise on your wife's arm like that, you damned swine," I muttered, " I'll first break your arm —so," and, by Gad ! Bill, as near as makes no odds I broke it then, so that he let out a squawk of pain—" and then I'll flog you till you scream for mercy."

" ' There was murder in his face when I left him, and I cursed myself for a fool. His fury was bound to be vented on Joan. And on the way up in the boat train I made up my mind : I'd take her away. I felt pretty certain that she'd come. And when she rang me up at the Carlton Hotel in Jo'burg I wasn't surprised.

" ' " I can't stand it, Jack," she said. " He's become a devil incarnate. He—he thrashed me last night."

" ' God ! old man—that finished it.

" " " Pack what you want, dear," I said, " and come to the Carlton. We leave for Durban to-night. I'm going to see your husband now."

" ' I rang off before she could say anything, and went round to his office. There was some meeting on, but I went straight into his private office. I suppose I looked a bit wild, for he rose to his feet and started opening a drawer in his desk. And I got to him just before he drew his gun.

" " " Shall we discuss this matter with or without an audience ? " I remarked.

" ' The audience settled that and left rapidly.

" " " You thrashed your wife last night, Kreseltein," I said quietly. " We will now have a hair of the dog that bit her."

" ' Well, Bill, I broke the stick on him, and it was a stoutish weapon. And when I'd finished with him I told him I was taking her to Durban that night. He lay there huddled up in his chair with the malevolence of all hell in his eyes.

" " " I shall not divorce her," he croaked. " And in addition to that I shall make it my business to have you followed wherever you go, so that your relationship may be known."

" ' I was on the point of starting in on him again, when he suddenly sat up and stared at me.

" " " I admit that you are stronger than I am, Mr. Burnham," he said, " but there are other ways of settling affairs of this sort. Unless you're afraid."

" ' " Get on with it," I snapped at him.

" " " I suggest revolvers," he remarked. " A shooting trip in Rhodesia—from which one of us will not return."

" " " I agree," I said instantly. " And we start at once."

" ' A sardonic smile twitched round his lips.

" " " To-night," he answered, and with that I left him.

" ' It was Joan who interpreted that smile.

" " " My dear," she said ; " it's murder. Otto is supposed to be one of the half-dozen best revolver shots in the world."

" " " I guessed he'd probably shot before when he suggested it," I laughed. " But, don't you see, dear heart, that it's the only way. You know I'm not a complete dud myself."

" ' And so I pacified her as best I could, though, to tell you the truth, I wasn't feeling too easy myself. I *am* a good revolver shot, but I lay no claim to being an expert.'

" He lit another cigarette, and his face was grim.

" ' We staged it well, Bill ; no one suspected. And four days later we met in a belt of scrub and desert about fifty miles north of Bulawayo. We were to stand back to back at thirty paces, and at the word " Fire " we were to swing round and shoot. We tossed for who was to speak—he won. And I, like a fool, trusted him. He plugged me through the back before he spoke. I heard the report ; felt the sharp, searing pain go through me, and even as my knees gave from under me and I crashed, for the second time I cursed myself for a fool. I thought it was the end, Bill ; I couldn't see clearly, though he was standing over me shaking with laughter. And then there occurred the most amazing thing. The scene seemed to fade out from my mind, and I was back again in that Arab graveyard. But this time I was the corpse. I tell you, I could see the ring of natives around me, and that dreadful woman coming at me. I could see her shining and luminous ; I could hear the chanting; I could feel her as she threw herself on me. And suddenly—it's incredible, I know, but it is so—I felt strength come into my arms which had previously been numb and powerless. I felt my right arm lift, until it pointed at the woman's heart. And dimly, as if from a great distance, I heard a report. Then everything faded out, though the last act had still to come.

" ' The dream came back. I saw Joan beckoning to me, with that same dear, elusive smile, and then she faded away and I knew the horror was coming. Something came flapping round my head, buffeting me in the face, and I beat at it as always. The stench of carrion was ghastly ; the smothering feeling more overpowering than ever before. On and on it went, that dream, and I couldn't wake up. Until at last my eyes forced themselves open and I was awake. Vultures, Bill—dozens of them. One great brute on my chest, and others flapping around me. And a few yards away was something that lay on the ground covered with them.

" ' And then everything grew hazy again. I have a dim recollection of the filthy brutes suddenly hopping away—of seeing the thing they had left behind them—of realising it was what was left of Kreseltein. I saw Joan's face too : imagined she was leaning over me. And Bill—she was. That wasn't a dream, as I found out later. She'd followed us, and she saved my life.

" ' Somehow she got me to a native kraal—the men carried me, and there I lay for three months. As soon as I was fit to be left she went back to Johannesburg, and there later on I joined her. For she'd been with me to the end, and the horror had passed away.

" ' Can you account for it, Bill ? '

" I couldn't—and to this day I can't. He married her, of course, and there has never been any return of the horror. But what was the strange power that entered the arm of a man wellnigh dead, and directed the aim of his revolver at the heart of Otto Kreseltein ? "

Reprinted with the Author's permission from *Word of Honour*.

DOROTHY SAYERS
Absolutely Elsewhere

¶ DOROTHY SAYERS was born at
Oxford, and left Somerville College with
a first-class Honours degree in French.
She then taught for a while, before
turning (with a sigh of relief) to pub-
lishing and advertising work. Later
the writing of detective stories, at first
her hobby, became, to her content, her
profession.

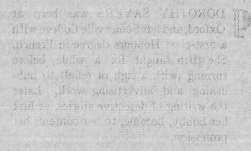

ABSOLUTELY ELSEWHERE

LORD PETER WIMSEY sat with Chief-Inspector Parker of the C.I.D. and Inspector Henley of the Baldock Police in the library at The Lilacs.

" So you see," said Parker, " that all the obvious suspects were elsewhere at the time."

" What do you mean by ' elsewhere ' ? " demanded Wimsey, peevishly. Parker had hauled him down to Wapley on the Great North Road without his breakfast, and his temper had suffered. " Do you mean that they couldn't have reached the scene of the murder without travelling at over 186,000 miles a second ? Because, if you don't mean that, they weren't absolutely elsewhere. They were only relatively and apparently elsewhere.

" For Heaven's sake, don't go all Eddington. Humanly speaking, they were elsewhere, and if we're going to nail one of them we shall have to do it without going into their Fitzgerald contractions and coefficients of spherical curvature. I think, Inspector, we had better have them in one by one, so that I can hear all their stories again. You can check them up if they depart from their original statements at any point. Let's take the butler first."

The inspector put his head out into the hall and said : " Hamworthy."

The butler was a man of middle age, whose spherical curvature was certainly worthy of consideration. His large face was pale and puffy, and he looked unwell. However, he embarked on his story without hesitation.

" I have been in the late Mr. Grimbold's service for twenty years, gentlemen, and have always found him a good master. He was a strict gentleman, but very just. I know he was considered very hard in business matters, but I suppose he had to be that. He was a bachelor, but he brought up his two nephews, Mr. Harcourt and Mr. Neville, and was very good to them. In his private life I should call him a kind

857

and considerate man. His profession ? Yes, I suppose you would call him a moneylender.

"About the events of last night, sir, yes. I shut up the house at 7.30 as usual. Everything was done exactly to time, sir—Mr. Grimbold was very regular in his habits. I locked all the windows on the ground floor, as was customary during the winter months. I am quite sure I didn't miss anything out. They all have burglar-proof bolts and I should have noticed if they had been out of order. I also locked and bolted the front door and put up the chain."

"How about the conservatory door ? "

"That, sir, is a Yale lock. I tried it, and saw that it was shut. No, I didn't fasten the catch. It was always left that way, sir, in case Mr. Grimbold had business which kept him in Town late, so that he could get in without disturbing the household."

"But he had no business in Town last night ? "

"No, sir, but it was always left that way. Nobody could get in without the key, and Mr. Grimbold had that on his ring."

"Is there no other key in existence ? "

"I believe——" the butler coughed—"I believe, sir, though I do not know, that there is *one*, sir—in the possession of—of a lady, sir, who is at present in Paris."

"I see. Mr. Grimbold was about sixty years old, I believe. Just so. What is the name of this lady ? "

"Mrs. Winter, sir. She lives at Wapley, but since her husband died last month, sir, I understand she has been residing abroad."

"I see. Better make a note of that, Inspector. Now, how about the upper rooms and the back door ? "

"The upper room windows were all fastened in the same way, sir, except Mr. Grimbold's bedroom and the cook's room and mine, sir ; but they couldn't be reached without a ladder, and the ladder is locked up in the tool-shed."

"That's all right," put in Inspector Henley. "We went into that last night. The shed was locked and, what's more, there were unbroken cobwebs between the ladder and the wall."

"I went through all the rooms at half-past seven, sir, and there was nothing out of order."

"You may take it from me," said the inspector, again,

"that there was no interference with any of the locks.
Carry on, Hamworthy."

"Yes, sir. While I was seeing to the house, Mr. Grimbold
came down into the library for his glass of sherry. At
7.45 the soup was served and I called Mr. Grimbold to dinner.
He sat at the end of the table as usual, facing the serving-
hatch."

"With his back to the library door," said Parker, making
a mark on a rough plan of the rooms, which lay before him.
"Was that door shut?"

"Oh, yes, sir. All the doors and windows were shut."

"It looks a dashed draughty room," said Wimsey.
"Two doors and a serving-hatch and two french windows."

"Yes, my lord ; but they are all very well-fitting, and the
curtains were drawn."

His lordship moved across to the connecting door and
opened it.

"Yes," he said, "good and heavy, and moves in sinister
silence. I like these thick carpets, but the pattern's a bit
fierce." He shut the door noiselessly and returned to his
seat.

"Mr. Grimbold would take about five minutes over his
soup, sir. When he had done, I removed it and put on the
fish. I did not have to leave the room ; everything comes
through the serving-hatch. The wine—that is, the Chablis
—was already on the table. That course was only a small
portion of turbot, and would take Mr. Grimbold about five
minutes again. I removed that, and put on the roast
pheasant. I was just about to serve Mr. Grimbold with the
vegetables, when the telephone-bell rang. Mr. Grimbold
said : ' You'd better see who it is. I'll help myself.' It was
not the cook's business, of course, to answer the telephone."

"Are there no other servants?"

"Only the woman who comes in to clean during the day,
sir. I went out to the instrument, shutting the door behind
me."

"Was that this telephone or the one in the hall?"

"The one in the hall, sir. I always used that one, unless
I happened to be actually in the library at the time. The
call was from Mr. Neville Grimbold in Town, sir. He and
Mr. Harcourt have a flat in Jermyn Street. Mr. Neville

spoke, and I recognised his voice. He said : ' Is that you,
Hamworthy ? Wait a moment. Mr. Harcourt wants you.'
He put the receiver down and then Mr. Harcourt came on.
He said : ' Hamworthy, I want to run down to-night to
see my uncle, if he's at home.' I said : ' Yes, sir, I'll tell
him.' The young gentlemen often come down for a night
or two. We keep their bedrooms ready for them. Mr.
Harcourt said he would be starting at once and expected
to get down by about half-past nine. While he was speaking
I heard the big grandfather-clock up in their flat chime the
quarters and strike eight, and immediately after, our own
hall-clock struck, and then I heard the Exchange say, ' Three
minutes.' So the call must have come through at three
minutes to eight, sir."

" Then there's no doubt about the time. That's a comfort. What next, Hamworthy ? "

" Mr. Harcourt asked for another three minutes and said :
' Mr. Neville has got something to say,' and then Mr. Neville
came back to the 'phone. He said he was going to Scotland
shortly, and wanted me to send up a country suit and some
stockings and shirts that he had left down here. He wanted
the suit sent to the cleaner's first, and there were various
other instructions, so that he asked for another three
minutes. That would be at eight-three, sir, yes. And about
a minute after that, while he was still speaking, the front-
door bell rang. I couldn't very well leave the 'phone, so
the caller had to wait, and at five past eight he rang the bell
again. I was just going to ask Mr. Neville to excuse me,
when I saw Cook come out of the kitchen and go through the
hall to the front door. Mr. Neville asked me to repeat his
instructions, and then the Exchange interrupted us again,
so he rang off, and when I turned round I saw Cook just
closing the library door. I went to meet her, and she said :
' Here's that Mr. Payne again, wanting Mr. Grimbold.
I've put him in the library, but I don't like the looks of
him.' So I said : ' All right ; I'll fix him,' and Cook went
back to the kitchen."

" One moment," said Parker. " Who's Mr. Payne ? "

" He's one of Mr. Grimbold's clients, sir. He lives about
five minutes away, across the fields, and he's been here before, making trouble. I think he owes Mr. Grimbold money,
sir, and wanted more time to pay."

" He's here, waiting in the hall," added Henley.

" Oh ? " said Wimsey. " The unshaven party with the scowl and the ash-plant, and the blood-stained coat ? "

" That's him, my lord," said the butler. " Well, sir "— he turned to Parker again—" I started to go along to the library, when it came over me sudden-like that I'd never taken in the claret and Mr. Grimbold would be getting very annoyed. So I went back to my pantry—you see where that is, sir—and fetched it from where it was warming before the fire. I had a little hunt then for the salver, sir, till I found I had put down my evening paper on top of it, but I wasn't more than a minute, sir, before I got back into the dining-room. And then, sir "—the butler's voice faltered—" then I saw Mr. Grimbold fallen forward on the table, sir, all across his plate, like. I thought he must have been took ill, and I hurried up to him and found—I found he was dead, sir, with a dreadful wound in his back."

" No weapon anywhere ? "

" Not that I could see, sir. There was a terrible lot of blood. It made me feel shockingly faint, sir, and for a minute I didn't hardly know what to do. As soon as I could think of anything, I rushed over to the serving-hatch and called Cook. She came hurrying in and let out an awful scream when she saw the master. Then I remembered Mr. Payne and opened the library door. He was sitting there, and he began at once, asking how long he'd have to wait. So I said : ' Here's an awful thing ! Mr. Grimbold has been murdered ! ' and he pushed past me into the dining-room, and the first thing he said was : ' How about those windows ? ' He pulled back the curtain of the one nearest the library, and there was the window standing open. ' This is the way he went,' he said, and started to rush out. I said, ' No, you don't '—thinking he meant to get away, and I hung on to him. He called me a lot of names, and then he said : ' Look here, my man, be reasonable. The fellow's getting away all this time. We must have a look for him.' So I said, ' Not without I go with you,' and he said, ' All right.' So I told Cook not to touch anything, but to ring up the police, and Mr. Payne and I went out after I'd washed the poor master's blood off my hands and fetched my torch from the pantry."

" Did Payne go with you while you did all that ? "

" Yes, sir. Well, him and me went out and we searched about in the garden, but we couldn't see any footprints or anything, because it's an asphalt path all round the house and down to the gate. And we couldn't see any weapon, either. So then he said : ' We'd better go back and get the car and search the roads,' but I said : ' No, he'll be away by then,' because it's only a quarter of a mile from our gate to the Great North Road, and it would take us five or ten minutes before we could start. So Mr. Payne said : ' Perhaps you're right,' and came back to the house with me. Well, then, sir, the constable came from Wapley, and after a bit the inspector here and Dr. Crofts from Baldock, and they made a search and asked a lot of questions, which I answered to the best of my ability, and I can't tell you no more, sir."

" Did you notice," asked Parker, " whether Mr. Payne had any stains of blood about him ? "

" No, sir—I can't say that he had. When I first saw him, he was sitting in here, right under the light, and I think I should have seen it if there was anything, sir. I can't say fairer than that."

" Of course, you've searched this room, Inspector, for bloodstains or a weapon or for anything such as gloves or a cloth, or anything that might have been used to protect the murderer from bloodstains ? "

" Yes, Mr. Parker. We searched very carefully."

" Could anybody have come downstairs while you were in the dining-room with Mr. Grimbold ? "

" Well, sir, I suppose they might. But they'd have to have got into the house before half-past seven, sir, and hidden themselves somewhere. Still, there's no doubt it might have happened that way. They couldn't come down by the back stairs, of course, because they'd have had to pass the kitchen, and Cook would have heard them, the passage being flagged, sir, but the front stairs—well, I don't know hardly what to say about that."

" That's how the man got in, depend upon it," said Parker. " Don't look so distressed, Hamworthy. You can't be expected to search all the cupboards in the house every evening for concealed criminals. Now I think I had better see the two nephews. I suppose they and their uncle got on together all right ? "

" Oh, yes, sir. Never had a word of any sort. It's been a great blow to them, sir. They were terribly upset when Mr. Grimbold was ill in the summer——"

" He was ill, was he ? "

" Yes, sir, with his heart, last July. He took a very bad turn, sir, and we had to send for Mr. Neville. But he pulled round wonderfully, sir—only he never seemed to be quite such a cheerful gentleman afterwards. I think it made him feel he wasn't getting younger, sir. But I'm sure nobody ever thought he'd be cut off like this."

" How is his money left ? " asked Parker.

" Well, sir, that I don't know. I believe it would be divided between the two gentlemen, sir—not but what they have plenty of their own. But Mr. Harcourt would be able to tell you, sir. He's the executor."

" Very well, we'll ask him. Are the brothers on good terms ? "

" Oh, yes, indeed, sir. Most devoted. Mr. Neville would do anything for Mr. Harcourt—and Mr. Harcourt for him, I'm sure. A very pleasant pair of gentlemen, sir. You couldn't have nicer."

" Thanks, Hamworthy. That will do for the moment, unless anybody else has anything to ask ? "

" How much of the pheasant was eaten, Hamworthy ? "

" Well, my lord, not a great deal of it—I mean, nothing like all of what Mr. Grimbold had on his plate. But he'd ate some of it. It might have taken three or four minutes or so to eat what he had done, my lord, judging by what I helped him to."

" There was nothing to suggest that he had been interrupted, for example, by somebody coming to the windows, or of his having got up to let the person in ? "

" Nothing at all, my lord, that I could see."

" The chair was pushed in close to the table when I saw him," put in the inspector, " and his napkin was on his knees and the knife and fork lying just under his hands, as though he had dropped them when the blow came. I understand that the body was not disturbed."

" No, sir. I never moved it—except, of course, to make sure that he was dead. But I never felt any doubt of that, sir, when I saw that dreadful wound in his back. I just lifted his head and let it fall forward again, same as before."

" All right, then, Hamworthy. Ask Mr. Harcourt to
come in."

Mr. Harcourt Grimbold was a brisk-looking man of about
thirty-five. He explained that he was a stockbroker and his
brother Neville an official in the Ministry of Public Welfare,
and that they had been brought up by their uncle from the
ages of eleven and ten respectively. He was aware that his
uncle had had many business enemies, but for his own part
he had received nothing from him but kindness.

" I'm afraid I can't tell you much about this terrible
business, as I didn't get here till 9.45 last night, when, of
course, it was all over."

" That was a little later than you hoped to be here ? "

" Just a little. My tail-lamp went out between Welwyn
Garden City and Welwyn, and I was stopped by a bobby.
I went to a garage in Welwyn, where they found that the
lead had come loose. They put it right, and that delayed
me for a few minutes more."

" It's about forty miles from here to London ? "

" Just over. In the ordinary way, at that time of night,
I should reckon an hour and a quarter from door to door.
I'm not a speed-merchant."

" Did you drive yourself ? "

" Yes. I have a chauffeur, but I don't always bring him
down here with me."

" When did you leave London ? "

" About 8.20, I should think. Neville went round to the
garage and fetched the car as soon as he'd finished telephoning, while I put my toothbrush and so on in my bag."

" You didn't hear about the death of your uncle before
you left ? "

" No. They didn't think of ringing me up, I gather, till
after I had started. The police tried to get Neville later on,
but he'd gone round to the club, or something. I 'phoned
him myself after I got here, and he came down this morning."

" Well, now, Mr. Grimbold, can you tell us anything about
your late uncle's affairs ? "

" You mean his will ? Who profits, and that kind of
thing ? Well, I do, for one, and Neville, for another. And
Mrs. —— Have you heard of a Mrs. Winter ? "

" Something, yes."

" Well, she does, for a third. And then, of course, old Hamworthy gets a nice little nest-egg, and the cook gets something, and there is a legacy of £500 to the clerk at my uncle's London office. But the bulk of it goes to us and to Mrs. Winter. I know what you're going to ask—how much is it ? I haven't the faintest idea, but I know it must be something pretty considerable. The old man never let on to a soul how much he really was worth, and we never bothered about it. I'm turning over a good bit, and Neville's salary is a heavy burden on a long-suffering public, so we only had a mild, academic kind of interest in the question."

" Do you suppose Hamworthy knew he was down for a legacy ? "

" Oh, yes—there was no secret about that. He was to get one hundred pounds and a life-interest in two hundred pounds a year, provided, of course, he was still in my uncle's service when he—my uncle, I mean—died."

" And he wasn't under notice, or anything ? "

" N-no. No. Not more than usual. My uncle gave everybody notice about once a month to keep them up to the mark. But it never came to anything. He was like the Queen of Hearts in ' Alice '—he never executed nobody, you know."

" I see. We'd better ask Hamworthy about that, though. Now, this Mrs. Winter. Do you know anything about her ? "

" Oh, yes. She's a nice woman. Of course, she was Uncle William's mistress for donkeys' years, but her husband was practically potty with drink, and you could scarcely blame her. I wired her this morning and here's her reply, just come."

He handed Parker a telegram, despatched from Paris, which read : " Terribly shocked and grieved. Returning immediately. Love and sympathy. Lucy."

" You are on friendly terms with her, then ? "

" Good Lord, yes. Why not ? We were always damned sorry for her. Uncle William would have taken her away with him somewhere, only she wouldn't leave Winter. In fact, I think they had practically settled that they were to

28

get married now that Winter has had the grace to peg out.
She's only about thirty-eight, and it's time she had some
sort of show in life, poor thing ! "

" So, in spite of the money, she hadn't really very much
to gain by your uncle's death ? "

" Not a thing. Unless, of course, she wanted to marry
somebody younger, and was afraid of losing the cash. But
I believe she was honestly fond of the old boy. Anyhow,
she couldn't have done the murder, because she's in
Paris."

" H'm ! " said Parker. " I suppose she is. We'd better
make sure, though. I'll ring through to the Yard and have
her looked out for at the ports. Is this 'phone through to
the Exchange ? "

" Yes," said the inspector. " It doesn't have to go
through the hall 'phone ; they're connected in parallel."

" All right. Well, I don't think we need trouble you
further, at the moment, Mr. Grimbold. I'll put my call
through, and after that we'll send for the next witness . . .
Give me Whitehall 1212, please . . . I suppose the time of
Mr. Harcourt's call from Town has been checked, Inspector ? "

" Yes, Mr. Parker. It was put in at 7.57 and renewed at
8 o'clock and 8.3. Quite an expensive little item. And
we've also checked up on the constable who spoke to him
about his lights and the garage that put them right for him.
He got into Welwyn at 9.5 and left again about 9.15. The
number of the car is right, too."

" Well, he's out of it in any case, but it's just as well to
check all we can . . . Hullo ! is that Scotland Yard ? Put
me through to Chief-Inspector Hardy. Chief-Inspector
Parker speaking."

As soon as he had finished with his call, Parker sent for
Neville Grimbold. He was rather like his brother, only a
little slimmer and a little more suave in speech, as befitted a
civil servant. He had nothing to add, except to confirm
his brother's story and to explain that he had gone to a
cinema from 8.20 to about 10 o'clock, and then on to his
club, so that he had heard nothing about the tragedy till
later in the evening.

The cook was the next witness. She had a great deal to
say, but nothing very convincing to tell. She had not hap-

pened to see Hamworthy go to the pantry for the claret,
otherwise she confirmed his story. She scouted the idea that
somebody had been concealed in one of the upper rooms,
because the daily woman, Mrs. Crabbe, had been in the house
till nearly dinner-time, putting camphor-bags in all the
wardrobes ; and, anyhow, she had no doubt but . what
" that Payne " had stabbed Mr. Grimbold—" a nasty,
murdering beast." After which it only remained to interview the murderous Mr. Payne.

Mr. Payne was almost aggressively frank. He had been
treated very harshly by Mr. Grimbold. What with exor-
bitant usury and accumulated interest added to the principal he had already paid back about five times the original
loan, and now Mr. Grimbold had refused him any more time
to pay and had announced his intention of foreclosing on the
security, namely, Mr. Payne's house and land. It was all
the more brutal because Mr. Payne had every prospect of
being able to pay off the entire debt in six months' time,
owing to some sort of interest or share in something or other
which was confidently expected to turn up trumps. In
his opinion, old Grimbold had refused to renew on purpose,
so as to prevent him from paying—what *he* wanted was the
property. Grimbold's death was the saving of the situation,
because it would postpone settlement till after the con-
fidently-expected trumps had turned up. Mr. Payne would
have murdered old Grimbold with pleasure, but he hadn't
done so, and, in any case, he wasn't the sort of man to stab
anybody in the back, though if the moneylender had been a
younger man, he, Payne, would have been happy to break all
his bones for him. There it was, and they could take it or
leave it. If that old fool, Hamworthy, hadn't got in his
way, he'd have laid hands on the murderer all right—if
Hamworthy was a fool, which he doubted. Blood ? yes,
there was blood on his coat. He had got that in struggling
with Hamworthy at the window. Hamworthy's hands had
been all over blood when he made his appearance in the
library. No doubt he had got it from the corpse. He,
Payne, had taken care not to change his clothes, because, if
he had done so, somebody would have tried to make out that
he was hiding something. Actually, he had not been home,
or asked to go home, since the murder. Mr. Payne added
that he objected strongly to the attitude taken up by the

local police, who had treated him with undisguised hostility. To which Inspector Henley replied that Mr. Payne was quite mistaken.

" Mr. Payne," said Lord Peter, " will you tell me one thing ? When you heard the commotion in the dining-room, and the cook screaming, and so on, why didn't you go in at once to find out what was the matter ? "

" Why ? " retorted Mr. Payne. " Because I never heard anything of the sort, that's why. The first thing I knew about it was seeing the butler-fellow standing there in the doorway, waving his bloody hands about and gibbering."

" Ah ! " said Wimsey. " I thought it was a good, solid door. Shall we ask the lady to go in and scream for us now, with the dining-room window open ? "

The inspector departed on this errand, while the rest of the company waited anxiously to count the screams. Nothing happened, however, till Henley put his head in and asked, " What about it ? "

" Nothing," said Parker.

" It's a well-built house," said Wimsey. " I suppose any sound coming through the window would be muffled by the conservatory. Well, Mr. Payne, if you didn't hear the screams it's not surprising that you didn't hear the murderer. Are those all your witnesses, Charles ? Because I've got to get back to London to see a man about a dog. But I'll leave you two suggestions, with my blessing. One is, that you should look for a car which was parked within a quarter of a mile of this house last night between 7.30 and 8.15 ; the second is, that you should all come and sit in the dining-room to-night, with the doors and windows shut, and watch the french windows. I'll give Mr. Parker a ring about eight. Oh, and you might lend me the key of the conservatory door. I've got a theory about it."

The Chief-Inspector handed over the key, and his lordship departed.

The party assembled in the dining-room was in no very companionable mood. In fact, all the conversation was supplied by the police, who kept up a chatty exchange of fishing reminiscences, while Mr. Payne glowered, the two Grimbolds smoked cigarette after cigarette, and the cook and butler balanced themselves nervously on the extreme edges of their chairs. It was a relief when the telephone-bell rang.

Parker glanced at his watch as he got up to answer it. " Seven fifty-seven," he observed, and saw the butler pass his handkerchief over his twitching lips. " Keep your eye on the windows." He went out into the hall.

" Hullo ! " he said.

" Is that Chief-Inspector Parker ? " asked a voice he knew well. " This is Lord Peter Wimsey's man speaking from his lordship's rooms in London. Would you hold the line a moment ? His lordship wishes to speak to you."

Parker heard the receiver set down and lifted again. Then Wimsey's voice came through : " Hullo, old man ? Have you found that car yet ? "

" We've heard of *a* car," replied the Chief-Inspector, cautiously, " at a Road House on the Great North Road, about five minutes' walk from the house."

" Was the number TBJ 28 ? "

" Yes. How did you know ? "

" I thought it might be. It was hired from a London garage at five o'clock yesterday afternoon and brought back just before ten. Have you traced Mrs. Winter ? "

" Yes, I think so. She landed from the Calais boat this evening. So apparently she's O.K."

" I thought she might be. Now, listen. Do you know that Harcourt Grimbold's affairs are in a bit of a mess ? He nearly had a crisis last July, but somebody came to his rescue—possibly Uncle, don't you think ? All rather fishy, my informant saith. And I'm told, very confidentially, that he's got badly caught over the Biggars-Whitlow crash. But of course he'll have no difficulty in raising money now, on the strength of Uncle's will. But I imagine the July business gave Uncle William a jolt. I expect——"

He was interrupted by a little burst of tinkling music, followed by the eight silvery strokes of a bell.

" Hear that ? Recognise it ? That's the big French clock in my sitting-room. What ? All right, Exchange, give me another three minutes. Bunter wants to speak to you again."

The receiver rattled, and the servant's suave voice took up the tale.

"His lordship asks me to ask you, sir, to ring off at once and go straight into the dining-room."

Parker obeyed. As he entered the room, he got an instantaneous impression of six people sitting as he had left them, in an expectant semi-circle, their eyes strained towards the french windows. Then the library door opened noiselessly and Lord Peter Wimsey walked in.

"Good God!" exclaimed Parker, involuntarily. "How did you get here?" The six heads jerked round suddenly.

"On the back of the light waves," said Wimsey, smoothing back his hair. "I have travelled eighty miles to be with you, at 186,000 miles a second."

"It was rather obvious, really," said Wimsey, when they had secured Harcourt Grimbold (who fought desperately), and his brother Neville (who collapsed and had to be revived with brandy). "It had to be those two ; they were so very much elsewhere—almost absolutely elsewhere. The murder could only have been committed between 7.57 and 8.6, and there had to be a reason for that prolonged 'phone-call about something that Harcourt could very well have explained when he came. And the murderer had to be in the library before 7.57, or he would have been seen in the hall—unless Grimbold had let him in by the french window, which didn't appear likely.

"Here's how it was worked. Harcourt set off from Town in a hired car about six o'clock, driving himself. He parked the car at the Road House, giving some explanation. I suppose he wasn't known there?"

"No ; it's quite a new place ; only opened last month."

"Ah! Then he walked the last quarter-mile on foot, arriving here at 7.45. It was dark, and he probably wore goloshes, so as not to make a noise coming up the path. He let himself into the conservatory with a duplicate key."

"How did he get that?"

"Pinched Uncle William's key off his ring last July, when the old boy was ill. It was probably the shock of hearing that his dear nephew was in trouble that caused the illness. Harcourt was here at the time—you remember it was only Neville that had to be ' sent for '—and I suppose Uncle paid up then, on conditions. But I doubt if he'd have done as much again—especially as he was thinking of getting married. And I expect, too, Harcourt thought that Uncle might easily alter his will after marriage. He might even have founded a family, and what would poor Harcourt do then, poor thing ? From every point of view, it was better that Uncle should depart this life. So the duplicate key was cut and the plot thought out, and Brother Neville, who would ' do anything for Mr. Harcourt,' was roped in to help. I'm inclined to think that Harcourt must have done something rather worse than merely lose money, and Neville may have troubles of his own. But where was I ? "

" Coming in at the conservatory door."

" Oh, yes—that's the way I came to-night. He'd take cover in the garden and would know when Uncle William went into the dining-room, because he'd see the library light go out. Remember, he knew the household. He came in, in the dark, locking the outer door after him, and waited by the telephone till Neville's call came through from London. When the bell stopped ringing, he lifted the receiver in the library. As soon as Neville had spoken his little piece, Harcourt chipped in. Nobody could hear him through these sound-proof doors, and Hamworthy couldn't possibly tell that his voice wasn't coming from London. In fact, it *was* coming from London, because, as the 'phones are connected in parallel, it could only come by way of the Exchange. At eight o'clock the grandfather-clock in Jermyn Street struck —further proof that the London line was open. The minute Harcourt heard that, he called on Neville to speak again, and hung up under cover of the rattle of Neville's receiver. Then Neville detained Hamworthy with a lot of rot about a suit, while Harcourt walked into the dining-room, stabbed his uncle, and departed by the window. He had five good minutes in which to hurry back to his car and drive off—and Hamworthy and Payne actually gave him a few minutes more by suspecting and hampering one another."

" Why didn't he go back through the library and conservatory ? "

" He hoped everybody would think that the murderer had come in by the window. In the meantime, Neville left London at 8.20 in Harcourt's car, carefully drawing the attention of a policeman and a garage man to the licence number as he passed through Welwyn. At an appointed place outside Welwyn he met Harcourt, primed him with his little story about tail-lights, and changed cars with him. Neville returned to town with the hired 'bus ; Harcourt came back here with his own car. But I'm afraid you'll have a little difficulty in finding the weapon and the duplicate key and Harcourt's blood-stained gloves and coat. Neville probably took them back, and they may be anywhere. There's a good big river in London."

"SEAMARK"

Jungle Whispers
On the Trap-hatch
Bojun the Mad

❡ The late AUSTIN J. SMALL ("SEAMARK") began writing short stories and novels after an early life spent wandering in all parts of the world. He was in turn gold-miner, cow-puncher and boxer, and during the War he served in the Navy and held the middle-weight boxing championship of the Service. Many of his tremendously popular books of mystery and adventure have given their titles to successful films.

28*

JUNGLE WHISPERS

CRAYNE CORRAY sat back in a vilely creaking wicker chair under a sweat-dripping verandah and mentally cursed the heat and the diaphanous gold god that had brought him in from the sea to this fetid strip of the heat-stricken West Coast.

At every fifty miles or so along that dreaded littoral the black fellow has built himself little, reeking, sewerless townships, and all the way from Konakry through the Bight of Benin to Kamerun those townships have become living mausoleums to the whites. Their names are dainty and inviting—Bolama, Sinu, Cape Palmas, Cavalla, Sekondi, Akassa, and so on through to Duala—but the curse of Boma rests on them all. The black fellow who first chose the sites has been pushed back into the primeval jungle which steps down blatantly to the back doors of the one-storey shanties, or subjugated to the service of the all-conquering white people who rule where they cannot even live.

Occasionally big money is to be made in those stenchant villages. It has to be made quickly—five years is the allotted span for a white man on the Gold Coast—and Crayne Corray had wearied of the weight of the Old Man of the Sea, who demands such exacting labours of his slaves yet grants fortune to none. So he came into Kanassi, which squats in the gloom of the lone Sierras, and set about making his fortune quickly. For two years he cultivated the black-fellows' friendship and made money fast. Then Africa got him.

The Old Man of the Sea slid off his shoulders with a disgusted flop and the Old Man of the Jungle climbed up in his stead. The swamp and the gloom and the silent, brooding mystery of Africa entered his soul. He had got over the stage when a man cries like a child in the night for icebergs and tidal waves of Arctic waters ; twice he had presented himself to the devil by standing naked in the steaming

875

downpour of the three-o'clock rains. Each time he had successfully induced a high fever, which boosted his temperature to dangerous heights, but sometimes gave him delicious surcease in the short recurrent spells of cold shivering. Oh, to be cold in that living hot-house !

But that phase had passed. Malaria and dysentery had taught him sullen lessons. Gradually he found that he could withstand the morbid heats and killing noon hours of the tropic swamps without undue relapse, and he began to chum up to the Old Man of the Jungle. There were twenty-three white men in Kanassi, and of them all he was the only one who didn't violently pray for the fleshpots of temperate climes, for the dear, sweet beauty of English girls, and for the cold nights when a warm eiderdown is an added allurement to a comfortable bed.

He counted out five grains of quinine into a half-tumbler of whiskey, added half a bottle of Antilaria, and gulped it down. Now and then a great humming thing boomed into the verandah, caught a baleful whiff of lime chloride, and boomed out again, petulant and annoyed. He swatted a couple of huge mosquitoes that foolishly made their coming known, and then watched another silently alight on the back of his hand. He waited until the thing had seesawed its body sufficiently to push its sucker-sting into his flesh, and then suddenly flexed his fist. The insect struggled frantically, but the tight constriction of the skin across the back of his hand held its sucker as though in a vice. He was going to kill it with the lighted stub of his cigar, but with a grim chuckle he released it. It rose with a faint hum of vicious wings and settled under the verandah roof.

" Little blighter ! " he mused. " I wonder just what niche you occupy in the scheme of things. Does a 'skeeter really know that he's nothing but a bunch of wings and legs and irritation to every other living thing in the universe ? But there ! I s'pose the law of life makes mosquitoes of us all. Elephants and kings, bacilli and beggars, we've all got to live—on someone else. Maybe the white man's sting is just as irritant and absolute, only we don't realise it. Ah, you little thug." The mosquito left its humid perch and circled away behind Corray's head. In ten seconds he felt the fluffy tickle of his legs as he landed, and his hand smacked home with the deft precision of long practice.

" Once, my son," he muttered, " is quite sufficient ; twice is once too often. Only fools and the favourites of the gods trespass twice on forbidden ground."

There came a soft padding on the hot earth outside, and a black head, covered with a wiry mat of tiny black curls, passed by the rails of the verandah. Okompo came impassively before him and broke into a maudlin sing-song of information :

" Boss, Missim Tenyah, I no can find her. I look alla time, one time, but I no can find her. White boss Minchin say she gone long time, no come back long time. Boss, I make look on sishor', but I no find her."

" Okompo, you very wise person. I acknowledge you done your best one time. Very wise. Thank you."

The black's unlovely lips wreathed across his teeth in a delighted smile. The other twenty-two white inhabitants of Kanassi would have vented their heat-rotted tempers on his head with a boot or anything handy to the grasp, but Crayne Corray alone among them had the entrée to the blackfellows' confidence, and he always treated them according to his own ideas. The others were just plain white men— colonial whites—of a dozen nationalities ; men who upheld the sovereignty of colour with the despotism of superiority.

How could the black, with his puny thirty ounces of brain, hope to combat or even think up to the white man with his massive forty ? The black was deficient in the all-important ten ; the ten that ruled and thought and pioneered. He had sampled that ten. The coming of the whites was his first intimation. The fact that they stayed and died and kept on coming was his second. Then the big steamships loomed out of the dawn and iron railways began to snake and twine among the almost inaccessible fastnesses of the vast interior. Bullets that whistled the song of death and came with the speed of anger hummed from the white man's outstretched arm and substantiated the existence of that other ten.

Even with their own primitive weapons the whites had established an ascendancy. Scotty, the old doctor, and an old-time javelin champion in the field events back in England, had astonished them all by throwing a spear fifty feet clear of the best throw of their own champion. Their own black kings had been lavish with the use of the whip, but even they, with all their experience, could not handle a rawhide with the precise skill of a white boss.

But Corray was different from the rest. He doffed his white crown when he entered Kanassi, and he only retained thirty-two ounces of his grey matter when he held converse with the Kroomen. He talked with them instead of at them. He ruled the blacks without showing it, and therefore he ruled Kanassi. Because of it he was not popular with the rest of Kanassi. They accused him of lese-majesty and ascribed the rate at which he made his money to his regrettable familiarity with the lesser breed. But Corray had little in common with the rest of Kanassi—in fact, his only real friend was the consul, Tony Minchin, the only other Englishman.

So he praised Okompo because praise was due, and he sent the child-man off in a welter of delight. Those few words pleased Okompo far more than would a dollar from a Dutchman—the Dutch did not praise ; they merely rewarded merit with a small gift. They held that it was debasing to be friendly with inferiors, but Corray only grinned at them with his eyes and spoke with the blacks much and often.

Gusteg, a fat fruit agent who had decamped from Senegal because a thousand incensed black-fellows were hot for vengeance, said that Corray ought to be spoken to. He averred that Crayne was far too thick with the black devils to be good for the white man's prestige, and he tabulated his reasons for thinking so. There was that awful scourge of tarantulas which poured into Kanassi and made existence a terrified burden. Men could only walk about in double swathes of heavy netting, and the foul things squelched underfoot at every step. They invaded every little tumble-down dwelling in Kanassi—except Corray's. And when the whites fled to Corray's for sanctuary they invaded every room and hammock—except Corray's. There was that terrible time last year when the monthly coast-freighter called and left their supplies on the landing jetty, and every single grain of precious quinine was perished and rotten—except Corray's.

Why was it, he demanded, that a thousand mosquitoes could sting him and yet not sting him ? Why was it, when other tortured whites were walking about with puffed faces and swollen eyes, Corray never even slept under a mosquito-net, let alone used the vinegar dab? Oh yes, he admitted that they settled on him all right, but they left no sting. Hadn't they seen him pick up a green centipede—most secure of all deaths—and nonchalantly fling it out of the window, and then as nonchalantly pick four legs out of his flesh? An ordinary man could have slashed off that hand with a sterilised chopper and then not saved his life. Why didn't Corray die?

And again, why was he so chummy with N'Gopo, the filthiest medicine-man from Rufisqui to Kunde? And why was he so feverishly anxious to send Laurice Tennier away from Kanassi—she who was the life and the soul of life in this heat-blasted incubator which the controller of circumstances deemed fit for human habitation? Ever since she had come out from England to learn the native dances at first hand for a big West-End drama he had urged her instant return.

Yet she, with her fresh girlhood and dainty ways, was the only living thing in Kanassi that made life bearable. And she could sing, too. Thus she made their evenings passing pleasant. There was not such a thing as a piano within a hundred miles, of course, but Grusonne was no mean performer on the violin, and Stennesborg, who had migrated from the Polynesians, could handle the ukulele with no little artistry.

What a picture she presented, in the sweltering heat-glow of the African night as they sat under the orchid-crowded flamboyants, singing little medleys of minstrel songs; she with the fireflies darting white lines of fire around the wax-like flowers in her hair; Grusonne with his bearded chin caressing his violin; Stennesborg with his thick fingers picking sweet melodies from the heart of the ukulele, and all of them madly in love with Laurice.

And she was vivacious, too. That fact alone was sufficient to pluck at their heart-strings, for vivacity dies young on the Equatorial coast; it cannot live in the heat zone. All grace and charm and eagerness are submerged in the listless flood of heat weariness that becomes a component part of the Coast character. But Laurice was too young to lose her sparkle yet. Everything was still a garden of novelty to her. The heat was merely tiresome, quinine was a minor nuisance, and crawling things a bit of an annoyance. But the great flaming flowers, the hot-house fruits, the black boys, the riot of green vegetation, the livid sunsets and the pulsing nights with the stars hanging down like diamond lamps in the black velvet sky, the everlasting play of the blue night lightnings on the silhouetted summits of the Lone Sierras, and the gentle, tremulous dawns with the soft sigh of the warm blue seas murmuring gently on the silver beach, were to her an enchantment from which she had no intention of tearing herself away.

Crayne Corray sat back and frowned.

" Where in blazes has she gone now ? " he demanded wrathfully of himself. " If she isn't on the beach she must be inland, which means that she is poking her silly little nose where it has no business to be. The only way through the jungle is by the native paths, and native paths only lead to native villages. Silly little fathead," he added. " She will learn such a lesson one of these days that all the golden dawns of ten Africas won't stop her from hitting the trail back to civilisation."

Minchin strolled up.

" 'Lo," he said listlessly. " Your boy came round to my place to find your gal, but I'm afraid she——"

Crayne smiled indulgently.

" She's not my girl," he said. " How did you get that idea ? "

The consul sat down wearily.

" Oh, cheese it ! " he snapped. " As if all the mighty city of Kanassi and all its myriad inhabitants don't know she's your gal."

He mopped his forehead with a blazing bandana and shouted for a raw lime.

Crayne looked at him square in the eyes.

" Minchin," he said, " I swear violently and honestly that Laurice Tennier is no more to me than the ugliest, fattest mammy inside Cancer and Capricorn. Why, I have only one thought in connection with Miss Tennier, and that is to get her out of this blistering country as soon as circumstances permit. If she stays on, as she vows to do, she will become a sun-dried, tired old woman of twenty-two, like the rest of our white daughters of the sun. But she won't go."

" Don't you believe it," replied Minchin with colonial

assurance. "You've only got to say to her, 'Laurice, my gal, go and pack up your frills and fal-de-lals in time to catch the next fruit freighter when she calls; I've an idea I'd like to marry you,' for her to go scampering off to her shack and start packing her traps like a prospector getting wind of a gold stampede."

"Do you really believe that?" Corray asked the question sharply.

Minchin flung him a look of withering pity.

"Your eyesight wants renewing," he said bluntly. "If you looked at the matter as deeply as you look for trouble with the niggers, you could see it with only one eye. You two are cut out for each other, and every blighter in Kanassi knows it—except old Gusteg—and he swears to have her himself."

Corray looked up quickly.

"Does he, by Jove!" he blurted.

Minchin guffawed.

"Haw-haw! Enter the spirit of competition," he orated. "See how the hero's heart awakens from a comatose slumber! See how his pulses quicken!"

"Oh, shut up!" barked Corray. "You don't understand, man. Gusteg is beyond the pale. The Ju-Ju has marked him down. She mustn't be seen by the blacks alone with him, she——"

The consul was staring at him with a puzzled frown. He put out a hand gently to pacify the wild outburst of the sun-worried man before him.

"There, there!" he said. "Forget it! Forget it, old man! I was forgetting myself. None of us know quite how conversant you are with the hidden lives of these niggers, but surely there is no harm in her being seen with Gusteg?"

Corray relapsed with a weary sigh.

"Minchin," he said almost tonelessly, "you don't know just how frightful is the volcano smouldering in the heart of that reeking jungle over there. I'm a good deal nearer the heart of the blacks than even you imagine. Oh, I know you think I enjoy a certain amount of immunity from all sorts of tropical annoyances which normally beset other men, but I will tell you that there are greater forces hidden in that jungle there than even N'Gopo dreams, and I've seen him do some devilishly queer things. Minchin, if the blacks rose to-night—oh, don't look so startled, man ; assegais are being hammered even now in the Hills of Silence—Gusteg would be the first to go. His would not be a pleasant death. You and I know that he fled from Senegal, and that is all we know about him, even though close inquiries were made among the whites in Senegal. These poor devils here in all their awful ignorance knew the inside story within an hour of his landing here."

" But—but——"

" Don't ask me how. How in blazes do I know how ? I only know that they did know. Call it Ju-Ju if you like, and let your questioning soul go to sleep ; it's sleeping well on the crater's edge. Tony, there are impis gathering over yonder that make the Zulu hordes look like little squads of children playing at soldiers. Africa will writhe when the eruption comes. No, they have no mysterious cannon, no wonderful new death-dealing devices ; theirs is the oldest and newest tactic of all. Numbers ! Heaven, Minchin, their numbers are appalling. The men-children go as soon as they can pick a spoor through a forest. The women have but one function in life ; a sterile woman is relegated to the wood-gatherers for the forges in the Hills of Silence.

" Ah, I know you smile at Ju-Ju, and yet you yourself live on Faith. Man alive, the black's faith is Ju-Ju, and his faith is so tremendous that he can almost move mountains. It's useless your smiling—I've seen what I've seen. I've seen N'Gopo doing the Devil Dance of the Snake Kings, playing on that horrible pan-pipe of his ; you can't hear the tune, you can only feel it. Maybe you've heard a big gun fired miles out at sea ? You know that the thing has gone off, and yet there was no sound—only a kind of faint woom ! on the tympanum. That's how his damned piping sounds. It's an ether disturbance—handled by an ignorant savage.

" The result ? Oh, about two thousand jet-black king-snakes rustling towards him through the undergrowth. They come gliding in from every point, heads erect and bodies almost straight ; hundreds of them all writhing and constricting in a seething black mass round his legs in the Glade of Snakes. Faugh ! He made me take my boots off ; he himself trod them underfoot like so many magnified garden worms. King-snakes, mind you ! He pitched a handful of stuff on a raised fire, and a thick, oily smoke literally fell off the fire in slow, coiling cascades and spread round the clearing. In five minutes there was not a live snake among the whole awful mass. Three or four trembling women came out and decapitated them, sealed up their heads in coco-nut husks, and away they went to the men who work at the forges, two thousand miles into the interior. There are whisperings in the jungle, Minchin, but only those who will can hear them. Did you ever hear of the Dead Emperor ? "

" The giant baobab in the clearing ? "

" Yes. Eight weeks ago, as you know, it was a thing of living beauty. We sat under its shade ; we built a permanent seat under it, because it was such a beauty. We gave it individuality by calling it the Emperor. N'Gopo heard about it, and smiled at the name we gave it. When the news came through that Cetewayo was dead, he pointed fiercely at the bole of the great tree, and spat out a torrent of words which sent the only two blacks within earshot grovelling on their faces in a transport of terror. I am the only living white who saw that little scene. Pilhaus was with me at the time and also heard N'Gopo's clicking hiss as he passed us : ' All emperors die ! ' That tree died in the night, as also did Pilhaus. Old Scotty—you'll admit he's as clever an old sawbones as ever chewed the Lotus—could ascribe no cause ; so far as he could see, Pilhaus just lay down and died. The Dead Emperor stands there gaunt and grim enough to convince even you. That is the kernel of only one little story of which I could tell you dozens.

" Tisaka the headman told me that Gusteg is already dead. Lord knows what he meant. I've given up trying to think along their lines. They're too deep for me, Minchin. He said, ' Boss Gusteg—him dead, alla time now. All same Dead Emperor ; dead. When him Emperor die him killed Gusteg alla same time.' You know their pidgin as well as I do. Couldn't have it plainer, could you ? Gusteg died with the death of the giant baobab. In our philosophy, the mere fact that he is still alive gives them the lie. In the black-fellow's code, it means nothing—theirs is an eternal patience."

" H'm ! I rather fancy lightning snuffed the Dead Emperor's life," said Minchin dubiously.

" Lightning ? Nonsense ! You know perfectly well

there was no lightning that night. And even so, how do you account for the ants ? "

" Ants ? "

" Yes, ants, red ants. I found them the very next morning ; a dozen colonies already installed in the huge trunk. Who in blazes ever heard of red ants nesting in trees before ? There they were, though ; countless millions of them. And old Gusteg shuns the tree like the very devil."

" What did he do out in Senegal, Corray ? You seem to know most things about the black-fellows' secrets. What was his crime ? "

" I don't know. He's an unlovable beast, and you may be sure it had nothing to do with the male sex. He's been up to his old games here with Tisaka's daughter. You know her, I suppose ? An extremely good-looking little kid —as far as black beauty goes. Her name's Kistie, and her father is chief of all the Kroos. Tisaka holds a big palaver with N'Gopo to-night about it. Gusteg's a blind fool. He may be an all-conquering white, but he's right up against it when he meddles with reigning chiefs' daughters. I expect there will be half hell let loose in the Dark Swamp to-night."

" My God, Corray ! Don't tell me there is such a place as the Dark Swamp ! I—I thought it was only——"

" Travellers' tales ? No ! The Dark Swamp is there in that jungle right enough, and within ten miles of us, too. There are one or two people in this world gifted with the knack of gaining the black man's confidence. All the black man's human love and respect for great workers goes out to them. I am one of them. They set no eyes on world dominion or any of the fool fetishes of the civilised people, but they live and slave for the day when Africa shall be the reconquered home of the black people. Their little tribal feuds still continue, Temanae boys still fight with Kroos, and the Madingo still squabble with the Bassa ; but at stated periods the whole shooting match link arm in arm, to go up and parley with the tribes a thousand miles away. Zulus come south to the Basutos ; Kroomen mate with the Matabeles. Tom-toms drone on the hillsides in the far-back blocks, where only the blacks can hear. The Congo basin alone shelters millions. Vast tracts of this mighty land are still unexplored, and unconnected by telegraphic systems, yet the blacks are in constant touch throughout the territory. They count in spears. One length of railway metal makes five hundred and thirty spears, and how many miles of railway steel have been torn up in the last two years ? So the tom-toms continue to roll and rumble on the hillsides—and you live on in faith at the crater's edge."

" And you ? "

" Oh, I'm all right. One of the jungle's whispers is that I am safe within it. I could walk through the forest to-night sheer down to the drinking-pool, which is a veritable Zoo at midnight, and walk back again without as much as a gnat bite. But the unseen eyes of the jungle would be everywhere. The holocaust is coming, Minchin, as sure as the jungle obliterates a clearing in the night."

" Then why don't you pack up and go home ? "

Corray smiled.

" India was full of Doubting Thomases before Cawnpore. Cawnpore died, but the doubters lived. Africa will have its Cawnpore before many years are sped. But I have no need to go home. I am beyond the pale, too—but on the right side of it."

Minchin twisted uncomfortably in his chair.

" I'm not casting any aspersions, old man," he said, " but you ought to get away south to Durban or Cape Town, and get the heat out of your body."

But Corray merely smiled again, and twisted the conversation.

" Which way did Laurice go ? " he asked.

" Dunno. One of my boys told me she had gone off with Gusteg. I should have a yarn with her, if I were you, Crayne. She's new, she's fresh ; she hasn't grasped the perspective yet. Life out here is one big joke to her. She can't realise that she is playing with fire, the way she teases the niggers. They're only queer, harmless toys to her, and she's taking her passion for getting their weird dances off too far. I saw her imitating one of their tribal hops the other day, and some of the nigs looked queer and sideways at her. She merely said that her art demanded a perfect reproduction of their dances for her show back in London. The niggers don't worry about Black Magics nowadays—for all you try to kid me—they've got a White Magic now, that we taught 'em. And Laurice wouldn't be over-anxious to face her friends again in London if some of those boys got hold of her in the jungle."

" Who told you she had gone into the jungle ? "

" Nobody. I don't say she has. I merely tip you the wink to tell her about it. To the niggers, the way she mimics their religious dances is like jazzing ragtime in Westminster Abbey to us. She's your gal, and it's up to you."

Corray looked away over the clearing to where the jungle sprawled like a flat ogre over the humid earth, and Minchin got up and strolled off the verandah.

" S'long," he said casually. " 'Fraid I shan't be able to come over to-night for the usual rubber—drafting the monthly consular for the next boat."

Corray heard the soft pad of his boots turn past his bungalow and head away towards the ramshackle club-house.

" Okompo ! " he called. (Other men yelled out " Boy ! ")

The Krooman came in with a stolid face, quietly as a cat.

" Yes, boss ? "

" You savvy white Boss Minchin's servant ? "

" Yes, boss."

" Go find him ; ask him where white Missim Tenyah go along. Tellum white Boss Corray send you one time. Savvy ? "

" Yes, boss ! " Okompo turned and slid off the verandah.

The shadows were lengthening across the beach and a red, fiery ball of sun was slipping down into the sea. A crimson drugget stretched down from the sky-rim to the foreshore, where tiny wavelets pushed themselves unceasingly up the beach. To the left, and round in a wide arc, stretched the forest, primeval, unchanged, unchanging ; as stark and unrelenting as when it rose at the dawn of time, a loathly thing harbouring loathly things to its bosom. The blood-red sunset hovered above it, and a rising, greenish vapour shaded it. A hoarse battalion of giant bullfrogs croaked stridently from its hidden swamps, and the insistent hum, as of a thousand invisible fans, gradually toned with the accretion of night to the faint drone of the awaking nocturnal insects ; but the half-silence was intensified and made more sullen by the loud bellowings and harsh animal calls which struck out of its depths with abrupt suddenness.

The remnant of daylight switched out as suddenly as one

turns out the gas in a half-lighted room. It was past ten
o'clock when Okompo came back, and he came hurriedly.

" Ah, boss, Missim Tenyah gone along Ju-Ju ! " he
quavered.

" What ? "

" Boss Minchin's black boy say she go see Devil Dance all
along Boss Gusteg. He say she——"

But Corray was gone—flying down the matted track as
hard as he could run. He hustled Minchin away from the
draft of his consular report, and together they raced up the
jungle path.

" Got your gun ? " Minchin panted. " I forgot mine ! "

Corray held his breath, and in his heart pitied the man
who placed his trust in fire-arms on a Ju-Ju night. Suddenly
the great trees met overhead, and an utter blackness welled
up about them. They went slower. A great, clinging liana
might be a great, clinging liana, or it might be a pendant
python ; a blacker shadow in the high, motionless grasses
might be just that, or something foully different. A huge
bird above their heads flapped away on heavy, ungainly
pinions, cannoning against the contorted boughs and
squawking resentfully. Green eyes, sullen and watchful,
peered at them from the encompassing walls of opaque
foliage ; warm beads of sweat dripped ponderously from the
interlaces above, and the steam and stench of the inner
jungle filled the air. The heat was oppressive ; growing
nature had gone moribund. Their clothes hung about them
in warm, sodden folds, and a ghastly feeling of foreboding
descended on them—on the one because he knew what lay
ahead, and on the other because he didn't. A creeping
terror stalked abreast of Minchin ; he felt himself giving way
to a compelling desire to scream aloud, to turn and fly back
along the way he had come ; anywhere so long as it was away
from the brooding horror of that sweltering jungle. They
stumbled into a mangrove swamp, and squelched out of it
again. Unseen things scurried out of their way at every
turn and twist of the path. Sometimes the lianas and
moving vines had crept right across the trail in the few hours
that had elapsed since it was last used, and a dozen times
they went sprawling. For two hours they struggled along
through an anarchy of vegetation.

" Little fool ! " Corray panted. " She doesn't know what

she's butting into ; it's the dance of the tribal sacrifice
to-night ! " Something flopped on them from above, and
Minchin almost screamed. He bit his lips without realising
it and stumbled onward. The black darkness grew more
intense. Faint rustlings came from the undergrowth, and
something broke heavily through the canebrake to the left.
From far ahead came a faint throbbing, so thin and vague
as to be almost a figment of imagination. Corray cursed.
" Run, man, run ! " he gasped. " N'Gopo's dancing ! " A
matted wall of thorn bush upreared before them, but they
tore through it and emerged scratched and bleeding. The
throbbing grew more distinct.

They rounded a bend in the jungle path, and lights began
to glitter through the creeper-choked trees. The throbbing
resolved itself into the grisly drumming of a tom-tom and a
gruesome murmuring rose on the torpid air to meet it.
Together they raced down the path until only a dozen yards
separated them from the edge of the clearing where the flare-
lights blazed. Cautiously they approached, and peered
through the tangled riot of fetid vegetation. Minchin
recoiled in horror. " Oh, Heavens ! The Dark Swamp,"
he gasped.

" Shut up, fool ! " hissed Corray, and began to work round
the boundary of the circle. There were ten great gourds
filled with resinous oil, placed at intervals round the foul
arena which flared and blazed with a ghostly white light ;
the flames leaping high to the vast dome of interlocked
branches overhead. Inside the ring of lights was the Dark
Swamp, a reeking, depthless marsh of aqueous vegetation
and malarious slime. It was one of those evil spots peculiar
to the tropic jungles, scarcely fifty yards across, yet as
bottomless as the pit—a vent-hole for all the noisome gases
generated in the moving bogs under the jungle. Kneeling
on a tiny raft in the centre of the swamp was Kistie, the
cursed daughter of Chief Tisaka. Listless with horror and
hypnotised with fear, she was staring vacantly at N'Gopo,
the medicine-man, who was whirling to the bestial rhythm
of the Death Dance. Naked, except for the chains of
human teeth and patella bones hung on threads of skin
round his loins, and the circlets of bleached eye-sockets
round his ankles, he was working himself into a frenzy. All
round, squatting on the edge of the seething swamp sat the

Kroos, broad-shouldered and thin-hipped, swaying and gibbering to the beat of the tom-tom. N'Gopo yelled, and a responsive shudder flickered round the circle of blacks, their eyes rolling and dilating with religious fear. The blazing fires gleamed on their shiny skins, and cast deeper shadows among the dim recesses of the trees. Here and there a broad spear-head caught and reflected a shaft of light.

"Assegais ! " whispered Minchin. "Kroomen using assegais ! "

Corray stopped suddenly. " Look ! " he hissed. " Look ! Over there by the altar ! "

Minchin stared and drew in his breath sharply. Laurice was standing there behind a dense thicket of bloated greenery and flaming orchids, gazing raptly at the scene. But she was alone. Gusteg had gone. Minchin noted with a feeling of revulsion that she was swaying to the rhythm of the Death Dance and that her right hand was unconsciously imitating the beat of the tom-tom. To her the scene held nothing of horror or grimness. She could not realise that death was brooding over the writhing waters of the Dark Swamp. The blacks to her were only jolly old niggers, quite happy and very inoffensive. To her it was nothing more than a weirdly staged spectacle, a scene from the scenario of a film play. Corray saw the eager intensity in her eyes, saw the delighted smile that parted her lips and showed the tips of her teeth, and he muttered savagely to himself. He silently picked his way over the spongy ground towards her, Minchin creeping doggedly at his heels.

Suddenly the tom-tom quickened its beat, and the whole assembly broke into a weird chant that blended with the dull thumping of the drum with uncanny effect. N'Gopo whirled on madly before the Altar of Death, and with a burst of wild incantation the whole circle began to sway from side to side on their haunches. Beads of perspiration glistened on the black skin of the medicine-man, and his anklets clicked like castanets against his flesh. Laurice, too, was dancing quicker behind her screen, her eyes bright with the joy of this new-found delight. Corray could not help noticing with a thrill of admiration that her craze for realism was tempered by a vast amount of ability—her steps were almost perfect. He tried to signal his presence to her, but she was too deeply engrossed in her study of the wild gestures of the medicine-man.

From the rear of the Altar of Death a dozen concealed tom-toms broke out with a stomach-sinking monody—tum-tum-tum, ti-tum-tum-tum—and the girl in the thicket picked up the quickened metre with her hand as though strumming an invisible tom-tom herself. At every few seconds N'Gopo flung himself high in the air and uttered a long, dog-like howl. At each leap the swaying tribe shuddered and gibbered afresh, and at each horrible howl the doomed girl on the raft trembled convulsively and gazed helplessly at the surface of the Dark Swamp. As N'Gopo neared the climax old Tisaka's voice rose in a senile piping. Instantly ten Kroos rose to their feet and flung something into the blazing gourds. The white flames leaped higher in a momentary burst of incandescence and then slowly turned to a pale green.

" Ah, the Green Death," muttered Corray.

Kistie screamed, and the whole chanting tribe uprose and prostrated themselves towards the altar. With a final leap and a loud-yelled " Kahali ! " N'Gopo dropped, gasping, to the ground. As though at a signal, the flames half died and a convulsive shudder shook the bodies of the prone blacks. Kistie screamed again, shrilly and in mortal terror, for the surface of the green ooze swirled and boiled and a dozen long green snouts arose, skimming across the top. Swiftly they closed on the frail raft, and there came a horrible clamping of jaws, a shriek that was cut off short, and Kistie was gone.

Then it was that the actress in the thicket saw Africa in all its grimness. Its whispers had passed her unheeded, but its stridently uplifted voice penetrated to her brain with a violent shock. For a brief moment she stood there dazed and helpless while the whole glut of facts sank into her consciousness. Corray came up quietly behind her, with one arm outstretched, but he was too late. Laurice shrieked —a long-drawn, terror-filled shriek, in which was distilled all the horror that gripped her soul. She completely lost her grip on herself ; the thing had been so sudden and, to her, so unexpected that the surging reaction submerged her. A second scream was killed in its infancy by the bone-hard hand of Corray closing on her mouth.

"Be quiet, you little fool!" he hissed. "Do you want the whole insane tribe on our——"

His voice was drowned in the angry roar that went up from the outraged blacks. They swept across the clearing in a tumultuous uproar of fierce screeching, animal in its very intensity. Assegais flashed, and a vast tide of black bodies crashed through the canebrake, the pad of their bare feet making the Dark Swamp quiver ; but even as they rushed round the thicket N'Gopo's voice rose shrilly above the din :

"Hold! Kattah! Back! I am N'Gopo, in whom rests the spirit of the Great Black Ju-Ju, whose father raised Tchaka, whose mother bore Lobengula. In my mouth the Great Black Ju-Ju speaks—the Ju-Ju will punish. Back! Thus speaketh——"

Laurice trembled on the verge of delirium. She felt the pressure of Corray's fingers in her ears blotting out the boom of N'Gopo's voice as he proclaimed the punishment ; there came a sharp twitching in her shoulder, and a blacker darkness than even that of the jungle closed about her. . . .

It was almost dawn when she came to. Her head was aching terribly, and the back of her throat seemed raw. A queer tremor was running down her right arm, and all sense of feeling had gone out of it. She strove to regain her faculties. Recollection of the scenes of a few hours before came gradually back, and she shuddered. She heard a voice speaking very near her in the darkness, and she tried to answer, but her throat was as dry and harsh as leather. She feebly realised that she was being carried. Her feet were on Minchin's shoulders and her head on Corray's. Strange how her shoulder kept twitching. Never mind— must be the awkward way they were carrying her. She gave up trying to think coherently and waited with a kind of dull apathy for dawn and the end of the dream. Again came a low voice from the darkness :

"Corray, look! The Dead Emperor ; he's down!"

They were rounding the clearing in front of Corray's house, and she willed her heavy eyelids to open. Faintly through the gloom she could see the vast bulk of the giant baobab prone across the clearing. Minchin was right enough, the Dead Emperor was dead indeed. She shook herself ; the silly twitching in her shoulder annoyed her.

Then another thought planted itself on her inner con-

sciousness. She could still hear the faint, distant drumming
of a tom-tom. As though from the edge of the world it
came—tum-tum-tum, ti-tum-tum-tum. A shiver went
through her body. Surely those devils weren't still mocking
that poor girl's death in that loathsome jungle ? Yet there
it was, as distinct and insistent as though the instrument
were just under her nose, and yet as vague and undefined as
though a whole lifetime stretched between her and the drum.
Strange ! The distance between wasn't so much a matter of
space as time. The two men mounted the verandah steps
and passed into the bungalow. She felt herself being laid on
a rickety old settee that had been fashioned by Corray's
Temanae boys as a mark of high esteem.

Suddenly Corray's voice bit through the gloom :

" Laurice, are you awake ? "

Somewhat to her own surprise, she heard herself say :
" Yes, Crayne."

There came a slight pause, in which she could hear two
men breathing heavily. Oh, hang that silly twitching
shoulder ! Corray's voice sounded again :

" Do you think you could refrain from—from hysterics if
I struck a light ? "

" Hysterics ? Why, what's the matter with me ? Why
should I go into hysterics ? " There was querulous doubt
in her voice.

Corray's voice became hard and incisive.

" You little fool ! Why in blazes did you meddle with
things beyond your ken ? "

The actress almost broke down.

" Oh, Crayne," she said in a half-frighted whisper, " I
didn't dream that Kistie was to——"

" Well, you know now, don't you ? " the bitter voice cut
in. " Now perhaps you'll leave Devil Dances out of your
repertoire."

" Oh, Crayne, don't scold me. What's the matter with
my shoulder ? Did I get a spear in it ? "

Minchin blundered out with a half-strangled sob, but
Corray's voice was very steady when he spoke :

" No, my girl, you didn't get a spear in your shoulder.
God alone knows what you got in it—or the devil——"

" Crayne, what do you mean ? Why don't you strike a
light ? "

"Because I'm hoping that N'Gopo gets here before a light is struck."

She started up. "N'Gopo? Oh, Crayne, don't bring that awful beast here. He's still dancing. I can hear the beat of the tom-tom."

"Or is it the echo, little lady? Listen now, try to get a grip on yourself; force your will to obey you. You will realise in a minute what has happened. There is something the matter with you. For the time being the Ju-Ju—which is Africa—has got you, but it will be all right again as soon as N'Gopo gets here. Okompo met us in the jungle, and I sent him on to the village with orders to the medicine-man to be here before the dawn."

There came a little gasp from the darkness.

"Crayne! My hand! It's moving!" The words came tumbling out of her mouth as though they hurt her to keep them in. "Moving! Oh, Crayne, what is the matter with it—my hand! Look! My hand! Ah-h!"

And a loud, pulsing scream rang round the bungalow, and Corray knew, with a thrill of callous horror, that it was the exact counterpart of her first awful scream at the edge of the Dark Swamp that night. He fought to reassure her, but shriek after shriek burst from her constricted lips. She clutched madly at her right hand with her left, but as soon as her flesh connected all power seemed to vanish from both her arms. A sickly horror gripped at her heart with icy fingers; for her right hand was ceaselessly beating, beating, beating; drumming the hellish tattoo of the Death Dance on a drum that was not there. And she could hear it! Tum-tum-tum, ti-tum-tum-tum. She stared with wide-eyed terror at the hand that drummed of its own volition, and from the edge of the world throbbed the sound of that distant tom-tom, dinning into her ears from a region that was bounded not so much by space as by time.

"Crayne, help me, help me!" she gibbered, hysterical laughter alternating with gusts of soul-stricken screams.

Corray tried to force her to think rationally, but she blundered round the room and fell into a corner in a limp, shuddering heap.

The dawn broke with a faint flood of light across the shimmering sea, and Corray sat down by the shivering bundle of nerves and fear in the corner. Gradually the light grew stronger, and Laurice collapsed when she saw her hand in all its ghastly reality beating relentlessly on a tom-tom that existed only in the sound reception cells of her brain.

" Thank Heavens ! " gulped Corray as she rolled over in a limp heap. He got up and hurried outside. Over by the clearing two lone figures were standing by the Dead Emperor, Minchin and N'Gopo. The medicine-man was glaring maliciously at a skeleton pinned in the branches of the fallen tree. The red ants are voracious devils, and Gusteg would lead no more chief's daughters to the Altar of Death. Minchin had fetched his revolver, and he was pointing it in a direct line with N'Gopo's knee-caps. " If you ain't inside that bungalow in two minutes, I'll blow enough pain into your legs as will last——"

" N'Gopo ! "

The black turned.

" Yes, boss ? "

" Come here—quickly ! "

The huge savage grinned at Minchin contemptuously and went into the bungalow with Corray. The girl was still in a dead faint, and Corray pointed to her.

" You'll stop that hand business right now," he said ominously.

N'Gopo looked hard at the white man.

" Your gal ? " he asked insolently.

Corray swallowed.

" Yes ! " he said.

" All right, boss. Go 'way ! "

Corray went outside and sat down with Minchin. N'Gopo came out after a few minutes with an evil smile on his face.

" Good gal, dat white missim," he said as he swung down the track. At the clearing he paused. " Boss ! " he called, " you take her long way 'way, eh ? "

" Sure," answered Corray.

" All right, boss—you alla same moskeeter now. You savvy ? "

Corray didn't answer, but mentally he wondered whether he was a fool or a favourite of the gods.

Laurice was very white and agitated when he went in again, but her hand had ceased its ghastly motion.

Three days later the coast freighter called, and on the decrepit landing-stage Corray pulled out a ring. In full view of all Kanassi, who had come down in a body to give them a send-off, he slid it on her finger.

"Tisaka gave it to me for this occasion," he said smilingly. " He insists on your wearing it—always."

It was a beautifully carved crocodile in gold, joined at the snout and tail by two mosquitoes. She blushed furiously and happily as they ascended the gangway, and the little knot of empire builders on the jetty howled a delirious farewell—it was the first romance Kanassi had ever known.

Behind the whites was a little group of blacks, keeping haughtily isolated in the background. Corray put his arm round her and pointed them out as the old steamer slipped her moorings.

"Look ! " he said. " Memories of old Kanassi ! "

Laurice looked, and all the old thrilling grip of the silent mysteries of Africa swept back upon her. For the little group of Kroos, Okompo, Tisaka, and N'Gopo were gazing stolidly away from the old coast freighter back over the jungle towards the Dark Swamp, where, for no apparent reason a scintillating curtain of mosquitoes rose, cloud on cloud to the density of a white mist, and slowly dissolved into the upper air.

ON THE TRAP-HATCH

MR. HILARY LYNDON, a gentleman if ever there was one, met Dago Nye on the trap-hatch of the *Fit and Proper*, at sea.

That fact in itself was wholly remarkable. In the bluntness of its happening, in the suavity of its occurrence, it stood as the keystone and capstone of a deftly manipulated miracle. When those two met they stared destiny straight in the eyes, and destiny itself surpassed ninety per cent. of its own previous attainments. When they sat on the edge of the hatch, looked at each other and spoke, that old archplotter of the ages, jealously guarding and zealously scheming, must have sat back on his haunches and grinned in high glee, proudly content in the knowledge that in bringing them together he had brought off the million-to-one chance.

For these were the odds against.

Ten thousand miles of sea and land stretched wide between the cities of their birth. Windswept dune and far-ranging mountain, sun-blistered desert and greeny-foul jungle, cold-running oceans and oven-dry bushlands swung out illimitable between their town and town, stepped away gigantically under and beyond vast horizons. And there were yet mightier wardens holding the barriers between. Kings, creeds and castes ; colours, class and tongues ; empires, parallels of latitude, ruled and rolled between them when their mothers' pain was ended.

There was Mr. Hilary Lyndon, born to the rights and titlements of all the Northern Line. A noble, splendid heritage. Twenty ships and a thousand men, a line of docks and a row of wharves, a stately home on the wooded hills kneeling down to the Channel's glitter, a name that was known and honoured in office and bourse and mart, and goodwill beyond price of purchase in the trading cities at the uttermost ends of the merchant routes around and across the earth. Stout keels crossing the round of the oceans, bulky with cargoes above and below the line, running their courses to spread-eagled markets, homing to harbour at hard-stated intervals laden with credit and burthened with cash, all heading full-steam to the vaults of his sires. That was the Lyndon heritage, the standing, hard-wrought heirloom of all the Lyndon line.

A goodly portion for even a gentleman to open his infant eyes upon. But that was not quite all. One other thing passed down to him through the iron-bound laws of inheritance. Had his sire been engined half so soundly as his league-eating steamers, young Hilary would never have got it. As it was, a leaky valve pumped unreliably in the tiny heart. Thus at the very outset destiny made quite sure that Hilary Lyndon would ultimately go sailing on the *Fit and Proper.*

And there was Dago Nye, born of a Greek woman to a captain out of Port o' Spain in a tramp that linked land to land at an uncertain speed of six knots—a deep-chested, red-rusted, shovel-nosed tramp running her easting down through the isles beyond the Horn. And destiny took him by the ear from the cradle, took him, most like, by the finger and thumb of acute distaste and steered him thenceforth steadily and inexorably towards the trap-hatch of a ship that was half of her still in the mines and half of her still spreading on the hillsides.

In the years that followed David Pedrigo Nye did many things. He came to be something only a little higher than an animal. By a slow and manifold process he acquired a hatred towards the rest of mankind that grew and grew until he attained to the trap-hatch. By devious routes he came to be that most repulsive of all creatures, a vicious beast, destitute of decency *and proud of it.* A sea sloth, he went ranging and quartering over the world to the beat of a million criss-cross miles, puncturing his halts with sullen-eyed rum-swillings in the sailor towns along the coasts. He robbed and stole and plundered. He built up a name for himself that was snarled at in fo'c'sle and tradeport and tavern. He did not merely envy those above him, he *hated* them, with a savage and bitter ferocity that was born of his own unreasoning ignorance. He achieved so black a sourness that it marched ahead of him a cable's length. He made the discovery that behind his back men had done the

29

obvious thing ; they flattened out the decent-sounding
" David Pedrigo " into plain, unvarnished " Dago." Which
he was.

Mr. Hilary Lyndon did more than that ; and considerably
less. He grew up. He grew up sane and reasonable. He
accepted the things as they were and honoured the powers
that bound him, shook hands with the forces that governed
and admitted their equity. He buried his father. He
proved himself a gentlemanly employer—his thousand men
mentally touched a forelock when they spoke of him. He
studied the needs of the Northern Line and added six ships
to the fleet. He found that his league-eaters needed food,
so he bought them a colliery of their own. On the six per
cent. increase of profit which accrued he bettered the conditions of his ships. He installed refrigerators that the fresh
meat might outlast the longest run ; paid good cooks good
wages that the seamen's meal-hours might be something
more than a mere matter of routine ; he raised the standard
wage of all and remedied their grievances from cabin-boy to
commodore. He chose his captains as much for their
humanity as their seamanship. He worked and strove and
laboured to make the Northern Line the happiest ships on
the tradeways. He played too hard on the leaky valve, and
the leaky valve turned on him and flung him out to the
curtain's hem. And destiny, bowing and scraping, inveigled
him a little nearer to the trap-hatch of the *Fit and Proper*.

" Er—eh ! Precisely," said His Dreadfulness the Cardiac
Consultant with perfectly restrained asperity. " I—er—I
must ask you to listen very carefully to what I—er—have
to tell you. You must take things very quietly indeed for
a considerable number of weeks. That is to say, a whole
year, if you—er—are wise. I—ah—I warned you last year,
if you remembah. Quite. You've been overdoing it—
drawing too heavily on a strength you—ah—haven't got.
Undoubtedly. You must get out of harness. Completely
out. No half measures. Long sea voyage. Not South.
North. Go North. Norway. Iceland, if you like. Yes,
Iceland. In Septembah. Quite. You've had a very close
call."

" But, doctor, I——"

" My *dear* Mr. Lyndon. You must please yourself entirely whether you accept or reject my advice. I merely

acquaint you with the facts you have—ah—paid me to tell you. Quite. The law of human resistance has, in your case, bedrocked itself down to a single phrase. Thus far and no farther. You have gone as far as you may."

Thus destiny, after uncountable manœuvres on the chessboard of life, fingered her pieces for the final check.

Mr. Hilary Lyndon, wrapped hugely in a great bear-fur coat, sat himself down on the edge of the trap-hatch and cast an admiring eye over the swart figure of Dago Nye beside him. Had he the slightest idea of the beastly loutishness, the inconceivable boorishness of the man, he would never have opened his lips. He was not to know that in Dago Nye he was looking at a man who was drenched and drugged with the bitterest virus of class-hatred.

Therefore he nodded affably and said, " Good morning. How are you ? I don't think I have seen you on deck before, have I ? "

Dago Nye removed a broken clay from among a clutter of broken teeth and turned and surveyed Mr. Lyndon. There was offensive disapproval in every line of him, crude insolence in the very curl of his lip. He spat on the deck.

" I don't suppose you 'ave," he growled. " I works for my damn livin'."

Mr. Lyndon winced and looked his surprise. He wasn't used to bullies ; and it was a new experience for him to see a sincerely friendly overture flung back in his teeth with a surly curse for no reason at all. Certainly one meets with all sorts and conditions on shipboard. Mr. Lyndon shrugged his shoulders and hoped that he had been mistaken in the note in the man's voice, hoped it was just the man's way. Sailors are queer folk.

" Well, well, work has its compensations in these latitudes," he said with a wry smile. " What is your special line—fireman ? "

Nye regarded the passenger with eyes that oozed antipathy and contemptuous hate.

" Now do I look like a clinker-knocker ? " he demanded. " Eh ? Do I look like a mat-faced oily wad to be bossed around by a perishin' crowd o' greasers ? "

" I—I'm awfully sorry," gasped Mr. Lyndon in a tone of shocked apology. " I'm afraid I don't understand much about the ranks and distinctions in the fo'c'sle."

" Then keep your blamed mouth shut."

" But—my dear friend—I wasn't being rude to you——"

" Yes, you was, blast you ! You're all the same, you and your crowd. *Passengers !* Ridin' first-class round the world on the backs of the likes o' me. Hire a berth for a trip and thinks you own the damned line. High-falutin crowd o' washouts—y'oughter be made to work for your livin's the same as I 'as to."

" But—but——" Mr. Lyndon stopped, completely jolted out of his groove.

Dago Nye wheeled on him savagely. " There's a rule in this 'ere hooker against passengers associatin' with the crew —and I'll trouble you to observe it," he snarled. " You've got no rights a' settin' on this trap-hatch at all ; this is a bit of the crew's quarters. Your deck space is for'ard of that funnel, and why the hell you can't stay there beats me flat. I never invited you along here, and I never spoke to you. And I ain't likely to. When I gets a hankerin' for the company of the likes o' you, I'll drown myself." He hunched his shoulders, glared out over the quarter at a mammoth berg that went sliding by like a great chunk broken out of a glass mountain, and spat again in an endeavour to demonstrate to the full his rabid aversion to the entire passenger breed, especially Mr. Lyndon, who was entered on the passenger list as ordinary Mr. Hilary.

Mr. Lyndon, mild and friendly Mr. Lyndon, blinked at the hulking brute in blank surprise. Nye was an entirely new type to him. For a moment he thought he must surely be joking—pulling his leg in one of those grotesque, far-fetched ways that are the birthright of the deep-water man. But a glance, a half-scared glance at the scowling face with the sullen, smouldering eyes, was quite sufficient to dispel that. Humour and Dago Nye had never met.

He couldn't understand it all. He had spoken to a dozen different seamen during the trip, had held technical converse with hundreds since he succeeded to the headship of the line, and always he had found the average sailor a remarkably friendly individual, a little too prone to pepper his English with expletives, perhaps, but certainly none the worse for that, since swearing is a fifth of the vocabulary of the sea.

Cordiality between master and man was part and parcel of the Lyndon ideal. He himself had never been known to be discourteous to even his most junior clerk, and he was a little aggrieved to think that anyone would be so gratuitously insulting to him. Nye was quite wrong about the rule forbidding passengers to associate with the crew ; the rule was framed with exactly the opposite intention—that members of the crew should not obtrude themselves on the passengers. Lyndon knew it. It was a rule that was a paragraph in every sailor's training, a rule that held fixed and rigid in every ship from tropics to iceblink.

Almost unconsciously his mind began to grope back along the conversation, seeking to discover the something he must have said which so blatantly angered the seaman. He must have touched him on the raw somehow, he reasoned—men don't go whizzing off the handle like that for nothing. And the tolerance that was an innate part of his own nature made him quite sure that he himself was to blame. Something he must have said.

Ah ! That was it. He had asked the man if he were a fireman. Very foolish of him. He ought to have remembered that, to each other, fireman and seaman are as water to oil. There is a pride of profession between them as hidebound and as inexplicable as the castes of India. The sailor regards the fireman in exactly the same light as the coachman regards the motorist. The fireman, for his part, looks upon the seaman as an unfortunate necessity ; his presence *is* rather essential to the smooth running of the ship, but the fact is admitted and regretted in the same breath.

Mr. Lyndon realised that he had undoubtedly given the man cause for offence. He was hurt about it—hurt because he had done it all unconsciously and because it seemed such an anæmic point on which to hang bitterness.

He fished out a flat leather case. A good smoke is a wonderful opener of doors.

" Here, old chap, I'm awfully sorry about that. Have a cigar," he said.

Dago Nye turned his head four inches and squinted at the cigars out of the corner of his eye. Mr. Lyndon held them out to him, perfectly moulded Henry Clays. " Take a handful," he said, " and ask your chums to smoke my health with you."

Nye looked at Lyndon eye to eye for two deliberate seconds. Without the slightest sign of hurry he put out a great nail-bitten hand and selected one. He flexed his great tarry fingers round it and smashed it to frayed leaves. Then he put it under his heel and ground it to fragments with a twist of his great sea-boot.

" You go to hell ! " he rasped, and went lurching away aft with his hands deep in his coat pockets.

Mr. Lyndon, his eyes blinking in dazed unbelief at such incredible brutishness, watched him go through a great bulkhead door into his own quarters.

" Extraordinary ! " he muttered, and looked down at the mangled cigar as though to assure himself that his imagination wasn't going the way of his heart.

" If you take my advice, sir, you won't have too much to say to that swipe," said a keen, reliable voice in his ear. The shipowner looked round and saw the clear-eyed face of Vincent, the third mate of the ship, looking down at him.

" Who on earth is he, Mr. Vincent ? "

" Chap name of Dago Nye, sir—an impossible beast. A dogfish, no good to himself or to anybody else. Sort of complete Bolshevist ; kill all kings, smash up all constitutions, annihilate all law and order—you know the sort of thing I mean—down with everybody and everything ; but why, heaven alone knows—he doesn't. Picks quarrels with everyone on board, except, of course, the gentlemen touched with the tar-brush, who happen to be as artistic in the use of the knife as he is himself. Type of swine who ought to be strangled at birth. I'd never have shipped him, only we were two hands short at Copenhagen, and it isn't easy to find men willing to sign on for a two months' Iceland run."

" You appear to know him pretty well."

" Oh, bless you, yes, sir ! He's a known character. If he had the ability to pass for his ticket he'd be a second Bully Hayes. But he won't, thank heaven. He's the most ignorant pig from Borneo to Bering Strait. When we get to Trondhjem I'll get the engineer to pay him off."

" The who, Mr. Vincent ? "

" The engineer, sir. Dago Nye comes under his department."

" But really ? What is he ? "

" A fireman, sir."

That night in his cabin Mr. Hilary Lyndon pondered long and earnestly on the inscrutable perversities of the night-born. A drumming in his temples and a tightness in his chest warned him that Dago Nye would be a good man to keep away from for a while. His methods were too primitive to suit the delicate dictates of a murmurous ventricle.

One thing, one little sidelight of the affair, persisted with him, against his will, rather tickled him : " Hire a berth for a trip and think you own the damned line."

" Oh, that was very good—very good indeed," he muttered to himself. " I wonder how he would have acted had he known I do own this—er—condemned line ? Probably have nailed me with a sheaf of grievances about this particular unit of it. Pity he didn't. I'd much rather have done something for him than have him think unfairly of me. Ah, well, I hope he finds a ship to suit him when we get to Trondhjem."

An hour later he was still pondering the incident and wondering why sleep did not come. All through the night he heard the far-away voice of the crow's-nest man, " Ice awa-a-ay-ay ; port she bears." And the acknowledging hail piping back from the bridge. For the summer was cracking the ice away from the stark land-edges beyond the Circle and the floes were drifting down on wind and tide in sullen, stately battalions. In his cabin Lyndon could hear those that passed close, crackling like volleys of musket-fire with the great lumps splitting away and the new fissures breaking open in them.

Bad nights those for captains at sea. They whiten the temples and gnaw the confidence till the nerves are dancing on their own raw-ragged edges and one is ready to believe that even the chronometer and compass-card are playing tricks in league with the ice.

He heard the middle watchmen take over their reliefs, thick, heavy boots clumping by overhead, the quiet tread of the second officer past his door on his way up to the bridge.

Then came the fog—and the *Fit and Proper* never got to Trondhjem. She never even got within hail of land. Out of the pulseless night it came, with awful violence, the white horror in the black darkness of the middle watch. A vast hill of ice, its summit reaching far up into the night above the mastheads, suddenly swirled up out of the wreathing mists and smashed its way down her sides. The tumult of its impact was as the screeching of ten thousand demoniacal furies turned loose over the belly of the deep. There was a horrific screaming of mountainous ice pounding through the pygmy strength of armour steel—and the plates were crushed and rolled back like strips of waterlogged cardboard. Her side was torn out, ripped away as completely as though a colossal battle-axe had shorn it out at a single stroke.

The *Fit and Proper* fell over on her wounded side in the water as though trying to hide the ghastly thing that had happened to her. Then the steam-pipes burst and the lights went out.

Mr. Hilary Lyndon was flung out of his bunk when the ship canted over. Trembling in the darkness, he stood and listened to the dreadful thunder of the inrushing water. He fumbled for matches and tried to get his bearings. Something had gone wrong with his cabin. Its centre of gravity had shifted. He was standing on the wall among a chaos of broken crockery and piled-up furniture. He struck a match and looked round for the cabin door. He was standing on it. He had to lift it open like a trap-door of a cellar. Then he dropped down into the cabin passage-way. Somebody passed him, rushing like a maddened bull through the darkness, pounding on the cabin doors. One of the doors was open. There was crash below, a whimpering gasp and silence. Mr. Lyndon groped his way to the main passenger hatch. He had the uncanny experience of walking *along* the stairway instead of up it.

The rails and boats were awash on the starboard side, the boats all smashed and shattered, hanging like dead cattle from the torn davits. Great convulsions were shaking the ship as huge air-bubbles gulped out from under her side. The crackle of musketry astern grew faint and fainter ; and the icehill marched stolidly on into the darkness. The port ratlines snapped away from the straining mast. A twisted tangle of three-inch wire descended on the syren-lanyard and jammed it. Above the shouts and cries and blasphemies arose the steamer's swan-song, the tortured moan of her last protest against the wanton injustice of the thing the sea had done to her, the senseless cruelty and callousness of it. The crow's-nest touched down to the water, and Mr. Lyndon saw the look-out man scrambling desperately back astride the mast towards the upright deck. He heard the muffled booming of the bulkheads giving way. One by one they burst under the giant pressure of the settling ship. Door after door went like the thudding of distant cannon.

Mr. Hilary Lyndon did not know it, but his one great concern at that moment was his heart. It was a source of hazy wonderment to him ; it puzzled him tremendously. He himself was too dazed, too stunned to be able to do anything or think anything rationally. He was a hopelessly bewildered unit of an irresponsible whole, unable to grasp at realities or to focus his faculties. His normal being had suddenly ceased to be ; it had stopped functioning. He was just a nebulous nothing that clung to a horizontal bollard and waited . . . and waited, with an incurious patience, wondering in a dim sort of maze how it was his heart still pumped. That was the most remarkable thing of all ; that leaky, renegade valve of his was defying even its own weakness.

Then the hatches went, blew out with a roar that echoed thunderously back from the rolling banks of fog.

And that was the end of it. He was in the water. Somebody chucked him in. Mr. Vincent he thought it was. It was his voice, anyway. It howled in his ear, " Swim, you damned fool—she's going ! "

Mr. Lyndon thought it an excellent idea, once he was in the water. The fearful frigid coldness of it struck into his very narrow. The shock of it, instead of closing down for all time that valve of his, jolted his brain into some definite orientation of sanity. He struck out manfully into the fog. There were moans and shrieks and curses coming out of the sea, all on a level with his own listening ear and his own shouting mouth.

He broke his finger-nails against something that loomed up out of the darkness ahead. He grabbed it and clung to it. Half a boat, rocking gently in the icy swell ; the stern half of a whaler, with a provision locker under the coxwain's seat.

" Dear me ; half a boat," he mumbled. " Now I know something about half a boat. What is it now ? Half a boat is better than—better than—eh ?—not ' no bread ' ; that's silly. Better than—what the dickens is it better than ? My God, what am I saying ? What on earth has happened ? Oh, of course. I remember. Iceberg hit us. Must

29*

have done. Perfectly logical. We went down like a ——"
Something hit him ; a gentle nudging bump at the back
of his head. He let go his clutch on the rocking piece of
boat and gripped his fingers on the new-comer. It seemed
remarkably stable. After ten minutes' frantic struggling
he got atop of it, a great flat, rafty-looking affair, square and
a hundred times safer than any of the mangled boats. He
began to cry out his good news to the others. Holding on
grimly to the tiller lines of the broken boat, he shouted like
a maniac, bawling aloud insensate phrases at the echoing
night :

"Here I am ! Here ! Here ! Swim towards me !
Better than ! Better than ! I can save you ! Swim, you
damned old fools ! I've got food here ! You'll be all right !
You'll be safe ! Better than ! Come on ! Listen to me !
I'm here ! It's my ship ! Come on ! I own the damned
line ! "

White-hot stabs were shooting about in his chest, and
about his eyes was a blackness that was even blacker than
the pall of the night. But for a manful, heroic hour he kept
it up ; through chattering teeth and constricting jaws he
howled his messages into the night. And all around him
the cries grew less and less insistent, less hopeful, less loud.
They petered away into a vast silence. And still the man
with the rackety heart, kneeling on all fours at the edge of
the raft, croaked his encouragement at the blanketing fog,
staring wild-eyed at the place where his ship had gone down.

Then a dim arm rose up out of the sea and clutched at the
raft. A face slowly lifted above it and a hoarse voice muttered : " Gimme a hand up, guv'nor."

Lyndon crawled to him and helped him up. He was exhausted. He collapsed on the planking and lay there gasping, with the water streaming away from him over the
woodwork. He spat.

Dago Nye !

And in an intuitive flash Mr. Hilary Lyndon realised where
they were. They were sprawling on the trap-hatch of the
Fit and Proper.

The dawn broke dull and freezingly cold. A few lone
bergs sat about in the sea in solitary grandeur. The iceblink winked and flickered along the horizon. The fog had

gone, save for little patches, dead white, that hung about the sea like steam columns. And that was all, the whole wide sweep of the sea was tenantless save for the two on the trap-hatch. An empty sea under an empty sky.

The two men looked at each other.

" Good morning," said Mr. Lyndon. " Lucky the sea isn't very rough, isn't it ? "

Nye spat on the hatch and looked over at the whaler's provision locker, tied down on the trap by the tiller ropes.

" Where ja git that ? " he demanded.

" Out of a half-smashed boat. I transhipped it during the night. You were fagged out, fast asleep."

Nye nodded. " There's rum in there," he said flatly. " Two tins o' biscuits, two kegs o' water and a jar o' rum. Fetch it out."

" Good idea. We'll both have a peg. Warm us up."

The fireman glared at him. " You'll drink water—and not so blamed much o' that," he growled.

" I beg your pardon ? "

" That rum's mine. I claims it in loo of wages due. You bein' only a blasted passenger, you got no call on it." Nye got up and kicked at the tin till he had smashed the lock. Mr. Lyndon could have wept. The smashing of the tin meant that there would be no protection for the precious little stock of biscuits ; the sea-water would make them un-eatable in less than twenty-four hours.

Nye drank rum and Mr. Lyndon drank water. The water had been in the kegs for days and was brackish. It tasted mousy, dusty. He nibbled a stone-hard biscuit and prayed for smoke on the freezing sky-rim.

The Dago grinned at him. It was a grin that held murder in it, a compound of hate and devilish inhumanity. He had eight pints of rum hugged against his stomach and a cursed passenger to taunt. Under the conditions, life was being profoundly generous to him.

" Ey ! " he said. " All that crowd's dead. Dead as last year's salt cod. Passengers ! That's all the good they are. Serve 'em right. They're all right when they're ridin' round on someone else's back. But they're no damned good at all when they've got to sink or swim on their own hook, are they ? Drat 'em ! Drownin's all they're fit for."

Mr. Lyndon sighed and gazed helplessly round the friend-
less horizon. He took off a great woolly sweater and wrung
the water out of it.

" Gimme that ! "

Mr. Lyndon gazed at the fireman in dumb dismay.

" But, my dear fellow, I——"

Nye hit him across the mouth, a savage blow that sent him
staggering across the hatch with his lips cut against his
teeth. " Blast your eyes, don't argue wi' *me* ! " snarled the
Dago and climbed into the big sweater.

By nightfall Nye was rolling drunk and hiccupping his
defiance to the stars and the blazing lights on the northern
wall of the night. Lyndon was gasping with cramp in his
thighs. His suppressed groaning irritated the fireman.

" Shut up, you ! " he roared, and began crawling towards
him on all fours, mouthing his passionate ravings as he went.
For two desperate hours they scrambled about over the
pitching hatch, a ghastly game of hide and seek, played on
a flat and heaving hatch-top twelve feet square that threatened to hurl them both into the water at any minute, hunter
and hunted.

But Nye was too drunk to get his hands on him. Sometimes Lyndon jumped right over him when the Dago got
him into a corner. And when at last the fireman fell over
in a drunken stupor, Mr. Lyndon took the other tiller rope
and tied him down to a cleat to save him from falling off.

The minutes and hours dragged themselves into days—
weary, dreadful days that had to be lived and endured to
their very last second ; days that alternated clear cold sunlight with close-packed banks of fog ; days when it seemed
to Lyndon that all warmth had fled from off the face of the
earth.

He had never dreamed that life could be so achingly void
of all that makes life bearable. Warmth had vanished, it
did not exist. He was numbed in body and soul.

Great wide-winged solan geese and full-feathered gannets
wheeled and screamed around them ; kittiwakes perched on
the raft-edge and mewed through the horror-filled nights.
Once they heard a trawler's fog-bell clanging through the
gloom. It came and went ; and the next day dawned on a
sea that was pitilessly empty.

Nye, with vermin cunning, had learnt a lesson from his

first night's rum-guzzle. He had drunk three pints of the
neat spirit and was mad about it. He loudly accused
Lyndon of having drunk it behind his back, and he thumped
him unmercifully to prove his words. But thereafter he
allowed himself just enough to keep the warmth in his body,
while Lyndon sat on the edge of the hatch with his jaws
chattering out of control.

On the fourth day Nye claimed the remainder of the provisions for himself, and told Lyndon to starve or drown.
" If you touch another biscuit or another drop of water I'll
kill you," he threatened.

Lyndon looked at the fireman as though unable to believe
his own ears.

" Grub's gettin' short," explained Nye. " And what's left
is mine. And I want it. I don't mind you lodgin' on this
'ere hatch, but you ain't goin' to board with me, too."

" But—but—Nye ! " said Lyndon incredulously, " there's
over eighty biscuits still left and—and nearly two gallons of
water."

" If I'd done the proper thing and drowned you off four
days ago there'd have been more ! "

Mr. Hilary Lyndon wept. He saw the Dago's idea—
plain, cool, deliberate murder.

He realised later that they were both slowly going mad.
He saw it in the red, despotic devilry that blazed in the fireman's eyes ; in the way he fixed his every movement with
his wicked, merciless gaze ; in the way he counted his biscuits over one by one like a miser fondling his gold ; in the
way he would suddenly shriek aloud and send biscuit after
biscuit flying with frightful thuds against the beautiful white
breasts of the following gulls ; in the way he gloated over
the passenger's helplessness. He saw it in himself in the
convulsive twitching that had suddenly set up in his limbs
and eyes ; in the absurd things he found himself saying
aloud—almost as though he was talking in his sleep ; in the
way he whimpered and wept for warmth ; in the raw
seablisters that he could not feel, but which galled him to
fits of hysteria ; in the terrible animosity between them
that had suddenly become a live thing, no longer one-sided,
but mutual.

On the sixth night Mr. Lyndon either went completely
mad or completely sane. He marched up to the provision

locker and ate biscuit after biscuit. They were pappy with fog and spindrift. He crammed them down, ravenously, feverishly. Then he tipped up the water-keg and drained it. As he lowered it he saw Dago Nye within a yard of him clawing towards him with screaming murder in his eyes. " Thought I was asleep, did you ? " he mouthed.

Lyndon shied the keg at him in a panic. It bounced emptily off his head into the water. Nye rolled over on his side and a wail of disappointment rose from the swooping gulls round the keg.

That night a yelling squall slashed down at them out of the north-east. It swept the provision locker overboard. Big, racing waves toppled upon them and drenched them to the skin with bitter water. They hung on to the side ring-bolts like flat crabs, while the hatch jerked about under them as though it were being kicked by great battering-rams. All night long the high winds shook them. Squall after squall drove down at them, whistling and whining in crazy-eyed fury across the smothering water.

Dawn found them tossing on a wild, tempestuous sea, weak from hunger and sickness. Both of them were three parts insane from sleeplessness. Lyndon looked at Nye and saw that he was swaying on the borderland. They lay and glared at each other on the pitching hatch, too weak even to stand up and vent their hate in action.

Along towards noon they drifted into the sheltering lee of a great ice-floe and the raft floated as flat as on a summer lake. The fireman reared up and staggered over at Lyndon. He got his hands locked round his throat and they fell to-gether.

" Die, die, damn you ! " croaked Nye. " What do you keep livin' for, eh ! Why are you still lastin' out ? "

Mr. Lyndon blessed the years he had lived clean. He shook Nye off. Nye was too feeble ; he couldn't even *push* the older man off the raft, though he tried till he exhausted himself. When the great test came it was the strong man who cracked up.

So they played the waiting game on each other. Flat on their faces on the trap-hatch they lay and waited for each other to fall asleep. Half a score of times Lyndon found himself dozing off. But always his own excited gabblings jolted him back to wakefulness. He was lying full across the middle of the hatch between the two great doors. And Nye waited—waited with the dreadful, unwinking patience of an animal. His foot was outstretched to the great steel bolt that held the doors rigid.

Nye never quite remembered the exact moment when he accomplished his coup. Things had been going very badly with him, and there was a vague, tiresome haze across his brain. All he knew was that he was quite sure he had twitched his foot and that the bolt had slipped ; and he was quite sure that the two great doors had sunk away and that the hated passenger had pitched through them into the water.

The rest was a slow, enormous drifting, drifting towards the shore. Stark and grim the great battlements of the land reared up from the sea, with the breakers thudding white at their feet. It seemed an uncountable number of days before that blessed vision rose ahead. But he saw it, saw it with delirious, victory-filled eyes. The onward rush of the shore-ward breakers caught him up in their stride and flung him ashore as though they were glad and thankful to be rid of the loathly thing.

And the warmth came to him at last—warmth in high and wonderful abundance, the dear delightful dream of all the castaways of the sea. Warmth ! Hot, rosy, comfortable warmth, in a great fur-dowered bunk piled high with blankets and a sheet-iron stove roaring away white-hot beside him. He revelled in it, soaked in it, let it permeate and drench him through.

Big, bony men came and looked at him—great, strong fellows, well-fitting that gaunt, forbidding land. They fried him unlimited flapjacks, cooked him great cans of beef-tea, joked with him, chatted with him, laughed with him. Oh, life was a great and splendid thing ! It was yielding his greatest desires, fulfilling his ears, his eyes and his senses with all he had prayed for and dreamed about in those hellish days on the trap-hatch.

And there was one of them who stayed with him always. The big, muscular nurse, self-appointed. He watched over him like a mother over an ailing child, worked for him, slaved for him, and never even showed resentment at his most imperious demands.

Nye didn't quite know whether he liked him or not. For

there was one extraordinary thing about him that worried
and pained and puzzled him. His voice. It was the voice
of Lyndon, gabbling away oddly to himself as he made up
the fire, warmed up hot rum, fed him with flapjacks, heated
the blankets and remade the bunk. Always and all the time
he kept up that incessant gabble of foolish, disjointed mutterings that burbled out of Lyndon's mouth on the trap-hatch.
But it was not the gabblings so much as the voice—it was
the voice of Lyndon.

There were days and days of it. Every one exactly and
entirely alike. Nye felt himself giving way again. It was
getting on his nerves. It rasped till he wanted to rear up
and take that great throat in his two hands and choke the
life out of it, to wring it into silence. He screamed at him
once and demanded his name. But the fool never said a
word. All he did was to continue his endless pottering
about round the cabin and mutter idiotically to himself.

The breaking-point came. It was bound to. It came
one morning when the great, hefty fool looked at him eye
to eye and coldly and deliberately offered him a cigar.

Dago Nye hissed. He rose up in the bunk, took that
great throat in his two hands and choked the life out of it.

And then the others came in. Frantic, furious devils they
were. For a minute they went mad round him. Then all
of a sudden they quietened down. They glared at him
silently, with a cold, malignant ferocity that appalled him.
There was a deep and terrible silence for a minute—a silence
that seemed to merge itself and become part of the gloom
in the shack.

The oldest of them stepped forward and looked round the
circle of faces.

" The rope ? " he asked, in a great booming voice.

The others nodded and four of them stood guard over
Nye. In a little while they all came back and dragged him
out on to the great black headland.

There were white clouds driving across it and Nye couldn't
see where he was till they halted at some wooden steps.

" We've built you a proper drop," said one, and the others
laughed. They trussed him up and one of them held his
hands over his eyes while they adjusted the noose.

Nye whimpered—somebody had started gabbling again
in Lyndon's voice, right in his ear.

The hands were taken away and he saw where he was. He shrieked. The vague, tiresome haze suddenly cleared from his brain and a convulsive kick of rebellion shot through him. He was standing on the trap-hatch of the *Fit and Proper*.

. . . .

His own kick knocked out the bolts and he dropped. The water swirled and closed over him.

Mr. Hilary Lyndon woke with a start, the echo of a shriek in his ears. The pitching had rolled him clear of the two great doors. There was a great square of water where the doors had been.

And ahead, stark and grim, the great battlements of the land reared up from the sea, with the breakers thudding white at their feet.

BOJUN THE MAD

AN ALEUTIAN LEGEND

AT St. Michaels by the Bering Sea they tell of the story yet : of Bojun the Mad and the story he told and his last tremendous telling of it.   When the driven snows are smoking along the barrens in head-high billows and the drifts are mounting up past the windward windows, they sit at the fires and tell of it yet, pointing to the gold medallion in proof of it.

They begin with the story of Ragnar the Swede, who died and yet did not die ; of Hellfire Buckley who killed him and yet was killed by him ; of the Lost Island of a Million Seals ; of the last amazing voyage of the *Golden Gate* and of all that happened thereon.

In the long nights, when midwinter gales are streaming down from the polar seas and the floe-ice is piled into Norton Sound like a vast city of glittering blue cathedrals, they tell of those things that happened in the far days when Swede and Saxon, Russian, Dane and Dutchman fought rail to rail in the fogs of Kotzebue Sound, slaying fiercely for the sake of the glossy black pelts bulking heavy in the holds. They tell of grim battles with the great Bowhead, when the sea mammoths died spitefully ; of the awesome day when the cod, outraging every tribal law of its kind, suddenly shoaled, millions and billions of them and, in a mile-wide chaos of hissing water, turned on the Eskimo fishing-boats and sank them ; of the day when the iceberg toppled and thrust up its mangled secret to the sky ; of the year when the east-wind failed, and the floe-ice choked the Bay till all the settlements along the Norton coast were mausoleums of starved and frozen dead.

Of all these things they tell ; but always they come back to the story of Ragnar the Swede.   For that is the story of Bojun the Mad, and he links it with all the rest.

Thirty odd they number, those men whom the ceaseless call of the sea for the strength of the young and vigorous has driven back from the ships to the cold land-edges where the sealers and the whalers crawl in to mend their hurts with hammer and chisel and welding iron. Swart, bony men they are, taciturn and much given to chewing bits of skin-hide as they sit and listen to the stories they know by heart.

Bojun's voice is a singsong monody and sometimes he stumbles for a word ; for Bojun is old and the north wind has bitten his brain. They nod their heads in appreciative content as the tales draw in to their familiar endings, or, when he stumbles, jerk the right word at him, lest he lose his thread altogether.

When the hundred and thirty miles of bergs have screamed and pounded their way out to sea and the Bay is open again, they will tell those same legends to the men of the whalers, and, quite probably, pick up a new one. The new one will be forgotten almost before the last impatient captain has paid his bill and is gone. Certainly it will be forgotten past all remembrance by the time the boats are back and the Bowheads clutter the beaches, black and ponderous as the hulls of overturned barquentines.

"Ah-he ! " mutters Sverik the Dane, " Bojun is too old. Why doesn't he die ? Thrice he failed in the story of how the walrus colonies fought till all the Bay was black and red with the frenzy of the fighting ; and twice again he failed when he told of Ig-nuk the Hunter, who trapped the Baldface with coiled springs of whalebone inside his baits of block-fat. Pah ! he is too old ! "

" Old and foolish. He talks like a child." Buckley the Sullen, son of Hellfire Buckley of the far days, gets his taunts in with a snarling sneer on his bearded lip. " See ! he itches to tell the story of Ragnar the Swede—of things that never happened. Let him tell it : it pleases him, liar and madman that he is. How does *he* know of things that happened on the last voyage of the *Golden Gate*—she went down with all hands. None came back to tell of it. How can *he* know, maniac that he is ? "

" Aye, but let him tell it. Bojun, madman, tell the story you remember."

Thus the story had always started. For winters out of memory Bojun had begun his story to that incentive. And at the end of it Buckley the Sullen would curse and revile him for a liar and a lunatic. And Bojun would glower at him and say, "Ah-he! mad, yes! But I know what I know, Buckley the Sullen. It is told to me that the sons shall die, even as the fathers did—die and yet not die, kill and yet be killed. Beware, lest the son of Ragnar find you!"

And Buckley would glare murderously at him while the thirty odd would declare it a great tale, worthy the telling, and that Bojun the Mad undoubtedly had something up his sleeve.

But that night Bojun told his story differently. There was a change. It came abruptly; with a jolt: like the shock of an electric discharge in the bunk-house. Bojun, with vibrant voice and red-smouldering eyes, was on his feet and into his story almost before they knew it. Gone the plaintive singsong drone, gone the cow-like disinterest in his own story. He flung at them so ferociously that Buckley the Sullen cowered back against the wall-bunks, staring tight-lipped at the teller, wheeled on them so fiercely that the thirty odd sat stiffly on their stools with tense faces thrust forward, mute with the wonderment of incredulity.

His first words knocked the placid calm headlong out of the bunk-house and sent a tingling prickle of anticipation down their spines.

"Aye, hear you the words of Bojun the Mad!" he cried. "I, Bojun, *who came back to tell the story when the* Golden Gate *went down!*"

He thundered the words direct at Buckley, who shied away from him, open mouthed. "It's a lie—a lie!" he screamed.

"'Tis no lie. I tell you of the last voyage of that hell-ship when she sailed out of here fifty years ago. I alone came back. I alone out of thirty-eight. Fourteen was the tally of my years when your father, son of the damned that he is, hocussed me aboard his ship. A boy-baby, a stripling, kidnapped away to a life of terror and torment by the vilest bully on the northern coasts. He robbed me of my boyhood, plundered me of my youth. Ye hear that, son of his? Your father kicked me into the fears and toils of manhood before I was even old enough to know the ways of my own birth. But what cared he for the birthrights of youth—

Buckley would have shanghaied his own mother were he short of men.

" You—you who were here in the far days, and you others who have heard the song of the singers and listened to the Eskimo *shamans*—you know what manner of ship she was. She was such that men, with the sea running liquid in their veins, men who *desired* the sea with the yearning of a man for his mate, picked up their dunnage and put the width of the Yukon between them and him when the *Golden Gate* swung her black nose into Norton Sound. Back they went, back from the sea to the river at St. Josephs, and across the river to Deminti : strong men, fearful yet unashamed ; for there is no shame in running from misery with a human beast from whose brain every cell of humanity has gone.

" And there came that night, here in the bunk-house of St. Michaels, when Buckley made his last effort to get Ragnar. For twenty years he had been trying to get Ragnar. Here by this very stove he and the mate of the *Golden Gate* made their last effort. But Ragnar was in ahead of them. He was quickest to the draw. He held on to his liberty by the snout of his gun, and men called him fool for not pulling the trigger.

" So Buckley took me, the brat who washed the pots and scrubbed the dishes. Aye ! he hauled me by the scruff of the neck to his ship out there in the anchorage. And when Ragnar heard of it, he, man among men that he was, offered himself as a hostage. He delivered himself up to Buckley that the brat might go free. But was that Buckley's way ? Hey ? I'll tell you that when the *Golden Gate* cleared to the open sea in the dawn, Buckley had claimed us both—the man and the brat.

" We were six weeks making to the sealing grounds. Mother of Mercy ! did ever a brat pass through six such weeks of terror and live to tell of it ? I have told you that we started with thirty-eight. Before Stuart Island had sunk astern we were thirty-seven, and before Nome had risen ahead another had gone the way of the first. Two in the first two hundred miles ! And all for no reason. Buckley did it with less heed than a hunter clubs a seal, with less pity than a sailor thumbs a weevil. He did it, as he always did it, to hammer his sovereignty into the heads of the others. ' And see you here,' he roared from the bridge,

' I can run this ship on twenty-four—and there's room in the sea ! '

" For eighteen days out of St. Michaels there were never less than three men flat on the bunks with faces battered and bruised. What can you say of a man who bashes the last man down from the yards, when there *must* be a last man down from the yards ? Hey, you ! son of the dead, what can you say ?

" On the seventh day out we were thirty-five. A Finn jumped overboard. Ye hear that ? A Finn. On the seventh day ! With two dead already on the log ! And we knew then we were a ship of the damned. The big seas came, the wild seas, the great green seas alive with the anger of the deeps—and the bell tolling all night at the heel of the mast. The raging armies of the sea drove us back, back past Cape Lisburne and Seppings, back through Kotzebue and Bering Sound. They mauled us and smashed us and shook us. They roared inboard in sullen green surges, eddying white where they raced round the masts, loud with the tumult of their own might. They plunged across the decks like avenging gods, thundering against the for'ard bulkheads with righteous anger. It was the uprising of the green devils of the sea against the ship that insulted their strength. It was a rebellion : the children of the Old Woman of the Sea were pounding on the doors of the *Golden Gate*, a death-warrant in the fingers of every sea that crashed aboard.

" Aie ! the sea had turned against Buckley at last. And who can stand against the sea ? He had outraged her ways since the first day he broke from the land ; and the Old Woman was calling for him. She had named him. We should all have gone to our doom that night had not I, the brat, done the proper thing. On the urging of the crew, I, the youngest, threw my Bible to the waters. And the seas went down. They were still angry and spilling over with resentment, but they went down. They wanted Buckley.

" We were worn out with fatigue, skeletons of men who slept in wet blankets on dripping bunks ; and Hellfire Buckley made the cook douse his fires so that we lacked even the warmth of hot cocoa. That was the way of the man. Up on the yards he drove us, to battle and toil at the ice-hard canvas, till our nails were smashed and our finger-ends burst.

"And then he tacked. With the men still up there, clinging for life to the frozen man-ropes, he put the helm up and let the yards thud over in the wind. Strained shoulder-blades and torn muscles for every man aloft—and a lump of galley-coal in a tarpaulin shirt for the fool who fell. And Buckley jeering at them from the bridge, in Dago. Not man but devil, I tell you, and the sea was after him. Kaspar the Pole, who was a warlock and knew the ways of death in the sea, said he was already dead. The sea had already claimed him and was only biding its time."

Bojun paused in his tempest of words and glared heatedly round the circle of staring faces. The look in his eyes was at once a taunt and a challenge.

"Will you laugh to-night when I tell of the gold medal-lion "—he blazed—" you, who have always grinned at me from behind your eyes when I speak of the medal that Ragnar wore ? Aie ! to-night I will show you that medal ! "

Dumb, silent faces stared a sober response. They were awed by a feeling, deep-grounded in their hearts, that tragedy, swift and stark, was rushing up behind Bojun's melodrama. He was racing it to a climax. They saw it in the passionate vehemence of his wild new story, in the ring of truth vibrating through it, in the animal yammering that suddenly leapt to the mouth of Buckley the Sullen when Bojun made mention of the gold medallion.

Bojun spun round on Sverik the Dane. "You have harried the seal on the breeding-grounds," he declared. "You have sat at the fires in all the settlements from Point Barrow to Unalaska, and you have heard the tales they tell. Eskimo, Russian, Aleut, and Sitka, they all tell their tales. All the way through on the frozen coasts. And they all give mention to the Lost Island of a Million Seals. Is it not so ? It has been handed down in the legends ; therefore there is truth in it. Somewhere up there in the smoky seas that no man ever sails is the Lost Isle of a Million Seals. It is the great breeding-ground for all the seal-herds of all the North. It is the Seal Home, the great centre from which the colonies emigrate. Up there beyond the Circle. Is that not so ? "

Sverik nodded a ponderous affirmation, chewing rapidly at his skin-hide.

" That island was found by a whaling captain back in the far days. He was blown out of his course and sheltered in the lee of her. Thus he found one of the secrets of the sea, a secret the sea had a right to keep. The seals belong to the sea ; they are hers. Man plunders them season by season, those she lets go ; but the secret of the main womb of her seals was a secret she had a right to keep. She kept it. Of that crew only three came back, and they left their brains on the island. They came back softies, knowing naught of what had happened, save one, who, before the madness got him, stamped the bearings of that island into a gold medallion. And Ragnar nursed him. But he died. They all died. And Ragnar came by the medal.

" Ragnar was a good man. He honoured the sea as he believed in his God. He acknowledged her lawful rights and he let her keep the secret of the seals. See you ! One single journey to that island would have filled his house with riches beyond the power of his spending. But Ragnar never went ; for there are some secrets that must not be tampered with. But somewhere up there is the fountainhead of all the herds—and Ragnar had its dead reckonings.

" That was why for twenty years Buckley had schemed to get Ragnar. When he got him he did that to him which condemned his own immortal soul. Buckley pitted his greed against the might and power of the sea. For four weeks Buckley hounded and harried the Swede to wring his secret from him. Days there were when Ragnar could not talk for the blows of Buckley's fists. And then Buckley did the mad thing : he killed Ragnar.

" For an hour they fought on the bridge. Ragnar went down. He always went down. In a wild and stormy sea, on a plunging, reeling bridge, they fought till Ragnar could fight no more. And Buckley threw him overboard.

" Aie ! but that was a death any sailor could die. We have all come near to death that way, close in the soul of the sea. But the way Ragnar went out was a devilry the sea was bound to avenge. Buckley *towed* him on the end of a line.

" He and the mate dragged him aft and propped him against the stern rail. ' Scandiwegian,' he said, ' you get your last chance to eat wisdom. Give me that medal and I'll split profits with you.'

" And Ragnar looked at him through eyes that were puffed near to blindness. Buckley held out his hand for the medal. But all he got was the voice of Ragnar, cold and dogged, which said, ' I would not trust your word, you spawn of Satan's first mate, not if all your dead ancestors were lined up behind you, standing bond for the oath you took ; not if your own mother was tottering on the brink of death, waiting for the breaking of your oath to push her over, I wouldn't trust you, not if your own son——'

" But Buckley, with his eyes showing white in the frenzy of his passion, leapt in upon him. He caught him up by the middle and threw him into the tumbling waters astern. The drag of the tow took him down, down. Only once he came up, shooting high out of the water with the speed of the pull. And I, the brat, hauled in the limp line when the killers got him. I was crying as I did it, weeping cold tears of fear, overwhelmed with the awfulness of the thing they had thrust before my eyes. I could not see the rope for the horror of it, but as I hauled it in I felt the scorching burn of the medal under my heel. Ragnar had thrust it upon me to hide in my boot.

" That was how Ragnar died. I have told you the story fair. And now all you who have listened shall hear how Ragnar came back.

" He came back that night, at midnight with the bell clanging of its own accord, echoing the dread of death through the timbers of the *Golden Gate*. Hand over hand over the stern he came, all wet and dripping with the tears of the sea. With the broken rope still tight round his waist and his eyes wide open, he walked across the reeling deck and up the companion-way to the bridge. The helmsman turned at the binnacle and saw him, Ragnar the Swede, with the sea-water streaming from him, come back to take his trick at the wheel.

" He ran from the wheel-house with a face of chalk. I was in my bunk on the wall in the black darkness of the f'c'sle, but I heard the rush of his boots along the deck outside, heard him fall sprawling into the scuppers as the ship kicked against a sea. Then he rushed in through the fo'c'sle door and flung himself under the sodden blankets on his bunk.

" ' What ails you, Karl,' I whispered, scared in the darkness.

" ' Mercy, have mercy on us ! There's a dead man at the wheel. Ragnar is up there at the binnacle.'

" Kaspar the warlock heard it and rocked on his bunk. ' We're all dead men,' he moaned. ' Ragnar will come every night till the sea takes us.'

" We felt the ship staggering off to port. Ragnar was putting us on the course of a madman. We had sail out on every mast and near half a gale was streaming down from the north. Great seas thundered broadside against us and we heeled over to the press of the wind. The mate ran up from his cabin with a pistol in his hand and murder in his eyes. But he found nothing. Only a ship that held dead on its mad course—and a wheel that spun useless in his hands.

" All night long the watch worked and slaved at the wheel. Every connection to the rudder was out of gear, broken. And all night long the *Golden Gate* held on to her course. North by west she headed—and the log-line telling of a ceaseless twelve knots rolled out with the steadiness of an ocean liner.

" By noon the seas were running bridge high and the wind was droning a death-song in the rigging. But on she plunged with her lee rails awash and her canvas bursting to ribbons like cannon shots up on the yards. Did Buckley falter ? Did he draw back ? Aie ! He drove us up on the yards with a sealing club to spread more canvas and to trim it against the wind. That ceaseless twelve knots maddened him. Mile by mile it was taking us out of the known sealing courses ; and he swore he'd put a brake on it if he cracked the masts out of her. We rove strengthening guys to the mastheads and trimmed the sails into wind.

" Thus Buckley tried to pit his seamanship against the Old Woman herself. And what happened ? Hey ? What did the Old Woman do ? She shifted the wind. A hurricane flailed down at us from dead ahead, a hurricane that piled the seas over our fo'c'sle in great rolling hills. The masts snapped out like icicles struck by a mushpole. They crashed in a tangled litter of wires and spars and cordage, cluttering the decks in a tugging, straining mass, dragging yard by yard over the side. We rushed to chop away the wreckage. And the *Golden Gate*, without a stick or a spar, drove on into the hurricane as though she were working on

boilers and churning screws. Ye hear that ? A bare hull,
without a mast or a sail, logging twelve knots against a gale.
" We fled to the fo'c'sle. Neither fists nor boots could
drive us out. We were dead with fear. So Buckley and
the mate worked at the wheel alone.

" And at midnight Ragnar came again. He saw what
they had done ; and he jammed the wheel. He jammed it
so that fourteen men, heaving at it with the fear of death
in their muscles, could not move it. I crawled aft and
peered down over the stern. The rudder was swinging aimlessly in the little pool of idle water behind the sternpost.
Thus we went on night after night, with Ragnar coming
aboard each middle watch to take his bearings and trim her
course.

" Sometimes the seas were so hungry for us that we hung
stationary on our course with the seas making twelve knots
under us. For days there was no sun, only a half-light over
the smothering waters, a dim gloom that scarce lit the frenzy
of the sea-armies. Alone in an empty sea, with a dead man
at the wheel, we drove along sheer into the face of the wind.
There was no look-out, no helm, no crew, no captain : just
a ship of the dead careering along to her doom. Buckley
and the mate locked themselves in the cabin, drinking their
fears deeper into their souls. We stayed huddled in the
galley, with ropes round our waists to the galley stanchions.
We were rolling rails under, and heavy with the weight of
water in the holds.

" The end came in the blackness of the night. Spindrift
was lashing along the bare decks in long, smothering lines,
and the combers were breaking aboard. Through the galley
scuttles we saw Ragnar pass on his way up to the bridge.
He did not look at us, but with his eyes straight ahead and
the broken tow-rope trailing behind him, he went up the
companion-way and was lost in the blackness above. Then
Buckley went up. He must have seen him come aboard.
He had a gun in his hand and he was shouting drunk.

" We struck as he got to the wheel-house. With a crash
that flung us all against the galley lockers, she drove ashore.
There was a smashing and a rending and a bursting of
timbers, a mighty grinding of wood against granite, and
then the seas began to burst over us. The crew ran out
and the sea madness got them. One screamed that he could

see the lights of a city through the darkness. They jumped overboard with their faces turned to lights that were not there. Four of them stayed to make a raft before they, too, went out to meet the Old Woman of the Sea.

I crawled up to the chart-house and fired a signal rocket. It roared up into the night and burst high up in the darkness. A blood-red glare streamed out, falling slow. Aie, my skin prickled all over. For out of the darkness around came a bellowing roar that swelled and grew until it seemed that all the devils and furies that ever died in the night were trumpeting in millions around us. I heard the clamour and din of it and I knew what we had struck. We were pounding our fo'c'sle to pulp on the granite fangs of Lost Island and the dog-seals were giving tongue. Aie ! the devil himself must have laughed aloud when Ragnar put us on that course.

" Hey, Buckley the Sullen ! D'ye know the way of your father's death ? I found him strangled next morning in the wheel-house. There were three turns of rope round his neck. Ragnar had done it with the bit of tow-rope. Ya ! that was the way of Hellfire Buckley's death, up there in the smoky seas, by the hand of the last man he killed.

" For four weeks I was on that island, alone with the seals and the screaming gulls. And, Buckley the Sullen, I came back ! I came back because the Old Woman of the Sea helped me. I stayed on the *Golden Gate* till the seas went down. She calmed them quickly. The third morning broke fair and fine. The Old Woman was appeased. She did not want me. I had given her my Bible.

" I got one of the sealing boats and mended it. She washed planks ashore from the *Golden Gate* to me, that I might do it quickly and well. For four weeks I toiled at the boat. Then I filled it with food and ballasted it with water. When I hoisted the stuns'l and sped away to the south-east she gave me a soft wind and a following sea.

" You, you who have sailed with the northbound whalers, you have knowledge of the *Valdespar* ? She picked me up on the tenth day. She was running her course down from Nuwuk and I was asleep in the boat.

" Will you grin at me now from behind your eyes when I tell of these things : I, who came back ? See you ! I will tell you there is one among you, loudest in his scoffings, who has always believed in these things. He has believed in them so well that a hundred times he has tried to steal my medal."

He paused and glared full in the eyes of Buckley the Sullen. " That," he blazed, " is the story of Ragnar the Swede, the story of Jan Ragnar, *my father* ! "

Buckley yelped aloud with fear and fright. He crawled backwards to the angle of the bunk-house, whimpering with his hand on his breast pocket.

Then, like the crack of a pistol, the question shot across the bunk-house : " Buckley, what have you done with my father's medal ? "

Before a hand could be raised to stop him, Buckley pulled his gun. With a dry gasp in his throat, he fired at the son of Ragnar. Like whip-cracks the bullets leapt across between. The thirty odd saw the shock of them hitting into Bojun's body. The powder smoke gouted from the gun muzzle in quick, abrupt puffs. And Bojun the Mad, with the bullets spitting into him, walked unsteadily towards them. One, two, three, four, five, six, seven, the bullets smashed across the bunk-house, and, then, the hammer clicked sharply on the empty chambers. Buckley, with the spent gun hanging limp in his hand, stared wildly at the advancing figure.

" Even as the fathers died," said Bojun, with his eyes glazing. He swayed against the sheet-iron stove and his hand went slowly down to his own gun.

Buckley screamed and leapt, but the bullet met him half-way, a single shot that went clean through his breast and made him spin round before he fell. The thirty odd swear that Bojun's eyes were already closed in death when his finger tightened on the trigger.

But at St. Michaels by the Bering Sea they tell of the story yet, pointing to the little gold medallion in proof of it : the little gold medallion, with a bullet-hole clean through the centre, which they took from the breast pocket of Buckley the Sullen.

EDGAR WALLACE

The Magic of Fear
The Man who Sang in Church
The Poetical Policeman

¶ The late EDGAR WALLACE'S life-
story was one of the most exciting of
any that an author has been able to tell.
He started life in a London slum, was
educated in a Board school, and sold
newspapers in the street. After being
a soldier and correspondent in the
Boer War, he turned to novel writing,
The Four Just Men appearing in 1906.
But it was not until after the War that
his fame as a writer of "thrillers"
spread throughout the world.

THE MAGIC OF FEAR

I

ALL this happened in the interim between excellencies, or it could hardly have happened at all.

His Excellency, the retiring Administrator of the Reserved Territories, had departed amidst the banging of guns and the playing of the National Anthem by a small band of near-white musicians, all of whom, and especially the cornet, had a tendency to play flat. The new Excellency was enduring the agony of gout at his house in Budleigh Salterton in Devon, and his departure from home was indefinitely postponed.

A change of administration made little or no difference to the people of the big river, and Captain Hamilton of the King's Houssas, for one, was hardly conscious of the lacuna as he strode savagely towards the hut which housed his youthful second in command.

His annoyance was well warranted, for Lieutenant Tibbetts had committed the unpardonable crime of writing to the newspapers—a weakness of his. Hamilton was moist and furious, for the afternoon sun blistered the world, and as he crossed the yellow oven-floor called a parade ground, the heat of it came through the soles of his boots and tortured him.

The barrack hutments which formed one side of the square danced and shimmered in the heat haze ; he saw the fronds of the Isisi palms in a blur ; even the weaver birds were silent : when it grows too hot for the weavers to talk, it is very hot indeed.

Kicking open the door of Lieutenant Tibbetts's hut, he stepped in and snorted his disgust. Mr. Tibbetts, whose other name was Bones, lay face upward on the top of his bed ; and he was arrayed in a costume beyond forgiveness, for not Solomon in all his glory wore purple pyjamas with alternate green and ochre stripes.

Hamilton flung down upon the table the paper he had been carrying as Bones opened one eye.

" 'Morning, sir," he said, slightly dazed. " Is it still raining ? "

" 'Morning ! " snapped Hamilton. " It is within an hour of dinner, and I've something to say to you, Bones ! "

Bones relapsed into slumber.

" Wake up, and hide your hideous feet ! "

The eyelids of the sleeper fluttered ; he murmured something about not seeing the point—he had at least seen the newspaper, and recognised the Gothic title-piece.

" The point is, Bones," said Hamilton awfully, " nobody knows better than you that it is an offence for *any* officer to write to the newspapers on *any* subject ! This "—he smacked the folded newspaper on the table—" this is an outrage ! "

" *Surrey Star and Middlesex Plain Dealer*, sir," murmured Bones, his eyes closed, a picture of patience, forbearance and resignation, " with which, sir, is incorporated the *Sunbury Herald and Molesey Times*, sir."

His long body was stretched luxuriously, his hands were clasped beneath his head, his large red feet overhung the end of the bed. He had the air and manner of one who was deeply wronged but forgave his enemies.

" It doesn't matter *what* paper you write to——"

" ' To which you write,' dear old officer," murmured Bones. " Let us be jolly old grammarians, sir, an' superior ; don't let us go around debasin' the language——"

" Get up, you insubordinate devil, and stand on your big feet ! " hissed the Captain of Houssas ; but Lieutenant Tibbetts did not so much as open his eyes.

" Is this a friendly discussion, or isn't it, dear old sir ? " he pleaded. " Is it a friendly call or a council of war, dear old Ham ? "

Hamilton gripped him by the silk collar of his pyjama coat and jerked him to his feet.

" Assault ! " said Bones quietly. " Mad with envy, captain strikes risin' an' brilliant young officer. Court martial finds jolly old captain guilty, and he takes poison ! "

" A newspaper man you will never be," said Hamilton. (Here Bones bowed gravely.) " You can't spell, for one thing ! "

" Neither could dear old Napoleon," said Bones firmly,
" nor dinky old Washington—spellin' is a sign of a weak
mind. You're a good speller, I admit it, dear old Demos-
thenes——"

" The point is this—and I'm perfectly serious "—Hamilton pushed his junior on to the bed, and he collapsed
obediently—" you really must not write political articles,
suggesting that the Secretary of State should come and ' see
with his own eyes ' "—Hamilton sought for the offending
paragraph and read it—" ' . . . the work that is being
carried out by young officers unknown (except by the in-
digenous natives, who adore them) and unhonoured . . .'—
of all the rubbish ! "

Bones shrugged his narrow shoulders : his silence was
offensively respectful.

" You'll not write any more of these self-advertising
letters, Bones—either to the *Star*, the *Comet*, the *Moon*, the
Sun, or any other member of the solar system."

" Let us keep religion out of the discussion, dear old
Ham," said Bones in a hushed voice.

It is doubtful whether Mr. Nickerson Haben had even
heard of the existence of that organ of public conscience, the
Surrey Star and Middlesex Plain Dealer. He was not the
type of man who gave a thought to any newspaper that had
a circulation of less than half a million.

And yet, the appearance of this literary effort of Bones'
coincided with a peculiar moment of crisis in his life, and
the sequel almost excused the subsequent jubilation of the
Surrey Star and went far to consolidate the editor's claim
that " What the *Star* thinks to-day, the Government does
to-morrow ! "

For Nickerson Haben went almost at once to examine the
Territories with his own eyes. He was in the middle thirties
and had the globe at his feet. How this came to be the case,
nobody troubled to consider.

A narrow-chested and pallid man with heavy raven hair,
one lock of which hung over his forehead in moments of
oratorical excess, he was deep-eyed, thin-lipped, hollow-
faced, and had hands white and long. Nickerson was swept
into the House of Commons in a whirlwind of oratory that
blew down a phalanx of sober men and conservative citizens
which stood between. Silver-tongued, or glib, according to

your political prejudices, he carried his powers of suasion
and criticism into the chaste and unemotional atmosphere
of Parliament. So that ministers squirmed uneasily under
the razor-edge of his gibes, and the whips, foregathering in
the lobby, grew pettish at the mention of his name. A
party man, he never fell into the error of wounding the
susceptibilities of his own leaders ; if he criticised them at
all, he merely repeated, in tones of finality, the half-con-
fessions of fallacies they had already made.

When a Government fell, Mr. Haben, deserting a safe seat,
fought West Monrouth County, turned out the sitting member and returned to Westminster in triumph.

The new Government made him an under-secretary, first
of Agriculture, then of Foreign Affairs. He had married
the widow of Cornelius Beit, an American lady, fifteen years
his senior—a clever woman with a violent temper and a
complete knowledge of men. Their home life, though it was
lived at Carlton House Terrace, was not happy. She knew
him rather too well ; his own temper was none of the sweetest. He had all the arrogance of a self-made man who had
completed the process just a little too young. She once told
a near friend that Nickerson had a streak of commonness
which she found it difficult to endure, and there was even
talk of a divorce.

That was just before her operation for appendicitis. The
best surgeon in England performed ; her recovery was never
in doubt. Nickerson, under the spell of her recovery, went
down to the House and delivered the best speech of his life
on the subject of Baluchistan.

Three days later she was dead—there had occurred one of
those curious relapses which are so inexplicable to the lay-
man, so dreaded by the medical profession.

Haben was like a man stunned. Those who hated him—
many—wondered what he would do now, with the principal source of income departed. They had time for no
further than a brief speculation, the matter being decided
when the will was read, leaving him everything—except for
a legacy to a maid.

This tragedy occurred between excellencies, an opportunity seized upon by a sympathetic chief. Nickerson
Haben went out on the first African mail-boat, to combine
business with recreation ; to find flaws and forgetfulness.

Lieutenant Tibbetts, of the King's Houssas, was the news-man of head-quarters. The lank legs of this thin, monocled lad had brought many tidings of joy and calamity, mostly exaggerated.

Now he came flying across the lemon sands of the beach, a mail-bag in his hand, his helmet at the back of his head, surprising truth in his mouth.

He took the five steps of the stoep in one stride, dashed into the big, cool dining-room where Hamilton sat at break-fast, and dropped the bag into his superior's lap at the pre-cise moment when Captain Hamilton's coffee-cup was delicately poised.

" Bones ! You long-legged beach-hound ! " snarled Hamilton, fishing for his handkerchief to mop the hot Mocha from his white duck trousers.

" He's coming, Ham ! " gasped Bones. " Saw my letter, dear old sir, packed his jolly old grip, took the first train ! . . ."

Hamilton looked up sharply for symptoms of sunstroke.

" Who is coming, you left-handed oaf ? " he asked, between wrath and curiosity.

" Haben, old sir. . . . Under-Secretary, dear old Ham ! " Bones was a little incoherent. " Saw my letter in the jolly old *Star* . . . he's at Administration now ! This means a C.B. for me, Ham, old boy ; but I'm not goin' to take any-thing unless they give old Ham the same——"

Hamilton pointed sternly to a chair.

" Sit down and finish your hysteria. Who has been stuffing you with this yarn ? "

It was the second officer of the *Bassam*, he who had brought ashore the mails. Haben was already at Adminis-trative Head-quarters, having travelled on the same ship. For the moment Hamilton forgot his coffee-stained ducks.

" This is darned awkward," he said, troubled. " With Sanders up-country . . . what is he like, this Haben man ? "

Bones, for his own purpose, desired to give a flattering account of the visitor ; he felt that a man who could respond so instantly to a newspaper invitation appearing over his name must have some good in him. He had asked the same question of the second officer, and the second officer, with all a seaman's bluntness, had answered in two words, one of which was Rabelaisian and the other unprintable. For Mr.

Haben did not shine in the eyes of his social inferiors. Servants hated him ; his private secretaries came and went monthly. A horsey member of the Upper House summed him up when he said that " Haben can't carry corn."

" Not so bad," said Bones mendaciously.

Early the next morning Sergeant Ahmet Mahmed brought a grey pigeon to Hamilton, and the captain of Houssas wrote a message on a cigarette paper :

" Haben, Foreign Office tourist, en route. He is at A.H.Q. raising hell. Think you had better come back and deal with him."

Hamilton had gone out in a surf-boat to interview the captain, and the character of Mr. Nickerson Haben was no longer a mystery to him.

He fastened the paper to the red leg of the pigeon and flung it up into the hot air.

" 'Ware hawks, little friend of soldiers," he said conventionally.

II

Linked very closely with the life and fate of Mr. Nickerson Haben, Under-Secretary of State, (this he did not dream) was that of Agasaka, the Chimbiri woman. Mr. Haben was dressed by the best tailor in Savile Row ; Agasaka wore no clothes at all except for the kilt of dried grass which hung from her beautiful waist.

A tall maiden, very slim of body and very grave of eyes, no lover for any man, having a great love for something more imponderable than man ; terribly wise, too, in the ways of ghosts and devils ; straight-backed, small-breasted, beloved of children, so strong in the arm and skilled in her strength that she could put a spear beyond the range of young men's throw—this was Agasaka, the Chimbiri woman, daughter of N'kma-n'kimi, the dead woodman.

She was elderly for a virgin, being seventeen ; had been wooed by men in their every mood ; had kindness for all, generosity for none.

She lived with her brother, M'suru, the hunting man ; and his women hated her, for she never spoke a lie and was frank to her elderly brothers on the matter of their numerous lovers. They would have beaten her, but that they knew the strength of her throwing arm. Where hands did not dare, tongues were more reckless, but none of their mud stuck. Few men were so poor in mind that they would admit others had succeeded where they had failed.

She had lived for many years with her father in the deep of the forest in the abiding place of M'shimba M'shamba, the fearfully boisterous devil who tears up trees with each hand, whilst his mouth drips molten fire ; and other mighty ones dwelt near by. N'guro, the headless dog, and Chikalaka-m'bofunga, the eater of moons—indeed, all except the Fire Lizard, whose eyes talk death. And N'kema had taught her the mysteries of life and the beginning of life and the ground where life is sown. She knew men in their rawness and in their strength. N'kema taught her the way in which she might be more wonderful than any other woman ; the magic handed down from mouth to mouth—the magic which was old when they laid the first deep stones of the Pyramids. . . .

Men were afraid of her ; even Oboro, the witch-doctor, avoided her.

For this was her strangest magic : that she had the power to bring before the eyes of men and women that which they desired least to see.

Once, a small chief stalked her by the river path where the grass is chin-high, having certain plans with her. And at the right and lonely moment he slipped from cover, dropping his spears in the grass, and caught her by the arms so that, strong as she was, she could not move.

" Agasaka," he said, " I have a hut in this forest that has never heard a woman's voice——"

He got so far and then, over her silken shoulder, he saw three black leopards walking flank by flank along the narrow path. Their heads hung low, their golden eyes shone hungrily.

In an instant he released her and fled to his spears.

When he turned again, leopards and woman were gone.

Aliki, the huntsman of her village, neither feared nor cared, for he was familiar with magics of all kinds and often walked in the woods communing with devils. One night he saw a vision in the fire, a great red lizard that blinked its heavy eyelids. Aliki looked round his family circle in a cold-blooded search for a victim. Calichi, the fire-lizard, is the most benevolent of devils and will accept a deputy for the man or woman to whom, with its red and blinking eyes, it has given its warning of death.

This Aliki saw his three wives and his father and an uncle who had come many days' journey on a hunting trip, and none of these, save the youngest wife, was well enough favoured for the purpose. Calichi is a fastidious devil ; nothing short of the best and the most beautiful will please him. Beyond the group sitting about the red fire and eating from the big pot that stood in the embers, were other groups. The village street of Chimbiri-Isisi runs from the forest to the river, a broad avenue fringed with huts ; and before each hut burnt a fire, and about each fire squatted the men and women of the house.

Dark had come ; above the tall gum trees the sky was encrusted with bright stars that winked and blinked as Clichi, but more rapidly.

Aliki saw the stars, and rubbed his palms in the dust for luck ; and at that moment into his vision came the second wife of his neighbour, a tall woman of eighteen, a nymph carved in mahogany, straight and supple of back, naked to the waistline of her grass skirt. And Aliki knew that he had found a proper substitute and said her name under his breath as he caught the lizard's eyes. Thereupon the beast faded and died away, and Aliki knew that the fire-god approved his choice.

Later that night, when Loka, the wife of M'suru the hunts-man, went down to the river to draw water for the first wife's needs, Aliki intercepted her.

" There is nobody so beautiful as you, Loka," he said, " for you have the legs of a lion and the throat of a young deer."

He enumerated other physical perfections, and Loka laughed and listened. She had quarrelled that day with the first wife of her husband, and M'suru had beaten her. She was terribly receptive to flattery and ripe for such adventure as women enjoy.

" Have you no wives, Aliki ? " she asked, pleased. " Now I will give you Agasaka, the sister of my husband, who is very beautiful and has never touched the shoulder of a man."

This she said in spite, for she hated Agasaka, and it is a way of women to praise, to strangers, the qualities of the sisters they loathe.

" As to Agasaka—and wives "—he made a gesture of contempt—" there is no such wife as you, not even in the hut of the old king beyond the mountains, which are the end of the world," said Aliki, and Loka laughed again.

" Now I know that you are mad, as M'suru says. Also that you see strange sights which are not there to see," she said in her deep, gurgling voice. " And not M'suru alone, but all men, say that you have the sickness *mongo*."

It was true that Aliki was sick and had shooting pains in his head. He saw other things than lizards.

" M'suru is an old man and a fool," he said. " I have a ju-ju who gives me eyes to see wonders. Come with me into the forest, Loka, and I will tell you magic and give you love such as an old man cannot give."

She put down her gourd, hiding it in a patch of elephant grass near the river's edge, and walked behind him into the forest. There, eventually, he killed her. And he lit a fire and saw the lizard, who seemed satisfied. Aliki washed himself in the river and went back to his hut and to sleep.

When he awoke in the morning he was sorry he had killed Loka, for of all the women in the world she had been most beautiful in his eyes. The village was half empty, for Loka's gourd had been found and trackers had gone into the woods searching for her. Her they found ; but nobody had seen her walking to death. Some people thought she had been taken by Ochori fishermen, others favoured a devil notorious for his amorous tricks. They brought the body back along the village street, and all the married women made skirts of green leaves and stamped the Death Dance, singing strangely.

Aliki, squatting before his fire, watched the procession with incurious eyes. He was sorry he had killed the Thing that was carried shoulder high, and, dropping his gaze to the dull fire, was even more sorry, for the hot lizard was leering up at him, his bulging eyelids winking at a great rate.

So he had taken the wrong sacrifice.

His eyes rose, rested on the slim figure of a woman, one hand gripping the door-post of her brother's hut. And there came to Aliki a tremendous conviction.

30*

The lizard had vanished from the heart of the fire when he looked down.

No time was to be lost ; he rose and went towards the virgin of Chimbiri.

" I see you, Agasaka," he said. " Now this is a terrible shame to come to your brother's house, for men say that this woman Loka had a lover who killed her."

She turned her big eyes slowly towards him. They were brown and filled with a marvellous luminosity that seemed to quiver as she looked.

" Loka died because she was a fool," she said, " but he who killed her was a bigger. Her pain is past ; his to come. Soon Sandi *malaka* will come, the brown butcher bird, and he will pick the eyes of the man who did this thing."

Aliki hated her, but he was clever to nod his agreement.

" I am wise, Agasaka," he said. " I see wonders which no man sees. Now before Sandi comes with his soldiers, I will show you a magic that will bring this wicked man to the door of your brother's hut when the moon is so and the river is so."

Her grave eyes were on his ; the sound of the singing women was a drone of sound at the far end of the village. A dog barked wheezily in the dark of the hut and all faces were turned towards the river where the body was being laid in a canoe before it was ferried to the little middle island where the dead lie in their shallow graves.

" Let us go," she said, and walked behind him through an uneven field of maize, gained the shelter of the wood behind the village, and by awkward paths reached the outliers of the forest, where there was no maize, for this place was too sad for the weaver birds and too near to the habitation of man for the little monkeys who have white beards. Still he walked on until they made a patch of yellow flowers growing in a clearing. Here the trees were very high, and ten men might have stood on one another's heads against the smooth boles, and the topmost alone could have touched the lowermost branch.

He stopped and turned. At that second came an uneasy stirring of the tree tops, a cold wind and the rumbling of thunder.

" Let us sit down," he said. " First I will talk to you of women who loved me, and of how I would not walk before

them because of my great thoughts for you. Then we will
be lovers——"

"There is no magic in that, Aliki," she said, and he saw
that she was against him and lifted his spear.

"You die, as Loka died, because of the word which the
lizard of fire brought to me," he said, and his shoulder
hunched back for the throw.

"I *am* Loka!" said the girl, and he looked and his jaw
dropped. For she was truly Loka, the woman he had killed.
Loka with her sly eyes and long fingers. And she had
Loka's way of putting a red flower behind her ear, and Loka's
long, satiny legs.

"Oh ko!" he said in distress, and dropped his spear.

Agasaka bent in the middle and picked it up, and in that
moment became herself again. There was no flower and
her fingers were shorter, and where the sly smile had been,
was the gravity of death.

"This is my magic," she said. "Now walk before me,
Aliki, killer of Loka, for I am not made for love, but for
strange power."

Without a word the bemused man walked back the way
he had come and Agasaka followed, and, following, felt the
edge of the spear's broad blade. Though she touched
lightly, there was a line of blood on her thumb where blade
and skin had met. The wood was growing dark, the wind
was alternately a shriek and a whimper of sound.

Near the pool at the edge of the forest she swung the spear
backward over her left shoulder as a cavalry soldier would
swing his sword, and he half turned at the sound of the
whistle it made. . . .

The first wife of her brother was by the pool gathering
manioc root from a place where it had been left to soak—
the head of Aliki fell at her feet as the first flash of lightning
lit the gloom of the world.

III

The sun was four hours old when a river gunboat, a white
and glittering thing, came round the bluff which is called
The Fish because of its shape. The black waters of the river
were piled up around its bows, a glassy hillock of water,
tinged red at its edges, for the *Zaire* was driving against a

six-knot current. Every river from the Isisi to the Mokalibi
was in spate, and there were sand shoals where deeps had
been, and deeps in the places where the crocodiles had slept
open-mouthed the last time Mr. Commissioner Sanders had
come that way.

He stood by the steersman, a slim and dapper figure in
spotless white, his pith helmet at a rakish angle, for an
elephant fly had bitten him on the forehead the night before,
and the lump it had induced was painful to the touch.
Between his regular, white teeth was a long, black cheroot.
He had breakfasted, and an orderly was clearing away the
silver coffee-pot and the fruit-plates. Overhead the sky was
a burning blue, but the glass was falling with alarming
rapidity, and he desired the safe harbourage of a deep bank
and the shelter of high trees which a little bay south of
Chimbiri would give to him.

" Lo'ba, ko'lo ka ! A fathom of water by the mercy of
God ! "

The sleepy-eyed boy sitting in the bow of the boat drew
up his wet sounding-rod.

Sanders's hand shot out to the handle of the telegraph and
pulled, and Yoka the engineer sent a clanging acknowledg-
ment.

" Half a fathom."

Thump !

The boat slowed of itself, its wheel threshing astern, but
the nose was in sand and a side-swinging current drove the
stern round until it was broadside to the sand-reef. Then,
as the wheel reversed, the *Zaire* began to move towards the
right bank of the river, skirting the shoal until the nose
found deep water again.

" Lord," said the steersman, virtuously annoyed, " this
bank has come up from hell, for it has never been here since
I was without clothing."

" Think only of the river, man," said Sanders, not inclined
for gossip.

And now, above the tree-tops ahead, Sanders saw the
rolling smoke of clouds—yellow clouds that tumbled and
tossed and threw out tawny banners before the wind.

And the still surface of the river was ripped into little
white shreds that leapt and scattered in spray. Sanders
moved his cigar from one side of his mouth to the other, took

"His jaw dropped, for she was truly Loka, the woman he had killed."

Fig. 474.—Savage life in the tropics. [illegible caption]

it out, looked at it regretfully and threw it over the side. His servant was behind him with an oilskin invitingly held ; he struggled into the coat, passed his helmet back and took in exchange the sou'wester which he fastened under his chin. The heat was intolerable. The storm was driving a furnace blast of hot air to herald its fury. He was wet to the skin, his clothes sticking to him.

A ribbon of blinding light leapt across the sky, and split into a tracery of branches. The explosion of the thunder was deafening ; it seemed as if a heavy weight was pressing down on his head ; again the flash, and again and again. Now it showed bluely on either bank, vivid blue shrieks of light that ran jaggedly from sky to earth. The yellow clouds had become black ; the darkness of night was on the world, a darkness intensified by the ghastly sideways light that came from a distant horizon where the clouds were broken.

" Port," said Sanders curtly ; " now starboard again— now port ! "

They had reached the shelter of the bank as the first rain fell. Sanders sent a dozen men overboard with the fore and aft hawser and made fast to the big gums that grew down to the river-side.

In a second the deck was running with water and the Commissioner's white shoes had turned first to dove-grey and then to slate. He sent for Yoka the engineer, who was also his headman.

" Put out another hawser and keep a full head of steam." He spoke in coast Arabic, which is a language allowing of nice distinctions.

" Lord, shall I sound the *oopa-oopa* [1] ? " he asked. " For I see that these thieving Akasava people are afraid to come out into the rain to welcome your lordship."

Sanders shook his head.

" They will come in their time—the village is a mile away, and they would not hear your *oopa-oopa* ! " he said, and went to his cabin to recover his breath. A ninety-knot wind had been blowing into his teeth for ten minutes, and ten minutes is a long time when you are trying to breathe.

The cabin had two long windows, one at each side. That

---

[1] Siren : On the river most words describing novel things are onoma-topœic.

to the left above the settee on which he dropped gave him a view of the forest path along which, sooner or later, a villager would come and inevitably carry a message to the chief.

The lightning was still incessant ; the rain came down in such volume that he might well think he had anchored beneath a small waterfall, but the light had changed, and ahead the black of clouds had become a grey opacity.

Sanders pulled open the doors he had closed behind him ; the wind was gusty but weaker. He reached out for a cheroot and lit it, patient to wait. The river was running eight knots ; he would need hand-towing to the beach of the village. He hoped they had stacked wood for him. The Chimbiri folk were lazy, and the last time he had tied they showed him a wood stack—green logs, and few of them.

Yoka and his crew loved to hear the devil whoop of the *oopa-oopa*—Sanders knew just how much steam a siren wasted.

His eyes sought the river-side path—and at the critical moment. For he saw eight men walking two and two, and they carried on their shoulders a trussed figure.

An electric chrysanthemum burst into blinding bloom as he leapt to the bank—its dazzling petals, twisting every way through the dark clouds, made light enough to see the burden very clearly, long before he reached the path to stand squarely in the way of eight sullen men and the riff-raff which had defied the storm to follow at a distance.

" O men," said Sanders softly—he showed his teeth when he talked that way—" who are you that you put the ghost mark on this woman's face ? "

For the face of their passenger was daubed white with clay. None spoke : he saw their toes wriggling, all save those of one man, and him he addressed.

" M'suru, son of N'kema, what woman is this ? "

M'suru cleared his throat.

" Lord, this woman is the daughter of my own mother ; she killed Aliki, also she killed first my wife Loka."

" Who saw this ? "

" Master, my first wife, who is a true woman to me since her lover was drowned, she saw the head of Aliki fall. Also she heard Agasaka say ' Go, man, where I sent Loka, as you know best, who saw me slay her.' "

Sanders was not impressed.

" Let loose this woman that she may stand in my eyes,"
he said, and they untied the girl and by his order wiped the
joke of death from her face.

" Tell me," said Sanders.

She spoke very simply and her story was good.   Yet——

" Bring me the woman who heard her say these evil
things."

The wife was found in the tail of the procession and came
forward important—frightened—for the cold eyes of Sanders
were unnerving.   But she was voluble when she had discovered her voice.

The man in the streaming oilskins listened, his head bent.
Agasaka, the slim woman, stood grave, unconscious of
shame—the grass girdle had gone and she was as her mother
had first seen her.   Presently the first wife came to the end
of her story.

" Sandi, this is the truth, and if I speak a lie may the
' long ones ' take me to the bottom of the river and feed me
to the snakes ! "

Sanders, watching her, saw the brown skin go dull and
grey ; saw the mouth open in shocking fear.

What he did not see was the " long one "—the yellow
crocodile that was creeping through the grass towards the
perjurer, his little eyes gleaming, his wet mouth open to
show the cruel white spikes of teeth.

Only the first wife of M'suru saw this, and fell screaming
and writhing at her husband's feet, clasping his knees.

Sanders said nothing, but heard much that was in con-
tradiction of the earlier story.

" Come with me, Agasaka, to my fine ship," he said, for
he knew that trouble might follow if the girl stayed with her
people.   Wars have started for less cause.

He took her to the *Zaire* ; she followed meekly at his
heels, though meekness was not in her.

That night came a tired pigeon from headquarters, and
Sanders, reading the message, was neither pleased nor sorry.

High officials, especially the arm-chair men, worried him
a little, but those he had met were such charming and understanding gentlemen that he had lost some of his fear of them.
What worried him more were the reports which reached him
from reliable sources of Agasaka's strange powers.   He had
seen many queer things on the river ; the wonder of the

lokali that hollowed the tree trunk by which messages might be relayed across a continent was still something of a puzzle to him. Magic inexplicable, sometimes revolting, was an everyday phenomenon. Some of it was crude hypnotism, but there were higher things beyond his understanding. Many of these had come down through the ages from Egypt and beyond; Abraham had brought practices from the desert lands about Babylon which were religious rites amongst people who had no written language.

The *Zaire* was steaming for home the next day when he sent for Abiboo, his orderly.

" Bring me this woman of Chimbiri," he said, and they brought her from the little store-cabin where she was both guest and prisoner.

" They tell me this and that about you, Agasaka," he said, giving chapter and verse of his authority.

" Lord, it is true," said Agasaka when he had finished. " These things my father taught me, as his father taught him. For, lord, as he was the son of M'kufusu, the son of Bonfongu-m'lini, the son of N'sambi. . . ."

She recited thirty generations before he stopped her—roughly four hundred years. Even Sanders was staggered, though he had once met an old man of the N'gombi who told him intimate details about a man who had lived in the days of Saladin.

" Show me your magic, woman," he said, and to his surprise she shook her head.

" Lord, this one magic only comes when I am afraid."

Sanders dropped his hand to his Browning and half drew it from its leather holster.

He was sitting under an awning spread over the bridge. The steersman was at the wheel, in the bow the *kano* boy with his long sounding rod. Purposely he did not look at the woman, fixing his eyes on the steersman's back.

His hand had scarcely closed on the brown grip when, almost at his feet, he saw the one thing in all the world that he loathed—an English puff adder, mottled and swollen, its head thrown back to strike.

Twice his pistol banged—the steersman skipped to cover with a yell and left the *Zaire* yawing in the strong current.

There was nothing—nothing but two little holes in the deck, so close together that they overlapped. Sanders sprang to the wheel and straightened the boat, and then, when the steersman had been called back and the sounding boy retrieved from the cover of the wood pile where he crouched and trembled, Sanders returned to his chair, waving away Abiboo, who had arrived, rifle in hand, to the rescue of his master.

"Woman," said Sanders quietly, "you may go back to your little house."

And Agasaka went without the evidence of triumph a lesser woman might have felt. He had not looked at her—there was no mesmerism here.

He stooped down and examined the bullet holes, too troubled to feel foolish.

That afternoon he sent for her again and gave her chocolate to eat, talking of her father. She was sitting on the deck at his feet, and once, when he thought he had gained her confidence, he dropped his hand lightly on her head as he had dropped his hand on so many young heads.

The puff adder was there—within striking distance, his spade head thrown back, his coils rigid.

Sanders stared at the thing and did not move his hand, and then, through the shining body, he saw the deck planks, and the soft bitumen where plank joined plank, and then the viper vanished.

"You do not fear?" he asked quietly.

"Lord . . . a little ; but now I do not fear, for I know that you would not hurt women."

The *Zaire*, with its strange passenger, came alongside the residency wharf two hours before sundown on the third day. Captain Hamilton was waiting, a fuming, angry man, for he had been the unwilling host of one who lacked something in manners.

IV

"He's pure swine," said Hamilton. "Nothing is good enough for him ; he raised hell when he found you weren't here to meet him. Bones mollified him a little. The silly ass had a guard of honour drawn up on the beach. I only found this out just before the boat landed, and it was too late to send the men to quarters. But apparently it was the right thing to do ; Nickerson Esquire expected it—and more. Flags and things and a red carpet for his hooves and a band to play ' Here comes the bride ! ' "

All this between wharf and residency garden. A figure in white stretched languidly in a deep chair turned his head but did not trouble to rise. Still less was he inclined to exchange the cool of the broad veranda for the furnace of space open to a red-hot sun.

Sanders saw a white face that looked oddly dirty in contrast with the spotless purity of a duck jacket. Two deep, suspicious eyes, a long, untidy wisp of hair lying lankly on a high forehead—a pink, almost bloodless mouth.

" You're Sanders ? "

Mr. Haben looked up at the trim figure.

" I am the Commissioner, sir," said Sanders.

" Why weren't you here to meet me ; you knew that I was due ? "

Sanders was more shocked than nettled by the tone. A coarse word in the mouth of a woman would have produced the same effect. Secretaries and under-secretaries of state were god-like people who employed a macrology of their own, wrapping their reproofs in the silver tissue of stilted diction which dulled the sting of their rebukes.

" Do you hear me, sir ? "

The man on the chair sat up impatiently.

Hamilton, standing by, was near to kicking him off the stoep.

" I heard you. I was on a visit to the Chimbiri country. No notice of your arrival or your pending arrival was received."

Sanders spoke very carefully ; he was staring down at the scowling Nickerson.

Mr. Haben had it on the tip of his tongue to give him the lie. There was, as the late Mrs. Haben had said, a streak of commonness in him ; but there was a broader streak of discretion. The gun still hung at the Commissioner's hip ; the grip was shiny with use.

" H'm ! " said Mr. Under-Secretary Haben, and allowed himself to relax in his chair.

He was clever enough, Sanders found ; knew the inside story of the territories ; was keen for information. He thought the country was not well run. The system was wrong, the taxes fell short of the highest possible index. In all ways his attitude was antagonistic. Commissioners were lazy people, intent on having a good time and " their shooting." Sanders, who had never shot a wild beast in his life, save for the pot or to rid himself of a pressing danger, said nothing.

" A thoroughly nasty fellow," said Hamilton.

But it was Bones who suffered the heaviest casualty to his amour-propre.

Left alone with the visitor in the hour before dinner, Bones cunningly led the conversation towards the *Surrey Star and Middlesex Plain Dealer.*

" I suppose, sir, when you read my jolly old letter, you thought I had a fearful nerve ? "

" Your letter ? " Mr. Haben allowed his head to fall in Bones's direction.

" . . . about seeing the place with your own holy old eyes," and Bones went on, unconscious of the doom which awaited him, and explained fully his reason for writing, the thought that led him to write, the incident that induced the thought.

" My good young man, you don't imagine that His Majesty's Government would send a Minister of State flying off to Africa because an empty-headed subaltern wrote letters to an obscure county journal, do you ? "

Bones opened and closed his eyes very quickly.

" I came—but why should I tell you ? " asked Nickerson Haben wearily. " You may be assured that your letter had nothing to do with my coming. As I said before, you officers have too much time on your hands. It is a matter which requires looking into."

But it was at dinner that he touched the zenith of his boorishness. The dinner was bad ; he hated palm-nut chop ; sweet potatoes made him ill ; the chicken was tough, the coffee vile. Happily he had brought his own cigars.

Bones spent that trying hour wondering what would happen to him if he leant across the table and batted an Under-Secretary with a cut-glass salt-cellar.

Only Sanders showed no sign of annoyance. Not a muscle of his face moved when Mr. Nickerson Haben made the most unforgivable of all suggestions. He did this out of sheer ignorance and because of that streak of commonness which was his very own.

" A native woman is a native woman," said Sanders quietly. " Happily, I have only had gentlemen under my control, and that complication has never arisen."

Mr. Haben smiled sceptically ; he was sourest when he smiled.

" Very noble," he said dryly, " and yet one has heard of such things happening."

Hamilton was white with rage. Bones stared open-mouthed, like a boy who only dimly understood. The pale man asked a question and, to the amazement of the others, Sanders nodded.

" Yes, I brought a girl down from Chimbiri," he said ; " she is at present in the Houssa lines with the wife of Sergeant Abiboo. I hardly know what to do with her."

" I suppose not," more dryly yet, " a prisoner, I suppose ? "

" N-no "—Sanders hesitated—seemed confused in Haben's eyes. " She has a peculiar brand of magic which rather confounds me——"

Here Mr. Nickerson Haben laughed.

" That stuff ! " he said contemptuously. " Let me see your magician."

Bones was sent to fetch her—he swore loudly all the way across the dark square.

" That is what we complain about," said Mr. Haben in the time of waiting. " You fellows are in the country so long that you get niggerised." (Sanders winced. " Nigger " is a word you do not use in Africa.) " You absorb their philosophies and superstitions. Magic—good God ! "

He waggled his long head hopelessly.

" My poor wife believed in the same rubbish—she came from one of the southern states—had a black mammy who did wonderful things with chicken bones ! "

Sanders had not credited him with a wife. When he learnt that the poor lady had died he felt that worse things could happen to a woman.

" Appendicitis—an operation . . . fool of a doctor." Mr. Haben unbent so far as to scatter these personal items. " As I said before, you people—hum . . ."

Agasaka stood in the doorway, " missionary dressed " as they say. Her figure was concealed in a blue cotton " cloth " wrapped and pinned about her to the height of her breast.

" This is the lady, eh ?   Come here ! "   He beckoned her
and she came to him.   " Let us see her magic . . . speak
to her ! "

Sanders nodded.

" This man wishes to see your magic, Agasaka ; he is a
great chief amongst my people."

She did not answer.

" Not bad-looking," said Nickerson, and did a thing
which amazed these men, for he rose and, putting his hand
under her chin, raised her face to his.   And there was something in his queer, hard eyes that she read, as we may read
the printed word.   The streak of commonness was abominably broad and raw-edged.

" You're not so bad for a nig . . ."

He dropped his hands suddenly ; they saw his face
pucker hideously.   He was looking at a woman, a handsome
woman with deep shadows under her eyes.   It was the face
he often saw and always tried to forget.   A dead white face.
She wore a silk nightdress, rather high to the throat . . .

And she spoke.

" Won't you wait until the nurse comes back, Nick ?   I
don't think I ought to drink ice-water—the doctor says——"

" Damn the doctor ! " said Nickerson Haben between his
teeth, and the three men heard him, saw his hand go up
holding an imaginary glass, saw his eyes fall to the level of
an imaginary pillow.

" I'm sick of you—sick of you !   Make a new will, eh ?
Like hell ! "

He stared and stared, and then slowly turned his drawn
face to Sanders.

" My wife "—he pointed to space and mumbled the words
—" I—I killed her——"

And then he realised that he was Nickerson Haben,
Under-Secretary of State, and these were three very unim-
portant officials—and a black woman who was regarding
him gravely.   But this discovery of his was just the flash of
a second too late.

" Go to your room, sir," said Sanders, and spent the
greater part of the night composing a letter to the Foreign
Secretary.

Reprinted by permission from *Sanders*.

THE MAN WHO SANG IN CHURCH

To Leon Gonsalez went most of the cases of blackmail which came the way of the Three Just Men.

And yet, from the views he had so consistently expressed, he was the last man in the world to whom such problems should have gone, for in that famous article of his entitled " Justification," which put up the sales of a quarterly magazine by some thousand per cent., he offered the following opinion :

" . . . as to blackmail, I see no adequate punishment but death in the case of habitual offenders. You cannot parley with the type of criminal who specialises in this loathsome form of livelihood. Obviously there can be no side of him to which appeal can be made : no system of reformation can affect him. He is dehumanised, and may be classified with the secret poisoner, the baby-farmer and . . ."

He mentioned a trade as unwholesome.

Leon found less drastic means of dealing with these pests ; yet we may suppose that the more violent means which distinguished the case of Miss Brown and the man who sang in church had his heartiest approval.

There are so many types of beauty that even Leon Gonsalez, who had a passion for classification, gave up at the eighteenth subdivision of the thirty-third category of brunettes. By which time he had filled two large quarto notebooks.

If he had not wearied of his task before he met Miss Brown, he would assuredly have recognised its hopelessness, for she fell into no category, nor had he her peculiar attractions catalogued in any of his sub-sections. She was dark and slim and elegant. Leon hated the word, but he was compelled to admit this characteristic. The impression she left was one of delicate fragrance. Leon called her the Lavender

Girl. She called herself Brown, which was obviously not her name ; also, in the matter of simulations, she wore one of those closely-fitting hats that came down over a woman's eyes and might make subsequent identification extremely difficult.

She timed her visit for the half-light of dusk—the cigarette hour that follows a good dinner, when men are inclined rather to think than to talk, and to doze than either.

Others had come at this hour to the little house in Curzon Street, where the silver triangle on the door marked the habitation of the Three Just Men, and when the bell rang George Manfred looked up at the clock.

" It is too early for the post—see who it is, Raymond : and before you go, I will tell you. It is a young lady in black, rather graceful of carriage, very nervous and in bad trouble."

Leon grinned as Poiccart rose heavily from his chair and went out.

" Clairvoyance rather than deduction," he said, " and observation rather than either : from where you sit you can see the street. Why mystify our dear friend ? "

George Manfred sent a ring of smoke to the ceiling.

" He is not mystified," he said lazily. " He has seen her also. If you hadn't been so absorbed in your newspaper you would have seen her, too. She has passed up and down the street three times on the other side. And on each occasion she has glanced toward this door. She is rather typical, and I have been wondering exactly what variety of blackmail has been practised on her."

Here Raymond Poiccart came back.

" She wishes to see one of you," he said. " Her name is Miss Brown—but she doesn't look like a Miss Brown ! "

Manfred nodded to Leon.

" It had better be you," he said.

Gonsalez went to the little front drawing-room, and found the girl standing with her back to the window, her face in shadow.

" I would rather you did not put on the light, please," she said, in a calm, steady voice. " I do not wish to be recognised if you meet me again."

Leon smiled.

" I had no intention of touching the switch," he said. " You see, Miss——" he waited expectantly.

" Brown," she replied, so definitely that he would have known she desired anonymity even if she had not made her request in regard to the light. " I told your friend my name."

" You see, Miss Brown," he went on, " we have quite a number of callers who are particularly anxious not to be recognised when we meet them again. Will you sit down ? I know that you have not much time, and that you are anxious to catch a train out of town."

She was puzzled.

" How did you know that ? " she asked.

Leon made one of his superb gestures.

" Otherwise you would have waited until it was quite dark before you made your appointment. You have, in point of fact, left it just as late as you could."

She pulled a chair to the table and sat down slowly, turning her back to the window.

" Of course that is so," she nodded—" Yes, I have to leave in time, and I have cut it fine. Are you Mr. Manfred ? "

" Gonsalez," he corrected her.

" I want your advice," she said.

She spoke in an even, unemotional voice, her hands lightly clasped before her on the table. Even in the dark, and unfavourably placed as she was for observation, he could see that she was beautiful. He guessed from the maturity of her voice that she was in the region of twenty-four.

" I am being blackmailed. I suppose you will tell me I should go to the police, but I am afraid the police would be of no assistance, even if I were willing to risk an appearance in Court, which I am not. My father—" she hesitated—" is a Government official. It would break his heart if he knew. What a fool I have been ! "

" Letters ? " asked Leon, sympathetically.

" Letters and other things," she said. " About six years ago I was a medical student at St. John's Hospital. I did not take my final exam. for reasons which you will understand. My surgical knowledge has not been of very much use to me, except . . . well, I once saved a man's life, though I doubt if it was worth saving. He seems to think it was, but that has nothing to do with the case. When I was at St. John's I got to know a fellow-student, a man whose name will not interest you, and, as girls of my age sometimes do, I fell desperately in love with him. I did not know that he was married, although he told me this before our friendship reached a climax.

" For all that followed I was to blame. There were the usual letters——"

" And these are the basis of the blackmail ? " asked Leon.

She nodded.

" I was worried ill about the . . . affair. I gave up my work and returned home ; but that doesn't interest you, either."

" Who is blackmailing you ? " asked Leon.

She hesitated.

" The man. It is horrible, isn't it ? But he has gone down and down. I have money of my own—my mother left me £2,000 a year—and of course I have paid."

" When did you see this man last ? "

She was thinking of something else, and she did not answer him. As he repeated the question, she looked up quickly.

" Last Christmas Day—only for a moment. He was not staying with us—I mean it was at the end of . . ."

She had become suddenly panic-stricken, confused, and was almost breathless as she went on :

" I saw him by accident. Of course he did not see me, but it was a great shock. . . . It was his voice. He always had a wonderful tenor voice."

" He was singing ? " suggested Leon, when she paused, as he guessed, in an effort to recover her self-possession.

" Yes, in church," she said, desperately. " That is where I saw him."

She went on speaking with great rapidity, as though she were anxious not only to dismiss from her mind that chance encounter, but to make Leon also forget.

" It was two months after this that he wrote to me—he wrote to our old address in town. He said he was in desperate need of money, and wanted £500. I had already given him more than £1,000, but I was sane enough to write and tell him I intended to do no more. It was then that he horrified me by sending a photograph of the letter—of one of the letters—I had sent him. Mr. Gonsalez, I have met another man, and . . . well, John had read the news of my engagement."

" Your fiancé knows nothing about this earlier affair ? "
She shook her head.

" No, nothing, and he mustn't know. Otherwise everything would be simple. Do you imagine I would allow myself to be blackmailed any further but for that ? "

Leon took a slip of paper from one pocket and a pencil from another.

" Will you tell me the name of this man ? John——? "
" John Letheritt, 27, Lion Row, Whitechurch Street. It is a little room that he has rented, as an office, and a sleeping-place. I have already had inquiries made."
Leon waited.

" What is the crisis—why have you come now ? " he asked.
She took from her bag a letter, and he noted that it was in a clean envelope ; evidently she had no intention that her real name and address should be known.

He read it, and found it a typical communication. The letter demanded £3,000 by the third of the month, failing which the writer intended putting " papers " in " certain hands." There was just that little touch of melodrama which for some curious reason the average blackmailer adopts in his communiques.

" I will see what I can do—how am I to get in touch with you ? " asked Leon. " I presume that you do not wish that either your real name or your address should be known even to me."

She did not answer until she had taken from her bag a number of banknotes, which she laid on the table.
Leon smiled.

" I think we will discuss the question of payment when we have succeeded. What is it you want me to do ? "

" I want you to get the letters, and, if it is possible, I want you so to frighten this man that he will not trouble me again. As to the money, I shall feel so much happier if you will let me pay you now ! "

" It is against the rules of the firm ! " said Leon cheerfully.
She gave him a street and a number which he guessed was an accommodation address.

" Please don't see me to the door," she said, with a half-glance at the watch on her wrist.

He waited till the door closed behind her, and then went upstairs to his companions.

" I know so much about this lady that I could write a monograph on the subject," he said.

" Tell us a little," suggested Manfred. But Leon shook his head.

That evening he called at Whitechurch Street. Lion Row was a tiny, miserable thoroughfare, more like an alley than anything, and hardly deserved its grand designation. In one of those ancient houses which must have seen the decline of Alsatia, at the top of three rickety flights of stairs, he found a door, on which had been recently painted : " J. LETHERITT, EXPORTER."

His knock produced no response.

He knocked again more heavily, and heard the creaking of a bed, and a harsh voice asking on the other side who was there. It took some time before he could persuade the man to open the door, and then Leon found himself in a very long, narrow room, lighted by a shadeless electric table-lamp. The furniture consisted of a bed, an old washstand and a dingy desk piled high with unopened circulars.

He guessed the man who confronted him, dressed in a soiled shirt and trousers, to be somewhere in the region of thirty-five ; he certainly looked older. His face was un-shaven and there was in the room an acrid stink of opium.

. " What do you want ? " growled John Letheritt, glaring suspiciously at the visitor.

With one glance Leon had taken in the man—a weakling, he guessed—one who had found and would always take the easiest way. The little pipe on the table by the bed was a direction post not to be mistaken.

Before he could answer, Letheritt went on :

" If you have come for letters you won't find them here, my friend." He shook a trembling hand in Leon's face. " You can go back to dear Gwenda and tell her that you are no more successful than the last gentleman she sent ! "

" A blackmailer, eh ? You are the dirtiest little black-mailer I ever met," mused Leon. " I suppose you know the young lady intends to prosecute you ? "

" Let her prosecute. Let her get a warrant and have me pinched ! It won't be the first time I've been inside. Maybe she can get a search warrant, then she will be able to have her letters read in Court. I'm saving you a lot of trouble. I'll save Gwenda trouble, too ! Engaged, eh ? You're not the prospective bridegroom ? " he sneered.

" If I were, I should be wringing your neck," said Leon calmly. " If you are a wise man——"

" I am not wise," snarled the other. " Do you think I would be living in this pigsty if I were ? I . . . a man with a medical degree ? "

Then, with a sudden rage, he pushed his visitor towards the door.

" Get out and stay out ! "

Leon was so surprised by this onslaught that he was listening to the door being locked and bolted against him before he had realised what had happened.

From the man's manner, he was certain that the letters were in that room—there were a dozen places where they might be hidden : he could have overcome the degenerate with the greatest ease, bound him to the bed and searched the room, but in these days the Three Just Men were very law-abiding people.

Instead he came back to his friends late that night with the story of his partial failure.

" If he left the house occasionally, it would be easy—but he never goes out. I even think that Raymond and I could, without the slightest trouble, make a very thorough search of the place. Letheritt has a bottle of milk left every morning, and it should not be difficult to put him to sleep if we reached the house a little after the milkman."

Manfred shook his head.

" You'll have to find another way ; it's hardly worth while antagonising the police," he said.

" Which is putting it mildly," murmured Poiccart. " Who's the lady ? "

Leon repeated almost word for word the conversation he had had with Miss Brown.

" There are certain remarkable facts in her statement, and I am pretty sure they *were* facts, and that she was not trying to deceive me," he said. " Curious item No. 1 is that the lady heard this man singing in church last Christmas Day. Is Mr. Letheritt the kind of person one would expect to hear exercising his vocal organs on Christmas carols ? My brief acquaintance with him leads me to suppose that he isn't.

Curious item No. 2 was the words : ' He was not staying with us,' or something of that sort ; and he was ' nearing the end '—of what ? Those three items are really remarkable ! "

" Not particularly remarkable to me," growled Poiccart. " He was obviously a member of a house-party somewhere, and she did not know he was staying in the neighbourhood, until she saw him in church. It was near the end of his visit."

Leon shook his head.

" Letheritt has been falling for years. He has not reached his present state since Christmas ; therefore he must have been as bad—or nearly as bad—nine months ago. I really have taken a violent dislike to him, and I must get those letters."

Manfred looked at him thoughtfully.

" They would hardly be at his bankers, because he wouldn't have a banker ; or at his lawyers, because I should imagine that he is the kind of person whose acquaintance with law begins and ends in the Criminal Courts. I think you are right, Leon ; the papers are in his room."

Leon lost no time. Early the next morning he was in Whitechurch Street, and watched the milkman ascend to the garret where Letheritt had his foul habitation. He waited till the milkman had come out and disappeared, but, sharp as he was, he was hardly quick enough. By the time he had reached the top floor, the milk had been taken in, and the little phial of colourless fluid which might have acted as a preservative to the milk was unused.

The next morning he tried again, and again he failed.

On the fourth night, between the hours of one and two, he managed to gain an entry into the house, and crept noiselessly up the stairs. The door was locked from the inside, but he could reach the end of the key with a pair of narrow pliers he carried.

There was no sound from within when he snapped back the lock and turned the handle softly. He had forgotten the bolts.

The next day he came again, and surveyed the house from the outside. It was possible to reach the window of the room, but he would need a very long ladder, and after a brief consultation with Manfred, he decided against this method.

Manfred made a suggestion.

" Why not send him a wire, asking him to meet your Miss Brown at Liverpool Street Station ? You know her Christian name ? "

Leon sighed wearily.

" I tried that on the second day, my dear chap, and had little Lew Leveson on hand to ' whizz ' him the moment he came into the street in case he was carrying the letters on him."

" By ' whizz ' you mean to pick his pocket ? I can't keep track of modern thief slang," said Manfred. " In the days when I was actively interested, we used to call it ' dip.' "

" You are *démodé*, George ; ' whizz ' is the word. But of course the beggar didn't come out. If he owed rent I could get the brokers put in ; but he does not owe rent. He is breaking no laws, and is living a fairly blameless life— except, of course, one could catch him for being in possession of opium. But that would not be much use, because the police are rather chary of allowing us to work with them."

He shook his head.

" I am afraid I shall have to give Miss Brown a very bad report."

It was not until a few days later that he actually wrote to the agreed address, having first discovered that it was, as he suspected, a small stationer's shop where letters could be called for.

A week later Superintendent Meadows, who was friendly with the Three, came down to consult Manfred on a matter of a forged Spanish passport, and since Manfred was an authority on passport forgeries and had a fund of stories about Spanish criminals, it was long after midnight when the conference broke up.

Leon, who needed exercise, walked to Regent Street with Meadows, and the conversation turned to Mr. John Letheritt.

" Oh, yes, I know him well. I took him two years ago on a false pretence charge, and got him eighteen months at the London Assizes. A real bad egg, that fellow, and a bit of a ' squeaker,' too. He's the man who put away Joe Lenthall, the cleverest cat burglar we've had for a generation. Joe got ten years, and I shouldn't like to be this fellow when he comes out ! "

Suddenly Leon asked a question about Letheritt's imprisonment, and when the other had answered, his companion stood stock-still in the middle of the deserted Hanover Square and doubled up with silent laughter.

" I don't see the joke."

" But I do," chuckled Leon. " What a fool I've been ! And I thought I understood the case ! "

" Do you want Letheritt for anything ? I know where he lives," said Meadows.

Leon shook his head.

" No, I don't want him : but I should very much like to have ten minutes in his room ! "

Meadows looked serious.

" He's blackmailing, eh ? I wondered where he was getting his money from."

But Leon did not enlighten him. He went back to Curzon Street and began searching certain works of reference, and followed this by an inspection of a large-scale map of the Home Counties. He was the last to go to bed, and the first to awaken, for he slept in the front of the house and heard the knocking at the door.

It was raining heavily as he pulled up the window and looked out ; and in the dim light of dawn he thought he recognised Superintendent Meadows. A second later he was sure of his visitor's identity.

" Will you come down ? I want to see you."

Gonsalez slipped into his dressing-gown, ran downstairs and opened the door to the Superintendent.

" You remember we were talking about Letheritt last night ? " said Meadows as Leon ushered him into the little waiting-room.

The Superintendent's voice was distinctly unfriendly, and he was eyeing Leon keenly.

" Yes—I remember."

" You didn't by any chance go out again last night ? "

" No. Why ? "

Again that look of suspicion.

" Only Letheritt was murdered at half-past one this morning, and his room ransacked."

Leon stared at him.

31

"Murdered ? Have you got the murderer ? " he asked at last.

"No, but we shall get him all right. He was seen coming down the rainpipe by a City policeman. Evidently he had got into Letheritt's room through the window, and it was this discovery by the constable which led to a search of the house. The City Police had to break in the door, and they found Letheritt dead on the bed. He had evidently been hit on the head with a jemmy, and ordinarily that injury would not have killed him, according to the police doctor ; but in his state of health it was quite enough to put him out. A policeman went round the house to intercept the burglar, but somehow he must have escaped into one of the little alleys that abound in this part of the city, and he was next seen by a constable in Fleet Street, driving a small car, the number-plate of which had been covered with mud."

"Was the man recognised ? "

"He hasn't been—yet. What he did was to leave three finger-prints on the window, and as he was obviously an old hand at the game, that is as good as a direct identification. The City Detective Force called us in, but we have not been able to help them except to give them particulars of Letheritt's past life. Incidentally, I supplied them with a copy of your finger-prints. I hope you don't mind."

Leon grinned.

"Delighted ! " he said.

After the officer had left, Leon went upstairs to give the news to his two friends.

But the most startling intelligence was to come when they were sitting at breakfast. Meadows arrived. They saw his car draw up at the door, which Poiccart went out to open to him. He strode into the little room, his eyes bulging with excitement.

"Here's a mystery which even you fellows will never be able to solve," he said. "Do you know that this is a day of great tragedy for Scotland Yard and for the identification system ? It means the destruction of a method that has been laboriously built up . . ."

"What are you talking about ? " asked Manfred quickly.

"The finger-print system," said Meadows, and Poiccart,

to whom the finger-print method was something God-like, gaped at him.

" We've found a duplicate," said Meadows. " The prints on the glass were undoubtedly the prints of Joe Lenthall— and Joe Lenthall is in Wilford County Gaol serving the first part of twelve years' penal servitude ! "

Something made Manfred turn his head toward his friend. Leon's eyes were blazing, his thin face wreathed in one joyous smile.

" The man who sang in church ! " he said, softly. " This is the prettiest case that I have ever dealt with. Now sit down, my dear Meadows, and eat ! No, no ; sit down. I want to hear about Lenthall—is it possible for me to see him ? "

Meadows stared at him.

" What use would that be ? I tell you this is the biggest blow we have ever had. And what is more, when we showed the City policeman a photograph of Lenthall, he recognised him as the man he had seen coming down the rainpipe ! I thought Lenthall had escaped, and 'phoned the prison. But he's there all right."

" Can I see Lenthall ? "

Meadows hesitated.

" Yes—I think it could be managed. The Home Office is rather friendly with you, isn't it ? "

Friendly enough, apparently. By noon, Leon Gonsalez was on his way to Wilford Prison, and, to his satisfaction, he went alone.

Wilford Gaol is one of the smaller convict establishments, and was brought into use to house long-time convicts of good character and who were acquainted with the book-binding and printing trade. There are several " trade " prisons in England—Maidstone is the " printing " prison, Shepton Mallet the " dyeing " prison—where prisoners may exercise their trades.

The Chief Warder whom Leon interviewed told him that Wilford was to be closed soon, and its inmates transferred to Maidstone. He spoke regretfully of this change.

" We've got a good lot of men here—they give us no trouble, and they have an easy time. We've had no cases of indiscipline for years. We only have one officer on night-duty—that will give you an idea how quiet we are."

"Who was the officer last night ? " asked Leon, and the unexpectedness of the question took the Chief Warder by surprise.

"Mr. Bennett," he said; "he's gone sick to-day by the way—a bilious attack. Curious thing you should ask the question : I've just been to see him. We had an inquiry about the man you've come to visit. Poor old Bennett is in bed with a terrible headache."

"Can I see the Governor ? " asked Leon

The Chief Warder shook his head.

"He has gone to Dover with Miss Folian—his daughter. She's gone off to the Continent."

"Miss Gwenda Folian ? " and when the Chief Warder nodded :

"Is she the lady who was training to be a doctor ? "

"She *is* a doctor," said the other, emphatically. "Why, when Lenthall nearly died from a heart attack, she saved his life—he works in the Governor's house, and I believe he'd cut off his right hand to serve the young lady. There's a lot of good in some of these fellows ! "

They were standing in the main prison hall. Leon gazed along the grim vista of steel balconies and little doors.

"This is where the night warder sits, I suppose ? " he asked, as he laid his hand on the high desk near where they were standing ; "and that door leads——? "

"To the Governor's quarters."

"And Miss Gwenda often slips through there with a cup of coffee and a sandwich for the night man. I suppose ? " he added, carelessly.

The Chief Warder was evasive.

"It would be against regulations if she did," he said. "Now you want to see Lenthall ? "

Leon shook his head.

"I don't think so," he said quietly.

.   .   .   .   .

"Where could a blackguard like Letheritt be singing in church on Christmas Day ? " asked Leon when he was giving the intimate history of the case to his companions. "In only one place—a prison. Obviously our Miss Brown was in that prison : the Governor and his family invariably attend church. Letheritt was 'not staying'—it was the end of his sentence, and he had been sent to Wilford for discharge.   Poor Meadows !   With all his faith in finger-prints gone astray because a released convict was true to his word and went out to get the letters that I missed, whilst the doped Mr. Bennett slept at his desk and Miss Gwenda Folian took his place ! "

Reprinted by permission from *Again the Three*.

THE POETICAL POLICEMAN

THE day Mr. Reeder arrived at the Public Prosecutor's office was indeed a day of fate for Mr. Lambton Green, Branch Manager of the London Scottish and Midland Bank.

That branch of the bank which Mr. Green controlled was situate at the corner of Pell Street and Firling Avenue on the " country side " of Ealing. It is a fairly large building and, unlike most suburban branch offices, the whole of the premises were devoted to banking business, for the bank carried very heavy deposits, the Lunar Traction Company, with three thousand people on its pay-roll, the Associated Novelties Corporation, with its enormous turnover, and the Laraphone Company being only three of the L.S.M.'s customers.

On Wednesday afternoons, in preparation for the pay days of these corporations, large sums in currency were brought from the head office and deposited in the steel and concrete strong-room, which was immediately beneath Mr. Green's private office, but admission to which was gained through a steel door in the general office. This door was observable from the street, and to assist observation there was a shaded lamp fixed to the wall immediately above, which threw a powerful beam of light upon the door. Further security was ensured by the employment of a night watchman, Arthur Malling, an army pensioner.

The bank lay on a restricted police beat which had been so arranged that the constable on patrol passed the bank every forty minutes. It was his practice to look through the window and exchange signals with the night watchman, his orders being to wait until Malling appeared.

On the night of October 17th Police-Constable Burnett stopped as usual before the wide peep-hole and glanced into the bank. The first thing he noticed was that the lamp above the strong-room door had been extinguished. The night watchman was not visible, and, his suspicions aroused, the officer did not wait for the man to put in an appearance as he would ordinarily have done, but passed the window to the door, which, to his alarm, he found ajar. Pushing it open, he entered the bank, calling Malling by name. There was no answer.

Permeating the air was a faint, sweet scent which he could not locate. The general offices were empty and, entering the manager's room, in which a light burnt, he saw a figure stretched upon the ground. It was the night watchman. His wrists were handcuffed, two straps had been tightly buckled about his knees and ankles.

The explanation for the strange and sickly aroma was now clear. Above the head of the prostrate man was suspended, by a wire hooked to the picture-rail, an old tin can, the bottom of which was perforated so that there fell an incessant trickle of some volatile liquid upon the thick cotton pad which covered Malling's face.

Burnett, who had been wounded in the war, had instantly recognised the smell of chloroform and, dragging the unconscious man into the outer office, snatched the pad from his face and, leaving him only long enough to telephone to the police-station, sought vainly to bring him to consciousness.

The police reserves arrived within a few minutes, and with them the divisional surgeon who, fortunately, had been at the station when the alarm came through. Every effort to restore the unfortunate man to life proved unavailing.

" He was probably dead when he was found," was the police doctor's verdict. " What those scratches are on his right palm is a mystery."

He pulled open the clenched fist and showed half a dozen little scratches. They were recent, for there was a smear of blood on the palm.

Burnett was sent at once to arouse Mr. Green, the manager, who lived in Firling Avenue, at the corner of which the bank stood ; a street of semi-detached villas of a pattern familiar enough to the Londoner. As the officer walked through the little front garden to the door he saw a light through the panels, and he had hardly knocked before the door was opened and Mr. Lambton Green appeared, fully dressed and, to the officer's discerning eye, in a state of considerable agitation. Constable Burnett saw on a hall chair a big bag, a travelling rug and an umbrella.

The little manager listened, pale as death, whilst Burnett told him of his discovery.

" The bank robbed ?　Impossible ! " he almost shrieked. " My God ! this is awful ! "

He was so near the point of collapse that Burnett had to assist him into the street.

" I—I was going away on a holiday," he said incoherently, as he walked up the dark thoroughfare towards the bank premises. " The fact is—I was leaving the bank. I left a note—explaining to the directors."

Into a circle of suspicious men the manager tottered. He unlocked the drawer of his desk, looked and crumpled up.

" They're not here ! " he said wildly. " I left them here —my keys—with the note ! "

And then he swooned. When the dazed man recovered he found himself in a police cell and, later in the day, he drooped before a police magistrate, supported by two constables, and listened, like a man in a dream, to a charge of causing the death of Arthur Malling, and further, of converting to his own use the sum of £100,000.

It was on the morning of the first remand that Mr. John G. Reeder, with some reluctance, for he was suspicious of all Government departments, transferred himself from his own office on Lower Regent Street to a somewhat gloomy bureau on the top floor of the building which houses the Public Prosecutor. In making this change he advanced only one stipulation : that he should be connected by private telephone wire with his old bureau.

He did not demand this—he never demanded anything. He asked, nervously and apologetically. There was a certain wistful helplessness about John G. Reeder that made people feel sorry for him, that caused even the Public Prosecutor a few uneasy moments of doubt as to whether he had been quite wise in substituting this weak-appearing man of middle age for Inspector Holford—bluff, capable and heavily mysterious.

Mr. Reeder was something over fifty, a long-faced gentleman with sandy-grey hair and a slither of side whiskers that mercifully distracted attention from his large outstanding ears. He wore half-way down his nose a pair of steel-rimmed pince-nez, through which nobody had ever seen him look—they were invariably removed when he was reading. A high and flat-crowned bowler hat matched and yet did not match a frock-coat tightly buttoned across his sparse chest. His boots were square-toed, his cravat—of the broad, chest-protector pattern—was ready-made and buckled into place behind a Gladstonian collar. The neatest appendage to Mr. Reeder was an umbrella rolled so tightly that it might be mistaken for a frivolous walking-cane. Rain or shine, he carried this article hooked to his arm, and within living memory it had never been unfurled.

Inspector Holford (promoted now to the responsibilities of Superintendent) met him in the office to hand over his duties, and a more tangible quantity in the shape of old furniture and fixings.

" Glad to know you, Mr. Reeder. I haven't had the pleasure of meeting you before, but I've heard a lot about you. You've been doing Bank of England work, haven't you ? "

Mr. Reeder whispered that he had had that honour, and sighed as though he regretted the drastic sweep of fate that had torn him from the obscurity of his labours. Mr. Holford's scrutiny was full of misgivings.

" Well," he said awkwardly, " this job is different, though I'm told that you are one of the best informed men in London, and if that is the case this will be easy work. Still, we've never had an outsider—I mean, so to speak, a private detective—in this office before, and naturally the Yard is a bit——"

" I quite understand," murmured Mr. Reeder, hanging up his immaculate umbrella. " It is very natural. Mr. Bolond expected the appointment. His wife is annoyed—very properly. But she has no reason to be. She is an ambitious woman. She has a third interest in a West End dancing club that might be raided one of these days."

Holford was staggered. Here was news that was little more than a whispered rumour at Scotland Yard.

" How the devil do you know that ? " he blurted.

Mr. Reeder's smile was one of self-depreciation.

" One picks up odd scraps of information," he said apologetically. " I—I see wrong in everything. That is my curious perversion—I have a criminal mind ! "

Holford drew a long breath.

31*

" Well—there is nothing much doing. That Ealing case is pretty clear. Green is an ex-convict, who got a job at the bank during the war and worked up to manager. He has done seven years for conversion."

" Embezzlement and conversion," murmured Mr. Reeder. " I—er—I'm afraid I was the principal witness against him : bank crimes were rather—er—a hobby of mine. Yes, he got into difficulties with money-lenders. Very foolish—extremely foolish. And he doesn't admit his error." Mr. Reeder sighed heavily. " Poor fellow ! With his life at stake one may forgive and indeed condone his pitiful prevarications."

The inspector stared at the new man in amazement.

" I don't know that there is much ' poor fellow ' about him. He has cached £100,000 and told the weakest yarn that I've ever read—you'll find copies of the police reports here, if you'd like to read them. The scratches on Malling's hand are curious—they've found several on the other hand. They are not deep enough to suggest a struggle. As to the yarn that Green tells——"

Mr. J. G. Reeder nodded sadly.

" It was not an ingenious story," he said, almost with regret. " If I remember rightly, his story was something like this : he had been recognised by a man who served in Dartmoor with him, and this fellow wrote a blackmailing letter telling him to pay or clear out. Sooner than return to a life of crime, Green wrote out all the facts to his directors, put the letter in the drawer of his desk with his keys, and left a note for his head cashier on the desk itself, intending to leave London and try to make a fresh start where he was unknown."

" There were no letters in or on the desk, and no keys," said the inspector decisively. " The only true part of the yarn was that he had done time."

" Imprisonment," suggested Mr. Reeder plaintively. He had a horror of slang. " Yes, that was true."

Left alone in his office, he spent a very considerable time at his private telephone, communing with the young person who was still a young person, although the passage of time had dealt unkindly with her. For the rest of the morning he was reading the depositions which his predecessor had put on the desk.

It was late in the afternoon when the Public Prosecutor strolled into his room and glanced at the big pile of manuscript through which his subordinate was wading.

" What are you reading—the Green business ? " he asked, with a note of satisfaction in his voice. " I'm glad that is interesting you—though it seems a fairly straightforward case. I have had a letter from the president of the man's bank, who for some reason seems to think Green was telling the truth."

Mr. Reeder looked up with that pained expression of his which he invariably wore when he was puzzled.

" Here is the evidence of Policeman Burnett," he said. " Perhaps you can enlighten me, sir. Policeman Burnett stated in his evidence—let me read it :

" ' Some time before I reached the bank premises I saw a man standing at the corner of the street, immediately outside the bank. I saw him distinctly in the light of a passing mail van. I did not attach any importance to his presence, and I did not see him again. It was possible for this man to have gone round the block and come to 120, Firling Avenue without being seen by me. Immediately after I saw him, my foot struck against a piece of iron on the sidewalk. I put my lamp on the object and found it was an old horseshoe ; I had seen children playing with this particular shoe earlier in the evening. When I looked again towards the corner, the man had disappeared. He would have seen the light of my lamp. I saw no other person, and so far as I can remember, there was no light showing in Green's house when I passed it.' "

Mr. Reeder looked up.

" Well ? " said the Prosecutor. " There's nothing remarkable about that. It was probably Green who dodged round the block and came in at the back of the constable."

Mr. Reeder scratched his chin.

" Yes," he said thoughtfully, " ye-es." He shifted uncomfortably in his chair. " Would it be considered indecorous if I made a few inquiries, independent of the police ? " he asked nervously. " I should not like them to think that a mere dilettante was interfering with their lawful functions."

" By all means," said the Prosecutor heartily. " Go down and see the officer in charge of the case : I'll give you a note to him—it is by no means unusual for my officer to conduct a separate investigation, though I am afraid you will discover very little. The ground has been well covered by Scotland Yard."

" It would be permissible to see the man ? " hesitated Reeder.

" Green ? Why, of course ! I will send you up the necessary order."

The light was fading from a grey, blustering sky, and rain was falling fitfully, when Mr. Reeder, with his furled umbrella hooked to his arm, his coat collar turned up, stepped through the dark gateway of Brixton Prison and was led to the cell where a distracted man sat, his head upon his hands, his pale eyes gazing into vacancy.

" It's true ; it's true ! Every word." Green almost sobbed the words.

A pallid man, inclined to be bald, with a limp yellow moustache, going grey. Reeder, with his extraordinary memory for faces, recognised him the moment he saw him, though it was some time before the recognition was mutual.

" Yes, Mr. Reeder, I remember you now. You were the gentleman who caught me before. But I've been as straight as a die. I've never taken a farthing that didn't belong to me. What my poor girl will think——"

" Are you married ? " asked Mr. Reeder sympathetically.

" No, but I was going to be—rather late in life. She's nearly thirty years younger than me, and the best girl that ever——"

Reeder listened to the rhapsody that followed, the melancholy deepening in his face.

" She hasn't been into the court, thank God, but she knows the truth. A friend of mine told me that she has been absolutely knocked out."

" Poor soul ! " Mr. Reeder shook his head.

" It happened on her birthday, too," the man went on bitterly.

" Did she know you were going away ? "

" Yes, I told her the night before. I'm not going to bring her into the case. If we'd been properly engaged it would be different ; but she's married and is divorcing her husband, but the decree hasn't been made absolute yet. That's why I never went about with her or saw much of her. And of course, nobody knew about our engagement, although we lived in the same street."

" Firling Avenue ? " asked Reeder, and the bank manager nodded despondently.

" She was married when she was seventeen to a brute. It was pretty galling for me, having to keep quiet about it—I mean, for nobody to know about our engagement. All sorts of rotten people were making up to her, and I had just to grind my teeth and say nothing. Impossible people ! Why, that fool Burnett, who arrested me, he was sweet on her ; used to write her poetry—you wouldn't think it possible in a policeman, would you ? "

The outrageous incongruity of a poetical policeman did not seem to shock the detective.

" There is poetry in every soul, Mr. Green," he said gently, " and a policeman is a man."

Though he dismissed the eccentricity of the constable so lightly, the poetical policeman filled his mind all the way home to his house in the Brockley Road, and occupied his thoughts for the rest of his waking time.

It was a quarter to eight o'clock in the morning, and the world seemed entirely populated by milkmen and whistling newspaper boys, when Mr. J. G. Reeder came into Firling Avenue.

He stopped only for a second outside the bank, which had long since ceased to be an object of local awe and fearfulness, and pursued his way down the broad avenue. On either side of the thoroughfare ran a row of pretty villas— pretty although they bore a strong family resemblance to one another ; each house with its little forecourt, sometimes laid out simply as a grass plot, sometimes decorated with flower-beds. Green's house was the eighteenth in the road on the right-hand side. Here he had lived with a cook-housekeeper, and apparently gardening was not his hobby, for the forecourt was covered with grass that had been allowed to grow at its will.

Before the twenty-sixth house in the road Mr. Reeder paused and gazed with mild interest at the blue blinds which covered every window. Evidently Miss Magda Grayne was a lover of flowers, for geraniums filled the window-boxes and were set at intervals along the tiny border under the bow window. In the centre of the grass plot was a circular flower-bed with one flowerless rose tree, the leaves of which were drooping and brown.

As he raised his eyes to the upper window, the blind went up slowly, and he was dimly conscious that there was a figure behind the white lace curtains. Mr. Reeder walked hurriedly away, as one caught in an immodest act, and resumed his peregrinations until he came to the big nursery gardener's which formed the corner lot at the far end of the road.

Here he stood for some time in contemplation, his arm resting on the iron railings, his eyes staring blankly at the vista of green-houses. He remained in this attitude so long that one of the nurserymen, not unnaturally thinking that a stranger was seeking a way into the gardens, came over with the laborious gait of the man who wrings his living from the soil, and asked if he was wanting anybody.

" Several people," sighed Mr. Reeder ; " several people ! "

Leaving the resentful man to puzzle out his impertinence, he slowly retraced his steps. At No. 412 he stopped again, opened the little iron gate and passed up the path to the front door. A small girl answered his knock and ushered him into the parlour.

The room was not well furnished ; it was scarcely furnished at all. A strip of almost new linoleum covered the passage ; the furniture of the parlour itself was made up of wicker chairs, a square of art carpet and a table. He heard the sound of feet above his head, feet on bare boards, and then presently the door opened and a girl came in.

She was pretty in a heavy way, but on her face he saw the marks of sorrow. It was pale and haggard ; the eyes looked as though she had been recently weeping.

" Miss Magda Grayne ? " he asked, rising as she came in. She nodded.

" Are you from the police ? " she asked quickly.

" Not exactly the police," he corrected carefully. " I hold an—er—an appointment in the office of the Public Prosecutor, which is analogous to, but distinct from, a position in the Metropolitan Police Force."

She frowned, and then :

" I wondered if anybody would come to see me," she said. " Mr. Green sent you ? "

" Mr. Green told me of your existence : he did not send me."

There came to her face in that second a look which almost startled him. Only for a fleeting space of time, the expression had dawned and passed almost before the untrained eye could detect its passage.

" I was expecting somebody to come," she said. Then : " What made him do it ? " she asked.

" You think he is guilty ? "

" The police think so." She drew a long sigh. " I wish to God I had never seen—this place ! "

He did not answer ; his eyes were roving round the apartment. On a bamboo table was an old vase which had been clumsily filled with golden chrysanthemums, of a peculiarly beautiful variety. Not all, for amidst them flowered a large Michaelmas daisy that had the forlorn appearance of a parvenu that had strayed by mistake into noble company.

" You're fond of flowers ? " he murmured.

She looked at the vase indifferently.

" Yes, I like flowers," she said. " The girl put them in there." Then : " Do you think they will hang him ? "

The brutality of the question, put without hesitation, pained Reeder.

" It is a very serious charge," he said. And then : " Have you a photograph of Mr. Green ? "

She frowned.

" Yes ; do you want it ? "

He nodded.

She had hardly left the room before he was at the bamboo table and had lifted out the flowers. As he had seen through the glass, they were roughly tied with a piece of string. He examined the ends, and here again his first observation had been correct : none of these flowers had been cut ; they had been plucked bodily from their stalks. Beneath the string was the paper which had been first wrapped about the stalks. It was a page torn from a notebook ; he could see the red lines, but the pencilled writing was indecipherable.

As her foot sounded on the stairs, he replaced the flowers

in the vase, and when she came in he was looking through the window into the street.

"Thank you," he said, as he took the photograph from her.

It bore an affectionate inscription on the back.

"You're married, he tells me, madam?"

"Yes, I am married, and practically divorced," she said shortly.

"Have you been living here long?"

"About three months," she answered. "It was his wish that I should live here."

He looked at the photograph again.

"Do you know Constable Burnett?"

He saw a dull flush come to her face and die away again.

"Yes, I know the sloppy fool!" she said viciously. And then, realising that she had been surprised into an expression which was not altogether ladylike, she went on, in a softer tone: "Mr. Burnett is rather sentimental, and I don't like sentimental people, especially—well, you understand, Mr. ——"

"Reeder," murmured that gentleman.

"You understand, Mr. Reeder, that when a girl is engaged and in my position, those kind of attentions are not very welcome."

Reeder was looking at her keenly. Of her sorrow and distress there could be no doubt. On the subject of the human emotions, and the ravages they make upon the human countenance, Mr. Reeder was almost as great an authority as Mantegazza.

"On your birthday," he said. "How very sad! You were born on the seventeenth of October. You are English, of course?"

"Yes, I'm English," she said shortly. "I was born in Walworth—in Wallington. I once lived in Walworth."

"How old are you?"

"Twenty-three," she answered.

Mr Reeder took off his glasses and polished them on a large silk handkerchief.

"The whole thing is inexpressibly sad," he said. "I am glad to have had the opportunity of speaking with you, young lady. I sympathise with you very deeply."

And in this unsatisfactory way he took his departure.

She closed the door on him, saw him stop in the middle of the path, and pick up something from a border bed and wondered, frowning, why this middle-aged man had picked up the horseshoe she had thrown through the window the night before. Into Mr. Reeder's tail pocket went this piece of rusted steel, and then he continued his thoughtful way to the nursery gardens, for he had a few questions to ask.

The men of Section 10 were parading for duty when Mr. Reeder came timidly into the charge room and produced his credentials to the inspector in charge.

" Oh, yes, Mr. Reeder," said that officer affably. " We have had a note from the P.P.'s office, and I think I had the pleasure of working with you on that big slush [1] case a few years ago. Now what can I do for you ? . . . Burnett ? Yes, he's here."

He called the man's name and a young and good-looking officer stepped from the ranks.

" He's the man who discovered the murder—he's marked for promotion," said the inspector. " Burnett, this gentleman is from the Public Prosecutor's office and he wants a little talk with you. Better use my office, Mr. Reeder."

The young policeman saluted and followed the shuffling figure into the privacy of the inspector's office. He was a confident young man : already his name and portrait had appeared in the newspapers, the hint of promotion had become almost an accomplished fact, and before his eyes was the prospect of a supreme achievement.

" They tell me that you are something of a poet, officer," said Mr. Reeder.

Burnett blushed.

" Why, yes, sir. I write a bit," he confessed.

" Love poems, yes ? " asked the other gently. " One finds time in the night—er—for such fancies. And there is no inspiration like—er—love, officer."

Burnett's face was crimson.

" I've done a bit of writing in the night, sir," he said, " though I've never neglected my duty."

" Naturally," murmured Mr. Reeder. " You have a poetical mind. It was a poetical thought to pluck flowers in the middle of the night——"

Slush = forged Bank of England notes.

" The nurseryman told me I could take any flowers I wanted," Burnett interrupted hastily. " I did nothing wrong."

Reeder inclined his head in agreement.

" That I know. You picked the flowers in the dark—by the way, you inadvertently included a Michaelmas daisy with your chrysanthemums—tied up your little poem to them and left them on the doorstep with—er—a horseshoe. I wondered what had become of that horseshoe."

" I threw them up on to her—to the lady's window-sill," corrected the uncomfortable young man. " As a matter of fact, the idea didn't occur to me until I had passed the house——"

Mr. Reeder's face was thrust forward.

" This is what I want to confirm," he said softly. " The idea of leaving the flowers did not occur to you until you had passed her house ? The horseshoe suggested the thought ? Then you went back, picked the flowers, tied them up with the little poem you had already written, and tossed them up to her window—we need not mention the lady's name."

Constable Burnett's face was a study.

" I don't know how you guessed that, but it is a fact. If I've done anything wrong——"

" It is never wrong to be in love," said Mr. J. G. Reeder soberly. " Love is a very beautiful experience—I have frequently read about it."

Miss Magda Grayne had dressed to go out for the afternoon and was putting on her hat, when she saw the queer man who had called so early that morning, walking up the tessellated path. Behind him she recognised a detective engaged in the case. The servant was out ; nobody could be admitted except by herself. She walked quickly behind the dressing-table into the bay of the window and glanced up and down the road. Yes, there was the taxicab which usually accompanies such visitations, and, standing by the driver, another man, obviously a " busy."

She pulled up the overlay of her bed, took out the flat pad of bank-notes that she found, and thrust them into her handbag, then, stepping on tiptoe, she went out to the landing, into the unfurnished back room, and, opening the window, dropped to the flat roof of the kitchen. In another

minute she was in the garden and through the back gate.
A narrow passage divided the two lines of villas that backed
on one another. She was in High Street and had boarded a
car before Mr. Reeder grew tired of knocking. To the best
of his knowledge Mr. Reeder never saw her again.

. . . . .

At the Public Prosecutor's request, he called at his chief's
house after dinner and told his surprising story.

" Green, who had the unusual experience of being promoted to his position over the heads of his seniors, for special
services he rendered during the war, was undoubtedly an
ex-convict, and he spoke the truth when he said that he
had received a letter from a man who had served a period
of imprisonment with him. The name of this blackmailer is,
or rather was, Arthur George Crater, whose other name was
Malling ! "

" Not the night watchman ? " said the Public Prosecutor,
in amazement.

Mr. Reeder nodded.

" Yes, sir, it was Arthur Malling. His daughter, Miss
Magda Crater, was, as she very truly said, born at Walworth
on the 17th of October, 1900. She said Wallington after,
but Walworth first. One observes that when people adopt
false family names, they seldom change their given names,
and the ' Magda ' was easy to identify.

" Evidently Malling had planned this robbery of the bank
very carefully. He had brought his daughter, in a false
name, to Ealing, and had managed to get her introduced
to Mr. Green. Magda's job was to worm her way into
Green's confidence and learn all that she could. Possibly
it was part of her duty to secure casts of the keys. Whether
Malling recognised in the manager an old prison acquaintance, or whether he obtained the facts from the girl, we shall
never know. But when the information came to him, he
saw, in all probability, an opportunity of robbing the bank
and of throwing suspicion upon the manager.

" The girl's rôle was that of a woman who was to be
divorced, and I must confess this puzzled me until I realised
that in no circumstances would Malling wish his daughter's
name to be associated with the bank manager.

" The night of the seventeenth was chosen for the raid.
Malling's plan to get rid of the manager had succeeded.

He saw the letter on the table in Green's private office, read it, secured the keys—although he had in all probability a duplicate set—and at a favourable moment cleared as much portable money from the bank vaults as he could carry, hurried them round to the house in Firling Avenue, where they were buried in the central bed of the front garden, under a rose bush—I rather imagined there was something interfering with the nutrition of that unfortunate bush the first time I saw it. I can only hope that the tree is not altogether dead, and I have given instructions that it shall be replanted and well fertilised."

"Yes, yes," said the Prosecutor, who was not at all interested in horticulture.

"In planting the tree, as he did in some haste, Malling scratched his hand. Roses have thorns—I went to Ealing to find the rose bush that had scratched his hand. Hurrying back to the bank, he waited, knowing that Constable Burnett was due at a certain time. He had prepared the can of chloroform, the handcuffs and straps were waiting for him, and he stood at the corner of the street until he saw the flash of Burnett's lamp ; then, running into the bank and leaving the door ajar, he strapped himself, fastened the handcuffs and lay down, expecting that the policeman would arrive, find the open door and rescue him before much harm was done.

"But Constable Burnett had had some pleasant exchanges with the daughter. Doubtless she had received instructions from her father to be as pleasant to him as possible. Burnett was a poetical young man, knew it was her birthday, and as he walked along the street his foot struck an old horseshoe and the idea occurred to him that he should return, attach the horseshoe to some flowers, which the nurseryman had given him permission to pick, and leave his little bouquet, so to speak, at his lady's feet—a poetical idea, and one worthy of the finest traditions of the Metropolitan Police Force. This he did, but it took some time ; and all the while this young man was philandering—Arthur Crater was dying !

"In a few seconds after lying down he must have passed from consciousness . . . the chloroform still dripped, and when the policeman eventually reached the bank, ten minutes after he was due, the man was dead ! "

The Public Prosecutor sat back in his padded chair and frowned at his new subordinate.

"How on earth did you piece together all this?" he asked in wonder.

Mr. Reeder shook his head sadly.

"I have that perversion," he said. "It is a terrible misfortune, but it is true. I see evil in everything . . . in dying rose bushes, in horseshoes—in poetry even. I have the mind of a criminal. It is deplorable!"

Reprinted by permission from *The Mind of Mr. J. G. Reeder.*

VALENTINE WILLIAMS

The Pigeon Man
The Alibi

¶ Mr. WILLIAMS was Berlin correspondent of Reuter's until 1909. He later became the first accredited correspondent at the British headquarters in Flanders during the World War. And it was from the experience he gained as foreign correspondent that his famous spy character, Clubfoot, emerged. More recently, however, he has taken to the straight detective story, where he has scored several big successes: notably, *The Clock Ticks On* and *The Portcullis Room*.

THE PIGEON MAN

I

FLANDERS in '18, and March coming in like a lion. With a purr that, nearer the front, might have been confused with the thudding of distant drum-fire the icy rain beat against the panes. At the streaming window of a dingy bedroom of the Hôtel du Commerce a girl stood gazing listlessly into the street below. Outside, over the gleaming cobbles of the little Belgian town, the great grey lorries, splashed hood-high with Flanders mud, slithered along in an endless train, swerving from the road's greasy crown only to make way for the snorting Staff cars that, freighted with begoggled officers in field-grey, from time to time came roaring down the street. In and out of the traffic, despatch-riders on motor-cycles whirled and rattled, staying their progress with trailing, gaitered leg to inquire the location of Operations or Intelligence offices of the Corps established there. In the hotel bedroom the crockery on the washstand jingled to the din of the street.

Without turning round from her observation post, the girl flung a question across her shoulder. She was tall, and the black frock she wore emphasised her slimness. Her shining red hair, loosely coiled about her well-shaped head, was the only blur of positive colour among the neutral shades of the room.

" Am I to wait the convenience of the Corps Intelligence office all day ? " she demanded sullenly. At a table against the wall an officer in field-grey sat reading the *Kölnische Zeitung*. He did not lift his eyes from his newspaper at the girl's question.

" Such were Colonel von Trompeter's orders, *meine Gnädige*," he retorted.

She stamped her foot and faced the speaker. " This room stifles me, do you hear ? " she exclaimed tensely. " I don't mind the rain : I'm going out ! "

985

" No ! " said the officer.

" Do I understand that I'm a prisoner ? "

The officer shrugged his shoulders as, stretching forth his arms, he folded back the paper. " You're of the Service, Fräulein Sylvia," he rejoined placidly. " You've got to obey orders like the rest of us ! "

" Agreed," she cried. " But they can trust me, can't they ? "

The officer shrugged his shoulders again. " Doubtless the Colonel had his reasons for not wishing civilians to roam about Corps Headquarters. . . ."

" Bah ! " she broke in contemptuously. " Do you think I'm blind ? Do you really imagine, Captain Pracht, that I don't know "—she waved a slim hand towards the window and the sounding street beyond—" what all this movement means ? Every railhead from the North Sea to the Vosges is pouring forth men and guns ; your troops released by the Russian Revolution are gathering to deal the Allies the final——"

Pracht sprang to his feet. " *Um Gottes Willen*, mind what you're saying ! You speak of things that are known to but a handful of us——"

" Quite so, my friend. But will you please remember that I am of that handful ? My sources in Brussels are excellent——" She broke off and contemplated her companion's face. " Why has Colonel von Trompeter sent for me ? "

" There I can answer you quite frankly," said the Captain. " I don't know."

" And if you did, you wouldn't tell me ? "

The officer bowed. " It would be hard to refuse so charming a lady anything. . . ."

She shook herself impatiently. " Words, merely words ! " she cried.

She let her eyes rest meltingly on his face. They were strange eyes, madder-brown under dark lashes. " Have you ever been in love, Captain Pracht ? "

The officer's face set doggedly, so that two small vertical lines appeared on either side of his thin lips under the clipped brown moustache. " Never on duty, *gnädiges Fräulein*—that is "—he paused, then added—" unless commanded."

" Why, then," she put in merrily, " I might have spared myself the trouble of locking my door last night."

Captain Pracht flushed darkly, and a little pulse began to beat at his temple. She looked at him fixedly and laughed. " You have a charming *métier*, Herr Hauptmann ! "

An ugly look crept into his face. " The same as yours, *meine Gnädige* ! "

A patch of colour crept into her pale cheeks. " Not quite ! " Her voice vibrated a little. " Men know how to protect themselves. They go into these things with their eyes open. But almost every woman, even in the Secret Service, is blinded by love . . . once . . ." she sighed and added, " the first time. . . ."

" The gracious lady speaks from personal experience, no doubt," the officer hazarded. His manner was unpleasant. With calm disdain she looked him up and down.

" Yes," she answered simply.

" I have always said," the Captain announced ponderously, " that women were too emotional for Secret Service work. Especially foreigners."

" Rumanians, for instance ? " suggested the girl sweetly.

" I was not speaking personally," retorted the officer huffily. " If we must have women spies, then why not Germans ? Our German women have an ingrained sense of discipline, a respect for orders . . ."

The girl's gurgling laugh pealed through the room. " But their taste in nighties is dreadful," she broke in. " You must remember, my dear Captain Pracht, that our battle-field is the boudoir——"

At that moment the door was flung back. An orderly, in a streaming cape, stood there. " Colonel von Trompeter's compliments," he bawled out of a wooden face, saluting with a stamp that shook the floor, " and will the Herr Hauptmann bring Fräulein Averescu to the office immediately."

II

" The trouble about this job of ours, young Horst," said Colonel von Trompeter, " is to recognise the truth when you find it ! "

A heavy man, the Herr Oberst, but handsome still with his fearless eyes of the brightest blue, straight nose, and trim white moustache. The blue and silver Hussar cap which, in defiance of all clothing regulations, he insisted on wearing with his Staff uniform, was the only evidence that he had started his army career in the light cavalry, for advancing years had endowed him with the body of a heavy dragoon. His big form, muscular yet under its swelling curves, was moulded in his well-fitting service dress of grey, frogged with the brandenbourgs of the Hussars, and the broad pink stripe of the Great General Staff, together with the glossy brown field-boot into which it disappeared, set off admirably his length of leg.

A fine blade, the Herr Oberst, with a naturally intuitive mind sharpened by the intensive training of War School and Great General Staff, a gift of lightning decision and a notable aptitude for languages. But, more than this, he was a man of rugged character, of unflinching moral courage, and as such ranged head and shoulders above the swarm of silver-laced sycophants at Headquarters who assiduously lick-spittled to His Excellency Lieutenant-General Baron Haase von dem Hasenberg, the Corps Commander. For His Excellency, a choleric old party with the brains of a louse and the self-control of a gorilla, was His Majesty's friend who with supple spine had genuflected his way up the rough road of promotion under the approving eye of the All-Highest War Lord.

His Excellency detested his Chief of Intelligence. He might have forgiven Colonel von Trompeter his outstanding ability, for brains are an asset on the staff of a Corps Commander when awkward incidents have to be covered up ; and Baron Haase had not been a lucky leader. But His Excellency was enraged by the Colonel's habit of invariably speaking his mind. It infuriated him that Colonel von Trompeter should have made his career in spite of his brutal candour. When only a Major, acting as assistant umpire at Kaiser manœuvres, had he not curtly replied to the Emperor himself, enthusiastically seeking praise for a cavalry charge led in the All-Highest Person against a nest of machine-guns : " All dead to the last horse, Your Majesty ! " and been promptly exiled to an East Prussian frontier garrison for his pains ?

Yet, although the victim of the All-Highest displeasure had lived the incident down, he had learned nothing by experience. To the Corps Commander's resentful fury, he flatly refused to curry favour with his immediate Chief by lending himself to the great conspiracy of eyewash by means of which, in war as in peace, the War Lord was justified of his appointments to the high commands.

And so a state of open warfare existed between His Excellency—and that signified the bulk of the Headquarters Staff—and his Chief of Intelligence. Only the Intelligence Staff, who worshipped Trompeter to a man, less for his brilliant ability than for his sturdy championship of his subordinates even in the face of the epileptic ravings of His Excellency, stood by their Chief. For the rest, every imaginable form of chicane and sabotage was employed in the attempt to drive Colonel von Trompeter into seeking a transfer. In almost every branch of Corps Headquarters, save only the Intelligence, it became as important to defeat Colonel von Trompeter and his assistants as to beat the English who held the line in this part of Flanders. And His Excellency proclaimed at least thrice a day to all who would hear him that Trompeter was " *ein taktloser Kerl.*"

When, therefore, on this wet March morning, " the old man," as his staff called Trompeter, delivered himself of the apothegm set forth above, Lieutenant Horst, his youngest officer, who was examining a sheaf of aeroplane photographs at his desk in a corner of the office, glanced up with troubled eyes. It was rare, indeed, that " the old man " allowed the daily dose of pinpricks to get under his skin. But to-day the Chief was restless. Ever since breakfast he had been pacing like a caged lion up and down the wet track left by the boots of visitors on the strip of matting between the door and his desk.

" Operations are making trouble about the shelling of the 176th divisional area last night," the Colonel continued.

" With permission, Herr Oberst," Horst put in diffidently, " these fresh troops carry on as though they were still in Russia. Their march discipline is deplorable. They were probably spotted by aircraft——"

The Herr Oberst shook his grizzled poll. " Won't wash, my boy. They went in after dark. *That* explanation we put up to Operations when the 58th Division had their dumps shelled last week. Operations won't swallow it again. Humph——"

He grunted and turned to stare out into the rain. A battalion was passing up the street, rank on rank of soaked and weary men. Their feet hammered out a melancholy tattoo on the cobbles. There was no brave blare of music to help them on their way. The band marched in front with instruments wrapped up against the wet. " Fed—up," " Fed—up," the crunching feet seemed to say.

The Colonel's voice suddenly cut across the rhythmic tramping. " What time is Ehrhardt arriving with that prisoner from the 91st Division ? " he asked.

" He was ordered for eleven, Herr Oberst ! "

" It's after that now——"

" The roads are terribly congested, Herr Oberst !

The Colonel made no reply. His fingers drummed on the window-pane. Then he said : " Our English cousins are concentrating on the Corps area, young Horst. They've got a pigeon man out. That much was clear when that basket of pigeons was picked up in Fleury Wood last week."

" A pigeon man, Herr Oberst ? "

" I was forgetting ; you're new to the game. So you don't know what a pigeon man is, young Horst ? "

" No, Herr Oberst ! "

" Then let me tell you something : if you ever meet a pigeon man, you can safely take your hat off to him, for you're meeting a hero. It's a job that means almost certain death. A pigeon man is a Secret Service officer who's landed by an aeroplane at some quiet spot in the enemy lines with a supply of carrier-pigeons. His job is to collect the reports which spies have already left for him at agreed hiding-places. He fastens these messages to the legs of his birds and releases them to fly back to their loft. . . ."

" Does the aeroplane wait, Herr Oberst ? "

The Colonel laughed shortly. " *I wo !* The pigeon man has to make his way home the best he çan. They usually head for the Dutch frontier. . . ."

" He's in plain clothes, then ? "

" Of course. That's why I say the job means almost certain death. Even we Huns, as they call us, are justified in shooting an officer caught in plain clothes behind our lines."

The young man pursed up his lips in a silent whistle.

whispered across the desk, " although he seems to hear all right."

" Wait ! " Trompeter bade him. He spoke to the prisoner again.

" Any civilian found wandering in the military zone without proper papers is liable to be shot," he said sternly. " Do you realise that ? "

The tramp grinned feebly and made a gurgling noise like an infant. The Colonel repeated his warning in Flemish.

" Grr . . . goo . . . grr ! " gibbered the prisoner.

Trompeter went round the desk and looked the man in the eye. " See his hands, Herr Oberst," said Ehrhardt in an undertone. The tramp's hands were coarse and horny, with blackened and broken nails. " Are those the hands of an officer ? "

The Colonel grunted, but made no other comment.

There was a smart rap at the door. Reinhold, the orderly, appeared with a tray. On it were set out a pot of coffee, a jug of milk, sugar, a plate of ham, and a hunk of greyish war bread. The Colonel signed to the man to put the tray down on a side table. Then he turned to the prisoner. " Eat ! " he bade him.

The idiot grinned broadly and broke into a cackling laugh. Then, while the two officers watched him from a distance, he fell upon the victuals. It was horrible to see him wolf the food. He tore the ham with his hands and thrust great fragments into his mouth ; he literally buried his face in the bread, wrenching off great lumps with his teeth ; he emptied the milk-pot at a draught, spilling a good deal of the milk down his jacket in the process. He made animal noises as he ate and drank, stuffing himself until he gasped for breath.

" Could an officer eat like that ? " Ehrhardt whispered in his Chief's ear. But again the Colonel proffered no remark. When the last of the food had disappeared he said to his subordinate : " Take the prisoner outside now, and when I ring three times send him in—alone. Alone, do you understand ? "

" *Zu Befehl*, Herr Oberst ! "

Left alone, Colonel von Trompeter strode across to the window and stood for an instant looking out. In the street a gang of British prisoners of war, their threadbare khaki sodden with the rain, scraped away at the mud with broom

" Brave fellows ! Do we send out pigeon men too, Herr Oberst ? "

His Chief shook his head. " They wouldn't stand an earthly. The pigeon man can only operate successfully among a friendly civilian population. Well ? "

An orderly had bounced into the office, and, stiff as a ramrod, now fronted the Colonel. " Hauptmann Ehrhardt is here to report to the Herr Oberst."

The clear blue eyes snapped into alertness. " Has he brought a prisoner with him, Reinhold ? "

" *Jawohl*, Herr Oberst."

" Send him in ! Prisoner and escort remain outside." He turned to Horst as the orderly withdrew. " Herr Leutnant, a certain lady is waiting at the Hôtel du Commerce in charge of Captain Pracht, of the Brussels command. I may ask you to send for her presently. You will not say anything to her about this prisoner, and you will be responsible to me that no one approaches him in the meantime. And see that I'm not disturbed."

Then with bowed head the Colonel resumed his pacing up and down.

III

" As the Herr Oberst will see for himself," said Ehrhardt, rocking slightly as he stood stiffly at attention before his Chief—he was a secondary-school teacher in civil life and the military still overawed him—" the prisoner is practically a half-wit. If you speak to him, he only grins idiotically and dribbles. He looks half-starved, and as for his body—well, with respect, he's fairly crawling. God knows how long he's been wandering about the Bois des Corbeaux, where the fatigue party ran across him in the early hours of this morning. According to the Herr Oberst's orders, I had advised all units that any civilian caught in our lines was to be brought straightway to me at the Divisional Intelligence office. When this man was sent in I rang the Herr Oberst up at once. I haven't overlooked the possibility that the fellow may be acting a part ; but I'm bound to say that he seems to me to be what he looks like—a half-witted Flemish peasant. Speaking ethnologically——"

A brusque gesture cut short the imminent deadly treatise

on the psychology of the Flemings. The Colonel pointed to a chair beside the desk and pushed across a box of cigars. "Ehrhardt," said he, "information of the most exact description is being sent back regularly. Our troop movements are known. The 176th Division had two hundred casualties getting into their billeting area last night. These are no haphazard notes of regimental numbers jotted down at railway stations, or of movements of isolated units strung together by ignorant peasants. They are accurate reports prepared with intelligence by someone with a thorough grasp of the military situation. The English have a star man operating on this front. Who he is or what he looks like we don't know; but what we do know is that correspondence of a very secret nature which fell into the hands of one of our agents at The Hague speaks with enthusiasm of the accuracy of the reports sent by an unnamed agent concerning our present troop movements in Belgium. You are aware of my belief that an English pigeon man has been at work here"—he bent his white-tufted brows at his companion, who was gazing intently at him through gold-rimmed spectacles. "Supposing our friend outside is the man I'm looking for . . ."

Very positively Captain Ehrhardt shook his head. "Of course," he said in his pedantic fashion. "I must bow to the Herr Oberst's experience in these matters. But for me the hypothesis is out of the question. This fellow may be a spy; but in that case he's an agent of the lowest order, a brutish Belgian peasant—not a man of the calibre you mention, an educated individual, possibly a regular officer."

"Certainly a regular officer," the Colonel's calm voice broke in.

"*Ausgeschlossen*, Herr Oberst! The thing's impossible, as you'll realise the moment you see him!"

"Wait, my friend! The English have an extraordinary fellow, with whom we of the Great General Staff are well acquainted, at least by repute from pre-war days. We never managed to ascertain his name or get his photograph; but we know him for a man who is a marvellous linguist, with a most amazing knowledge of the Continent and Continental peoples. Dialect is one of his specialities. What is more to the point, he is a magnificent actor, and his skill in disguises is legendary. Again and again we were within an

ace of catching him, but he always contrived to slip through our fingers. We used to call him 'N,' the Unknown Quantity. Do you see what I'm driving at?"

"*Gewiss, gewiss,* Herr Oberst!" Ehrhardt wagged his head dubiously. "But this lout is no English officer."

"Well," said the Colonel, "let's look at him, anyway." He pressed a button on the desk, and presently, between two stolid figures in field-grey, a woebegone and miserable-looking tramp shambled in.

His clothes were a mass of rags. On his head a torn and shapeless cloth cap was stuck askew, and from beneath its tattered peak a pair of hot, dark eyes stared stupidly out of a face that was clotted with grime and darkened, as to the lower part, with a stiff growth of beard. A straggling moustache trembled above a pendulous under-lip that gleamed redly through bubbles that frothed at the mouth and dripped down the chin. His skin glinted yellowly through great rents in jacket and trousers, and his bare feet were thrust into clumsy, broken boots, one of which was swathed round with a piece of filthy rag. As he stood framed between the fixed bayonets of the escort, long shudders shook him continually.

Without looking up, the Colonel scribbled something on a writing-pad, tore off the slip and gave it to Horst. "Let the escort remain outside," he ordered. Horst and the guards clumped out. Then only did Trompeter, screwing his monocle in his eye, favour the prisoner with a long and challenging stare. The man did not budge. He continued to gaze into space, with his head rocking slightly to and fro and the saliva running down his chin.

The Colonel spoke in an aside to Ehrhardt. "You say you found nothing on him when you searched him?"

"Only a clasp-knife, some horse-chestnuts, and a piece of string, Herr Oberst."

"No papers?"

"No, Herr Oberst."

The Colonel addressed the prisoner in French. "Who are you and where do you come from?" he demanded.

Very slowly the man turned his vacuous gaze towards the speaker. He smiled feebly and dribbled, but did not speak.

"It struck me that he might be dumb," Ehrhardt

and spade. A voice at the door brought the Colonel about. Horst was there.

" Herr Oberst, the lady has arrived ! "

" She's not seen the prisoner, I trust ? "

" No, Herr Oberst. I put her to wait in the orderlies' room."

Trompeter nodded approval. " Good. I'll see her at once . . . alone."

As Horst went away he moved to the desk and turned the chair which Ehrhardt had vacated so that it faced the door. He himself remained standing, his hands resting on the desk at his back. With his long fingers he made sure that the bell-push in its wooden bulb was within his reach.

IV

It was commonly said of Colonel von Trompeter that he had a card-index mind. He forgot no name, no face, no date, that came into his day's work, and he had an uncanny facility at need of opening, as it were, a drawer in his brain and drawing forth a file of data.

As he helped Sylvia Averescu out of her wrap and invited her to be seated he was mentally glancing over her record. Nineteen hundred and twelve it had been when Steuben had brought her away from the Russians at Bucharest and installed her at Brussels, that clearing-house of international espionage. For a woman, the Colonel condescendingly reflected, she had proved her worth. That affair of the signalling-book of H.M.S. *Queen* had been her doing ; and it was she who had laid the information which had led to the arrest of the English spy, Barton, at Wilhelmshaven.

" Madame," was Trompeter's opening when he had given her a cigarette, " I have ventured to bring you out from Brussels in this terrible weather because I need your help."

Sylvia Averescu looked at him coldly. Her wait in a freezing cubby-hole full of damp and strongly flavoured orderlies had not improved her temper. She had entered the room resolved to give this Colonel von Trompeter a piece of her mind. Yet, somehow, his personality cowed her. Against her will she was favourably impressed by his direct gaze, good looks and charming manners. She saw at once that he was a regular officer of the old school, a man of breeding, not a commercial traveller stuffed into uniform, like Pracht. She was flattered by the way he handed her to a chair and assisted her out of her furs as though she were a Duchess. And the Latin in her, which had always squirmed at the " Frau " and " Fräulein " of her German associates, was grateful for " Madame " as a form of address.

Still, the recollection of that icy vigil yet grated on her, and she replied rather tartly, " I don't know in what way I can be of any assistance to you, Herr Oberst." The Colonel's blue eyes rested for an instant on her handsome, rather discontented face. Then, brushing the ash from the end of his cigarette, he said : " When you were in Brussels before the war, you knew the British Secret Service people pretty well, I believe ? "

She shrugged her shoulders. " It was what I was paid for."

" You were acquainted with some of their principal agents, I take it : the star turns, I mean—men like Francis Oke-wood or Philip Brewster, or "—he paused—" even our friend ' N,' the mysterious Unknown Quantity ? "

She laughed on a hard note. " If you'll tell me who ' N ' was—or is," she returned, " I'll tell you if I knew him. I've met the other two you mentioned." She leaned back in her chair and blew out luxuriantly a cloud of smoke. " ' The Unknown Quantity,' eh ? What a dance he led you, Colonel ! I've often wondered which of the boys he was."

The Colonel's hand groped behind him until he found the bell. Thrice his thumb pushed the button. His eyes were on the woman as she reclined gracefully in her chair staring musingly at the ceiling. His watchful gaze did not quit her face even when the door was suddenly thrust open and a tatterdemalion figure hobbled into the room.

Trompeter, his face a mask of steel, saw how, at the sound of the door closing, the woman at his side looked up—saw, too, the little furrow of perplexity that suddenly appeared between her narrow, arching eyebrows. But the swift, suspicious glance she shot at her companion found him apparently intent on studying the end of his cigarette, yet even as her gaze switched back to the outcast, cowering in forlorn abandonment in the centre of the floor, the Colonel's bright blue eyes were quick to note the expression of horror-struck amazement which for one fleeting instant flickered across her regular features.

But the next moment she was bored and listless as before. So swift was her reaction that it was as though her face had never lost its wonted air of rather sulky indifference. She darted an amused glance at the impassive visage gazing down upon her and laughed.

" You have some queer visitors, Herr Oberst," she said. " Tell me "—she indicated the tramp with a comic movement of the head—" is he one of us ? "

" No," replied Trompeter, with quiet emphasis.

" Then who is he ? "

" I was hoping you would be able to tell me that."

She stared at him for a moment, then suddenly broke into a peal of merry laughter.

" Oh, my dear Colonel," she exclaimed, " you do their ingenuity too much honour."

" And yet," observed Trompeter quietly, " he's one of their star men." His eyes were on the prisoner as he spoke. But the tramp, leering idiotically, stared into space and dribbled feebly.

Sylvia Averescu laughed incredulously. " Then they've changed their methods. All the British Secret Service aces I've known were serving officers, or ex-officers. You're not going to claim that this miserable creature is an English gentleman, Colonel. Why, his hands alone give you the lie ! "

" Specially roughened for the job ! "

" What job ? "

But the Colonel left the question unanswered. " The English are devilish thorough," he added. " I'll grant them that ! "

The woman left her chair and went boldly up to the idiot. With a pointing finger she indicated a " V " of yellow skin that appeared below his uncollared neck between the lapels of his jacket.

" Look," she vociferated in disgust, " the man's filthy. He hasn't had a bath for years ! " She turned about to face Trompeter, who had followed her. " If this man is what you say, he would have a white skin, a properly tended body, under his rags. But this creature is disgusting ! "

Trompeter stepped swiftly up to the prisoner and with

brutal hands ripped the ragged jacket apart. The man wore no shirt ; his coat was buttoned across his naked body. The Colonel recoiled a pace and clapped his handkerchief to his nose. " *Pfui Deibel !* " he muttered.

Something had rattled smartly on the floor. Trompeter stooped quickly with groping fingers ; then, drawing himself erect, stared fixedly at the prisoner. The outside pocket of the idiot's jacket had been almost ripped away in the vigour of the Colonel's action and hung lamentably down. Trompeter's hand darted into the torn pocket and explored the lining. His fingers dredged up some tiny invisible thing, which he transferred to the palm of his other hand.

With an air of triumph he swung round to the woman. " Well," he remarked roughly, " he's for it, anyway. If he were a friend of yours, I should tell you to kiss him goodbye."

At that she faltered ever so slightly. " What do you mean ? " Her voice was rather hoarse.

" What I mean," Trompeter gave her back brutally, " is that he's the pigeon man we've been looking for. He'll go before the court in the morning, and by noon he'll be snugly under the sod ! "

So saying, he unfolded his clenched hand and thrust it close under her face. Two little shining yellow grains reposed in the open palm. " Maize," he announced grimly. " Food for the birds. Pigeon men always carry it."

With that, he shut his hand and joined it to its fellow behind his back, while he dropped his square chin on his breast and sternly surveyed her.

" And do you mean to say," she questioned unsteadily, " that the military court would send him to his death on no other evidence than that ? "

" Certainly. There was an identical case last month. Two English flying officers. They shot them in the riding school at Charleroi. Game lads they were, too ! "

" But this poor devil may have picked up some maize somewhere and kept it for food. He looks half-starved, anyway."

Trompeter shrugged his shoulders. " That's his look-out. We're not taking any chances on pigeon men. They're too dangerous, my dear. Not that I want the poor devil shot. I'd rather have him identified."

The woman raised her head and gazed curiously at the Colonel. " Why ? " she asked, almost in a whisper.

Trompeter drew her to the window, out of earshot of the prisoner. Outside, the whole town seemed to reverberate to the passage of heavy guns, monsters, snouting under their tarpaulins, that thundered by in the wake of their tractors.

" Because," he said in an undertone, " I can use him to mislead the enemy. Our dear English cousins shall get their pigeon service all right, but after this the birds will carry my reports instead of our friend's. For this I must have the fellow's name." He paused and bent his bushy eyebrows at her. " You know this man ? "

" Wait," she bade him, rather breathless. " Let us get this clear. If this man were identified, you would spare his life ? "

The Colonel nodded curtly. His eyes never left her face.

" What guarantee have I that you will keep your word ? "

" I shall hand over to you the only evidence there is against him."

" You mean the maize ? "

" Yes."

She cast a timorous glance across the room to where the prisoner was standing, his head lolling on his shoulder. He had not changed his position. His eyes were half-closed and his tongue hung out under the ragged moustache. The reek of him was pungent in the room.

Silently she held out her hand to Trompeter. Without hesitation he dropped the two grains of maize into the slender palm. She ran to the stove and dropped them in. Impassively the Colonel watched her from the window. The maps on the walls trembled in the din of gun-wheels in the street.

Slowly the woman returned to the Colonel's side. He noticed how pale her face appeared against the flame of her hair. She looked at him intently, then said, in a sort of breathless whisper, " You're right, I know him."

A steely light glittered in the quick blue eyes. " Ah ! Who is it ? "

" Dunlop. Captain Dunlop."

Trompeter leaned forward swiftly. " Not ' The Unknown Quantity ' ? "

She made a little movement of the shoulders. " I can't

tell you. He never attempted to disguise himself with me."

" Did you meet him in Brussels ? "

She nodded. " He used to come over from London almost every week-end. . . ."

The Colonel grunted assent. " Yes, that was the way they did it before the war." He flashed her a scrutinising glance. " Did you know him well ? You're sure you're not making a mistake ? "

She shook her head, and there was something wistful in the gesture. " He was my lover. . . ."

Trompeter smiled broadly. " Ah," he murmured, " Steuben always managed that sort of thing so cleverly. . . ."

" Steuben had nothing to do with it," came back her hot whisper. " No one knew him for a secret agent—at least, not until I found him out. He told me he was an English engineer who came to Brussels on business ; I was jealous of him, and one day I discovered he was visiting another woman, a Belgian. Then—then I followed things up and found out the rest. He was frank enough when I confronted him—the English are, you know. He told me he had only been carrying out his orders. And I "—she faltered—" I was part of those orders too. . . ."

She clenched her hands tensely, and turned to stare forlornly out at the rain.

" You were fond of him, Madame ? "

" My feelings have nothing to do with the business between you and me, Colonel," she told him glacially over her shoulder.

He bowed. " I beg your pardon. And you have told me all you know ? What is his full name ? "

" James, I think. I called him Jimmy."

" How did he sign his reports ? Can you tell me that ? "

She nodded. " ' J. Dunlop,' " she answered.

" How do you know this ? "

" Because I made it my business to find out . . . afterwards ! " she answered passionately, and was silent.

" And he is a regular officer ? "

" Of the Royal Engineers." She turned to the Colonel. " And now, if you don't mind, I should like to go back to my hotel. I—I don't feel very well. I expect I must have caught a chill. This awful weather . . ."

The Colonel rang. " I'll send for Captain Pracht——"

Like a fury she rounded on him. " For the love of God ! " she burst forth, " am I never to be left alone again ? Can't I go back to the hotel by myself ? "

Trompeter bowed. " Certainly, if you promise to go straight there. It's in your own interest I say it. The P.M. is very strict about civilians just now."

" I'll go straight back," she retorted impatiently. " And you'll keep to our bargain, Colonel ? "

The officer inclined his head.

" What—what will you do with *him* ? " she asked, rather unsteadily.

" Oh, prisoners of war camp, I suppose," was the brisk answer.

She said no more, but moved slowly towards the door. There she paused and let her eyes rest for an instant on the scarecrow shape that mowed and gibbered between them. The Colonel saw her put forth one little hand towards the pigeon man and stand thus as though she hoped that he might turn and greet her. But the tramp with his melancholy imbecile stare paid no heed. She seemed to droop as she turned and passed out.

Then Trompeter went up to the prisoner and clapped him encouragingly on the shoulder. " It's a wonderful disguise, Dunlop," he said pleasantly and in flawless English, " and I don't mind telling you that you nearly took me in. But the game's up, my friend ! You're spotted. Let's have a friendly talk. I don't expect you to give anything away, but I'm anxious for news of Colonel Ross, my esteemed opposite number on the other side of No Man's Land. I heard he'd been down with this damnable *grippe*. . . ."

" Goo . . . ! " mumbled the tramp, and the bubbles frothed at his mouth. The telephone on the desk rang. The Colonel left the prisoner to answer it. A well-bred voice said : " His Excellency desires to speak with Colonel von Trompeter." The next instant a high-pitched, furious voice came ringing over the wire.

" Is that Trompeter ? So, Herr Oberst, a new division can't come into the corps area without being shelled to ribbons ! What the devil are your people doing ? What's that you say ? You're investigating. Investigating be damned ! I want action—action, do you understand ?

32*

The whole Corps knows that there's a spy in the area sending information back, and when I ask you what you propose to do about it you tell me you're investigating ! *Verdammt nochmal !* what I expect you to do is to catch the lousy fellow and shoot him, and by God if you don't, I'll have the collar off your back, and don't you forget it ! *Himmelkreuz-sakrament !* I'll show you who's in command here, you and your investigation ! You'll report to me in person at six o'clock this afternoon, and I shall expect to hear then that you've laid hands on this spy. If you fail me this time, Herr Oberst, I give you fair warning that I'll get somebody I can rely upon to carry out my wishes. And you are to understand that the General is extremely dissatisfied with you. Is that clear ? "

" *Zu Befehl, Excellenz !* " replied the Colonel stiffly, and hung up the receiver. He lit a cigarette and sat at the desk for a full minute, contemplating through a swathe of blue smoke the wretched-looking outcast before him.

" Sorry, Dunlop," he said at last. " I'd have saved you if I could, but charity begins at home. My General demands a victim, and my head is the price. I'm a poor man, my friend, with no private means and a family to support. I've got powerful enemies, and if I lose this job my career's over. As God is my judge, Dunlop, I can't afford to keep my pledged word." He paused and pressed his handkerchief to his lips. " If there's anything I can do about letting your people know . . ."

He broke off expectantly, but the pigeon man made no sign. With his head cocked in the air his whole attention appeared to be directed to a fly buzzing round the wire of the electric light.

" You'll at least give me the honour," Trompeter went on rather tremulously, " of shaking hands with a brave man ? "

But the pigeon man did not even look at him. His grimy right hand stole furtively under his tattered jacket and he writhed beneath his verminous rags. His gaze remained immutably distant, as though he were peering down some long vista. Slowly the grizzled head at the desk drooped and there was a moment's pregnant hush in the room.

Then the Colonel stood up, a stalwart figure, and moved

resolutely to a press in the wall. He opened the door and disclosed, neatly hung on pegs, his steel helmet, revolver, Thermos flask, map-case and saddle-bags. He unstrapped one of the saddle-bags, and, dipping in his hand, brought away in his fingers a few shining orange grains. Then he rang and told the orderly to send in Captain Ehrhardt. The officer recoiled at the grim severity of his Chief's expression.

" *Also*, Herr Hauptmann," was the Colonel's greeting, " you searched the prisoner, did you ? "

" *Jawohl*, Herr Oberst ! " said Ehrhardt, in a quaking voice.

" And found nothing, I think you told me ? "

" Nothing—that is, except the articles I enumerated, Herr Oberst, namely——"

The stern voice interrupted him. " Would it surprise you to learn that I discovered maize in the prisoner's pocket when I searched him ? See ! " The Colonel's hand opened and spilled a few grains of maize on the blotter. " It appears to me, Herr Hauptmann, that you have grossly neglected your duty. You've got to wake yourself up, or one of these mornings you'll find yourself back in the trenches with your regiment. Now pay attention to me ! The prisoner goes before the tribunal to-morrow. You will have him washed and disinfected and issued with clean clothes immediately, and hand him over to the Provost Marshal. Horst will warn the P.M. The prisoner can have anything he likes in the way of food or drink or smokes. Your evidence will be required at the trial, so you'll have to stay the night. See Horst about a bed. March the prisoner out ! "

The door shut and the escort's ringing tramp died away. Grimly the Colonel shook his balled fist at the telephone.

" Break me, would you, you old sheep's-head ! " he muttered through his teeth. " But my pigeon man will spike your guns, my boy ! *Verdammt*, though, the price is high ! "

Then, drawing himself up to his full height, he brought his heels together with a jingle of spurs and gravely saluted the door through which the pigeon man had disappeared between the fixed bayonets of his guards.

V

A week later, in an unobtrusive office at Whitehall, high
above the panorama of London threaded by the silver
Thames, a large, quiet man sat at his desk and frowned
down at a typewritten sheet he held in his hand.

"Well," he said, addressing an officer in khaki who stood
in an expectant attitude before him, "they've nabbed
Tony, Carruthers!"

"Oh, sir!" ejaculated Carruthers in dismay. "You
were right, then?"

"'Fraid so. I knew they'd pinched him when Corps
forwarded those Dunlop messages that kept reachin' 'em by
pigeon. Prendergast, of Rotterdam, says here he has word
from a trustworthy source in Belgium that at Roulers on
the 6th the Boches shot a half-witted tramp on a charge of
espionage. The trial, of course, was held in secret, but the
rumour in the town is that the tramp was a British officer.
That'd be Tony, all right. God bless my soul, what an
actor the fellow was! I'd never have lent him for this job,
only G.H.Q. were so insistent. Well, he had a good run for
his money, anyway. Our friends on the other side used to
call him 'N,' the Unknown Quantity. They never managed
to identify him, you see. My hat! old Tony must be
smilin' to think that he managed to take his incognito down
to the grave with him."

"But did he?"

"Obviously, otherwise the old Boches would have signed
his real name to those pigeon messages of theirs which have
so much amused Ross and his young men at Corps Headquarters."

"By why 'Dunlop,' sir?"

The large man smiled enigmatically. "Ah," he remarked,
"you weren't in the Service before the war, Carruthers, or
you'd have known that 'Dunlop' was one of our accommodation names in the office. Most of us were Captain Dunlop
at one time or another. I've been Captain Dunlop myself.
We run up against some rum coves in this business, and it
ain't a bad plan to have a sort of general *alias*. It prevents
identification, and all manner of awkwardness, when the
double-crossin' begins." He broke off to chuckle audibly.
"Let's see, it's old Trompeter on that front, ain't it? I

wonder where he got hold of the office *alias*, the foxy old devil ! He's probably put up another Iron Cross over this ! He'd be kickin' himself if he knew the truth. That's the catch about this job of ours, my boy—to recognise the truth when you find it ! "

So saying, the large man unlocked his desk and, taking out a book, turned to a list of names. With the red pencil he scored out, slowly and methodically, a name that stood there.

THE ALIBI

BOISTEROUSLY the March wind drove the rain across the desolation of the square. The plane trees, waiting naked, like beggars, at the gates of spring, shivered above the head of King Walters as he loitered by the iron railings in the centre and, under cover of the cars parked along the kerb, watched the policeman saunter past the doorway into which old Corling had just disappeared.

How slowly it moved, the stalwart figure, waterproof cape reflecting the yellow blur of the street lamps ! He must have a tranquil mind, the policeman, King told himself, a tranquil mind, not a brain which was like a dart of steel sharpened in the white-hot furnace of resolve. Even when one has waited six years, six seconds can seem an eternity ; and King Walters, peering from behind the cars at the white beam of the constable's lamp rising and falling on door and window of the old Georgian houses, felt as though his vigil would never end.

This was the third night now since his arrival in London that he had spied upon that door, waiting for old Corling to come home. Robert, the old man's servant, King had seen ; but Corling himself not at all. That is, not until that breathless, exhilarating, triumphant moment, a bare three minutes since, when he had descried the well-known figure breasting the spring gale that howled round the corner of the square.

The old man, of course, had been lying low. No doubt he felt safe in spending a week-end in town. Maybe, though, it was only that he had a pressing business engagement in London on the Sunday ; old Corling would always be too mean to go to an hotel.

Suddenly the door under the wooden portico groaned protestingly, opened, then shut with a slam that seemed to echo down the roaring corridor of the wind. King's heart went sick with disappointment. But the next instant it began to thud noisily in his ears. Not Corling but his man emerged from the house, old Robert, as gnarled and as crabbed as his master, an umbrella in one hand, a small bag in the other. He put up the umbrella and, bowing to the storm, paddled away. King had a sudden thrill of exultation. Old Robert —over the vista of six gaunt years memory rushed back— old Robert was in the habit of going home to his wife for week-ends.

Under the shabby raincoat the watcher was shaking with eagerness. How wise he had been to wait! On catching sight a few instants before of this man who had betrayed him, his impulse had been to spring forward and bar his passage, crying aloud in that aged, brutal face: " *Hullo, Corling! Here's King Walters back from the dead!* "

How wise to have waited! The watcher forgot his weary vigil, forgot the damp chill that pierced him through and through under his suit of shoddy, forgot the time, the place. He knew only that he was master of the hour.

Master of the hour!

Upstairs in his lonely flat, isolated on the top of this office building which none would visit before Monday morning, was Corling, alone, unable to escape!

The policeman had passed on ; the square was very quiet. King Walters darted across the road. At the house door his hand fumbled in his pocket, there was a slight " click," and then a funnel of stuffy blackness swallowed him up. Noiselessly the door swung to and the wind was left to rage round the square alone.

Upward in the dark, landing after landing, the man mounted with sure and silent strides, nor halted till the staircase ended before a door. Lightly his gloved fingers sought out the protuberance of the lock, there was a little scratching sound such as a mouse might make behind the wainscot. King Walters found himself gazing along the obscurity of a narrow hall at a line of yellow light beneath a door.

He stood still ; and there fell upon his ears the pompous ticking of a clock. No other sound. But it was not to listen that he had paused, or yet to rest after his rapid climb ; men were in the pink of physical fitness where King Walters had come from. It was to taste to the full the savour of this moment for which during six endless twelve months he had hungered that he paused, paused as will pause in ecstasy a lover before the offering of his mistress's red lips.

He was alone in that flat, old Corling's flat, with his ravenous appetite for revenge, and at the end of the passage, behind that closed door, in that room with the solemn clock, was his quarry. . . .

Until he had lost all sense of time King Walters stood there in the cold, dark lobby, thinking of the wasted years, of Queenie torn from his arms, of this old Corling who had smashed to bits a young man's life but was now going to pay. " At last ! At last ! " the clock seemed to be repeating ; " At last ! At last ! " thumped King Walters's heart in his ears. Yes, Corling was going to pay. He was good for a steady income, if not . . .

With money, King told himself, he could look up Queenie again and resume the old life. Not that she, good sort that she was, would mind if he were penniless and shabby. But he had his pride ; and he had made up his mind not to see her until he had had this reckoning with Corling.

And now Corling was there, separated from his raving, red imagination only by a door. King felt that his luck was in. The night would bring him money ; that meant soft linen, decent clothes, a gold watch, cigars, all these half-forgotten luxuries . . . and Queenie. The blood hammered at his temples as his memory brought back to him all manner of little things about her, the softness of her arms entwined about his neck, the warm and subtle fragrance of her welling masses of hair . . . He caught his breath and began to creep along the dim hall-way.

Now he was at the door. Noiselessly he turned the handle. Of a sudden the ticking of the clock was portentously loud, and with it the sound of gentle breathing. Within the room a reading-lamp on the desk spilled from under its green shade a pool of light that dimly illuminated the familiar setting : the old man's study as King had seen it on the night before the great betrayal of six years ago, with scarce a dusty document moved, one might believe, from its place on the littered desk, with the same shabby furniture, the same battered safe, the same fly-blown engravings on the walls, the same smug marble clock on the mantelpiece, and yes, by God ! Corling himself asleep in his chair before the fire.

He slept the death-like slumber of the old, his head fallen
forward on his chest as though he had collapsed and died in
the deep arm-chair. His toothless mouth was open and the
high ridge of his beak-like nose glistened white in the firelight. " He's aged ! " was King's thought as he gazed down
upon his sleeping enemy. Then he caught sight of himself
in the dingy glass above the fireplace, dark hair flecked with
grey, crow's-feet at the eyes, bitter lines from nose to jaw
and grim folds about the mouth. Anger flamed up within
him. " Corling ! " he cried, and walked sharply up to the
hearth. His heavy tread set the old-fashioned chandelier
a-jangling.

The old man awoke gently as though he had but closed his
eyes. Bolt upright he sat and peered at the clock. " A
quarter past ten ! " he mumbled. " I must a' dropped
off. . . ."

Then in the dim mirror behind the clock his eye fell upon
the reflection of his visitor. King Walters's heart leaped
high within him as he saw the terror distort that yellowing,
wrinkled countenance. Gripping the arms of his chair, the
old man hauled himself into a standing posture and remained
thus, one skinny hand picking irresolutely at his mouth, his
rheumy eyes fixed on the grim visage that confronted him
icily out of the looking-glass. Very slowly, at last, old
Corling swung round.

" 'Ow did yer . . . 'oo let yer in ? " he demanded in a
voice that quavered peevishly.

King grinned maliciously.

" Love laughs at locksmiths, Corling," he rejoined.
" Well, so does hate ! Don't worry about how I got in.
The essential fact is that I'm here ! "

Gradually he leaned forward until his hard and bony jaw
all but grazed the old man's chin.

" Wot . . . wot d'yer want with me ? " the other
faltered.

King's massive fingers, gnarled and blackened with rough
labour, were pressed against his palms until the knuckles
stood out whitely in front of his balled fists.

" What I want I know I can't get," he retorted in a
voice made hoarse by resentment, " and that would be to
have you as a young man with all your life before you, and
pluck you out of the sunshine and flowers and the busy hum

of life, away from the woman you love, and stuff you into a cold, grey hell of silence and watching eyes, of clanging bolts and stone walls, and there let you rot, damn you, damn you. . . ."

From head to foot he trembled, his eyes darkly hot, his stern face livid with passion. Inch by inch the old man shrank back until he had to stem himself by one claw-like hand thrust behind him into the seat of his chair. In the breathless silence that fell between the two men the voice of the clock was heard, ticking the inexorable seconds away.

It was King Walters who broke the hush. He drew a deep breath, opened and shut his hands, laughed shortly.

" Dreams," he murmured, " the idle dreams of a prison cell. Stand up, Corling, and listen to me ! " Unceremoniously he laid hold of the other's necktie and dragged him erect.

" When I lifted those jewels for you in Chesterfield Street," he said, " and things suddenly looked ugly, you sold me to the police for the insurance reward. . . ."

" It's a lie ! " the old man piped wildly. " S'welp me, King, you ain't got it right. . . ."

" What I *know* is good enough for me," was the stern rejoinder. " Five hundred pounds you got from the insurance, wasn't it ? I'll have that now to be going on with ! " And he pointed at the safe.

A little colour was creeping into the ivory cheeks. Nervously old Corling rubbed his palms together.

" You're . . . you're a good lad, King," he wheezed, " one o' the very best, as always I 'ave maintained. But you don't want to be 'ot-'eaded, boy. No young feller never gained nothin' by being 'ot-'eaded. I ain't a-denyin' as 'ow you was treated rough. But it worn't no fault o' mine. The p'lice was one too many fer us that time. I never see nothin' of the reward, and if any one says the contrairey he's a liar. I must 'ave bin a tenner out o' pocket on that job." He wagged his head deprecatingly, then, catching King's eye, rather hastily added : " Still, me an' a few friends 'as got it all planned out to do the right thing by you, boy. Now that you're back in London I'll 'ave to see wot the others is willin' to put up, but if the loan of . . ."—the lizard eyes shot a shrewdly mustering glance at the other—" of a couple o' thick 'uns, say . . ."

King Walters was biting his forefinger and moodily staring at the speaker.

" Five hundred, I said," he now interrupted. " Get a move on, will you ? I'm in a hurry. . . ."

With a senile smile old Corling balanced his head from side to side.

" Five 'undred quid ? " he cackled. " Oh dear, oh dear, you'll be the death o' me ! Why do yer talk so silly ? W'ere in 'ell d'yer think I'd get all that money from, boy ? "

" I don't want any more of your play-acting," said King. " You've got thousands stored away in that safe of yours, you old screw. Are you going to fetch the money out or am I ? " Menacingly he took a pace forward.

" If I 'ave a few 'undreds in the safe," croaked Corling, drawing back in alarm, " it ain't mine, King. Trust funds, that's wot they are, money deposited for safe keeping by good friends o' mine, like yerself. You wouldn't 'ave me go back on me pals, boy ? Lemme see now if I can't lay me 'ands on me note-case. I might 'ave a fiver 'andy. . . ." Tremblingly he began to pat his pockets.

" Open that safe ! "

The order rang out like the crack of a whip.

" I 'aven't the key ! " squealed the old man suddenly. " I left it in me other soot. Strike me blind if that ain't the truth. . . ."

" Open that safe ! "

The convict stood before him. His right hand now grasped a long, black, pear-shaped object, with a strap slung about his muscular wrist.

Out of his lashless eyes old Corling darted a quick look to right and left. He affected not to see the life-preserver in the other's hand, but turned to the desk and began pitching the papers about.

" You'll ruin me ! " he grumbled. " It's blackmail, that's wot it is. . ."

And then his hand found the pistol for which he had been groping, and in a flash he had swung round, pointing the weapon at the intruder and screaming, in a voice made fluty by rage and fear : " Put up your hands ! "

But King Walters was too quick for him. With a lightning sweep of the arm he brushed the lamp from the desk, and as with a tinkle of broken glass the room was plunged into darkness, leaped at the old man's throat.

There was one horrid, unnatural cry that began on a scream and ended on a whistling gurgle; some heavy weight crashed into the fender with a thud that shook the floor; and thereafter the only sounds were the slither of two forms, tightly locked together, that heaved and swayed before the reddish glow of the fire, and the hiss of laboured breathing. . . .

It was King Walters who at length raised himself erect and scratched a match. He found and lit a candle which stood in a tray smeared with sealing-wax. Holding the light aloft, he seemed to seek for something on the carpet. Then he stooped and picked up the pistol, which had fallen to the ground. " Unloaded ! " he muttered to himself. " I thought as much ! "

He laid the pistol down upon the table and, raising his head, listened. The silence in the house was profound. Some sixth sense, developed in his convict's cell maybe, seemed to tell him that the quietness of the room was abnormal, the silence incomplete; for his eyes sought at once the mantelpiece.

The clock had ceased its ticking, as though it had breathed its last when the old man died. There was a vacant space, marked out in dust, on the chimney-piece, and the clock lay face upward in the fender, cheek by jowl with old Corling stretched out on the hearth-rug. Walters, remembering the reverberating crash he had heard, realised that, as he sprang forward, his elbow must have caught the massive clock and knocked it to the ground. The marble was cracked across; but, miraculously, glass and dial were intact.

The hands had stopped at twenty minutes past ten.

Stupidly the man stared at the clock, rubbing his thighs, mechanically, irresolutely, with his gloved hands. Suddenly he appeared to become aware of the discoloured face which, with mouth awry and wide-open eyes, grinned up at him from the floor.

He stumbled blindly from the room, leaving the candle to gutter on the desk, shedding its trembling ray upon the two blank faces on the hearth. . . .

Time stands still at Dartmoor, and King Walters knew nothing of the rejuvenating magic of modern fashions. The woman who, in answer to his ring, opened the front door of the quiet house in Mayfair had a slim, girlish figure, close-cropped auburn hair, and a jade-green evening frock that scarcely covered her knees. On seeing the gaunt stranger standing under the dripping porch she gave a little gasping cry and flung herself into his arms.

" At last ! " she murmured. " Oh, why did you make me wait ? All the six years put together did not seem so long as these last three days and nights I've watched for you, knowing you were free, and you never came ! I was afraid there'd been some mistake, that you'd had to go back. Darling, why ever didn't you come before ? It was cruel of you not to let me meet you, and then to send no word, to leave me in suspense ! " She snuggled her face to his, straining him to her. " Oh, honey, it's good to have you back. . . ."

With crooning words of endearment she drew him into the warm and well-lit hall and closed the door. But when the light fell upon his face she gave a little moaning sob and buried her face against his coat. " Your poor suffering eyes," she exclaimed brokenly, " I can't bear to see them ! "

Then she stepped back, glancing down at her frock.

" Gosh ! " she declared. " I declare you're sopping ! Where have you come from, King ? Did you walk here ? On a night like this ? "

With a hunted air he was gazing about him. Hats and coats were stacked about the dainty hall ; and from the staircase drifted down the murmur of voices, the aroma of cigars.

" I've been walking about for hours," he answered gruffly. " Have you got a party on, Queenie ? "

" Only some of the boys sitting in on a poker game. Jack Meldon's here, and Benny Isaacs. They'll sure be glad to see you, King. . . ."

He scowled. " I've got to talk to you, Queenie. And I'm dying for a drink. Do you still keep the whisky in here ? "

He pushed open a door and switched on a light, which gleamed on the nude mahogany of a small dining-room. The woman ran to the sideboard and measured the man a drink from the decanter which stood there on a tray, flanked by siphon and glasses. As he drank she turned to a lacquer mirror that hung on the wall and began patting her shining crop to rights.

" You haven't noticed that I've shingled my hair," she observed coquettishly over her shoulder. " It was brown when you went away. Masses of it I had, do you remember ? coiled in two long plaits round my head. How do you think red suits me ? And do you like me bobbed . . . ? "

" Corling's dead," said King as he put down his glass.

Astonished, she swung about.

" Dead ? " she repeated. " It was sudden, wasn't it ? Why, Benny Isaacs saw him on the street only yesterday. He was telling us upstairs just now. . . ."

" I killed him to-night," said King.

She showed no dismay. Her grey eyes grew thoughtful and a little pucker fended her smooth forehead between the delicately pencilled half-moons of her eyebrows. As he looked at her, he recognised at last the Queenie he had left behind. Grit all through was Mayfair Queenie, as they called her. She was never " faized," as she called it in her native idiom, never lost her nerve, never made mistakes.

" It was he that sold you, then ? " was her only comment. King nodded grimly. " Bully for you ! " she told him and grasped his hand. She drew him to her. " Tell me ! " she bade him.

" I didn't mean to kill him. I went to get money out of him. He pulled a gun on me and I saw red. When I took my hands away from his throat he was dead. . . ." A long shudder shook his powerful frame.

She patted his shoulder. " Easy, son. . . ."

" I'm not the man I was, kid," he muttered with a dry sob. " They break your spirit in clink. . . ."

" That's all right, boy," she soothed him. " You leave this to Mum." Briskly she looked at her wrist-watch. " At what time did it happen ? "

" At twenty past ten."

" Are you sure of the time ? "

He nodded. " We knocked the clock over in the mix-up and it stopped. I let it lie. I'd have set it going again if I hadn't lost my head. . . ."

" Leave any tracks ? "

He shook his head.

" Prints ? "

He showed her his gloved hands. Swiftly she scrutinised them.

" Those wax-marks look fresh," she observed. She pointed at the gloves. " Take 'em off ! " He peeled them from his hands and gave them to her. From the plate-basket on the sideboard she took a knife and sawed off the buttons, which she slipped into her bag. The gloves she flung on the fire. Then,

" Did you come straight here ? " she asked.

He stared at her weakly. " I don't know what I did. I seem to have been wandering about in the rain for ages. Suddenly I found myself in Berkeley Square and so I thought I'd come to you. . . . "

" Poor old boy ! If you'd stopped to think, you'd have made a bee-line for your old Queenie. Still," she went on, with another look at her wrist, " you haven't been so long. It's only five past eleven now." Thoughtfully she pinched her chin. " It'll have to be an alibi," she announced at length. " Listen here, honey ! If you'll sit tight and do as Queenie says, everything's going to be as right as right. When the busies come round here after you, as come they surely will directly the body's found, you're going to hand them an ab-so-loote-ly unbustable alibi. Now don't ask questions, but cut along upstairs to your old room and clean up. You'll find a new suit laid out on the bed—oh, and all the fixings that go with it ; that was my little surprise for my boy. But, say, you want to make it snappy, honey : I can only allow you five minutes. As soon as you're ready you come down to the drawing-room and leave the rest to me ! Now beat it ! "

She kissed him on the forehead and shooed him out of the room. " Kids," she murmured, addressing her pleasing vision in the mirror, " kids, that's all they are. But Gosh ! like kids, they surely do get a hold of your heart-strings ! "

Then she switched off the light and went back to her guests.

A dense cloud of tobacco smoke, shaded lights, a knot of men in their shirt-sleeves, ties and collars loosened or laid aside, seated about a table where, amid glasses and brimming ash-trays, the high lights of playing-cards gleamed on the green cloth, and in the background the chaste elegance of Queenie's Pompadour drawing-room :—the scene plunged King Walters headlong back into that world of his which he thought he had forgotten. The new clothes seemed to have given him back his self-assurance, and the neat blue suit, though it hung a trifle loosely on him, contrived to lend him the quiet and distinguished air familiar to his old associates.

Of these he found but two in the party round the poker-table : Benny Isaacs, who in his excitable Jewish way gave him clamorous greeting, and old Jack Meldon, who through teeth clenched on cigar growled out, affably enough : " Glad to see you back, son ! " The rest were strangers : a sunburnt Colonial addressed as " Mac " ; a red-faced, fat man with a Lancashire burr ; a sleek youth who was not quite sober ; two or three others. Queenie, who did the honours, rolled out a string of names. Then she summarily propelled King towards the end of the room, where a cold buffet was laid out.

" You must be ravenous," she said. " Whatever time is it, for pity's sake ? " Before King could explain that he had no watch, she had called out down the long room : " Hey, you, Gerry Lomax, you can see the clock, what's the time ? "

It was the red-faced, fat man whom she thus addressed. King's appearance had momentarily suspended the game. Mr. Lomax was standing in front of the fire, thoughtfully picking his teeth. On hearing Queenie's question he raised his eyes to the dainty Louis Quinze clock that faced him on the mantelpiece.

" Five minutes past ten, me dear ! " he answered. Then, turning round to the table, he said, addressing the others : " Eh, chaaps, ain't we ever going t'eat again ? "

King Walters had moved forward instinctively until he could see the clock's face.

The gilt hands pointed to five minutes past ten.

" Well, I should say so," cried Queenie gaily from the end of the room. " There are sandwiches and lobster mayonnaise and I don't know what else back here on the table. Why don't you make a break and eat ? "

" A' could do wi' a snack," observed Mr. Lomax, easing

his collar. " Ten o'clock, eh, an' a'. 'ad me dinner at won ! "

" Aw to. hell, Gerry," growled Jack Meldon," get on with the game. . . ."

" Sit down, brother, and let's go !." said Benny.

With a wistful glance down the room, Mr. Lomax resumed his seat.

" Well, I declare," cried Queenie, " if it isn't a shame ! It's ten o'clock and none of you have had any dinner. And when poor old Gerry says he's hungry you won't stop for five minutes to let him have a snack. . . ."

" Aw, pshaw, Queenie," grunted Jack Meldon, who was dealing, " what's the matter with shooting the eats along over here ? "

" That's the ticket," ejaculated Mr. Lomax with a brightening eye. " Bring t' groob over 'ere, lass, bring t' groob over 'ere ! "

. With the delicate air with which she did everything the woman carried two plates of sandwiches across the room and dumped them down among the ash-trays and the matches masquerading as chips. Then she drew King Walters away towards the buffet. " Come over here and talk to me, King," she said. " Wait ! You must have a glass of champagne. . . ."

They halted at the side-table, outside the circle of light and the murmur of voices round the cards. As she poured out the wine King said under his breath :

" You're a wonder, Queenie ! "

- She reddened with pleasure and smiled happily at him across the creaming wine.

. " Squared 'em, have you ? " He jerked his head in the direction of the players.

Her eyes said no. " Those who don't know can't split ! " she affirmed demurely.

He wrinkled up his forehead. " Wouldn't it be safer to let Jack and Benny in on this ? We can trust them anyway, and maybe they could fix the others. If one of those chaps over there happens to look at his watch we're busted, Queenie. D'you realise that ? "

She made a little disdainful grimace. " I should worry. Those guys sat down to play at four this afternoon, and they'll keep it up the round of the clock, I shouldn't wonder.

You know how it is. Once they get going they lose all sense of time. I don't have to tell you that, King. Many a night I was the poker widow before you went away. . . ."

But with sombre doggedness he stuck to his point. " It seems risky to me. . . ."

" Risky . . . nothing ! I'm not afraid of their remembering the time. What scares me stiff is that they won't remember it. I started out by telling myself that one of the bunch has got to be dead sure of the time at which you are supposed to have turned up. I went out after that. I chose my man and concentrated on him. . . ."

" You mean what's his name ? . . . Lomax ? "

She smiled teasingly. " Isn't he the bright boy ! Yes, honey, Lomax is my strong suit. He's sober, which is more than you can say of young Pilchard or of Mac ; and, so far as I know, he's never been in trouble. He's a hick from Wigan, or some ghastly place in the north, having a whirl in town. Jack picked him up in a bar down the Strand somewheres. The police will have nothing on him. He's good, respectable evidence, that bird. . . ."

But King was not yet satisfied. He was still suspicious, fretful.

" How do you know that he'll remember the time ? "

She laughed rather contemptuously. " I impressed it on his mind through his stomach. That's the kind of bozo this is. He may forget your name, but he's not likely to forget that he missed his dinner and didn't eat until ten o'clock when you came in and I produced the sandwiches. That's psychology, son ! You leave it all to Queenie and psychology, and there's not a split in this old burg who'll bust the alibi ! " She leaned forward and touched her glass to his. " Welcome home, honey. . . ."

. . . .

King had joined the game and was at the table with the others when the challenge came. The close-curtained windows were rimmed in hodden grey, and in the weeping dawn outside the Sabbath morning was reluctantly breaking. On that hushed room, beneath its canopy of fragrant tobacco smoke, the strident summons of the front-door bell broke like the crash of a pistol-shot.

Queenie was crouched on the divan at the end of the room, her knees drawn up to her chin, listening to the fuddled inanities of young Mr. Pilchard, who had been finding his finishing course of poker, conducted by those eminent professors, Messrs. Meldon and Isaacs, somewhat expensive, and was denouncing his wretched luck. As the loud pealing of the bell rang through the house, King checked an impulse to turn and see if Queenie had the same presentiment as himself. He kept his eyes on the table, aware that the game had come to a standstill amid desultory chaff about Queenie's early morning visitor, aware also, without intercepting it, of the swift glance which Jack and Benny interchanged ; of the men present only they knew where King Walters had spent the last six years of his life.

Together he and Queenie had concocted the tale he was to tell, should occasion arise, of the way he had spent the previous evening. Now as, to steady his nerves, he made an elaborate business of choosing a fresh cigar from the box at his elbow, he went over the story, link by link, in his mind. Yes, it rang sound and convincing ; and Queenie—once more he raised his eyes to the chimney-piece to make sure— had put the clock forward again to the right time. She had waited a good hour, and then, under cover of powdering her face before the mirror over the fireplace, had moved the hands on. So surely, so swiftly had she acted that nobody detected the operation ; nor, in the upshot, had any one remarked the change.

Now there was the buzz of voices, the sound of feet, upon the stairs. King was conscious that Queenie had left the room. " I'll count ten," he promised himself as he pinched the end of his cigar, " and then I'll look towards the door." But he had not reached five when the door was plucked open and a voice cried fiercely : " You stay out of this, my girl ! "

King knew that voice, deep and hard and subtly menacing, a voice which seemed to set rejangling in the very depths of his being strings that once the hand of bitter experience had swept. As in a dream he heard Benny Isaacs's sarcastically polite, " Why, if it isn't Mr. Manderton ! Good morning, Inspector ! "

Very deliberately King Walters blew out the match with which he had just lit his cigar and looked up. It was six years since he had heard that stern voice or seen that burly, self-contained figure. Manderton hadn't changed an atom ; down to his very tie he looked the same stolid individual who, in the stuffy hush of the Old Bailey, at the end of a long day's trial, had given the red-robed judge, waiting to pass sentence, the plain blunt facts of King Walters's criminal career.

" I want you, Walters," said the detective.

King stood up at once and went to the door. Below in the hall he heard Queenie's voice, shrill and angry : " Keep your filthy hands off me, blast you ! " Then a door slammed and he was left on the landing face to face with the inspector.

At Dartmoor they teach you to keep your eyes on the ground when speaking to those in authority. It gave the convict a sort of thrill of defiance to be able to raise his head and boldly meet the detective's long and searching glance.

" Where were you last night, Walters ? "

" Here ! "

" What time did you come ? "

" Just before ten ! "

" Where had you spent the evening ? "

The convict stuck his cigar in his mouth and shot the other a challenging look.

" Can't the police ever let a man be ? " he demanded. " What are you hounding me for ? Why do you come butting into a quiet poker party with all these questions ? "

" Richard Corling was found murdered in his flat last night, that's why," was the impassive answer.

King had wanted to deny all acquaintanceship with Corling. But Queenie had said no ; he mustn't give the police the chance of catching him out in a lie. So King, facing the detective calmly, rejoined :

" I know nothing about it. I haven't seen Corling since I came out."

" Where did you spend last evening ? " Unimpressed by the denial, the inspector repeated his previous question.

With an assumption of indifference King told his story. He had left his room in Bayswater at six, had a cup of coffee at the Corner House and gone to a cinema in Leicester Square. Because he was hard up, he had fought shy of calling on Queenie, but on coming out of the cinema he felt he couldn't face his shabby bedroom and so had walked through the rain to Mayfair. From time to time during the recital Manderton scratched a note in his book.

" Am I to take it that you've no proof other than your own word as to where you were from six until ten ? " presently asked the detective.

" You don't have to give your name and address to get a cup of coffee," the other retorted, " or to buy a seat at the pictures ! "

" Perhaps you can tell me the name of the picture you saw ? " demanded Manderton evenly.

" I don't remember the name," was the candid reply. " But Alice Joyce was in it. And there was a comic thing of Harold Lloyd's. . . ."

With warm gratitude his heart thrilled to the recognition of Queenie's uncanny prevision. Foreseeing the question, she had primed him with details of a picture-show she had visited in Leicester Square on the evening before the murder.

The detective grunted. " You say you arrived here at ten. Any proof ? "

" Ask Queenie. . . ."

" Proof, I said," repeated the inspector with sarcastic emphasis.

King shrugged his shoulders.

" Why not ask the others ? "

Mr. Manderton gave him a sharp glance, then called a name over the stairs. A plain-clothes man came up.

" There's to be no communication between him and the woman below," he snapped. Then he went into the drawing-room and shut the door behind him. King sat down on the stairs to finish his cigar.

The inspector was not long away. When he came out of the drawing-room he walked downstairs without taking any notice of the convict. The plain-clothes man, at a nod from his Chief, followed after. From the hall King heard Queenie's furious protest : " Say, what d'you think you're doing, shutting me up here alone with this man-ape ? What are my guests going to think of me ? You've gotta nerve, busting into a private party. If you're coming to call on King Walters every time a guy gets bumped off under your noses you'd better have a latch-key, hadn't you ? "

There was a rumble of deep laughter, then Manderton's voice : " Keep your hair on, Queenie ! We're not going to take King away this time. . . ."

The front door slammed, a motor-engine roared outside in the street. Queenie came flying upstairs.

"You're safe," she whispered as King caught her to him. "I made that boob downstairs spill me the whole story while Manderton was talking to you. Old Robert found the body. When he went home last night he carried off by mistake the letters that came by the night mail. He brought them back and must have reached the house soon after you left. Manderton, who's one of those scientific busies, has taken the evidence of the clock as proof of the time at which the murder was committed. Old Robert's dithering and they can't get a word out of him, this plain-clothes bird told me, but Corling's clerk says the clock was going and the old man was always fussy about keeping it right. The alibi's solid, honey! Didn't I tell you to leave it to Queenie?"

He crushed her in his arms. "You're a wonderful kid!" Then he sought her lips. "Get rid of the boys!" he bade her presently. She nodded happily and he went upstairs.

. . . . . .

Noon was past, and the Sunday bells had ceased to ring out across the mild and spring-like morning as King Walters sat at breakfast with Queenie in the little dining-room over the coffee and scrambled eggs which Queenie herself had prepared. With inimitable humour she was describing the detective's interview with Mr. Lomax as she had gathered it from the lips of her guest. In vain the inspector had sought to shake the other's recollection of the time of King's arrival.

"'I don't often 'ave to go wi'out ma sooper,'" Queenie proclaimed in a fantastic imitation of Mr. Lomax's sing-song burr, "'but w'en it dus 'aappen, ba goom! I remember it. Five minutes passt ten it wor, w'en t' chaap arrived and t'lass produced t' groob. . . .'"

A shadow darkened the window as, engine throbbing, a car drew up outside the house. The next instant the front-door bell pealed. The man and woman exchanged a silent glance. Queenie went softly to the window and peered through the curtains.

"It's Manderton come back," she said. Again the bell trilled. "We must let him in," she added, and, drawing